Norman Spinrad is the author of five science fiction novels, including *Bug Jack Barron* and *The Iron Dream*, and editor of *The New Tomorrows*, an anthology of post-1965 science fiction. He has been a critic, an agent, and a sometime lecturer in the science fiction field, and for two years has been vice-president of the Science Fiction Writers of America.

MODERN SCIENCE FICTION

Modern Science Fiction

Edited by
NORMAN SPINRAD

ANCHOR BOOKS
Anchor Press/Doubleday GARDEN CITY, NEW YORK 1974

The Anchor Books edition is the first publication of *Modern Science Fiction*.

Anchor Books edition: 1974

Library of Congress Cataloging in Publication Data

Spinrad, Norman, comp.
  Modern science fiction.

  Includes bibliographies.
  CONTENTS: The golden age: Campbell, J. W. Twilight. Van Vogt, A. E. The enchanted village. Del Rey, L. Helen O'Loy. Asimov, I. Nightfall.—The postwar awakening: Clarke, A. C. The star. Sturgeon, T. Affair with a green monkey. Knight, D. Stranger station. Godwin, T. The cold equations. Kornbluth, C. M. The marching morons. Bester, A. 5,271,009. [etc.]
  1. Science fiction, American. 2. Science fiction, English. I. Title.
PZ1.S758Mo [PS648.S3]   813'.0876
ISBN 0-385-02263-8
Library of Congress Catalog Card Number 73-18782

ACKNOWLEDGMENTS

"Twilight" by John W. Campbell, Jr. Copyright 1934 by Street & Smith Publications, Inc. Copyright renewed 1962 by John W. Campbell, Jr. Reprinted by permission of the author and the author's agents, Scott Meredith Literary Agency, Inc., 580 Fifth Avenue, New York, New York 10036.

"The Enchanted Village" by A. E. Van Vogt. Copyright © 1950 by Clark Publishing Company. Reprinted by permission of the author and the author's agent, Forrest J. Ackerman.

and the author's agents, Scott Meredith Literary Agency, Inc., 580 Fifth Avenue, New York, New York 10036.

"Faith of Our Fathers" by Philip K. Dick. Copyright © 1967 by Harlan Ellison. Reprinted by permission of the author and the author's agents, Scott Meredith Literary Agency, Inc, 580 Fifth Avenue, New York, New York 10036.

"Aye, and Gomorrah . . ." by Samuel R. Delany. Copyright © 1967 by Harlan Ellison. Reprinted by permission of the author and Henry Morrison, Inc., his agents.

"At the Mouse Circus" by Harlan Ellison. Copyright © 1971 by Harlan Ellison. Reprinted with permission of the author and the author's agents, Robert P. Mills, Ltd., New York.

"In Entropy's Jaws" by Robert Silverberg. Copyright © 1971 by Lancer Books, Inc. Reprinted by permission of the author and the author's agents, Scott Meredith Literary Agency, Inc., 580 Fifth Avenue, New York, New York 10036.

"Nine Lives" by Ursula K. Le Guin. Reprinted from a story which originally appeared in *Playboy* magazine, copyright © 1969 by *Playboy;* since revised by the author. Reprinted by permission of *Playboy*, the author, and the author's agent, Virginia Kidd.

For Philip K. Dick

CONTENTS

FOREWORD

The aim of this book is to provide the reader unfamiliar with science fiction with an orientation in the field, with a large body of short fiction which reflects the breadth and scope of modern science fiction, and with suggestions for further reading in the literature. The reader more familiar with science fiction will realize that many fine science fiction writers—Robert A. Heinlein, Ray Bradbury, Brian W. Aldiss, John Brunner, A. J. Budrys, Cordwainer Smith, and others—do not have work appearing here. Problems with rights forced the exclusion of some writers, space limitations forced the exclusion of others. It would have taken a book three or four times as long as this one to include stories by all significant modern science fiction writers.

Therefore, in addition to the list of selected works after each author's story, I have also included at the end of the book a list of significant works by science fiction writers whose work, for one reason or another, I was not able to include. Most of the books on this list and the majority of books listed after the author's stories are novels (all, in fact, are novels unless otherwise noted). Since *Modern Science Fiction* offers what I consider to be a good general introduction to short science fiction, I felt it would be more useful to the reader to concentrate on novels in these lists. I have deviated from this practice and listed only collections of short stories when the contributors are primarily or wholly short-story writers.

I wish to thank the following people for their help in the preparation of *Modern Science Fiction:* Bill Strachan, my editor at Anchor for his smooth and sure co-operation; Harlan Ellison, George Clayton Johnson, Hank Stine, Paul Turner, Theodore Sturgeon, and others too diffuse and subliminal to mention for suggesting possible stories; Dona Sadock for her encouragement and help in preparing the final draft of my essays; and particularly David Hartwell, for his hospitality, the use of his library, and his many useful suggestions.

Norman Spinrad

New York, N.Y.
November, 1973

INTRODUCTION —
MODERN SCIENCE FICTION

It seems mandatory to begin any discussion of modern science fiction with a definition of science fiction, or with a definition of the alternate term for the literature which has recently come into some currency, speculative fiction. So let's dispose of the terminology at the outset.

Everything from *2001* to *1984*, from Vladimir Nabokov's *Ada* to *Star Trek*, from *Gray Matters* to *The Space Barbarians*, from *Seven Days in May* to *THX 1138*, from *Naked Lunch* to *Space Cadet*, and yes, giant green bugs on Mars too, is speculative fiction. Speculative fiction is exactly what the words imply—any fiction containing a speculative element, anything at all written about the could-be-but-isn't.

Science fiction, on the other hand, is a special case of speculative fiction. It's a school of literature, a commercial genre with its own strange history and an attendant subculture. It's all those tacky old pulp magazines and murky-looking paperbacks, but it's also a rather large body of literature that can hold its own in respectable company—the novels of Brian W. Aldiss and Philip K. Dick, Alfred Bester's *The Demolished Man*, the short stories of Ray Bradbury and Theodore Sturgeon, *A Canticle for Leibowitz* by Walter M. Miller, Jr., *Behold the Man* by Michael Moorcock.

For complex reasons which we will shortly begin to explore, most speculative fiction published in the United States is published as "science fiction." I myself have coined what I believe to be the only valid definition of science fiction: "Science fiction is anything published as science fiction." Which is only a specific case of "the medium is the message."

"Science fiction" is a publisher's marketing category like "westerns" or "gothics" or "nurse novels"—a packaging definition. When you walk through a supermarket, you can tell the breakfast cereals from the detergents at a glance, even though they come in boxes of roughly the same size and shape. This near-subliminal recognition is accomplished by consistency of packaging style. Otherwise, you might inadvertently pour yourself a bowlful of Bold and throw a cup of Kellogg's Corn Flakes into the washing machine. Thus it is with the racks of paperback books on the newsstands, all roughly the same size and shape. People who regularly read westerns don't want to pick up science fiction by mistake, so the publishers package science fiction with space ships, peeled eyeballs, and tentacled goo, and they package westerns with horses, sagebrush, and blazing six-shooters.

Thus, at the point of sale, a serious novel by Philip K. Dick looks just like the latest adventure of Brak the Barbarian, and a collection of the outstanding short stories of Theodore Sturgeon looks like *Giant Green Slime from Outer Space*. In fact, some paperback houses have even been known to change the titles of novels to make them more "science fictiony." *Tiger, Tiger* becomes *The Stars My Destination*, *The Dragon in the Sea* becomes *21st Century Sub*, and *The Man Who Counts* becomes *War of the Wing-Men*.

In the United States today, almost all speculative fiction gets squeezed into this commercial bed of Procrustes. Therefore, a best-selling science fiction novel is a contradiction in terms, for as soon as a potential best-selling science fiction novel is delivered to a publisher—*Seven Days in May*, *The Andromeda Strain*, *The Child Buyer*, et al.—it is put into the packaging category of "best seller," not "science fiction." A novel from a "serious writer" with speculative content—*Tunc*, *Nova Express*, or *Ada* —gets packaged as a "serious novel."

As a result, any novel with speculative content that

isn't by an already well-known "serious" writer or that the publisher hasn't decided to push as a potential "best seller" is a "science fiction novel," period, and off it goes to be embellished with rocketships and monsters.

Science fiction writers have complained that serious literary critics automatically ignore their work, no matter what its merits, and sometimes have spun elaborate theories about the snobbishness of the "literary establishment." But after all, how *can* a serious, conscientious literary critic sort through the year's mountain-high pile of tacky-looking science fiction paperbacks to find a few real jewels buried in this heap of literary mediocrity? He knows what a potentially important book looks like as an artifact, as a physical package, because publishers have consistently packaged most of these books in an identifiable style. He may even realize that one soap box out of twenty contains breakfast cereal, but is he going to chomp through nineteen boxes of soap to find it? Certainly not. He's going to open a box labeled breakfast cereal.

Why then, do so many serious-minded and talented writers continue to write speculative fiction? The answer, I believe, is to be found not in the personal rewards offered by the genre, but in the artistic imperatives of our time. Speculative fiction is the only fiction that deals with modern reality in the only way that it can be comprehended—as the interface between a rapidly evolving and fissioning environment and the resultant continuously mutating human consciousness. Speculative fiction is surfacing into popular culture from every direction because it reflects the condition of the modern mind. It is the only fiction that confronts and explores the modern zeitgeist and is therefore inherently the literature of our times.

Further, what is called "mainstream" fiction in contradistinction to speculative fiction is really a very restricted and special case of speculative fiction, limited to what "really" was and what "really" is right here right now, which, paradoxically, makes it anachronistic in a modern context.

Originally, all fiction was speculative fiction. People weren't so sure that they knew what was real and what was not until the eighteenth century, in what its inheritors were pleased to call the Age of Reason. Cyrano de Bergerac could fly to the moon on the morning dew, Gilgamesh could live forever, Odysseus could stagger around a Mediterranean filled with more unearthly creatures than the population of the special effects studio at American International, and nobody in the audience at the time could be sure that any of it was impossible or even untrue. Who knew?

Today, we call such stories "fantasies" because we know (or think we know) that such things are clearly beyond the realm of the possible. But the people who wrote these "fantasies" were writing in the spirit of speculative fiction. *They* didn't think they were writing about the impossible; from their viewpoint, they were exploring the terra incognita of their time, the frontiers of the possible. Since much of the world was unexplored, and many of the forces that move it not clearly understood until well into the Age of Reason, it was virtually impossible to write anything *but* speculative fiction. There was too much uncertainty even in the here-and-now for artists to delude themselves that they could deal definitively and exclusively with the way things "really are." Before the Age of Reason, "reality" was a quicksilver witch's brew, not the contents of the Encyclopaedia Britannica.

The "realistic," here-and-now, single-reality fiction now considered "mainstream" developed as a mutation of speculative fiction sometime in the early nineteenth century as a result of the Victorian mind's ability to convince itself that it had the nature of the universe pinned down in nice neat formulas, that life was real, life was earnest, and vice versa.

Today, after Einstein, Freud, psychedelics, quantum mechanics, McLuhan, cybernetics, the Heisenberg Uncertainty Principle, systems analysis, and a few hundred other little vision-expanders, we're back where we were before the Victorians defined reality as a rigid Tinker Toy construct. We know that a literature which pretends that it is somehow more relevant to the "real world" than speculative fiction because it deals with the "here-and-now" is putting itself on. There is no fixed "here" and no fixed "now," only the continuous kaleidoscopic explosion of the evolving human mind in a total space-time universe that is itself evolving new realities around us faster than we can catch our breath.

To restrict your scope to one arbitrary reality at one thin moment of space-time is to strike a sputtering match in the infinite blackness and call it a star. So-called "mainstream" fiction is something that you write either by accident or by deliberately closing your mind to the multifaceted nature of modern reality.

How then did speculative fiction, this ancient and primal literature of the infinite possible, get squeezed and stunted and shoehorned half moribund into the "science fiction" genre? And what happens next, now that this literature is bubbling forth into the contemporary consciousness, despite a long period of critical scorn and mountains of bug-eyed monsters and bad packaging?

Literature-as-art cannot be divorced from the reality of art as the product of cranky human beings attempting to cope with an imperfect chameleon reality. Even if you live in an ivory tower, you've got to pay the rent, and the rent is always outrageous.

Art is the product of the interaction between the artist's mind and his environment as he staggers about like any other man, trying to maintain a favorable self-image, pay the bills, get laid, live like a king if he can, find love, destroy his enemies, keep his friends safe from harm, and carve some beauty out of the void as best he can. Everyone's life is a work of art—good or bad; heroic, comic, or tragic—and every work of art is the product of someone's life. That's why *great* art hits us where we really live.

So to understand what science fiction and speculative fiction are, how they got that way, what they are doing to us and we to them, and in what direction the whole gestalt is evolving, you've got to look at it for what it is in total reality: art flowing from the lives of human beings under evolutionary pressure.

"THE GOLDEN AGE"

While speculative fiction has a history as man's primal literature, science fiction as a commercial and packaging literary genre can trace its origins back to one man at one time in one place. In 1926, in New York City, a transplanted Luxembourger, Hugo Gernsback, started a magazine called *Amazing Stories,* dedicated to what he called "scientifiction." It was a classic, noble, Victorian idea. Since adolescent boys were forever reading trashy pulp magazines instead of "good literature" or scientific treatises, Papa Gernsback would sneak some scientific knowledge into their innocent little heads by incorporating the latest scientific notions into formula pulp adventure fiction.

Thus "scientifiction," first conceived as a thin adventure sugar-coating for the scientific enlightenment of the callow masses. In a similar frame of mind, years later, Hugo Gernsback would found a magazine called *Sexology,* aimed at bringing simple sexual enlightenment to poor benighted folk who almost literally didn't know their asses from their elbows. Noblesse oblige.

But what Gernsback didn't quite reckon with was that when you paid 1¢ or less a word for commercial adventure fiction, the stories were written by penny-a-word commercial hacks. The basic pulp adventure plot can be summarized quite simply: bad guy threatens to beat good guy, good guy finally wins. Run this through sagebrush and six-shooters, and you've got a western. Crank it through sleuth and murderer and you've got a detective story. The boys that first started writing "scientifiction" had been writing this way for years. When the new market opened up, these pulp hacks simply started grinding the same basic plot through spaceships,

alien planets, robots, and mad scientists. The rustlers
became space pirates or alien creatures, the private
eye became the upright young scientist or spaceman,
the minister's lovely daughter turned into the absent-
minded professor's daughter or assistant, and the
pulp machine rolled on.

Hugo Gernsback, for the most part, was not
really getting what he wanted. He wanted scientific
enlightenment packaged in adventure fiction, and
what he mainly got was adventure fiction with
pseudo-scientific trappings.

However, the fiction Gernsback actually called into
being *was* popular with readers, and competing
magazines began to spring up. There was something
about this crude "scientifiction" that struck a deep
chord in some young souls and drew them toward it
like a moth to a flame, like a knight to the Holy
Grail. By 1929 these readers were already organizing
themselves into science fiction fan clubs.

The "good literature" of the 1920s was out of touch
with the popular spirit of the times. The here-and-now
fixed-reality fiction which had dominated the
nineteenth century as the expression of the Victorian
mind's high opinion of itself had cast speculative
fiction and even fantasy into disrepute as "idle
rubbish." But fantasy is the natural state of human
consciousness. To maintain its opposite—absolutely
rigid literal-mindedness—takes tremendous and painful
effort, like constipating oneself by sheer act of will.
Everything we see or hear or feel flashes us associated
memories of other sounds or sights or feelings, so
that almost all sensory experience is colored by
emotion and rendered subjective. Further, our perceptions can be distorted by alcohol, drugs, fear, fatigue,
or joy. We walk at every moment through a wonderland
of living metaphor. Freud understood this sourly in
his grim nineteenth-century way, and James Joyce,
who gave this reality a direct and spontaneous

expression, was one of the early psychic citizens of the twentieth century.

But the literary establishment of the day had no brighter view of James Joyce than of "scientifiction," and perhaps the basic reason was the same, though the dirty names thrown were different. Scientifiction, like fantasy, like surrealism, and like Joyce, opened the door to anything. By so doing, scientifiction created an aesthetic effect that was totally alien to the Victorian mind: an ecstatic appreciation of the infinite possibilities of a universe that bubbled with at least as many realities as could be conceived of by the mind of man.

The literary critics of the day had no term for this mind-blowing, consciousness-expanding literary effect, but the early science fiction fans had a good one. They called it "Sense of Wonder."

Sense of Wonder was simultaneously a throwback to the basic appeal of the speculative fiction that had been dominant before the Age of Reason repressed the external expression of the internal human landscape and an early forerunner of the new style of consciousness which would come into full flower in the 1960s. Prior to the Age of Reason, fantasy, speculative fiction, expressed the existential position of the human mind as it interacted with a fairly stable environment full of knowable unknowns. In the true post-Age-of-Reason period, the 1960s and 1970s, speculative fiction would express the existential position of the human mind as it interacted with and was *constantly changed by* a well-known and well-understood world that began to go through changes so rapidly that realities began to overlap and coexist.

The single-reality fiction of the nineteenth century was an evolutionary digression, a dead end. By the 1920s and 1930s there was a generation of young Americans whose minds had been formed in an era of rapid and dramatic technological development.

Airplanes! Automobiles! Radio! Talking pictures!
Color photography! Early television! Magic had
re-entered the world through science and technology
and the only real literary expression of this drastic
reorientation of human consciousness was that
dreadfully written, formula-plotted adolescent
garbage—"science fiction."

Sense of Wonder was nothing less than the
charge the twentieth century produced as it blew
its way through the cobwebs and constrictions of
the nineteenth-century mind. No wonder science
fiction turned these kids on!

A scarce three years after its birth as a commercial
genre, science fiction had much more than a loyal
circle of readers. An embryo cult, a self-contained
subculture, had already begun to evolve around
it. There were already people who considered
themselves "science fiction fans," who published
amateur magazines called "fanzines," and who were
members of a nationwide tribe which called itself
"science fiction fandom."

Science fiction fandom was an utterly unique
development at the time. No school of literature, no
literary movement, had ever generated a subculture
before, creating a tribe out of its most dedicated
readers. Its birth was another distant forerunner of
the revolutions of the 1960s, when tribes and subcultures
formed around gurus and theories, rock music and
drugs, and even a single science fiction novel,
Stranger in a Strange Land by Robert A. Heinlein.

In the 1920s and 1930s science fiction was the
literature of the future in more ways than one.

Please understand, this first-generation science
fiction was godawful stuff. Not only was it crudely
written pulp adventure fiction, but the so-called
"scientific content" was mostly hot air. The pulp
writers simply took the scientific speculations of their
day, fictionalized them into artifacts, and used them

as props in their stories. When this got dull, they evolved the genre of "space opera": pseudo-Wagnerian, superpowered hugger-mugger, exploding planets, combat between whole galaxies, mythic conflicts between superhuman beings—Jungian fantasy, the straight uncut stuff.

Science fiction was beginning to appeal to two powerful forces in the minds of the youth of the day: the emerging technological spirit of the twentieth century and the urge to externalize inner mythic archetypal imagery which, in another place, was giving rise to that ultimate and ghastly Wagnerian space opera, Nazi Germany.

Frequently it appealed to both urges in the same individual. Magic and science were beginning to mate in the dark shrubbery in the minds of these early science fiction fans.

The midwife at the strange birth that resulted was John W. Campbell, Jr.

John W. Campbell, Jr., was the editor of *Astounding Science Fiction* and its later transmogrification, *Analog*, from 1937 till his death in 1971, and is generally considered the father of the so-called "Golden Age of Science Fiction" of the 1930s and 1940s. Of course, this "Golden Age" existed primarily in the minds of the aging fans of the 1950s and 1960s who had been young at the time. What Campbell actually did was call into being the first full-fledged modern science fiction.

Campbell was not a hack writer by profession. Rather, he came to the field from a different direction. He was trained as an engineer, but never actually worked in technology or science. As an editor of science fiction, he carried on a forty-year, love-hate-contempt-envy affair with the scientific establishment. Campbell's ideal (and no doubt his vision of himself) was the scientific visionary, the lone hero advancing the course of man's understanding and mastery of the universe through inspired personal effort: Faust as an existential hero in a reality, without a Mephistopheles.

Throughout the years Campbell championed dubious scientific and pseudo-scientific causes—extrasensory perception, anti-gravity devices, dowsing, space travel, astrological prediction of the weather, Dianetics—sometimes proving to be a genuine visionary, sometimes running up some blind alley. He was constantly sensitive to the scorn of "real" scientists whom he both envied and held in a kind of lofty contempt, but he was adamant in his support of what he believed were legitimate areas of scientific inquiry which the scientific establishment was stupidly and willfully ignoring.

Obviously, as the editor of a lurid pulp magazine filled with space fantasy that called itself "science fiction," Campbell was wide open to ridicule for the "science" in the fiction he printed. While the space opera that sold the magazine offended his sensibilities and embarrassed him, he knew that the straight Gernsbackian "scientifiction" would bore his readers silly.

Therefore, he lent his full and formidable charismatic powers to the fusion of space opera with true scientific speculation. He demanded that his writers justify the scientific credibility of every imaginary device they put in their stories. When they were not up to the task, he frequently supplied the scientific speculation for them and ultimately taught many writers to think this way themselves. He also demanded that plot and theme flow out of the scientific speculation in the stories, that human action and lives be shown as changed by the advance of science and technology. He was not above pulp plotting or pulp-level prose, but he wouldn't go for space-cattle rustlers on Mars. In Campbell's early story "Twilight," we have virtually a capsule of the ideas and thinking that filled over thirty years of *Astounding* and *Analog*, ideas that

Campbell freely donated to other writers when he gave up his writing career to become the first of science fiction's editorial giants, perhaps the single most influential editor in the history of the genre. How many of the multitude of ideas in this single short story have reappeared down through the years as premises for short stories, novelettes, and even whole novels!

Twilight

JOHN W. CAMPBELL, JR.

"Speaking of hitch-hikers," said Jim Bendell in a rather be-wildered way, "I picked up a man the other day that cer-tainly was a queer cuss." He laughed, but it wasn't a real laugh. "He told me the queerest yarn I ever heard. Most of them tell you how they lost their good jobs and tried to find work out here in the wide spaces of the West. They don't seem to realize how many people we have out here. They think all this great beautiful country is uninhabited."

Jim Bendell's a real estate man, and I knew how he could go on. That's his favorite line, you know. He's real worried because there's a lot of homesteading plots still open out in our state. He talks about the beautiful country, but he never went further into the desert than the edge of town. 'Fraid of it actually. So I sort of steered him back on the track.

"What did he claim, Jim? Prospector who couldn't find land to prospect?"

"That's not very funny, Bart. No; it wasn't only what he claimed. He didn't even claim it, just said it. You know, he didn't say it was true, he just said it. That's what gets me. I know it ain't true, but the way he said it— Oh, I don't know."

By which I knew he didn't. Jim Bendell's usually pretty careful about his English—real proud of it. When he slips, that means he's disturbed. Like the time he thought the rat-tlesnake was a stick of wood and wanted to put it on the fire.

Jim went on: And he had funny clothes, too. They looked like silver, but they were soft as silk. And at night they glowed just a little.

I picked him up about dusk. Really picked him up. He was lying off about ten feet from the South Road. I thought, at first, somebody had hit him, and then hadn't stopped. Didn't see him very clearly, you know. I picked him up, put him in the car, and started on. I had about three hundred miles to go, but I thought I could drop him at Warren Spring with Doc Vance. But he came to in about five minutes, and opened his eyes. He looked straight off, and he looked first at the car, then at the Moon. "Thank God!" he says, and then looks at me. It gave me a shock. He was beautiful. No; he was handsome.

He wasn't either one. He was magnificent. He was about six feet two, I think, and his hair was brown, with a touch of red-gold. It seemed like fine copper wire that's turned brown. It was crisp and curly. His forehead was wide, twice as wide as mine. His features were delicate, but tremendously impressive; his eyes were gray, like etched iron, and bigger than mine—a lot.

That suit he wore—it was more like a bathing suit with pajama trousers. His arms were long and muscled smoothly as an Indian's. He was white, though, tanned lightly with a golden, rather than a brown, tan.

But he was magnificent. Most beautiful man I ever saw. I don't know, damn it!

"Hello!" I said. "Have an accident?"

"No; not this time, at least."

And his voice was magnificent, too. It wasn't an ordinary voice. It sounded like an organ talking, only it was human.

"But maybe my mind isn't quite steady yet. I tried an experiment. Tell me what the date is, year and all, and let me see," he went on.

"Why—December 9, 1932," I said.

And it didn't please him. He didn't like it a bit. But the wry grin that came over his face gave way to a chuckle.

"Over a thousand—" he says reminiscently. "Not as bad as seven million. I shouldn't complain."

"Seven million what?"

"Years," he said, steadily enough. Like he meant it. "I tried an experiment once. Or I will try it. Now I'll have to try again. The experiment was—in 3059. I'd just finished the release experiment. Testing space then. Time—it wasn't that,

I still believe. It was space. I felt myself caught in that field, but I couldn't pull away. Field gamma-H 481, intensity 935 in the Pellman range. It sucked me in, and I went out.

"I think it took a short cut through space to the position the solar system will occupy. Through a higher dimension, effecting a speed exceeding light and throwing me into the future plane."

He wasn't telling me, you know. He was just thinking out loud. Then he began to realize I was there.

"I couldn't read their instruments, seven million years of evolution changed everything. So I overshot my mark a little coming back. I belong in 3059.

"But tell me, what's the latest scientific invention of this year?"

He startled me so, I answered almost before I thought.

"Why, television, I guess. And radio and airplanes."

"Radio—good. They will have instruments."

"But see here—who are you?"

"Ah—I'm sorry. I forgot," he replied in that organ voice of his. "I am Ares Sen Kenlin. And you?"

"James Waters Bendell."

"Waters—what does that mean? I do not recognize it."

"Why—it's a name, of course. Why should you recognize it?"

"I see—you have not the classification, then. 'Sen' stands for science."

"Where did you come from, Mr. Kenlin?"

"Come from?" He smiled, and his voice was slow and soft. "I came out of space across seven million years or more. They had lost count—the men had. The machines had eliminated the unneeded service. They didn't know what year it was. But before that—my home is in Neva'th City in the 3059."

That's when I began to think he was a nut.

"I was an experimenter," he went on. "Science, as I have said. My father was a scientist, too, but in human genetics. I myself am an experiment. He proved his point, and all the world followed suit. I was the first of the new race.

"The new race—oh, holy destiny—what has—what will—

"What is its end? I have seen it—almost. I saw them—the little men—bewildered—lost. And the machines. Must it be—can't anything sway it?

"Listen—I heard this song."

He sang the song. Then he didn't have to tell me about the people. I knew them. I could hear their voices, in the queer, crackling, un-English words. I could read their bewildered longings. It was in a minor key, I think. It called, it called and asked, and hunted hopelessly. And over it all the steady rumble and whine of the unknown, forgotten machines.

The machines that couldn't stop, because they had been started, and the little men had forgotten how to stop them, or even what they were for, looking at them and listening —and wondering. They couldn't read or write any more, and the language had changed, you see, so that the phonic records of their ancestors meant nothing to them.

But that song went on, and they wondered. And they looked out across space and they saw the warm, friendly stars—too far away. Nine planets they knew and inhabited. And locked by infinite distance, they couldn't see another race, a new life.

And through it all—two things. The machines. Bewildered forgetfulness. And maybe one more. Why?

That was the song, and it made me cold. It shouldn't be sung around people of today. It almost killed something. It seemed to kill hope. After that song—I—well, I believed him.

When he finished the song, he didn't talk for a while. Then he sort of shook himself.

You won't understand (he continued). Not yet—but I have seen them. They stand about, like misshapen men with huge heads. But their heads contain only brains. They had machines that could think—but somebody turned them off a long time ago, and no one knew how to start them again. That was the trouble with them. They had wonderful brains. Far better than yours or mine. But it must have been millions of years ago when they were turned off, too, and they just haven't thought since then. Kindly little people. That was all they knew.

When I slipped into that field it grabbed me like a gravitational field whirling a space transport down to a planet.
It sucked me in—and through. Only the other side must have
been seven million years in the future. That's where I was.
It must have been in exactly the same spot on Earth's surface,
but I never knew why.

It was night then, and I saw the city a little way off. The
Moon was shining on it, and the whole scene looked wrong.
You see, in seven million years, men had done a lot with the
positions of the planetary bodies, what with moving space
liners, clearing lanes through the asteroids, and such. And
seven million years is long enough for natural things to
change positions a little. The Moon must have been fifty
thousand miles farther out. And it was rotating on its axis.
I lay there awhile and watched it. Even the stars were different.

There were ships going out of the city. Back and forth,
like things sliding along a wire, but there was only a wire of
force, of course. Part of the city, the lower part, was brightly
lighted with what must have been mercury vapor glow, I
decided. Blue-green. I felt sure men didn't live there—the
light was wrong for eyes. But the top of the city was so
sparsely lighted.

Then I saw something coming down out of the sky. It
was brightly lighted. A huge globe, and it sank straight to
the center of the great black-and-silver mass of the city.

I don't know what it was, but even then I knew the city
was deserted. Strange that I could even imagine that, I who
had never seen a deserted city before. But I walked the
fifteen miles over to it and entered it. There were machines
going about the streets, repair machines, you know. They
couldn't understand that the city didn't need to go on functioning, so they were still working. I found a taxi machine
that seemed fairly familiar. It had a manual control that I
could work.

I don't know how long that city had been deserted. Some
of the men from the other cities said it was a hundred and
fifty thousand years. Some went as high as three hundred
thousand years. Three hundred thousand years since human

foot had been in that city. The taxi machine was in perfect condition, functioned at once. It was clean, and the city
was clean and orderly. I saw a restaurant and I was hungry.
Hungrier still for humans to speak to. There were none, of
course, but I didn't know.

The restaurant had the food displayed directly, and I made
a choice. The food was three hundred thousand years old,
I suppose, I didn't know, and the machines that served it to
me didn't care, for they made things synthetically, you see,
and perfectly. When the builders made those cities, they
forgot one thing. They didn't realize that things shouldn't go
on forever.

It took me six months to make my apparatus. And near
the end I was ready to go; and, from seeing those machines
go blindly, perfectly, on in orbits of their duties with the
tireless, ceaseless perfection their designers had incorporated in them, long after those designers and their sons, and
their sons' sons had no use for them—

When Earth is cold, and the Sun has died out, those machines will go on. When Earth begins to crack and break,
those perfect, ceaseless machines will try to repair her—

I left the restaurant and cruised about the city in the taxi.
The machine had a little, electric-power motor, I believe,
but it gained its power from the great central power radiator.
I knew before long that I was far in the future. The city was
divided into two sections, a section of many strata where
machines functioned smoothly, save for a deep humming beat
that echoed through the whole city like a vast unending song
of power. The entire metal framework of the place echoed
with it, transmitted it, hummed with it. But it was soft
and restful, a reassuring beat.

There must have been thirty levels above ground, and
twenty more below, a solid block of metal walls and metal
floors and metal and glass and force machines. The only
light was the blue-green glow of the mercury vapor arcs.
The light of mercury vapor is rich in high-energy-quanta,
which stimulate the alkali metal atoms to photo-electric activity. Or perhaps that is beyond the science of your day? I
have forgotten.

But they had used that light because many of their worker machines needed sight. The machines were marvelous. For five hours I wandered through the vast power plant on the very lowest level, watching them, and because there was motion, and that pseudo-mechanical life, I felt less alone.

The generators I saw were a development of the release I had discovered—when? The release of the energy of matter, I mean, and I knew when I saw that for what countless ages they could continue.

The entire lower block of the city was given over to the machines. Thousands. But most of them seemed idle, or, at most, running under light load. I recognized a telephone apparatus, and not a single signal came through. There was no life in the city. Yet when I pressed a little stud beside the screen on one side of the room, the machine began working instantly. It was ready. Only no one needed it any more. The men knew how to die, and be dead, but the machines didn't.

Finally I went up to the top of the city, the upper level. It was a paradise.

There were shrubs and trees and parks, glowing in the soft light that they had learned to make in the very air. They had learned it five million years or more before. Two million years ago they forgot. But the machines didn't, and they were still making it. It hung in the air, soft, silvery light, slightly rosy, and the gardens were shadowy with it. There were no machines here now, but I knew that in daylight they must come out and work on those gardens, keeping them a paradise for masters who had died, and stopped moving, as they could not.

In the desert outside the city it had been cool, and very dry. Here the air was soft, warm and sweet with the scent of blooms that men had spent several hundreds of thousands of years perfecting.

Then somewhere music began. It began in the air, and spread softly through it. The Moon was just setting now, and as it set, the rosy-silver glow waned and the music grew stronger.

It came from everywhere and from nowhere. It was within

me. I do not know how they did it. And I do not know how such music could be written.

Savages make music too simple to be beautiful, but it is stirring. Semisavages write music beautifully simple, and simply beautiful. Your Negro music was your best. They knew music when they heard it and sang it as they felt it. Semicivilized peoples write great music. They are proud of their music, and make sure it is known for great music. They make it so great it is top-heavy.

I had always thought our music good. But that which came through the air was the song of triumph, sung by a mature race, the race of man in its full triumph! It was man singing his triumph in majestic sound that swept me up; it showed me what lay before me; it carried me on.

And it died in the air as I looked at the deserted city. The machines should have forgotten that song. Their masters had, long before.

I came to what must have been one of their homes; it was a dimly-seen doorway in the dusky light, but as I stepped up to it, the lights which had not functioned in three hundred thousand years illuminated it for me with a green-white glow, like a firefly, and I stepped into the room beyond. Instantly something happened to the air in the doorway behind me; it was as opaque as milk. The room in which I stood was a room of metal and stone. The stone was some jet-black substance with the finish of velvet, and the metals were silver and gold. There was a rug on the floor, a rug of just such material as I am wearing now, but thicker and softer. There were divans about the room, low and covered with these soft metallic materials. They were black and gold and silver, too.

I had never seen anything like that. I never shall again, I suppose, and my language and yours were not made to describe it.

The builders of that city had right and reason to sing that song of sweeping triumph, triumph that swept them over the nine planets and the fifteen habitable moons.

But they weren't there any more, and I wanted to leave. I thought of a plan and went to a subtelephone office to examine a map I had seen. The old World looked much the same. Seven or even seventy million years don't mean much to old Mother Earth. She may even succeed in wearing down those marvelous machine cities. She can wait a hundred million or a thousand million years before she is beaten.

I tried calling different city centers shown on the map. I had quickly learned the system when I examined the central apparatus.

I tried once—twice—thrice—a round dozen times. Yawk City, Lunon City, Paree, Shkago, Singpor, others. I was beginning to feel that there were no more men on all earth. And I felt crushed, as at each city the machines replied and did my bidding. The machines were there in each of those far vaster cities, for I was in the Neva City of their time. A small city. Yawk City was more than eight hundred kilometers in diameter.

In each city I tried several numbers. Then I tried San Frisco. There was someone there, and a voice answered and the picture of a human appeared on the little glowing screen. I could see him start and stare in surprise at me. Then he started speaking to me. I couldn't understand, of course. I can understand your speech, and you mine, because your speech of this day is largely recorded on records of various types and has influenced our pronunciation.

Some things are changed; names of cities, particularly, because names of cities are apt to be polysyllabic, and used a great deal. People tend to elide them, shorten them. I am in—Nee-vah-dah—as you would say? We say only Neva. And Yawk State. But it is Ohio and Iowa still. Over a thousand years, effects were small on words, because they were recorded.

But seven million years had passed, and the men had forgotten the old records, used them less as time went on, and their speech varied till the time came when they could no longer understand the records. They were not written any more, of course.

Some men must have arisen occasionally among that last of the race and sought for knowledge, but it was denied them. An ancient writing can be translated if some basic rule is found. An ancient voice though—and when the race has forgotten the laws of science and the labor of mind.

So his speech was strange to me as he answered over that circuit. His voice was high in pitch, his words liquid, his tones sweet. It was almost a song as he spoke. He was excited and called others. I could not understand them, but I knew where they were. I could go to them.

So I went down from the paradise gardens, and as I prepared to leave, I saw dawn in the sky. The strange-bright stars winked and twinkled and faded. Only one bright rising star was familiar—Venus. She shone golden now. Finally, as I stood watching for the first time that strange heaven, I began to understand what had first impressed me with the wrongness of the view. The stars, you see, were all different.

In my time—and yours, the solar system is a lone wanderer that by chance is passing across an intersection point of Galactic traffic. The stars we see at night are the stars of moving clusters, you know. In fact our system is passing through the heart of the Ursa Major group. Half a dozen other groups center within five hundred light-years of us.

But during those seven millions of years, the Sun had moved out of the group. The heavens were almost empty to the eye. Only here and there shone a single faint star. And across the vast sweep of black sky swung the band of the Milky Way. The sky was empty.

That must have been another thing those men meant in their songs—felt in their hearts. Loneliness—not even the close, friendly stars. We have stars within half a dozen light-years. They told me that their instruments, which gave directly the distance to any star, showed that the nearest was one hundred and fifty light-years away. It was enormously bright. Brighter even than Sirius of our heavens. And that made it even less friendly, because it was a blue-white supergiant. Our sun would have served as a satellite for that star.

I stood there and watched the lingering rose-silver glow die as the powerful blood-red light of the Sun swept over the horizon. I knew by the stars now, that it must have been several millions of years since my day; since I had last seen the

Sun sweep up. And that blood-red light made me wonder if the Sun itself was dying.

An edge of it appeared, blood-red and huge. It swung up, and the color faded, till in half an hour it was the familiar yellow-gold disk.

It hadn't changed in all that time.

I had been foolish to think that it would. Seven million years —that is nothing to Earth, how much less to the Sun? Some two thousand thousand thousand times it had risen since I last saw it rise. Two thousand thousand thousand days. If it had been that many years—I might have noticed a change.

The universe moves slowly. Only life is not enduring; only life changes swiftly. Eight short millions of years. Eight days in the life of Earth—and the race was dying. It had left something: machines. But they would die, too, even though they could not understand. So I felt. I—may have changed that. I will tell you. Later.

For when the Sun was up, I looked again at the sky and the ground, some fifty floors below. I had come to the edge of the city.

Machines were moving on that ground, leveling it, perhaps. A great wide line of gray stretched off across the level desert straight to the east. I had seen it glowing faintly before the Sun rose—a roadway for ground machines. There was no traffic on it.

I saw an airship slip in from the east. It came with a soft, muttering whine of air, like a child complaining in sleep; it grew to my eyes like an expanding balloon. It was huge when it settled in a great port-slip in the city below. I could hear now the clang and mutter of machines, working on the materials brought in, no doubt. The machines had ordered raw materials. The machines in other cities had supplied. The freight machines had carried them here.

San Frisco and Jacksville were the only two cities on North America still used. But the machines went on in all the others, because they couldn't stop. They hadn't been ordered to.

Then high above, something appeared, and from the city beneath me, from a center section, three small spheres rose. They, like the freight ship, had no visible driving mechanisms. The point in the sky above, like a black star in a blue space, had grown to a moon. The three spheres met it high above. Then together they descended and lowered into the center of the city, where I could not see them.

It was freight transport from Venus. The one I had seen land the night before had come from Mars, I learned.

I moved after that and looked for some sort of a taxi-plane. They had none that I recognized in scouting about the city. I searched the higher levels, and here and there saw deserted ships, but far too large for me, and without controls.

It was nearly noon—and I ate again. The food was good.

I knew then that this was a city of the dead ashes of human hopes. The hopes not of *a* race, not the whites, nor the yellows, nor the blacks, but the human race. I was mad to leave the city. I was afraid to try the ground road to the east, for the taxi I drove was powered from some source in the city, and I knew it would fail before many miles.

It was afternoon when I found a small hangar near the outer wall of the vast city. It contained three ships. I had been searching through the lower strata of the human section—the upper part. There were restaurants and shops and theatres there. I entered one place where, at my entrance, soft music began, and colors and forms began to rise on a screen before me.

They were the triumph songs in form and sound and color of a mature race, a race that had marched steadily upward through five millions of years—and didn't see the path that faded out ahead, when they were dead and stopped, and the city itself was dead—but hadn't stopped. I hastened out of there—and the song that had not been sung in three hundred thousand years died behind me.

But I found the hangar. It was a private one, likely. Three ships. One must have been fifty feet long and fifteen in diameter. It was a yacht, a space yacht, probably. One was some fifteen feet long and five feet in diameter. That must have been the family air machine. The third was a tiny thing, little more than ten feet long and two in diameter. I had to lie down within it, evidently.

There was a periscope device that gave me a view ahead

and almost directly above. A window that permitted me to
see what lay below—and a device that moved a map under
a frosted-glass screen and projected it onto the screen in such
a way that the cross-hairs of the screen always marked my
position.

I spent half an hour attempting to understand what the
makers of that ship had made. But the men who made that
were men who held behind them the science and knowledge
of five millions of years and the perfect machines of those
ages. I saw the release mechanism that powered it. I understood the principles of that and, vaguely, the mechanics.
But there were no conductors, only pale beams that pulsed
so swiftly you could hardly catch the pulsations from the corner of the eye. They had been glowing and pulsating, some
half dozen of them, for three hundred thousand years at
least; probably more.

I entered the machine, and instantly half a dozen more
beams sprang into being; there was a slight suggestion of a
quiver, and a queer strain ran through my body. I understood in an instant, for the machine was resting on gravity
nullifiers. That had been my hope when I worked on the
space fields I discovered after the release.

But they had had it for millions of years before they built
that perfect deathless machine. My weight entering it had
forced it to readjust itself and simultaneously to prepare for
operation. Within, an artificial gravity equal to that of Earth
had gripped me, and the neutral zone between the outside
and the interior had caused the strain.

The machine was ready. It was fully fueled. You see they
were equipped to tell automatically their wants and needs.
They were almost living things, every one. A caretaker machine kept them supplied, adjusted, even repaired them when
need be, and when possible. If it was not, I learned later, they
were carried away in a service truck that came automatically;
replaced by an exactly similar machine; and carried to the
shops where they were made, and automatic machines made
them over.

The machine waited patiently for me to start. The controls
were simple, obvious. There was a lever at the left that you

pushed forward to move forward, pulled back to go back. On the right a horizontal, pivoted bar. If you swung it left, the ship spun left; if right, the ship spun right. If tipped up, the ship followed it, and likewise for all motions other than backward and forward. Raising it bodily raised the ship, as depressing it depressed the ship.

I lifted it slightly, a needle moved a bit on a gauge comfortably before my eyes as I lay there, and the floor dropped beneath me. I pulled the other control back, and the ship gathered speed as it moved gently out into the open. Releasing both controls into neutral, the machine continued till it stopped at the same elevation, the motion absorbed by air friction. I turned it about, and another dial before my eyes moved, showing my position. I could not read it, though. The map did not move, as I had hoped it would. So I started toward what I felt was west.

I could feel no acceleration in that marvelous machine. The ground simply began leaping backward, and in a moment the city was gone. The map unrolled rapidly beneath me now, and I saw that I was moving south of west. I turned northward slightly, and watched the compass. Soon I understood that, too, and the ship sped on.

I had become too interested in the map and the compass, for suddenly there was a sharp buzz and, without my volition, the machine rose and swung to the north. There was a mountain ahead of me; I had not seen, but the ship had.

I noticed then what I should have seen before—two little knobs that could move the map. I started to move them and heard a sharp clicking, and the pace of the ship began decreasing. A moment and it had steadied at a considerably lower speed, the machine swinging to a new course. I tried to right it, but to my amazement the controls did not affect it.

It was the map, you see. It would either follow the course, or the course would follow it. I had moved it and the machine had taken over control of its own accord. There was a little button I could have pushed—but I didn't know. I couldn't control the ship until it finally came to rest and lowered itself to a stop six inches from the ground in the center of what

must have been the ruins of a great city. Sacramento, probably.

I understood now, so I adjusted the map for San Frisco,
and the ship went on at once. It steered itself around a mass
of broken stone, turned back to its course, and headed on, a
bullet-shaped, self-controlled dart.

It didn't descend when it reached San Frisco. It simply
hung in the air and sounded a soft musical hum. Twice. Then
I waited, too, and looked down.

There were people here. I saw the humans of that age for
the first time. They were little men—bewildered—dwarfed,
with heads disproportionately large. But not extremely so.

Their eyes impressed me most. They were huge, and when
they looked at me there was a power in them that seemed
sleeping, but too deeply to be roused.

I took the manual controls then and landed. And no
sooner had I got out, than the ship rose automatically and
started off by itself. They had automatic parking devices.
The ship had gone to a public hangar, the nearest, where it
would be automatically serviced and cared for. There was a
little call set I should have taken with me when I got out.
Then I could have pressed a button and called it to me—
wherever I was in that city.

The people about me began talking—singing almost—
among themselves. Others were coming up leisurely. Men
and women—but there seemed no old and few young. What
few young there were, were treated almost with respect,
carefully taken care of lest a careless footstep on their toes
or a careless step knock them down.

There was reason, you see. They lived a tremendous
time. Some lived as long as three thousand years. Then—they
simply died. They didn't grow old, and it never had been
learned why people died as they did. The heart stopped, the
brain ceased thought—and they died. But the young children,
children not yet mature, were treated with the utmost care.
But one child was born in the course of a month in that city
of one hundred thousand people. The human race was growing sterile.

And I have told you that they were lonely? Their loneliness

was beyond hope. For, you see, as man strode toward maturity, he destroyed all forms of life that menaced him. Disease. Insects. Then the last of the insects, and finally the last of the man-eating animals.

The balance of nature was destroyed then, so they had to go on. It was like the machines. They started them—and now they can't stop. They started destroying life—and now it wouldn't stop. So they had to destroy weeds of all sorts, then many formerly harmless plants. Then the herbivora, too, the deer and the antelope and the rabbit and the horse. They were a menace, they attacked man's machine-tended crops. Man was still eating natural foods.

You can understand. The thing was beyond their control. In the end they killed off the denizens of the sea, also, in self-defense. Without the many creatures that had kept them in check, they were swarming beyond bounds. And the time had come when synthetic foods replaced natural. The air was purified of all life about two and a half million years after our day, all microscopic life.

That meant that the water, too, must be purified. It was— and then came the end of life in the ocean. There were minute organisms that lived on bacterial forms, and tiny fish that lived on the minute organisms, and small fish that lived on the tiny fish, and big fish that lived on the small fish—and the beginning of the chain was gone. The sea was devoid of life in a generation. That meant about one thousand and five hundred years to them. Even the sea plants had gone.

And on all Earth there was only man and the organisms he had protected—the plants he wanted for decoration, and certain ultra-hygienic pets, as long-lived as their masters. Dogs. They must have been remarkable animals. Man was reaching his maturity then, and his animal friend, the friend that had followed him through a thousand millenniums to your day and mine, and another four thousand millenniums to the day of man's early maturity, had grown in intelligence. In an ancient museum—a wonderful place, for they had, perfectly preserved, the body of a great leader of mankind who had died five and a half million years before I saw him—in that museum, deserted then, I saw one of those canines. His skull was nearly as large as mine. They had simple ground machines that dogs could be trained to drive, and they held races in which the dogs drove those machines.

Then man reached his full maturity. It extended over a period of a full million years. So tremendously did he stride ahead, the dog ceased to be a companion. Less and less were they wanted. When the million years had passed, and man's decline began, the dog was gone. It had died out.

And now this last dwindling group of men still in the system had no other life form to make its successor. Always before when one civilization toppled, on its ashes rose a new one. Now there was but one civilization, and all other races, even other species, were gone save in the plants. And man was too far along in his old age to bring intelligence and mobility from the plants. Perhaps he could have in his prime.

Other worlds were flooded with man during that million years—the million years. Every planet and every moon of the system had its quota of men. Now only the planets had their populations, the moons had been deserted. Pluto had been left before I landed, and men were coming from Neptune, moving in toward the Sun, and the home planet, while I was there. Strangely quiet men, viewing, most of them, for the first time, the planet that had given their race life.

But as I stepped from that ship and watched it rise away from me, I saw why the race of man was dying. I looked back at the faces of those men, and on them I read the answer. There was one single quality gone from the still-great minds—minds far greater than yours or mine. I had to have the help of one of them in solving some of my problems. In space, you know, there are twenty coordinates, ten of which are zero, six of which have fixed values, and the four others represent our changing, familiar dimensions in space-time. That means that integrations must proceed in not double, or triple, or quadruple—but ten integrations.

It must have taken me too long. I would never have solved all the problems I must work out. I could not use their mathematics machines; and mine, of course, were seven million years in the past. But one of those men was interested and helped me. He did quadruple and quintuple integration, even quadruple integration between varying exponential limits—in his head.

When I asked him to. For the one thing that had made man great had left him. As I looked in their faces and eyes on landing I knew it. They looked at me, interested at this rather unusual-looking stranger—and went on. They had come to see the arrival of a ship. A rare event, you see. But they were merely welcoming me in a friendly fashion. They were not curious! Man had lost the instinct of curiosity.

Oh, not entirely! They wondered at the machines, they wondered at the stars. But they did nothing about it. It was not wholly lost to them yet, but nearly. It was dying. In the six short months I stayed with them, I learned more than they had learned in the two or even three thousand years they had lived among the machines.

Can you appreciate the crushing loneliness it brought to me? I, who love science, who see in it, or have seen in it, the salvation, the raising of mankind—to see those wondrous machines, of man's triumphant maturity, forgotten and misunderstood. The wondrous, perfect machines that tended, protected, and cared for those gentle, kindly people who had—forgotten.

They were lost among it. The city was a magnificent ruin to them, a thing that rose stupendous about them. Something not understood, a thing that was of the nature of the world. It was. It had not been made; it simply was. Just as the mountains and the deserts and the waters of the seas.

Do you understand—can you see that the time since those machines were new was longer than the time from our day to the birth of the race? Do we know the legends of our first ancestors? Do we remember their lore of forest and cave? The secret of chipping a flint till it had a sharp-cutting edge? The secret of trailing and killing a saber-toothed tiger without being killed oneself?

They were now in similar straits, though the time had been longer, because the languages had taken a long step toward perfection, and because the machines maintained everything for them through generation after generation.

Why, the entire planet of Pluto had been deserted—yet on Pluto the largest mines of one of their metals were located; the machines still functioned. A perfect unity existed throughout the system. A unified system of perfect machines.

And all those people knew was to do a certain thing to a certain lever produced certain results. Just as men in the Middle Ages knew that to take a certain material, wood, and place it in contact with other pieces of wood heated red, would cause the wood to disappear, and become heat. They did not understand that wood was being oxidized with the release of the heat of formation of carbon dioxide and water. So those people did not understand the things that fed and clothed and carried them.

I stayed with them there for three days. And then I went to Jacksville. Yawk City, too. That was enormous. It stretched over—well, from well north of where Boston is today to well south of Washington—that was what they called Yawk City.

I never believed that, when he said it, said Jim, interrupting himself. I knew he didn't. If he had I think he'd have bought land somewhere along there and held for a rise in value. I know Jim. He'd have the idea that seven million years was something like seven hundred, and maybe his great-grandchildren would be able to sell it.

Anyway, went on Jim, he said it was all because the cities had spread so. Boston spread south. Washington, north. And Yawk City spread all over. And the cities between grew into them.

And it was all one vast machine. It was perfectly ordered and perfectly neat. They had a transportation system that took me from the North End to the South End in three minutes. I timed it. They had learned to neutralize acceleration.

Then I took one of the great space liners to Neptune. There were still some running. Some people, you see, were coming the other way.

The ship was huge. Mostly it was a freight liner. It floated up from Earth, a great metal cylinder three quarters of a mile long, and a quarter of a mile in diameter. Outside the atmosphere it began to accelerate. I could see Earth dwindle. I have ridden one of our own liners to Mars, and it took me, in

3048, five days. In half an hour on this liner Earth was just a star, with a smaller, dimmer star near it. In an hour we passed Mars. Eight hours later we landed on Neptune. M'reen was the city. Large as the Yawk City of my day—and no one living there.

The planet was cold and dark—horribly cold. The sun was a tiny, pale disk, heatless and almost lightless. But the city was perfectly comfortable. The air was fresh and cool, moist with the scent of growing blossoms, perfumed with them. And the whole giant metal framework trembled just slightly with the humming, powerful beat of the mighty machines that had made and cared for it.

I learned from records I deciphered, because of my knowledge of the ancient tongue that their tongue was based on, and the tongue of that day when man was dying, that the city was built three million, seven hundred and thirty thousand, one hundred and fifty years after my birth. Not a machine had been touched by the hand of man since that day.

Yet the air was perfect for man. And the warm, rose-silver glow hung in the air here and supplied the only illumination.

I visited some of their other cities where there were men. And there, on the retreating outskirts of man's domain, I first heard the Song of Longings, as I called it.

And another, The Song of Forgotten Memories. Listen:

He sang another of those songs. There's one thing I know, declared Jim. That bewildered note was stronger in his voice, and by that time I guess I pretty well understood his feelings. Because, you have to remember, I heard it only secondhand from an ordinary man, and Jim had heard it from an eye-and-ear witness that was not ordinary, and heard it in that organ voice. Anyway, I guess Jim was right when he said: "He wasn't any ordinary man." No ordinary man could think of those songs. They weren't right. When he sang that song, it was full of more of those plaintive minors. I could feel him searching his mind for something he had forgotten, something he desperately wanted to remember—something he knew he should have known—and I felt it eternally elude him. I felt it get further away from him as he sang. I heard that lonely, frantic searcher attempting to recall that thing—that thing that would save him.

And I heard him give a little sob of defeat—and the song ended. Jim tried a few notes. He hasn't a good ear for music —but that was too powerful to forget. Just a few hummed notes. Jim hasn't much imagination, I guess, or when that man of the future sang to him he would have gone mad. It shouldn't be sung to modern men; it isn't meant for them. You've heard those heart-rending cries some animals give, like human cries, almost? A loon, now—he sounds like a lunatic being murdered horribly.

That's just unpleasant. That song made you feel just exactly what the singer meant—because it didn't just sound human—it was human. It was the essence of humanity's last defeat, I guess. You always feel sorry for the chap who loses after trying hard. Well, you could feel the whole of humanity trying hard—and losing. And you knew they couldn't afford to lose, because they couldn't try again.

He said he'd been interested before. And still not wholly upset by these machines that couldn't stop. But that was too much for him.

I knew after that, he said, that these weren't men I could live among. They were dying men, and I was alive with the youth of the race. They looked at me with the same longing, hopeless wonder with which they looked at the stars and the machines. They knew what I was, but couldn't understand.

I began to work on leaving.

It took six months. It was hard because my instruments were gone, of course, and theirs didn't read in the same units. And there were few instruments, anyway. The machines didn't read instruments; they acted on them. They were sensory organs to them.

But Reo Lantal helped where he could. And I came back.

I did just one thing before I left that may help. I may even try to get back there sometime. To see, you know.

I said they had machines that could really think? But that someone had stopped them a long time ago, and no one knew how to start them?

I found some records and deciphered them. I started one

of the last and best of them and started it on a great problem. It is only fitting it should be done. The machine can work on it, not for a thousand years, but for a million, if it must.

I started five of them actually, and connected them together as the records directed.

They are trying to make a machine with something that man had lost. It sounds rather comical. But stop to think before you laugh. And remember that Earth as I saw it from the ground level of Neva City just before Reo Lantal threw the switch.

Twilight—the sun has set. The desert out beyond, in its mystic, changing colors. The great, metal city rising straight-walled to the human city above, broken by spires and towers and great trees with scented blossoms. The silvery-rose glow in the paradise of gardens above.

And all the great city-structure throbbing and humming to the steady gentle beat of perfect, deathless machines built more than three million years before—and never touched since that time by human hands. And they go on. The dead city. The men that have lived, and hoped, and built—and died to leave behind them those little men who can only wonder and look and long for a forgotten kind of companionship. They wander through the vast cities their ancestors built, knowing less of them than the machines themselves.

And the songs. Those tell the story best, I think. Little, hopeless, wondering men amid vast unknowing, blind machines that started three million years before—and just never know how to stop. They are dead—and can't die and be still.

So I brought another machine to life, and set it to a task which, in time to come, it will perform.

I ordered it to make a machine which would have what man had lost. A curious machine.

And then I wanted to leave quickly and go back. I had been born in the first full light of man's day. I did not belong in the lingering, dying glow of man's twilight.

So I came back. A little too far back. But it will not take me long to return—accurately this time.

"Well, that was his story," Jim said. "He didn't *tell* me it was true—didn't say anything about it. And he had me thinking so hard I didn't even see him get off in Reno when we stopped for gas.

"But—he wasn't an ordinary man," repeated Jim, in a rather belligerent tone.

Jim claims he doesn't believe the yarn, you know. But he does; that's why he always acts so determined about it when he says the stranger wasn't an ordinary man.

No, he wasn't, I guess. I think he lived and died, too, probably, sometime in the thirty-first century. And I think he saw the twilight of the race, too.

by JOHN W. CAMPBELL, JR.
Who Goes There?
The Astounding Science Fiction Reader (editor)

By the beginning of the 1940s John Campbell had created a stable of writers that was something new under the sun: not pulp hacks cynically churning out scientifiction and space opera like yard goods, nor yet writers fully conscious of general literary values, but idealistic science fiction writers writing science fiction. During the 1930s and 1940s Campbell had nurtured this first generation of truly dedicated science fiction writers, men who viewed it as more than a way to make a precarious living, as something of absolute importance.

A strange and unconventional crew they were, too, these so-called "Giants of the Golden Age of Science Fiction." A. E. Van Vogt wrote a novel called *Slan* which fused Campbell's predilection for extrasensory perception with the Nietzschean superman and produced one of the new archetypes of science fiction, the human mutant, the next step after man. While Van Vogt's prose left much to be desired and his plots tended to be supercomplicated and internally self-contradictory at novel length, his work dealt with the forefronts of human evolution, and he caused science fiction to look not merely at the future evolution of science and technology but at the future of the human mind and the human species. His short stories, of which "The Enchanted Village" is perhaps the best, often had a clarity and focus which many of his novels lacked.

Robert A. Heinlein was a former naval officer, trained in engineering and perhaps the closest to Campbell in his ambivalence towards authority. An authoritarian personality by inclination and training, he nevertheless betrayed in his work a feeling that the rightful place of the world's natural aristocrats had been usurped by fools and parvenus. Although his prose was utterly pedestrian and his characterization shallow even for science fiction, his amazing faculty for visualizing the myriad details of future worlds enabled him to draw the reader into his fictional universes with a near-schizoid power that transcended mere literary effect. If a reader was the least bit prone to schizoid musings (and who isn't at one time or another), Heinlein could warp him into a fictional reality, send him on a trip. He sent a lot of people on a trip in the 1960s with a book called *Stranger in a Strange Land.* Heinlein introduced the messianic hero and the messianic novel into the repertoire of science fiction, and the world hasn't been the same since.

Isaac Asimov worked his way through college to a Ph.D. in chemistry by writing science fiction. He first made his mark with a long, multi-episode space opera, *The Foundation Trilogy,* which fictionalized the millennial rise, decline, and rebirth of a galactic empire along overtly Spenglerian lines. Later, he wrote a long series of short stories and novels about robots which, with occasional exceptions like Lester del Rey's powerfully human "Helen O'Loy," froze the subject into a rather sterile Asimovian iconography for nearly twenty years. Ironically, his best novels, such as *The Naked Sun* and *The Caves of Steel,* and his best short story, "Nightfall," never quite achieved the fame of the more superficial work which generated his huge reputation.

The husband-and-wife team of Henry Kuttner and C. L. Moore, writing under numerous pseudonyms, churned out a lot of superficial work, but also produced short fiction of great sophistication and power. Toward the end of the 1930s Theodore Sturgeon's early work began to appear.

The "Golden Age" of the 1930s and 1940s may not have been the pinnacle of science fiction that the aging science fiction fans of the 1950s and 1960s viewed it as through the golden haze of nostalgia's hindsight, but it did mark the emergence of writers of some substance within the science fiction genre, and it did produce some works which will live on. Rather than a fulfillment of science fiction's promise, it was the dawn of truly modern science fiction, the first tentative reawakenings of serious speculative fiction within the commercial genre created by Hugo Gernsback.

The Enchanted Village

A. E. VAN VOGT

"Explorers of a new frontier" they had been called before they left for Mars.

For a while, after the ship crashed into a Martian desert, killing all on board except—miraculously—this one man, Bill Jenner spat the words occasionally into the constant, sand-laden wind. He despised himself for the pride he had felt when he first heard them.

His fury faded with each mile that he walked, and his black grief for his friends became a gray ache. Slowly he realized that he had made a ruinous misjudgment.

He had underestimated the speed at which the rocketship had been traveling. He'd guessed that he would have to walk three hundred miles to reach the shallow, polar sea he and the others had observed as they glided in from outer space. Actually, the ship must have flashed an immensely greater distance before it hurtled down out of control.

The days stretched behind him, seemingly as numberless as the hot, red, alien sand that scorched through his tattered clothes. A huge scarecrow of a man, he kept moving across the endless, arid waste—he would not give up.

By the time he came to the mountain, his food had long been gone. Of his four water bags, only one remained, and that was so close to being empty that he merely wet his cracked lips and swollen tongue whenever his thirst became unbearable.

Jenner climbed high before he realized that it was not just another dune that had barred his way. He paused, and as he gazed up at the mountain that towered above him, he cringed a little. For an instant he felt the hopelessness of this mad race he was making to nowhere—but he reached the top. He saw that below him was a depression surrounded by hills as high as, or higher than, the one on which he stood. Nestled in the valley they made was a village.

He could see trees and the marble floor of a courtyard. A score of buildings was clustered around what seemed to be a central square. They were mostly low-constructed, but there were four towers pointing gracefully into the sky. They shone in the sunlight with a marble luster.

Faintly, there came to Jenner's ears a thin, high-pitched whistling sound. It rose, fell, faded completely, then came up again clearly and unpleasantly. Even as Jenner ran toward it, the noise grated on his ears, eerie and unnatural.

He kept slipping on smooth rock, and bruised himself when he fell. He rolled halfway down into the valley. The buildings remained new and bright when seen from nearby. Their walls flashed with reflections. On every side was vegetation—reddish-green shrubbery, yellow-green trees laden with purple and red fruit.

With ravenous intent, Jenner headed for the nearest fruit tree. Close up, the tree looked dry and brittle. The large red fruit he tore from the lowest branch, however, was plump and juicy.

As he lifted it to his mouth, he remembered that he had been warned during his training period to taste nothing on Mars until it had been chemically examined. But that was meaningless advice to a man whose only chemical equipment was in his own body.

Nevertheless, the possibility of danger made him cautious. He took his first bite gingerly. It was bitter to his tongue, and he spat it out hastily. Some of the juice which remained in his mouth seared his gums. He felt the fire on it, and he reeled from nausea. His muscles began to jerk, and he lay down on the marble to keep himself from falling. After what seemed like hours to Jenner, the awful trembling finally went out of his body and he could see again. He looked up despisingly at the tree.

The pain finally left him, and slowly he relaxed. A soft breeze rustled the dry leaves. Nearby trees took up that gentle clamor, and it struck Jenner that the wind here in the valley was only a whisper of what it had been on the flat desert beyond the mountain.

There was no other sound now. Jenner abruptly remembered the high-pitched, ever-changing whistle he had heard. He lay very still, listening intently, but there was only the rustling of the leaves. The noisy shrilling had stopped. He wondered if it had been an alarm, to warn the villagers of his approach.

Anxiously he climbed to his feet and fumbled for his gun. A sense of disaster shocked through him. It wasn't there. His mind was a blank, and then he vaguely recalled that he had first missed the weapon more than a week before. He looked around him uneasily, but there was not a sign of creature life. He braced himself. He couldn't leave, as there was nowhere to go. If necessary, he would fight to the death to remain in the village.

Carefully Jenner took a sip from his water bag, moistening his cracked lips and his swollen tongue. Then he replaced the cap and started through a double line of trees toward the nearest building. He made a wide circle to observe it from several vantage points. On one side a low, broad archway opened into the interior. Through it, he could dimly make out the polished gleam of a marble floor.

Jenner explored the buildings from the outside, always keeping a respectful distance between him and any of the entrances. He saw no sign of animal life. He reached the far side of the marble platform on which the village was built, and turned back decisively. It was time to explore interiors.

He chose one of the four tower buildings. As he came within a dozen feet of it, he saw that he would have to stoop low to get inside.

Momentarily, the implications of that stopped him. These buildings had been constructed for a life form that must be very different from human beings.

He went forward again, bent down, and entered reluctantly, every muscle tensed.

He found himself in a room without furniture. However, there were several low marble fences projecting from one marble wall. They formed what looked like a group of four wide, low stalls. Each stall had an open trough carved out of the floor.

The second chamber was fitted with four inclined planes of marble, each of which slanted up to a dais. Altogether there were four rooms on the lower floor. From one of them a circular ramp mounted up, apparently to a tower room.

Jenner didn't investigate the upstairs. The earlier fear that he would find alien life was yielding to the deadly conviction that he wouldn't. No life meant no food or chance of getting any. In frantic haste he hurried from building to building, peering into the silent rooms, pausing now and then to shout hoarsely.

Finally there was no doubt. He was alone in a deserted village on a lifeless planet, without food, without water—except for the pitiful supply in his bag—and without hope.

He was in the fourth and smallest room of one of the tower buildings when he realized that he had come to the end of his search. The room had a single stall jutting out from one wall. Jenner lay down wearily in it. He must have fallen asleep instantly.

When he awoke he became aware of two things, one right after the other. The first realization occurred before he opened his eyes—the whistling sound was back; high and shrill, it wavered at the threshold of audibility.

The other was that a fine spray of liquid was being directed down at him from the ceiling. It had an odor, of which technician Jenner took a single whiff. Quickly he scrambled out of the room, coughing, tears in his eyes, his face already burning from chemical reaction.

He snatched his handkerchief and hastily wiped the exposed parts of his body and face.

He reached the outside and there paused, striving to understand what had happened.

The village seemed unchanged.

Leaves trembled in a gentle breeze. The sun was poised on a mountain peak. Jenner guessed from its position that it was morning again and that he had slept at least a dozen hours. The glaring white light suffused the valley. Half hidden by trees and shrubbery, the buildings flashed and shimmered.

He seemed to be in an oasis in a vast desert. It was an oasis, all right, Jenner reflected grimly, but not for a human being. For him, with its poisonous fruit, it was more like a tantalizing mirage.

He went back inside the building and cautiously peered into the room where he had slept. The spray of gas had stopped, not a bit of odor lingered, and the air was fresh and clean.

He edged over the threshold, half inclined to make a test. He had a picture in his mind of a long-dead Martian creature lazing on the floor in the stall while a soothing chemical sprayed down on its body. The fact that the chemical was deadly to human beings merely emphasized how alien to man was the life that had spawned on Mars. But there seemed little doubt of the reason for the gas. The creature was accustomed to taking a morning shower.

Inside the "bathroom," Jenner eased himself feet first into the stall. As his hips came level with the stall entrance, the solid ceiling sprayed a jet of yellowish gas straight down upon his legs. Hastily Jenner pulled himself clear of the stall. The gas stopped as suddenly as it had started.

He tried it again, to make sure it was merely an automatic process. It turned on, then shut off.

Jenner's thirst-puffed lips parted with excitement. He thought, "If there can be one automatic process, there may be others."

Breathing heavily, he raced into the outer room. Carefully he shoved his legs into one of the two stalls. The moment his hips were in, a steaming gruel filled the trough beside the wall.

He stared at the greasy-looking stuff with a horrified fascination—food—and drink. He remembered the poison fruit and felt repelled, but he forced himself to bend down and put his finger into the hot, wet substance. He brought it up, dripping, to his mouth.

It tasted flat and pulpy, like boiled wood fiber. It trickled viscously into his throat. His eyes began to water and his lips drew back convulsively. He realized he was going to be sick, and ran for the outer door—but didn't quite make it.

When he finally got outside, he felt limp and unutterably listless. In that depressed state of mind, he grew aware again of the shrill sound.

He felt amazed that he could have ignored its rasping even for a few minutes. Sharply he glanced about, trying to determine its source, but it seemed to have none. Whenever he approached a point where it appeared to be loudest, then it would fade or shift, perhaps to the far side of the village.

He tried to imagine what an alien culture would want with a mind-shattering noise—although, of course, it would not necessarily have been unpleasant to them.

He stopped and snapped his fingers as a wild but nevertheless plausible notion entered his mind. Could this be music?

He toyed with the idea, trying to visualize the village as it had been long ago. Here a music-loving people had possibly gone about their daily tasks to the accompaniment of what was to them beautiful strains of melody.

The hideous whistling went on and on, waxing and waning. Jenner tried to put buildings between himself and the sound. He sought refuge in various rooms, hoping that at least one would be soundproof. None were. The whistle followed him wherever he went.

He retreated into the desert, and had to climb halfway up one of the slopes before the noise was low enough not to disturb him. Finally, breathless but immeasurably relieved, he sank down on the sand and thought blankly:

What now?

The scene that spread before him had in it qualities of both heaven and hell. It was all too familiar now—the red sands, the stony dunes, the small, alien village promising so much and fulfilling so little.

Jenner looked down at it with his feverish eyes and ran his parched tongue over his cracked, dry lips. He knew that he was a dead man unless he could alter the automatic food-making machines that must be hidden somewhere in the walls and under the floors of the buildings.

In ancient days, a remnant of Martian civilization had survived here in this village. The inhabitants had died off, but the village lived on, keeping itself clean of sand, able to provide refuge for any Martian who might come along. But there were no Martians. There was only Bill Jenner, pilot of the first rocketship ever to land on Mars.

He had to make the village turn out food and drink that he could take. Without tools, except his hands, with scarcely any knowledge of chemistry, he must force it to change its habits.

Tensely he hefted his water bag. He took another sip and fought the same grim fight to prevent himself from guzzling it down to the last drop. And, when he had won the battle once more, he stood up and started down the slope.

He could last, he estimated, not more than three days. In that time he must conquer the village.

He was already among the trees when it suddenly struck him that the "music" had stopped. Relieved, he bent over a small shrub, took a good firm hold of it—and pulled.

It came up easily, and there was a slab of marble attached to it. Jenner stared at it, noting with surprise that he had been mistaken in thinking the stalk came up through a hole in the marble. It was merely stuck to the surface. Then he noticed something else—the shrub had no roots. Almost instinctively, Jenner looked down at the spot from which he had torn the slab of marble along with the plant. There was sand there.

He dropped the shrub, slipped to his knees, and plunged his fingers into the sand. Loose sand trickled through them. He reached deep, using all his strength to force his arm and hand down; sand—nothing but sand.

He stood up and frantically tore up another shrub. It also came up easily, bringing with it a slab of marble. It had no roots, and where it had been was sand.

With a kind of mindless disbelief, Jenner rushed over to a fruit tree and shoved at it. There was a momentary resistance, and then the marble on which it stood split and lifted slowly into the air. The tree fell over with a swish and a crackle as its dry branches and leaves broke and crumbled into a thousand pieces. Underneath where it had been was sand.

Sand everywhere. A city built on sand. Mars, planet of sand. That was not completely true, of course. Seasonal vegetation had been observed near the polar icecaps. All but the hardiest of it died with the coming of summer. It had been intended that the rocketship land near one of those shallow, tideless seas.

By coming down out of control, the ship had wrecked more than itself. It had wrecked the chances for life of the only survivor of the voyage.

Jenner came slowly out of his daze. He had a thought then. He picked up one of the shrubs he had already torn loose, braced his foot against the marble to which it was attached, and tugged, gently at first, then with increasing strength.

It came loose finally, but there was no doubt that the two were part of a whole. The shrub was growing out of the marble.

Marble? Jenner knelt beside one of the holes from which he had torn a slab, and bent over an adjoining section. It was quite porous—calciferous rock, most likely, but not true marble at all. As he reached toward it, intending to break off a piece, it changed color. Astounded, Jenner drew back. Around the break, the stone was turning a bright orange-yellow. He studied it uncertainly, then tentatively he touched it.

It was as if he had dipped his fingers into searing acid. There was a sharp, biting, burning pain. With a gasp, Jenner jerked his hand clear.

The continuing anguish made him feel faint. He swayed and moaned, clutching the bruised members to his body. When the agony finally faded and he could look at the injury, he saw that the skin had peeled and that blood blisters had formed already. Grimly Jenner looked down at the break in the stone. The edges remained bright orange-yellow.

The village was alert, ready to defend itself from further attacks.

Suddenly weary, he crawled into the shade of a tree. There was only one possible conclusion to draw from what had happened, and it almost defied common sense. This lonely village was alive.

As he lay there, Jenner tried to imagine a great mass of living substance growing into the shape of buildings, adjusting itself to suit another life form, accepting the role of servant in the widest meaning of the term.

If it would serve one race, why not another? If it could adjust to Martians, why not to human beings?

There would be difficulties, of course. He guessed wearily that essential elements would not be available. The oxygen for water could come from the air . . . thousands of compounds could be made from sand. . . . Though it meant death if he failed to find a solution, he fell asleep even as he started to think about what they might be.

When he awoke it was quite dark.

Jenner climbed heavily to his feet. There was a drag to his muscles that alarmed him. He wet his mouth from his water bag and staggered toward the entrance of the nearest building. Except for the scraping of his shoes on the "marble," the silence was intense.

He stopped short, listened, and looked. The wind had died away. He couldn't see the mountains that rimmed the valley, but the buildings were still dimly visible, black shadows in a shadow world.

For the first time, it seemed to him that, in spite of his new hope, it might be better if he died. Even if he survived, what had he to look forward to? Only too well he recalled how hard it had been to rouse interest in the trip and to raise the large amount of money required. He remembered the colossal problems that had had to be solved in building the ship, and some of the men who had solved them were buried somewhere in the Martian desert.

It might be twenty years before another ship from Earth would try to reach the only other planet in the Solar System that had shown signs of being able to support life.

During those uncountable days and nights, those years, he would be here alone. That was the most he could hope for— if he lived. As he fumbled his way to a dais in one of the rooms, Jenner considered another problem: How did one let a living village know that it must alter its processes? In a way, it must already have grasped that it had a new tenant. How could he make it realize he needed food in a different chemical combination than that which it had served in the past; that he liked music, but on a different scale system; and that he could use a shower each morning—of water, not of poison gas?

He dozed fitfully, like a man who is sick rather than sleepy. Twice he wakened, his lips on fire, his eyes burning, his body bathed in perspiration. Several times he was startled into consciousness by the sound of his own harsh voice crying out in anger and fear at the night.

He guessed, then, that he was dying.

He spent the long hours of darkness tossing, turning, twisting, befuddled by waves of heat. As the light of morning came, he was vaguely surprised to realize that he was still alive. Restlessly he climbed off the dais and went to the door.

A bitingly cold wind blew, but it felt good to his hot face. He wondered if there were enough pneumococci in his blood for him to catch pneumonia. He decided not.

In a few moments he was shivering. He retreated back into the house, and for the first time noticed that, despite the doorless doorway, the wind did not come into the building at all. The rooms were cold but not draughty.

That started an association: Where had his terrible body heat come from? He teetered over to the dais where he spent the night. Within seconds he was sweltering in a temperature of about one hundred and thirty.

He climbed off the dais, shaken by his own stupidity. He estimated that he had sweated at least two quarts of moisture out of his dried-up body on that furnace of a bed.

This village was not for human beings. Here even the beds were heated for creatures who needed temperatures far beyond the heat comfortable for men.

Jenner spent most of the day in the shade of a large tree. He felt exhausted, and only occasionally did he even remember that he had a problem. When the whistling started, it bothered him at first, but he was too tired to move away from it. There were long periods when he hardly heard it, so dulled were his senses.

Late in the afternoon he remembered the shrubs and the trees he had torn up the day before and wondered what had happened to them. He wet his swollen tongue with the last few drops of water in his bag, climbed lackadaisically to his feet, and went to look for the dried-up remains.

There weren't any. He couldn't even find the holes where he had torn them out. The living village had absorbed the dead tissue into itself and had repaired the breaks in its "body."

That galvanized Jenner. He began to think again . . . about mutations, genetic readjustments, life forms adapting to new environments. There'd been lectures on that before the ship left Earth, rather generalized talks designed to acquaint the explorers with the problems men might face on an alien planet. The important principle was quite simple: adjust or die.

The village had to adjust to him. He doubted if he could seriously damage it, but he could try. His own need to survive must be placed on as sharp and hostile a basis as that.

Frantically Jenner began to search his pockets. Before leaving the rocket he had loaded himself with odds and ends of small equipment. A jackknife, a folding metal cup, a printed radio, a tiny superbattery that could be charged by spinning an attached wheel—and for which he had brought along, among other things, a powerful electric fire lighter.

Jenner plugged the lighter into the battery and deliberately scraped the red-hot end along the surface of the "marble." The reaction was swift. The substance turned an angry purple this time. When an entire section of the floor had changed color, Jenner headed for the nearest stall trough, entering far enough to activate it.

There was a noticeable delay. When the food finally flowed into the trough, it was clear that the living village had realized the reason for what he had done. The food was a pale, creamy color, where earlier it had been a murky gray.

Jenner put his finger into it but withdrew it with a yell and wiped his finger. It continued to sting for several moments. The vital question was: Had it deliberately offered him food that would damage him, or was it trying to appease him without knowing what he could eat?

He decided to give it another chance, and entered the adjoining stall. The gritty stuff that flooded up this time was yellower. It didn't burn his finger, but Jenner took one taste and spat it out. He had the feeling that he had been offered a soup made of a greasy mixture of clay and gasoline.

He was thirsty now with a need heightened by the unpleasant taste in his mouth. Desperately he rushed outside and tore open the water bag, seeking the wetness inside. In his fumbling eagerness, he spilled a few precious drops onto the courtyard. Down he went on his face and licked them up.

Half a minute later, he was still licking, and there was still water.

The fact penetrated suddenly. He raised himself and gazed wonderingly at the droplets of water that sparkled on the smooth stone. As he watched, another one squeezed up from the apparently solid surface and shimmered in the light of the sinking sun.

He bent, and with the tip of his tongue sponged up each visible drop. For a long time he lay with his mouth pressed to the "marble," sucking up the tiny bits of water that the village doled out to him.

The glowing white sun disappeared behind a hill. Night fell, like the dropping of a black screen. The air turned cold, then icy. He shivered as the wind keened through his ragged clothes. But what finally stopped him was the collapse of the surface from which he had been drinking.

Jenner lifted himself in surprise, and in the darkness gingerly felt over the stone. It had genuinely crumbled. Evidently the substance had yielded up its available water and had disintegrated in the process. Jenner estimated that he had drunk altogether an ounce of water.

It was a convincing demonstration of the willingness of the village to please him, but there was another, less satisfying, implication. If the village had to destroy a part of itself every time it gave him a drink, then clearly the supply was not unlimited.

Jenner hurried inside the nearest building, climbed onto a dais—and climbed off again hastily, as the heat blazed up at him. He waited, to give the Intelligence a chance to realize he wanted a change, then lay down once more. The heat was as great as ever.

He gave that up because he was too tired to persist and too sleepy to think of a method that might let the village know he needed a different bedroom temperature. He slept on the floor with an uneasy conviction that it could *not* sustain him for long. He woke up many times during the night and thought, "Not enough water. No matter how hard it tries—" Then he would sleep again, only to wake once more, tense and unhappy.

Nevertheless, morning found him briefly alert; and all his steely determination was back—that iron will power that had brought him at least five hundred miles across an unknown desert.

He headed for the nearest trough. This time, after he had activated it, there was a pause of more than a minute; and then about a thimbleful of water made a wet splotch at the bottom.

Jenner licked it dry, then waited hopefully for more. When none came he reflected gloomily that somewhere in the village an entire group of cells had broken down and released their water for him.

Then and there he decided that it was up to the human being, who could move around, to find a new source of water for the village, which could not move.

In the interim, of course, the village would have to keep him alive, until he had investigated the possibilities. That meant, above everything else, he must have some food to sustain him while he looked around.

He began to search his pockets. Toward the end of his food supply, he had carried scraps and pieces wrapped in small bits of cloth. Crumbs had broken off into the pocket, and he had searched for them often during those long days in the desert. Now, by actually ripping the seams, he discovered tiny particles of meat and bread, little bits of grease and other unidentifiable substances.

Carefully he leaned over the adjoining stall and placed the scrapings in the trough there. The village would not be able to offer him more than a reasonable facsimile. If the spilling of a few drops on the courtyard could make it aware of his need for water, then a similar offering might give it the clue it needed as to the chemical nature of the food he could eat.

Jenner waited, then entered the second stall and activated it. About a pint of thick, creamy substance trickled into the bottom of the trough. The smallness of the quantity seemed evidence that perhaps it contained water.

He tasted it. It had a sharp, musty flavor and a stale odor. It was almost as dry as flour—but his stomach did not reject it.

Jenner ate slowly, acutely aware that at such moments as this the village had him at its mercy. He could never be sure that one of the food ingredients was not a slow-acting poison.

When he had finished the meal he went to a food trough in another building. He refused to eat the food that came up, but activated still another trough. This time he received a few drops of water.

He had come purposefully to one of the tower buildings. Now he started up the ramp that led to the upper floor. He paused only briefly in the room he came to, as he had already discovered that they seemed to be additional bedrooms. The familiar dais was there in a group of three.

What interested him was that the circular ramp continued to wind on upward. First to another, smaller room that seemed to have no particular reason for being. Then it wound on up to the top of the tower, some seventy feet above the ground. It was high enough for him to see beyond the rim of all the surrounding hilltops. He had thought it might be, but he had been too weak to make the climb before. Now he looked out to every horizon. Almost immediately the hope that had brought him up faded.

The view was immeasurably desolate. As far as he could see was an arid waste, and every horizon was hidden in a mist of wind-blown sand.

Jenner gazed with a sense of despair. If there were a Martian sea out there somewhere, it was beyond his reach.

Abruptly he clenched his hands in anger against his fate,

which seemed inevitable now. At the very worst, he had hoped he would find himself in a mountainous region. Seas and mountains were generally the two main sources of water. He should have known, of course, that there were very few mountains on Mars. It would have been a wild coincidence if he had actually run into a mountain range.

His fury faded because he lacked the strength to sustain any emotion. Numbly he went down the ramp.

His vague plan to help the village ended as swiftly and finally as that.

The days drifted by, but as to how many he had no idea. Each time he went to eat, a smaller amount of water was doled out to him. Jenner kept telling himself that each meal would have to be his last. It was unreasonable for him to expect the village to destroy itself when his fate was certain now.

What was worse, it became increasingly clear that the food was not good for him. He had misled the village as to his needs by giving it stale, perhaps even tainted, samples, and prolonged the agony for himself. At times after he had eaten, Jenner felt dizzy for hours. All too frequently his head ached and his body shivered with fever.

The village was doing what it could. The rest was up to him, and he couldn't even adjust to an approximation of Earth food.

For two days he was too sick to drag himself to one of the troughs. Hour after hour he lay on the floor. Some time during the second night the pain in his body grew so terrible that he finally made up his mind.

"If I can get to a dais," he told himself, "the heat alone will kill me; and in absorbing my body, the village will get back some of its lost water."

He spent at least an hour crawling laboriously up the ramp of the nearest dais, and when he finally made it, he lay as one already dead. His last waking thought was: "Beloved friends, I'm coming."

The hallucination was so complete that momentarily he seemed to be back in the control room of the rocketship, and all around him were his former companions.

With a sigh of relief Jenner sank into a dreamless sleep.

He woke to the sound of a violin. It was a sad-sweet music that told of the rise and fall of a race long dead.

Jenner listened for a while and then, with abrupt excitement, realized the truth. This was a substitute for the whistling—the village had adjusted its music to him!

Other sensory phenomena stole in upon him. The dais felt comfortably warm, not hot at all. He had a feeling of wonderful physical well-being.

Eagerly he scrambled down the ramp to the nearest food stall. As he crawled forward, his nose close to the floor, the trough filled with a steamy mixture. The odor was so rich and pleasant that he plunged his face into it and slopped it up greedily. It had the flavor of thick, meaty soup and was warm and soothing to his lips and mouth. When he had eaten it all, for the first time he did not need a drink of water.

"I've won!" thought Jenner. "The village has found a way!"

After a while he remembered something and crawled to the bathroom. Cautiously, watching the ceiling, he eased himself backward into the shower stall. The yellowish spray came down, cool and delightful.

Ecstatically Jenner wriggled his four-foot-tail and lifted his long snout to let the thin streams of liquid wash away the food impurities that clung to his sharp teeth.

Then he waddled out to bask in the sun and listen to the timeless music.

by A. E. VAN VOGT
Slan
The World of Null-A
Voyage of the Space Beagle (collection of short stories)

Helen O'Loy

LESTER DEL REY

I am an old man now, and I can still see Helen as Dave un-packed her, and still hear him gasp as he looked her over.

"Man, isn't she a beauty?"

She was beautiful, a dream in spun plastics and metals, something Keats might have seen dimly when he wrote his sonnet. If Helen of Troy had looked like that the Greeks must have been pikers when they launched only a thousand ships; at least, that's what I told Dave.

"Helen of Troy, eh?" He looked at her tag. "At least it beats this thing—K2W88. Helen . . . Mmmm . . . Helen of Alloy."

"Not much swing to that, Dave. Too many unstressed syl-lables in the middle. How about Helen O'Loy?"

"Helen O'Loy she is, Phil." And that's how it began—one part beauty, one part dream, one part science; add a stereo broadcast, stir mechanically, and the result is chaos.

Dave and I hadn't gone to college together, but when I came to Messina to practice medicine, I found him downstairs in a little robot repair shop. After that, we began to pal around, and when I started going with one twin, he found the other equally attractive, so we made it a foursome.

When our business grew better, we rented a house near the rocket field—noisy but cheap, and the rockets discouraged apartment building. We liked room enough to stretch our-selves. I suppose, if we hadn't quarreled with them, we'd have married the twins in time. But Dave wanted to look over the latest Venus-rocket attempt when his twin wanted to see a display stereo starring Larry Ainslee, and they were both stubborn. From then on, we forgot the girls and spent our evenings at home.

But it wasn't until "Lena" put vanilla on our steak instead of salt that we got off on the subject of emotions and robots. While Dave was dissecting Lena to find the trouble, we naturally mulled over the future of the mechs. He was sure that the robots would beat men some day, and I couldn't see it.

"Look here, Dave," I argued. "You know Lena doesn't think—not really. When those wires crossed, she could have corrected herself. But she didn't bother; she followed the mechanical impulse. A man might have reached for the vanilla, but when he saw it in his hand, he'd have stopped. Lena has sense enough, but she has no emotions, no consciousness of self."

"All right, that's the big trouble with the mechs now. But we'll get around it, put in some mechanical emotions, or something." He screwed Lena's head back on, turned on her juice. "Go back to work, Lena, it's nineteen o'clock."

Now I specialized in endocrinology and related subjects. I wasn't exactly a psychologist, but I did understand the glands, secretions, hormones, and miscellanies that are the physical causes of emotions. It took medical science three hundred years to find out how and why they worked, and I couldn't see men duplicating them mechanically in much less time.

I brought home books and papers to prove it, and Dave quoted the invention of memory coils and veritoid eyes. During that year we swapped knowledge until Dave knew the whole theory of endocrinology, and I could have made Lena from memory. The more we talked, the less sure I grew about the impossibility of *homo mechanensis* as the perfect type.

Poor Lena. Her cuproberyl body spent half its time in scattered pieces. Our first attempts were successful only in getting her to serve fried brushes for breakfast and wash the dishes in oleo oil. Then one day she cooked a perfect dinner with six wires crossed, and Dave was in ecstasy.

He worked all night on her wiring, put in a new coil, and taught her a fresh set of words. And the next day she flew into a tantrum and swore vigorously at us when we told her she wasn't doing her work right.

"It's a lie," she yelled, shaking a suction brush. "You're all liars. If you so-and-so's would leave me whole long enough, I might get something done around the place."

When we calmed her temper and got her back to work, Dave ushered me into the study. "Not taking any chances with Lena," he explained. "We'll have to cut out that adrenal pack and restore her to normalcy. But we've got to get a better robot. A housemaid mech isn't complex enough."

"How about Dillard's new utility models? They seem to combine everything in one."

"Exactly. Even so, we'll need a special one built to order, with a full range of memory coils. And out of respect to old Lena, let's get a female case for its works."

The result, of course, was Helen. The Dillard people had performed a miracle and put all the works in a girl-modeled case. Even the plastic and rubberite face was designed for flexibility to express emotions, and she was complete with tear glands and taste buds, ready to simulate every human action, from breathing to pulling hair. The bill they sent with her was another miracle, but Dave and I scraped it together; we had to turn Lena over to an exchange to complete it, though, and thereafter we ate out.

I'd performed plenty of delicate operations on living tissues, and some of them had been tricky, but I still felt like a pre-med student as we opened the front plate of her torso and began to sever the leads of her "nerves." Dave's mechanical glands were all prepared, complex little bundles of radio tubes and wires that heterodyned on the electrical thought impulses and distorted them as adrenalin distorts the reaction of human minds.

Instead of sleeping that night, we pored over the schematic diagrams of her structures, tracing the thoughts through mazes of her wiring, severing the leaders, implanting the heterones, as Dave called them. And while we worked, a mechanical tape fed carefully prepared thoughts of consciousness and awareness of life and feeling into an auxiliary memory coil. Dave believed in leaving nothing to chance.

It was growing light as we finished, exhausted and exultant. All that remained was the starting of her electrical power; like all the Dillard mechs, she was equipped with a tiny atomotor instead of batteries, and once started would need no further attention.

Dave refused to turn her on. "Wait until we've slept and rested," he advised. "I'm as eager to try her as you are, but we can't do much studying with our minds half dead. Turn in, and we'll leave Helen until later."

Even though we were both reluctant to follow it, we knew the idea was sound. We turned in, and sleep hit us before the air-conditioner could cut down to sleeping temperature. And then Dave was pounding on my shoulders.

"Phil! Hey, snap out of it!"

I groaned, turned over, and faced him. "Well? . . . Uh! What is it? Did Helen—"

"No, it's old Mrs. van Styler. She 'visored to say her son has an infatuation for a servant girl, and she wants you to come out and give counter-hormones. They're at the summer camp in Maine."

Rich Mrs. van Styler! I couldn't afford to let that account down, now that Helen had used up the last of my funds. But it wasn't a job I cared for.

"Counter-hormones! That'll take two weeks' full time. Anyway, I'm no society doctor, messing with glands to keep fools happy. My job's taking care of serious trouble."

"And you want to watch Helen." Dave was grinning, but he was serious, too. "I told her it'd cost her fifty thousand!"

"*Huh?*"

"And she said okay, if you hurried."

Of course, there was only one thing to do, though I could have wrung fat Mrs. van Styler's neck cheerfully. It wouldn't have happened if she'd used robots like everyone else—but she had to be different.

Consequently, while Dave was back home puttering with Helen, I was racking my brain to trick Archy van Styler into getting the counter-hormones, and giving the servant girl the same. Oh, I wasn't supposed to, but the poor kid was crazy about Archy. Dave might have written, I thought, but never a word did I get.

It was three weeks later instead of two when I reported

that Archy was "cured," and collected on the line. With that money in my pocket, I hired a personal rocket and was back in Messina in half an hour. I didn't waste time in reaching the house.

As I stepped into the alcove, I heard a light patter of feet, and an eager voice called out, "Dave, dear?" For a minute I couldn't answer, and the voice came again, pleading, "Dave?"

I don't know what I expected, but I didn't expect Helen to meet me that way, stopping and staring at me, obvious disappointment on her face, little hands fluttering up against her breast.

"Oh," she cried. "I thought it was Dave. He hardly comes home to eat now, but I've had supper waiting hours." She dropped her hands and managed a smile. "You're Phil, aren't you? Dave told me about you when . . . at first. I'm so glad to see you home, Phil."

"Glad to see you doing so well, Helen." Now what does one say for light conversation with a robot? "You said something about supper?"

"Oh, yes. I guess Dave ate downtown again, so we might as well go in. It'll be nice having someone to talk to around the house, Phil. You don't mind if I call you Phil, do you? You know, you're sort of a godfather to me."

We ate. I hadn't counted on such behavior, but apparently she considered eating as normal as walking. She didn't do much eating, at that; most of the time she spent staring at the front door.

Dave came in as we were finishing, a frown a yard wide on his face. Helen started to rise, but he ducked toward the stairs, throwing words over his shoulder.

"Hi, Phil. See you up here later."

There was something radically wrong with him. For a moment, I'd thought his eyes were haunted, and as I turned to Helen, hers were filling with tears. She gulped, choked them back, and fell to viciously on her food.

"What's the matter with him . . . and you?" I asked.

"He's sick of me." She pushed her plate away and got up hastily. "You'd better see him while I clean up. And there's nothing wrong with me. And it's not my fault, anyway." She grabbed the dishes and ducked into the kitchen; I could have sworn she was crying.

Maybe all thought is a series of conditioned reflexes—but she certainly had picked up a lot of conditioning while I was gone. Lena in her heyday had been nothing like this. I went up to see if Dave could make any sense out of the hodge-podge.

He was squirting soda into a large glass of apple brandy, and I saw that the bottle was nearly empty. "Join me?" he asked.

It seemed like a good idea. The roaring blast of an iron rocket overhead was the only familiar thing left in the house. From the look around Dave's eyes, it wasn't the first bottle he'd emptied while I was gone, and there were more left. He dug out a new bottle for his own drink.

"Of course, it's none of my business, Dave, but that stuff won't steady your nerves any. What's gotten into you and Helen? Been seeing ghosts?"

Helen was wrong; he hadn't been eating downtown—nor anywhere else. His muscles collapsed into a chair in a way that spoke of fatigue and nerves, but mostly of hunger. "You noticed it, eh?"

"Noticed it? The two of you jammed it down my throat."

"Uhmmm." He swatted at a non-existent fly, and slumped further down in the pneumatic. "Guess maybe I should have waited with Helen until you got back. But if that stereo cast hadn't changed . . . anyway, it did. And those mushy books of yours finished the job."

"Thanks. That makes it all clear."

"You know, Phil, I've got a place up in the country . . . fruit ranch. My dad left it to me. Think I'll look it over."

And that's the way it went. But finally, by much liquor and more perspiration, I got some of the story out of him before I gave him an amytal and put him to bed. Then I hunted up Helen and dug the rest of the story from her, until it made sense.

Apparently as soon as I was gone, Dave had turned her on and made preliminary tests, which were entirely satisfactory. She had reacted beautifully—so well that he decided to leave her and go down to work as usual.

Naturally, with all her untried emotions, she was filled with curiosity and wanted him to stay. Then he had an inspiration. After showing her what her duties about the house would be, he set her down in front of the stereovisor, tuned in a travelogue, and left her to occupy her time with that.

The travelogue held her attention until it was finished, and the station switched over to a current serial with Larry Ainslee, the same cute emoter who'd given us all the trouble with the twins. Incidentally, he looked something like Dave.

Helen took to the serial like a seal to water. This play acting was a perfect outlet for her newly excited emotions. When that particular episode finished, she found a love story on another station, and added still more to her education. The afternoon programs were mostly news and music, but by then she'd found my books; and I do have rather adolescent taste in literature.

Dave came home in the best of spirits. The front alcove was neatly swept, and there was the odor of food in the air that he'd missed around the house for weeks. He had visions of Helen as the super-efficient housekeeper.

So it was a shock to him to feel two strong arms around his neck from behind and hear a voice all a-quiver coo into his ear, "Oh, Dave, darling, I've missed you so, and I'm so *thrilled* that you're back." Helen's technique may have lacked polish, but it had enthusiasm, as he found when he tried to stop her from kissing him. She had learned fast and furiously —also, Helen was powered by an atomotor.

Dave wasn't a prude, but he remembered that she was only a robot, after all. The fact that she felt, acted, and looked like a young goddess in his arms didn't mean much. With some effort, he untangled her and dragged her off to supper, where he made her eat with him to divert her attention.

After her evening work, he called her into the study and gave her a thorough lecture on the folly of her ways. It must have been good, for it lasted three solid hours, and covered her station in life, the idiocy of stereos, and various other miscellanies. When he finished, Helen looked up with dewy eyes and said wistfully, "I know, Dave, but I still love you."

That's when Dave started drinking.

It grew worse each day. If he stayed downtown, she was crying when he came home. If he returned on time, she fussed over him and threw herself at him. In his room, with the door locked, he could hear her downstairs pacing up and down and muttering; and when he went down, she stared at him reproachfully until he had to go back up.

I sent Helen out on a fake errand in the morning and got Dave up. With her gone, I made him eat a decent breakfast and gave him a tonic for his nerves. He was still listless and moody.

"Look here, Dave," I broke in on his brooding. "Helen isn't human, after all. Why not cut off her power and change a few memory coils? Then we can convince her that she never was in love and couldn't get that way."

"You try it. I had the idea, but she put up a wail that would wake Homer. She says it would be murder—and the hell of it is that I can't help feeling the same about it. Maybe she isn't human, but you wouldn't guess it when she puts on that martyred look and tells you to go ahead and kill her."

"We never put in substitutes for some of the secretions present in man during the love period."

"I don't know what we put in. Maybe the heterones backfired or something. Anyway, she's made this idea so much a part of her thoughts that we'd have to put in a whole new set of coils."

"Well, why not?"

"Go ahead. You're the surgeon of this family. I'm not used to fussing with emotions. Matter of fact, since she's been acting this way, I'm beginning to hate work on any robot. My business is going to blazes."

He saw Helen coming up the walk and ducked out the back door for the monorail express. I'd intended to put him back in bed, but let him go. Maybe he'd be better off at his shop than at home.

"Dave's gone?" Helen did have that martyred look now.

"Yeah. I got him to eat, and he's gone to work."

"I'm glad he ate." She slumped down in a chair as if she were worn out, though how a mech could be tired beat me. "Phil?"

"Well, what is it?"

"Do you think I'm bad for him? I mean, do you think he'd be happier if I weren't here?"

"He'll go crazy if you keep acting this way around him."

She winced. Those little hands were twisting about pleadingly, and I felt like an inhuman brute. But I'd started, and I went ahead. "Even if I cut out your power and changed your coils, he'd probably still be haunted by you."

"I know. But I can't help it. And I'd make him a good wife, really I would, Phil."

I gulped; this was getting a little too far. "And give him strapping sons to boot, I suppose. A man wants flesh and blood, not rubber and metal."

"Don't, please! I can't think of myself that way; to me, I'm a woman. And you know how perfectly I'm made to imitate a real woman . . . in all ways. I couldn't give him sons, but in every other way . . . I'd try so hard, I know I'd make him a good wife."

I gave up.

Dave didn't come home that night, nor the next day. Helen was fussing and fuming, wanting me to call the hospitals and the police, but I knew nothing had happened to him. He always carried identification. Still, when he didn't come on the third day, I began to worry. And when Helen started out for his shop, I agreed to go with her.

Dave was there, with another man I didn't know. I parked Helen where he couldn't see her, but where she could hear, and went in as soon as the other fellow left.

Dave looked a little better and seemed glad to see me. "Hi, Phil—just closing up. Let's go eat."

Helen couldn't hold back any longer, but came trooping in. "Come on home, Dave. I've got roast duck with spice stuffing, and you know you love that."

"Scat!" said Dave. She shrank back, turned to go. "Oh, all right, stay. You might as well hear it, too. I've sold the shop. The fellow you saw just bought it, and I'm going up to the old fruit ranch I told you about, Phil. I can't stand the mechs any more."

"You'll starve to death at that," I told him.

"No, there's a growing demand for old-fashioned fruit, raised out of doors. People are tired of this water-culture stuff. Dad always made a living out of it. I'm leaving as soon as I can get home and pack."

Helen clung to her idea. "I'll pack, Dave, while you eat. I've got apple cobbler for dessert." The world was toppling under her feet, but she still remembered how crazy he was for apple cobbler.

Helen was a good cook; in fact she was a genius, with all the good points of a woman and a mech combined. Dave ate well enough, after he got started. By the time supper was over, he'd thawed out enough to admit he liked the duck and cobbler, and to thank her for packing. In fact, he even let her kiss him good-bye, though he firmly refused to let her go to the rocket field with him.

Helen was trying to be brave when I got back, and we carried on a stumbling conversation about Mrs. van Styler's servants for a while. But the talk began to lull, and she sat staring out of the window at nothing most of the time. Even the stereo comedy lacked interest for her, and I was glad to have her go off to her room. She could cut her power down to simulate sleep when she chose.

As the days slipped by, I began to realize why she couldn't believe herself a robot. I got to thinking of her as a girl and companion myself. Except for odd intervals when she went off by herself to brood, or when she kept going to the telescript for a letter that never came, she was as good a companion as a man could ask. There was something homey about the place that Lena had never put there.

I took Helen on a shopping trip to Hudson and she giggled and purred over wisps of silk and glassheen that were the fashion, tried on endless hats, and conducted herself as any normal girl might. We went trout fishing for a day, where she proved to be as good a sport and as sensibly silent as a man. I thoroughly enjoyed myself and thought she was forgetting Dave. That was before I came home unexpectedly and found her doubled up on the couch, threshing her legs up and down and crying to the high heavens.

It was then I called Dave. They seemed to have trouble in reaching him, and Helen came over beside me while I waited. She was tense and fidgety as an old maid trying to propose. But finally they located Dave.

"What's up, Phil?" he asked as his face came on the viewplate. "I was just getting my things together to—"

I broke him off. "Things can't go on the way they are, Dave. I've made up my mind. I'm yanking Helen's coils tonight. It won't be worse than what she's going through now."

Helen reached up and touched my shoulder. "Maybe that's best, Phil. I don't blame you."

Dave's voice cut in. "Phil, you don't know what you're doing!"

"Of course I do. It'll all be over by the time you can get here. As you heard, she's agreeing."

There was a black cloud sweeping over Dave's face. "I won't have it, Phil. She's half mine and I forbid it!"

"Of all the—"

"Go ahead, call me anything you want. I've changed my mind. I was packing to come home when you called."

Helen jerked around me, her eyes glued to the panel. "Dave, do you . . . are you—"

"I'm just waking up to what a fool I've been, Helen. Phil, I'll be home in a couple of hours, so if there's anything—"

He didn't have to chase me out. But I heard Helen cooing something about loving to be a rancher's wife before I could shut the door.

Well, I wasn't as surprised as they thought. I think I knew when I called Dave what would happen. No man acts the way Dave had been acting because he hates a girl; only because he thinks he does—and thinks wrong.

No woman ever made a lovelier bride or a sweeter wife. Helen never lost her flare for cooking and making a home. With her gone, the old house seemed empty, and I began to drop out to the ranch once or twice a week. I suppose they had trouble at times, but I never saw it, and I know the neighbors never suspected they were anything but normal man and wife.

Dave grew older, and Helen didn't, of course. But
us, we put lines in her face and grayed her hair withou
ting Dave know that she wasn't growing old with him; he
forgotten that she wasn't human, I guess.

I practically forgot, myself. It wasn't until a letter came
from Helen this morning that I woke up to reality. There,
in her beautiful script, just a trifle shaky in places, was the
inevitable that neither Dave nor I had seen.

Dear Phil,

As you know, Dave has had heart trouble for several
years now. We expected him to live on just the same,
but it seems that wasn't to be. He died in my arms just
before sunrise. He sent you his greetings and farewell.

I've one last favor to ask of you, Phil. There is only
one thing for me to do when this is finished. Acid will
burn out metal as well as flesh, and I'll be dead with
Dave. Please see that we are buried together, and that
the morticians do not find my secret. Dave wanted it
that way, too.

Poor, dear Phil. I know you loved Dave as a brother,
and how you felt about me. Please don't grieve too much
for us, for we have had a happy life together, and both
feel that we should cross this last bridge side by side.

With love and thanks from,

Helen.

It had to come sooner or later, I suppose, and the first shock
has worn off now. I'll be leaving in a few minutes to carry
out Helen's last instructions.

Dave was a lucky man, and the best friend I ever had.
And Helen— Well, as I said, I'm an old man now, and can
view things more sanely; I should have married and raised
a family, I suppose. But . . . there was only one Helen
O'Loy.

by LESTER DEL REY
Nerves
Pstalemate

"If the stars should appear one night in a thousand years, how would men believe and adore, and preserve for many generations the remembrance of the city of God!"—Emerson

Aton 77, director of Saro University, thrust out a belligerent lower lip and glared at the young newspaperman in a hot fury.

Theremon 762 took that fury in his stride. In his earlier days, when his now widely syndicated column was only a mad idea in a cub reporter's mind, he had specialized in "impossible" interviews. It had cost him bruises, black eyes, and broken bones; but it had given him an ample supply of coolness and self-confidence.

So he lowered the outthrust hand that had been so pointedly ignored and calmly waited for the aged director to get over the worst. Astronomers were queer ducks, anyway, and if Aton's actions of the last two months meant anything, this same Aton was the queer-duckiest of the lot.

Aton 77 found his voice, and though it trembled with restrained emotion, the careful, somewhat pedantic, phraseology, for which the famous astronomer was noted, did not abandon him.

"Sir," he said, "you display an infernal gall in coming to me with that impudent proposition of yours."

The husky telephotographer of the Observatory, Beenay 25, thrust a tongue's tip across dry lips and interposed nervously, "Now, sir, after all—"

The director turned to him and lifted a white eyebrow.

"Do not interfere, Beenay. I will credit you with good intentions in bringing this man here; but I will tolerate no insubordination now."

Theremon decided it was time to take a part. "Director Aton, if you'll let me finish what I started saying I think—"

"I don't believe, young man," retorted Aton, "that anything you could say now would count much as compared with your daily columns of these last two months. You have led a vast newspaper campaign against the efforts of myself and my colleagues to organize the world against the menace which it is now too late to avert. You have done your best with your highly personal attacks on me to make the staff of this Observatory objects of ridicule."

The director lifted the copy of the Saro City *Chronicle* on the table and shook it at Theremon furiously. "Even a person of your well-known impudence should have hesitated before coming to me with a request that he be allowed to cover today's events for his paper. Of all newsmen, you!"

Aton dashed the newspaper to the floor, strode to the window and clasped his arms behind his back.

"You may leave," he snapped over his shoulder. He stared moodily out at the skyline where Gamma, the brightest of the planet's six suns, was setting. It had already faded and yellowed into the horizon mists, and Aton knew he would never see it again as a sane man.

He whirled. "No, wait, come here!" He gestured peremptorily. "I'll give you your story."

The newsman had made no motion to leave, and now he approached the old man slowly. Aton gestured outward, "Of the six suns, only Beta is left in the sky. Do you see it?"

The question was rather unnecessary. Beta was almost at zenith; its ruddy light flooding the landscape to an unusual orange as the brilliant rays of setting Gamma died. Beta was at aphelion. It was small; smaller than Theremon had ever seen it before, and for the moment it was undisputed ruler of Lagash's sky.

Lagash's own sun, Alpha, the one about which it revolved, was at the antipodes; as were the two distant companion pairs. The red dwarf Beta—Alpha's immediate companion—was alone, grimly alone.

Aton's upturned face flushed redly in the sunlight. "In just under four hours," he said, "civilization, as we know it, comes to an end. It will do so because, as you see, Beta is the only sun in the sky." He smiled grimly. "Print that! There'll be no one to read it."

"But if it turns out that four hours pass—and another four —and nothing happens?" asked Theremon softly.

"Don't let that worry you. Enough will happen."

"Granted! And *still*—if nothing happens?"

For a second time, Beenay 25 spoke, "Sir, I think you ought to listen to him."

Theremon said, "Put it to a vote, Director Aton."

There was a stir among the remaining five members of the Observatory staff, who till now had maintained an attitude of wary neutrality.

"That," stated Aton flatly, "is not necessary." He drew out his pocket watch. "Since your good friend, Beenay, insists so urgently, I will give you five minutes. Talk away."

"Good! Now, just what difference would it make if you allowed me to take down an eyewitness account of what's to come? If your prediction comes true, my presence won't hurt; for in that case my column would never be written. On the other hand, if nothing comes of it, you will just have to expect ridicule or worse. It would be wise to leave that ridicule to friendly hands."

Aton snorted. "Do you mean yours when you speak of friendly hands?"

"Certainly!" Theremon sat down and crossed his legs. "My columns may have been a little rough at times, but I gave you people the benefit of the doubt every time. After all, this is not the century to preach 'the end of the world is at hand' to Lagash. You have to understand that people don't believe the 'Book of Revelations' any more, and it annoys them to have scientists turn about face and tell us the Cultists are right after all—"

"No such thing, young man," interrupted Aton. "While a

great deal of our data has been supplied us by the Cult, our results contain none of the Cult's mysticism. Facts are facts, and the Cult's so-called 'mythology' *has* certain facts behind it. We've exposed them and ripped away their mystery. I assure you that the Cult hates us now worse than you do."

"I don't hate you. I'm just trying to tell you that the public is in an ugly humor. They're angry."

Aton twisted his mouth in derision. "Let them be angry."

"Yes, but what about tomorrow?"

"There'll be no tomorrow!"

"But if there is. Say that there is—just to see what happens. That anger might take shape into something serious. After all, you know, business has taken a nose dive these last two months. Investors don't really believe the world is coming to an end, but just the same they're being cagey with their money until it's all over. Johnny Public doesn't believe you, either, but the new spring furniture might as well wait a few months—just to make sure.

"You see the point. Just as soon as this is all over, the business interests will be after your hide. They'll say that if crackpots—begging your pardon—can upset the country's prosperity any time they want simply by making some cockeyed prediction—it's up to the planet to prevent them. The sparks will fly, sir."

The director regarded the columnist sternly. "And just what were you proposing to do to help the situation?"

"Well," grinned Theremon, "I was proposing to take charge of the publicity. I can handle things so that only the ridiculous side will show. It would be hard to stand, I admit, because I'd have to make you all out to be a bunch of gibbering idiots, but if I can get people laughing at you, they might forget to be angry. In return for that, all my publisher asks is an exclusive story."

Beenay nodded and burst out, "Sir, the rest of us think he's right. These last two months we've considered everything but the million-to-one chance that there is an error somewhere in our theory or in our calculations. We ought to take care of that, too."

There was a murmur of agreement from the men grouped

about the table, and Aton's expression became that of one who found his mouth full of something bitter and couldn't get rid of it.

"You may stay if you wish, then. You will kindly refrain, however, from hampering us in our duties in any way. You will also remember that I am in charge of all activities here, and in spite of your opinions as expressed in your columns, I will expect full co-operation and full respect—"

His hands were behind his back, and his wrinkled face thrust forward determinedly as he spoke. He might have continued indefinitely but for the intrusion of a new voice.

"Hello, hello, hello!" It came in a high tenor, and the plump cheeks of the newcomer expanded in a pleased smile. "What's this morgue-like atmosphere about here? No one's losing his nerve, I hope."

Aton started in consternation and said peevishly, "Now what the devil are you doing here, Sheerin? I thought you were going to stay behind in the Hideout."

Sheerin laughed and dropped his tubby figure into a chair. "Hideout be blowed! The place bored me. I wanted to be here, where things are getting hot. Don't you suppose I have my share of curiosity? I want to see these Stars the Cultists are forever speaking about." He rubbed his hands and added in a soberer tone, "It's freezing outside. The wind's enough to hang icicles on your nose. Beta doesn't seem to give any heat at all, at the distance it is."

The white-haired director ground his teeth in sudden exasperation, "Why do you go out of your way to do crazy things, Sheerin? What kind of good are you around here?"

"What kind of good am I around there?" Sheerin spread his palms in comical resignation. "A psychologist isn't worth his salt in the Hideout. They need men of action and strong, healthy women that can breed children. Me? I'm a hundred pounds too heavy for a man of action, and I wouldn't be a success at breeding children. So why bother them with an extra mouth to feed? I feel better over here."

Theremon spoke briskly, "Just what is the Hideout, sir?"

Sheerin seemed to see the columnist for the first time. He

frowned and blew his ample cheeks out. "And just who in Lagash are you, redhead?"

Aton compressed his lips and then muttered sullenly, "That's Theremon 762, the newspaper fellow. I suppose you've heard of him."

The columnist offered his hand. "And, of course, you're Sheerin 501 of Saro University. I've heard of you." Then he repeated, "What is this Hideout, sir?"

"Well," said Sheerin, "we have managed to convince a few people of the validity of our prophecy of—er—doom, to be spectacular about it, and those few have taken proper measures. They consist mainly of the immediate members of the families of the Observatory staff, certain of the faculty of Saro University and a few outsiders. Altogether, they number about three hundred, but three quarters are women and children."

"I see! They're supposed to hide where the Darkness and the—er—Stars can't get at them, and then hold out when the rest of the world goes poof."

"If they can. It won't be easy. With all of mankind insane; with the great cities going up in flames—environment will not be conducive to survival. But they have food, water, shelter, and weapons—"

"They've got more," said Aton. "They've got all our records, except for what we will collect today. Those records will mean everything to the next cycle, and *that's* what must survive. The rest can go hang."

Theremon whistled a long, low whistle and sat brooding for several minutes. The men about the table had brought out a multichess board and started a six-member game. Moves were made rapidly and in silence. All eyes bent in furious concentration on the board. Theremon watched them intently and then rose and approached Aton, who sat apart in whispered conversation with Sheerin.

"Listen," he said, "let's go somewhere where we won't bother the rest of the fellows. I want to ask some questions."

The aged astronomer frowned sourly at him, but Sheerin chirped up, "Certainly. It will do me good to talk. It always does. Aton was telling me about your ideas concerning world reaction to a failure of the prediction—and I agree with you. I read your column pretty regularly, by the way, and as a general thing I like your views."

"Please, Sheerin," growled Aton.

"Eh? Oh, all right. We'll go into the next room. It has softer chairs, anyway."

There *were* softer chairs in the next room. There were also thick red curtains on the windows and a maroon carpet on the floor. With the bricky light of Beta pouring in, the general effect was one of dried blood.

Theremon shuddered, "Say, I'd give ten credits for a decent dose of white light for just a second. I wish Gamma or Delta were in the sky."

"What are your questions?" asked Aton. "Please remember that our time is limited. In a little over an hour and a quarter we're going upstairs, and after that there will be no time to talk."

"Well, here it is." Theremon leaned back and folded his hands on his chest. "You people seem so all-fired serious about this that I'm beginning to believe you. Would you mind explaining what it's all about?"

Aton exploded, "Do you mean to sit there and tell me that you've been bombarding us with ridicule without even finding out what we've been trying to say?"

The columnist grinned sheepishly. "It's not that bad, sir. I've got the general idea. You say that there is going to be a world-wide Darkness in a few hours and that all mankind will go violently insane. What I want now is the science behind it."

"No, you don't. No, you don't," broke in Sheerin. "If you ask Aton for that—supposing him to be in the mood to answer at all—he'll trot out pages of figures and volumes of graphs. You won't make head or tail of it. Now if you were to ask *me*, I could give you the layman's standpoint."

"All right; I ask you."

"Then first I'd like a drink." He rubbed his hands and looked at Aton.

"Water?" grunted Aton.

"Don't be silly!"

"Don't you be silly. No alcohol today. It would be too easy to get my men drunk. I can't afford to tempt them."

The psychologist grumbled wordlessly. He turned to Theremon, impaled him with his sharp eyes, and began.

"You realize, of course, that the history of civilization on Lagash displays a cyclic character—but I mean, *cyclic!*"

"I know," replied Theremon cautiously, "that that is the current archeological theory. Has it been accepted as a fact?"

"Just about. In this last century it's been generally agreed upon. This cyclic character is—or, rather, was—one of *the* great mysteries. We've located series of civilizations, nine of them definitely, and indications of others as well, all of which have reached heights comparable to our own, and all of which, without exception, were destroyed by fire at the very height of their culture.

"And no one could tell why. All centers of culture were thoroughly gutted by fire, with nothing left behind to give a hint as to the cause."

Theremon was following closely. "Wasn't there a Stone Age, too?"

"Probably, but as yet, practically nothing is known of it, except that men of that age were little more than rather intelligent apes. We can forget about that."

"I see. Go on!"

"There have been explanations of these recurrent catastrophes, all of a more or less fantastic nature. Some say that there are periodic rains of fire; some that Lagash passes through a sun every so often; some even wilder things. But there is one theory, quite different from all of these, that has been handed down over a period of centuries."

"I know. You mean this myth of the 'Stars' that the Cultists have in their 'Book of Revelations.' "

"Exactly," rejoined Sheerin with satisfaction. "The Cultists said that every two thousand and fifty years Lagash entered a huge cave, so that all the suns disappeared, and there came *total darkness all over the world!* And then, they say, things called Stars appeared, which robbed men of their souls and left them unreasoning brutes, so that they destroyed the civilization they themselves had built up. Of course, they mix all this up with a lot of religio-mystic notions, but that's the central idea."

There was a short pause in which Sheerin drew a long breath. "And now we come to the Theory of Universal Gravitation." He pronounced the phrase so that the capital letters sounded—and at that point Aton turned from the window, snorted loudly, and stalked out of the room.

The two stared after him, and Theremon said, "What's wrong?"

"Nothing in particular," replied Sheerin. "Two of the men were due several hours ago and haven't shown up yet. He's terrifically short-handed, of course, because all but the really essential men have gone to the Hideout."

"You don't think the two deserted, do you?"

"Who? Faro and Yimot? Of course not. Still, if they're not back within the hour, things would be a little sticky." He got to his feet suddenly, and his eyes twinkled. "Anyway, as long as Aton is gone—"

Tiptoeing to the nearest window, he squatted, and from the low window box beneath withdrew a bottle of red liquid that gurgled suggestively when he shook it.

"I *thought* Aton didn't know about this," he remarked as he trotted back to the table. "Here! We've only got one glass so, as the guest you can have it. I'll keep the bottle." And he filled the tiny cup with judicious care.

Theremon rose to protest, but Sheerin eyed him sternly. "Respect your elders, young man."

The newsman seated himself with a look of pain and anguish on his face. "Go ahead, then, you old villain."

The psychologist's Adam's apple wobbled as the bottle upended, and then, with a satisfied grunt and a smack of the lips, he began again.

"But what do you know about gravitation?"

"Nothing, except that it is a very recent development, not too well established, and that the math is so hard that only twelve men in Lagash are supposed to understand it."

"*Tcha!* Nonsense! Boloney! I can give you all the essential math in a sentence. The Law of Universal Gravitation states that there exists a cohesive force among all bodies of the universe, such that the amount of this force between any two given bodies is proportional to the product of their masses divided by the square of the distance between them."

"Is that all?"

"That's enough! It took four hundred years to develop it."

"Why that long? It sounded simple enough, the way you said it."

"Because great laws are not divined by flashes of inspiration, whatever you may think. It usually takes the combined work of a world full of scientists over a period of centuries. After Genovi 41 discovered that Lagash rotated about the sun Alpha, rather than vice versa—and that was four hundred years ago—astronomers have been working. The complex motions of the six suns were recorded and analyzed and unwoven. Theory after theory was advanced and checked and counterchecked and modified and abandoned and revived and converted to something else. It was a devil of a job."

Theremon nodded thoughtfully and held out his glass for more liquor. Sheerin grudgingly allowed a few ruby drops to leave the bottle.

"It was twenty years ago," he continued after remoistening his own throat, "that it was finally demonstrated that the Law of Universal Gravitation accounted exactly for the orbital motions of the six suns. It was a great triumph."

Sheerin stood up and walked to the window, still clutching his bottle. "And now we're getting to the point. In the last decade, the motions of Lagash about Alpha were computed according to gravity, and *it did not account for the orbit observed;* not even when all perturbations due to the other suns were included. Either the law was invalid, or there was another, as yet unknown, factor involved."

Theremon joined Sheerin at the window and gazed out past the wooded slopes to where the spires of Saro City gleamed bloodily on the horizon. The newsman felt the tension of uncertainty grow within him as he cast a short glance at Beta. It glowered redly at zenith, dwarfed and evil.

"Go ahead, sir," he said softly.

Sheerin replied, "Astronomers stumbled about for years,

each proposed theory more untenable than the one before —until Aton had the inspiration of calling in the Cult. The head of the Cult, Sor 5, had access to certain data that simplified the problem considerably. Aton set to work on a new track.

"What if there were another nonluminous planetary body such as Lagash? If there were, you know, it would shine only by reflected light, and if it were composed of bluish rock, as Lagash itself largely is, then in the redness of the sky, the eternal blaze of the suns would make it invisible— drown it out completely."

Theremon whistled, "What a screwy idea!"

"You think *that's* screwy? Listen to this: Suppose this body rotated about Lagash at such a distance and in such an orbit and had such a mass that its attraction would exactly account for the deviations of Lagash's orbit from theory—do you know what would happen?"

The columnist shook his head.

"Well, sometimes this body would get in the way of a sun." And Sheerin emptied what remained in the bottle at a draft.

"And it does, I suppose," said Theremon flatly.

"Yes! But only one sun lies in its plane of revolutions." He jerked a thumb at the shrunken sun above. "Beta! And it has been shown that the eclipse will occur only when the arrangement of the suns is such that Beta is alone in its hemisphere and at a maximum distance, at which time the moon is invariably at minimum distance. The eclipse that results, with the moon seven times the apparent diameter of Beta, covers all of Lagash and lasts well over half a day, so that no spot on the planet escapes the effect. *That eclipse comes once every two thousand and forty-nine years.*"

Theremon's face was drawn into an expressionless mask. "And that's my story?"

The psychologist nodded. "That's all of it. First the eclipse —which will start in three quarters of an hour—then universal Darkness, and, maybe, these mysterious Stars—then madness, and end of the cycle."

He brooded. "We had two months' leeway—we at the

Observatory—and that wasn't enough time to persuade Lagash of the danger. Two centuries might not have been enough. But our records are at the Hideout, and today we photograph the eclipse. The next cycle will *start off* with the truth, and when the *next* eclipse comes, mankind will at last be ready for it. Come to think of it, that's part of your story, too."

A thin wind ruffled the curtains at the window as Theremon opened it and leaned out. It played coldly with his hair as he stared at the crimson sunlight on his hand. Then he turned in sudden rebellion.

"What is there in Darkness to drive *me* mad?"

Sheerin smiled to himself as he spun the empty liquor bottle with abstracted motions of his hand. "Have you ever experienced Darkness, young man?"

The newsman leaned against the wall and considered. "No. Can't say I have. But I know what it is. Just—uh—" He made vague motions with his fingers, and then brightened. "Just no light. Like in caves."

"Have you ever been in a cave?"

"In a *cave!* Of course not!"

"I thought not. *I* tried last week—just to see—but I got out in a hurry. I went in until the mouth of the cave was just visible as a blur of light, with black everywhere else. I never thought a person my weight could run that fast."

Theremon's lip curled. "Well, if it comes to that, I guess I wouldn't have run, if I had been there."

The psychologist studied the young man with an annoyed frown.

"My, don't you talk big! I dare you to draw the curtain."

Theremon looked his surprise and said, "What for? If we had four or five suns out there we might want to cut the light down a bit for comfort, but now we haven't enough light as it is."

"That's the point. Just draw the curtain; then come here and sit down."

"All right." Theremon reached for the tasseled string and jerked. The red curtain slid across the wide window, the brass rings hissing their way along the crossbar, and a dusk-red shadow clamped down on the room.

Theremon's footsteps sounded hollowly in the silence as he made his way to the table, and then they stopped halfway. "I can't see you, sir," he whispered.

"Feel your way," ordered Sheerin in a strained voice.

"But I can't see you, sir." The newsman was breathing harshly. "I can't see anything."

"What did you expect?" came the grim reply. "Come here and sit down!"

The footsteps sounded again, waveringly, approaching slowly. There was the sound of someone fumbling with a chair. Theremon's voice came thinly, "Here I am. I feel . . . *ulp* . . . all right."

"You like it, do you?"

"N-no. It's pretty awful. The walls seem to be—" He paused. "They seem to be closing in on me. I keep wanting to push them away. But I'm not going *mad!* In fact, the feeling isn't as bad as it was."

"All right. Draw the curtain back again."

There were cautious footsteps through the dark, the rustle of Theremon's body against the curtain as he felt for the tassel, and then the triumphant *ro-o-osh* of the curtain slithering back. Red light flooded the room, and with a cry of joy Theremon looked up at the sun.

Sheerin wiped the moistness off his forehead with the back of a hand and said shakily, "And that was just a dark room."

"It can be stood," said Theremon lightly.

"Yes, a dark room can. But were you at the Jonglor Centennial Exposition two years ago?"

"No, it so happens I never got around to it. Six thousand miles was just a bit too much to travel, even for the exposition."

"Well, I was there. You remember hearing about the 'Tunnel of Mystery' that broke all records in the amusement area —for the first month or so, anyway?"

"Yes. Wasn't there some fuss about it?"

"Very little. It was hushed up. You see, that Tunnel of Mystery was just a mile-long tunnel—with no lights. You got into a little open car and jolted along through Darkness for fifteen minutes. It was very popular—while it lasted."

"Popular?"

"Certainly. There's a fascination in being frightened *when it's part of a game*. A baby is born with three instinctive fears: of loud noises, of falling, and of the absence of light. That's why it's considered so funny to jump at someone and shout 'Boo!' That's why it's such fun to ride a roller coaster. And that's why that Tunnel of Mystery started cleaning up. People came out of that Darkness shaking, breathless, half dead with fear, but they kept on paying to get in."

"Wait awhile, I remember now. Some people came out dead, didn't they? There were rumors of that after it shut down."

The psychologist snorted. "Bah! Two or three died. That was nothing! They paid off the families of the dead ones and argued the Jonglor City Council into forgetting it. After all, they said, if people with weak hearts want to go through the tunnel, it was at their own risk—and besides, it wouldn't happen again. So they put a doctor in the front office and had every customer go through a physical examination before getting into the car. That actually *boosted* ticket sales."

"Well, then?"

"But, you see, there was something else. People sometimes came out in perfect order, except that they refused to go into buildings—any buildings; including palaces, mansions, apartment houses, tenements, cottages, huts, shacks, lean-tos, and tents."

Theremon looked shocked. "You mean they refused to come in out of the open. Where'd they sleep?"

"In the open."

"They should have *forced* them inside."

"Oh, they did, they did. Whereupon these people went into violent hysterics and did their best to bat their brains out against the nearest wall. Once you got them inside, you couldn't keep them there without a strait jacket and a shot of morphine."

"They must have been crazy."

"Which is exactly what they were. One person out of every ten who went into that tunnel came out that way. They called in the psychologists, and we did the only thing possible. We closed down the exhibit." He spread his hands.

"What was the matter with those people?" asked Theremon finally.

"Essentially the same thing that was the matter with you when you thought the walls of the room were crushing in on you in the dark. There is a psychological term for mankind's instinctive fear of the absence of light. We call it 'claustrophobia,' because the lack of light is always tied up with inclosed places, so that fear of one is fear of the other. You see?"

"And those people of the tunnel?"

"Those people of the tunnel consisted of those unfortunates whose mentality did not quite possess the resiliency to overcome the claustrophobia that overtook them in the Darkness. Fifteen minutes without light is a long time; you only had two or three minutes, and I believe you were fairly upset.

"The people of the tunnel had what is called a 'claustrophobic fixation.' Their latent fear of Darkness and inclosed places had crystallized and become active, and, as far as we can tell, permanent. *That's* what fifteen minutes in the dark will do."

There was a long silence, and Theremon's forehead wrinkled slowly into a frown. "I don't believe it's that bad."

"You mean you don't want to believe," snapped Sheerin. "You're afraid to believe. Look out the window!"

Theremon did so, and the psychologist continued without pausing, "Imagine Darkness—everywhere. No light, as far as you can see. The houses, the trees, the fields, the earth, the sky—*black!* And Stars thrown in, for all I know—whatever *they* are. Can you conceive it?"

"Yes, I can," declared Theremon truculently.

And Sheerin slammed his fist down upon the table in sudden passion. "You lie! You can't conceive that. Your brain wasn't built for the conception any more than it was built for the conception of infinity or of eternity. You can only talk about it. A fraction of the reality upsets you, and when the real thing comes, your brain is going to be presented with a phenomenon outside its limits of comprehension. You will go mad, completely and permanently! There is no question of it!"

He added sadly, "And another couple of millenniums of painful struggle comes to nothing. Tomorrow there won't be a city standing unharmed in all Lagash."

Theremon recovered part of his mental equilibrium. "That doesn't follow. I still don't see that I can go looney just because there isn't a Sun in the sky—but even if I did, and everyone else did, how does that harm the cities? Are we going to blow them down?"

But Sheerin was angry, too. "If you were in Darkness, what would you want more than anything else; what would it be that every instinct would call for? Light, damn you, *light!*"

"Well?"

"And how would you get light?"

"I don't know," said Theremon flatly.

"What's the *only* way to get light, short of the sun?"

"How should I know?"

They were standing face to face and nose to nose.

Sheerin said, "You burn something, mister. Ever see a forest fire? Ever go camping and cook a stew over a wood fire? Heat isn't the only thing burning wood gives off, you know. It gives off light, and people know that. And when it's dark they want light, and they're going to *get it.*"

"So they burn wood?"

"So they burn whatever they can get. They've got to have light. They've got to burn something, and wood isn't handy —so they'll burn whatever is nearest. They'll have their light— and every center of habitation goes up in flames!"

Eyes held each other as though the whole matter were a personal affair of respective will powers, and then Theremon broke away wordlessly. His breathing was harsh and ragged, and he scarcely noted the sudden hubbub that came from the adjoining room behind the closed door.

Sheerin spoke, and it was with an effort that he made it sound matter-of-fact. "I think I heard Yimot's voice. He and Faro are probably back. Let's go in and see what kept them."

"Might as well!" muttered Theremon. He drew a long breath and seemed to shake himself. The tension was broken.

The room was in an uproar, with members of the staff clustering about two young men who were removing outer garments even as they parried the miscellany of questions being thrown at them.

Aton bustled through the crowd and faced the newcomers angrily. "Do you realize that it's less than half an hour before deadline? Where have you two been?"

Faro 24 seated himself and rubbed his hands. His cheeks were red with the outdoor chill. "Yimot and I have just finished carrying through a little crazy experiment of our own. We've been trying to see if we couldn't construct an arrangement by which we could simulate the appearance of Darkness and Stars so as to get an advance notion as to how it looked."

There was a confused murmur from the listeners, and a sudden look of interest entered Aton's eyes. "There wasn't anything said of this before. How did you go about it?"

"Well," said Faro, "the idea came to Yimot and myself long ago, and we've been working it out in our spare time. Yimot knew of a low one-story house down in the city with a domed roof—it had once been used as a museum, I think. Anyway, we bought it—"

"Where did you get the money?" interrupted Aton peremptorily.

"Our bank accounts," grunted Yimot 70. "It cost two thousand credits." Then, defensively, "Well, what of it? Tomorrow, two thousand credits will be two thousand pieces of paper. That's all."

"Sure," agreed Faro. "We bought the place and rigged it up with black velvet from top to bottom so as to get as perfect a Darkness as possible. Then we punched tiny holes in the ceiling and through the roof and covered them with little metal caps, all of which could be shoved aside simultaneously at the close of a switch. At least, we didn't do that part ourselves; we got a carpenter and an electrician and some others—money didn't count. The point was that we could get the light to shine through those holes in the roof, so that we could get a starlike effect."

Not a breath was drawn during the pause that followed. Aton said stiffly:

"You had no right to make a private—"

Faro seemed abashed. "I know, sir—but, frankly, Yimot and I thought the experiment was a little dangerous. If the effect really worked, we half expected to go mad—from what Sheerin says about all this, we thought that would be rather likely. We wanted to take the risk ourselves. Of course, if we found we could retain sanity, it occurred to us that we might develop immunity to the real thing, and then expose the rest of you to the same thing. But things didn't work out at all—"

"Why, what happened?"

It was Yimot who answered. "We shut ourselves in and allowed our eyes to get accustomed to the dark. It's an extremely creepy feeling because the total Darkness makes you feel as if the walls and ceiling are crushing in on you. But we got over that and pulled the switch. The caps fell away and the roof glittered all over with little dots of light—"

"Well?"

"Well—nothing. That was the whacky part of it. Nothing happened. It was just a roof with holes in it, and that's just what it looked like. We tried it over and over again—that's what kept us so late—but there just isn't any effect at all."

There followed a shocked silence, and all eyes turned to Sheerin, who sat motionless, mouth open.

Theremon was the first to speak. "You know what this does to this whole theory you've built up, Sheerin, don't you?" He was grinning with relief.

But Sheerin raised his hand. "Now wait awhile. Just let me think this through." And then he snapped his fingers, and when he lifted his head there was neither surprise nor uncertainty in his eyes. "Of course—"

He never finished. From somewhere up above there

sounded a sharp clang, and Beenay, starting to his feet, dashed up the stairs with a "What the devil!"

The rest followed after.

Things happened quickly. Once up in the dome, Beenay cast one horrified glance at the shattered photographic plates and at the man bending over them; and then hurled himself fiercely at the intruder, getting a death grip on his throat. There was a wild threshing, and as others of the staff joined in, the stranger was swallowed up and smothered under the weight of half a dozen angry men.

Aton came up last, breathing heavily. "Let him up!"

There was a reluctant unscrambling and the stranger, panting harshly with his clothes torn and his forehead bruised, was hauled to his feet. He had a short yellow beard curled elaborately in the style affected by the Cultists.

Beenay shifted his hold to a collar grip and shook the man savagely. "All right, rat, what's the idea? These plates—"

"I wasn't after *them*," retorted the Cultist coldly. "That was an accident."

Beenay followed his glowering stare and snarled, "I see. You were after the cameras themselves. The accident with the plates was a stroke of luck for you, then. If you had touched Snapping Bertha or any of the others, you would have died by slow torture. As it is—" He drew his fist back.

Aton grabbed his sleeve. "Stop that! Let him go!"

The young technician wavered, and his arm dropped reluctantly. Aton pushed him aside and confronted the Cultist. "You're Latimer, aren't you?"

The Cultist bowed stiffly and indicated the symbol upon his hip. "I am Latimer 25, adjutant of the third class to his serenity, Sor 5."

"And"—Aton's white eyebrows lifted—"you were with his serenity when he visited me last week, weren't you?"

Latimer bowed a second time.

"Now, then, what do you want?"

"Nothing that you would give me of your own free will."

"Sor 5 sent you, I suppose—or is this your own idea?"

"I won't answer that question."

"Will there be any further visitors?"

"I won't answer that, either."

Aton glanced at his timepiece and scowled. "Now, man, what is it your master wants of me? I have fulfilled my end of the bargain."

Latimer smiled faintly, but said nothing.

"I asked him," continued Aton angrily, "for data only the Cult could supply, and it was given to me. For that, thank you. In return, I promised to prove the essential truth of the creed of the Cult."

"There was no need to prove that," came the proud retort. "It stands proven by the 'Book of Revelations.'"

"For the handful that constitute the Cult, yes. Don't pretend to mistake my meaning. I offered to present scientific backing for your beliefs. And I did!"

The Cultist's eyes narrowed bitterly. "Yes, you did—with a fox's subtlety, for your pretended explanation backed our beliefs, and at the same time removed all necessity for them. You made of the Darkness and of the Stars a natural phenomenon, and removed all its real significance. That was blasphemy."

"If so, the fault isn't mine. The facts exist. What can I do but state them?"

"Your 'facts' are a fraud and a delusion."

Aton stamped angrily. "How do *you* know?"

And the answer came with the certainty of absolute faith. "I *know!*"

The director purpled and Beenay whispered urgently. Aton waved him silent. "And what does Sor 5 want us to do? He still thinks, I suppose, that in trying to warn the world to take measures against the menace of madness, we are placing innumerable souls in jeopardy. We aren't succeeding, if that means anything to him."

"The attempt itself has done harm enough, and your vicious effort to gain information by means of your devilish instruments must be stopped. We obey the will of their Stars, and I only regret that my clumsiness prevented me from wrecking your infernal devices."

"It wouldn't have done you too much good," returned Aton. "All our data, except for the direct evidence we intend collecting right now, is already safely cached and well beyond possibility of harm." He smiled grimly. "But that does not affect your present status as an attempted burglar and criminal."

He turned to the men behind him. "Someone call the police at Saro City."

There was a cry of distaste from Sheerin. "Damn it, Aton, what's wrong with you? There's no time for that. Here"—he bustled his way forward—"let me handle this."

Aton stared down his nose at the psychologist. "This is not the time for your monkeyshines, Sheerin. Will you please let me handle this my own way? Right now you are a complete outsider here, and don't forget it."

Sheerin's mouth twisted eloquently. "Now why should we go to the impossible trouble of calling the police—with Beta's eclipse a matter of minutes from now—when this young man here is perfectly willing to pledge his word of honor to remain and cause no trouble whatsoever?"

The Cultist answered promptly, "I will do no such thing. You're free to do what you want, but it's only fair to warn you that just as soon as I get my chance I'm going to finish what I came out here to do. If it's my word of honor you're relying on, you'd better call the police."

Sheerin smiled in a friendly fashion. "You're a determined cuss, aren't you? Well, I'll explain something. Do you see that young man at the window? He's a strong, husky fellow, quite handy with his fists, and he's an outsider besides. Once the eclipse starts there will be nothing for him to do except keep an eye on you. Besides him, there will be myself—a little too stout for active fisticuffs, but still able to help."

"Well, what of it?" demanded Latimer frozenly.

"Listen and I'll tell you," was the reply. "Just as soon as the eclipse starts, we're going to take you, Theremon and I, and deposit you in a little closet with one door, to which is attached one giant lock and no windows. You will remain there for the duration."

"And afterward," breathed Latimer fiercely, "there'll be no one to let me out. I know as well as you do what the coming of the Stars means—I know it far better than you. With all your minds gone, you are not likely to free me. Suffocation or slow starvation, is it? About what I might have expected from a group of scientists. But I don't give my word. It's a matter of principle, and I won't discuss it further."

Aton seemed perturbed. His faded eyes were troubled. "Really, Sheerin, locking him—"

"Please!" Sheerin motioned him impatiently to silence. "I don't think for a moment things will go that far. Latimer has just tried a clever little bluff, but I'm not a psychologist just because I like the sound of the word." He grinned at the Cultist. "Come now, you don't really think I'm trying anything as crude as slow starvation. My dear Latimer, if I lock you in the closet, you are not going to see the Darkness, and you are not going to see the Stars. It does not take much of a knowledge of the fundamental creed of the Cult to realize that for you to be hidden from the Stars when they appear means the loss of your immortal soul. Now, I believe you to be an honorable man. I'll accept your word of honor to make no further effort to disrupt proceedings if you'll offer it."

A vein throbbed in Latimer's temple, and he seemed to shrink within himself as he said thickly, "You have it!" And then he added with swift fury, "But it is my consolation that you will all be damned for your deeds of today." He turned on his heel and stalked to the high three-legged stool by the door.

Sheerin nodded to the columnist. "Take a seat next to him, Theremon—just as a formality. Hey, Theremon!"

But the newspaperman didn't move. He had gone pale to the lips. "Look at that!" The finger he pointed toward the sky shook, and his voice was dry and cracked.

There was one simultaneous gasp as every eye followed the pointing finger and, for one breathless moment, stared frozenly.

Beta was chipped on one side!

The tiny bit of encroaching blackness was perhaps the width of a fingernail, but to the staring watchers it magnified itself into the crack of doom.

Only for a moment they watched, and after that there was a shrieking confusion that was even shorter of duration and which gave way to an orderly scurry of activity—each man at his prescribed job. At the crucial moment there was no time for emotion. The men were merely scientists with work to do. Even Aton had melted away.

Sheerin said prosaically, "First contact must have been made fifteen minutes ago. A little early, but pretty good considering the uncertainties involved in the calculation." He looked about him and tiptoed to Theremon, who still remained staring out the window, and dragged him away gently.

"Aton is furious," he whispered, "so stay away. He missed first contact on account of this fuss with Latimer, and if you get in his way he'll have you thrown out the window."

Theremon nodded shortly and sat down. Sheerin stared in surprise at him.

"The devil, man," he exclaimed, "you're shaking."

"Eh?" Theremon licked dry lips and then tried to smile. "I don't feel very well, and that's a fact."

The psychologist's eyes hardened. "You're not losing your nerve?"

"No!" cried Theremon in a flash of indignation. "Give me a chance, will you? I haven't really believed this rigmarole—not way down beneath, anyway—till just this minute. Give me a chance to get used to the idea. *You've* been preparing yourself for two months or more."

"You're right, at that," replied Sheerin thoughtfully. "Listen! Have you got a family—parents, wife, children?"

Theremon shook his head. "You mean the Hideout, I suppose. No, you don't have to worry about that. I have a sister, but she's two thousand miles away. I don't even know her exact address."

"Well, then, what about yourself? You've got time to get there, and they're one short anyway, since I left. After all, you're not needed here, and you'd make a darned fine addition—"

Theremon looked at the other wearily. "You think I'm scared stiff, don't you? Well, get this, mister, I'm a newspaperman and I've been assigned to cover a story. I intend covering it."

There was a faint smile on the psychologist's face. "I see. Professional honor, is that it?"

"You might call it that. But, man, I'd give my right arm for another bottle of that sockeroo juice even half the size of the one *you* hogged. If ever a fellow needed a drink, I do."

He broke off. Sheerin was nudging him violently. "Do you hear that? Listen!"

Theremon followed the motion of the other's chin and stared at the Cultist, who oblivious to all about him, faced the window, a look of wild elation on his face, droning to himself the while in singsong fashion.

"What's he saying?" whispered the columnist.

"He's quoting 'Book of Revelations,' fifth chapter," replied Sheerin. Then, urgently, "Keep quiet and listen, I tell you."

The Cultist's voice had risen in a sudden increase of fervor:

"'And it came to pass that in those days the Sun, Beta, held lone vigil in the sky for ever longer periods as the revolutions passed; until such time as for full half a revolution, it alone, shrunken and cold, shone down upon Lagash.

"'And men did assemble in the public squares and in the highways, there to debate and to marvel at the sight, for a strange depression had seized them. Their minds were troubled and their speech confused, for the souls of men awaited the coming of the Stars.

"'And in the city of Trigon, at high noon, Vendret 2 came forth and said unto the men of Trigon, "Lo ye sinners! Though ye scorn the ways of righteousness, yet will the time of reckoning come. Even now the Cave approaches to swallow Lagash; yea, and all it contains."

"'And even as he spoke the lip of the Cave of Darkness passed the edge of Beta so that to all Lagash it was hidden from sight. Loud were the cries of men as it vanished, and great the fear of soul that fell upon them.

"'It came to pass that the Darkness of the Cave fell upon Lagash, and there was no light on all the surface of Lagash. Men were even as blinded, nor could one man see his neighbor, though he felt his breath upon his face.

" 'And in this blackness there appeared the Stars, in countless numbers, and to the strains of ineffable music of a beauty so wondrous that the very leaves of the trees turned to tongues that cried out in wonder.

" 'And in that moment the souls of men departed from them, and their abandoned bodies became even as beasts; yea, even as brutes of the wild; so that through the blackened streets of the cities of Lagash they prowled with wild cries.

" 'From the Stars there then reached down the Heavenly Flame, and where it touched, the cities of Lagash flamed to utter destruction, so that of man and of the works of man nought remained.

" 'Even then—' "

There was a subtle change in Latimer's tone. His eyes had not shifted, but somehow he had become aware of the absorbed attention of the other two. Easily, without pausing for breath, the timbre of his voice shifted and the syllables became more liquid.

Theremon, caught by surprise, stared. The words seemed on the border of familiarity. There was an elusive shift in the accent, a tiny change in the vowel stress; nothing more —yet Latimer had become thoroughly unintelligible.

Sheerin smiled slyly. "He shifted to some old-cycle tongue, probably their traditional second cycle. That was the language in which the 'Book of Revelations' had originally been written, you know."

"It doesn't matter; I've heard enough." Theremon shoved his chair back and brushed his hair back with hands that no longer shook. "I feel much better now."

"You do?" Sheerin seemed mildly surprised.

"I'll say I do. I had a bad case of jitters just a while back. Listening to you and your gravitation and seeing that eclipse start almost finished me. But this"—he jerked a contemptuous thumb at the yellow-bearded Cultist—"*this* is the sort of thing my nurse used to tell me. I've been laughing at that sort of thing all my life. I'm not going to let it scare me *now*."

He drew a deep breath and said with a hectic gaiety, "But

if I expect to keep on the good side of myself, I'm going to turn my chair away from the window."

Sheerin said, "Yes, but you'd better talk lower. Aton just lifted his head out of that box he's got it stuck into and gave you a look that should have killed you."

Theremon made a mouth. "I forgot about the old fellow." With elaborate care he turned the chair from the window, cast one distasteful look over his shoulder and said, "It has occurred to me that there must be considerable immunity against this Star madness."

The psychologist did not answer immediately. Beta was past its zenith now, and the square of bloody sunlight that outlined the window upon the floor had lifted into Sheerin's lap. He stared at its dusky color thoughtfully and then bent and squinted into the sun itself.

The chip in its side had grown to a black encroachment that covered a third of Beta. He shuddered, and when he straightened once more his florid cheeks did not contain quite as much color as they had had previously.

With a smile that was almost apologetic, he reversed his chair also. "There are probably two million people in Saro City that are all trying to join the Cult at once in one gigantic revival." Then, ironically, "The Cult is in for an hour of un-exampled prosperity. I trust they'll make the most of it. Now, what was it you said?"

"Just this. How do the Cultists manage to keep the 'Book of Revelations' going from cycle to cycle, and how on Lagash did it get written in the first place? There must have been some sort of immunity, for if everyone had gone mad, who would be left to write the book?"

Sheerin stared at his questioner ruefully. "Well, now, young man, there isn't any eyewitness answer to that, but we've got a few damned good notions as to what happened. You see, there are three kinds of people who might remain relatively unaffected. First, the very few who don't see the Stars at all; the blind, those who drink themselves into a stupor at the beginning of the eclipse and remain so to the end. We leave them out—because they aren't really witnesses.

"Then there are children below six, to whom the world

as a whole is too new and strange for them to be too frightened at Stars and Darkness. They would be just another item in an already surprising world. You see that, don't you?"

The other nodded doubtfully. "I suppose so."

"Lastly, there are those whose minds are too coarsely grained to be entirely toppled. The very insensitive would be scarcely affected—oh, such people as some of our older, work-broken peasants. Well, the children would have fugitive memories, and that, combined with the confused, incoherent babblings of the half-mad morons, formed the basis for the 'Book of Revelations.'

"Naturally, the book was based, in the first place, on the testimony of those least qualified to serve as historians; that is, children and morons; and was probably extensively edited and re-edited through the cycles."

"Do you suppose," broke in Theremon, "that they carried the book through the cycles the way we're planning on handing on the secret of gravitation?"

Sheerin shrugged. "Perhaps, but their exact method is unimportant. They do it, somehow. The point I was getting at was that the book can't help but be a mass of distortion, even if it is based on fact. For instance, do you remember the experiment with the holes in the roof that Faro and Yimot tried —the one that didn't work?"

"Yes."

"You know why it didn't w—" He stopped and rose in alarm, for Aton was approaching, his face a twisted mask of consternation. *"What's happened?"*

Aton drew him aside and Sheerin could feel the fingers on his elbow twitching.

"Not so loud!" Aton's voice was low and tortured. "I've just gotten word from the Hideout on the private line."

Sheerin broke in anxiously. "They are in trouble?"

"Not *they*." Aton stressed the pronoun significantly. "They sealed themselves off just a while ago, and they're going to stay buried till day after tomorrow. They're safe. But the *city*, Sheerin—it's a shambles. You have no idea—" He was having difficulty in speaking.

"Well?" snapped Sheerin impatiently. "What of it? It will get worse. What are you shaking about?" Then, suspiciously, "How do you feel?"

Aton's eyes sparked angrily at the insinuation, and then faded to anxiety once more. "You don't understand. The Cultists are active. They're rousing the people to storm the Observatory—promising them immediate entrance into grace, promising them salvation, promising them anything. What are we to do, Sheerin?"

Sheerin's head bent, and he stared in long abstraction at his toes. He tapped his chin with one knuckle, then looked up and said crisply, "Do? What is there to do? Nothing at all! Do the men know of this?"

"No, of course not!"

"Good! Keep it that way. How long till totality?"

"Not quite an hour."

"There's nothing to do but gamble. It will take time to organize any really formidable mob, and it will take more time to get them out here. We're a good five miles from the city—"

He glared out the window, down the slopes to where the farmed patches gave way to clumps of white houses in the suburbs; down to where the metropolis itself was a blur on the horizon—a mist in the waning blaze of Beta.

He repeated without turning, "It will take time. Keep on working and pray that totality comes first."

Beta was cut in half, the line of division pushing a slight concavity into the still-bright portion of the Sun. It was like a gigantic eyelid shutting slantwise over the light of a world.

The faint clatter of the room in which he stood faded into oblivion, and he sensed only the thick silence of the fields outside. The very insects seemed frightened mute. And things were dim.

He jumped at the voice in his ear. Theremon said, "Is something wrong?"

"Eh? Er—no. Get back to the chair. We're in the way." They slipped back to their corner, but the psychologist did not speak for a time. He lifted a finger and loosened his collar. He twisted his neck back and forth but found no relief. He looked up suddenly.

"Are you having any difficulty in breathing?"

The newspaperman opened his eyes wide and drew two or three long breaths. "No. Why?"

"I looked out the window too long, I suppose. The dimness got me. Difficulty in breathing is one of the first symptoms of a claustrophobic attack."

Theremon drew another long breath. "Well, it hasn't got me yet. Say, here's another of the fellows."

Beenay had interposed his bulk between the light and the pair in the corner, and Sheerin squinted up at him anxiously. "Hello, Beenay."

The astronomer shifted his weight to the other foot and smiled feebly. "You won't mind if I sit down awhile and join in on the talk? My cameras are set, and there's nothing to do till totality." He paused and eyed the Cultist, who fifteen minutes earlier had drawn a small, skin-bound book from his sleeve and had been poring intently over it ever since. "That rat hasn't been making trouble, has he?"

Sheerin shook his head. His shoulders were thrown back and he frowned his concentration as he forced himself to breathe regularly. He said, "Have you had any trouble breathing, Beenay?"

Beenay sniffed the air in his turn. "It doesn't seem stuffy to me."

"A touch of claustrophobia," explained Sheerin apologetically.

"Oh-h-h! It worked itself differently with me. I get the impression that my eyes are going back on me. Things seem to blur and—well, nothing is clear. And it's cold, too."

"Oh, it's cold, all right. That's no illusion." Theremon grimaced. "My toes feel as if I've been shipping them cross country in a refrigerating car."

"What we need," put in Sheerin, "is to keep our minds busy with extraneous affairs. I was telling you a while ago, Theremon, why Faro's experiments with the holes in the roof came to nothing."

"You were just beginning," replied Theremon. He encircled a knee with both arms and nuzzled his chin against it.

"Well, as I started to say, they were misled by taking the 'Book of Revelations' literally. There probably wasn't any sense in attaching any physical significance to the Stars. It might be, you know, that in the presence of total Darkness, the mind finds it absolutely necessary to create light. This illusion of light might be all the Stars there really are."

"In other words," interposed Theremon, "you mean the Stars are the results of the madness and not one of the causes. Then, what good will Beenay's photographs be?"

"To prove that it is an illusion, maybe; or to prove the opposite, for all I know. Then again—"

But Beenay had drawn his chair closer, and there was an expression of sudden enthusiasm on his face. "Say, I'm glad you two got on to this subject." His eyes narrowed and he lifted one finger. "I've been thinking about these Stars and I've got a really cute notion. Of course, it's strictly ocean foam, and I'm not trying to advance it seriously, but I think it's interesting. Do you want to hear it?"

He seemed half reluctant, but Sheerin leaned back and said, "Go ahead! I'm listening."

"Well, then, supposing there were other suns in the universe." He broke off a little bashfully. "I mean suns that are so far away that they're too dim to see. It sounds as if I've been reading some of that fantastic fiction, I suppose."

"Not necessarily. Still, isn't that possibility eliminated by the fact that, according to the Law of Gravitation, they would make themselves evident by their attractive forces?"

"Not if they were far enough off," rejoined Beenay, "really far off—maybe as much as four light years, or even more. We'd never be able to detect perturbations then, because they'd be too small. Say that there were a lot of suns that far off; a dozen or two, maybe."

Theremon whistled melodiously. "What an idea for a good Sunday supplement article. Two dozen suns in a universe eight light years across. Wow! That would shrink *our* universe into insignificance. The readers would eat it up."

"Only an idea," said Beenay with a grin, "but you see the

point. During eclipse, these dozen suns would become visible, because there'd be no *real* sunlight to drown them out. Since they're so far off, they'd appear small, like so many little marbles. Of course, the Cultists talk of millions of Stars, but that's probably exaggeration. There just isn't any place in the universe you could put a million suns—unless they touch one another."

Sheerin had listened with gradually increasing interest. "You've hit something there, Beenay. And exaggeration is just exactly what would happen. Our minds, as you probably know, can't grasp directly any number higher than five; above that there is only the concept of 'many.' A dozen would become a million just like that. A damn good idea!"

"And I've got another cute little notion," Beenay said. "Have you ever thought what a simple problem gravitation would be if only you had a sufficiently simple system? Supposing you had a universe in which there was a planet with only one sun. The planet would travel in a perfect ellipse and the exact nature of the gravitational force would be so evident it could be accepted as an axiom. Astronomers on such a world would start off with gravity probably before they even invent the telescope. Naked-eye observation would be enough."

"But would such a system be dynamically stable?" questioned Sheerin doubtfully.

"Sure! They call it the 'one-and-one' case. It's been worked out mathematically, but it's the philosophical implications that interest me."

"It's nice to think about," admitted Sheerin, "as a pretty abstraction—like a perfect gas or absolute zero."

"Of course," continued Beenay, "there's the catch that life would be impossible on such a planet. It wouldn't get enough heat and light, and if it rotated there would be total Darkness half of each day. You couldn't expect life—which is fundamentally dependent upon light—to develop under those conditions. Besides—"

Sheerin's chair went over backward as he sprang to his feet in a rude interruption. "Aton's brought out the lights."

Beenay said, "Huh," turned to stare, and then grinned halfway around his head in open relief.

There were half a dozen foot-long, inch-thick rods cradled in Aton's arms. He glared over them at the assembled staff members.

"Get back to work, all of you. Sheerin, come here and help me!"

Sheerin trotted to the older man's side and, one by one, in utter silence, the two adjusted the rods in makeshift metal holders suspended from the walls.

With the air of one carrying through the most sacred item of a religious ritual, Sheerin scraped a large, clumsy match into spluttering life and passed it to Aton, who carried the flame to the upper end of one of the rods.

It hesitated there awhile, playing futilely about the tip, until a sudden, crackling flare cast Aton's lined face into yellow highlights. He withdrew the match and a spontaneous cheer rattled the window.

The rod was topped by six inches of wavering flame! Methodically, the other rods were lighted, until six independent fires turned the rear of the room yellow.

The light was dim, dimmer even than the tenuous sunlight. The flames reeled crazily, giving birth to drunken, swaying shadows. The torches smoked devilishly and smelled like a bad day in the kitchen. But they emitted yellow light.

There is something to yellow light—after four hours of somber, dimming Beta. Even Latimer had lifted his eyes from his book and stared in wonder.

Sheerin warmed his hands at the nearest, regardless of the soot that gathered upon them in a fine, gray powder, and muttered ecstatically to himself. "Beautiful! Beautiful! I never realized before what a wonderful color yellow is."

But Theremon regarded the torches suspiciously. He wrinkled his nose at the rancid odor, and said, "What are those things?"

"Wood," said Sheerin shortly.

"Oh, no, they're not. They aren't burning. The top inch is charred and the flame just keeps shooting up out of nothing."

"That's the beauty of it. This is a really efficient artificial-light mechanism. We made a few hundred of them, but most went to the Hideout, of course. You see"—he turned and wiped his blackened hands upon his handkerchief—"you take the pithy core of coarse water reeds, dry them thoroughly and soak them in animal grease. Then you set fire to it and the grease burns, little by little. These torches will burn for almost half an hour without stopping. Ingenious, isn't it? It was developed by one of our own young men at Saro University."

After the momentary sensation, the dome had quieted. Latimer had carried his chair directly beneath a torch and continued reading, lips moving in the monotonous recital of invocations to the Stars. Beenay had drifted away to his cameras once more, and Theremon seized the opportunity to add to his notes on the article he was going to write for the Saro City *Chronicle* the next day—a procedure he had been following for the last two hours in a perfectly methodical, perfectly conscientious and, as he was well aware, perfectly meaningless fashion.

But, as the gleam of amusement in Sheerin's eyes indicated, careful note taking occupied his mind with something other than the fact that the sky was gradually turning a horrible deep purple-red, as if it were one gigantic, freshly peeled beet; and so it fulfilled its purpose.

The air grew, somehow, denser. Dusk, like a palpable entity, entered the room, and the dancing circle of yellow light about the torches etched itself into ever-sharper distinction against the gathering grayness beyond. There was the odor of smoke and the presence of little chuckling sounds that the torches made as they burned; the soft pad of one of the men circling the table at which he worked, on hesitant tiptoes; the occasional indrawn breath of someone trying to retain composure in a world that was retreating into the shadow.

It was Theremon who first heard the extraneous noise. It was a vague, unorganized *impression* of sound that would have gone unnoticed but for the dead silence that prevailed within the dome.

The newsman sat upright and replaced his notebook. He held his breath and listened; then, with considerable reluctance, threaded his way between the solarscope and one of Beenay's cameras and stood before the window.

The silence ripped to fragments at his startled shout: *"Sheerin!"*

Work stopped! The psychologist was at his side in a moment. Aton joined him. Even Yimot 70, high in his little lean-back seat at the eyepiece of the gigantic solarscope, paused and looked downward.

Outside, Beta was a mere smoldering splinter, taking one last desperate look at Lagash. The eastern horizon, in the direction of the city, was lost in Darkness, and the road from Saro to the Observatory was a dull-red line bordered on both sides by wooden tracts, the trees of which had somehow lost individuality and merged into a continuous shadowy mass.

But it was the highway itself that held attention, for along it there surged another, and infinitely menacing, shadowy mass.

Aton cried in a cracked voice, "The madmen from the city! They've come!"

"How long to totality?" demanded Sheerin.

"Fifteen minutes, but . . . but they'll be here in five."

"Never mind, keep the men working. We'll hold them off. This place is built like a fortress. Aton, keep an eye on our young Cultist just for luck. Theremon, come with me."

Sheerin was out the door, and Theremon was at his heels. The stairs stretched below them in tight, circular sweeps about the central shaft, fading into a dank and dreary grayness.

The first momentum of their rush had carried them fifty feet down, so that the dim, flickering yellow from the open door of the dome had disappeared and both up above and down below the same dusky shadow crushed in upon them.

Sheerin paused, and his pudgy hand clutched at his chest. His eyes bulged and his voice was a dry cough. "I can't . . . breathe . . . go down . . . yourself. Close all doors—"

Theremon took a few downward steps, then turned. "Wait!

Can you hold out a minute?" He was panting himself. The air passed in and out his lungs like so much molasses, and there was a little germ of screeching panic in his mind at the thought of making his way into the mysterious Darkness below by himself.

Theremon, after all, was afraid of the dark!

"Stay here," he said. "I'll be back in a second." He dashed upward two steps at a time, heart pounding—not altogether from the exertion—tumbled into the dome and snatched a torch from its holder. It was foul smelling, and the smoke smarted his eyes almost blind, but he clutched that torch as if he wanted to kiss it for joy, and its flame streamed backward as he hurtled down the stairs again.

Sheerin opened his eyes and moaned as Theremon bent over him. Theremon shook him roughly. "All right, get a hold on yourself. We've got light."

He held the torch at tiptoe height and, propping the tottering psychologist by an elbow, made his way downward in the middle of the protecting circle of illumination.

The offices on the ground floor still possessed what light there was, and Theremon felt the horror about him relax.

"Here," he said brusquely, and passed the torch to Sheerin. "You can hear *them* outside."

And they could. Little scraps of hoarse, wordless shouts.

But Sheerin was right; the Observatory was built like a fortress. Erected in the last century, when the neo-Gavottian style of architecture was at its ugly height, it had been designed for stability and durability, rather than for beauty.

The windows were protected by the grillework of inch-thick iron bars sunk deep into the concrete sills. The walls were solid masonry that an earthquake couldn't have touched, and the main door was a huge oaken slab reinforced with iron at the strategic points. Theremon shot the bolts and they slid shut with a dull clang.

At the other end of the corridor, Sheerin cursed weakly. He pointed to the lock of the back door which had been nearly jimmied into uselessness.

"That must be how Latimer got in," he said.

"Well, don't stand there," cried Theremon impatiently.

"Help drag up the furniture—and keep that torch out of my eyes. The smoke's killing me."

He slammed the heavy table up against the door as he spoke, and in two minutes had built a barricade which made up for what it lacked in beauty and symmetry by the sheer inertia of its massiveness.

Somewhere, dimly, far off, they could hear the battering of naked fists upon the door; and the screams and yells from outside had a sort of half reality.

That mob had set off from Saro City with only two things in mind: the attainment of Cultist salvation by the destruction of the Observatory, and a maddening fear that all but paralyzed them. There was no time to think of ground cars, or of weapons, or of leadership, or even of organization. They made for the Observatory on foot and assaulted it with bare hands.

And now that they were there, the last flash of Beta, the last ruby-red drop of flame, flickered feebly over a humanity that had left only stark, universal fear!

Theremon groaned, "Let's get back to the dome!"

In the dome, only Yimot, at the solarscope, had kept his place. The rest were clustered about the cameras, and Beenay was giving his instructions in a hoarse, strained voice.

"Get it straight, all of you. I'm snapping Beta just before totality and changing the plate. That will leave one of you to each camera. You all know about . . . about times of exposure—"

There was a breathless murmur of agreement.

Beenay passed a hand over his eyes. "Are the torches still burning? Never mind, I see them!" He was leaning hard against the back of a chair. "Now remember, don't . . . don't try to look for good shots. Don't waste time trying to get t-two stars at a time in the scope field. One is enough. And . . . and if you feel yourself going, *get away from the camera.*"

At the door, Sheerin whispered to Theremon, "Take me to Aton. I don't see him."

The newsman did not answer immediately. The vague

form of the astronomers wavered and blurred, and the torches overhead had become only yellow splotches.

"It's dark," he whimpered.

Sheerin held out his hand, "Aton." He stumbled forward. "Aton!"

Theremon stepped after and seized his arm. "Wait, I'll take you." Somehow he made his way across the room. He closed his eyes against the Darkness and his mind against the chaos within it.

No one heard them or paid attention to them. Sheerin stumbled against the wall. "Aton!"

The psychologist felt shaking hands touching him, then withdrawing, and a voice muttering, "Is that you, Sheerin?"

"Aton!" He strove to breathe normally. "Don't worry about the mob. The place will hold them off."

Latimer, the Cultist, rose to his feet, and his face twisted in desperation. His word was pledged, and to break it would mean placing his soul in mortal peril. Yet that word had been forced from him and had not been given freely. The Stars would come soon; he could not stand by and allow— And yet his word was pledged.

Beenay's face was dimly flushed as it looked upward at Beta's last ray, and Latimer, seeing him bend over his camera, made his decision. His nails cut the flesh of his palms as he tensed himself.

He staggered crazily as he started his rush. There was nothing before him but shadows; the very floor beneath his feet lacked substance. And then someone was upon him and he went down with clutching fingers at his throat.

He doubled his knee and drove it hard into his assailant. "Let me up or I'll kill you."

Theremon cried out sharply and muttered through a blinding haze of pain, "You double-crossing rat!"

The newsman seemed conscious of everything at once. He heard Beenay croak, "I've got it. At your cameras, men!" and then there was the strange awareness that the last thread of sunlight had thinned out and snapped.

Simultaneously he heard one last choking gasp from

Beenay, and a queer little cry from Sheerin, a hysterical giggle that cut off in a rasp—and a sudden silence, a strange, deadly silence from outside.

And Latimer had gone limp in his loosening grasp. Theremon peered into the Cultist's eyes and saw the blankness of them, staring upward, mirroring the feeble yellow of the torches. He saw the bubble of froth upon Latimer's lips and heard the low animal whimper in Latimer's throat.

With the slow fascination of fear, he lifted himself on one arm and turned his eyes toward the blood-curdling blackness of the window.

Through it shone the Stars!

Not Earth's feeble thirty-six hundred Stars visible to the eye—Lagash was in the center of a giant cluster. Thirty thousand mighty suns shone down in a soul-searing splendor that was more frighteningly cold in its awful indifference than the bitter wind that shivered across the cold, horribly bleak world.

Theremon staggered to his feet, his throat constricting him to breathlessness, all the muscles of his body writhing in a tensity of terror and sheer fear beyond bearing. He was going mad, and knew it, and somewhere deep inside a bit of sanity was screaming, struggling to fight off the hopeless flood of black terror. It was very horrible to go mad and know that you were going mad—to know that in a little minute you would be here physically and yet all the real essence would be dead and drowned in the black madness. For this was the Dark—the Dark and the Cold and the Doom. The bright walls of the universe were shattered and their awful black fragments were falling down to crush and squeeze and obliterate him.

He jostled someone crawling on hands and knees, but stumbled somehow over him. Hands groping at his tortured throat, he limped toward the flame of the torches that filled all his mad vision.

"Light!" he screamed.

Aton, somewhere, was crying, whimpering horribly like a terribly frightened child. "Stars—all the Stars—we didn't know at all. We didn't know anything. We thought six stars is a

universe is something the Stars didn't notice is Darkness forever and ever and ever and the walls are breaking in and
we didn't know we couldn't know and anything—"

Someone clawed at the torch, and it fell and snuffed out.
In the instant, the awful splendor of the indifferent Stars
leaped nearer to them.

On the horizon outside the window, in the direction of
Saro City, a crimson glow began growing, strengthening in
brightness, that was not the glow of a sun.

The long night had come again.

by ISAAC ASIMOV
The Foundation Trilogy (*Foundation, Foundation and Em-
pire, Second Foundation*)
I, Robot (collection of short stories)
The Caves of Steel
The Naked Sun

Van Vogt wrote about the superman, Heinlein wrote messianic novels about messianic figures, and Asimov wrote Spenglerian fantasies on a grand scale, but L. Ron Hubbard, another of Campbell's writers, *became* a facsimile of a Van Vogtian superman and a Heinlein messiah, founding a mass religion, Dianetics (later to become "Scientology"), which today claims a world-wide following of over ten million people.

Dianetics was a kind of computer-theory reworking of Freud, the goal of which was to produce a "Clear," a psychic Van Vogtian superman devoid of "engrams," or mental blocks caused by chains of past trauma. When Hubbard decided to live out the messiah role instead of writing a novel about it, it really wasn't very surprising that A. E. Van Vogt got involved and that Campbell took up the crusade in *Astounding* for a while.

Nor was it surprising that Dianetics found ready initial converts in the microcosm of science fiction fandom, for Golden Age science fiction was working on something much deeper and more powerful than conventional literary appeal. In fact, it had little conventional literary appeal at all, with its for the most part wooden prose, characterization that was either cardboard stereotypical or unselfconsciously pathological, and structure that was usually the basic pulp plot. Only in theme and idea did this work crackle with originality and mesmerize with archetypal power.

But for many people, especially the young, that was more than enough. Wolfe, Woolf, Faulkner, Steinbeck, & Co. didn't have the all-involving intricacy and narcissistic fantasies of Van Vogt or the schizoid power of Heinlein, and perhaps a Hemingway might not, even in the most private recesses of his being, dream of becoming his own messianic character like L. Ron Hubbard.

Science fiction was doing something beyond playing with words. Half unconsciously, these writers were writing fiction that moved susceptible readers deep within their Jungian unconscious structure. They were feeding back murky adolescent longings for power, strength, peer-group solidarity, and mystic transcendence, and by so doing were drawing together tribal cults around their works, creating pocket universes of which they were the little gods and thereby altering reality itself. Hubbard was only the most blatant example of this, and Scientology only an instance of this phenomenon outgrowing the bounds of the microcosm of science fiction and bursting upon the world at large.

Remember that this messianic literature was being unleashed on the adolescent mind in an era that began with the Great Depression, produced Nazi Germany, and climaxed in the technological Götterdämmerung of World War II. By the time the war was over, there was a tight subculture of perhaps 2,000 science fiction fans nationwide. There were fan magazines by the score, and annual World Science Fiction Conventions were soon to follow. The motto "Fans Are Slans" came into being, not without its master race overtones. Forrest J. Ackerman, Donald A. Wollheim, Sam Moskowitz, and similar figures were national celebrities in the microcosm of science fiction fandom as "Big Name Fans"—in effect, fan politicians, rather than writers.

All this empire building was going on within a national core group of maybe a twentieth or less of the total readership of science fiction, but what is significant is that by the end of the war this was the community in which most science fiction writers lived, as its aristocracy. This community, by and large, produced most of the post-Golden Age generation of science fiction writers. Writers like Ray Bradbury, Philip José Farmer, Frederik Pohl, and C. M. Kornbluth grew up under the literary influence of Campbell, Heinlein, and Van Vogt, *not* the classics or even the well-known writers of the day.

Many of them had been drawn into the h___ of science fiction fandom before they became ___ and began writing as converted members of this ___ subculture. Most of the others could hardly resist the lure of a subculture which venerated their work and canonized their beings at a time when the literary world at large sneered at them, if they were noticed at all.

Thus by the end of World War II, science fiction as an evolving literature had become largely cut off from any larger literary context and was primarily being written by cult writers who led lives circumscribed by the subculture of their own groupies. In fact, the groupies were becoming the writers. The literary world at large held science fiction in contempt, and the feeling was quite mutual.

But while science fiction drifted further and further into its own schizoid narcissistic reality, the world outside was going through a series of revolutions which, paradoxically, were loosing waves of consciousness-changing that were beginning to create a multiplex reality, a science fiction universe in realtime.

THE POSTWAR AWAKENING

Nineteen forty-five marked a series of great divides. The end of World War II gave birth to the United Nations and the Cold War and sounded the death knell of the great colonial empires. The mushroom cloud over Hiroshima ushered in an unprecedented era, the Nuclear Age, in which man for the first time held the ultimate power of life and death for the planet. The advent of commercial television was about to change our perception of the world. The meteoric rise of paperback book publishing was about to transform our reading habits and admit a few fresh breezes into the hermetically sealed world of genre science fiction.

Science fiction time had come—the multireality world was upon us. World War II was a cataclysm that shattered generations of frozen world-lines and freed bottled-up social and psychological forces to interact with each other in new and ever-mutating ways. Reality lost its fixed, single-value character and became the multiplex, constantly evolving bouillabaisse in which we live today.

Inside science fiction as well as outside, people were sticking their noses up out of the rubble of past certainties and sniffing tentatively at the altered air.

In the late 1940s and early 1950s some of the people who had come up through the science fiction subculture began to produce work of genuine literary merit. Arthur C. Clarke, with his early roots in the bolts-and-grommets scientifiction school, began to write about the interaction of science and mysticism, producing *Childhood's End*, a vision of the future of man from a Buddhist viewpoint, a novel of great power and some subtlety, as well as short stories like his classic "The Star."

Theodore Sturgeon, who had been discovered by Campbell, and who had developed entirely inside the closed world of the science fiction genre, faced up to the realization that his major topic of interest was neither technological gadgetry nor geopolitical thud and blunder but the possible variations of human and inhuman love. He began to produce a long series of short science fiction stories of unusual sensitivity and unique vision that may very well have been the best short stories being written by anyone at the time. "Affair with a Green Monkey" displays both Sturgeon's peculiar viewpoint and his psychological subtlety. It is inconceivable that such a story could have been published in any of the prewar genre science fiction magazines or that any Golden Age science fiction writer would have dreamed of writing it.

Inspired by Sturgeon, a young science fiction fan-turned-writer named Ray Bradbury began writing science fiction as prose poetry. Bradbury rapidly became a stylist, then a fine stylist, the only true stylist that science fiction had thus far produced.

Another young fan-turned-writer, Damon Knight, became the first critic of any worth within the genre, mercilessly exposing some of the hollow "classics" of the Golden Age for what they were, and began to write short stories that concentrated on psychological depth and developmental precision, stories like "Stranger Station."

Random bolides of creativity like Edgar Pangborn, Thomas Scortia, Chad Oliver, and Tom Godwin streaked erratically across the science fiction firmament with sui-generis gems like "The Cold Equations" and "Sea Change." Growth and change were in the air.

The Star

ARTHUR C. CLARKE

It is three thousand light-years to the Vatican. Once, I believed that space could have no power over faith, just as I believed that the heavens declared the glory of God's handiwork. Now I have seen that handiwork, and my faith is sorely troubled. I stare at the crucifix that hangs on the cabin wall above the Mark VI Computer, and for the first time in my life I wonder if it is no more than an empty symbol.

I have told no one yet, but the truth cannot be concealed. The facts are there for all to read, recorded on the countless miles of magnetic tape and the thousands of photographs we are carrying back to Earth. Other scientists can interpret them as easily as I can, and I am not one who would condone that tampering with the truth which often gave my order a bad name in the olden days.

The crew are already sufficiently depressed: I wonder how they will take this ultimate irony. Few of them have any religious faith, yet they will not relish using this final weapon in their campaign against me—that private, good-natured, but fundamentally serious, war which lasted all the way from Earth. It amused them to have a Jesuit as chief astrophysicist: Dr. Chandler, for instance, could never get over it (why are medical men such notorious atheists?). Sometimes he would meet me on the observation deck, where the lights are always low so that the stars shine with undiminished glory. He would come up to me in the gloom and stand staring out of the great oval port, while the heavens crawled slowly around us as the ship turned end over end with the residual spin we had never bothered to correct.

"Well, Father," he would say at last, "it goes on forever

and forever, and perhaps *Something* made it. But how you can believe that Something has a special interest in us and our miserable little world—that just beats me." Then the argument would start, while the stars and nebulae would swing around us in silent, endless arcs beyond the flawlessly clear plastic of the observation port.

It was, I think, the apparent incongruity of my position that caused most amusement to the crew. In vain I would point to my three papers in the *Astrophysical Journal,* my five in the *Monthly Notices of the Royal Astronomical Society.* I would remind them that my order has long been famous for its scientific works. We may be few now, but ever since the eighteenth century we have made contributions to astronomy and geophysics out of all proportion to our numbers. Will my report on the Phoenix Nebula end our thousand years of history? It will end, I fear, much more than that.

I do not know who gave the nebula its name, which seems to me a very bad one. If it contains a prophecy, it is one that cannot be verified for several billion years. Even the word nebula is misleading: this is a far smaller object than those stupendous clouds of mist—the stuff of unborn stars—that are scattered throughout the length of the Milky Way. On the cosmic scale, indeed, the Phoenix Nebula is a tiny thing—a tenuous shell of gas surrounding a single star.

Or what is left of a star . . .

The Rubens engraving of Loyola seems to mock me as it hangs there above the spectrophotometer tracings. What would *you,* Father, have made of this knowledge that has come into my keeping, so far from the little world that was all the universe you knew? Would your faith have risen to the challenge, as mine has failed to do?

You gaze into the distance, Father, but I have traveled a distance beyond any that you could have imagined when you founded our order a thousand years ago. No other survey ship has been so far from Earth: we are at the very frontiers of the explored universe. We set out to reach the Phoenix Nebula, we succeeded, and we are homeward bound with our burden of knowledge. I wish I could lift that burden from my shoulders, but I call to you in vain across the centuries and the light-years that lie between us.

On the book you are holding the words are plain to read. AD MAIOREM DEI GLORIAM, the message runs, but it is a message I can no longer believe. Would you still believe it, if you could see what we have found?

We knew, of course, what the Phoenix Nebula was. Every year, in our galaxy alone, more than a hundred stars explode, blazing for a few hours or days with thousands of times their normal brilliance before they sink back into death and obscurity. Such are the ordinary novae—the commonplace disasters of the universe. I have recorded the spectrograms and light curves of dozens since I started working at the Lunar Observatory.

But three or four times in every thousand years occurs something beside which even a nova pales into total insignificance.

When a star becomes a *supernova*, it may for a little while outshine all the massed suns of the galaxy. The Chinese astronomers watched this happen in A.D. 1054, not knowing what it was they saw. Five centuries later, in 1572, a supernova blazed in Cassiopeia so brilliantly that it was visible in the daylight sky. There have been three more in the thousand years that have passed since then.

Our mission was to visit the remnants of such a catastrophe, to reconstruct the events that led up to it, and, if possible, to learn its cause. We came slowly in through the concentric shells of gas that had been blasted out six thousand years before, yet were expanding still. They were immensely hot, radiating even now with a fierce violet light, but were far too tenuous to do us any damage. When the star had exploded, its outer layers had been driven upward with such speed that they had escaped completely from its gravitational field. Now they formed a hollow shell large enough to engulf a thousand solar systems, and at its center burned the tiny, fantastic object which the star had now become—a White Dwarf, smaller than the Earth, yet weighing a million times as much.

The glowing gas shells were all around us, banishing the

normal night of interstellar space. We were flying into the center of a cosmic bomb that had detonated millennia ago and whose incandescent fragments were still hurtling apart. The immense scale of the explosion, and the fact that the debris already covered a volume of space many billions of miles across, robbed the scene of any visible movement. It would take decades before the unaided eye could detect any motion in these tortured wisps and eddies of gas, yet the sense of turbulent expansion was overwhelming.

We had checked our primary drive hours before, and were drifting slowly toward the fierce little star ahead. Once it had been a sun like our own, but it had squandered in a few hours the energy that should have kept it shining for a million years. Now it was a shrunken miser, hoarding its resources as if trying to make amends for its prodigal youth.

No one seriously expected to find planets. If there had been any before the explosion, they would have been boiled into puffs of vapor, and their substance lost in the greater wreckage of the star itself. But we made the automatic search, as we always do when approaching an unknown sun, and presently we found a single small world circling the star at an immense distance. It must have been the Pluto of this vanished solar system, orbiting on the frontiers of the night. Too far from the central sun ever to have known life, its remoteness had saved it from the fate of all its lost companions.

The passing fires had seared its rocks and burned away the mantle of frozen gas that must have covered it in the days before the disaster. We landed, and we found the Vault.

Its builders had made sure that we should. The monolithic marker that stood above the entrance was now a fused stump, but even the first long-range photographs told us that here was the work of intelligence. A little later we detected the continent-wide pattern of radio-activity that had been buried in the rock. Even if the pylon above the Vault had been destroyed, this would have remained, an immovable and all but eternal beacon calling to the stars. Our ship fell toward this gigantic bull's-eye like an arrow into its target.

The pylon must have been a mile high when it was built, but now it looked like a candle that had melted down into a puddle of wax. It took us a week to drill through the fused rock, since we did not have the proper tools for a task like this. We were astronomers, not archaeologists, but we could improvise. Our original purpose was forgotten: this lonely monument, reared with such labor at the greatest possible distance from the doomed sun, could have only one meaning. A civilization that knew it was about to die had made its last bid for immortality.

It will take us generations to examine all the treasures that were placed in the Vault. They had plenty of time to prepare, for their sun must have given its first warnings many years before the final detonation. Everything that they wished to preserve, all the fruit of their genius, they brought here to this distant world in the days before the end, hoping that some other race would find it and that they would not be utterly forgotten. Would we have done as well, or would we have been too lost in our own misery to give thought to a future we could never see or share?

If only they had had a little more time! They could travel freely enough between the planets of their own sun, but they had not yet learned to cross the interstellar gulfs, and the nearest solar system was a hundred light-years away. Yet even had they possessed the secret of the Transfinite Drive, no more than a few millions could have been saved. Perhaps it was better thus.

Even if they had not been so disturbingly human as their sculpture shows, we could not have helped admiring them and grieving for their fate. They left thousands of visual records and the machines for projecting them, together with elaborate pictorial instructions from which it will not be difficult to learn their written language. We have examined many of these records, and brought to life for the first time in six thousand years the warmth and beauty of a civilization that in many ways must have been superior to our own. Perhaps they only showed us the best, and one can hardly blame them. But their worlds were very lovely, and their cities were built with a grace that matches anything of man's. We have watched them at work and play, and listened to their musical speech sounding across the centuries. One scene is still before my eyes—a group of children on a beach of strange blue sand, playing in the waves as children play on Earth. Curious whip-like trees line the shore, and some very large animal is wading in the shadows yet attracting no attention at all.

And sinking into the sea, still warm and friendly and life-giving, is the sun that will soon turn traitor and obliterate all this innocent happiness.

Perhaps if we had not been so far from home and so vulnerable to loneliness, we should not have been so deeply moved. Many of us had seen the ruins of ancient civilizations on other worlds, but they had never affected us so profoundly. This tragedy was unique. It is one thing for a race to fail and die, as nations and cultures have done on Earth. But to be destroyed so completely in the full flower of its achievement, leaving no survivors—how could that be reconciled with the mercy of God?

My colleagues have asked me that, and I have given what answers I can. Perhaps you could have done better, Father Loyola, but I have found nothing in the *Exercitia Spiritualia* that helps me here. They were not an evil people: I do not know what gods they worshiped, if indeed they worshiped any. But I have looked back at them across the centuries, and have watched while the loveliness they used their last strength to preserve was brought forth again into the light of their shrunken sun. They could have taught us much: why were they destroyed?

I know the answers that my colleagues will give when they get back to Earth. They will say that the universe has no purpose and no plan, that since a hundred suns explode every year in our galaxy, at this very moment some race is dying in the depths of space. Whether that race has done good or evil during its lifetime will make no difference in the end: there is no divine justice, for there is no God.

Yet, of course, what we have seen proves nothing of the sort. Anyone who argues thus is being swayed by emotion, not logic. God has no need to justify His actions to man. He who built the universe can destroy it when He chooses. It is arrogance—it is perilously near blasphemy—for us to say what He may or may not do.

This I could have accepted, hard though it is to look upon whole worlds and peoples thrown into the furnace. But there comes a point when even the deepest faith must falter, and now, as I look at the calculations lying before me, I know I have reached that point at last.

We could not tell, before we reached the nebula, how long ago the explosion took place. Now, from the astronomical evidence and the record in the rocks of that one surviving planet, I have been able to date it very exactly. I know in what year the light of this colossal conflagration reached our Earth. I know how brilliantly the supernova whose corpse now dwindles behind our speeding ship once shone in terrestrial skies. I know how it must have blazed low in the east before sunrise, like a beacon in that oriental dawn.

There can be no reasonable doubt: the ancient mystery is solved at last. Yet, oh God, there were so many stars you could have used. What was the need to give these people to the fire, that the symbol of their passing might shine above Bethlehem?

by ARTHUR C. CLARKE
Childhood's End
The City and the Stars
The Nine Billion Names of God (collection of short stories)

Affair with a Green Monkey

THEODORE STURGEON

There was this trained nurse who retired at 24 to marry a big guy, six foot seven, top brass in a Government agency. He was home only weekends. His name was Fritz Rhys. About sick people, wrong people, different people, he was a very understanding guy. It was his business to understand them.

So one night he went for a walk with his wife Alma down to this little park on the river front where they could get some air. There was a fountain and a bench where they could sit and see the lights across the water and flower-beds and all that, and this particular Sunday night there was a bunch of punks, eight of them, kicking someone to death over by the railing. Fritz Rhys understood right away what was happening and what to do, and in three big jumps he was right in the middle of it. He snatched a hunk of broom-handle away from one of the kids just before it got buried in the victim, and then they all saw him and that was the end of that. They cut out of there, ducking around Alma where she stood as if she was dangerous too.

Alma ran over to where Fritz knelt and helped him turn the man over. She got Fritz's display handkerchief and sponged the blood and broken teeth out of the slack mouth and turned the head to one side, and did the other things trained nurses are trained to do.

"Anything broken?"

She said yes. "His arm. Maybe internal injuries too. We'd better get an ambulance."

"Home's quicker. Hey boy! You're all right now. *Up* you go!" So by the time the man got his eyes open Fritz had him on his feet.

They half carried him up the steps and over the footbridge that crosses the Drive, and Fritz was right, they had him back to their apartment forty minutes sooner than it would have taken to call a wagon.

She was going to phone but he stopped her. "We can handle it. Get some pajamas." He looked at the injured man draped over one big arm. "Get some of yours. He won't mind."

They cleaned him up and splinted the arm. It wasn't so bad. Bruises on the ribs and buttocks, and then the face, but he was lucky. "Give him one week and one dentist and you'll never know it happened."

"He will."

"Oh, that," Fritz said.

She said, "What do you suppose they did it for?"

"Green monkey."

"Oh," she said, and they left the man sleeping and went to bed. At five in the morning Fritz rose quietly and got dressed and she didn't wake up until he thumped his suitcase down by the bed and bent over to kiss her goodbye.

She gave him his kiss and then came all the way awake and said, "Fritz! You're not just—leaving, like always?"

He wanted to know why not, and she pointed at the guest room. "Leave me with—"

He laughed at her. "Believe me, honey, you haven't got a thing to worry about."

"But he . . . I . . . oh, Fritz!"

"If anything happens you can call me."

"In *Washington?*" She sat up and sort of hugged the sheet around her. "Oh, why can't I just send him to a hospital where—"

He had a way sometimes of being so patient it was insulting. He said, "Because I want to talk to him, help him, when he's better, and you know what hospitals are. You just keep him happy and tell him not to leave until I can have a talk with him." Then he said something so gentle and careful that she knew when to shut up: "And let's say no more about it, shall we?" so she said no more about it and he went back to Washington.

The pajamas were small for him but not much and he was about her age, too. (Fritz Rhys was quite a bit older.) He had a name that she got fond of saying, and small strong hands. All day Monday he was kind of dazed and didn't say much, only smiled thanks for the eggnog and bouillon and bedpan and so on. Tuesday he was up and about. His clothes were back from the cleaners and mended and he put them on and they sat around the whole day talking. Alma read books a good deal and she read aloud to him. She played a lot of music on the phonograph too. Whatever she liked, he liked even better. Wednesday she took him to the dentist, once in the morning to get the stubs ground down and impressions, and again in the afternoon to have the temporary acrylic caps cemented in. By this time the lip swelling was all but gone, and with the teeth fixed up she found herself spending a lot of time just looking at his mouth. His hair shone in the sun and she half believed it would shine in the dark too. He somehow never answered her when she wanted to know where he came from. Maybe there was too much laughing going on at the time. They laughed a whole lot together. Anyway it was some place where you couldn't get spaghetti. She took him to an Italian restaurant for dinner and had to teach him how to spin it on his fork. They had a lot of fun with that and he ate plenty of it.

On Wednesday night—late—she phoned her husband.

"Alma! What is it? Are you all right?"

She did not answer until he called her name twice again, and then she said, all whispery, "Yes, Fritz. I'm all right. Fritz, I'm *frightened!*"

"Of what?"

She didn't say anything, though he could hear her trying.

"Is it the . . . what's his name, anyway?"

"Loolyo."

"Julio?"

She sang: "Lool-yo."

"Well, then. What's he done?"

"N-nothing."

"Well then—are you afraid of anything he might do?"

"Oh, *no!*"

"You're so right. I understood that when I left, or he wouldn't be there. Now then: he hasn't done anything, and you're sure he won't, and I'm sure he won't, so—why call me up at this time of night?"

She didn't say anything.

"Alma?"

"Fritz," she said. She was swift, hoarse: "Come home. Come right home."

"Act your age!"

"Your three minutes are up. Signal when through please."

"Yes operator."

"Alma! Are you calling from an outside phone? Why aren't you home?"

"I couldn't bear to have him hear me," she whispered. "Goodbye, Fritz." He might have said something more to her, but she hung up and went home.

On Thursday she phoned for the car and packed a picnic and they went to the beach. It was too cold to swim but they sat on the sand most of the day and talked, and sang some. "I'm frightened," she said again, but she said it to herself. Once they talked about Fritz. She asked him why those boys had clobbered him and he said he didn't know. She said Fritz knew. "He says you're a green monkey," and she explained it: "He says if you catch a monkey in the jungle and paint it green, all the other monkeys will tear it to pieces because it's different. Not dangerous, just different."

"Different how?" Loolyo asked, in a quiet voice, about himself.

She had a lot of answers to that, but they were all things of her own and she didn't mention them. She just said again that Fritz knew. "He's going to help you."

He looked at her and said, "He must be a good man."

She thought that over and said, "He's a very understanding man."

"What does he do in Washington?"

"He's an expert on rehabilitation programs."

"Rehabilitation of what?"

"People."

"Oh. . . . I'm looking forward to Saturday."

She told him, "I love you." He turned to her as she sat round-eyed, all her left knuckles in her mouth so that the ring hurt her.

"You don't mean that."

"I didn't mean to say it."

After that, and on Friday, they stayed together, but like the wires on your lamp cord, never touching. They went to the zoo, where Loolyo looked at the animals excited as a child, except the monkeys, which made them be quiet and go quickly to something else. The longer the day got the quieter they were together, and at dinner they said almost nothing, and after that they even stopped looking at each other. That night when it was darkest she went to his room and opened the door and closed it again behind her. She did not turn on the light. She said, "I don't care . . ." and again, "I don't care," and wept in a whisper.

Loolyo was alone in the apartment when Fritz came home. "Shopping," he answered the big man's question. "Good afternoon, Mr. Rhys. I'm glad to see you."

"Fritz," instructed Fritz. "You're looking chipper. Alma been good to you?"

Loolyo smiled enough to light up the place.

"What'd you say your name was? Julio? Oh yeh, Loolyo, I remember. Well, Lou m'lad, let's have our little talk. Sit down over there and let me have a good look at you." He took a good long look and then grunted and nodded, satisfied. "You ashamed of yourself, boy?"

"Wh . . . ? Ashamed? Uh—no, I don't think so."

"Good! That means this doesn't have to be a long talk at all. Just to make it even shorter, I want you to know from the start that I know what you are and you don't have to hide it and it doesn't matter a damn to me and I'm not going to pry. Okay?"

"You *know*?"

Fritz boomed a big laugh. "Don't *worry* so, Louie! Everybody you meet doesn't see what I see. It's my business to see these things and understand them."

Loolyo shifted nervously. "What things are you talking about?"

"Shape of the hands. Way you walk, way you sit, way you show your feelings, sound of your voice. Lots more. All small things, any one or two or six might mean nothing. But all together—I'm on to you, I understand you. I'm not asking, I'm telling. And I don't *care*. It's just that I can tell you how to behave so you don't get mobbed again. You want to hear it or don't you?"

Loolyo didn't look a thing in the world but puzzled. Fritz stood up and pulled off his jacket and shirt and threw them on the corner of the couch and fell back in the big chair, altogether relaxed. He began to talk like a man who loves talking and who knows what to say because he's said it all before, knows he's right, knows he says it well. "A lot of people live among people all their lives and never find out this one simple thing about people: human beings cease to be human when they congregate, and a mob is a monster. If you think of a mob as a living thing and you want to get its I.Q., take the average intelligence of the people there and divide it by the number of people there. Which means that a mob of fifty has somewhat less intelligence than an earthworm. No one person could sink to its level of cruelty and lack of principle. It thinks that anything that is different is dangerous, and it thinks it's protecting itself by tearing anything that's different to small bloody bits. The difference-which-is-dangerous changes with the times. Men have been mob-murdered for wearing beards, and for not wearing beards. For saying the right series of words in what the mob thinks is the wrong order. For wearing or not wearing this or that article of clothing, or tattoo, or piece of skin."

"That's . . . ugly," Loolyo said.

" 'That's . . . ugly,' " Fritz repeated, with completely accurate and completely insulting mimicry, then made his big roar of laughter and told Loolyo not to get mad. "You've just made a point for me, but wait a bit till I get to it." He leaned back and went on with his speech. "Now, of all 'dangerous' differences which incite the mob, the one that hits 'em hardest, quickest and nastiest is any variation in sex. It devolves upon every human being to determine which sex he belongs to and then to *be* that as loud as possible for as long as he lives. To the smallest detail men dress like men and women dress like women, and God help them if they cross the line. A man has got to look and act like a man. That isn't a right. It's a duty. And no matter how weird mankind gets in its rules and regulations—whether manhood demands shoulder-length hair for a Cavalier or waist-length for a Sikh or a crew-cut for a Bavarian, the rules must be followed or bloody well else.

"Now, as for you people," Fritz said, sitting up and flipping his long index finger down and forward, like a sharpshooter practicing a snap shot, "you are what you are just like everybody else. But I'm not talking about what you are—that's self-evident—only about how you're treated.

"The only big difference between you and normal people, in those terms, is that they must display their sex and insist on it, and you may not. But I mean, you one hundred percent by God *may* not, not in public. Among your own kind you can camp and scream and giggle to your heart's content, but don't let yourself get caught at it. It would be better not to do it at all."

"Now wait, wait, wait," Loolyo barked. "Hold on here. What has this got to do with me?"

Fritz opened his eyes big and round and then closed them and slumped into the cushions. He said in a very very tired voice, "Aw, now lookit. You're not going to bust into the middle of this and make me go all the way back to the beginning."

"I just want to know what makes you think—"

"Sit down and shut up!" Fritz bellowed, and he was the man who could do it. "Do you or do you not want to know how to go about among human beings without getting your girlish face kicked down your throat?"

Loolyo stood for a while, pale, his bright eyes drawn down to angry slits. It was as if Fritz's question didn't reach him all at once, but had to percolate in. Slowly he sat down again. "Go ahead then."

Fritz nodded approvingly. "I hate a bad liar, Louie, and

you were about to try the one lie you could never get away with. Not with anyone who understands you. . . . All right then. My advice to you: Be a man. Not any old man, not mankind, but manhood. To do this you don't need to play pro football and grow hair on your chest and seduce every third woman you meet long as she's female. All you have to do is hunt, fish (or talk sense about 'em as if you had) and go bug-eyed when the girls go by. If a sunset moves you so much you *have* to express yourself, do it with a grunt and a dirty word. Or you say, 'That Beethoven, he blows a cool symphony.' Never champion a real underdog unless it's a popular type, like a baseball team. Always treat other men as if you were sore at something and will wipe it off on them if they give you the slightest excuse. I mean sore, Louie, not vexed or in a snit. And stay away from women. They have an intuition that'll find you out nine times out of ten. The tenth time she falls for you, and there's nothing funnier."

"I think," Loolyo said after a time, "that you hate human beings."

"I understand 'em, that's all. Do you think I hate you?"

"Maybe you should. I'm not what you think I am."

Fritz Rhys shook his head and quietly cursed. "All right. Wear your cellophane mask if it makes you feel better. I don't give a damn about you or what you do. Do what I tell you and you can live in a man's world. Go on the way you are and in that last split second before they kick your brains in, you'll admit I was right."

"I'm glad you told me. It's what I came here to find out," Loolyo said finally.

At the sound of a key in the lock Fritz sprang up and ran to the door. It was Alma. Fritz took her packages and kissed her. While he was kissing her she looked past him to the living room and Loolyo, and as soon as he was finished she went and stood in the doorway. Fritz stood behind her, watching. Loolyo raised his head slowly and saw her and started and smiled shyly.

Fritz stepped up and took her shoulder and turned her around because just then he had to see her face. When he saw it he gently bit his lower lip and said, "Oh," and went back to his chair. He was a man who understood things real quick.

Alma ignored him, all eyes for Loolyo. "What has he been saying to you?"

He didn't answer. He looked at the carpet. Fritz jumped up and rapped, "Well, are you willing to tell the lady?"

"Why?"

"Promise me you will, every word, and I'll let her take the car and give you a lift out of town. You are from out of town? Yes. Well, I think you owe it to each other. What do you say, Louie?"

"Fritz! Have you gone cr—"

"You better persuade him to play it that way, honey. It's the last chance you'll have to see him alone."

"Loolyo . . ." she whispered, "come on, then."

Loolyo stared at the big man. Fritz grinned and said, "Every God damned word, mind. I'll quiz her when she gets back and take it out on her if you don't. Alma, try not to make it more'n two, three hours. Okay?"

"Come on then," she said stiffly, and they went out. Fritz went and got a beer and came back and flopped in the chair, drinking and laughing and scratching his chest.

In the car he said only "Uptown, over the bridge," and then fell into a silence that lasted clear to the toll-booths. They turned north and at last he began to talk. He told her all about it. She said nothing until he had quite finished; then: "How could you let him suggest such a filthy thing?"

He laughed bitterly. "Let him? . . . When he understands something, that—is—it."

There was nothing she could say to this; she knew it better than anything in life. He said, "But I guess I'm a green monkey anyhow. Well . . . I should be grateful. He told me where my kind can hide, and how to act when we're out in the open. I'd about given up."

"What do you mean?" He would not answer her, but rode with his face turned away. He seemed to be scanning the roadside to the right.

Suddenly: "Here," he said. "Stop here."

Startled, she pulled off the pavement and stopped. There's a new parkway north of the bridge, and for miles it parallels the old road. Between them is a useless strip of land, mauled by construction machines, weedy and deserted. She looked at it and at him, and if she was going to speak again the expression on his face stopped her. It was filled with sadness and longing and something else, a sort of blue-mood laughter. He said, "I'm going home now."

She looked at her hands on the wheel and suddenly could not see them. He touched her arm and said gently, "You'll have to get over it, Alma. It can't work. Nothing could make it work. It would kill you. Try to get back with your husband. He's better equipped for you. I'm not, not at all."

"Stop it," she whispered. "Stop it, stop it."

Loolyo sighed deeply, put his arms around her and kissed her, rough, gentle, thorough, face, mouth, tongue, ears, neck, touching her body hungrily while he did it. She clung to him and cried. He put her arms from him and pressed something into her hand and vaulted out of the car, ran across the shoulder, jumped over the retaining wall and disappeared. It was only a low wall. He didn't disappear behind anything or into anything or in the distance. He just disappeared. She called him twice and then got out and ran to the wall. Nothing— weeds, broken ground, a bush or two. She wrung her hands and became conscious of the object he had given her. It was a transparent disk, about like a plain flat flashlight lens. She turned it over twice, then impulsively looked through it.

She saw Loolyo crouched in a . . . machine.

She saw the machine leave, and when it was gone, her glass disk ceased to exist also, so that she had nothing of his any more. For a while she thought she could not survive that. And in its time came the thing known to everyone who has had grief enough: that no matter what you've lost, the lungs and the heart go on, and all around, birds fly, cars pass, people make a buck and lose their souls and get hernia and happy and their hair cut just like before.

When she came through the other side of this, it was quite a bit later. She was weak and numb but she could drive again, so she did, very carefully, and soon she was able to think again, so she did, just as carefully, and by the time she got home her rehearsed "Hel-*lo!*" was perfect and easy.

Maybe she forgot to rehearse her face. Fritz Rhys, shirtless, huge and understanding, came up out of the big chair like a cresting wave of muscles and kindliness. He took her hand and laughed quietly and brought her to the couch. She cowered back into the corner cushions and just sat, waiting for him to wash over her any way he wanted. He sat on the edge of the couch close to her, leaning forward to wall her away from the world, his heavy forearm and fist on the end table next to the couch; singlehandedly he surrounded her: "Alma . . ." he whispered, and waited, waited, until at last she met his eyes.

"I'm not angry," he told her. "Believe me, honey, I'm glad you can . . . love someone that much. It only means you're alive and . . . compassionate and—Alma." He laughed the quiet laugh again. "Of course I'll admit I'm glad he turned out to be a—one of the girls. I don't know what I'd do if you ever felt that way about a real man."

Her eyes had been fixed on his all the while, and now she moved them, let them drop to the heavy naked forearm which lay across the polished wood of the end table. She watched it with increasing fascination as he talked. "So let's chalk up one for the statistical mind, namely me, versus feminine intuition which sort of let you down. What are you staring at?"

She was staring at the forearm. Almost in spite of herself she reached for it. She didn't answer. He said, "It could have been worse. Imagine living with him. Imagine getting right to the point, drunk on poetry and shiny hair, and just when you were . . . ah, why go on. It would be impossible."

"It was impossible," she said in a low voice. She put her hand on his forearm, looked up and saw him watching her, and snatched the hand away self-consciously. She couldn't seem to keep her eyes off his arm. She began to smile, looking at it. He was a big man, and his forearm was about seventeen inches long and perhaps five and a half inches thick. "Quite impossible," she murmured, "and that's about the size of it." *Damn near exactly the size of it,* she thought wildly.

"Good girl!" he said heartily. "And now I'll give you forty-eight hours mooning time and then we'll be—"

His voice trailed off weakly as he watched the wildness transfer itself from somewhere inside her to her face and turn to laughter, floods, arrows, flights, peals, bullets of laughter.

"Alma!"

Her laughter ceased instantly but left her lips curled and her eyes glittering. "You better go back to killing the green monkeys," she said in a flat hard voice. "You've given them a beachhead."

"What?"

"There's something awfully small about you, Fritz Rhys," she said, and again the laughter, more and more of it, and he couldn't croon it down, he couldn't shout it down, and he couldn't stand it. He got dressed and packed his bag and said from the door, into the blare and blaze of her laughter, "I don't understand you. I don't understand you at all," and he went back to Washington.

Stranger Station

DAMON KNIGHT

The clang of metal echoed hollowly down through the Station's many vaulted corridors and rooms. Paul Wesson stood listening for a moment as the rolling echoes died away. The maintenance rocket was gone, heading back to Home; they had left him alone in Stranger Station.

Stranger Station! The name itself quickened his imagination. Wesson knew that both orbital stations had been named a century ago by the then British administration of the satellite service: "Home" because the larger, inner station handled the traffic of Earth and its colonies; "Stranger" because the outer station was designed specifically for dealings with foreigners . . . beings from outside the solar system. But even that could not diminish the wonder of Stranger Station, whirling out here alone in the dark—waiting for its once-in-two-decades visitor. . . .

One man, out of all Sol's billions, had the task and privilege of enduring the alien's presence when it came. The two races, according to Wesson's understanding of the subject, were so fundamentally different that it was painful for them to meet. Well, he had volunteered for the job, and he thought he could handle it—the rewards were big enough.

He had gone through all the tests, and against his own expectations he had been chosen. The maintenance crew had brought him up as dead weight, drugged in a survival hamper; they had kept him the same way while they did their work, and then had brought him back to consciousness. Now they were gone. He was alone.

. . . But not quite.

"Welcome to Stranger Station, Sergeant Wesson," said a

pleasant voice. "This is your alpha network speaking. I'm here to protect and serve you in every way. If there's anything you want, just ask me."

Wesson had been warned, but he was still shocked at the human quality of it. The alpha networks were the last word in robot brains—computers, safety devices, personal servants, libraries, all wrapped up in one, with something so close to "personality" and "free will" that experts were still arguing the question. They were rare and fantastically expensive; Wesson had never met one before.

"Thanks," he said now, to the empty air. "Uh—what do I call you, by the way? I can't keep saying, 'Hey, alpha network.'"

"One of your recent predecessors called me Aunt Nettie."

Wesson grimaced. Alpha network—Aunt Nettie. He hated puns; that wouldn't do. "The Aunt part is all right," he said. "Suppose I call you Aunt Jane. That was my mother's sister; you sound like her, a little bit."

"I am honored," said the invisible mechanism politely. "Can I serve you any refreshments now? Sandwiches? A drink?"

"Not just yet," said Wesson.

He turned away. That seemed to end the conversation as far as the network was concerned. A good thing; it was all right to have it for company, speaking when spoken to, but if it got talkative . . .

The human part of the Station was in four segments: bedroom, living room, dining room, bath. The living room was comfortably large and pleasantly furnished in greens and tans: the only mechanical note in it was the big instrument console in one corner. The other rooms, arranged in a ring around the living room, were tiny: just space enough for Wesson, a narrow encircling corridor, and the mechanisms that would serve him. The whole place was spotlessly clean, gleaming and efficient in spite of its twenty-year layoff.

This is the gravy part of the run, Wesson told himself. The month before the alien came—good food, no work, and an alpha network for conversation. "Aunt Jane, I'll have a small steak now," he said to the network. "Medium rare, with hash-brown potatoes, onions and mushrooms, and a glass of lager. Call me when it's ready."

"Right," said the voice pleasantly. Out in the dining room, the autochef began to hum and cluck self-importantly. Wesson wandered over and inspected the instrument console. Airlocks were sealed and tight, said the dials; the air was cycling. The Station was in orbit, and rotating on its axis with a force at the perimeter, where Wesson was, of one g. The internal temperature of this part of the Station was an even 73°.

The other side of the board told a different story; all the dials were dark and dead. Sector Two, occupying a volume some eighty-eight thousand times as great as this one, was not yet functioning.

Wesson had a vivid mental image of the Station, from photographs and diagrams—a 500-foot duralumin sphere, onto which the shallow 30-foot disk of the human section had been stuck apparently as an afterthought. The whole cavity of the sphere, very nearly—except for a honeycomb of supply and maintenance rooms, and the all-important, recently enlarged vats—was one cramped chamber for the alien. . . .

The steak was good, bubbling crisp outside the way he liked it, tender and pink inside. "Aunt Jane," he said with his mouth full, "this is pretty soft, isn't it?"

"The steak?" asked the voice, with a faintly anxious note.

Wesson grinned. "Never mind," he said. "Listen, Aunt Jane, you've been through this routine . . . how many times? Were you installed with the Station, or what?"

"I was not installed with the Station," said Aunt Jane primly. "I have assisted at three contacts."

"Um. Cigarette," said Wesson, slapping his pockets. The autochef hummed for a moment, and popped a pack of G.I.'s out of a vent. Wesson lit up. "All right," he said, "you've been through this three times. There are a lot of things you can tell me, right?"

"Oh, yes, certainly. What would you like to know?"

Wesson smoked, leaning back reflectively, green eyes narrowed. "First," he said, "read me the Pigeon report—you know, from the *Brief History*. I want to see if I remember it right."

"Chapter Two," said the voice promptly. "First contact with a non-Solar intelligence was made by Commander Ralph C. Pigeon on July 1, 1987, during an emergency landing on Titan. The following is an excerpt from his official report:

"'*While searching for a possible cause for our mental disturbance, we discovered what appeared to be a gigantic construction of metal on the far side of the ridge. Our distress grew stronger with the approach to this construction, which was polyhedral and approximately five times the length of the* Cologne.

"'*Some of those present expressed a wish to retire, but Lt. Acuff and myself had a strong sense of being called or summoned in some indefinable way. Although our uneasiness was not lessened, we therefore agreed to go forward and keep radio contact with the rest of the party while they returned to the ship.*

"'*We gained access to the alien construction by way of a large, irregular opening . . . The internal temperature was minus seventy-five degrees Fahrenheit; the atmosphere appeared to consist of methane and ammonia . . . Inside the second chamber, an alien creature was waiting for us. We felt the distress which I have tried to describe, to a much greater degree than before, and also the sense of summoning or pleading . . . We observed that the creature was exuding a thick yellowish fluid from certain joints or pores in its surface. Though disgusted, I managed to collect a sample of this exudate, and it was later forwarded for analysis . . .'*

"The second contact was made ten years later by Commodore Crawford's famous Titan Expedition—"

"No, that's enough," said Wesson. "I just wanted the Pigeon quote." He smoked, brooding. "It seems kind of chopped off, doesn't it? Have you got a longer version in your memory banks anywhere?"

There was a pause. "No," said Aunt Jane.

"There was more to it when I was a kid," Wesson complained nervously. "I read that book when I was twelve, and

I remember a long description of the alien . . . that is, I remember its being there." He swung around. "Listen, Aunt Jane—you're a sort of universal watchdog, that right? You've got cameras and mikes all over the Station?"

"Yes," said the network, sounding—was it Wesson's imagination?—faintly injured.

"Well, what about Sector Two—you must have cameras up there, too, isn't that so?"

"Yes."

"All right, then you can tell me. What do the aliens look like?"

There was a definite pause. "I'm sorry, I can't tell you that," said Aunt Jane.

"No," said Wesson, "I didn't think you could. You've got orders not to, I guess, for the same reason those history books have been cut since I was a kid. Now, what would the reason be? Have you got any idea, Aunt Jane?"

There was another pause. "Yes," the voice admitted.

"Well?"

"I'm sorry, I can't—"

"—tell you that," Wesson repeated along with it. "All right. At least we know where we stand."

"Yes, sergeant. Would you like some dessert?"

"No dessert. One other thing. *What happens to Station watchmen, like me, after their tour of duty?*"

"They are upgraded to Class Seven, students with unlimited leisure, and receive outright gifts of seven thousand stellors, plus free Class One housing—"

"Yeah, I know all that," said Wesson, licking his dry lips. "But here's what I'm asking you. The ones you knew—what kind of shape were they in when they left here?"

"The usual human shape," said the voice brightly. "Why do you ask, sergeant?"

Wesson made a discontented gesture. "Something I remember from a bull session at the Academy. I can't get it out of my head; I know it had something to do with the Station. Just a part of a sentence—*'blind as a bat, and white bristles all over.'* Now, would that be a description of the alien . . . or the watchman when they came to take him away?"

Aunt Jane went into one of her heavy pauses. "All right, I'll save you the trouble," said Wesson. "You're sorry, you can't tell me that."

"I *am* sorry," said the robot, sincerely.

Aunt Jane was a model companion. She had a record library of thousands of hours of music; she had films to show him, and micro-printed books that he could read on the scanner in the living room; or if he preferred, she would read to him. She controlled the Station's three telescopes, and on request would give him a view of Earth, or the Moon, or Home. . . .

But there was no news. Aunt Jane would obligingly turn on the radio receiver if he asked her, but nothing except static came out. That was the thing that weighed most heavily on Wesson, as time passed: the knowledge that radio silence was being imposed on all ships in transit, on the orbital stations, and on the planet-to-space transmitters. It was an enormous, almost a crippling handicap. Some information could be transmitted over relatively short distances by photophone, but ordinarily the whole complex traffic of the spacelanes depended on radio.

But this coming alien contact was so delicate a thing that even a radio voice, out here where the Earth was only a tiny disk twice the size of the Moon, might upset it. It was so precarious a thing, Wesson thought, that only one man could be allowed in the Station while the alien was there, and to give that man the company that would keep him sane, they had to install an alpha network. . . .

"Aunt Jane?"

The voice answered promptly, "Yes, Paul."

"This distress that the books talk about—you wouldn't know what it is, would you?"

"No, Paul."

"Because robot brains don't feel it, right?"

"Right, Paul."

"So tell me this—why do they need a man here at all? Why can't they get along with just you?"

A pause. "I don't know, Paul." The voice sounded faintly wistful.

He got up from the living-room couch and paced restlessly back and forth. "Let's have a look at Earth," he said. Obediently, the viewing screen on the console glowed into life: there was the blue Earth, swimming deep below him, in its first quarter, jewel-bright. "Switch it off," Wesson said.

"A little music?" suggested the voice, and immediately began to play something soothing, full of woodwinds.

"*No*," said Wesson. The music stopped.

Wesson's hands were trembling; he had a caged and frustrated feeling.

The fitted suit was in its locker beside the air lock. Wesson had been topside in it once or twice; there was nothing to see up there, just darkness and cold. But he had to get out of this squirrel-cage. He took the suit down.

"Paul," said Aunt Jane anxiously, "are you feeling nervous?"

"Yes," he snarled.

"Then don't go into Sector Two," said Aunt Jane.

"Don't tell me what to do, you hunk of tin!" said Wesson with sudden anger. He zipped up the front of his suit.

Aunt Jane was silent.

The air lock, an upright tube barely large enough for one man, was the only passage between Sector One and Sector Two. It was also the only exit from Sector One; to get here in the first place, Wesson had had to enter the big lock at the "south" pole of the sphere, and travel all the way down inside by drop-hole and catwalk. He had been drugged unconscious at the time, of course. When the time came, he would go out the same way; neither the maintenance rocket nor the tanker had any space, or time, to spare.

At the "north" pole opposite, there was a third air lock, this one so huge it could easily have held an interplanet freighter. But that was nobody's business—no human being's.

In the beam of Wesson's helmet lamp, the enormous central cavity of the Station was an inky gulf that sent back only remote, mocking glimmers of light. The near walls sparkled with hoar-frost. Sector Two was not yet pressurized; there was only a diffuse vapor that had leaked through the airseal, and had long since frozen into the powdery deposit that lined the walls. The metal rang cold under his shod feet; the vast emptiness of the chamber was the more depressing because it was airless, unwarmed and unlit. *Alone,* said his footsteps; *alone . . .*

He was thirty yards up the catwalk when his anxiety suddenly grew stronger. Wesson stopped in spite of himself, and turned clumsily, putting his back to the wall. The support of the solid wall was not enough. The catwalk seemed threatening to tilt underfoot, dropping him into the gulf.

Wesson recognized this drained feeling, this metallic taste at the back of his tongue. It was fear.

The thought ticked through his head, *They want me to be afraid.* But why? Why now? Of what?

Equally suddenly, he knew. The nameless pressure tightened, like a great fist closing, and Wesson had the appalling sense of something so huge that it had no limits at all, descending, with a terrible endless swift slowness. . . .

His first month was up.

The alien was coming.

As Wesson turned, gasping, the whole huge structure of the Station around him seemed to dwindle to the size of an ordinary room . . . and Wesson with it, so that he seemed to himself like a tiny insect, frantically scuttling down the walls toward safety.

Behind him as he ran, the Station *boomed.*

In the silent rooms, all the lights were burning dimly. Wesson lay still, looking at the ceiling. Up there, his imagination formed a shifting, changing image of the alien—huge, shadowy, formlessly menacing.

Sweat had gathered in globules on his brow. He stared, unable to look away.

"That was why you didn't want me to go topside, huh, Aunt Jane?"

"Yes. The nervousness is the first sign. But you gave me a direct order, Paul."

"I know it," he said vaguely, still staring fixedly at the ceiling. "A funny thing . . . Aunt Jane?"

"Yes, Paul."

"You won't tell me what it looks like, right?"

"*No*, Paul."

"I don't want to know. Lord, I don't *want* to know . . . Funny thing, Aunt Jane, part of me is just pure funk—I'm so scared, I'm nothing but a jelly—"

"I know," said the voice gently.

"—and part is real cool and calm, as if it didn't matter. Crazy, the things you think about. You know?"

"What things, Paul?"

He tried to laugh. "I'm remembering a kids' party I went to twenty . . . twenty-five years ago. I was, let's see, I was nine. I remember, because that was the same year my father died.

"We were living in Dallas then, in a rented mobilehouse, and there was a family in the next tract with a bunch of redheaded kids. They were always throwing parties; nobody liked them much, but everybody always went."

"Tell me about the party, Paul."

He shifted on the couch. "This one, this one was a Hallowe'en party. I remember the girls had on black and orange dresses, and the boys mostly wore spirit costumes. I was about the youngest kid there, and I felt kind of out of place. Then all of a sudden one of the redheads jumps up in a skull mask, hollering, 'C'mon, everybody get ready for hiden-seek.' And he grabs *me*, and says, '*You* be it,' and before I can even move, he shoves me into a dark closet. And I hear that door lock behind me."

He moistened his lips. "And then—you know, in the darkness—I feel something hit my *face*. You know, cold and clammy, like, I don't know, something dead. . . .

"I just hunched up on the floor of that closet, waiting for that thing to touch me again. You know? That thing, cold and kind of gritty, hanging up there. You know what it was?

A cloth glove, full of ice and bran cereal. A joke. Boy, that was one joke I never forgot. . . . Aunt Jane?"

"Yes, Paul."

"Hey, I'll bet you alpha networks make great psychs, huh? I could lie here and tell you anything, because you're just a machine—right?"

"Right, Paul," said the network sorrowfully.

"Aunt Jane, Aunt Jane . . . It's no use kidding myself along, I can *feel* that thing up there, just a couple of yards away."

"I know you can, Paul."

"I can't stand it, Aunt Jane."

"You can if you think you can, Paul."

He writhed on the couch. "It's—it's dirty, it's clammy. My God, is it going to be like that for *five months?* I can't, it'll kill me, Aunt Jane."

There was another thunderous boom, echoing down through the structural members of the Station. "What's that?" Wesson gasped. "The other ship—casting off?"

"Yes. Now he's alone, just as you are."

"Not like me. He can't be feeling what I'm feeling. Aunt Jane, you don't know . . ."

Up there, separated from him only by a few yards of metal, the alien's enormous, monstrous body hung. It was that poised weight, as real as if he could touch it, that weighed down his chest.

Wesson had been a space-dweller for most of his adult life, and knew even in his bones that if an orbital station ever collapsed, the "under" part would not be crushed but would be hurled away by its own angular momentum. This was not the oppressiveness of planetside buildings, where the looming mass above you seemed always threatening to fall: this was something else, completely distinct, and impossible to argue away.

It was the scent of danger, hanging unseen up there in the dark, waiting, cold and heavy. It was the recurrent nightmare of Wesson's childhood—the bloated unreal shape, no-color, no-size, that kept on hideously falling toward his face. . . . It was the dead puppy he had pulled out of the creek, that summer in Dakota . . . wet fur, limp head, cold, cold, *cold*. . . .

With an effort, Wesson rolled over on the couch and lifted himself to one elbow. The pressure was an insistent chill weight on his skull; the room seemed to dip and swing around in slow circles.

Wesson felt his jaw muscles contorting with the strain as he knelt, then stood erect. His back and legs tightened; his mouth hung painfully open. He took one step, then another, timing them to hit the floor as it came upright.

The right side of the console, the one that had been dark, was lighted. Pressure in Sector Two, according to the indicator, was about one and a third atmospheres. The air lock indicator showed a slightly higher pressure of oxygen and argon; that was to keep any of the alien atmosphere from contaminating Sector One, but it also meant that the lock would no longer open from either side.

"Lemme see Earth," he gasped.

The screen lighted up as he stared into it. "It's a long way down," he said. A long, long way down to the bottom of that well. . . . He had spent ten featureless years as a servo tech in Home Station. Before that, he'd wanted to be a pilot, but had washed out the first years—couldn't take the math. But he had never once thought of going back to Earth.

"Aunt Jane, Aunt Jane, it's beautiful," he mumbled.

Down there, he knew, it was spring; and in certain places, where the edge of darkness retreated, it was morning: a watery blue morning like the sea light caught in an agate, a morning with smoke and mist in it; a morning of stillness and promise. Down there, lost years and miles away, some tiny dot of a woman was opening her microscopic door to listen to an atom's song. Lost, lost, and packed away in cotton wool, like a specimen slide: one spring morning on Earth.

Black miles above, so far that sixty Earths could have been piled one on another to make a pole for his perch, Wesson swung in his endless circle within a circle. Yet, vast as was the gulf beneath him, all this—Earth, Moon, orbital stations, ships; yes, the Sun and all the rest of his planets, too—was the merest sniff of space, to be pinched up between thumb and finger.

Beyond—there was the true gulf. In that deep night, galaxies lay sprawled aglitter, piercing a distance that could only be named in a meaningless number, a cry of dismay: O,O,O. . . .

Crawling and fighting, blasting with energies too big for them, men had come as far as Uranus. But if a man had been tall enough to lie with his boots toasting in the Sun and his head freezing at Pluto, still he would have been too small for that overwhelming emptiness. Here, not at Pluto, was the outermost limit of man's empire: here the Outside funneled down to meet it, like the pinched waist of an hourglass: here, and only here, the two worlds came near enough to touch. Ours—and Theirs.

Down at the bottom of the board, now, the golden dials were faintly alight, the needles trembling ever so little on their pins.

Deep in the vats, the vats, the golden liquid was trickling down: *"Though disgusted, I took a sample of the exudate and it was forwarded for analysis. . . ."*

Space-cold fluid, trickling down the bitter walls of the tubes, forming little pools in the cups of darkness; goldenly agleam there, half-alive. The golden elixir. One drop of the concentrate would arrest aging for twenty years—keep your arteries soft, tonus good, eyes clear, hair pigmented, brain alert.

That was what the tests of Pigeon's sample had showed. That was the reason for the whole crazy history of the "alien trading post"—first a hut on Titan, then later, when people understood more about the problem, Stranger Station.

Once every twenty years, an alien would come down out of Somewhere, and sit in the tiny cage we had made for him, and make us rich beyond our dreams—rich with life . . . and still we did not know why.

Above him, Wesson imagined he could see that sensed body a-wallow in the glacial blackness, its bulk passively turning with the Station's spin, bleeding a chill gold into the lips of the tubes: drip, drop.

Wesson held his head. The pressure inside made it hard to think; it felt as if his skull were about to fly apart. "Aunt Jane," he said.

"Yes, Paul." The kindly, comforting voice: like a nurse. The nurse who stands beside your cot while you have painful, necessary things done to you.

"Aunt Jane," said Wesson, "do you know why they keep coming back?"

"No," said the voice precisely. "It is a mystery."

Wesson nodded. "I had," he said, "an interview with Gower before I left Home. You know Gower? Chief of the Outworld Bureau. Came up especially to see me."

"Yes?" said Aunt Jane encouragingly.

"Said to me, 'Wesson, you got to find out. Find out if we can count on them to keep up the supply. You know? There's fifty million more of us,' he says, 'than when you were born. We need more of the stuff, and we got to know if we can count on it. Because,' he says, 'you know what would happen if it stopped?' Do you know, Aunt Jane?"

"It would be," said the voice, "a catastrophe."

"That's right," Wesson said respectfully. "It would. Like, he says to me, 'What if the people in the Nefud area were cut off from the Jordan Valley Authority? Why, there'd be millions dying of thirst in a week.

"'Or what if the freighters stopped coming to Moon Base. Why,' he says, 'there'd be thousands starving and smothering.'

"He says, 'Where the water is, where you can get food and air, people are going to settle, and get married, you know? and have kids.'

"He says, 'If the so-called longevity serum stopped coming . . .' Says, 'Every twentieth adult in the Sol family is due for his shot this year.' Says, 'Of those, almost twenty per cent are one hundred fifteen or older.' Says, 'The deaths in that group, in the first year, would be at least three times what the actuarial tables call for.'" Wesson raised a strained face. "I'm thirty-four, you know?" he said. "That Gower, he made me feel like a baby."

Aunt Jane made a sympathetic noise.

"Drip, drip," said Wesson hysterically. The needles of the tall golden indicators were infinitesimally higher. "Every twenty years, we need more of the stuff, so somebody like me has to come out and take it for five lousy months. And one of *them* has to come out and sit there, and *drip. Why,* Aunt Jane? What for? Why should it matter to them whether we live a long time or not? Why do they keep on coming back? What do they take *away* from here?"

But to these questions, Aunt Jane had no reply.

All day and every day, the lights burned cold and steady in the circular gray corridor around the rim of Sector One. The hard gray flooring had been deeply scuffed in that circular path before Wesson ever walked there: the corridor existed for that only, like a treadmill in a squirrel cage; it said "Walk," and Wesson walked. A man would go crazy if he sat still, with that squirming, indescribable pressure on his head; and so Wesson paced off the miles, all day and every day, until he dropped like a dead man in the bed at night.

He talked, too, sometimes to himself, sometimes to the listening alpha network; sometimes it was difficult to tell which. "Moss on a rock," he muttered, pacing. "Told him, wouldn't give twenty mills for any damn shell. . . . Little pebbles down there, all colors." He shuffled on in silence for a while. Abruptly: "I don't see *why* they couldn't have given me a cat."

Aunt Jane said nothing. After a moment Wesson went on, "Nearly everybody at Home has a cat, for God's sake, or a goldfish or something. You're all right, Aunt Jane, but I can't *see* you. My God, I mean if they couldn't send a man a woman for company, what I mean, my God, I never liked *cats.*" He swung around the doorway into the bedroom, and absent-mindedly slammed his fist into the bloody place on the wall.

"But a cat would have been *something,*" he said.

Aunt Jane was still silent.

"Don't pretend your damn feelings are hurt, I know you, you're only a damn machine," said Wesson. "Listen, Aunt Jane, I remember a cereal package one time that had a horse and a cowboy on the side. There wasn't much room, so about all you saw was their faces. It used to strike me funny how much they looked alike. Two ears on the top with hair in the middle. Two eyes. Nose. Mouth with teeth in it. I was thinking, we're kind of distant cousins, aren't we, us and the horses. But compared to that thing up there—we're *brothers*. You know?"

"Yes," said Aunt Jane, quietly.

"So I keep asking myself, why couldn't they have sent a horse, or a cat, *instead* of a man? But I guess the answer is, because only a man could take what I'm taking. God, only a man. Right?"

"Right," said Aunt Jane, with deep sorrow.

Wesson stopped at the bedroom doorway again and shuddered, holding onto the frame. "Aunt Jane," he said in a low, clear voice, "you take pictures of *him* up there, don't you?"

"Yes, Paul."

"And you take pictures of me. And then what happens? After it's all over, who looks at the pictures?"

"I don't know," said Aunt Jane humbly.

"You don't know. But whoever looks at 'em, it doesn't do any good. Right? We got to find out why, why, why . . . And we never do find out, do we?"

"No," said Aunt Jane.

"But don't they figure that if the man who's going through it could see him, he might be able to tell something? That other people couldn't? Doesn't that make sense?"

"That's out of my hands, Paul."

He sniggered. "That's funny. Oh, that's funny." He chortled in his throat, reeling around the circuit.

"Yes, that's funny," said Aunt Jane.

"Aunt Jane, tell me what happens to the watchmen."

". . . I can't tell you that, Paul."

He lurched into the living room, sat down before the console, beat on its smooth, cold metal with his fists. "What are you, some kind of monster? Isn't there any blood in your veins, damn it, or oil or *anything?*"

"Please, Paul—"

"Don't you see, all I want to know, can they talk? Can they tell anything after their tour is over?"

". . . No, Paul."

He stood upright, clutching the console for balance. "They can't? No, I figured. And you know why?"

"No."

"Up there," said Wesson obscurely. "Moss on the rock."

"Paul, what?"

"We get changed," said Wesson, stumbling out of the room again. "We get changed. Like a piece of iron next to a magnet. Can't help it. You—nonmagnetic, I guess. Goes right through you, huh, Aunt Jane? You don't get changed. You stay here, wait for the next one."

"Yes," said Aunt Jane.

"You know," said Wesson, pacing, "I can tell how he's lying up there. Head *that* way, tail the other. Am I right?"

". . . Yes," said Aunt Jane.

Wesson stopped. "Yes," he said intently. "So you *can* tell me what you see up there, can't you, Aunt Jane?"

"No. Yes. It isn't allowed."

"Listen, Aunt Jane, *we'll die* unless we can find out what makes those aliens tick! Remember that." Wesson leaned against the corridor wall, gazing up. "He's turning now—around this way. Right?"

"Right."

"Well, what else is he doing? Come on, Aunt Jane!"

A pause. "He is twitching his . . ."

"What?"

"I don't know the words."

"My God, my God," said Wesson, clutching his head, "of course there aren't any words." He ran into the living room, clutched the console and stared at the blank screen. He pounded the metal with his fist. "You've got to show me, Aunt Jane, come on and show me, show me!"

"It isn't allowed," Aunt Jane protested.

"You've got to do it just the same, or we'll *die*, Aunt Jane —millions of us, billions, and it'll be your fault, get it, *your fault*, Aunt Jane!"

"Please," said the voice. There was a pause. The screen

flickered to life, for an instant only. Wesson had a glimpse of something massive and dark, but half transparent, like a magnified insect—a tangle of nameless limbs, whiplike filaments, claws, wings . . .

He clutched the edge of the console.

"Was that all right?" Aunt Jane asked.

"Of course! What do you think, it'll kill me to look at it? Put it back, Aunt Jane, put it back!"

Reluctantly, the screen lighted again. Wesson stared, and went on staring. He mumbled something.

"What?" said Aunt Jane.

"Life of my love, I loathe thee," said Wesson, staring. He roused himself after a moment and turned away. The image of the alien stayed with him as he went reeling into the corridor again; he was not surprised to find that it reminded him of all the loathsome, crawling, creeping things the Earth was full of. That explained why he was not supposed to see the alien, or even know what it looked like—because that fed his hate. And it was all right for him to be afraid of the alien, but he was not supposed to hate it . . . why not? Why not?

His fingers were shaking. He felt drained, steamed, dried up and withered. The one daily shower Aunt Jane allowed him was no longer enough. Twenty minutes after bathing, the acid sweat dripped again from his armpits, the cold sweat was beaded on his forehead, the hot sweat was in his palms. Wesson felt as if there were a furnace inside him, out of control, all the dampers drawn. He knew that under stress, something of the kind did happen to a man: the body's chemistry was altered—more adrenalin, more glycogen in the muscles; eyes brighter, digestion retarded. That was the trouble —he was burning himself up, unable to fight the thing that tormented him, or to run from it.

After another circuit, Wesson's steps faltered. He hesitated, and went into the living room. He leaned over the console, staring. From the screen, the alien stared blindly up into space. Down in the dark side, the golden indicators had climbed: the vats were more than two-thirds filled.

. . . to *fight,* or *run* . . .

Slowly Wesson sank down in front of the console. He sat

hunched, head bent, hands squeezed tight between his knees, trying to hold onto the thought that had come to him.

If the alien felt a pain as great as Wesson's—or greater—

Stress might alter the alien's body chemistry, too.

Life of my love, I loathe thee.

Wesson pushed the irrelevant thought aside. He stared at the screen, trying to envisage the alien, up there, wincing in pain and distress—sweating a golden sweat of horror. . . .

After a long time, he stood up and walked into the kitchen. He caught the table edge to keep his legs from carrying him on around the circuit. He sat down.

Humming fondly, the autochef slid out a tray of small glasses—water, orange juice, milk. Wesson put the water glass to his stiff lips; the water was cool, and hurt his throat. Then the juice, but he could drink only a little of it; then he sipped the milk. Aunt Jane hummed approvingly.

Dehydrated—how long had it been since he had eaten, or drunk? He looked at his hands. They were thin bundles of sticks, ropy-veined, with hard yellow claws. He could see the bones of his forearms under the skin, and his heart's beating stirred the cloth at his chest. The pale hairs on his arms and thighs—were they blond, or white?

The blurred reflections in the metal trim of the dining room gave him no answers—only pale faceless smears of gray. Wesson felt light-headed and very weak, as if he had just ended a bout of fever. He fumbled over his ribs and shoulder-bones. He was thin.

He sat in front of the autochef for a few minutes more, but no food came out. Evidently Aunt Jane did not think he was ready for it, and perhaps she was right. *Worse for them than for us,* he thought dizzily. *That's why the Station's so far out; why radio silence, and only one man aboard. They couldn't stand it at all, otherwise. . . .* Suddenly he could think of nothing but sleep—the bottomless pit, layer after layer of smothering velvet, numbing and soft. . . . His leg muscles quivered and twitched when he tried to walk, but he managed to get to the bedroom and fall on the mattress. The resilient block seemed to dissolve under him. His bones were melting.

He woke with a clear head, very weak, thinking cold and clear: *When two alien cultures meet, the stronger must transform the weaker with love or hate.* "Wesson's Law," he said aloud. He looked automatically for pencil and paper, but there was none, and he realized he would have to tell Aunt Jane, and let her remember it.

"I don't understand," she said.

"Never mind, remember it anyway. You're good at that, aren't you?"

"Yes, Paul."

"All right. . . . I want some breakfast."

He thought about Aunt Jane, so nearly human, sitting up here in her metal prison, leading one man after another through the torments of hell . . . nursemaid, protector, torturer. They must have known that something would have to give. . . . But the alphas were comparatively new; nobody understood them very well. Perhaps they really thought that an absolute prohibition could never be broken.

. . . *the stronger must transform the weaker* . . .

I'm *the stronger*, he thought. *And that's the way it's going to be.* He stopped at the console, and the screen was blank. He said angrily, "Aunt Jane!" And with a guilty start, the screen flickered into life.

Up there, the alien had rolled again in his pain. Now the great clustered eyes were staring directly into the camera; the coiled limbs threshed in pain: the eyes were staring, asking, pleading . . .

"*No,*" said Wesson, feeling his own pain like an iron cap, and he slammed his hand down on the manual control. The screen went dark. He looked up, sweating, and saw the floral picture over the console.

The thick stems were like antennae, the leaves thoraxes, the buds like blind insect-eyes. The whole picture moved slightly, endlessly, in a slow waiting rhythm.

Wesson clutched the hard metal of the console and stared at the picture, with sweat cold on his brow, until it turned into a calm, meaningless arrangement of lines again. Then he went into the dining room, shaking, and sat down.

After a moment he said, "Aunt Jane, does it get worse?"

"No. From now on, it gets better."

"How long?" he asked vaguely.

"One month."

A month, getting "better" . . . that was the way it had always been, with the watchman swamped and drowned, his personality submerged. Wesson thought about the men who had gone before him—Class Seven citizenship, with unlimited leisure, and Class One housing, yes, sure . . . in a sanatorium.

His lips peeled back from his teeth, and his fists clenched hard. *Not me!* he thought.

He spread his hands on the cool metal to steady them. He said, "How much longer do they usually stay able to talk?"

"You are already talking longer than any of them."

Then there was a blank. Wesson was vaguely aware, in snatches, of the corridor walls moving past, and the console glimpsed, and of a thunderous cloud of ideas that swirled around his head in a beating of wings. The aliens: what did they want? And what happened to the watchmen in Stranger Station?

The haze receded a little, and he was in the dining room again, staring vacantly at the table. Something was wrong.

He ate a few spoonfuls of the gruel the autochef served him, then pushed it away; the stuff tasted faintly unpleasant. The machine hummed anxiously and thrust a poached egg at him, but Wesson got up from the table.

The Station was all but silent. The resting rhythm of the household machines throbbed in the walls, unheard. The blue-lit living room was spread out before him like an empty stage-setting, and Wesson stared as if he had never seen it before.

He lurched to the console and stared down at the pictured alien on the screen: heavy, heavy, asprawl with pain in the darkness. The needles of the golden indicators were high, the enlarged vats almost full. *It's too much for him,* Wesson thought with grim satisfaction. The peace that followed the pain had not descended as it was supposed to; no, not this time!

He glanced up at the painting over the console: heavy crustacean limbs that swayed gracefully.

He shook his head violently. *I won't let it; I won't give in!* He held the back of one hand close to his eyes. He saw the dozens of tiny cuneiform wrinkles stamped into the skin over the knuckles, the pale hairs sprouting, the pink shiny flesh of recent scars. *I'm human,* he thought. But when he let his hand fall onto the console, the bony fingers seemed to crouch like crustaceans' legs, ready to scuttle.

Sweating, Wesson stared into the screen. Pictured there, the alien met his eyes, and it was as if they spoke to each other, mind to mind, an instantaneous communication that needed no words. There was a piercing sweetness in it, a melting, dissolving luxury of change into something that would no longer have any pain. . . . A pull, a calling.

Wesson straightened up slowly, carefully, as if he held some fragile thing in his mind that must not be handled roughly, or it would disintegrate. He said hoarsely, "Aunt Jane!"

She made some responsive noise.

He said, "Aunt Jane, I've got the answer! The whole thing! Listen, now, wait—listen!" He paused a moment to collect his thoughts. *"When two alien cultures meet, the stronger must transform the weaker with love or hate.* Remember? You said you didn't understand what that meant. I'll *tell* you what it means. When these—monsters—met Pigeon a hundred years ago on Titan, *they knew* we'd have to meet again. They're spreading out, colonizing, and so are we. We haven't got interstellar flight yet, but give us another hundred years, we'll *get* it. *We'll wind up out there, where they are.* And they can't stop us. Because they're not killers, Aunt Jane, it isn't in them. They're *nicer* than us. See, they're like the missionaries, and we're the South Sea Islanders. *They* don't kill their enemies, oh no—perish the thought!"

She was trying to say something, to interrupt him, but he rushed on. "Listen! The longevity serum—that was a lucky accident. But they played it for all it's worth. Slick and smooth —they come and give us the stuff free—they don't ask for a thing in return. Why not? Listen.

"They come here, and the shock of that first contact makes them sweat out that golden gook we need. Then, the last month or so, the pain always eases off. Why? Because the two minds, the human and alien, they stop fighting each other. Something gives way, it goes soft and there's a mixing together. And that's where you get the human casualties of this operation—the bleary men that come out of here not even able to talk human language any more. Oh, I suppose they're happy—happier than I am!—because they've got something big and wonderful inside 'em. Something that you and I can't even understand. But if you took them and put them together again with the aliens who spent time here, *they could all live together—they're adapted.*

"That's what they're aiming for!" He struck the console with his fist. "Not now—but a hundred, two hundred years from now! When we start expanding out to the stars—when we go a-conquering—we'll have already been conquered! Not by weapons, Aunt Jane, not by hate—by love! Yes, love! *Dirty, stinking, low-down, sneaking love!*"

Aunt Jane said something, a long sentence, in a high, anxious voice.

"What?" said Wesson irritably. He couldn't understand a word.

Aunt Jane was silent. "What, what?" Wesson demanded, pounding the console. "Have you got it through your tin head, or not? *What?*"

Aunt Jane said something else, tonelessly. Once more, Wesson could not make out a single word.

He stood frozen. Warm tears started suddenly out of his eyes. "Aunt Jane—" he said. He remembered, *You are already talking longer than any of them.* Too late? Too late? He tensed, then whirled and sprang to the closet where the paper books were kept. He opened the first one his hand struck.

The black letters were alien squiggles on the page, little humped shapes, without meaning.

The tears were coming faster, he couldn't stop them: tears of weariness, tears of frustration, tears of hate. "*Aunt Jane!*" he roared.

But it was no good. The curtain of silence had come down over his head. He was one of the vanguard—the conquered men, the ones who would get along with their stranger brothers, out among the alien stars.

The console was not working any more; nothing worked when he wanted it. Wesson squatted in the shower stall, naked, with a soup bowl in his hands. Water droplets glistened on his hands and forearms; the pale short hairs were just springing up, drying.

The silvery skin of reflection in the bowl gave him back nothing but a silhouette, a shadow man's outline. He could not see his face.

He dropped the bowl and went across the living room, shuffling the pale drifts of paper underfoot. The black lines on the paper, when his eyes happened to light on them, were worm-shapes, crawling things, conveying nothing. He rolled slightly in his walk; his eyes were glazed. His head twitched, every now and then, sketching a useless motion to avoid pain.

Once the bureau chief, Gower, came to stand in his way. "You fool," he said, his face contorted in anger, "you were supposed to go on to the end, like the rest. Now look what you've done!"

"I found out, didn't I?" Wesson mumbled, and as he brushed the man aside like a cobweb, the pain suddenly grew more intense. Wesson clasped his head in his hands with a grunt, and rocked to and fro a moment, uselessly, before he straightened and went on. The pain was coming in waves now, so tall that at their peak his vision dimmed out, violet, then gray.

It couldn't go on much longer. Something had to burst.

He paused at the bloody place and slapped the metal with his palm, making the sound ring dully up into the frame of the Station: *rroom, rroom.*

Faintly an echo came back: *boooom.*

Wesson kept going, smiling a faint and meaningless smile. He was only marking time now, waiting. Something was about to happen.

The dining-room doorway sprouted a sudden sill and

tripped him. He fell heavily, sliding on the floor, and lay without moving beneath the slick gleam of the autochef.

The pressure was too great: the autochef's clucking was swallowed up in the ringing pressure, and the tall gray walls buckled slowly in. . . .

The Station lurched.

Wesson felt it through his chest, palms, knees and elbows: the floor was plucked away for an instant and then swung back.

The pain in his skull relaxed its grip a little. Wesson tried to get to his feet.

There was an electric silence in the Station. On the second try, he got up and leaned his back against a wall. *Cluck,* said the autochef suddenly, hysterically, and the vent popped open, but nothing came out.

He listened, straining to hear. What?

The Station bounced beneath him, making his feet jump like a puppet's; the wall slapped his back hard, shuddered and was still; but far off through the metal cage came a long angry groan of metal, echoing, diminishing, dying. Then silence again.

The Station held its breath. All the myriad clickings and pulses in the walls were suspended; in the empty rooms the lights burned with a yellow glare, and the air hung stagnant and still. The console lights in the living room glowed like witchfires. Water in the dropped bowl, at the bottom of the shower stall, shone like quicksilver, waiting.

The third shock came. Wesson found himself on his hands and knees, the jolt still tingling in the bones of his body, staring at the floor. The sound that filled the room ebbed away slowly and ran down into the silences: a resonant metallic hollow sound, shuddering away now along the girders and hull plates, rattling tinnily into bolts and fittings, diminishing, noiseless, gone. The silence pressed down again.

The floor leaped painfully under his body: one great resonant blow that shook him from head to foot.

A muted echo of that blow came a few seconds later, as if the shock had traveled across the Station and back.

The bed, Wesson thought, and scrambled on hands and

knees through the doorway, along a floor curiously tilted, until he reached the rubbery block.

The room burst visibly upward around him, squeezing the block flat. It dropped back as violently, leaving Wesson bouncing helpless on the mattress, his limbs flying. It came to rest, in a long reluctant groan of metal.

Wesson rolled up on one elbow, thinking incoherently, *Air, the air lock.* Another blow slammed him down into the mattress, pinched his lungs shut, while the room danced grotesquely over his head. Gasping for breath in the ringing silence, Wesson felt a slow icy chill rolling toward him across the room . . . and there was a pungent smell in the air. *Ammonia!* he thought; and the odorless, smothering methane with it.

His cell was breached. The burst membrane was fatal: the alien's atmosphere would kill him.

Wesson surged to his feet. The next shock caught him off balance, dashed him to the floor. He arose again, dazed and limping; he was still thinking confusedly, *The air lock, get out.*

When he was halfway to the door, all the ceiling lights went out at once. The darkness was like a blanket around his head. It was bitter cold now in the room, and the pungent smell was sharper. Coughing, Wesson hurried forward. The floor lurched under his feet.

Only the golden indicators burned now: full to the top, the deep vats brimming, golden-lipped, gravid, a month before the time. Wesson shuddered.

Water spurted in the bathroom, hissing steadily on the tiles, rattling in the plastic bowl at the bottom of the shower stall. The lights winked on and off again. In the dining room, he heard the autochef clucking and sighing. The freezing wind blew harder: he was numb with cold to the hips. It seemed to Wesson abruptly that he was not at the top of the sky at all, but down, *down* at the bottom of the sea . . . trapped in this steel bubble, while the dark poured in.

The pain in his head was gone, as if it had never been there, and he understood what that meant: Up there, the great body was hanging like butcher's carrion in the darkness. Its death struggles were over, the damage done.

Wesson gathered a desperate breath, shouted, "Help me! The alien's dead! He kicked the Station apart—the methane's coming in! Get help, do you hear me? *Do you hear me?*"

Silence. In the smothering blackness, he remembered: *She can't understand me any more. Even if she's alive.*

He turned, making an animal noise in his throat. He groped his way on around the room, past the second doorway. Behind the walls, something was dripping with a slow cold tinkle and splash, a forlorn night sound. Small, hard floating things rapped against his legs. Then he touched a smooth curve of metal: the air lock.

Eagerly he pushed his feeble weight against the door. It didn't move. And it didn't move. Cold air was rushing out around the door frame, a thin knife-cold stream, but the door itself was jammed tight.

The suit! He should have thought of that before. If he just had some pure air to breathe, and a little warmth in his fingers . . . But the door of the suit locker would not move, either. The ceiling must have buckled.

And that was the end, he thought, bewildered. There were no more ways out. But there *had* to be— He pounded on the door until his arms would not lift any more; it did not move. Leaning against the chill metal, he saw a single light blink on overhead.

The room was a wild place of black shadows and swimming shapes—the book leaves, fluttering and darting in the air stream. Schools of them beat wildly at the walls, curling over, baffled, trying again; others were swooping around the outer corridor, around and around: he could see them whirling past the doorways, dreamlike, a white drift of silent paper in the darkness.

The acrid smell was harsher in his nostrils. Wesson choked, groping his way to the console again. He pounded it with his open hand: he wanted to see Earth.

But when the little square of brightness leaped up, it was the dead body of the alien that Wesson saw.

It hung motionless in the cavity of the Station, limbs dangling stiff and still, eyes dull. The last turn of the screw had been too much for it: but Wesson had survived . . .

For a few minutes.

The dead alien face mocked him; a whisper of memory floated into his mind: *We might have been brothers. . . .* All at once, Wesson passionately wanted to believe it—wanted to give in, turn back. That passed. Wearily he let himself sag into the bitter *now,* thinking with thin defiance, *It's done —hate wins. You'll have to stop this big giveaway—can't risk this happening again. And we'll hate you for that—and when we get out to the stars—*

The world was swimming numbly away out of reach. He felt the last fit of coughing take his body, as if it were happening to someone else beside him.

The last fluttering leaves of paper came to rest. There was a long silence in the drowned room.

Then:

"Paul," said the voice of the mechanical woman brokenly; "Paul," it said again, with the hopelessness of lost, unknown, impossible love.

by DAMON KNIGHT

Hell's Pavement
Mindswap (*The Other Foot*)
In Deep (collection of short stories)
Far Out (collection of short stories)
Three Novels ("Rule Golden," "Natural State," "The Dying Man")

The Cold Equations

TOM GODWIN

He was not alone.

There was nothing to indicate the fact but the white hand of the tiny gauge on the board before him. The control room was empty but for himself; there was no sound other than the murmur of the drives—but the white hand had moved. It had been on zero when the little ship was launched from the *Stardust;* now, an hour later, it had crept up. There was something in the supplies closet across the room, it was saying, some kind of a body that radiated heat.

It could be but one kind of a body—a living, human body.

He leaned back in the pilot's chair and drew a deep, slow breath, considering what he would have to do. He was an EDS pilot, inured to the sight of death, long since accustomed to it and to viewing the dying of another man with an objective lack of emotion, and he had no choice in what he must do. There could be no alternative—but it required a few moments of conditioning for even an EDS pilot to prepare himself to walk across the room and coldly, deliberately, take the life of a man he had yet to meet.

He would, of course, do it. It was the law, stated very bluntly and definitely in grim Paragraph L, Section 8, of Interstellar Regulations: *Any stowaway discovered in an EDS shall be jettisoned immediately following discovery.*

It was the law, and there could be no appeal.

It was a law not of men's choosing but made imperative by the circumstances of the space frontier. Galactic expansion had followed the development of the hyperspace drive and as men scattered wide across the frontier there had come the problem of contact with the isolated first-colonies and exploration parties. The huge hyperspace cruisers were the product of the combined genius and effort of Earth and were long and expensive in the building. They were not available in such numbers that small colonies could possess them. The cruisers carried the colonists to their new worlds and made periodic visits, running on tight schedules, but they could not stop and turn aside to visit colonies scheduled to be visited at another time; such a delay would destroy their schedule and produce a confusion and uncertainty that would wreck the complex interdependence between old Earth and new worlds of the frontier.

Some method of delivering supplies or assistance when an emergency occurred on a world not scheduled for a visit had been needed and the Emergency Dispatch Ships had been the answer. Small and collapsible, they occupied little room in the hold of the cruiser; made of light metal and plastics, they were driven by a small rocket drive that consumed relatively little fuel. Each cruiser carried four EDS's and when a call for aid was received the nearest cruiser would drop into normal space long enough to launch an EDS with the needed supplies or personnel, then vanish again as it continued on its course.

The cruisers, powered by nuclear converters, did not use the liquid rocket fuel but nuclear converters were far too large and complex to permit their installation in the EDS's. The cruisers were forced by necessity to carry a limited amount of the bulky rocket fuel and the fuel was rationed with care; the cruiser's computers determining the exact amount of fuel each EDS would require for its mission. The computers considered the course coordinates, the mass of the EDS, the mass of pilot and cargo; they were very precise and accurate and omitted nothing from their calculations. They could not, however, foresee, and allow for, the added mass of a stowaway.

The *Stardust* had received the request from one of the exploration parties stationed on Woden; the six men of the party already being stricken with the fever carried by the green *kala* midges and their own supply of serum destroyed by the tornado that had torn through their camp. The *Star-*

dust had gone through the usual procedure; dropping into normal space to launch the EDS with the fever serum, then vanishing again in hyperspace. Now, an hour later, the gauge was saying there was something more than the small carton of serum in the supplies closet.

He let his eyes rest on the narrow white door of the closet. There, just inside, another man lived and breathed and was beginning to feel assured that discovery of his presence would now be too late for the pilot to alter the situation. It *was* too late—for the man behind the door it was far later than he thought and in a way he would find terrible to believe.

There could be no alternative. Additional fuel would be used during the hours of deceleration to compensate for the added mass of the stowaway; infinitesimal increments of fuel that would not be missed until the ship had almost reached its destination. Then, at some distance above the ground that might be as near as a thousand feet or as far as tens of thousands of feet, depending upon the mass of ship and cargo and the preceding period of deceleration, the unmissed increments of fuel would make their absence known; the EDS would expend its last drops of fuel with a sputter and go into whistling free fall. Ship and pilot and stowaway would merge together upon impact as a wreckage of metal and plastic, flesh and blood, driven deep into the soil. The stowaway had signed his own death warrant when he concealed himself on the ship; he could not be permitted to take seven others with him.

He looked again at the telltale white hand, then rose to his feet. What he must do would be unpleasant for both of them; the sooner it was over, the better. He stepped across the control room, to stand by the white door.

"Come out!" His command was harsh and abrupt above the murmur of the drive.

It seemed he could hear the whisper of a furtive movement inside the closet, then nothing. He visualized the stowaway cowering closer into one corner, suddenly worried by the possible consequences of his act and his self-assurance evaporating.

"I said *out!*"

He heard the stowaway move to obey and he waited with his eyes alert on the door and his hand near the blaster at his side.

The door opened and the stowaway stepped through it, smiling. "All right—I give up. Now what?"

It was a girl.

He stared without speaking, his hand dropping away from the blaster and acceptance of what he saw coming like a heavy and unexpected physical blow. The stowaway was not a man—she was a girl in her teens, standing before him in little white gypsy sandals with the top of her brown, curly head hardly higher than his shoulder, with a faint, sweet scent of perfume coming from her and her smiling face tilted up so her eyes could look unknowing and unafraid into his as she waited for his answer.

Now what? Had it been asked in the deep, defiant voice of a man he would have answered it with action, quick and efficient. He would have taken the stowaway's identification disk and ordered him into the air lock. Had the stowaway refused to obey, he would have used the blaster. It would not have taken long; within a minute the body would have been ejected into space—had the stowaway been a man.

He returned to the pilot's chair and motioned her to seat herself on the boxlike bulk of the drive-control units that set against the wall beside him. She obeyed, his silence making the smile fade into the meek and guilty expression of a pup that has been caught in mischief and knows it must be punished.

"You still haven't told me," she said. "I'm guilty, so what happens to me now? Do I pay a fine, or what?"

"What are you doing here?" he asked. "Why did you stow away on this EDS?"

"I wanted to see my brother. He's with the government survey crew on Woden and I haven't seen him for ten years, not since he left Earth to go into government survey work."

"What was your destination on the *Stardust?*"

"Mimir. I have a position waiting for me there. My brother has been sending money home all the time to us—my father and mother and I—and he paid for a special course in linguistics I was taking. I graduated sooner than expected and I was offered this job on Mimir. I knew it would be almost a year before Gerry's job was done on Woden so he could come on to Mimir and that's why I hid in the closet, there. There was plenty of room for me and I was willing to pay the fine. There were only the two of us kids—Gerry and I—and I haven't seen him for so long, and I didn't want to wait another year when I could see him now, even though I knew I would be breaking some kind of a regulation when I did it."

I knew I would be breaking some kind of a regulation— In a way, she could not be blamed for her ignorance of the law; she was of Earth and had not realized that the laws of the space frontier must, of necessity, be as hard and relentless as the environment that gave them birth. Yet, to protect such as her from the results of their own ignorance of the frontier, there had been a sign over the door that led to the section of the *Stardust* that housed EDS's; a sign that was plain for all to see and heed:

UNAUTHORIZED PERSONNEL
KEEP OUT!

"Does your brother know that you took passage on the *Stardust* for Mimir?"

"Oh, yes. I sent him a spacegram telling him about my graduation and about going to Mimir on the *Stardust* a month before I left Earth. I already knew Mimir was where he would be stationed in a little over a year. He gets a promotion then, and he'll be based on Mimir and not have to stay out a year at a time on field trips, like he does now."

There were two different survey groups on Woden, and he asked, "What is his name?"

"Cross—Gerry Cross. He's in Group Two—that was the way his address read. Do you know him?"

Group One had requested the serum; Group Two was eight thousand miles away, across the Western Sea.

"No, I've never met him," he said, then turned to the control board and cut the deceleration to a fraction of a gravity; knowing as he did so that it could not avert the ultimate end, yet doing the only thing he could do to prolong that ultimate end. The sensation was like that of the ship suddenly dropping and the girl's involuntary movement of surprise half lifted her from the seat.

"We're going faster now, aren't we?" she asked. "Why are we doing that?"

He told her the truth. "To save fuel for a little while."

"You mean, we don't have very much?"

He delayed the answer he must give her so soon to ask: "How did you manage to stow away?"

"I just sort of walked in when no one was looking my way," she said. "I was practicing my Gelanese on the native girl who does the cleaning in the Ship's Supply office when someone came in with an order for supplies for the survey crew on Woden. I slipped into the closet there after the ship was ready to go and just before you came in. It was an impulse of the moment to stow away, so I could get to see Gerry—and from the way you keep looking at me so grim, I'm not sure it was a very wise impulse.

"But I'll be a model criminal—or do I mean prisoner?" She smiled at him again. "I intended to pay for my keep on top of paying the fine. I can cook and I can patch clothes for everyone and I know how to do all kinds of useful things, even a little bit about nursing."

There was one more question to ask:

"Did you know what the supplies were that the survey crew ordered?"

"Why, no. Equipment they needed in their work, I supposed."

Why couldn't she have been a man with some ulterior motive? A fugitive from justice, hoping to lose himself on a raw new world; an opportunist, seeking transportation to the new colonies where he might find golden fleece for the taking; a crackpot, with a mission—

Perhaps once in his lifetime an EDS pilot would find such a stowaway on his ship; warped men, mean and selfish men, brutal and dangerous men—but never, before, a smiling, blue-eyed girl who was willing to pay her fine and work for her keep that she might see her brother.

He turned to the board and turned the switch that would signal the *Stardust*. The call would be futile but he could not, until he had exhausted that one vain hope, seize her and thrust her into the air lock as he would an animal—or a man. The delay, in the meantime, would not be dangerous with the EDS decelerating at fractional gravity.

A voice spoke from the communicator. "*Stardust*. Identify yourself and proceed."

"Barton, EDS 34G11. Emergency. Give me Commander Delhart."

There was a faint confusion of noises as the request went through the proper channels. The girl was watching him, no longer smiling.

"Are you going to order them to come back after me?" she asked.

The communicator clicked and there was the sound of a distant voice saying, "Commander, the EDS requests—"

"Are they coming back after me?" she asked again. "Won't I get to see my brother, after all?"

"Barton?" The blunt, gruff voice of Commander Delhart came from the communicator. "What's this about an emergency?"

"A stowaway," he answered.

"A stowaway?" There was a slight surprise to the question. "That's rather unusual—but why the 'emergency' call? You discovered him in time so there should be no appreciable danger and I presume you've informed Ship's Records so his nearest relatives can be notified."

"That's why I had to call you, first. The stowaway is still aboard and the circumstances are so different—"

"Different?" the commander interrupted, impatience in his voice. "How can they be different? You know you have a limited supply of fuel; you also know the law, as well as I do: 'Any stowaway discovered in an EDS shall be jettisoned immediately following discovery.'"

There was the sound of a sharply indrawn breath from the girl. "*What does he mean?*"

"The stowaway is a girl."

"*What?*"

"She wanted to see her brother. She's only a kid and she didn't know what she was really doing."

"I see." All the curtness was gone from the commander's voice. "So you called me in the hope I could do something?" Without waiting for an answer he went on. "I'm sorry—I can do nothing. This cruiser must maintain its schedule; the life of not one person but the lives of many depend on it. I know how you feel but I'm powerless to help you. You'll have to go through with it. I'll have you connected with Ship's Records."

The communicator faded to a faint rustle of sound and he turned back to the girl. She was leaning forward on the bench, almost rigid, her eyes fixed wide and frightened.

"What did he mean, to go through with it? To jettison me . . . to go through with it—what did he mean? Not the way it sounded . . . he couldn't have. What did he mean . . . what did he really mean?"

Her time was too short for the comfort of a lie to be more than a cruelly fleeting delusion.

"He meant it the way it sounded."

"*No!*" She recoiled from him as though he had struck her, one hand half upraised as though to fend him off and stark unwillingness to believe in her eyes.

"It will have to be."

"No! You're joking—you're insane! You can't mean it!"

"I'm sorry." He spoke slowly to her, gently. "I should have told you before—I should have, but I had to do what I could first; I had to call the *Stardust*. You heard what the commander said."

"But you can't—if you make me leave the ship, I'll *die*."

"I know."

She searched his face and the unwillingness to believe left her eyes, giving way slowly to a look of dazed terror.

"You—know?" She spoke the words far apart, numb and wonderingly.

"I know. It has to be like that."

"You mean it—you really mean it." She sagged back against

the wall, small and limp like a little rag doll and all the pro-
testing and disbelief gone.

"You're going to do it—you're going to make me die?"

"I'm sorry," he said again. "You'll never know how sorry
I am. It has to be that way and no human in the universe can
change it."

"You're going to make me die and I didn't do anything
to die for—I didn't *do* anything—"

He sighed, deep and weary. "I know you didn't, child. I
know you didn't—"

"EDS." The communicator rapped brisk and metallic. "This
is Ship's Records. Give us all information on subject's identification disk."

He got out of his chair to stand over her. She clutched the
edge of the seat, her upturned face white under the brown
hair and the lipstick standing out like a blood-red cupid's
bow.

"Now?"

"I want your identification disk," he said.

She released the edge of the seat and fumbled at the chain
that suspended the plastic disk from her neck with fingers
that were trembling and awkward. He reached down and
unfastened the clasp for her, then returned with the disk to
his chair.

"Here's your data, Records: Identification Number T837—"

"One moment," Records interrupted. "This is to be filed
on the gray card, of course?"

"Yes."

"And the time of the execution?"

"I'll tell you later."

"Later? This is highly irregular; the time of the subject's
death is required before—"

He kept the thickness out of his voice with an effort. "Then
we'll do it in a highly irregular manner—you'll hear the disk
read, first. The subject is a girl and she's listening to everything that's said. Are you capable of understanding that?"

There was a brief, almost shocked, silence, then Records
said meekly: "Sorry. Go ahead."

He began to read the disk, reading it slowly to delay the

inevitable for as long as possible, trying to help her by giving her what little time he could to recover from her first terror and let it resolve into the calm of acceptance and resignation.

"Number T8374 dash Y54. Name: Marilyn Lee Cross. Sex: Female. Born: July 7, 2160. *She was only eighteen.* Height: 5-3. Weight: 110. *Such a slight weight, yet enough to add fatally to the mass of the shell-thin bubble that was an EDS.* Hair: Brown. Eyes: Blue. Complexion: Light. Blood Type: O. *Irrelevant data.* Destination: Port City, Mimir. *Invalid data—*"

He finished and said, "I'll call you later," then turned once again to the girl. She was huddled back against the wall, watching him with a look of numb and wondering fascination.

"They're waiting for you to kill me, aren't they? They want me dead, don't they? You and everybody on the cruiser wants me dead, don't you?" Then the numbness broke and her voice was that of a frightened and bewildered child. "Everybody wants me dead and I didn't *do* anything. I didn't hurt anyone —I only wanted to see my brother."

"It's not the way you think—it isn't that way, at all," he said. "Nobody wants it this way; nobody would ever let it be this way if it was humanly possible to change it."

"Then why is it! I don't understand. Why is it?"

"This ship is carrying *kala* fever serum to Group One on Woden. Their own supply was destroyed by a tornado. Group Two—the crew your brother is in—is eight thousand miles away across the Western Sea and their helicopters can't cross it to help Group One. The fever is invariably fatal unless the serum can be had in time, and the six men in Group One will die unless this ship reaches them on schedule. These little ships are always given barely enough fuel to reach their destination and if you stay aboard your added weight will cause it to use up all its fuel before it reaches the ground. It will crash, then, and you and I will die and so will the six men waiting for the fever serum."

It was a full minute before she spoke, and as she considered his words the expression of numbness left her eyes.

"Is that it?" she asked at last. "Just that the ship doesn't have enough fuel?"

"Yes."

"I can go alone or I can take seven others with me—is that the way it is?"

"That's the way it is."

"And nobody wants me to have to die?"

"Nobody."

"Then maybe— Are you sure nothing can be done about it? Wouldn't people help me if they could?"

"Everyone would like to help you but there is nothing anyone can do. I did the only thing I could do when I called the *Stardust*."

"And it won't come back—but there might be other cruisers, mightn't there? Isn't there any hope at all that there might be someone, somewhere, who could do something to help me?"

She was leaning forward a little in her eagerness as she waited for his answer.

"No."

The word was like the drop of a cold stone and she again leaned back against the wall, the hope and eagerness leaving her face. "You're sure—you *know* you're sure?"

"I'm sure. There are no other cruisers within forty light-years; there is nothing and no one to change things."

She dropped her gaze to her lap and began twisting a pleat of her skirt between her fingers, saying no more as her mind began to adapt itself to the grim knowledge.

It was better so; with the going of all hope would go the fear; with the going of all hope would come resignation. She needed time and she could have so little of it. How much?

The EDS's were not equipped with hull-cooling units; their speed had to be reduced to a moderate level before entering the atmosphere. They were decelerating at .10 gravity; approaching their destination at a far higher speed than the computers had calculated on. The *Stardust* had been quite near Woden when she launched the EDS; their present velocity was putting them nearer by the second. There would be a critical point, soon to be reached, when he would have to resume deceleration. When he did so the girl's weight would be multiplied by the gravities of deceleration, would become, suddenly, a factor of paramount importance; the factor the computers had been ignorant of when they determined the amount of fuel the EDS should have. She would have to go when deceleration began; it could be no other way. When would that be—how long could he let her stay?

"How long can I stay?"

He winced involuntarily from the words that were so like an echo of his own thoughts. How long? He didn't know; he would have to ask the ship's computers. Each EDS was given a meager surplus of fuel to compensate for unfavorable conditions within the atmosphere and relatively little fuel was being consumed for the time being. The memory banks of the computers would still contain all data pertaining to the course set for the EDS; such data would not be erased until the EDS reached its destination. He had only to give the computers the new data; the girl's weight and the exact time at which he had reduced the deceleration to .10.

"Barton." Commander Delhart's voice came abruptly from the communicator, as he opened his mouth to call the *Stardust*. "A check with Records shows me you haven't completed your report. Did you reduce the deceleration?"

So the commander knew what he was trying to do.

"I'm decelerating at point ten," he answered. "I cut the deceleration at seventeen fifty and the weight is a hundred and ten. I would like to stay at point ten as long as the computers say I can. Will you give them the question?"

It was contrary to regulations for an EDS pilot to make any changes in the course or degree of deceleration the computers had set for him but the commander made no mention of the violation, neither did he ask the reason for it. It was not necessary for him to ask; he had not become commander of an interstellar cruiser without both intelligence and an understanding of human nature. He said only: "I'll have that given the computers."

The communicator fell silent and he and the girl waited, neither of them speaking. They would not have to wait long;

the computers would give the answer within moments of the asking. The new factors would be fed into the steel maw of the first bank and the electrical impulses would go through the complex circuits. Here and there a relay might click, a tiny cog turn over, but it would be essentially the electrical impulses that found the answer; formless, mindless, invisible, determining with utter precision how long the pale girl beside him might live. Then five little segments of metal in the second bank would trip in rapid succession against an inked ribbon and a second steel maw would spit out the slip of paper that bore the answer.

The chronometer on the instrument board read 18:10 when the commander spoke again.

"You will resume deceleration at nineteen ten."

She looked toward the chronometer, then quickly away from it. "Is that when . . . when I go?" she asked. He nodded and she dropped her eyes to her lap again.

"I'll have the course corrections given you," the commander said. "Ordinarily I would never permit anything like this but I understand your position. There is nothing I can do, other than what I've just done, and you will not deviate from these new instructions. You will complete your report at nineteen ten. Now—here are the course corrections."

The voice of some unknown technician read them to him and he wrote them down on the pad clipped to the edge of the control board. There would, he saw, be periods of deceleration when he neared the atmosphere when the deceleration would be five gravities—and at five gravities, one hundred ten pounds would become five hundred fifty pounds.

The technician finished and he terminated the contact with a brief acknowledgment. Then, hesitating a moment, he reached out and shut off the communicator. It was 18:13 and he would have nothing to report until 19:10. In the meantime, it somehow seemed indecent to permit others to hear what she might say in her last hour.

He began to check the instrument readings, going over them with unnecessary slowness. She would have to accept the circumstances and there was nothing he could do to help her into acceptance; words of sympathy would only delay it.

It was 18:20 when she stirred from her motionlessness and spoke.

"So that's the way it has to be with me?"

He swung around to face her. "You understand now, don't you? No one would ever let it be like this if it could be changed."

"I understand," she said. Some of the color had returned to her face and the lipstick no longer stood out so vividly red. "There isn't enough fuel for me to stay; when I hid on this ship I got into something I didn't know anything about and now I have to pay for it."

She had violated a man-made law that said KEEP OUT but the penalty was not of men's making or desire and it was a penalty men could not revoke. A physical law had decreed: *h amount of fuel will power an EDS with a mass of m safely to its destination;* and a second physical law had decreed: *h amount of fuel will not power an EDS with a mass of m plus x safely to its destination.*

EDS's obeyed only physical laws and no amount of human sympathy for her could alter the second law.

"But I'm afraid. I don't want to die—not now. I want to live and nobody is doing anything to help me; everybody is letting me go ahead and acting just like nothing was going to happen to me. I'm going to die and nobody *cares.*"

"We all do," he said. "I do and the commander does and the clerk in Ship's Records; we all care and each of us did what little he could to help you. It wasn't enough—it was almost nothing—but it was all we could do."

"Not enough fuel—I can understand that," she said, as though she had not heard his own words. "But to have to die for it. *Me,* alone—"

How hard it must be for her to accept the fact. She had never known danger of death; had never known the environments where the lives of men could be as fragile and fleeting as sea foam tossed against a rocky shore. She belonged on gentle Earth, in that secure and peaceful society where she could be young and gay and laughing with the others of her kind; where life was precious and well-guarded and there was always the assurance that tomorrow would come. She belonged in that world of soft winds and warm suns, music and moonlight and gracious manners and not on the hard, bleak frontier.

"How did it happen to me, so terribly quickly? An hour ago I was on the *Stardust*, going to Mimir. Now the *Stardust* is going on without me and I'm going to die and I'll never see Gerry and Mama and Daddy again—I'll never see anything again."

He hesitated, wondering how he could explain it to her so she would really understand and not feel she had, somehow, been the victim of a reasonlessly cruel injustice. She did not know what the frontier was like; she thought in terms of safe-and-secure Earth. Pretty girls were not jettisoned on Earth; there was a law against it. On Earth her plight would have filled the newscasts and a fast black Patrol ship would have been racing to her rescue. Everyone, everywhere, would have known of Marilyn Lee Cross and no effort would have been spared to save her life. But this was not Earth and there were no Patrol ships; only the *Stardust*, leaving them behind at many times the speed of light. There was no one to help her, there would be no Marilyn Lee Cross smiling from the newscasts tomorrow. Marilyn Lee Cross would be but a poignant memory for an EDS pilot and a name on a gray card in Ship's Records.

"It's different here; it's not like back on Earth," he said. "It isn't that no one cares; it's that no one can do anything to help. The frontier is big and here along its rim the colonies and exploration parties are scattered so thin and far between. On Woden, for example, there are only sixteen men—sixteen men on an entire world. The exploration parties, the survey crews, the little first-colonies—they're all fighting alien environments, trying to make a way for those who will follow after. The environments fight back and those who go first usually make mistakes only once. There is no margin of safety along the rim of the frontier; there can't be until the way is made for the others who will come later, until the new worlds are tamed and settled. Until then men will have to pay the penalty for making mistakes with no one to help them because there is no one *to* help them."

"I was going to Mimir," she said. "I didn't know about the frontier; I was only going to Mimir and *it's* safe."

"Mimir is safe but you left the cruiser that was taking you there."

She was silent for a little while. "It was all so wonderful at first; there was plenty of room for me on this ship and I would be seeing Gerry so soon . . . I didn't know about the fuel, didn't know what would happen to me—"

Her words trailed away and he turned his attention to the viewscreen, not wanting to stare at her as she fought her way through the black horror of fear toward the calm gray of acceptance.

Woden was a ball, enshrouded in the blue haze of its atmosphere, swimming in space against the background of star-sprinkled dead blackness. The great mass of Manning's Continent sprawled like a gigantic hourglass in the Eastern Sea with the western half of the Eastern Continent still visible. There was a thin line of shadow along the right-hand edge of the globe and the Eastern Continent was disappearing into it as the planet turned on its axis. An hour before the entire continent had been in view, now a thousand miles of it had gone into the thin edge of shadow and around to the night that lay on the other side of the world. The dark blue spot that was Lotus Lake was approaching the shadow. It was somewhere near the southern edge of the lake that Group Two had their camp. It would be night there, soon, and quick behind the coming of night the rotation of Woden on its axis would put Group Two beyond the reach of the ship's radio.

He would have to tell her before it was too late for her to talk to her brother. In a way, it would be better for both of them should they not do so but it was not for him to decide. To each of them the last words would be something to hold and cherish, something that would cut like the blade of a knife yet would be infinitely precious to remember, she for her own brief moments to live and he for the rest of his life.

He held down the button that would flash the grid lines on the view-screen and used the known diameter of the planet to estimate the distance the southern tip of Lotus Lake had yet to go until it passed beyond radio range. It was approximately five hundred miles. Five hundred miles; thirty minutes—and the chronometer read 18:30. Allowing for error in estimating, it could not be later than 19:05 that the turning of Woden would cut off her brother's voice.

The first border of the Western Continent was already in sight along the left side of the world. Four thousand miles across it lay the shore of the Western Sea and the Camp of Group One. It had been in the Western Sea that the tornado had originated, to strike with such fury at the camp and destroy half their prefabricated buildings, including the one that housed the medical supplies. Two days before the tornado had not existed; it had been no more than great gentle masses of air out over the calm Western Sea. Group One had gone about their routine survey work, unaware of the meeting of the air masses out at sea, unaware of the force the union was spawning. It had struck their camp without warning; a thundering, roaring destruction that sought to annihilate all that lay before it. It had passed on, leaving the wreckage in its wake. It had destroyed the labor of months and had doomed six men to die and then, as though its task was accomplished, it once more began to resolve into gentle masses of air. But for all its deadliness, it had destroyed with neither malice nor intent. It had been a blind and mindless force, obeying the laws of nature, and it would have followed the same course with the same fury had men never existed.

Existence required Order and there was order; the laws of nature, irrevocable and immutable. Men could learn to use them but men could not change them. The circumference of a circle was always pi times the diameter and no science of Man would ever make it otherwise. The combination of chemical A with chemical B under condition C invariably produced reaction D. The law of gravitation was a rigid equation and it made no distinction between the fall of a leaf and the ponderous circling of a binary star system. The nuclear conversion process powered the cruisers that carried men to the stars; the same process in the form of a nova would destroy a world with equal efficiency. The laws *were*, and the universe moved in obedience to them. Along the frontier were arrayed all the forces of nature and sometimes they destroyed those who were fighting their way outward from Earth. The men of the frontier had long ago learned the bitter futility of cursing the forces that would destroy them for the forces were blind and deaf; the futility of looking to the heavens for mercy, for the stars of the galaxy swung in their long, long sweep of two hundred million years, as inexorably controlled as they by the laws that knew neither hatred nor compassion.

The men of the frontier knew—but how was a girl from Earth to fully understand? *H amount of fuel will not power an EDS with a mass of m plus x safely to its destination.* To himself and her brother and parents she was a sweet-faced girl in her teens; to the laws of nature she was x, the unwanted factor in a cold equation.

She stirred again on the seat. "Could I write a letter? I want to write to Mama and Daddy and I'd like to talk to Gerry. Could you let me talk to him over your radio there?"

"I'll try to get him," he said.

He switched on the normal-space transmitter and pressed the signal button. Someone answered the buzzer almost immediately.

"Hello. How's it going with you fellows now—is the EDS on its way?"

"This isn't Group One; this is the EDS," he said. "Is Gerry Cross there?"

"Gerry? He and two others went out in the helicopter this morning and aren't back yet. It's almost sundown, though, and he ought to be back right away—in less than an hour at the most."

"Can you connect me through to the radio in his 'copter?"

"Huh-uh. It's been out of commission for two months—some printed circuits went haywire and we can't get any more until the next cruiser stops by. Is it something important —bad news for him, or something?"

"Yes—it's very important. When he comes in get him to the transmitter as soon as you possibly can."

"I'll do that; I'll have one of the boys waiting at the field with a truck. Is there anything else I can do?"

"No, I guess that's all. Get him there as soon as you can and signal me."

He turned the volume to an inaudible minimum, an act that would not affect the functioning of the signal buzzer, and unclipped the pad of paper from the control board. He tore off the sheet containing his flight instructions and handed the pad to her, together with pencil.

"I'd better write to Gerry, too," she said as she took them. "He might not get back to camp in time."

She began to write, her fingers still clumsy and uncertain in the way they handled the pencil and the top of it trembling a little as she poised it between words. He turned back to the viewscreen, to stare at it without seeing it.

She was a lonely little child, trying to say her last good-by, and she would lay out her heart to them. She would tell them how much she loved them and she would tell them to not feel badly about it, that it was only something that must happen eventually to everyone and she was not afraid. The last would be a lie and it would be there to read between the sprawling, uneven lines; a valiant little lie that would make the hurt all the greater for them.

Her brother was of the frontier and he would understand. He would not hate the EDS pilot for doing nothing to prevent her going; he would know there had been nothing the pilot could do. He would understand, though the understanding would not soften the shock and pain when he learned his sister was gone. But the others, her father and mother—they would not understand. They were of Earth and they would think in the manner of those who had never lived where the safety margin of life was a thin, thin line—and sometimes not at all. What would they think of the faceless, unknown pilot who had sent her to her death?

They would hate him with cold and terrible intensity but it really didn't matter. He would never see them, never know them. He would have only the memories to remind him;

only the nights to fear, when a blue-eyed girl in gypsy sandals would come in his dreams to die again—

He scowled at the viewscreen and tried to force his thoughts into less emotional channels. There was nothing he could do to help her. She had unknowingly subjected herself to the penalty of a law that recognized neither innocence nor youth nor beauty, that was incapable of sympathy or leniency. Regret was illogical—and yet, could knowing it to be illogical ever keep it away?

She stopped occasionally, as though trying to find the right words to tell them what she wanted them to know, then the pencil would resume its whispering to the paper. It was 18:37 when she folded the letter in a square and wrote a name on it. She began writing another, twice looking up at the chronometer as though she feared the black hand might reach its rendezvous before she had finished. It was 18:45 when she folded it as she had done the first letter and wrote a name and address on it.

She held the letters out to him. "Will you take care of these and see that they're enveloped and mailed?"

"Of course." He took them from her hand and placed them in a pocket of his gray uniform shirt.

"These can't be sent off until the next cruiser stops by and the *Stardust* will have long since told them about me, won't it?" she asked. He nodded and she went on, "That makes the letters not important in one way but in another way they're very important—to me, and to them."

"I know. I understand, and I'll take care of them."

She glanced at the chronometer, then back to him. "It seems to move faster all the time, doesn't it?"

He said nothing, unable to think of anything to say, and she asked, "Do you think Gerry will come back to camp in time?"

"I think so. They said he should be in right away."

She began to roll the pencil back and forth between her palms. "I hope he does. I feel sick and scared and I want to hear his voice again and maybe I won't feel so alone. I'm a coward and I can't help it."

"No," he said, "you're not a coward. You're afraid, but you're not a coward."

"Is there a difference?"

He nodded. "A lot of difference."

"I feel so alone. I never did feel like this before; like I was all by myself and there was nobody to care what happened to me. Always, before, there was Mama and Daddy there and my friends around me. I had lots of friends, and they had a going-away party for me the night before I left."

Friends and music and laughter for her to remember—and on the viewscreen Lotus Lake was going into the shadow.

"Is it the same with Gerry?" she asked. "I mean, if he should make a mistake, would he have to die for it, all alone and with no one to help him?"

"It's the same with all along the frontier; it will always be like that so long as there is a frontier."

"Gerry didn't tell us. He said the pay was good and he sent money home all the time because Daddy's little shop just brought in a bare living but he didn't tell us it was like this."

"He didn't tell you his work was dangerous?"

"Well—yes. He mentioned that, but we didn't understand. I always thought danger along the frontier was something that was a lot of fun; an exciting adventure, like in the three-D shows." A wan smile touched her face for a moment. "Only it's not, is it? It's not the same at all, because when it's real you can't go home after the show is over."

"No," he said. "No, you can't."

Her glance flicked from the chronometer to the door of the air lock then down to the pad and pencil she still held. She shifted her position slightly to lay them on the bench beside, moving one foot out a little. For the first time he saw that she was not wearing Vegan gypsy sandals but only cheap imitations; the expensive Vegan leather was some kind of grained plastic, the silver buckle was gilded iron, the jewels were colored glass. *Daddy's little shop just brought in a bare living—* She must have left college in her second year, to take the course in linguistics that would enable her to make her own way and help her brother provide for her parents, earning what she could by part-time work after classes were over.

Her personal possessions on the *Stardust* would be taken back to her parents—they would neither be of much value nor occupy much storage space on the return voyage.

"Isn't it—" She stopped, and he looked at her questioningly. "Isn't it cold in here?" she asked, almost apologetically. "Doesn't it seem cold to you?"

"Why, yes," he said. He saw by the main temperature gauge that the room was at precisely normal temperature. "Yes, it's colder than it should be."

"I wish Gerry would get back before it's too late. Do you really think he will, and you didn't just say so to make me feel better?"

"I think he will—they said he would be in pretty soon." On the viewscreen Lotus Lake had gone into the shadow but for the thin blue line of its western edge and it was apparent he had overestimated the time she would have in which to talk to her brother. Reluctantly, he said to her, "His camp will be out of radio range in a few minutes; he's on that part of Woden that's in the shadow"—he indicated the viewscreen—"and the turning of Woden will put him beyond contact. There may not be much time left when he comes in—not much time to talk to him before he fades out. I wish I could do something about it—I would call him right now if I could."

"Not even as much time as I will have to stay?"

"I'm afraid not."

"Then—" She straightened and looked toward the air lock with pale resolution. "Then I'll go when Gerry passes beyond range. I won't wait any longer after that—I won't have anything to wait for."

Again there was nothing he could say.

"Maybe I shouldn't wait at all. Maybe I'm selfish—maybe it would be better for Gerry if you just told him about it afterward."

There was an unconscious pleading for denial in the way she spoke and he said, "He wouldn't want you to do that, to not wait for him."

"It's already coming dark where he is, isn't it? There will

be all the long night before him, and Mama and Daddy don't know yet that I won't ever be coming back like I promised them I would. I've caused everyone I love to be hurt, haven't I? I didn't want to—I didn't intend to."

"It wasn't your fault," he said. "It wasn't your fault at all. They'll know that. They'll understand."

"At first I was so afraid to die that I was a coward and thought only of myself. Now, I see how selfish I was. The terrible thing about dying like this is not that I'll be gone but that I'll never see them again; never be able to tell them that I didn't take them for granted; never be able to tell them I knew of the sacrifices they made to make my life happier, that I knew all the things they did for me and that I loved them so much more than I ever told them. I've never told them any of those things. You don't tell them such things when you're young and your life is all before you—you're afraid of sounding sentimental and silly.

"But it's so different when you have to die—you wish you had told them while you could and you wish you could tell them you're sorry for all the little mean things you ever did or said to them. You wish you could tell them that you didn't really mean to ever hurt their feelings and for them to only remember that you always loved them far more than you ever let them know."

"You don't have to tell them that," he said. "They will know—they've always known it."

"Are you sure?" she asked. "How can you be sure? My people are strangers to you."

"Wherever you go, human nature and human hearts are the same."

"And they will know what I want them to know—that I love them?"

"They've always known it, in a way far better than you could ever put in words for them."

"I keep remembering the things they did for me, and it's the little things they did that seem to be the most important to me, now. Like Gerry—he sent me a bracelet of fire-rubies on my sixteenth birthday. It was beautiful—it must have cost him a month's pay. Yet, I remember him more for what he did the night my kitten got run over in the street. I was only six years old and he held me in his arms and wiped away my tears and told me not to cry, that Flossy was gone for just a little while, for just long enough to get herself a new fur coat and she would be on the foot of my bed the very next morning. I believed him and quit crying and went to sleep dreaming about my kitten coming back. When I woke up the next morning, there was Flossy on the foot of my bed in a brand-new white fur coat, just like he had said she would be.

"It wasn't until a long time later that Mama told me Gerry had got the pet-shop owner out of bed at four in the morning and, when the man got mad about it, Gerry told him he was either going to go down and sell him the white kitten right then or he'd break his neck."

"It's always the little things you remember people by; all the little things they did because they wanted to do them for you. You've done the same for Gerry and your father and mother; all kinds of things that you've forgotten about but that they will never forget."

"I hope I have. I would like for them to remember me like that."

"They will."

"I wish—" She swallowed. "The way I'll die—I wish they wouldn't ever think of that. I've read how people look who die in space—their insides all ruptured and exploded and their lungs out between their teeth and then, a few seconds later, they're all dry and shapeless and horribly ugly. I don't want them to ever think of me as something dead and horrible, like that."

"You're their own, their child and their sister. They could never think of you other than the way you would want them to; the way you looked the last time they saw you."

"I'm still afraid," she said. "I can't help it, but I don't want Gerry to know it. If he gets back in time, I'm going to act like I'm not afraid at all and—"

The signal buzzer interrupted her, quick and imperative.

"Gerry!" She came to her feet. "It's Gerry, now!"

He spun the volume control knob and asked: "Gerry Cross?"

"Yes," her brother answered, an undertone of tenseness to his reply. "The bad news—what is it?"

She answered for him, standing close behind him and leaning down a little toward the communicator, her hand resting small and cold on his shoulder.

"Hello, Gerry." There was only a faint quaver to betray the careful casualness of her voice. "I wanted to see you—"

"Marilyn!" There was sudden and terrible apprehension in the way he spoke her name. "What are you doing on that EDS?"

"I wanted to see you," she said again. "I wanted to see you, so I hid on this ship—"

"You *hid* on it?"

"I'm a stowaway . . . I didn't know what it would mean—"

"*Marilyn!*" It was the cry of a man who calls hopeless and desperate to someone already and forever gone from him. "What have you done?"

"I . . . it's not—" Then her own composure broke and the cold little hand gripped his shoulder convulsively. "Don't, Gerry—I only wanted to see you; I didn't intend to hurt you. Please, Gerry, don't feel like that—"

Something warm and wet splashed on his wrist and he slid out of the chair, to help her into it and swing the microphone down to her own level.

"Don't feel like that— Don't let me go knowing you feel like that—"

The sob she had tried to hold back choked in her throat and her brother spoke to her. "Don't cry, Marilyn." His voice was suddenly deep and infinitely gentle, with all the pain held out of it. "Don't cry, Sis—you mustn't do that. It's all right, Honey—everything is all right."

"I—" Her lower lip quivered and she bit into it. "I didn't want you to feel that way—I just wanted us to say good-by because I have to go in a minute."

"Sure—sure. That's the way it will be, Sis. I didn't mean to sound the way I did." Then his voice changed to a tone of quick and urgent demand. "EDS—have you called the *Stardust?* Did you check with the computers?"

"I called the *Stardust* almost an hour ago. It can't turn back, there are no other cruisers within forty light-years, and there isn't enough fuel."

"Are you sure that the computers had the correct data— sure of everything?"

"Yes—do you think I could ever let it happen if I wasn't sure? I did everything I could do. If there was anything at all I could do now, I would do it."

"He tried to help me, Gerry." Her lower lip was no longer trembling and the short sleeves of her blouse were wet where she had dried her tears. "No one can help me and I'm not going to cry any more and everything will be all right with you and Daddy and Mama, won't it?"

"Sure—sure it will. We'll make out fine."

Her brother's words were beginning to come in more faintly and he turned the volume control to maximum. "He's going out of range," he said to her. "He'll be gone within another minute."

"You're fading out, Gerry," she said. "You're going out of range. I wanted to tell you—but I can't, now. We must say good-by so soon—but maybe I'll see you again. Maybe I'll come to you in your dreams with my hair in braids and crying because the kitten in my arms is dead; maybe I'll be the touch of a breeze that whispers to you as it goes by; maybe I'll be one of those gold-winged larks you told me about, singing my silly head off to you; maybe, at times, I'll be nothing you can see but you will know I'm there beside you. Think of me like that, Gerry; always like that and not—the other way."

Dimmed to a whisper by the turning of Woden, the answer came back:

"Always like that, Marilyn—always like that and never any other way."

"Our time is up, Gerry—I have to go now. Good—" Her voice broke in mid-word and her mouth tried to twist into crying. She pressed her hand hard against it and when she spoke again the words came clear and true:

"Good-by, Gerry."

Faint and ineffably poignant and tender, the last words came from the cold metal of the communicator:

"Good-by, little sister—"

She sat motionless in the hush that followed, as though listening to the shadow-echoes of the words as they died away, then she turned away from the communicator, toward the air lock, and he pulled the black lever beside him. The inner door of the air lock slid swiftly open, to reveal the bare little cell that was waiting for her, and she walked to it.

She walked with her head up and the brown curls brushing her shoulders, with the white sandals stepping as sure and steady as the fractional gravity would permit and the gilded buckles twinkling with little lights of blue and red and crystal. He let her walk alone and made no move to help her, knowing she would not want it that way. She stepped into the air lock and turned to face him, only the pulse in her throat to betray the wild beating of her heart.

"I'm ready," she said.

He pushed the lever up and the door slid its quick barrier between them, inclosing her in black and utter darkness for her last moments of life. It clicked as it locked in place and he jerked down the red lever. There was a slight waver to the ship as the air gushed from the lock, a vibration to the wall as though something had bumped the outer door in passing, then there was nothing and the ship was dropping true and steady again. He shoved the red lever back to close the door on the empty air lock and turned away, to walk to the pilot's chair with the slow steps of a man old and weary.

Back in the pilot's chair he pressed the signal button of the normal-space transmitter. There was no response; he had expected none. Her brother would have to wait through the night until the turning of Woden permitted contact through Group One.

It was not yet time to resume deceleration and he waited while the ship dropped endlessly downward with him and the drives purred softly. He saw that the white hand of the supplies closet temperature gauge was on zero. A cold equation had been balanced and he was alone on the ship. Something shapeless and ugly was hurrying ahead of him, going to Woden where its brother was waiting through the night, but the empty ship still lived for a little while with the presence of the girl who had not known about the forces that killed with neither hatred nor malice. It seemed, almost, that she still sat small and bewildered and frightened on the metal box beside him, her words echoing hauntingly clear in the void she had left behind her:

I didn't do anything to die for—I didn't do anything—

To fully understand the changes that came over science fiction in the 1950s, one must be willing to examine the grubby economics of the genre with a cold eye. At the end of World War II most science fiction was published in a few pulp magazines with circulations of not more than 50,000 copies per issue. A few specialty houses like Gnome Press published a few hardcover science fiction titles, but by and large science fiction meant short stories and serials in low-circulation pulp magazines whose notion of a princely wage was about 2¢ a word. What this meant was that the writing of science fiction novels was not economically encouraged and that science fiction writers had to write at a lunatic clip to keep from starving to death. That so many of them still chose to write science fiction on the ragged edge of survival is a tribute to their dedication to the genre.

But it also explains why they seldom, if ever, could even think in terms of a well-crafted literary product. The rent was always two months overdue, and the bill collectors were howling in the night. To slow down, produce better work, and thus break this vicious circle was not realistic because there was no place to publish better science fiction at rates that would permit it to be written. Instead, the science fiction writers turned necessity into virtue, developed a machismo of production, and worshiped the Great God Speed.

But by the early 1950s that too was changing. There were two new and different science fiction magazines.

The Magazine of Fantasy and Science Fiction was edited by Anthony Boucher and J. Francis McComas, and later by Boucher alone. Boucher was determined to bring at least a modicum of literary respectability to science fiction. He demanded good writing for its own sake, featured tasteful covers rather than lurid space-monsters, paid the modest top of the line for stories, and made *Fantasy and Science Fiction* the first science fiction magazine oriented toward presenting the best available science fiction to the world at large, toward creating a science fiction that the general reader and the literary world would deem worthy of notice.

Horace Gold, the editor of the other new magazine, *Galaxy,* still oriented his publication toward the traditional science fiction readership, but paid the highest rate in the field and favored heavily sociologically and psychologically oriented stories.

Fantasy and Science Fiction encouraged attention to style, *Galaxy* encouraged psychological depth, and most of the best writers—Sturgeon, Fritz Leiber, Robert Sheckley, Philip K. Dick, Damon Knight, Philip José Farmer, Alfred Bester—were writing for both magazines.

Then, too, paperback book publishing had become big business and paperback publishers like Ace and Ballantine found the economics of science fiction very attractive. Since magazine rates were so low, science fiction writers found the offer of, say, a $1,500 advance for a science fiction paperback novel quite an improvement over what they were used to. Since the magazines had circulations in the range of 40–50,000 copies per issue, the paperback publishers could count on similar average sales figures for science fiction books. At the royalty rates they were paying, they were guaranteed a decent profit before the books even earned out their minimal advances.

What these new economic imperatives meant creatively was that science fiction writers were being encouraged to pay attention to style, craftsmanship, and character and that they were being encouraged to write novels for the first time.

The result was that writers like Sturgeon, Clarke, Kornbluth, Farmer, Dick, Knight, and others began to develop, began to become self-conscious and contemplative about their own work.

There was a rash of fine science fiction novels and

also a growth of depth and sophistication in the science
fiction short story, which itself began to become more
"novelistic," more concerned with development and
detail. Sturgeon wrote *More Than Human, The Dreaming Jewels, Some of Your Blood,* and many of his finest
short stories. Frederik Pohl and C. M. Kornbluth wrote
The Space Merchants, a mordant satire on the
advertising industry, which reflected Kornbluth's incredibly biting viewpoint. Kornbluth's cosmically cynical
instinct for the sociological jugular reached full force
in short stories like "The Marching Morons" and "The
Advent on Channel Twelve." Walter M. Miller wrote
the classic *A Canticle for Leibowitz,* Edgar Pangborn
wrote *A Mirror for Observers,* and Philip K. Dick began
to develop the talent that would make him one of the
premier novelists of the 1960s and 1970s.

Perhaps the two ultimate science fiction novels of
the era were *The Demolished Man* and *The Stars
My Destination,* both by Alfred Bester. These were
filled with verbal wit, psychological and sociological
sophistication, typographical inventiveness, structural
cleverness, color, dash, and an energy and momentum
that verged on the preternatural. "5,271,009" is a
Bester novel-in-miniature and gives a fair picture of
this writer's maturity and panache, unheard of at that
time in the genre and seldom equaled since.

A list of the fine novels and short stories of this
period could go on endlessly and pointlessly, for science
fiction writers were learning how to really *write.* They
had discovered the novel, and they completely eclipsed
all the so-called "Golden Age" science fiction. Science
fiction writers were learning that they didn't have to be
commercial hacks, that they could be serious writers
who wrote science fiction, that their art could have
something of absolute value for the world at large.

The Marching Morons

C. M. KORNBLUTH

Some things had not changed. A potter's wheel was still a potter's wheel and clay was still clay. Efim Hawkins had built his shop near Goose Lake, which had a narrow band of good fat clay and a narrow beach of white sand. He fired three bottle-nosed kilns with willow charcoal from the wood lot. The wood lot was also useful for long walks while the kilns were cooling; if he let himself stay within sight of them, he would open them prematurely, impatient to see how some new shape or glaze had come through the fire, and—*ping!*— the new shape or glaze would be good for nothing but the shard pile back of his slip tanks.

A business conference was in full swing in his shop, a modest cube of brick, tile-roofed, as the Chicago–Los Angeles "rocket" thundered overhead—very noisy, very swept-back, very fiery jets, shaped as sleekly swift-looking as an airborne barracuda.

The buyer from Marshall Fields was turning over a black-glazed one liter carafe, nodding approval with his massive, handsome head. "This is real pretty," he told Hawkins and his own secretary, Gomez-Laplace. "This has got lots of what ya call real est'etic principles. Yeah, it is real pretty."

"How much?" the secretary asked the potter.

"Seven-fifty each in dozen lots," said Hawkins. "I ran up fifteen dozen last month."

"They are real est'etic," repeated the buyer from Fields. "I will take them all."

"I don't think we can do that, doctor," said the secretary. "They'd cost us $1,350. That would leave only $532 in our quarter's budget. And we still have to run down to East Liverpool to pick up some cheap dinner sets."

"Dinner sets?" asked the buyer, his big face full of wonder.

"Dinner sets. The department's been out of them for two months now. Mr. Garvy-Seabright got pretty nasty about it yesterday. Remember?"

"Garvy-Seabright, that meat-headed bluenose," the buyer said contemptuously. "He don't know nothin' about est'etics. Why for don't he lemme run my own department?" His eye fell on a stray copy of *Whambozambo Comix* and he sat down with it. An occasional deep chuckle or grunt of surprise escaped him as he turned the pages.

Uninterrupted, the potter and the buyer's secretary quickly closed a deal for two dozen of the liter carafes. "I wish we could take more," said the secretary, "but you heard what I told him. We've had to turn away customers for ordinary dinnerware because he shot the last quarter's budget on some Mexican piggy banks some equally enthusiastic importer stuck him with. The fifth floor is packed solid with them."

"I'll bet they look mighty est'etic."

"They're painted with purple cacti."

The potter shuddered and caressed the glaze of the sample carafe.

The buyer looked up and rumbled, "Ain't you dummies through yakkin' yet? What good's a seckertary for if'n he don't take the burden of *de*-tail off'n my back, harh?"

"We're all through, doctor. Are you ready to go?"

The buyer grunted peevishly, dropped *Whambozambo Comix* on the floor and led the way out of the building and down the log corduroy road to the highway. His car was waiting on the concrete. It was, like all contemporary cars, too low-slung to get over the logs. He climbed down into the car and started the motor with a tremendous sparkle and roar.

"Gomez-Laplace," called out the potter under cover of the noise, "did anything come of the radiation program they were working on the last time I was on duty at the Pole?"

"The same old fallacy," said the secretary gloomily. "It stopped us on mutation, it stopped us on culling, it stopped us on segregation, and now it's stopped us on hypnosis."

"Well, I'm scheduled back to the grind in nine days. Time

for another firing right now. I've got a new luster to try . . ."

"I'll miss you. I shall be 'vacationing'—running the drafting room of the New Century Engineering Corporation in Denver. They're going to put up a two hundred-story office building, and naturally somebody's got to be on hand."

"Naturally," said Hawkins with a sour smile.

There was an ear-piercingly sweet blast as the buyer leaned on the horn button. Also, a yard-tall jet of what looked like flame spurted up from the car's radiator cap; the car's power plant was a gas turbine, and had no radiator.

"I'm coming, doctor," said the secretary dispiritedly. He climbed down into the car and it whooshed off with much flame and noise.

The potter, depressed, wandered back up the corduroy road and contemplated his cooling kilns. The rustling wind in the boughs was obscuring the creak and mutter of the shrinking refractory brick. Hawkins wondered about the number two kiln—a reduction fire on a load of lusterware mugs. Had the clay chinking excluded the air? Had it been a properly smoky blaze? Would it do any harm if he just took one close—?

Common sense took Hawkins by the scruff of the neck and yanked him over to the tool shed. He got out his pick and resolutely set off on a prospecting jaunt to a hummocky field that might yield some oxides. He was especially low on coppers.

The long walk left him sweating hard, with his lust for a peek into the kiln quiet in his breast. He swung his pick almost at random into one of the hummocks; it clanged on a stone, which he excavated. A largely obliterated inscription said:

ERSITY OF CHIC
OGICAL LABO
ELOVED MEMORY OF
KILLED IN ACT

The potter swore mildly. He had hoped the field would turn out to be a cemetery, preferably a once-fashionable cemetery full of once-massive bronze caskets moldered into oxides of tin and copper.

Well, hell, maybe there was some around anyway.

He headed lackadaisically for the second largest hillock and sliced into it with his pick. There was a stone to under-cut and topple into a trench, and then the potter was very glad he'd stuck at it. His nostrils were filled with the bitter smell, and the dirt was tinged with the exciting blue of copper salts. The pick went *clang!*

Hawkins, puffing, pried up a stainless steel plate that was quite badly stained and was also marked with incised letters. It seemed to have pulled loose from rotting bronze; there were rivets on the back that brought up flakes of green patina. The potter wiped off the surface dirt with his sleeve, turned it to catch the sunlight obliquely, and read:

"HONEST JOHN BARLOW"

"Honest John," famed in university annuals repre-sents a challenge which medical science has not yet answered: revival of a human being accidentally thrown into a state of suspended animation.

In 1988 Mr. Barlow, a leading Evanston real estate dealer, visited his dentist for treatment of an impacted wisdom tooth. His dentist requested and received per-mission to use the experimental anesthetic Cyclopara-dimethanol-B-7, developed at the University.

After administration of the anesthetic, the dentist resorted to his drill. By freakish mischance, a short cir-cuit in his machine delivered 220 volts of 60-cycle cur-rent into the patient. (In a damage suit instituted by Mrs. Barlow against the dentist, the University and the makers of the drill, a jury found for the defendants.) Mr. Barlow never got up from the dentist's chair and was assumed to have died of poisoning, electrocution or both.

Morticians preparing him for embalming discovered, however, that their subject was—though certainly not living—just as certainly not dead. The University was notified and a series of exhaustive tests was begun, including attempts to duplicate the trance state on volunteers. After a bad run of seven cases which ended fatally, the attempts were abandoned.

Honest John was long an exhibit at the University museum, and livened many a football game as mascot of the University's Blue Crushers. The bounds of taste were overstepped, however, when a pledge to Sigma Delta Chi was ordered in '03 to "kidnap" Honest John from his loosely guarded glass museum case and introduce him into the Rachel Swanson Memorial Girls' Gymnasium shower room.

On May 22nd, 2003, the University Board of Regents issued the following order: "By unanimous vote, it is directed that the remains of Honest John Barlow be removed from the University museum and conveyed to the University's Lieutenant James Scott III Memorial Biological Laboratories and there be securely locked in a specially prepared vault. It is further directed that all possible measures for the preservation of these remains be taken by the Laboratory administration and that access to these remains be denied to all persons except qualified scholars authorized in writing by the Board. The Board reluctantly takes this action in view of recent notices and photographs in the nation's press which, to say the least, reflect but small credit upon the University."

It was far from his field, but Hawkins understood what had happened—an early and accidental blundering onto the bare bones of the Levantman shock anesthesia, which had since been replaced by other methods. To bring subjects out of Levantman shock, you let them have a squirt of simple saline in the trigeminal nerve. Interesting. And now about that bronze—

He heaved the pick into the rotting green salts, expecting no resistance, and almost fractured his wrist. *Something* down there was *solid*. He began to flake off the oxides.

A half hour of work brought him down to phosphor bronze, a huge casting of the almost incorruptible metal. It had weakened structurally over the centuries; he could fit the point of his pick under a corroded boss and pry off great creaking and grumbling striae of the stuff.

Hawkins wished he had an archeologist with him, but didn't dream of returning to his shop and calling one to take over the find. He was an all-around man: by choice and in his free time, an artist in clay and glaze; by necessity, an automotive, electronics, and atomic engineer who could also swing a project in traffic control, individual and group psychology, architecture, or tool design. He didn't yell for a specialist every time something out of his line came up; there were so few, with so much to do . . .

He trenched around his find, discovering that it was a great brick-shaped bronze mass with an excitingly hollow sound. A long strip of moldering metal from one of the long vertical faces pulled away, exposing red rust that went *whoosh* and was sucked into the interior of the mass.

It had been de-aired, thought Hawkins, and there must have been an inner jacket of glass which had crystallized through the centuries and quietly crumbled at the first clang of his pick. He didn't know what a vacuum would do to a subject of Levantman shock, but he had hopes; nor did he quite understand what a real estate dealer was, but it might have something to do with pottery. And *anything* might have a bearing on Topic Number One.

He flung his pick out of the trench, climbed out and set off at a dog-trot for his shop. A little rummaging turned up a hypo, and there was a plasticontainer of salt in the kitchen.

Back at his dig, he chipped for another half hour to expose the juncture of lid and body. The hinges were hopeless; he smashed them off.

Hawkins extended the telescopic handle of the pick for the best leverage, fitted its point into a deep pit, set its built-in fulcrum, and heaved. Five more heaves and he could see, inside the vault, what looked like a dusty marble statue. Ten more and he could see that it was the naked body of Honest John Barlow, Evanston real estate dealer, uncorrupted by time.

The potter found the apex of the trigeminal nerve with his needle's point and gave him 60 cc.

In an hour Barlow's chest began to pump.

In another hour, he rasped, "Did it work?"

"*Did* it!" muttered Hawkins.

Barlow opened his eyes and stirred, looked down, turned his hands before his eyes—

"I'll sue!" he screamed. "My clothes! My fingernails!" A horrid suspicion came over his face and he clapped his hands to his hairless scalp. "My hair!" he wailed. "I'll sue you for every penny you've got! That release won't mean a damned thing in court—I didn't sign away my hair and clothes and fingernails!"

"They'll grow back," said Hawkins casually. "Also your epidermis. Those parts of you weren't alive, you know, so they weren't preserved like the rest of you. I'm afraid the clothes are gone though."

"What is this—the University hospital?" demanded Barlow. "I want a phone. No, you phone. Tell my wife I'm all right, and tell Sam Immerman—he's my lawyer—to get over here right away. Greenleaf 7-4022. Ow!" He had tried to sit up, and a portion of his pink skin rubbed against the inner surface of the casket, which was powdered by the ancient cystallized glass. "What the hell did you guys do, boil me alive? Oh, you're going to pay for this!"

"You're all right," said Hawkins, wishing now he had a reference book to clear up several obscure terms. "Your epidermis will start growing immediately. You're not in the hospital. Look here."

He handed Barlow the stainless steel plate that had labeled the casket. After a suspicious glance, the man started to read. Finishing, he laid the plate carefully on the edge of the vault and was silent for a spell.

"Poor Verna," he said at last. "It doesn't say whether she was stuck with the court costs. Do you happen to know—"

"No," said the potter. "All I know is what was on the plate, and how to revive you. The dentist accidentally gave you a dose of what we call Levantman shock anesthesia. We haven't used it for centuries; it was powerful, but too dangerous."

"Centuries . . ." brooded the man. "Centuries . . . I'll bet Sam swindled her out of her eyeteeth. Poor Verna. How long ago was it? What year is this?"

Hawkins shrugged. "We call it 7-B-936. That's no help to you. It takes a long time for these metals to oxidize."

"Like that movie," Barlow muttered. "Who would have thought it? Poor Verna!" He blubbered and sniffled, reminding Hawkins powerfully of the fact that he had been found under a flat rock.

Almost angrily, the potter demanded, "How many children did you have?"

"None yet," sniffed Barlow. "My first wife didn't want them. But Verna wants one—wanted one—but we're going to wait until—we *were* going to wait until—"

"Of course," said the potter, feeling a savage desire to tell him off, blast him to hell and gone for his work. But he choked it down. There was The Problem to think of; there was always The Problem to think of, and this poor blubberer might unexpectedly supply a clue. Hawkins would have to pass him on.

"Come along," Hawkins said. "My time is short."

Barlow looked up, outraged. "How can you be so unfeeling? I'm a human being like—"

The Los Angeles–Chicago "rocket" thundered overhead and Barlow broke off in mid-complaint. "Beautiful!" he breathed, following it with his eyes. "Beautiful!"

He climbed out of the vault, too interested to be pained by its roughness against his infantile skin. "After all," he said briskly, "this should have its sunny side. I never was much for reading, but this is just like one of those stories. And I ought to make some money out of it, shouldn't I?" He gave Hawkins a shrewd glance.

"You want money?" asked the potter. "Here." He handed over a fistful of change and bills. "You'd better put my shoes on. It'll be about a quarter mile. Oh, and you're—uh, modest?"

—yes, that was the word. "Here." Hawkins gave him his pants, but Barlow was excitedly counting the money.

"Eighty-five, eighty-six—and it's dollars, too! I thought it'd be credits or whatever they call them. 'E Pluribus Unum' and 'Liberty'—just different faces. Say, is there a catch to this? Are these real, genuine, honest twenty-two-cent dollars like we had or just wallpaper?"

"They're quite all right, I assure you," said the potter. "I wish you'd come along. I'm in a hurry."

The man babbled as they stumped toward the shop. "Where are we going—The Council of Scientists, the World Coordinator or something like that?"

"Who? Oh, no. We call them 'President' and 'Congress.' No, that wouldn't do any good at all. I'm just taking you to see some people."

"I ought to make plenty out of this. *Plenty!* I could write books. Get some smart young fellow to put it into words for me and I'll bet I could turn out a best-seller. What's the setup on things like that?"

"It's about like that. Smart young fellows. But there aren't any best-sellers any more. People don't read much nowadays. We'll find something equally profitable for you to do."

Back in the shop, Hawkins gave Barlow a suit of clothes, deposited him in the waiting room, and called Central in Chicago. "Take him away," he pleaded. "I have time for one more firing, and he blathers and blathers. I haven't told him anything. Perhaps we should just turn him loose and let him find his own level, but there's a chance—"

"The Problem," agreed Central. "Yes, there's a chance."

The potter delighted Barlow by making him a cup of coffee with a cube that not only dissolved in cold water but heated the water to boiling point. Killing time, Hawkins chatted about the "rocket" Barlow had admired, and had to haul himself up short; he had almost told the real estate man what its top speed really was—almost, indeed, revealed that it was not a rocket.

He regretted, too, that he had so casually handed Barlow a couple of hundred dollars. The man seemed obsessed with fear that they were worthless, since Hawkins refused to take a note or I.O.U. or even a definite promise of repayment. But Hawkins couldn't go into details, and was very glad when a stranger arrived from Central.

"Tinny-Peete, from Algeciras," the stranger told him swiftly as the two of them met at the door. "Psychist for Poprob. Polasigned special overtake Barlow."

"Thank Heaven," said Hawkins. "Barlow," he told the man from the past, "this is Tinny-Peete. He's going to take care of you and help you make lots of money."

The psychist stayed for a cup of the coffee whose preparation had delighted Barlow, and then conducted the real estate man down the corduroy road to his car, leaving the potter to speculate on whether he could at last crack his kilns.

Hawkins, abruptly dismissing Barlow and The Problem, happily picked the chinking from around the door of the number two kiln, prying it open a trifle. A blast of heat and the heady, smoky scent of the reduction fire delighted him. He peered and saw a corner of a shelf glowing cherry-red, becoming obscured by wavering black areas as it lost heat through the opened door. He slipped a charred wood paddle under a mug on the shelf and pulled it out as a sample, the hairs on the back of his hand curling and scorching. The mug crackled and pinged, and Hawkins sighed happily.

The bismuth resinate luster had fired to perfection, a haunting film of silvery-black metal with strange bluish lights in it as it turned before the eyes, and the Problem of Population seemed very far away to Hawkins then.

Barlow and Tinny-Peete arrived at the concrete highway where the psychist's car was parked in a safety bay.

"What—a—*boat!*" gasped the man from the past.

"Boat? No, that's my car."

Barlow surveyed it with awe. Swept-back lines, deep-drawn compound curves, kilograms of chrome. He ran his hands futilely over the door—or was it the door?—in a futile search for a handle, and asked respectfully, "How fast does it go?"

The psychist gave him a keen look and said slowly, "Two hundred and fifty. You can tell by the speedometer."

"Wow! My old Chevy could hit a hundred on a straight-away, but you're out of my class, mister!"

Tinny-Peete somehow got a huge low door open and Barlow descended three steps into immense cushions, floundering over to the right. He was too fascinated to pay serious attention to his flayed dermis. The dashboard was a lovely wilderness of dials, plugs, indicators, lights, scales and switches.

The psychist climbed down into the driver's seat and did something with his feet. The motor started like lighting a blowtorch as big as a silo. Wallowing around in the cushions, Barlow saw through a rear-view mirror a tremendous exhaust filled with brilliant white sparkles.

"Do you like it?" yelled the psychist.

"It's terrific!" Barlow yelled back. "It's—"

He was shut up as the car pulled out from the bay into the road with a great *voo-ooo-ooom!* A gale roared past Barlow's head, though the windows seemed to be closed; the impression of speed was terrific. He located the speedometer on the dashboard and saw it climb past 90, 100, 150, 200.

"Fast enough for me," yelled the psychist, noting that Barlow's face fell in response. "Radio?"

He passed over a surprisingly light object, like a football helmet, with no trailing wires, and pointed to a row of buttons. Barlow put on the helmet, glad to have the roar of air stilled, and pushed a pushbutton. It lit up satisfyingly and Barlow settled back even farther for a sample of the brave new world's super-modern taste in ingenious entertainment.

"TAKE IT AND STICK IT!" a voice roared in his ears.

He snatched off the helmet and gave the psychist an injured look. Tinny-Peete grinned and turned a dial associated with the pushbutton layout. The man from the past donned the helmet again and found the voice had lowered to normal.

"The show of shows! The supershow! The super-duper show! The quiz of quizzes! *Take it and stick it!*"

There were shrieks of laughter in the background.

"Here we got the contes-tants all ready to go. You know

how we work it. I hand a contes-tant a triangle-shaped cutout and like that down the line. Now we got these here boards, they got cut-out places the same shape as the triangles and things, only they're all different shapes, and the first contes-tant that sticks the cutouts into the board, he wins.

"Now I'm gonna innaview the first contes-tant. Right here, honey. What's your name?"

"Name? Uh—"

"Hoddaya like that, folks? She don't remember her name! Hah? *Would you buy that for a quarter?*" The question was spoken with arch significance, and the audience shrieked, howled and whistled its appreciation.

It was dull listening when you didn't know the punch lines and catch lines. Barlow pushed another button, with his free hand ready at the volume control.

"—latest from Washington. It's about Senator Hull-Mendoza. He is still attacking the Bureau of Fisheries. The North California Syndicalist says he got affidavits that John Kingsley-Schultz is a bluenose from way back. He didn't publistat the affydavits, but he says they say that Kingsley-Schultz was saw at bluenose meetings in Oregon State College and later at Florida University. Kingsley-Schultz says he gotta confess he did major in fly-casting at Oregon and got his Ph.D. in gamefish at Florida.

"And here is a quote from Kingsley-Schultz: 'Hull-Mendoza don't know what he's talking about. He should drop dead.' Unquote. Hull-Mendoza says he won't publistat the affydavits, to pertect his sources. He says they was sworn by three former employees of the Bureau which was fired for in-competence and in-com-pat-ibility by Kingsley-Schultz.

"Elsewhere they was the usual run of traffic accidents. A three-way pileup of cars on Route 66 going outta Chicago took twelve lives. The Chicago–Los Angeles morning rocket crashed and exploded in the Mo-have—Mo-javvy—what-ever-you-call-it Desert. All the 94 people aboard got killed. A Civil Aeronautics Authority investigator on the scene says that the pilot was buzzing herds of sheep and didn't pull out in time.

"Hey! Here's a hot one from New York! A Diesel tug run

wild in the harbor while the crew was below and shoved in the port bow of the luck-shury liner *S. S. Placentia*. It says the ship filled and sank taking the lives of an es-ti-mated 180 passengers and 50 crew members. Six divers was sent down to study the wreckage, but they died, too, when their suits turned out to be fulla little holes.

"And here is a bulletin I just got from Denver. It seems—"

Barlow took off the headset uncomprehendingly. "He seemed so callous," he yelled at the driver. "I was listening to a newscast—"

Tinny-Peete shook his head and pointed at his ears. The roar of air was deafening. Barlow frowned baffledly and stared out of the window.

A glowing sign said:

MOOGS!
WOULD YOU BUY IT
FOR A QUARTER?

He didn't know what Moogs was or were; the illustration showed an incredibly proportioned girl, 99.9 per cent naked, writhing passionately in animated full color.

The roadside jingle was still with him, but with a new feature. Radar or something spotted the car and alerted the lines of the jingle. Each in turn sped along a roadside track, even with the car, so it could be read before the next line was alerted.

IF THERE'S A GIRL
YOU WANT TO GET
DEFLOCCULIZE
UNROMANTIC SWEAT.
"A*R*M*P*I*T*T*O"

Another animated job, in two panels, the familiar "Before and After." The first said, "Just Any Cigar?" and was illustrated with a two-person domestic tragedy of a wife holding her nose while her coarse and red-faced husband puffed a slimy-looking rope. The second panel glowed, "Or a VUELTA ABAJO?" and was illustrated with—

Barlow blushed and looked at his feet until they had passed the sign.

"Coming into Chicago!" bawled Tinny-Peete.

Other cars were showing up, all of them dreamboats.

Watching them, Barlow began to wonder if he knew what a kilometer was, exactly. They seemed to be traveling so slowly, if you ignored the roaring air past your ears and didn't let the speedy lines of the dreamboats fool you. He would have sworn they were really crawling along at twenty-five, with occasional spurts up to thirty. How much was a kilometer anyway?

The city loomed ahead, and it was just what it ought to be: towering skyscrapers, overhead ramps, landing platforms for helicopters—

He clutched at the cushions. Those two 'copters. They were going to—they were going to—they—

He didn't see what happened, because their apparent collision courses took them behind a giant building.

Screamingly sweet blasts of sound surrounded them as they stopped for a red light. "What the hell is going on here?" said Barlow in a shrill, frightened voice; because the braking time was just about zero, he wasn't hurled against the dashboard. "Who's kidding who?"

"Why, what's the matter?" demanded the driver.

The light changed to green and he started the pickup. Barlow stiffened as he realized that the rush of air past his ears began just a brief, unreal split-second before the car was actually moving. He grabbed for the door handle on his side.

The city grew on them slowly: scattered buildings, denser buildings, taller buildings, and a red light ahead. The car rolled to a stop in zero braking time, the rush of air cut off an instant after it stopped; and Barlow was out of the car and running frenziedly down a sidewalk one instant after that.

They'll track me down, he thought, panting. *It's a secret police thing. They'll get you—mind-reading machines, television eyes everywhere, afraid you'll tell their slaves about*

*freedom and stuff. They don't let anybody cross them, like
that story I once read.*

Winded, he slowed to a walk and congratulated himself
that he had guts enough not to turn around. That was what
they always watched for. Walking, he was just another
business-suited back among hundreds. He would be safe, he
would be safe—

A hand tumbled from a large, coarse, handsome face thrust
close to his: "Wassamatta bumpinninna people likeya owna
sidewalk gotta miner slamya inna mushya bassar!" It was
neither the mad potter nor the mad driver.

"Excuse me," said Barlow. "What did you say?"

"Oh, yeah?" yelled the stranger dangerously, and waited
for an answer.

Barlow with the feeling that he had somehow been suck-
ered into the short end of an intricate land-title deal, heard
himself reply belligerently, "Yeah!"

The stranger let go of his shoulder and snarled, "Oh, yeah?"

"Yeah!" said Barlow, yanking his jacket back into shape.

"Aaah!" snarled the stranger, with more contempt and disgust than ferocity. He added an obscenity current in Barlow's
time, a standard but physiologically impossible directive, and
strutted off hulking his shoulders and balling his fists.

Barlow walked on, trembling. Evidently he had handled
it well enough. He stopped at a red light while the long, low
dreamboats roared before him and pedestrians in the sidewalk
flow with him threaded their ways through the stream of cars.
Brakes screamed; fenders clanged and dented; hoarse cries
flew back and forth between drivers and walkers. He leaped
backward frantically as one car swerved over an arc of sidewalk to miss another.

The signal changed to green; the cars kept on coming
for about thirty seconds and then dwindled to an occasional
light-runner. Barlow crossed warily and leaned against a vend-
ing machine, blowing big breaths.

Look natural, he told himself. *Do something normal. Buy
something from the machine.*

He fumbled out some change, got a newspaper for a dime,

a handkerchief for a quarter and a candy bar for another quarter.

The faint chocolate smell made him ravenous suddenly. He clawed at the glassy wrapper printed "CRIGGLIES" quite futilely for a few seconds, and then it divided neatly by itself. The bar made three good bites, and he bought two more and gobbled them down.

Thirsty, he drew a carbonated orange drink in another one of the glassy wrappers from the machine for another dime. When he fumbled with it, it divided neatly and spilled all over his knees. Barlow decided he had been there long enough and walked on.

The shop windows were—shop windows. People still wore and bought clothes, still smoked and bought tobacco, still ate and bought food. And they still went to the movies, he saw with pleased surprise as he passed and then returned to a glittering place whose sign said it was THE BIJOU.

The place seemed to be showing a triple feature, *Babies Are Terrible, Don't Have Children,* and *The Canali Kid.*

It was irresistible; he paid a dollar and went in.

He caught the tail-end of *The Canali Kid* in three-dimensional, full-color, full-scent production. It appeared to be an interplanetary saga winding up with a chase scene and a reconciliation between estranged hero and heroine. *Babies Are Terrible* and *Don't Have Children* were fantastic arguments against parenthood—the grotesquely exaggerated dangers of painfully graphic childbirth, vicious children, old parents beaten and starved by their sadistic offspring. The audience, Barlow astoundedly noted, was placidly champing sweets and showing no particular signs of revulsion.

The *Coming Attractions* drove him into the lobby. The fanfares were shattering, the blazing colors blinding, and the added scents stomach-heaving.

When his eyes again became accustomed to the moderate lighting of the lobby, he groped his way to a bench and opened the newspaper he had bought. It turned out to be *The Racing Sheet,* which afflicted him with a crushing sense of loss. The familiar boxed index in the lower left hand corner of the front page showed almost unbearably that Churchill Downs and Empire City were still in business—

Blinking back tears, he turned to the Past Performances at Churchill. They weren't using abbreviations any more, and the pages because of that were single-column instead of double. But it was all the same—or was it?

He squinted at the first race, a three-quarter-mile maiden claimer for thirteen hundred dollars. Incredibly, the track record was two minutes, ten and three-fifths seconds. Any beetle in his time could have knocked off the three-quarter in one-fifteen. It was the same for the other distances, much worse for route events.

What the hell had happened to everything?

He studied the form of a five-year-old brown mare in the second and couldn't make head or tail of it. She'd won and lost and placed and showed and lost and placed without rhyme or reason. She looked like a front-runner for a couple of races and then she looked like a no-good pig and then she looked like a mudder but the next time it rained she wasn't and then she was a stayer and then she was a pig again. In a good five-thousand-dollar allowances event, too!

Barlow looked at the other entries and it slowly dawned on him that they were all like the five-year-old brown mare. Not a single damned horse running had the slightest trace of class.

Somebody sat down beside him and said, "That's the story."

Barlow whirled to his feet and saw it was Tinny-Peete, his driver.

"I was in doubts about telling you," said the psychist, "but I see you have some growing suspicions of the truth. Please don't get excited. It's all right, I tell you."

"So you've got me," said Barlow.

"*Got* you?"

"Don't pretend. I can put two and two together. You're the secret police. You and the rest of the aristocrats live in luxury on the sweat of these oppressed slaves. You're afraid of me because you have to keep them ignorant."

There was a bellow of bright laughter from the psychist

that got them blank looks from other patrons of the lobby. The laughter didn't sound at all sinister.

"Let's get out of here," said Tinny-Peete, still chuckling. "You couldn't possibly have it more wrong." He engaged Barlow's arm and led him to the street. "The actual truth is that the millions of workers live in luxury on the sweat of the handful of aristocrats. I shall probably die before my time of overwork unless—" He gave Barlow a speculative look. "You may be able to help us."

"I know that gag," sneered Barlow. "I made money in my time and to make money you have to get people on your side. Go ahead and shoot me if you want, but you're not going to make a fool out of me."

"You nasty little ingrate!" snapped the psychist, with a kaleidoscopic change of mood. "This damned mess is all your fault and the fault of people like you! Now come along and no more of your nonsense."

He yanked Barlow into an office building lobby and an elevator that, disconcertingly, went *whoost* loudly as it rose. The real estate man's knees were wobbly as the psychist pushed him from the elevator, down a corridor and into an office.

A hawk-faced man rose from a plain chair as the door closed behind them. After an angry look at Barlow, he asked the psychist, "Was I called from the Pole to inspect this— this—?"

"Unget updandered. I've deeprobed etfind quasichance ex-him Poprobattackline," said the psychist soothingly.

"Doubt," grunted the hawk-faced man.

"Try," suggested Tinny-Peete.

"Very well. Mr. Barlow, I understand you and your lamented had no children."

"What of it?"

"This of it. You were a blind, selfish stupid ass to tolerate economic and social conditions which penalized child-bearing by the prudent and foresighted. You made us what we are today, and I want you to know that we are far from satisfied. Damn-fool rockets! Damn-fool automobiles! Damn-fool cities with overhead ramps!"

"As far as I can see," said Barlow, "you're running down the best features of time. Are you crazy?"

"The rockets aren't rockets. They're turbo-jets—good turbo-jets, but the fancy shell around them makes for a bad drag. The automobiles have a top speed of one hundred kilometers per hour—a kilometer is, if I recall my paleolinguistics, three-fifths of a mile—and the speedometers are all rigged accordingly so the drivers will think they're going two hundred and fifty. The cities are ridiculous, expensive, unsanitary, wasteful conglomerations of people who'd be better off and more productive if they were spread over the countryside.

"We need the rockets and trick speedometers and cities because, while you and your kind were being prudent and foresighted and not having children, the migrant workers, slum dwellers and tenant farmers were shiftlessly and short-sightedly having children—breeding, breeding. My God, how they bred!"

"Wait a minute," objected Barlow. "There were lots of people in our crowd who had two or three children."

"The attrition of accidents, illness, wars, and such took care of that. Your intelligence was bred out. It is gone. Children that should have been born never were. The just-average, they'll-get-along majority took over the population. The average IQ now is 45."

"But that's far in the future—"

"So are you," grunted the hawk-faced man sourly.

"But who are *you* people?"

"Just people—real people. Some generations ago the geneticists realized at last that nobody was going to pay any attention to what they said, so they abandoned words for deeds. Specifically, they formed and recruited for a closed corporation intended to maintain and improve the breed. We are their descendants, about three million of us. There are five billion of the others, so we are their slaves.

"During the past couple of years, I've designed a skyscraper, kept Billings Memorial Hospital here in Chicago running, headed off war with Mexico, and directed traffic at La Guardia Field in New York."

"I don't understand! Why don't you let them go to hell in their own way?"

The man grimaced. "We tried it once for three months. We holed up at the South Pole and waited. They didn't notice it. Some drafting-room people were missing; some chief nurses didn't show up; minor government people on the non-policy level couldn't be located. It didn't seem to matter.

"In a week there was hunger. In two weeks there were famine and plague; in three weeks war and anarchy. We called off the experiment; it took us most of the next generation to get things squared away again."

"But why *didn't* you let them kill each other off?"

"Five billion corpses mean about five hundred million tons of rotting flesh."

Barlow had another idea. "Why don't you sterilize them?"

"Two and one half billion operations is a lot of operations. Because they breed continuously, the job would never be done."

"I see. Like the marching Chinese!"

"Who the devil are they?"

"It was a—uh, paradox of my time. Somebody figured out that if all the Chinese in the world were to line up four abreast, I think it was, and start marching past a given point, they'd never stop because of the babies that would be born and grow up before they passed the point."

"That's right. Only instead of 'a given point,' make it 'the largest conceivable number of operating rooms that we could build and staff.' There could never be enough."

"Say!" said Barlow. "Those movies about babies—was that your propaganda?"

"It was. It doesn't seem to mean a thing to them. We have abandoned the idea of attempting propaganda contrary to a biological drive."

"So if you work *with* a biological drive?"

"I know of none which is consistent with inhibition of fertility."

Barlow's face went poker-blank, the result of years of careful discipline. "You don't, huh? You're the great brains, and you can't think of any?"

"Why, no," said the psychist innocently. "Can you?"

"That depends. I sold ten thousand acres of Siberian tundra —through a dummy firm, of course—after the partition of Russia. The buyers thought they were getting improved building lots on the outskirts of Kiev. I'd say that was a lot tougher than this job."

"How so?" asked the hawk-faced man.

"Those were normal, suspicious customers, and these are morons, born suckers. You just figure out a con they'll fall for; they won't know enough to do any smart checking."

The psychist and the hawk-faced man had also had training; they kept themselves from looking with sudden hope at each other.

"You seem to have something in mind," said the psychist.

Barlow's poker face went blanker still. "Maybe I have. I haven't heard any offer yet."

"There's the satisfaction of knowing that you've prevented Earth's resources from being so plundered," the hawk-faced man pointed out, "that the race will soon become extinct."

"I don't know that," Barlow said bluntly. "All I have is your word."

"If you really have a method, I don't think any price would be too great," the psychist offered.

"Money," said Barlow.

"All you want."

"More than you want," the hawk-faced man corrected.

"Prestige," added Barlow. "Plenty of publicity. My picture and my name in the papers and over TV every day, statues to me, parks and cities and streets and other things named after me. A whole chapter in the history books."

The psychist made a facial sign to the hawk-faced man that meant, "Oh, brother!"

The hawk-faced man signaled back, "Steady, boy!"

"It's not too much to ask," the psychist agreed.

Barlow, sensing a seller's market, said, "Power!"

"Power?" the hawk-faced man repeated puzzledly. "Your own hydro station or nuclear pile?"

"I mean a world dictatorship with me as dictator!"

"Well, now—" said the psychist but the hawk-faced man interrupted, "It would take a special emergency act of Congress but the situation warrants it. I think that can be guaranteed."

"Could you give us some indication of your plan?" the psychist asked.

"Ever hear of lemmings?"

"No."

"They are—were, I guess, since you haven't heard of them —little animals in Norway, and every few years they'd swarm to the coast and swim out to sea until they drowned. I figure on putting some lemming urge into the population."

"How?"

"I'll save that till I get the right signatures on the deal."

The hawk-faced man said, "I'd like to work with you on it, Barlow. My name's Ryan-Ngana." He put out his hand.

Barlow looked closely at the hand, then at the man's face. "Ryan what?"

"Ngana."

"That sounds like an African name."

"It is. My mother's father was a Watusi."

Barlow didn't take the hand. "I thought you looked pretty dark. I don't want to hurt your feelings, but I don't think I'd be at my best working with you. There must be somebody else just as well qualified, I'm sure."

The psychist made a facial sign to Ryan-Ngana that meant, "Steady *yourself*, boy!"

"Very well," Ryan-Ngana told Barlow. "We'll see what arrangement can be made."

"It's not that I'm prejudiced, you understand. Some of my best friends—"

"Mr. Barlow, don't give it another thought. Anybody who could pick on the lemming analogy is going to be useful to us."

And so he would, thought Ryan-Ngana, alone in the office after Tinny-Peete had taken Barlow up to the helicopter stage. So he would. Poprob had exhausted every rational attempt and the new Poprobattacklines would have to be irrational or sub-rational. This creature from the past with his lemming legends and his improved building lots would be a fountain of precious vicious self-interest.

Ryan-Ngana sighed and stretched. He had to go and run the San Francisco subway. Summoned early from the Pole to study Barlow, he'd left unfinished a nice little theorem. Between interruptions, he was slowly constructing an n-dimensional geometry whose foundations and superstructure owed no debt whatsoever to intuition.

Upstairs, waiting for a helicopter, Barlow was explaining to Tinny-Peete that he had nothing against Negroes, and Tinny-Peete wished he had some of Ryan-Ngana's imperturbability and humor for the ordeal.

The helicopter took them to International Airport, where, Tinny-Peete explained, Barlow would leave for the Pole.

The man from the past wasn't sure he'd like a dreary waste of ice and cold.

"It's all right," said the psychist. "A civilized layout. Warm, pleasant. You'll be able to work more efficiently there. All the facts at your fingertips, a good secretary—"

"I'll need a pretty big staff," said Barlow, who had learned from thousands of deals never to take the first offer.

"I meant a private, confidential one," said Tinny-Peete readily, "but you can have as many as you want. You'll naturally have top-primary-top priority if you really have a workable plan."

"Let's not forget this dictatorship angle," said Barlow.

He didn't know that the psychist would just as readily have promised him deification to get him happily on the "rocket" for the Pole. Tinny-Peete had no wish to be torn limb from limb; he knew very well that it would end that way if the population learned from this anachronism that there was a small elite which considered itself head, shoulders, trunk and groin above the rest. The fact that this assumption was perfectly true and the fact that the elite was condemned by its superiority to a life of the most grinding toil would not be considered; the difference would.

The psychist finally put Barlow aboard the "rocket" with some thirty people—real people—headed for the Pole.

Barlow was airsick all the way because of a post-hypnotic suggestion Tinny-Peete had planted in him. One idea was to make him as averse as possible to a return trip, and another idea was to spare the other passengers from his aggressive, talkative company.

Barlow, during the first day at the Pole, was reminded of his first day in the army. It was the same now-where-the-hell-are-we-going-to-put-*you*? business until he took a firm line with them. Then instead of acting like supply sergeants they acted like hotel clerks.

It was a wonderful, wonderfully calculated buildup, and one that he failed to suspect. After all, in his time a visitor from the past would have been lionized.

At day's end he reclined in a snug underground billet with the 60 mile gales roaring yards overhead, and tried to put two and two together.

It was like old times, he thought—like a coup in real estate where you had the competition by the throat, like a 50-percent rent boost when you knew damned well there was no place for the tenants to move, like smiling when you read over the breakfast orange juice that the city council had decided to build a school on the ground you had acquired by a deal with the city council. And it was simple. He would just sell tundra building lots to eagerly suicidal lemmings, and that was absolutely all there was to solving The Problem that had these double-domes spinning.

They'd have to work out most of the details, naturally; but, what the hell, that was what subordinates were for. He'd need specialists in advertising, engineering, communications —did they know anything about hypnotism? That might be helpful. If not, there'd have to be a lot of bribery done, but he'd make sure—damned sure—there were unlimited funds.

Just selling building lots to lemmings . . .

He wished, as he fell asleep, that poor Verna could have been in on this. It was his biggest, most stupendous deal.

Verna—that sharp shyster Sam Immerman must have swindled her. . . .

It began the next day with people coming to visit him. He
knew the approach. They merely wanted to be helpful to
their illustrious visitor from the past and would he help fill
them in about his era, which unfortunately was somewhat
obscure historically, and what did he think could be done
about The Problem? He told them he was too old to be roped
any more, and they wouldn't get any information out of him
until he got a letter of intent from at least the Polar President,
and a session of the Polar Congress empowered to make him
dictator.

He got the letter and the session. He presented his program, was asked whether his conscience didn't revolt at its
callousness, explained succinctly that a deal was a deal and
anybody who wasn't smart enough to protect himself didn't
deserve protection—"*Caveat emptor*," he threw in for scholar-
ship, and had to translate it to "Let the buyer beware." He
didn't, he stated, give a damn about either the morons or
their intelligent slaves; he'd told them his price and that was
all he was interested in.

Would they meet it or wouldn't they?

The Polar President offered to resign in his favor, with certain temporary emergency powers that the Polar Congress
would vote him if he thought them necessary. Barlow demanded the title of World Dictator, complete control of world
finances, salary to be decided by himself, and the publicity
campaign and historical writeup to begin at once.

"As for the emergency powers," he added, "they are
neither to be temporary nor limited."

Somebody wanted the floor to discuss the matter, with
the declared hope that perhaps Barlow would modify his
demands.

"You've got the proposition," Barlow said. "I'm not knocking off even ten percent."

"But what if the Congress refuses, sir?" the President asked.

"Then you can stay up here at the Pole and try to work it
out yourselves. I'll get what I want from the morons. A

shrewd operator like me doesn't have to compromise; I haven't got a single competitor in this whole cockeyed moronic era."

Congress waived debate and voted by show of hands. Barlow won unanimously.

"You don't know how close you came to losing me," he said in his first official address to the joint Houses. "I'm not the boy to haggle; either I get what I ask or I go elsewhere. The first thing I want is to see designs for a new palace for me—nothing *un*ostentatious either—and your best painters and sculptors to start working on my portraits and statues. Meanwhile, I'll get my staff together."

He dismissed the Polar President and the Polar Congress, telling them that he'd let them know when the next meeting would be.

A week later, the program started with North America the first target.

Mrs. Garvy was resting after dinner before the ordeal of turning on the dishwasher. The TV, of course, was on and it said, "Ooooh!"—long, shuddery and ecstatic, the cue for the *Parfum Assault Criminale* spot commercial. "Girls," said the announcer hoarsely, "do you want your man? It's easy to get him—easy as a trip to Venus."

"Huh?" said Mrs. Garvy.

"Wassamatter?" snorted her husband, starting out of a doze.

"Ja hear that?"

"Wha'?"

"He said 'easy like a trip to Venus.'"

"So?"

"Well, I thought ya couldn't get to Venus. I thought they just had that one rocket thing that crashed on the Moon."

"Aah, women don't keep up with the news," said Garvy righteously, subsiding again.

"Oh," said his wife uncertainly.

And the next day, on *Henry's Other Mistress,* there was a new character who had just breezed in: Buzz Rentshaw, Master Rocket Pilot of the Venus run. On *Henry's Other Mis-*

tress, "the broadcast drama about you and your neighbors, *folksy* people, *ordinary* people, *real* people"! Mrs. Garvy listened with amazement over a cooling cup of coffee as Buzz made hay of her hazy convictions.

MONA: Darling, it's so good to see you again!

BUZZ: You don't know how I've missed you on that dreary Venus run.

SOUND: *Venetian blind run down; key turned in door lock.*

MONA: Was it *very* dull, dearest?

BUZZ: Let's not talk about my humdrum job, darling. Let's talk about us.

SOUND: *Creaking bed.*

Well, the program was back to normal at last. That evening Mrs. Garvy tried to ask again whether her husband was sure about those rockets, but he was dozing right through *Take It and Stick It,* so she watched the screen and forgot the puzzle.

She was still rocking with laughter at the gag line, "Would you buy it for a quarter?" when the commercial went on for the detergent powder she always faithfully loaded her dishwasher with on the first of every month.

The announcer displayed mountains of suds from a tiny piece of the stuff and coyly added: "Of course, Cleano don't lay around for you to pick up like the soap root on Venus, but it's pretty cheap and it's almost pretty near just as good. So for us plain folks who ain't lucky enough to live up there on Venus, Cleano is the real cleaning stuff!"

Then the chorus went into their "Cleano-is-the-stuff" jingle, but Mrs. Garvy didn't hear it. She was a stubborn woman, but it occurred to her that she was very sick indeed. She didn't want to worry her husband. The next day she quietly made an appointment with her family freud.

In the waiting room she picked up a fresh new copy of *Readers Pablum* and put it down with a faint palpitation. The lead article, according to the table of contents on the cover, was titled "The Most Memorable Venusian I Ever Met."

"The freud will see you now," said the nurse, and Mrs. Garvy tottered into his office.

His traditional glasses and whiskers were reassuring. She choked out the ritual: "Freud, forgive me, for I have neuroses."

He chanted the antiphonal: "Tut, my dear girl, what seems to be the trouble?"

"I got like a hole in the head," she quavered. "I seem to forget all kinds of things. Things like everybody seems to know and I don't."

"Well, that happens to everybody occasionally, my dear. I suggest a vacation on Venus."

The freud stared, open-mouthed, at the empty chair. His nurse came in and demanded, "Hey, you see how she scrammed? What was the matter with *her?*"

He took off his glasses and whiskers meditatively. "You can search me. I told her she should maybe try a vacation on Venus." A momentary bafflement came into his face and he dug through his desk drawers until he found a copy of the four-color, profusely illustrated journal of his profession. It had come that morning and he had lip-read it, though looking mostly at the pictures. He leafed through to the article *Advantages of the Planet Venus in Rest Cures.*

"It's right there," he said.

The nurse looked. "It sure is," she agreed. "Why shouldn't it be?"

"The trouble with these here neurotics," decided the freud, "is that they all the time got to fight reality. Show in the next twitch."

He put on his glasses and whiskers again and forgot Mrs. Garvy and her strange behavior.

"Freud, forgive me, for I have neuroses."

"Tut, my dear girl, what seems to be the trouble?"

Like many cures of mental disorders, Mrs. Garvy's was achieved largely by self-treatment. She disciplined herself sternly out of the crazy notion that there had been only one rocket ship and that one a failure. She could join without wincing, eventually, in any conversation on the desirability of Venus as a place to retire, on its fabulous floral profusion. Finally she went to Venus.

All her friends were trying to book passage with the Evening Star Travel and Real Estate Corporation, but naturally the demand was crushing. She considered herself lucky to get a seat at last for the two-week summer cruise. The spaceship took off from a place called Los Alamos, New Mexico. It looked just like all the spaceships on television and in the picture magazines, but was more comfortable than you would expect.

Mrs. Garvy was delighted with the fifty or so fellow-passengers assembled before takeoff. They were from all over the country, and she had a distinct impression that they were on the brainy side. The captain, a tall, hawk-faced, impressive fellow named Ryan-Something or other, welcomed them aboard and trusted that their trip would be a memorable one. He regretted that there would be nothing to see because, "due to the meteorite season," the ports would be dogged down. It was disappointing, yet reassuring that the line was taking no chances.

There was the expected momentary discomfort at takeoff, and then two monotonous days of droning travel through space to be whiled away in the lounge at cards or craps. The landing was a routine bump and the voyagers were issued tablets to swallow to immunize them against any minor ailments. When the tablets took effect, the lock was opened and Venus was theirs.

It looked much like a tropical island on Earth, except for a blanket of cloud overhead. But it had a heady, otherworldly quality that was intoxicating and glamorous.

The ten days of the vacation were suffused with a hazy magic. The soap root, as advertised, was free and sudsy. The fruits, mostly tropical varieties transplanted from Earth, were delightful. The simple shelters provided by the travel company were more than adequate for the balmy days and nights.

It was with sincere regret that the voyagers filed again into the ship, and swallowed more tablets doled out to counteract and sterilize any Venus illnesses they might unwittingly communicate to Earth.

Vacationing was one thing. Power politics was another.

At the Pole, a small man was in a soundproof room, his face deathly pale and his body limp in a straight chair.

In the American Senate Chamber, Senator Hull-Mendoza (Synd., N. Cal.) was saying: "Mr. President and gentlemen, I would be remiss in my duty as a legislature if'n I didn't bring to the attention of the au-gust body I see here a perilous situation which is fraught with peril. As is well known to members of this au-gust body, the perfection of space flight has brought with it a situation I can only describe as fraught with peril. Mr. President and gentlemen, now that swift American rockets now traverse the trackless void of space between this planet and our nearest planetarial neighbor in space—and, gentlemen, I refer to Venus, the star of dawn, the brightest jewel in fair Vulcan's diadome—now, I say, I want to inquire what steps are being taken to colonize Venus with a vanguard of patriotic citizens like those minutemen of yore.

"Mr. President and gentlemen! There are in this world nations, envious nations—I do not name Mexico—who by fair means or foul may seek to wrest from Columbia's grasp the torch of freedom of space; nations whose low living standards and innate depravity give them an unfair advantage over the citizens of our fair republic.

"This is my program: I suggest that a city of more than 100,000 population be selected by lot. The citizens of the fortunate city are to be awarded choice lands on Venus free and clear, to have and to hold and convey to their descendants. And the national government shall provide free transportation to Venus for these citizens. And this program shall continue, city by city, until there has been deposited on Venus a sufficient vanguard of citizens to protect our manifest rights in that planet.

"Objections will be raised, for carping critics we have always with us. They will say there isn't enough steel. They will call it a cheap giveaway. I say there *is* enough steel for *one* city's population to be transferred to Venus, and that is all that is needed. For when the time comes for the second city to be transferred, the first, emptied city can be wrecked for the needed steel! And is it a giveaway? Yes! It is the most

glorious giveaway in the history of mankind! Mr. President
and gentlemen, there is no time to waste—Venus must be
American!"

Black-Kupperman, at the Pole, opened his eyes and said
feebly, "The style was a little uneven. Do you think anybody'll notice?"

"You did fine, boy; just fine," Barlow reassured him.

Hull-Mendoza's bill became law.

Drafting machines at the South Pole were busy around the
clock and the Pittsburgh steel mills spewed millions of plates
into the Los Alamos spaceport of the Evening Star Travel and
Real Estate Corporation. It was going to be Los Angeles, for
logistic reasons, and the three most accomplished psycho-
kineticists went to Washington and mingled in the crowd at
the drawing to make certain that the Los Angeles capsule
slithered into the fingers of the blindfolded Senator.

Los Angeles loved the idea and a forest of spaceships began to blossom in the desert. They weren't very good spaceships, but they didn't have to be.

A team at the Pole worked at Barlow's direction on a mail
setup. There would have to be letters to and from Venus to
keep the slightest taint of suspicion from arising. Luckily Barlow remembered that the problem had been solved once
before—by Hitler. Relatives of persons incinerated in the fur-
naces of Lublin or Majdanek continued to get cheery postal
cards.

The Los Angeles flight went off on schedule, under tremendous press, newsreel, and television coverage. The world
cheered the gallant Angelenos who were setting off on their
patriotic voyage to the land of milk and honey. The forest of
spaceships thundered up, and up, and out of sight without
untoward incident. Billions envied the Angelenos, cramped
and on short rations though they were.

Wreckers from San Francisco, whose capsule came up second, moved immediately into the city of the angels for the
scrap steel their own flight would require. Senator Hull-
Mendoza's constituents could do no less.

The president of Mexico, hypnotically alarmed at this extension of *yanqui imperialismo* beyond the stratosphere, launched his own Venus-colony program.

Across the water it was England versus Ireland, France versus Germany, China versus Russia, India versus Indonesia. Ancient hatreds grew into the flames that were rocket ships assailing the air by hundreds daily.

Dear Ed, how are you? Sam and I are fine and hope you are fine. Is it nice up there like they say with food and close grone on trees? I drove by Springfield yesterday and it sure looked funny all the buildings down but of coarse it is worth it we have to keep the greasers in their place. Do you have any trouble with them on Venus? Drop me a line some time. Your loving sister, Alma.

Dear Alma, I am fine and hope you are fine. It is a fine place here fine climate and easy living. The doctor told me today that I seem to be ten years younger. He thinks there is something in the air here keeps people young. We do not have much trouble with the greasers here they keep to theirselves it is just a question of us outnumbering them and staking out the best places for the Americans. In South Bay I know a nice little island that I have been saving for you and Sam with lots of blanket trees and ham bushes. Hoping to see you and Sam soon, your loving brother, Ed.

Sam and Alma were on their way shortly.

Poprob got a dividend in every nation after the emigration had passed the halfway mark. The lonesome stay-at-homes were unable to bear the melancholy of a low population density; their conditioning had been to swarms of their kin. After that point it was possible to foist off the crudest stripped-down accommodations on would-be emigrants; they didn't care.

Black-Kupperman did a final job on President Hull-Mendoza, the last job that genius of hypnotics would ever do on any moron, important or otherwise.

Hull-Mendoza, panic-stricken by his presidency over an

emptying nation, joined his constituents. The *Independence*, aboard which traveled the national government of America, was the most elaborate of all the spaceships—bigger, more comfortable, with a lounge that was handsome, though cramped, and cloakrooms for Senators and Representatives. It went, however, to the same place as the others and Black-Kupperman killed himself, leaving a note that stated he "couldn't live with my conscience."

The day after the American President departed, Barlow flew into a rage. Across his specially built desk were supposed to flow all Poprob high-level documents and this thing—this outrageous thing—called Poprob*term* apparently had got into the executive stage before he had even had a glimpse of it!

He buzzed for Rogge-Smith, his statistician. Rogge-Smith seemed to be at the bottom of it. Poprobterm seemed to be about first and second and third derivatives, whatever they were. Barlow had a deep distrust of anything more complex than what he called an "average."

While Rogge-Smith was still at the door, Barlow snapped, "What's the meaning of this? Why haven't I been consulted? How far have you people got and why have you been working on something I haven't authorized?"

"Didn't want to bother you, Chief," said Rogge-Smith. "It was really a technical matter, kind of a final cleanup. Want to come and see the work?"

Mollified, Barlow followed his statistician down the corridor.

"You still shouldn't have gone ahead without my okay," he grumbled. "Where the hell would you people have been without me?"

"That's right, Chief. We couldn't have swung it ourselves; our minds just don't work that way. And all that stuff you knew from Hitler—it wouldn't have occurred to us. Like poor Black-Kupperman."

They were in a fair-sized machine shop at the end of a slight upward incline. It was cold. Rogge-Smith pushed a button that started a motor, and a flood of arctic light poured in as the roof parted slowly. It showed a small spaceship with the door open.

Barlow gaped as Rogge-Smith took him by the elbow and his other boys appeared: Swenson-Swenson, the engineer; Tsutsugimushi-Duncan, his propellants man; Kalb-French, advertising.

"In you go, Chief," said Tsutsugimushi-Duncan. "This is Poprobterm."

"But I'm the World Dictator!"

"You bet, Chief. You'll be in history, all right—but this is necessary, I'm afraid."

The door was closed. Acceleration slammed Barlow cruelly to the metal floor. Something broke, and warm, wet stuff, salty tasting, ran from his mouth to his chin. Arctic sunlight through a port suddenly became a fierce lancet stabbing at his eyes; he was out of the atmosphere.

Lying twisted and broken under the acceleration, Barlow realized that some things had not changed, that Jack Ketch was never asked to dinner however many shillings you paid him to do your dirty work, that murder will out, that crime pays only temporarily.

The last thing he learned was that death is the end of pain.

by C. M. KORNBLUTH
The Space Merchants (with Frederik Pohl)
The Syndic
The Marching Morons (collection of short stories)
The Other Side of the Moon (collection of short stories)

5,271,009

ALFRED BESTER

Take two parts of Beelzebub, two of Ishmael, one of Monte Cristo, one of Cyrano, mix violently, season with mystery, and you have Mr. Solon Aquila. He is tall, gaunt, sprightly in manner, bitter in expression, and when he laughs his dark eyes turn into wounds. His occupation is unknown. He is wealthy without visible means of support. He is seen everywhere and understood nowhere. There is something odd about his life.

This is what's odd about Mr. Aquila, and you can make what you will of it. When he walks, he is never forced to wait on a traffic signal. When he desires to ride, there is always a vacant taxi on hand. When he bustles into his hotel, an elevator always happens to be waiting. When he enters a store, a salesclerk is always free to serve him. There always happens to be a table available for Mr. Aquila in restaurants. There are always last-minute ticket returns when he craves entertainment at sold-out shows.

You can question waiters, hack drivers, elevator girls, salesmen, box-office men. There is no conspiracy. Mr. Aquila does not bribe or blackmail for these petty conveniences. In any case, it would not be possible for him to bribe or blackmail the automatic clock that governs the city traffic signal system. These things, which make life so convenient for him, simply happen. Mr. Solon Aquila is never disappointed. Presently we shall hear about his first disappointment and see what it led to.

Mr. Aquila has been seen fraternizing in low saloons, in middle saloons, in high saloons. He has been met in bagnios, at coronations, executions, circuses, magistrate's courts, and handbook offices. He has been known to buy antique cars, historic jewels, incunabula, pornography, chemicals, Porro prisms, polo ponies, and full-choke shotguns.

"HimmelHerrGottSeiDank! I'm crazy, man, crazy. Eclectic, by God," he told a flabbergasted department store president. "The Weltmann type, nicht wahr? My ideal: Goethe. Tout le monde. God damn."

He spoke a spectacular tongue of mixed metaphors and meanings. Dozens of languages and dialects came out in machine-gun bursts. Apparently he also lied *ad libitum.*

"Sacré bleu. Jeez!" he was heard to say once. "Aquila from the Latin. Means aquiline. O tempora O mores. Speech by Cicero. My ancestor."

And another time: "My idol: Kipling. Took my name from him. Aquila, one of his heroes. God damn. Greatest Negro writer since *Uncle Tom's Cabin.*"

On the morning that Mr. Solon Aquila was stunned by his first disappointment, he bustled into the atelier of Lagan & Derelict, dealers in paintings, sculpture, and rare objects of art. It was his intention to buy a painting. Mr. James Derelict knew Aquila as a client. He had already purchased a Frederick Remington and a Winslow Homer some time ago when, by another odd coincidence, he had bounced into the Madison Avenue shop one minute after the coveted paintings went up for sale. Mr. Derelict had also seen Mr. Aquila boat a prize striper at Montauk.

"Bon soir, bel esprit, God damn, Jimmy," Mr. Aquila said. He was on first name terms with everyone. "Here's a cool day for color, oui! Cool. Slang. I have in me to buy a picture."

"Good morning, Mr. Aquila," Derelict answered. He had the seamed face of a cardsharp, but his blue eyes were honest and his smile was disarming. However at this moment his smile seemed strained, as though the volatile appearance of Aquila had unnerved him.

"I'm in the mood for your man, by Jeez," Aquila said, rapidly opening cases, fingering ivories and tasting the porcelains. "What's his name, my old? Artist like Bosch. Like Heinrich Kley. You handle him, parbleu, exclusive. O si sic omnia, by Zeus!"

"Jeffrey Halsyon?" Derelict asked timidly.

"Oeil-de-boeuf!" Aquila cried. "What a memory. Chryselephantine. Exactly the artist I want. He is my favorite. A monochrome, preferably. A small Jeffrey Halsyon for Aquila, bitte. Wrap her up."

"I wouldn't have believed it," Derelict muttered.

"Ah! Ah-ha? This is not one-hundred-proof guaranteed Ming," Mr. Aquila exclaimed, brandishing an exquisite vase. "Caveat emptor, by damn. Well, Jimmy? I snap my fingers. No Halsyons in stock, old faithful?"

"It's extremely odd, Mr. Aquila." Derelict seemed to struggle with himself. "Your coming in like this. A Halsyon monochrome arrived not five minutes ago."

"You see? Tempo ist Richtung. Well?"

"I'd rather not show it to you. For personal reasons, Mr. Aquila."

"HimmelHerrGott! Pourquoi? She's bespoke?"

"N-no, sir. Not for my personal reasons. For your personal reasons."

"Oh? God damn. Explain myself to me."

"Anyway it isn't for sale, Mr. Aquila. It can't be sold."

"For why not? Speak, old fish and chips."

"I can't say, Mr. Aquila."

"Zut alors! Must I judo your arm, Jimmy? You can't show. You can't sell. Me, internally, I have pressurized myself for a Jeffrey Halsyon. My favorite. God damn. Show me the Halsyon or sic transit gloria mundi. You hear me, Jimmy?"

Derelict hesitated, then shrugged. "Very well, Mr. Aquila. I'll show you."

Derelict led Aquila past cases of china and silver, past lacquer and bronzes and suits of shimmering armor to the gallery in the rear of the shop, where dozens of paintings hung on the gray velour walls, glowing under warm spotlights. He opened a drawer in a Goddard breakfront and took out a manila envelope. On the envelope was printed BABYLON INSTITUTE. From the envelope Derelict withdrew a dollar bill and handed it to Mr. Aquila.

"Jeffrey Halsyon's, latest," he said.

With a fine pen and carbon ink, a cunning hand had drawn

another portrait over the face of George Washington on the dollar bill. It was a hateful, diabolic face set in a hellish background. It was a face to strike terror, in a scene to inspire loathing. The face was a portrait of Mr. Aquila.

"God damn," Mr. Aquila said.

"You see, sir? I didn't want to hurt your feelings."

"Now I must own him, big boy." Mr. Aquila appeared to be fascinated by the portrait. "Is she accident or for purpose? Does Halsyon know myself? Ergo sum."

"Not to my knowledge, Mr. Aquila. But in any event I can't sell the drawing. It's evidence of a felony . . . mutilating United States currency. It must be destroyed."

"Never!" Mr. Aquila returned the drawing as though he feared the dealer would instantly set fire to it. "Never, Jimmy. Nevermore, quoth the raven. God damn. Why does he draw on money, Halsyon? My picture, pfui. Criminal libels but n'importe. But pictures on money? Wasteful. Joci causa."

"He's insane, Mr. Aquila."

"No! Yes? Insane?" Aquila was shocked.

"Quite insane, sir. It's very sad. They've had to put him away. He spends his time drawing these pictures on money."

"God damn, mon ami. Who gives him money?"

"I do, Mr. Aquila, and his friends. Whenever we visit him, he begs for money for his drawings."

"Le jour viendra, by Jeez! Why you don't give him paper for drawings, eh, my ancient of days?"

Derelict smiled sadly. "We tried that, sir. When we gave Jeff paper, he drew pictures of money."

"HimmelHerrGott! My favorite artist. In the looney bin. Eh, bien. How in the holy hell am I to buy paintings from same if such be the case?"

"You won't, Mr. Aquila. I'm afraid no one will ever buy a Halsyon again. He's quite hopeless."

"Why does he jump his tracks, Jimmy?"

"They say it's a withdrawal, Mr. Aquila. His success did it to him."

"Ah? QED me, big boy. Translate."

"Well, sir, he's still a young man; in his thirties and very immature. When he became so very successful, he wasn't ready for it. He wasn't prepared for the responsibilities of his life and his career. That's what the doctors told me. So he turned his back on everything and withdrew into childhood."

"Ah? And the drawing on money?"

"They say that's his symbol of his return to childhood, Mr. Aquila. It proves he's too young to know what money is for."

"Ah? Oui. Ja. Astute, by cracky. And my portrait?"

"I can't explain that, Mr. Aquila, unless you have met him in the past and he remembers you somehow."

"Hmmm. Perhaps. So. You know something, my attic of Greece? I am disappointed. Je n'oublierai jamais. I am most severely disappointed. God damn. No more Halsyons ever? Merde. My slogan. We must do something about Jeffrey Halsyon. I will not be disappointed. We must do something."

Mr. Solon Aquila nodded his head emphatically, took out a cigarette, took out a lighter, then paused, deep in thought. After a long moment, he nodded again, this time with decision, and did an astonishing thing. He returned the lighter to his pocket, took out another, glanced around quickly, and lit it under Mr. Derelict's nose.

Mr. Derelict appeared not to notice. Mr. Derelict appeared, in one instant, without transition, to be stuffed. Allowing the lighter to burn, Mr. Aquila placed it carefully on a ledge in front of the art dealer, who stood before it without moving. The orange flame gleamed on his glassy eyeballs.

Aquila darted out into the shop, searched, and found a rare Chinese crystal globe. He took it from its case, warmed it against his heart, and peered into it. He mumbled. He nodded. He returned the globe to the case, went to the cashier's desk, took a pad and pencil, and began ciphering in symbols that bore no relationship to any language or any graphology. He nodded again, tore up the sheet of paper, and took out his wallet.

From the wallet he removed a dollar bill. He placed the bill on the glass counter, took an assortment of fountain pens from his vest pocket, selected one, and unscrewed it. Carefully shielding his eyes, he allowed one drop to fall from the penpoint onto the bill. There was a blinding flash of light. There was a humming vibration that slowly died.

Mr. Aquila returned the pens to his pocket, carefully picked up the bill by a corner, and ran back into the picture gallery, where the art dealer still stood staring glassily at the orange flame. Aquila fluttered the bill before the sightless eyes.

"Listen, my ancient," Aquila whispered. "You will visit Jeffrey Halsyon this afternoon. N'est-ce-pas? You will give him this very own coin of the realm when he asks for drawing materials. Eh? God damn." He removed Mr. Derelict's wallet from his pocket, placed the bill inside, and returned the wallet.

"And that is why you make the visit," Aquila continued. "It is because you have had an inspiration from le Diable Boiteux. Nolens volens, the lame devil has inspired you with a plan for healing Jeffrey Halsyon. God damn. You will show him samples of his great art of the past to bring him to his senses. Memory is the all-mother. HimmelHerrGott! You hear me, big boy? You do what I say. Go today, and devil take the hindmost."

Mr. Aquila picked up the burning lighter, lit his cigarette, and permitted the flame to go out. As he did so, he said, "No, my holy of holies! Jeffrey Halsyon is too great an artist to languish in durance vile. He must be returned to this world. He must be returned to me. E sempre l'ora. I will not be disappointed. You hear me, Jimmy? I will not!"

"Perhaps there's hope, Mr. Aquila," James Derelict said. "Something's just occurred to me while you were talking . . . a way to bring Jeff back to sanity. I'm going to try it this afternoon."

As he drew the face of the Faraway Fiend over George Washington's portrait on a bill, Jeffrey Halsyon dictated his autobiography to nobody.

"Like Cellini," he recited. "Line and literature simultaneously. Hand in hand, although all art is one art, holy brothers in barbiturate, near ones and dear ones in Nembutal. Very well. I commence: I was born. I am dead. Baby wants a dollar. No—"

He arose from the padded floor and raged from padded

wall to padded wall, envisioning anger as a deep purple
fury running into the pale lavenders of recrimination by the
magic of his brushwork, his chiaroscuro, by the clever blend-
ing of oil, pigment, light, and the stolen genius of Jeffrey
Halsyon torn from him by the Faraway Fiend whose hideous
face—

"Begin anew," he muttered. "We darken the highlights.
Start with the underpainting. . . ." He squatted on the floor
again, picked up the quill drawing pen whose point was warranted harmless, dipped it into carbon ink whose contents
were warranted poisonless, and applied himself to the monstrous face of the Faraway Fiend which was replacing the
first President on the dollar.

"I was born," he dictated to space while his cunning hand
wrought beauty and horror on the banknote paper. "I had
peace. I had hope. I had art. I had peace. Mama. Papa. Kin
I have a glass of water? Oooo! There was a big bad bogeyman who gave me a look; a big bad look and he fighta baby.
Baby's afraid. Mama! Baby wantsa make pretty pictures
onna pretty paper for Mama and Papa. Look, Mama. Baby
makin' a picture of the bad bogeyman who fighta baby with
a mean look, a black look with his black eyes like pools of
hell, like cold fires of terror, like faraway fiends from faraway fears—who's that!"

The cell door unbolted. Halsyon leaped into a corner and
cowered, naked and squalling, as the door was opened
for the Faraway Fiend to enter. But it was only the medicine man in his white jacket and a stranger man in black suit,
black Homburg, carrying a black portfolio with the initials
J D lettered on it in a bastard gold Gothic with ludicrous
overtones of Goudy and Baskerville.

"Well, Jeffrey?" the medicine man inquired heartily.

"Dollar?" Halsyon whined. "Kin baby have a dollar?"

"I've brought an old friend, Jeffrey. You remember Mr.
Derelict?"

"Dollar," Halsyon whined. "Baby wants a dollar."

"What happened to the last one, Jeffrey? You haven't
finished it yet, have you?"

Halsyon sat on the bill to conceal it, but the medicine man

was too quick for him. He snatched it up, and he and the stranger man examined it.

"As great as all the rest," Derelict sighed. "Greater. What a magnificent talent wasting away. . . ."

Halsyon began to weep. "Baby wants a dollar!" he cried.

The stranger man took out his wallet, selected a dollar bill, and handed it to Halsyon. As soon as he touched it, he heard it sing, and he tried to sing with it, but it was singing him a private song so he had to listen.

It was a lovely dollar; smooth but not too new, with a faintly matte surface that would take ink like kisses. George Washington looked reproachful but resigned, as though he were used to the treatment in store for him. And indeed he might well be, for he was much older on this dollar. Much older than on any other, for his serial number was 5,271,-009 which made him 5,000,000 years old and more, and the oldest he had ever been before was 2,000,000.

As Halsyon squatted contentedly on the floor and dipped his pen in the ink as the dollar told him to, he heard the medicine man say, "I don't think I should leave you alone, Mr. Derelict."

"No, we must be, Doctor. Jeff was always shy about his work. He could only discuss it with me when we were alone."

"How much time would you need?"

"Give me an hour."

"I doubt very much whether it'll do any good."

"But there's no harm trying?"

"I suppose not. All right, Mr. Derelict. Call the nurse when you're through."

The door opened; the door closed. The stranger man named Derelict put his hand on Halsyon's shoulder in a friendly, intimate way. Halsyon looked up at him and grinned cleverly, meanwhile waiting for the sound of the bolt in the door. It came; like a shot, like a final nail in a coffin.

"Jeff, I've brought some of your old work with me," Derelict said in a voice that was only approximately casual. "I thought you might like to look it over with me."

"Have you got a watch on you?" Halsyon asked.

Restraining his start of surprise at Halsyon's normal tone, the art dealer took out his pocket watch and displayed it.

"Lend it to me for a minute."

Derelict unchained the watch and handed it over. Halsyon took it carefully and said, "All right. Go ahead with the pictures."

"Jeff!" Derelict exclaimed. "This is you again, isn't it? This is the way you always—"

"Thirty," Halsyon interrupted. "Thirty-five, forty, forty-five, fifty, fifty-five, ONE." He concentrated on the flicking second hand with rapt expectation.

"No, I guess it isn't," the dealer muttered. "I only imagined you sounded—oh, well." He opened the portfolio and began sorting mounted drawings.

"Forty, forty-five, fifty, fifty-five, TWO."

"Here's one of your earliest, Jeff. Remember when you came into the gallery with the roughs, and we thought you were the new polisher from the agency? Took you months to forgive us. You always claimed we bought your first picture just to apologize. Do you still think so?"

"Forty, forty-five, fifty, fifty-five, THREE."

"Here's that tempera that gave you so many heartaches. I was wondering if you'd care to try another? I really don't think tempera is as inflexible as you claim, and I'd be interested to have you try again now that your technique's so much more matured. What do you say?"

"Forty, forty-five, fifty, fifty-five, FOUR."

"Jeff, put down that watch."

"Ten, fifteen, twenty, twenty-five . . ."

"What the devil's the point of counting minutes?"

"Well," Halsyon said reasonably, "sometimes they lock the door and go away. Other times they lock up and stay and spy on you. But they never spy longer than three minutes so I'm giving them five just to make sure. FIVE."

Halsyon gripped the small pocket watch in his big fist and drove the fist cleanly into Derelict's jaw. The dealer dropped without a sound. Halsyon dragged him to the wall, stripped him naked, dressed himself in his clothes, repacked the portfolio, and closed it. He picked up the dollar bill and pocketed it. He picked up the bottle of carbon ink warranted nonpoisonous and dashed the contents into his face.

Choking and shouting, he brought the nurse to the door.

"Let me out of here," Halsyon cried in a muffled voice. "That maniac tried to drown me. Threw ink in my face. I want out!"

The door was unbolted and opened. Halsyon shoved past the nurse man, cunningly mopping his blackened face with a hand that only smeared it more. As the nurse man started to enter the cell, Halsyon said, "Never mind Halsyon. He's all right. Get me a towel or something. Hurry!"

The nurse man locked the door again, turned, and ran down the corridor. Halsyon waited until he disappeared into a supply room, then turned and ran in the opposite direction. He went through the heavy doors to the main wing corridor, still cleverly mopping, still sputtering with cunning indignation. He reached the main building. He was halfway out and still no alarm. He knew those brazen bells. They tested them every Wednesday noon.

It's like a ring-a-levio game, he told himself. It's fun. It's games. It's nothing to be scared of. It's being safely, sanely, joyously a kid again and when we quit playing, I'm going home to Mama and dinner and Papa reading me the funnies and I'm a kid again, really a kid again, forever.

There still was no hue and cry when he reached the main floor. He complained about his indignity to the receptionist. He complained to the protection guards as he forged James Derelict's name in the visitors' book, and his inky hand smeared such a mess on the page that the forgery went undetected. The guard buzzed the final gate open. Halsyon passed through into the street, and as he started away, he heard the brass throats of the bells begin a clattering that terrified him.

He ran. He stopped. He tried to stroll. He could not. He lurched down the street until he heard the guards shouting. He darted around a corner, and another, tore up endless streets, heard cars behind him, sirens, bells, shouts, commands. It was a ghastly Catherine wheel of flight. Searching desperately for a hiding place, Halsyon darted into the hall-way of a desolate tenement.

Halsyon began to climb the stairs. He went up three at a clip, then two, then struggled step by step as his strength failed and panic paralyzed him. He stumbled at a landing and fell against a door. The door opened. The Faraway Fiend stood within, smiling briskly, rubbing his hands.

"Glückliche Reise," he said. "On the dot. God damn. You twenty-three skiddooed, eh? Enter, my old. I'm expecting you. Be it never so humble . . ."

Halsyon screamed.

"No, no, no! No Sturm and Drang, my beauty." Mr. Aquila clapped a hand over Halsyon's mouth, heaved him up, dragged him through the doorway, and slammed the door.

"Presto chango," he laughed. "Exit Jeffrey Halsyon from mortal ken. Dieu vous garde."

Halsyon freed his mouth, screamed again, and fought hysterically, biting and kicking. Mr. Aquila made a cluck-ing noise, dipped into his pocket, and brought out a package of cigarettes. He flipped one up expertly and broke it under Halsyon's nose. The artist at once subsided and suffered himself to be led to a couch, where Aquila cleansed the ink from his face and hands.

"Better, eh?" Mr. Aquila chuckled. "Nonhabit-forming. God damn. Drinks now called for."

He filled a shot glass from a decanter, added a tiny cube of purple ice from a fuming bucket, and placed the drink in Halsyon's hand. Compelled by a gesture from Aquila, the artist drank it off. It made his brain buzz. He stared around, breathing heavily. He was in what appeared to be the luxuri-ous waiting room of a Park Avenue physician. Queen Anne furniture. Axminster rug. Two Morelands and a Crome on the wall in gilt frames. They were genuine, Halsyon realized with amazement. Then, with even more amazement, he realized that he was thinking with coherence, with continuity. His mind was quite clear.

He passed a heavy hand over his forehead. "What's hap-pened?" he asked faintly. "There's like . . . something like a fever behind me. Nightmares."

"You have been sick," Aquila replied. "I am blunt, my old. This is a temporary return to sanity. It is no feat, God damn. Any doctor can do it. Niacin plus carbon dioxide. Id genus omne. We much search for something more permanent."

"What's this place?"

"Here? My office. Anteroom without. Consultation room within. Laboratory to left. In God we trust."

"I know you," Halsyon mumbled. "I know you from somewhere. I know your face."

"Oui. You have drawn and redrawn and tredrawn me in your fever. Ecce homo. But you have the advantage, Halsyon. Where have we met? I ask myself." Aquila put on a brilliant speculum, tilted it over his left eye, and let it shine into Halsyon's face. "Now I ask you. Where have we met?"

Blinded by the light, Halsyon answered dreamily. "At the Beaux Arts Ball. . . . A long time ago. . . . Before the fever. . . ."

"Ah? Si. It was half a year ago. I was there. An unfortunate night."

"No. A glorious night. . . . Gay, happy, fun. . . . Like a school dance . . . like a prom in costume. . . ."

"Always back to the childhood, eh?" Mr. Aquila murmured. "We must attend to that. Cetera desunt, young Lochinvar. Continue."

"I was with Judy. . . . We realized we were in love that night. We realized how wonderful life was going to be. And then you passed and looked at me. . . . Just once. You looked at me. It was horrible."

"Tk!" Mr. Aquila clicked his tongue in vexation. "Now I remember said incident. I was unguarded. Bad news from home. A pox on both my houses."

"You passed in red and black . . . satanic. Wearing no mask. You looked at me . . . a red and black look I never forgot. A look from black eyes like pools of hell, like cold fires of terror. And with that look you robbed me of everything . . . of joy, of hope, of love, of life. . . ."

"No, no!" Mr. Aquila said sharply. "Let us understand ourselves. My carelessness was the key that unlocked the door.

But you fell into a chasm of your own making. Nevertheless, old beer and skittles, we must alter same." He removed the speculum and shook his finger at Halsyon. "We must bring you back to the land of the living. Auxilium ab alto. Jeez. That is for why I have arranged this meeting. What I have done I will undone, eh? But you must climb out of your own chasm. Knit up the raveled sleave of care. Come inside."

He took Halsyon's arm, led him down a paneled hall, past a neat office, and into a spanking white laboratory. It was all tile and glass with shelves of reagent bottles, porcelain filters, an electric oven, stock jars of acids, bins of raw materials. There was a small round elevation in the center of the floor, a sort of dais. Mr. Aquila placed a stool on the dais, placed Halsyon on the stool, got into a white lab coat, and began to assemble apparatus.

"You," he chatted, "are an artist of the utmost. I do not dorer la pilule. When Jimmy Derelict told me you were no longer at work, God damn! We must return him to his muttons, I said. Solon Aquila must own many canvases of Jeffrey Halsyon. We shall cure him. Hoc age."

"You're a doctor?" Halsyon asked.

"No. Let us say, a warlock. Strictly speaking, a witch pathologist. Very high-class. No nostrums. Strictly modern magic. Black magic and white magic are passé, n'est-ce pas? I cover entire spectrum, specializing mostly in the fifteen-thousand-angstrom band."

"You're a witch doctor? Never!"

"Oh, yes."

"In this kind of place?"

"Ah-ha? You too are deceived, eh? It is our camouflage. Many a modern laboratory you think concerns itself with science is devoted to magic. But we are scientific, too. Parbleu! We move with the times, we warlocks. Witch's brew now complies with Pure Food and Drug Act. Familiars one hundred percent sterile. Sanitary brooms. Cellophane-wrapped curses. Father Satan in rubber gloves. Thanks to Lord Lister; or is it Pasteur? My idol."

The witch pathologist gathered raw materials, consulted

an ephemeris, ran off some calculations on an electronic computer, and continued to chat.

"Fugit hora," Aquila said. "Your trouble, my old, is loss of sanity. Oui? Lost in one damn flight from reality and one damn desperate search for peace brought on by one unguarded look from me to you. Hélas! I apologize for that, RSVP." With what looked like a miniature tennis linemarker, he rolled a circle around Halsyon on the dais. "But your trouble is, to wit: You search for the peace of infancy. You should be fighting to acquire the peace of maturity, n'est-pas? Jeez."

Aquila drew circles and pentagons with a glittering compass and rule, weighed out powders on a microbeam balance, dropped various liquids into crucibles from calibrated burettes, and continued. "Many warlocks do brisk trade in potions from fountains of youth. Oh, yes. Are many youths and many fountains; but none for you. No. Youth is not for artists. Age is the cure. We must purge your youth and grow you up, nicht wahr?"

"No," Halsyon argued. "No. Youth is the art. Youth is the dream. Youth is the blessing."

"For some, yes. For many, not. Not for you. You are cursed, my adolescent. We must purge you. Lust for power. Lust for sex. Injustice collecting. Escape from reality. Passion for revenges. Oh, yes, Father Freud is also my idol. We wipe your slate clean at very small price."

"What price?"

"You will see when we are finished."

Mr. Aquila deposited liquids and powders around the helpless artist in crucibles and petri dishes. He measured and cut fuses, set up a train from the circle to an electric timer which he carefully adjusted. He went to a shelf of serum bottles, took down a small Woulff vial numbered 5-271-009, filled a syringe, and meticulously injected Halsyon.

"We begin," he said, "the purge of your dreams. Voilà!"

He tripped the electric timer and stepped behind a lead shield. There was a moment of silence. Suddenly black music crashed from a concealed loudspeaker and a recorded voice began an intolerable chant. In quick succession, the powders and liquids around Halsyon burst into flame. He was engulfed in music and fire fumes. The world began to spin around him in a roaring confusion. . . .

The president of the United Nations came to him. He was tall and gaunt, sprightly but bitter. He was wringing his hands in dismay.

"Mr. Halsyon! Mr. Halsyon!" he cried. "Where you been, my cupcake? God damn. Hoc tempore. Do you know what has happened?"

"No," Halsyon answered. "What's happened?"

"After your escape from the looney bin. Bango! H-bombs everywhere. The two-hour war. It is over. Hora fugit, old faithful. Virility is over."

"What!"

"Hard radiation, Mr. Halsyon, has destroyed the virility of the world. God damn. You are the only man left capable of engendering children. No doubt on account of a mysterious mutant strain in your makeup which it makes you different. Jeez."

"No."

"Oui. It is your responsibility to repopulate the world. We have taken for you a suite at the Odeon. It has three bedrooms. Three, my favorite. A prime number."

"Hot dog!" Halsyon said. "This is my big dream."

His progress to the Odeon was a triumph. He was garlanded with flowers, serenaded, hailed, and cheered. Ecstatic women displayed themselves wickedly before him, begging for his attention. In his suite, Halsyon was wined and dined. A tall, gaunt man entered subserviently. He was sprightly but bitter. He had a list in his hand.

"I am World Procurer at your service, Mr. Halsyon," he said. He consulted his list. "God damn. Are 5,271,009 virgins clamoring for your attention. All guaranteed beautiful. Ewig-Weibliche. Pick a number from one to 5,000,000."

"We'll start with a redhead," Halsyon said.

They brought him a redhead. She was slender, boyish, with a small hard bosom. The next was fuller with a rollicking rump. The fifth was Junoesque and her breasts were like African pears. The tenth was a voluptuous Rembrandt. The twentieth was wiry. The thirtieth was slender and boyish with a small hard bosom.

"Haven't we met before?" Halsyon inquired.

"No," she said.

The next was fuller with a rollicking rump.

"The body is familiar," Halsyon said.

"No," she answered.

The fiftieth was Junoesque with breasts like African pears.

"Surely?" Halsyon said.

"Never," she answered.

The World Procurer entered with Halsyon's morning aphrodisiac.

"Never touch the stuff," Halsyon said.

"God damn," the Procurer exclaimed. "You are a veritable giant. An elephant. No wonder you are the beloved Adam. Tant soit peu. No wonder they all weep for love of you." He drank off the aphrodisiac himself.

"Have you noticed they're all getting to look alike?" Halsyon complained.

"But no! Are all different. Parbleu! This is an insult to my office."

"Oh, they're different from one to another, but the types keep repeating."

"Ah? This is life, my old. All life is a cyclic. Have you not, as an artist, noticed?"

"I didn't think it applied to love."

"To all things. Wahrheit und Dichtung."

"What was that you said about them weeping?"

"Oui. They all weep."

"Why?"

"For ecstatic love of you. God damn."

Halsyon thought over the succession of boyish, rollicking, Junoesque, Rembrandtesque, wiry, red, blond, brunette, white, black, and brown women.

"I hadn't noticed," he said.

"Observe today, my world father. Shall we commence?"

It was true. Halsyon hadn't noticed. They all wept. He was flattered but depressed.

"Why don't you laugh a little?" he asked.

They would not or could not.

Upstairs on the Odeon roof, where Halsyon took his afternoon exercise, he questioned his trainer, who was a tall, gaunt man with a sprightly but bitter expression.

"Ah?" said the trainer. "God damn. I don't know, old scotch and soda. Perhaps because it is a traumatic experience for them."

"Traumatic?" Halsyon puffed. "Why? What do I do to them?"

"Ah-ha? You joke, eh? All the world knows what you do to them."

"No, I mean . . . how can it be traumatic? They're all fighting to get to me, aren't they? Don't I come up to expectations?"

"A mystery. Tripotage. Now, beloved father of the world, we practice the pushups. Ready? Begin."

Downstairs, in the Odeon restaurant, Halsyon questioned the headwaiter, a tall, gaunt man with a sprightly manner but bitter expression.

"We are men of the world, Mr. Halsyon. Suo jure. Surely you understand. These women love you and can expect no more than one night of love. God damn. Naturally they are disappointed."

"What do they want?"

"What every woman wants, my gateway to the west. A permanent relationship. Marriage."

"Marriage!"

"Oui."

"All of them?"

"Oui."

"All right. I'll marry all 5,271,009."

But the World Procurer objected. "No, no, no, young Lochinvar. God damn. Impossible. Aside from religious difficulties there are human also. God damn. Who could manage such a harem?"

"Then I'll marry one."

"No, no, no. Pensez à moi. How could you make the choice? How could you select? By lottery, drawing straws, tossing coins?"

"I've already selected one."

"Ah? Which?"

"My girl," Halsyon said slowly. "Judith Field."

"So. Your sweetheart?"

"Yes."

"She is far down on the list of 5,000,000."

"She's always been number one on my list. I want Judith." Halsyon sighed. "I remember how she looked at the Beaux Arts Ball. . . . There was a full moon. . . ."

"But there will be no full moon until the twenty-sixth."

"I want Judith."

"The others will tear her apart out of jealousy. No, no, no, Mr. Halsyon, we must stick to the schedule. One night for all, no more for any."

"I want Judith . . . or else."

"It will have to be discussed in council. God damn."

It was discussed in the U. N. council by a dozen delegates, all gaunt, sprightly but bitter. It was decided to permit Jeffrey Halsyon one secret marriage.

"But no domestic ties," the World Procurer warned. "No faithfulness to your wife. That must be understood. We cannot spare you from our program. You are indispensable."

They brought the lucky Judith Field to the Odeon. She was a tall, dark girl with cropped curly hair and lovely tennis legs. Halsyon took her hand. The World Procurer tiptoed out.

"Hello, darling," Halsyon murmured.

Judith looked at him with loathing. Her eyes were wet, her face bruised from weeping.

"Hello, darling," Halsyon repeated.

"If you touch me, Jeff," Judith said in a strangled voice, "I'll kill you."

"Judy!"

"That disgusting man explained everything to me. He didn't seem to understand when I tried to explain to him . . . I was praying you'd be dead before it was my turn."

"But this is marriage, Judy."

"I'd rather die than be married to you."

"I don't believe you. We've been in love for—"

"For God's sake, Jeff, love's over for you. Don't you understand? Those women cry because they hate you. I hate you. The world loathes you. You're disgusting."

Halsyon stared at the girl and saw the truth in her face. In an excess of rage he tried to seize her. She fought him bitterly. They careened around the huge living room of the suite, overturning furniture, their breath hissing, their fury mounting. Halsyon struck Judith Field with his big fist to end the struggle once and for all. She reeled back, clutched at a drape, smashed through a French window, and fell fourteen floors to the street like a gyrating doll.

Halsyon looked down in horror. A crowd gathered around the smashed body. Faces upturned. Fists shook. An ominous growl began. The World Procurer dashed into the suite.

"My old! My blue!" he cried. "What have you done? Per conto. It is a spark that will ignite savagery. You are in very grave danger. God damn."

"Is it true they all hate me?"

"Hélas, then you have discovered the truth? That indiscreet girl. I warned her. Oui. You are loathed."

"But you told me I was loved. The new Adam. Father of the new world."

"Oui. You are the father, but what child does not hate his father? You are also a legal rapist. What woman does not hate being forced to embrace a man . . . even by necessity for survival? Come quickly, my rock and rye. Passim. You are in great danger."

He dragged Halsyon to a back elevator and took him down to the Odeon cellar.

"The army will get you out. We take you to Turkey at once and effect a compromise."

Halsyon was transferred to the custody of a tall, gaunt, bitter army colonel who rushed him through underground passages to a side street, where a staff car was waiting. The colonel thrust Halsyon inside.

"Jacta alea est," he said to the driver. "Speed, my corporal. Protect old faithful. To the airport. Alors!"

"God damn, sir," the corporal replied. He saluted and started the car. As it twisted through the streets at breakneck speed, Halsyon glanced at him. He was a tall, gaunt man, sprightly but bitter.

"Kulturkampf der Menschheit," the corporal muttered. "Jeez!"

A giant barricade had been built across the street, improvised of ash barrels, furniture, overturned cars, traffic stanchions. The corporal was forced to brake the car. As he slowed for a U-turn, a mob of women appeared from doorways, cellars, stores. They were screaming. Some of them brandished improvised clubs.

"Excelsior!" the corporal cried. "God damn." He tried to pull his service gun out of its holster. The women yanked open the car doors and tore Halsyon and the corporal out. Halsyon broke free, struggled through the wild clubbing mob, dashed to the sidewalk, stumbled, and dropped with a sickening yaw through an open coal chute. He shot down and spilled out into an endless black space. His head whirled. A stream of stars sailed before his eyes. . . .

And he drifted alone in space, a martyr, misunderstood, a victim of cruel injustice.

He was still chained to what had once been the wall of Cell 5, Block 27, Tier 100, Wing 9 of the Callisto Penitentiary until that unexpected gamma explosion had torn the vast fortress dungeon—vaster than the Château d'If—apart. That explosion, he realized, had been detonated by the Grssh.

His assets were his convict clothes, a helmet, one cylinder of O_2 his grim fury at the injustice that had been done him, and his knowledge of the secret of how the Grssh could be defeated in their maniacal quest for solar domination.

The Grssh, ghastly marauders from Omicron Ceti, space degenerates, space imperialists, cold-blooded, roachlike, depending for their metabolism upon the psychotic horrors which they engendered in man through mental control and upon which they fed, were rapidly conquering the galaxy. They were irresistible, for they possessed the power of simulkinesis . . . the ability to be in two places at the same time.

Against the vault of space, a dot of light moved, slowly, like a stricken meteor. It was a rescue ship, Halsyon realized, combing space for survivors of the explosion. He wondered whether the light of Jupiter, flooding him with rusty radiation, would make him visible to the rescuers. He wondered whether he wanted to be rescued at all.

"It will be the same thing again," Halsyon grated. "Falsely accused by Balorsen's robot . . . falsely convicted by Judith's father . . . and finally destroyed by Judith herself . . . jailed again . . . and finally destroyed by the Grssh as they destroy the last strongholds of Terra. Why not die now?"

But even as he spoke he realized he lied. He was the one man with the one secret that could save the earth and the very galaxy itself. He must survive. He must fight.

With indomitable will, Halsyon struggled to his feet, fighting the constricting chains. With the steely strength he had developed as a penal laborer in the Grssh mines, he waved and shouted. The spot of light did not alter its slow course away from him. Then he saw the metal link of one of his chains strike a brilliant spark from the flinty rock. He resolved on a desperate expedient to signal the rescue ship.

He detached the plastihose of the O_2 tank from his plastihelmet, and permitted the stream of life-giving oxygen to spurt into space. With trembling hands, he gathered the links of his leg chain and dashed them against the rock under the oxygen. A spark glowed. The oxygen caught fire. A brilliant geyser of white flame spurted for half a mile into space.

Husbanding the last oxygen in his plastihelmet, Halsyon twisted the cylinder slowly, sweeping the fan of flame back and forth in a last desperate bid for rescue. The atmosphere in his plastihelmet grew foul and acrid. His ears roared. His sight flickered. At last his senses failed. . . .

When he recovered consciousness he was in a plasticot in the cabin of a starship. The high frequency whine told him they were in overdrive. He opened his eyes. Balorsen stood before the plasticot, and Balorsen's robot, and High Judge Field, and his daughter Judith. Judith was weeping. The robot was in magnetic clamps and winced as General Balorsen lashed him again and again with a nuclear whip.

"Parbleu! God damn!" the robot grated. "It is true I framed Jeff Halsyon. Ouch! Flux de bouche. I was the space pirate

who space-hijacked the space freighter. God damn. Ouch!
The bartender in the spacemen's saloon was my accomplice.
When Jackson wrecked the helicab I went to the space garage
and X-beamed the sonic *before* Tantial murdered O'Leary.
Aux armes. Jeez. Ouch!"

"There you have the confession, Halsyon," General Balorsen grated. He was tall, gaunt, bitter. "By God. Ars est
celare artem. You are innocent."

"I falsely condemned you, old faithful," Judge Field grated.
He was tall, gaunt, bitter. "Can you forgive this Goddamn
fool? We apologize."

"We wronged you, Jeff," Judith whispered. "How can you
ever forgive us? Say you forgive us."

"You're sorry for the way you treated me," Halsyon grated.
"But it's only because on account of a mysterious mutant
strain in my makeup which it makes me different, I'm the
one man with the one secret that can save the galaxy from
the Grssh."

"No, no, no, old gin and tonic," General Balorsen pleaded.
"God damn. Don't hold grudges. Save us from the Grssh."

"Save us, faute de mieux, save us, Jeff," Judge Field put in.

"Oh, please, Jeff, please," Judith whispered. "The Grssh
are everywhere and coming closer. We're taking you to the
U. N. You must tell the council how to stop the Grssh from
being in two places at the same time."

The starship came out of overdrive and landed on Gover-
nor's Island, where a delegation of world dignitaries met the
ship and rushed Halsyon to the General Assembly room of
the U. N. They drove down the strangely rounded streets
lined with strangely rounded buildings which had all been
altered when it was discovered that the Grssh always appeared in corners. There was not a corner or an angle left on
all Terra.

The General Assembly was filled when Halsyon entered.
Hundreds of tall, gaunt, bitter diplomats applauded as he
made his way to the podium, still dressed in convict plasti-
clothes. Halsyon looked around resentfully.

"Yes," he grated. "You all applaud. You all revere me

now; but where were you when I was framed, convicted and jailed . . . an innocent man? Where were you then?"

"Halsyon, forgive us. God damn!" they shouted.

"I will not forgive you. I suffered for seventeen years in the Grssh mines. Now it's your turn to suffer."

"Please, Halsyon!"

"Where are your experts? Your professors? Your specialists? Where are your electronic calculators? Your superthinking machines? Let them solve the mystery of the Grssh."

"They can't, old whiskey and sour. Entre nous. They're stopped cold. Save us, Halsyon. Auf wiedersehen."

Judith took his arm. "Not for my sake, Jeff," she whispered. "I know you'll never forgive me for the injustice I did you. But for the sake of all the other girls in the galaxy who love and are loved."

"I still love you, Judy."

"I've always loved you, Jeff."

"Okay. I didn't want to tell them, but you talked me into it." Halsyon raised his hand for silence. In the ensuing hush he spoke softly. "The secret is this, gentlemen. Your calculators have assembled data to ferret out the secret weakness of the Grssh. They have not been able to find any. Consequently you have assumed that the Grssh have no secret weakness. *That was a wrong assumption.*"

The General Assembly held its breath.

"Here is the secret. *You should have assumed there was something wrong with the calculators.*"

"God damn!" The General Assembly cried. "Why didn't we think of that? God damn!"

"*And I know what's wrong!*"

There was a deathlike hush.

The door of the General Assembly burst open. Professor Deathhush, tall, gaunt, bitter, tottered in. "Eureka!" he cried. "I've found it. God damn. Something wrong with the thinking machines. Three comes *after* two, not before."

The General Assembly exploded into cheers. Professor Deathhush was seized and pummeled happily. Bottles were opened. His health was drunk. Several medals were pinned on him. He beamed.

"Hey!" Halsyon called. "That was my secret. I'm the one man who on account of a mysterious mutant strain in my—"

The ticker tape began pounding: ATTENTION. ATTENTION. HUSHENKOV IN MOSCOW REPORTS DEFECT IN CALCULATORS. 3 COMES AFTER 2 AND NOT BEFORE. REPEAT: AFTER (UNDERSCORE) NOT BEFORE.

A postman ran in. "Special delivery from Doctor Lifehush at Caltech. Says something's wrong with the thinking machines. Three comes after two, not before."

A telegraph boy delivered a wire: THINKING MACHINE WRONG STOP TWO COMES BEFORE THREE STOP NOT AFTER STOP. VON DREAMHUSH, HEIDELBERG.

A bottle was thrown through the window. It crashed on the floor revealing a bit of paper on which was scrawled: *Did you ever stopp to thinc that maibe the number 3 comes after 2 instead of in front? Down with the Grssh, Mr. Hush-Hush.*

Halsyon buttonholed Judge Field. "What the hell is this?" he demanded. "I thought I was the one man in the world with that secret."

"HimmelHerrGott." Judge Field replied impatiently. "You are all alike. You dream you are the one man with a secret, the one man with a wrong, the one man with an injustice, with a girl, without a girl, with or without anything. God damn. You bore me, you one-man dreamers. Get lost."

Judge Field shouldered him aside. General Balorsen shoved him back. Judith Field ignored him. Balorsen's robot sneakily tripped him into a corner where a Grssh, also in a corner on Neptune, appeared, did something unspeakable to Halsyon, and disappeared with him, screaming, jerking and sobbing into a horror that was a delicious meal for the Grssh but an agonizing nightmare for Halsyon. . . .

From which his mother awakened him and said, "This'll teach you not to sneak peanut-butter sandwiches in the middle of the night, Jeffrey."

"Mama?"

"Yes. It's time to get up, dear. You'll be late for school."

She left the room. He looked around. He looked at himself. It was true. True! The glorious realization came upon him. His dream had come true. He was ten years old again, in the flesh that was his ten-year-old body, in the home that was his boyhood home, in the life that had been his life in the nineteen thirties. And within his head was the knowledge, the experience, the sophistication of a man of thirty-three.

"Oh, joy!" he cried. "It'll be a triumph. A triumph!"

He would be the school genius. He would astonish his parents, amaze his teachers, confound the experts. He would win scholarships. He would settle the hash of that kid Rennahan who used to bully him. He would hire a typewriter and write all the successful plays and stories and novels he remembered. He would cash in on that lost opportunity with Judy Field behind the memorial in Isham Park. He would steal inventions, discoveries, get in on the ground floor of new industries, make bets, play the stock market. He would own the world by the time he caught up with himself.

He dressed with difficulty. He had forgotten where his clothes were kept. He ate breakfast with difficulty. This was no time to explain to his mother that he'd gotten into the habit of starting the day with coffee laced with rye. He missed his morning cigarette. He had no idea where his schoolbooks were. His mother had trouble starting him out.

"Jeff's in one of his moods," he heard her mutter. "I hope he gets through the day."

The day started with Rennahan laying for him on the corner opposite the boys' entrance. Halsyon remembered him as a big tough kid with a vicious expression. He was astonished to discover that Rennahan was skinny, harassed, and obviously compelled by some bedevilments to be omnivorously aggressive.

"Why, you're not hostile to me," Halsyon exclaimed. "You're just a mixed-up kid who's trying to prove something."

Rennahan punched him.

"Look, kid," Halsyon said kindly. "You really want to be friends with the world. You're just insecure. That's why you're compelled to fight."

Rennahan was deaf to spot analysis. He punched Halsyon harder. It hurt.

"Oh, leave me alone," Halsyon said. "Go prove yourself on somebody else."

Rennahan, with two swift motions, knocked Halsyon's books from under his arm and ripped his fly. There was nothing for it but to fight. Twenty years of watching films of the future Joe Louis did nothing for Halsyon. He was thoroughly licked. He was also late for school. Now was his chance to amaze his teachers.

"The fact is," he explained to Miss Ralph of the fifth grade, "I had a run-in with a neurotic. I can speak for his left hook, but I won't answer for his id."

Miss Ralph slapped him and sent him to the principal with a note, reporting unheard-of-insolence.

"The only thing unheard of in this school," Halsyon told Mr. Snider, "is psychoanalysis. How can you pretend to be competent teachers if you don't—"

"Dirty little boy!" Mr. Snider interrupted angrily. He was tall, gaunt, bitter. "So you've been reading dirty books, eh?"

"What the hell's dirty about Freud?"

"And using profane language, eh? You need a lesson, you filthy little animal."

He was sent home with a note requesting an immediate consultation with his parents regarding the withdrawal of Jeffrey Halsyon from school as a degenerate in desperate need of correction and vocational guidance.

Instead of going home he went to a newsstand to check the papers for events on which to get a bet down. The headlines were full of the pennant race. But who the hell won the pennant in 1931? And the series? He couldn't for the life of him remember. And the stock market? He couldn't remember anything about that either. He'd never been particularly interested in such matters as a boy. There was nothing planted in his memory to call upon.

He tried to get into the library for further checks. The librarian, tall, gaunt, bitter, would not permit him to enter until children's hour in the afternoon. He loafed on the streets. Wherever he loafed he was chased by gaunt and bitter adults. He was beginning to realize that ten-year-old boys had limited opportunities to amaze the world.

At lunch hour he met Judy Field and accompanied her home from school. He was appalled by her knobby knees and black corkscrew curls. He didn't like the way she smelled either. But he was rather taken with her mother who was the image of the Judy he remembered. He forgot himself with Mrs. Field and did one or two things that indeed confounded her. She drove him out of the house and then telephoned his mother, her voice shaking with indignation.

Halsyon went down to the Hudson River and hung around the ferry docks until he was chased. He went to a stationery store to inquire about typewriter rentals and was chased. He searched for a quiet place to sit, think, plan, perhaps begin the recall of a successful story. There was no quiet place to which a small boy would be admitted.

He slipped into his house at 4:30, dropped his books in his room, stole into the living room, sneaked a cigarette, and was on his way out when he discovered his mother and father ambushing him. His mother looked shocked. His father looked gaunt and bitter.

"Oh," Halsyon said. "I suppose Snider phoned. I'd forgotten about that."

"*Mister* Snider," his mother said.

"And Mrs. Field," his father said.

"Look," Halsyon began. "We'd better get this straightened out. Will you listen to me for a few minutes? I have something startling to tell you and we've got to plan what to do about it. I—"

He yelped. His father had taken him by the ear and was marching him down the hall. Parents did not listen to children for a few minutes. They did not listen at all.

"Pop. . . . Just a minute. . . . Please! I'm trying to explain. I'm not really ten years old. I'm thirty-three. There's been a freak in time, see? On account of a mysterious mutant strain in my makeup which—"

"Damn you! Be quiet!" his father shouted. The pain of his big hands, the suppressed fury in his voice silenced Halsyon. He suffered himself to be led out of the house, four agonizing blocks to the school, and up one flight to Mr. Snider's office, where a public school psychologist was waiting with the principal. He was a tall man, gaunt, bitter, but sprightly.

"Ah, yes, yes," he said. "So this is our little degenerate. Our Scarface Al Capone, eh? Come, we take him to the clinic, and there I shall take his journal intime. We will hope for the best. Nisi prius. He cannot be all bad."

He took Halsyon's arm. Halsyon pulled his arm away and said, "Listen, you're an adult, intelligent man. You'll listen to me. My father's got emotional problems that blind him to the—"

His father gave him a tremendous box on the ear, grabbed his arm, and thrust it back into the psychologist's grasp. Halsyon burst into tears. The psychologist led him out of the office and into the tiny school clinic. Halsyon was hysterical. He was trembling with frustration and terror.

"Won't anybody listen to me?" he sobbed. "Won't anybody try to understand? Is this what we're all like to kids? Is this what all kids go through?"

"Gently, my sausage," the psychologist murmured. He popped a pill into Halsyon's mouth and forced him to drink some water.

"You're all so damned inhuman," Halsyon wept. "You keep us out of your world, but you keep barging into ours. If you don't respect us, why don't you leave us alone?"

"You begin to understand, eh?" the psychologist said. "We are two different breeds of animals, childrens and adults. God damn. I speak to you with frankness. Les absents ont toujours tort. There is no meetings of the minds. Jeez. There is nothing but war. It is why all childrens grow up hating their childhoods and searching for revenges. But there is never revenges. Pari mutuel. How can there be? Can a cat insult a king?"

"It's . . . s'hateful," Halsyon mumbled. The pill was taking effect rapidly. "Whole world's hateful. Full of conflicts'n'insults 'at can't be r'solved . . . or paid back. . . . S'like a joke somebody's playin' on us. Silly joke without point. Isn't?"

As he slid down into darkness, he could hear the psychologist chuckle but couldn't for the life of him understand what he was laughing at. . . .

He picked up his spade and followed the first clown into the cemetery. The first clown was a tall man, gaunt, bitter, but sprightly.

"Is she to be buried in Christian burial that willfully seeks her own salvation?" the first clown asked.

"I tell thee she is," Halsyon answered. "And therefore make her grave straight: The crowner hath sat on her and finds it Christian burial."

"How can that be, unless she drowned herself in her own defense?"

"Why, 'tis found so."

They began to dig the grave. The first clown thought the matter over, then said, "It must be *se offendendo;* it cannot be else. For here lies the point: If I drown myself wittingly, it argues an act, and an act hath three branches; it is, to act, to do, to perform: argal, she drowned herself wittingly."

"Nay, but hear you, goodman delver—" Halsyon began.

"Give me leave," the first clown interrupted and went on with a tiresome discourse on quest law. Then he turned sprightly and cracked a few professional jokes. At last Halsyon got away and went down to Yaughan's for a drink. When he returned, the first clown was cracking jokes with a couple of gentlemen who had wandered into the graveyard. One of them made quite a fuss about a skull.

The burial procession arrived; the coffin, the dead girl's brother, the king and queen, the priests and lords. They buried her, and the brother and one of the gentlemen began to quarrel over her grave. Halsyon paid no attention. There was a pretty girl in the procession, dark, with cropped curly hair and lovely long legs. He winked at her. She winked back. Halsyon edged over toward her, speaking with his eyes, and she answered him saucily the same way.

Then he picked up his spade and followed the first clown into the cemetery. The first clown was a tall man, gaunt, with a bitter expression but a sprightly manner.

"Is she to be buried in Christian burial that willfully seeks her own salvation?" the first clown asked.

"I tell thee she is," Halsyon answered. "And therefore make her grave straight: The crowner hath sat on her and finds it Christian burial."

"How can that be, unless she drowned herself in her own defense?"

"Didn't you ask me that before?" Halsyon inquired.

"Shut up, old faithful. Answer the question."

"I could swear this happened before."

"God damn. Will you answer? Jeez."

"Why, 'tis found so."

They began to dig the grave. The first clown thought the matter over and began a long discourse on quest law. After that he turned sprightly and cracked trade jokes. At last Halsyon got away and went down to Yaughan's for a drink. When he returned there were a couple of strangers at the grave and then the burial procession arrived.

There was a pretty girl in the procession, dark, with cropped curly hair and lovely long legs. Halsyon winked at her. She winked back. Halsyon edged over toward her, speaking with his eyes, and she answering him the same way.

"What's your name?" he whispered.

"Judith," she answered.

"I have your name tattooed on me, Judith."

"You're lying, sir."

"I can prove it, madam. I'll show you where I was tattooed."

"And where is that?"

"In Yaughan's tavern. It was done by a sailor off the Golden Hind. Will you see it with me tonight?"

Before she could answer, he picked up his spade and followed the first clown into the cemetery. The first clown was a tall man, gaunt, with a bitter expression but a sprightly manner.

"For God's sake!" Halsyon complained. "I could swear this happened before."

"Is she to be buried in Christian burial that willfully seeks her own salvation?" the first clown asked.

"I just know we've been through all this."

"Will you answer the question!"

"Listen," Halsyon said doggedly. "Maybe I'm crazy; maybe not. But I've got a spooky feeling that all this happened before. It seems unreal. Life seems unreal."

The first clown shook his head. "HimmelHerrGott," he muttered. "It is as I feared. Lux et veritas. On account of a mysterious mutant strain in your makeup which it makes you different, you are treading on thin water. "Ewigkeit! Answer the question."

"If I've answered it once, I've answered it a hundred times."

"Old ham and eggs," the first clown burst out, "you have answered it 5,271,009 times. God damn. Answer again."

"Why?"

"Because you must. Pot au feu. It is the life we must live."

"You call this life? Doing the same things over and over again? Saying the same things? Winking at girls and never getting any further?"

"No, no, no, my Donner und Blitzen. Do not question. It is a conspiracy we dare not fight. This is the life every man lives. Every man does the same things over and over. There is no escape."

"Why is there no escape?"

"I dare not say; I dare not. Vox populi. Others have questioned and disappeared. It is a conspiracy. I'm afraid."

"Afraid of what?"

"Of our owners."

"What? We are owned?"

"Si. Ach, ja! All of us, young mutant. There is no reality. There is no life, no freedom, no will. God damn. Don't you realize? We are . . . we are all characters in a book. As the book is read, we dance our dances; when the book is read again, we dance again. E pluribus unum. Is she to be buried in Christian burial that willfully seeks her own salvation?"

"What are you saying?" Halsyon cried in horror. "We're puppets?"

"Answer the question."

"If there's no freedom, no free will, how can we be talking like this?"

"Whoever's reading our book is daydreaming, my capital of Dakota. Idem est. Answer the question."

"I will not. I'm going to revolt. I'll dance for our owners no longer. I'll find a better life. . . . I'll find reality."

"No, no! It's madness, Jeffrey! Cul-de-sac!"

"All we need is one brave leader. The rest will follow. We'll smash the conspiracy that chains us!"

"It cannot be done. Play it safe. Answer the question."

Halsyon answered the question by picking up his spade and bashing in the head of the first clown who appeared not to notice. "Is she to be buried in Christian burial that willfully seeks her own salvation?" he asked.

"Revolt!" Halsyon cried and bashed him again. The clown started to sing. The two gentlemen appeared. One said, "Has this fellow no feeling of business that he sings at grave-making?"

"Revolt! Follow me!" Halsyon shouted and swung his spade against the gentleman's melancholy head. He paid no attention. He chatted with his friend and the first clown. Halsyon whirled like a dervish, laying about with his spade. The gentleman picked up a skull and philosophized over some person or persons named Yorick.

The funeral procession approached. Halsyon attacked it, whirling and turning, around and around with the clotted frenzy of a man in a dream.

"Stop reading the book," he shouted. "Let me out of the pages. Can you hear me? Stop reading the book! I'd rather be in a world of my own making. Let me go!"

There was a mighty clap of thunder, as of the covers of a mighty book slamming shut. In an instant Halsyon was swept spinning into the third compartment of the seventh circle of the Inferno in the fourteenth Canto of the Divine Comedy where they who have sinned against art are tormented by flakes of fire which are eternally showered down upon them. There he shrieked until he had provided sufficient amusement. Only then was he permitted to devise a text of his own . . . and he formed a new world, a romantic world, a world of his fondest dreams. . . .

He was the last man on earth.

He was the last man on earth, and he howled.

The hills, the valleys, the mountains and streams were his, his alone, and he howled.

There were 5,271,009 houses for his shelter, and 5,271,009 beds were his for sleeping. The shops were his for the breaking and entering. The jewels of the world were his; the toys, the tools, the playthings, the necessities, the luxuries . . . all belonged to the last man on earth, and he howled.

He left the country mansion in the fields of Connecticut where he had taken up residence; he crossed into Westchester, howling; he ran south along what had once been the Hendrick Hudson Highway, howling; he crossed the bridge into Manhattan, howling; he ran downtown past lonely skyscrapers, department stores, amusement palaces, howling. He howled down Fifth Avenue, and at the corner of Fiftieth Street he saw a human being.

She was alive, breathing; a beautiful woman. She was tall and dark with cropped curly hair and lovely long legs. She wore a white blouse, tiger-skin riding breeches and patent leather boots. She carried a rifle. She wore a revolver on her hip. She was eating stewed tomatoes from a can and she stared at Halsyon in unbelief. He howled. He ran up to her.

"I thought I was the last human on earth," she said.

"You're the last woman," Halsyon howled. "I'm the last man. Are you a dentist?"

"No," she said. "I'm the daughter of the unfortunate Professor Field whose well-intentioned but ill-advised experiment in nuclear fission has wiped mankind off the face of the earth with the exception of you and me who, no doubt on account of some mysterious mutant strain in our makeup which it makes us different, are the last of the old civilization and the first of the new."

"Didn't your father teach you anything about dentistry?" Halsyon howled.

"No," she said.

"Then lend me your gun for a minute."

She unholstered the revolver and handed it to Halsyon, meanwhile keeping her rifle ready. Halsyon cocked the gun.

"I wish you'd been a dentist," he howled.

"I'm a beautiful woman with an IQ of one hundred forty-one, which is more important for the propagation of a brave new beautiful race of men to inherit the good green earth," she said.

"Not with my teeth it isn't," Halsyon howled.

He clapped the revolver to his temple and blew his brains out.

He awoke with a splitting headache. He was lying on the tile dais alongside the stool, his bruised temple pressed against the cold floor. Mr. Aquila had emerged from the lead shield and was turning on an exhaust fan to clear the air.

"Bravo, my liver and onions," he chuckled. "The last one you did by yourself, eh? No assistance from yours truly required. Meglio tarde che mai. But you went over with a crack before I could catch you. God damn."

He helped Halsyon to his feet and led him into the consultation room, where he seated him on a velvet chaise longue and gave him a glass of brandy.

"Guaranteed free of drugs," he said. "Noblesse oblige. Only the best spiritus frumenti. Now we discuss what we have done, eh? Jeez."

He sat down behind the desk, still sprightly, still bitter, and regarded Halsyon with kindliness. "Man lives by his decisions, n'est-ce-pas?" he began. "We agree, oui? A man has some five million two hundred seventy-one thousand and nine decisions to make in the course of his life. Peste! Is it a prime number? N'importe. Do you agree?"

Halsyon nodded.

"So, my coffee and doughnuts, it is the maturity of these decisions that decides whether a man is a man or a child. Nicht wahr? Malgré nous. A man cannot start making adult decisions until he has purged himself of the dreams of childhood. God damn. Such fantasies. They must go. Pfui."

"No," Halsyon said slowly. "It's the dreams that make my art . . . the dreams and fantasies that I translate into line and color. . . ."

"God damn! Yes. Agreed. Maître d'hôtel! But adult dreams,

not baby dreams. Baby dreams. Pfui! All men have them.
. . . To be the last man on earth and own the earth. . . . To
be the last fertile man on earth and own the women . . . To
go back in time with the advantage of adult knowledge and
win victories . . . To escape reality with the dream that life
is make-believe . . . To escape responsibility with a fantasy
of heroic injustice, of martyrdom with a happy ending . . .
And there are hundreds more, equally popular, equally
empty. God bless Father Freud and his merry men. He applies the quietus to such nonsense. Sic semper tyrannis.
Avaunt!"

"But if everybody has those dreams, they can't be bad,
can they?"

"For everybody read everybaby. Quid pro quo. God damn.
Everybody in fourteenth century had lice. Did that make it
good? No, my young, such dreams are for childrens. Too
many adults are still childrens. It is you, the artists, who
must lead them out as I have led you. I purge you; now you
purge them."

"Why did you do this?"

"Because I have faith in you. Sic vos non vobis. It will not
be easy for you. A long hard road and lonely."

"I suppose I ought to feel grateful," Halsyon muttered,
"but I feel . . . well . . . empty. Cheated."

"Oh, yes, God damn. If you live with one Jeez big ulcer
long enough, you miss him when he's cut out. You were hiding in an ulcer. I have robbed you of said refuge. Ergo: You
feel cheated. Wait! You will feel even more cheated. There
was a price to pay, I told you. You have paid it. Look."

Mr. Aquila held up a hand mirror. Halsyon glanced into it,
then started and stared. A fifty-year-old face stared back at
him: lined, hardened, solid, determined. Halsyon leaped to
his feet.

"Gently, gently," Mr. Aquila admonished. "It is not so bad.
It is damned good. You are still thirty-three in age of phy-
sique. You have lost none of your life . . . only all of your
youth. What have you lost? A pretty face to lure young
girls? Is that why you are wild?"

"Christ!" Halsyon cried.

"All right. Still gently, my child. Here you are, purged, disillusioned, unhappy, bewildered, one foot on the hard road to maturity. Would you like this to have happened or not have happened? Si. I can do. This can never have happened. Spurlos versenkt. It is ten seconds from your escape. You can have your pretty young face back. You can be recaptured. You can return to the safe ulcer of the womb . . . a child again. Would you like same?"

"You can't!"

"Sauve qui peut, my Pike's Peak. I can. There is no end to the fifteen thousand-angstrom band."

"Damn you! Are you Satan? Lucifer? Only the devil could have such powers."

"Or angels, my old."

"You don't look like an angel. You look like Satan."

"Ah? Ha? But Satan was an angel before he fell. He has many relations on high. Surely there are family resemblances. God damn." Mr. Aquila stopped laughing. He leaned across the desk, and the sprightliness was gone from his face. Only the bitterness remained. "Shall I tell you who I am, my chicken? Shall I explain why one unguarded look from this phizz toppled you over the brink?"

Halsyon nodded, unable to speak.

"I am a scoundrel, a black sheep, a scapegoat, a blackguard. I am a remittance man. Yes. God damn! I am a remittance man." Mr. Aquila's eyes turned into wounds. "By your standards I am the great man of infinite power and variety. So was the remittance man from Europe to naïve natives on the beaches of Tahiti. Eh? So am I to you as I comb the beaches of this planet for a little amusement, a little hope, a little joy to while away the weary desolate years of my exile. . . .

"I am bad," Mr. Aquila said in a voice of chilling desperation. "I am rotten. There is no place in my home that can tolerate me. And there are moments, unguarded, when my sickness and my despair fill my eyes and strike terror into your waiting souls. As I strike terror into you now. Yes?"

Halsyon nodded again.

"Be guided by me. It was the child in Solon Aquila that

destroyed him and led him into the sickness that destroyed his life. Oui. I too suffer from baby fantasies from which I cannot escape. Do not make the same mistake. I beg of you . . ." Mr. Aquila glanced at his wristwatch and leaped up. The sprightly returned to his manner. "Jeez. It's late. Time to make up your mind, old bourbon and soda. Which will it be? Old face or pretty face? The reality of dreams or the dream of reality?"

"How many decisions did you say we have to make in a lifetime?"

"Five million two hundred and seventy-one thousand and nine. Give or take a thousand. God damn."

"And which one is this for me?"

"Ah? Vérité sans peur. The two million six hundred and thirty-five thousand five hundred and fourth . . . offhand."

"But it's the big one."

"They are all big." Mr. Aquila stepped to the door, placed his hand on the buttons of a rather complicated switch, and cocked an eye at Halsyon.

"Voilà tout," he said. "It rests with you."

Halsyon paused, studied that obsidian eye, sighed. "I'll take it the hard way," he said.

by ALFRED BESTER

The Demolished Man
The Stars My Destination (*Tiger, Tiger*)
The Dark Side of the Earth (collection of short stories)

It would be gratifying to be able to say that this enormous awakening of creative energy and artistic consciousness within the science fiction genre was communicated to the outside world and broke down the walls of the ghetto in which the field had been imprisoned for so many years.

Unfortunately, the very conditions which had given rise to this newer, more sophisticated science fiction conspired to keep it from the attention of the public at large. Since the paperback publishers of science fiction could virtually assure themselves of a guaranteed profit by capitalizing on the same limited market that the science fiction magazines were reaching, they festooned all their science fiction books with the rocket-ships and alien slime that made the magazines so recognizable to the specialty market. From the publishers' point of view this packaging strategy was entirely successful, but it had the effect of turning off new readers, of artificially maintaining the ghetto walls.

Meanwhile, buoyed by the success of *Galaxy* and *Fantasy* and *Science Fiction,* and especially by the appearance of all those paperback science fiction novels on the newsstands, every cheap magazine publisher extant brought out his own pulp science fiction magazine. For a while, there were as many as forty science fiction magazines available. All of which created the science fiction boom of the mid-1950s.

For the most part, the rash of new magazines was filled with pretty dreadful stuff. With the sudden expansion of the market, every fan who fancied himself a writer was able to get anything halfway readable published. Hollywood was discovering monster movies, and the covers of the magazines were even more lurid than those of the books.

The meaningful work being done within the genre was utterly buried in an avalanche of giant ants, brass brassières, mindless space opera, and bubbling green slime. The great tragedy was that the larger literary scene seemed ready for serious science fiction. While writers like Sturgeon, Bester, Clarke, and Dick were producing fine science fiction novels like *Childhood's End, The Demolished Man, More Than Human* and *The Man in the High Castle,* speculative fiction was beginning to revive in the outside world after its hundred-year dormancy. George Orwell had written *1984,* William Burroughs was writing *Nova Express,* and novels like Thomas Pynchon's *V* and Nevil Shute's *On the Beach* were being read by wide audiences.

The time seemed right for a cross-pollination. The "mainstream" writers who were groping towards a rebirth of speculative fiction had a great deal to learn from writers like Dick, Clarke, Sturgeon, and Bester, who had dealt with similar subject matter in isolation and who had already solved many of the artistic problems arising out of it. The science fiction writers would have benefited enormously by the application of some absolute artistic criteria and learned a lot about prose from their stylistic betters. There were a few interesting hybrids. Ray Bradbury became a kind of "token science fiction writer" in the literary world at large. William Burroughs read the genre literature and translated it into his own unique idiom. Kurt Vonnegut, Jr., who had begun his career within the science fiction genre, took an adroit step sideways to where he is today, ensconced on the best seller list, a culture hero, and an object of critical approval.

On a whole, however, the fusion did not take place. The packaging controlled the public image of science fiction, and the public image of the genre was pulsing pseudopods and vaseline-colored ichor. This was more than enough to make anyone but

hardcore aficionados react with disgust without even
bothering to read the best works, which couldn't
readily be sorted out from the slime-pile without
prior knowledge. Novels which deserved
general attention were mummified, still kicking, in lurid
packages and sank out of sight with hardly a ripple
outside the genre.

Some of the better and more worldly-wise writers,
like Alfred Bester, quit science fiction in disgust and
despair; some, like Sturgeon, Farmer, and Dick, clung
on, heroic and windblown martyrs; some had their
creative lights blown out. A very few, like Bradbury,
Clarke, and Vonnegut, managed to free their work
from science fiction's putrid public image by one
ploy or another, but some potentially fine writers
became embittered, cynical hacks.

But when the boomlet inevitably burst, the exploitation magazines folded in droves, and the cynical
buck stopped being such an easy buck, the next
revolution in the genre began to emerge amidst
the debris.

THE FULL FLOWERING

The generation of Americans that came of age in the 1960s was the first to be simultaneously a product and a shaper of its times. Like other Americans of their generation, post-1960 science fiction writers lived through and took part in several cultural revolutions. Speculative fiction, too, had its revolution in the 1960s—it was called the "New Wave."

Between 1960 and 1965 an unusually large number of new writers began publishing their speculative fiction within the science fiction genre: Thomas M. Disch, Samuel R. Delany, Roger Zelazny, Piers Anthony, Michael Moorcock, James Sallis, Larry Niven, R. A. Lafferty, Barry Malzberg, Keith Laumer, myself, and at least a dozen others. A few, like Lafferty and Laumer, were older men who had turned to writing comparatively late in life. Others, like Ted White and Larry Niven, had come up through the subculture of science fiction in the manner of the generations of the 1940s and 1950s.

But young writers like Disch, Sallis, Delany, John T. Sladek, Malzberg, and myself were a new phenomenon. These writers had read a lot of science fiction in their teens, but for the most part had not had any contact with the subculture of science fiction fandom until after they became published writers. When they began to write—impelled by their own private demons—they were drawn to speculative fiction as a literary angle of attack, rather than to science fiction as a commercial genre-cum-subculture.

Although each of these new writers had his own subjective reason for writing speculative fiction, there was an over-all cultural reason for the total phenomenon as well. The multivalued, post-Age of Reason reality had been around for quite a while, but this was the first generation whose minds had been entirely

formed within this altered context. Linear, single-
reality, here-and-now fiction was simply out of sync
with the generational consciousness.

Of course, this is a somewhat post-factum
analysis of what at the time was a series of more or
less unconscious choices. These new writers simply
were drawn to the reading of all kinds of speculative
fiction—William Burroughs to Theodore Sturgeon,
Philip K. Dick to *E. C. Comics*, J. G. Ballard to
Anthony Burgess—the fiction of the might-be, which
cut across the arbitrary marketing definitions of "science
fiction" and "mainstream." Naturally, when readers
went on to become creators, they continued their
interest and began to write speculative fiction.

And found that almost all of it had to be published
as "science fiction."

It was perfectly natural to submit their work to
science fiction magazine and book publishers.
Since most speculative fiction in the United States was
published as science fiction, it would have been
entirely self-defeating for beginning writers to have
attempted to place speculative fiction with major
national magazines and first-line hardcover book
publishers. So, working largely in isolation from each
other, a new generation of writers began writing
science fiction, publishing it in science fiction magazines
and books, and thinking of themselves as "science
fiction writers." The commercial and subcultural
influences of science fiction began to mold the work
of the new writers towards the traditional norms of the
genre, without the writers being really aware that
such a process even existed. Some of the writers may
have felt an internal struggle going on, a vague
awareness that something was keeping them from
realizing the full artistic potential of speculative
fiction. Somehow they felt they were not dealing
adequately with the material, with the consciousness
that had brought them to science fiction in the first
place.

Inevitably, the new generation of writers began

to come into contact with each other, with older
science fiction writers, and with science fiction
fans. Things seemed terribly out of joint. Many of
the older men whose work the young writers had
deeply admired proved to be burnt-out cases. Many
had become bitter, cynical hacks concerned only with
how fast they could churn out the next paperback
potboiler. A few, like Philip José Farmer and Philip
K. Dick, were leading lives of desperate heroism,
still producing meaningful work but at enormous
economic and emotional cost. The majority of the
older writers seemed to be nothing more than
"grown-up science fiction fans" who had never
aspired to anything beyond sticky adulation from the
science fiction subculture.

The science fiction editors and publishers were,
with a few exceptions, commercial pragmatists who
dealt with the material in terms of wordage rates,
juvenile markets, sword-and-sorcery packages, selling
covers, library sales, and slippery contracts, instead of
literary values and thematic content.

Those marooned in this disaster area rapidly lost
their youthful naiveté. This being the 1960s, when
consciousness changes were impelling young people
everywhere to fight against the constrictions of
moribund social constructs, the result was not the
bitter and cynical resignation of the 1950s, but
nascent revolutionary awareness.

In England the situation had always been somewhat
different. While the phenomenon of the science fiction
subculture and the resulting isolation of much of
speculative fiction had been strongly transatlantic,
there had always been a number of speculative fiction
writers working entirely outside the "science fiction"
category: H. G. Wells, C. S. Lewis, Olaf Stapledon,
Mervyn Peake, George Orwell, Anthony Burgess,
and others. Hence, there was always a certain influence
from outside the science fiction genre and a somewhat
higher level of literary consciousness among its writers.

Brian Aldiss, for example, who began his career in the 1950s as a straightforward genre writer and was published as such, was also literary editor of the Oxford *Mail*.

One of the key figures in the so-called "New Wave" phenomenon was J. G. Ballard. Although his earlier work was fairly straightforward science fiction, he worked in isolation from the science fiction sub-culture and was more influenced by the literary avant-garde. By 1960 he was writing stories like "The Voices of Time," which seemed to fulfill all the genre requirements while at the same time clearly transcending them.

But the "New Wave" phenomenon itself was born when Michael Moorcock, a young British writer who had come up through the science fiction subculture, took over the editorship of *New Worlds*, a senior British pulp science fiction magazine.

Moorcock was easily the most influential editor the field had seen since John Campbell, and under Moorcock *New Worlds* underwent a rapid and deliberate evolution. Moorcock himself had evolved from a science fiction fan to a commercial genre writer to a sophisticated and self-conscious literary artist capable of writing stories like "The Pleasure Garden of Felipe Sagittarius." Now, looking backward with a new sophistication, he realized the process that had affected his own development, how the total phenomenon of science fiction had warped and stunted the literary possibilities of speculative fiction. Further, he understood that the linear, single-reality fiction that dominated the publishing media was a moribund anachronism. He set out not merely to give science fiction respectability, but to bring about a fusion between science fiction and mainstream fiction which would shatter the pulp shackles on the former, and breathe the reviving winds of change into the latter, creating a speculative fiction that would be the characteristic literature of our times.

The Voices of Time

J. G. BALLARD

I

Later Powers often thought of Whitby, and the strange grooves the biologist had cut, apparently at random, all over the floor of the empty swimming pool. An inch deep and twenty feet long, interlocking to form an elaborate ideogram like a Chinese character, they had taken him all summer to complete, and he had obviously thought about little else, working away tirelessly through the long desert afternoons. Powers had watched him from his office window at the far end of the Neurology wing, carefully marking out his pegs and string, carrying away the cement chips in a small canvas bucket. After Whitby's suicide no one had bothered about the grooves, but Powers often borrowed the supervisor's key and let himself into the disused pool, and would look down at the labyrinth of moldering gulleys, half-filled with water leaking in from the chlorinator, an enigma now past any solution.

Initially, however, Powers was too preoccupied with completing his work at the Clinic and planning his own final withdrawal. After the first frantic weeks of panic he had managed to accept an uneasy compromise that allowed him to view his predicament with the detached fatalism he had previously reserved for his patients. Fortunately he was moving down the physical and mental gradients simultaneously—lethargy and inertia blunted his anxieties, a slackening metabolism made it necessary to concentrate to produce a connected thought-train. In fact, the lengthening intervals of dreamless sleep were almost restful. He found himself beginning to look forward to them, made no effort to wake earlier than was essential.

At first he had kept an alarm clock by his bed, tried to compress as much activity as he could into the narrowing hours of consciousness, sorting out his library, driving over to Whitby's laboratory every morning to examine the latest batch of X-ray plates, every minute and hour rationed like the last drops of water in a canteen.

Anderson, fortunately, had unwittingly made him realize the pointlessness of this course.

After Powers had resigned from the Clinic he still continued to drive in once a week for his checkup, now little more than a formality. On what turned out to be the last occasion Anderson had perfunctorily taken his blood count, noting Powers' slacker facial muscles, fading pupil reflexes, the unshaven cheeks.

He smiled sympathetically at Powers across the desk, wondering what to say to him. Once he had put on a show of encouragement with the more intelligent patients, even tried to provide some sort of explanation. But Powers was too difficult to reach—neurosurgeon extraordinary, a man always out on the periphery, only at ease working with unfamiliar materials. To himself he thought: *I'm sorry, Robert. What can I say—"Even the sun is growing cooler—?"* He watched Powers drum his fingers restlessly on the enamel desk top, his eyes glancing at the spinal level charts hung around the office. Despite his unkempt appearance—he had been wearing the same unironed shirt and dirty white plimsoles a week ago—Powers looked composed and self-possessed, like a Conrad beachcomber more or less reconciled to his own weaknesses.

"What are you doing with yourself, Robert?" he asked. "Are you still going over to Whitby's lab?"

"As much as I can. It takes me half an hour to cross the lake, and I keep on sleeping through the alarm clock. I may leave my place and move in there permanently."

Anderson frowned. "Is there much point? As far as I could make out Whitby's work was pretty speculative—" He broke off, realizing the implied criticism of Powers' own disastrous work at the Clinic, but Powers seemed to ignore this, was examining the pattern of shadows on the ceiling. "Anyway, wouldn't it be better to stay where you are, among your own things, read through Toynbee and Spengler again?"

Powers laughed shortly. "That's the last thing I want to do. I want to *forget* Toynbee and Spengler, not try to remember them. In fact, Paul, I'd like to forget everything. I don't know whether I've got enough time, though. How much can you forget in three months?"

"Everything, I suppose, if you want to. But don't try to race the clock."

Powers nodded quietly, repeating this last remark to himself. Racing the clock was exactly what he had been doing. As he stood up and said goodbye to Anderson he suddenly decided to throw away his alarm clock, escape from his futile obsession with time. To remind himself he unfastened his wristwatch and scrambled the setting, then slipped it into his pocket. Making his way out to the car park he reflected on the freedom this simple act gave him. He would explore the lateral byways now, the side doors, as it were, in the corridors of time. Three months could be an eternity.

He picked his car out of the line and strolled over to it, shielding his eyes from the heavy sunlight beating down across the parabolic sweep of the lecture theater roof. He was about to climb in when he saw that someone had traced with a finger across the dust caked over the windshield:

96,688,365,498,721

Looking over his shoulder, he recognized the white Packard parked next to him, peered inside, and saw a lean-faced young man with blonde sun-bleached hair and a high cerebrotonic forehead watching him behind dark glasses. Sitting beside him at the wheel was a raven-haired girl whom he had often seen around the psychology department. She had intelligent but somehow rather oblique eyes, and Powers remembered that the younger doctors called her "the girl from Mars."

"Hello, Kaldren," Powers said to the young man. "Still following me around?"

Kaldren nodded. "Most of the time, Doctor." He sized

Powers up shrewdly. "We haven't seen very much of you recently, as a matter of fact. Anderson said you'd resigned, and we noticed your laboratory was closed."

Powers shrugged. "I felt I needed a rest. As you'll understand, there's a good deal that needs rethinking."

Kaldren frowned half-mockingly. "Sorry to hear that, Doctor. But don't let these temporary setbacks depress you." He noticed the girl watching Powers with interest. "Coma's a fan of yours. I gave her your papers from *American Journal of Psychiatry,* and she's read through the whole file."

The girl smiled pleasantly at Powers, for a moment dispelling the hostility between the two men. When Powers nodded to her she leaned across Kaldren and said: "Actually I've just finished Noguchi's autobiography—the great Japanese doctor who discovered the spirochete. Somehow you remind me of him—there's so much of yourself in all the patients you worked on."

Powers smiled wanly at her, then his eyes turned and locked involuntarily on Kaldren's. They stared at each other somberly for a moment, and a small tic in Kaldren's right cheek began to flicker irritatingly. He flexed his facial muscles, after a few seconds mastered it with an effort, obviously annoyed that Powers should have witnessed this brief embarrassment.

"How did the clinic go today?" Powers asked. "Have you had any more . . . headaches?"

Kaldren's mouth snapped shut, he looked suddenly irritable. "Whose care am I in, Doctor? Yours or Anderson's? Is that the sort of question you should be asking now?"

Powers gestured deprecatingly. "Perhaps not." He cleared his throat; the heat was ebbing the blood from his head and he felt tired and eager to get away from them. He turned toward his car, then realized that Kaldren would probably follow, either try to crowd him into the ditch or block the road and make Powers sit in his dust all the way back to the lake. Kaldren was capable of any madness.

"Well, I've got to go and collect something," he said, adding in a firmer voice: "Get in touch with me, though, if you can't reach Anderson."

He waved and walked off behind the line of cars. Reflected in the windows he could see Kaldren looking back and watching him closely.

He entered the Neurology wing, paused thankfully in the cool foyer, nodding to the two nurses and the armed guard at the reception desk. For some reason the terminals sleeping in the adjacent dormitory block attracted hordes of would-be sightseers, most of them cranks with some magical antinarcoma remedy, or merely the idly curious, but a good number of quite normal people, many of whom had traveled thousands of miles, impelled towards the Clinic by some strange instinct, like animals migrating to a pre-view of their racial graveyards.

He walked along the corridor to the supervisor's office overlooking the recreation deck, borrowed the key, and made his way out through the tennis courts and calisthenics rigs to the enclosed swimming pool at the far end. It had been disused for months, and only Powers' visits kept the lock free. Stepping through, he closed it behind him and walked past the peeling wooden stands to the deep end.

Putting a foot up on the diving board, he looked down at Whitby's ideogram. Damp leaves and bits of paper obscured it, but the outlines were just distinguishable. It covered almost the entire floor of the pool and at first glance appeared to represent a huge solar disc, with four radiating diamond-shaped arms, a crude Jungian mandala.

Wondering what had prompted Whitby to carve the device before his death, Powers noticed something moving through the debris in the center of the disc. A black, horny-shelled animal about a foot long was nosing about in the slush, heaving itself on tired legs. Its shell was articulated, and vaguely resembled an armadillo's. Reaching the edge of the disc, it stopped and hesitated, then slowly backed away into the center again, apparently unwilling or unable to cross the narrow groove.

Powers looked around, then stepped into one of the changing stalls and pulled a small wooden clothes locker off its

rusty wall bracket. Carrying it under one arm, he climbed
down the chromium ladder into the pool and walked carefully across the slithery floor toward the animal. As he approached it sidled away from him, but he trapped it easily,
using the lid to lever it into the box.

The animal was heavy, at least the weight of a brick.
Powers tapped its massive olive-black carapace with his
knuckle, noting the triangular warty head jutting out below
its rim like a turtle's, the thickened pads beneath the first
digits of the pentadactyl forelimbs.

He watched the three-lidded eyes blinking at him anxiously from the bottom of the box.

"Expecting some really hot weather?" he murmured.
"That lead umbrella you're carrying around should keep you
cool."

He closed the lid, climbed out of the pool, and made his
way back to the supervisor's office, then carried the box out
to his car.

". . . Kaldren continues to reproach me [*Powers wrote
in his diary*]. For some reason he seems unwilling to
accept his isolation, is elaborating a series of private
rituals to replace the missing hours of sleep. Perhaps
I should tell him of my own approaching zero, but he'd
probably regard this as the final unbearable insult, that I
should have in excess what he so desperately yearns
for. God knows what might happen. Fortunately the
nightmarish visions appear to have receded for the time
being . . ."

Pushing the diary away, Powers leaned forward across the
desk and stared out through the window at the white floor
of the lake bed stretching toward the hills along the horizon.
Three miles away, on the far shore, he could see the circular
bowl of the radio-telescope revolving slowly in the clear afternoon air, as Kaldren tirelessly trapped the sky, sluicing in
millions of cubic parsecs of sterile ether, like the nomads who
trapped the sea along the shores of the Persian Gulf.

Behind him the airconditioner murmured quietly, cooling
the pale blue walls half-hidden in the dim light. Outside the

air was bright and oppressive, the heat waves rippling up from the clumps of gold-tinted cacti below the Clinic blurring the sharp terraces of the twenty-story Neurology block. There, in the silent dormitories behind the sealed shutters, the terminals slept their long dreamless sleep. There were now over five hundred of them in the Clinic, the vanguard of a vast somnambulist army massing for its last march. Only five years had elapsed since the first narcoma syndrome had been recognized, but already huge government hospitals in the east were being readied for intakes in the thousands, as more and more cases came to light.

Powers felt suddenly tired, and glanced at his wrist, wondering how long he had to eight o'clock, his bedtime for the next week or so. Already he missed the dusk, soon would wake to his last dawn.

His watch was in his hip pocket. He remembered his decision not to use his timepieces, and sat back and stared at the bookshelves beside the desk. There were rows of green-covered AEC publications he had removed from Whitby's library, papers in which the biologist described his work out in the Pacific after the H-tests. Many of them Powers knew almost by heart, read a hundred times in an effort to grasp Whitby's last conclusions. Toynbee would certainly be easier to forget.

His eyes dimmed momentarily, as the tall black wall in the rear of his mind cast its great shadow over his brain. He reached for the diary thinking of the girl in Kaldren's car— Coma he had called her, another of his insane jokes—and her reference to Noguchi. Actually the comparison should have been made with Whitby, not himself; the monsters in the lab were nothing more than fragmented mirrors of Whitby's mind, like the grotesque radio-shielded frog he had found that morning in the swimming pool.

Thinking of the girl Coma, and the heartening smile she had given him, he wrote:

Woke 6:33 am. Last session with Anderson. He made it plain he's seen enough of me, and from now on I'm

better alone. To sleep 8:00? (These countdowns ter-
rify me.)

He paused, then added:

Goodbye, Eniwetok.

II

He saw the girl again the next day at Whitby's laboratory.
He had driven over after breakfast with the new specimen,
eager to get it into a vivarium before it died. The only previous armored mutant he had come across had nearly broken
his neck. Speeding along the lake road a month or so earlier
he had struck it with the offside front wheel, expecting the
small creature to flatten instantly. Instead its hard lead-
packed shell had remained rigid, even though the organism
within it had been pulped, had flung the car heavily into
the ditch. He had gone back for the shell, later weighed it
at the laboratory, found it contained over 600 grams of lead.

Quite a number of plants and animals were building up
heavy metals as radiological shields. In the hills behind the
beach house a couple of old-time prospectors were renovating
the derelict gold-panning equipment abandoned over eighty
years ago. They had noticed the bright yellow tints of the
cacti, run an analysis, and found that the plants were assim-
ilating gold in extractable quantities, although the soil
concentrations were unworkable. Oak Ridge was at last paying a dividend!!

Waking that morning just after 6:45—ten minutes later
than the previous day (he had switched on the radio, heard
one of the regular morning programs as he climbed out of
bed)—he had eaten a light unwanted breakfast, then spent
an hour packing away some of the books in his library, crat-
ing them up and taping on address labels to his brother.

He reached Whitby's laboratory half an hour later. This
was housed in a 100-foot wide geodesic dome built beside
his chalet on the west shore of the lake about a mile from
Kaldren's summer house. The chalet had been closed after

Whitby's suicide, and many of the experimental plants and animals had died before Powers had managed to receive permission to use the laboratory.

As he turned into the driveway he saw the girl standing on the apex of the yellow-ribbed dome, her slim figure silhouetted against the sky. She waved to him, then began to step down across the glass polyhedrons and jumped nimbly into the driveway beside the car.

"Hello," she said, giving him a welcoming smile. "I came over to see your zoo. Kaldren said you wouldn't let me in if he came so I made him stay behind."

She waited for Powers to say something while he searched for his keys, then volunteered: "If you like, I can wash your shirt."

Powers grinned at her, peered down ruefully at his dust-stained sleeves. "Not a bad idea. I thought I was beginning to look a little uncared-for." He unlocked the door, took Coma's arm. "I don't know why Kaldren told you that—he's welcome here any time he likes."

"What have you got in there?" Coma asked, pointing at the wooden box he was carrying as they walked between the gear-laden benches.

"A distant cousin of ours I found. Interesting little chap. I'll introduce you in a moment."

Sliding partitions divided the dome into four chambers. Two of them were storerooms, filled with spare tanks, apparatus, cartons of animal food, and test rigs. They crossed the third section, almost filled by a powerful X-ray projector, a giant 250-mega-amp G.E. Maxitron, angled onto a revolving table, concrete shielding blocks lying around ready for use like huge building bricks.

The fourth chamber contained Powers' zoo, the vivaria jammed together along the benches and in the sinks, big colored cardboard charts and memos pinned onto the draft hoods above them, a tangle of rubber tubing and power leads trailing across the floor. As they walked past the lines of tanks dim forms shifted behind the frosted glass, and at the far end of the aisle there was a sudden scurrying in a large-scale cage by Powers' desk.

Putting the box down on his chair, he picked a packet of peanuts off the desk and went over to the cage. A small black-haired chimpanzee wearing a dented jet pilot's helmet swarmed deftly up the bars to him, chirped happily, and then jumped down to a miniature control panel against the rear wall of the cage. Rapidly it flicked a series of buttons and toggles, and a succession of colored lights lit up like a juke box and jangled out a two-second blast of music.

"Good boy," Powers said encouragingly, patting the chimp's back and shoveling the peanuts into its hands. "You're getting much too clever for that one, aren't you?"

The chimp tossed the peanuts into the back of its throat with the smooth easy motions of a conjuror, jabbering at Powers in a singsong voice.

Coma laughed and took some of the nuts from Powers. "He's sweet. I think he's talking to you."

Powers nodded. "Quite right, he is. Actually he's got a two-hundred-word vocabulary, but his voice box scrambles it all up." He opened a small refrigerator by the desk, took out half a packet of sliced bread, and passed a couple of pieces to the chimp. It picked an electric toaster off the floor and placed it in the middle of a low wobbling table in the center of the cage, whipped the pieces into the slots. Powers pressed a tab on the switchboard beside the cage and the toaster began to crackle softly.

"He's one of the brightest we've had here, about as intelligent as a five-year-old child, though much more self-sufficient in a lot of ways." The two pieces of toast jumped out of their slots and the chimp caught them neatly, non-chalantly patting its helmet each time, then ambled off into a small ramshackle kennel and relaxed back with one arm out of a window, sliding the toast into its mouth.

"He built that house himself," Powers went on, switching off the toaster. "Not a bad effort, really." He pointed to a yellow polythene bucket by the front door of the kennel, from which a battered-looking geranium protruded. "Tends that plant, cleans up the cage, pours out an endless stream of wisecracks. Pleasant fellow all round."

Coma was smiling broadly to herself. "Why the space helmet, though?"

Powers hesitated. "Oh, it—er—it's for his own protection. Sometimes he gets rather bad headaches. His predecessors all—" He broke off and turned away. "Let's have a look at some of the other inmates."

He moved down the line of tanks, beckoning Coma with him. "We'll start at the beginning." He lifted the glass lid off one of the tanks, and Coma peered down into a shallow bath of water, where a small round organism with slender tendrils was nestling in a rockery of shells and pebbles.

"Sea anemone. Or was. Simple coelenterate with an open-ended body cavity." He pointed down to a thickened ridge of tissue around the base. "It's sealed up the cavity, converted the channel into a rudimentary notochord. Later the tendrils will knot themselves into a ganglion, but already they're sensitive to color. Look." He borrowed the violet handkerchief in Coma's breast pocket and spread it across the tank. The tendrils flexed and stiffened, began to weave slowly, as if they were trying to focus.

"The strange thing is that they're completely insensitive to white light. Normally the tendrils register shifting pressure gradients, like the tympanic diaphragms in your ears. Now it's almost as if they can *hear* primary colors, suggests it's readapting itself for a non-aquatic existence in a static world of violent color contrasts."

Coma shook her head, puzzled. "Why, though?"

"Hold on a moment. Let me put you in the picture first." They moved along the bench to a series of drum-shaped cages made of wire mosquito netting. Above the first was a large white cardboard screen bearing a blown-up microphoto of a tall pagodalike chain, topped by the legend: *"Drosophila: 15 roentgens/min."*

Powers tapped a small perspex window in the drum. "Fruit-fly. Its huge chromosomes make it a useful test vehicle." He bent down, pointed to a gray V-shaped honeycomb suspended from the roof. A few flies emerged from entrances, moving about busily. "Usually it's solitary, a nomadic scavenger. Now it forms itself into well-knit social groups, has begun to secrete a thin sweet lymph something like honey."

"What's this?" Coma asked, touching the screen.

"Diagram of a key gene in the operation." He traced a spray of arrows leading from a link in the chain. The arrows were labeled: *"Lymph gland"* and subdivided *"sphincter muscles, epithelium, templates."*

"It's rather like the perforated sheet music of a player piano," Powers commented, "or a computer punch tape. Knock out one link with an X-ray beam, lose a characteristic, change the score."

Coma was peering through the window of the next cage and pulling an unpleasant face. Over her shoulder Powers saw she was watching an enormous spiderlike insect, as big as a hand, its dark hairy legs as thick as fingers. The compound eyes had been built up so that they resembled giant rubies.

"He looks unfriendly," she said. "What's that sort of rope ladder he's spinning?" As she moved a finger to her mouth the spider came to life, retreated into the cage, and began spewing out a complex skein of interlinked gray thread which it slung in long loops from the roof of the cage.

"A web," Powers told her. "Except that it consists of nervous tissue. The ladders form an external neural plexus, an inflatable brain as it were, that he can pump up to whatever size the situation calls for. A sensible arrangement, really; far better than our own."

Coma backed away. "Gruesome. I wouldn't like to go into his parlor."

"Oh, he's not as frightening as he looks. Those huge eyes staring at you are blind. Or, rather, their optical sensitivity has shifted down the band; the retinas will only register gamma radiation. Your wristwatch has luminous hands. When you moved it across the window he started thinking. World War IV should really bring him into his element."

They strolled back to Powers' desk. He put a coffee pan over a Bunsen and pushed a chair across to Coma. Then he opened the box, lifted out the armored frog, and put it down on a sheet of blotting paper.

"Recognize him? Your old childhood friend, the common frog. He's built himself quite a solid little air raid shelter." He carried the animal across to a sink, turned on the tap, and let the water play softly over its shell. Wiping his hands on his shirt, he came back to the desk.

Coma brushed her long hair off her forehead, watched him curiously.

"Well, what's the secret?"

Powers lit a cigarette. "There's no secret. Teratologists have been breeding monsters for years. Have you ever heard of the 'silent pair'?"

She shook her head.

Powers stared moodily at the cigarette for a moment, riding the kick the first one of the day always gave him. "The so-called 'silent pair' is one of modern genetics' oldest problems, the apparently baffling mystery of the two inactive genes which occur in a small percentage of all living organisms, and appear to have no intelligible role in their structure or development. For a long while now biologists have been trying to activate them, but the difficulty is partly in identifying the silent genes in the fertilized germ cells of parents known to contain them, and partly in focusing a narrow enough X-ray beam which will do no damage to the remainder of the chromosome. However, after about ten years' work Dr. Whitby successfully developed a whole-body irradiation technique based on his observation of radiobiological damage at Eniwetok."

Powers paused for a moment. "He had noticed that there appeared to be more biological damage after the tests—that is, a greater transport of energy—than could be accounted for by direct radiation. What was happening was that the protein lattices in the genes were building up energy in the way that any vibrating membrane accumulates energy when it resonates—you remember the analogy of the bridge collapsing under the soldiers marching in step—and it occurred to him that if he could first identify the critical resonance frequency of the lattices in any particular silent gene he could then radiate the entire living organism, and not simply its germ cells, with a low field that would act selectively on the silent gene and cause no damage to the remainder of the chromosomes, whose lattices would resonate critically only at other specific frequencies."

Powers gestured around the laboratory with his cigarette. "You see some of the fruits of this 'resonance transfer' technique around you."

Coma nodded: "They've had their silent genes activated?"

"Yes, all of them. These are only a few of the thousands of specimens who have passed through here, and, as you've seen, the results are pretty dramatic."

He reached up and pulled across a section of the sun curtain. They were sitting just under the lip of the dome, and the mounting sunlight had begun to irritate him.

In the comparative darkness Coma noticed a stroboscope winking slowly in one of the tanks at the end of the bench behind her. She stood up and went over to it, examining a tall sunflower with a thickened stem and greatly enlarged receptacle. Packed around the flower, so that only its head protruded, was a chimney of gray-white stones, neatly cemented together and labeled: *"Cretaceous Chalk: 60,000,000 years."*

Beside it on the bench were three other chimneys, these labeled: *"Devonian Sandstone: 290,000,000 years"*, *"Asphalt: 20 years"*, *"Polyvinylchloride: 6 months."*

"Can you see those moist white discs on the sepals?" Powers pointed out. "In some way they regulate the plant's metabolism. It literally *sees* time. The older the surrounding environment, the more sluggish its metabolism. With the asphalt chimney it will complete its annual cycle in a week, with the PVC one in a couple of hours."

"Sees time," Coma repeated, wonderingly. She looked up at Powers, chewing her lower lip reflectively. "It's fantastic. Are these the creatures of the future, Doctor?"

"I don't know," Powers admitted. "But if they are their world must be a monstrous, surrealist one."

III

He went back to the desk, pulled two cups from a drawer, and poured out the coffee, switching off the Bunsen. "Some people have speculated that organisms possessing the silent pair of genes are the forerunners of a massive move up the evolutionary slope, that the silent genes are a sort of code, a divine message that we inferior organisms are carrying for our more highly developed descendants. It may well be true—perhaps we've broken the code too soon."

"Why do you say that?"

"Well, as Whitby's death indicates, the experiments in this laboratory have all come to a rather unhappy conclusion. Without exception the organisms we've irradiated have entered a final phase of totally disorganized growth, producing dozens of specialized sensory organs whose function we can't even guess. The results are catastrophic—the anemone will literally explode, the Drosophila cannibalize themselves, and so on. Whether the future implicit in these plants and animals is ever intended to take place, or whether we're merely extrapolating—I don't know. Sometimes I think, though, that the new sensory organs developed are parodies of their real intentions. The specimens you've seen today are all in an early stage of their secondary growth cycles. Later on they begin to look distinctly bizarre."

Coma nodded. "A zoo isn't complete without its keeper," she commented. "What about Man?"

Powers shrugged. "About one in every 100,000—the usual average—contains the silent pair. You might have them—or I. No one has volunteered yet to undergo whole-body irradiation. Apart from the fact that it would be classified as suicide, if the experiments here are any guide the experience would be savage and violent."

He sipped at the thin coffee, feeling tired and somehow bored. Recapitulating the laboratory's work had exhausted him.

The girl leaned forward. "You look awfully pale," she said solicitously. "Don't you sleep well?"

Powers managed a brief smile. "Too well," he admitted. "It's no longer a problem with me."

"I wish I could say that about Kaldren. I don't think he sleeps anywhere near enough. I hear him pacing around all night." She added, "Still, I suppose it's better than being a terminal. Tell me, Doctor, wouldn't it be worth trying this radiation technique on the sleepers at the Clinic? It might wake them up before the end. A few of them must possess the silent genes."

"They *all* do," Powers told her. "The two phenomena are very closely linked, as a matter of fact." He stopped, fatigue dulling his brain, and wondered whether to ask the girl to leave. Then he climbed off the desk and reached behind it, picked up a tape recorder.

Switching it on, he zeroed the tape and adjusted the speaker volume.

"Whitby and I often talked this over. Toward the end I took it all down. He was a great biologist, so let's hear it in his own words. It's absolutely the heart of the matter."

He flipped the table on, adding, "I've played it over to myself a thousand times, so I'm afraid the quality is poor."

An older man's voice, sharp and slightly irritable, sounded out above a low buzz of distortion, but Coma could hear it clearly.

(*Whitby*) . . . for heaven's sake, Robert, look at those FAO statistics. Despite an annual increase of five per-cent in acreage sown over the past fifteen years, world wheat crops have continued to decline by a factor of about two percent. The same story repeats itself ad nauseam. Cereals and root crops, dairy yields, ruminant fertility—are all down. Couple these with a mass of parallel symptoms, anything you care to pick from al-tered migratory routes to longer hibernation periods, and the overall pattern is incontrovertible.

(*Powers*) Population figures for Europe and North America show no decline, though.

(*Whitby*) Of course not, as I keep pointing out. It will take a century for such a fractional drop in fertility to have any effect in areas where extensive birth control provides an artificial reservoir. One must look at the countries of the Far East, and particularly at those where infant mortality has remained at a steady level. The

population of Sumatra, for example, has declined by
over fifteen percent in the last twenty years. A fabulous
decline! Do you realize that only two or three decades
ago the Neo-Malthusians were talking about a 'world
population explosion'? In fact, it's an implosion. Another
factor is—

Here the tape had been cut and edited, and Whitby's
voice, less querulous this time, picked up again.

. . . just as a matter of interest, tell me something: How
long do you sleep each night?

(*Powers*) I don't know exactly; about eight hours, I
suppose.

(*Whitby*) The proverbial eight hours. Ask anyone and
they say automatically, 'eight hours.' As a matter of fact
you sleep about ten and a half hours, like the majority
of people. I've timed you on a number of occasions. I
myself sleep eleven. Yet thirty years ago people did indeed sleep eight hours, and a century before that they
slept six or seven. In Vasari's *Lives* one reads of Michel-
angelo sleeping for only four or five hours, painting all
day at the age of eighty, and then working through the
night over his anatomy table with a candle strapped to
his forehead. Now he's regarded as a prodigy, but it was
unremarkable then. How do you think the ancients, from
Plato to Shakespeare, Aristotle to Aquinas, were able
to cram so much work into their lives? Simply because
they had an extra six or seven hours every day. Of
course, a second disadvantage under which we labor is
a lowered basal metabolic rate—another factor no one
will explain.

(*Powers*) I suppose you could take the view that the
lengthened sleep interval is a compensation device, a
sort of mass neurotic attempt to escape from the terrifying pressures of urban life in the late twentieth century.

(*Whitby*) You could, but you'd be wrong. It's simply a
matter of biochemistry. The ribonucleic acid templates

which unravel the protein chains in all living organisms
are wearing out, the dies enscribing the protoplasmic
signature have become blunted. After all, they've been
running now for over a thousand million years. It's time
to retool. Just as an individual organism's life span is
finite, or the life of a yeast colony or a given species, so
the life of an entire biological kingdom is of fixed duration. It's always been assumed that the evolutionary
slope reaches forever upward, but in fact the peak has
already been reached, and the pathway now leads downward to the common biological grave. It's a despairing
and at present unacceptable vision of the future, but it's
the only one. Five thousand centuries from now our
descendants, instead of being multibrained starmen, will
probably be naked prognathous idiots with hair on their
foreheads, grunting their way through the remains of
this Clinic like Neolithic men caught in a macabre in-
version of time. Believe me, I pity them, as I pity myself. My total failure, my absolute lack of any moral or
biological right to existence, is implicit in every cell of
my body . . .

The tape ended; the spool ran free and stopped. Powers
closed the machine, then massaged his face. Coma sat
quietly, watching him and listening to the chimp playing with
a box of puzzle dice.

"As far as Whitby could tell," Powers said, "the silent genes
represent a last desperate effort of the biological kingdom to
keep its head above the rising waters. Its total life period is
determined by the amount of radiation emitted by the sun,
and once this reaches a certain point the sure-death line
has been passed and extinction is inevitable. To compensate
for this, alarms have been built in which alter the form of
the organism and adapt it to living in a hotter radiological
climate. Soft-skinned organisms develop hard shells; these
contain heavy metals as radiation screens. New organs of
perception are developed too. According to Whitby, though,
it's all wasted effort in the long run—but sometimes I wonder."

He smiled at Coma and shrugged. "Well, let's talk about something else. How long have you known Kaldren?"

"About three weeks. Feels like ten thousand years."

"How do you find him now? We've been rather out of touch lately."

Coma grinned. "I don't seem to see very much of him either. He makes me sleep all the time. Kaldren has many strange talents, but he lives just for himself. You mean a lot to him, Doctor. In fact, you're my one serious rival."

"I thought he couldn't stand the sight of me."

"Oh, that's just a sort of surface symptom. He really thinks of you continuously. That's why we spend all our time following you around." She eyed Powers shrewdly. "I think he feels guilty about something."

"Guilty?" Powers exclaimed. "*He* does? I thought I was supposed to be the guilty one."

"Why?" she pressed. She hesitated, then said, "You carried out some experimental surgical technique on him, didn't you?"

"Yes," Powers admitted. "It wasn't altogether a success, like so much of what I seem to be involved with. If Kaldren feels guilty, I suppose it's because he feels he must take some of the responsibility."

He looked down at the girl, her intelligent eyes watching him closely. "For one or two reasons it may be necessary for you to know. You said Kaldren paced around all night and didn't get enough sleep. Actually he doesn't get any sleep at all."

The girl nodded. "You . . ." She made a snapping gesture with her fingers.

". . . narcotomized him," Powers completed. "Surgically speaking, it was a great success; one might well share a Nobel for it. Normally the hypothalamus regulates the period of sleep, raising the threshold of consciousness in order to relax the venous capillaries in the brain and drain them of accumulating toxins. However, by sealing off some of the control loops the subject is unable to receive the sleep cue, and the capillaries drain while he remains conscious. All he feels is a temporary lethargy, but this passes within three or four hours. Physically speaking, Kaldren has had another twenty years added to his life. But the psyche seems to need sleep for its own private reasons, and consequently Kaldren has periodic storms that tear him apart. The whole thing was a tragic blunder."

Coma frowned pensively. "I guessed as much. Your papers in the neurosurgery journals referred to the patient as K. A touch of pure Kafka that came all too true."

"I may leave here for good, Coma," Powers said. "Make sure that Kaldren goes to his clinics. Some of the deep scar tissue will need to be cleaned away."

"I'll try. Sometimes I feel I'm just another of his insane terminal documents."

"What are those?"

"Haven't you heard? Kaldren's collection of final statements about *Homo sapiens*. The complete works of Freud, Beethoven's deaf quartets, transcripts of the Nuremberg trials, an automatic novel, and so on." She broke off. "What's that you're drawing?"

"Where?"

She pointed to the desk blotter, and Powers looked down and realized he had been unconsciously sketching an elaborate doodle, Whitby's four-armed sun. "It's nothing," he said. Somehow, though, it had a strangely compelling force.

Coma stood up to leave. "You must come and see us, Doctor. Kaldren has so much he wants to show you. He's just got hold of an old copy of the last signals sent back by the Mercury Seven twenty years ago when they reached the moon, and can't think about anything else. You remember the strange messages they recorded before they died, full of poetic ramblings about the white gardens. Now that I think about it they behaved rather like the plants in your zoo here."

She put her hands in her pockets, then pulled something out. "By the way, Kaldren asked me to give you this."

It was an old index card from the observatory library. In the center had been typed the number:

$$96,688,365,498,720$$

"It's going to take a long time to reach zero at this rate," Powers remarked dryly. "I'll have quite a collection when we're finished."

After she had left he chucked the card into the waste bin and sat down at the desk, staring for an hour at the ideogram on the blotter.

Halfway back to his beach house the lake road forked to the left through a narrow saddle that ran between the hills to an abandoned Air Force weapons range on one of the remoter salt lakes. At the nearer end were a number of small bunkers and camera towers, one or two metal shacks, and a low-roofed storage hangar. The white hills encircled the whole area, shutting it off from the world outside, and Powers liked to wander on foot down the gunnery aisles that had been marked down the two-mile length of the lake toward the concrete sight-screens at the far end. The abstract patterns made him feel like an ant on a bone-white chessboard, the rectangular screens at one end and the towers and bunkers at the other like opposing pieces.

His session with Coma had made Powers feel suddenly dissatisfied with the way he was spending his last months. *Goodbye, Eniwetok*, he had written, but in fact systematically forgetting everything was exactly the same as remembering it, a cataloguing in reverse, sorting out all the books in the mental library and putting them back in their right places upside down.

Powers climbed one of the camera towers, leaned on the rail, and looked out along the aisles toward the sight-screens. Ricocheting shells and rockets had chipped away large pieces of the circular concrete bands that ringed the target bulls, but the outlines of the huge 100-yard-wide discs, alternately painted blue and red, were still visible.

For half an hour he stared quietly at them, formless ideas shifting through his mind. Then without thinking, he abruptly left the rail and climbed down the companionway. The storage hangar was fifty yards away. He walked quickly across to it, stepped into the cool shadows, and peered around the rusting electric trolleys and empty flare drums. At the far end, behind a pile of lumber and bales of wire, were a stack of unopened cement bags, a mound of dirty sand, and an old mixer.

Half an hour later he had backed the Buick into the hangar and hooked the cement mixer, charged with sand, cement, and water scavenged from the drums lying around outside, onto the rear bumper, then loaded a dozen more bags into the car's trunk and rear seat. Finally he selected a few straight lengths of timber, jammed them through the window, and set off across the lake toward the central target bull.

For the next two hours he worked away steadily in the center of the great blue disc, mixing up the cement by hand, carrying it across to the crude wooden forms he had lashed together from the timber, smoothing it down so that it formed a six-inch-high wall around the perimeter of the bull. He worked without pause, stirring the cement with a tire lever, scooping it out with a hubcap prized off one of the wheels.

By the time he finished and drove off, leaving his equipment where it stood, he had completed a thirty-foot long section of wall.

IV

JUNE 7: Conscious, for the first time, of the brevity of each day. As long as I was awake for over twelve hours I still orientated my time around the meridian; morning and afternoon set their old rhythms. Now, with just over eleven hours of consciousness left, they form a continuous interval, like a length of tape measure. I can see exactly how much is left on the spool and can do little to affect the rate at which it unwinds. Spend the time slowly packing away the library; the crates are too heavy to move and lie where they are filled.

Cell count down to 400,000.

Woke 8:10. To sleep 7:15. (Appear to have lost my

watch without realizing it; had to drive into town to buy another.)

JUNE 14: 9½ hours. Time races, flashing past like an expressway. However, the last week of a holiday always goes faster than the first. At the present rate there should be about four to five weeks left. This morning I tried to visualize what the last week or so—the final, 3, 2, 1, out —would be like, had a sudden chilling attack of pure fear, unlike anything I've ever felt before. Took me half an hour to steady myself enough for an intravenous.

Kaldren pursues me like my luminescent shadow, chalked up on the gateway '96,688,365,498,702.' Should confuse the mail man.

Woke 9:05. To sleep 6:36.

JUNE 19: 8¾ hours. Anderson rang up this morning. I nearly put the phone down on him, but managed to go through the pretense of making the final arrangements. He congratulated me on my stoicism, even used the word 'heroic.' Don't feel it. Despair erodes everything— courage, hope, self-discipline, all the better qualities. It's so damned difficult to sustain that impersonal attitude of passive acceptance implicit in the scientific tradition. I try to think of Galileo before the Inquisition, Freud surmounting the endless pain of his jaw cancer surgery.

Met Kaldren downtown, had a long discussion about the Mercury Seven. He's convinced that they refused to leave the moon deliberately, after the 'reception party' waiting for them had put them in the cosmic picture. They were told by the mysterious emissaries from Orion that the exploration of deep space was pointless, that they were too late as the life of the universe is now virtu- ally over!!! According to K. there are Air Force generals who take this nonsense seriously, but I suspect it's simply an obscure attempt on K.'s part to console me.

Must have the phone disconnected. Some contractor keeps calling me up about payment for fifty bags of cement he claims I collected ten days ago. Says he helped me load them onto a truck himself. I did drive

Whitby's pickup into town but only to get some lead screening. What does he think I'd do with all that cement? Just the sort of irritating thing you don't expect to hang over your final exit. (Moral: don't try too hard to forget Eniwetok.)

Woke 9:40. To sleep 4:15.

JUNE 25: 7½ hours. Kaldren was snooping around the lab again today. Phoned me there; when I answered a recorded voice he'd rigged up rambled out a long string of numbers, like an insane super-Tim. These practical jokes of his get rather wearing. Fairly soon I'll have to go over and come to terms with him, much as I hate the prospect. Anyway, Miss Mars is a pleasure to look at.

One meal is enough now, topped up with a glucose shot. Sleep is still "black," completely unrefreshing. Last night I took a 16-mm film of the first three hours, screened it this morning at the lab. The first true horror movie; I looked like a half-animated corpse.

Woke 10:25. To sleep 3:45.

JULY 3: 5¾ hours. Little done today. Deepening lethargy; dragged myself over to the lab, nearly left the road twice. Concentrated enough to feed the zoo and get the log up to date. Read through the operating manuals Whitby left for the last time, decided on a delivery rate of 40 roentgens/min., target distance of 350 cm. Everything is ready now.

Woke 11:05. To sleep 3:15.

Powers stretched, shifted his head slowly across the pillow, focusing on the shadows cast onto the ceiling by the blind. Then he looked down at his feet, saw Kaldren sitting on the end of the bed, watching him quietly.

"Hello, Doctor," he said, putting out his cigarette. "Late night? You look tired."

Powers heaved himself onto one elbow, glanced at his watch. It was just after eleven. For a moment his brain blurred, and he swung his legs around and sat on the edge of the bed, elbows on his knees, massaging some life into his face.

He noticed that the room was full of smoke. "What are you doing here?" he asked Kaldren.

"I came over to invite you to lunch." He indicated the bed-side phone. "Your line was dead so I drove round. Hope you don't mind me climbing in. Rang the bell for about half an hour. I'm surprised you didn't hear it."

Powers nodded, then stood up and tried to smooth the creases out of his cotton slacks. He had gone to sleep without changing for over a week, and they were damp and stale.

As he started for the bathroom door Kaldren pointed to the camera tripod on the other side of the bed. "What's this? Going into the blue movie business, Doctor?"

Powers surveyed him dimly for a moment, glanced at the tripod without replying, and then noticed his open diary on the bedside table. Wondering whether Kaldren had read the last entries, he went back and picked it up, then stepped into the bathroom and closed the door behind him.

From the mirror cabinet he took out a syringe and an ampoule, after the shot leaned against the door waiting for the stimulant to pick up.

Kaldren was in the lounge when he returned to him, reading the labels on the crates lying about in the center of the floor.

"O.K., then," Powers told him, "I'll join you for lunch." He examined Kaldren carefully. He looked more subdued than usual; there was an air almost of deference about him.

"Good," Kaldren said. "By the way, are you leaving?"

"Does it matter?" Powers asked curtly. "I thought you were in Anderson's care?"

Kaldren shrugged. "Please yourself. Come round at about twelve," he suggested, adding pointedly, "that'll give you time to clean up and change. What's that all over your shirt? Looks like lime."

Powers peered down, brushed at the white streaks. After Kaldren had left he threw the clothes away, took a shower, and unpacked a clean suit from one of the trunks.

Until this liaison with Coma, Kaldren lived alone in the old abstract summer house on the north shore of the lake. This was a seven-story folly originally built by an eccentric millionaire mathematician in the form of a spiraling concrete ribbon that wound around itself like an insane serpent, serving walls, floors, and ceilings. Only Kaldren had solved the building, a geometric model of $\sqrt{-1}$, and consequently he had been able to take it off the agents' hands at a comparatively low rent. In the evenings Powers had often watched him from the laboratory, striding restlessly from one level to the next, swinging through the labyrinth of inclines and terraces to the rooftop, where his lean angular figure stood out like a gallows against the sky, his lonely eyes sifting out radio lanes for the next day's trapping.

Powers noticed him there when he drove up at noon, poised on a ledge 150 feet above, head raised theatrically to the sky.

"Kaldren!" he shouted up suddenly into the silent air, half-hoping he might be jolted into losing his footing.

Kaldren broke out of his reverie and glanced down into the court. Grinning obliquely, he waved his right arm in a slow semicircle.

"Come up," he called, then turned back to the sky.

Powers leaned against the car. Once, a few months previously, he had accepted the same invitation, stepped through the entrance, and within three minutes lost himself helplessly in a second-floor cul de sac. Kaldren had taken half an hour to find him.

Powers waited while Kaldren swung down from his eyrie, vaulting through the wells and stairways, then rode up in the elevator with him to the penthouse suite.

They carried their cocktails through into a wide glass-roofed studio, the huge white ribbon of concrete uncoiling around them like toothpaste squeezed from an enormous tube. On the staged levels running parallel and across them rested pieces of gray abstract furniture, giant photographs on angled screens, carefully labeled exhibits laid out on low tables, all dominated by twenty-foot-high black letters on the rear wall which spelt out the single vast word:

YOU

Kaldren pointed to it. "What you might call the supra-liminal approach." He gestured Powers in conspiratorially, finishing his drink in a gulp. "This is *my* laboratory, Doctor," he said with a note of pride. "Much more significant than yours, believe me."

Powers smiled wryly to himself and examined the first exhibit, an old ECG tape traversed by a series of faded inky wriggles. It was labeled, *"Einstein, A.; Alpha Waves, 1922."*

He followed Kaldren around, sipping slowly at his drink, enjoying the brief feeling of alertness the amphetamine provided. Within two hours it would fade, leave his brain feeling like a block of blotting paper.

Kaldren chattered away, explaining the significance of the so-called Terminal Documents. "They're end-prints, Powers, final statements, the products of total fragmentation. When I've got enough together I'll build a new world for myself out of them." He picked a thick paperbound volume off one of the tables, riffled through its pages. "Association tests of the Nuremberg Twelve. I have to include these . . ."

Powers strolled on absently without listening. Over in the corner were what appeared to be three ticker-tape machines, lengths of tape hanging from their mouths. He wondered whether Kaldren was misguided enough to be playing the stock market, which had been declining slowly for twenty years.

"Powers," he heard Kaldren say. "I was telling you about the Mercury Seven." He pointed to a collection of typewritten sheets tacked to a screen. "These are transcripts of their final signals radioed back from the recording monitors."

Powers examined the sheets cursorily, read a line at random.

". . . *Blue* . . . *People* . . . *Recycle* . . . *Orion* . . . *Telemeters* . . ."

Powers nodded noncommittally. "Interesting. What are the ticker tapes for over there?"

Kaldren grinned. "I've been waiting for months for you to ask me that. Have a look."

Powers went over and picked up one of the tapes. The machine was labeled, *"Auriga 225-G. Interval: 69 hours."*

The tape read:

$$96,688,365,498,695$$
$$96,688,365,498,694$$
$$96,688,365,498,693$$
$$96,688,365,498,692$$

Powers dropped the tape. "Looks rather familiar. What does the sequence represent?"

Kaldren shrugged. "No one knows."

"What do you mean? It must replicate something."

"Yes, it does. A diminishing mathematical progression. A countdown, if you like."

Powers picked up the tape on the right, tabbed, *"Aries 44R951. Interval: 49 days."*

Here the sequence ran:

$$876,567,988,347,779,877,654,434$$
$$876,567,988,347,779,877,654,433$$
$$876,567,988,347,779,877,654,432$$

Powers looked round. "How long does it take each signal to come through?"

"Only a few seconds. They're tremendously compressed laterally, of course. A computer at the observatory breaks them down. They were first picked up at Jodrell Bank about twenty years ago. Nobody bothers to listen to them now."

Powers turned to the last tape.

$$6,554$$
$$6,553$$
$$6,552$$
$$6,551$$

"Nearing the end of its run," he commented. He glanced at the label on the hood, which read: *"Unidentified radio source, Canes Venatici. Interval: 97 weeks."*

He showed the tape to Kaldren. "Soon be over."

Kaldren shook his head. He lifted a heavy directory-sized volume off a table, cradled it in his hands. His face had suddenly become somber and haunted. "I doubt it," he said. "Those are only the last four digits. The whole number contains over 50 million."

He handed the volume to Powers, who turned to the title page. "*Master Sequence of Serial Signal received by Jodrell Bank Radio-Observatory, University of Manchester, England, 0012:59 hours, 21-5-72. Source: NGC 9743, Canes Venatici.*" He thumbed the thick stack of closely printed pages, millions of numerals, as Kaldren had said, running up and down across a thousand consecutive pages.

Powers shook his head, picked up the tape again, and stared at it thoughtfully.

"The computer only breaks down the last four digits," Kaldren explained. "The whole series comes over in each 15-second-long package, but it took IBM more than two years to unscramble one of them."

"Amazing," Powers commented. "But what is it?"

"A countdown, as you can see. NGC 9743, somewhere in Canes Venatici. The big spirals there are breaking up, and they're saying goodbye. God knows who they think we are but they're letting us know all the same, beaming it out on the hydrogen line for everyone in the universe to hear." He paused. "Some people have put other interpretations on them, but there's one piece of evidence that rules out everything else."

"Which is?"

Kaldren pointed to the last tape from Canes Venatici. "Simply that it's been estimated that by the time this series reaches zero the universe will have just ended."

Powers fingered the tape reflectively. "Thoughtful of them to let us know what the real time is," he remarked.

"I agree, it is," Kaldren said quietly. "Applying the inverse square law that signal source is broadcasting at a strength of about three million megawatts raised to the hundredth power. About the size of the entire Local Group. Thoughtful is the word."

Suddenly he gripped Powers' arm, held it tightly, and peered into his eyes closely, his throat working with emotion.

"You're not alone, Powers, don't think you are. These are the voices of time, and they're all saying goodbye to you. Think of yourself in a wider context. Every particle in your body, every grain of sand, every galaxy carries the same signature. As you've just said, you know what the time is now, so what does the rest matter? There's no need to go on looking at the clock."

Powers took his hand, squeezed it firmly. "Thanks, Kaldren. I'm glad you understand." He walked over to the window, looked down across the white lake. The tension between himself and Kaldren had dissipated; he felt that all his obligations to him had at last been met. Now he wanted to leave as quickly as possible, forget him as he had forgotten the faces of the countless other patients whose exposed brains had passed between his fingers.

He went back to the ticker machines, tore the tapes from their slots, and stuffed them into his pockets. "I'll take these along to remind myself. Say goodbye to Coma for me, will you."

He moved toward the door, when he reached it looked back to see Kaldren standing in the shadow of the three giant letters on the far wall, his eyes staring listlessly at his feet.

As Powers drove away he noticed that Kaldren had gone up onto the roof, watched him in the driving mirror waving slowly until the car disappeared around a bend.

V

The outer circle was now almost complete. A narrow segment, an arc about ten feet long, was missing, but otherwise the low perimeter wall ran continuously six inches off the concrete floor around the outer lane of the target bull, enclosing the huge rebus within it. Three concentric circles, the largest a hundred yards in diameter, separated from each other by ten-foot intervals, formed the rim of the device, divided into four segments by the arms of an enormous cross radiating from its center, where a small round platform had been built a foot above the ground.

Powers worked swiftly, pouring sand and cement into the mixer, tipping in water until a rough paste formed, then carried it across to the wooden forms and tamped the mixture down into the narrow channel.

Within ten minutes he had finished, quickly dismantled the forms before the cement had set, and slung the timbers into the back seat of the car. Dusting his hands on his trousers, he went over to the mixer and pushed it fifty yards away into the long shadow of the surrounding hills.

Without pausing to survey the gigantic cipher on which he had labored patiently for so many afternoons, he climbed into the car and drove off on a wake of bone-white dust, splitting the pools of indigo shadow.

He reached the laboratory at three o'clock, jumped from the car as it lurched back on its brakes. Inside the entrance he first switched on the lights, then hurried round, pulling the sun curtains down and shackling them to the floor slots, effectively turning the dome into a steel tent.

In their tanks behind him the plants and animals stirred quietly, responding to the sudden flood of cold fluorescent light. Only the chimpanzee ignored him. It sat on the floor of its cage, neurotically jamming the puzzle dice into the polythene bucket, exploding in bursts of sudden rage when the pieces refused to fit.

Powers went over to it, noticing the shattered glass fiber reinforcing panels bursting from the dented helmet. Already the chimp's face and forehead were bleeding from self-inflicted blows. Powers picked up the remains of the geranium that had been hurled through the bars, attracted the chimp's attention with it, then tossed a black pellet he had taken from a capsule in the desk drawer. The chimp caught it with a quick flick of the wrist, for a few seconds juggled the pellet with a couple of dice as it concentrated on the puzzle, then pulled it out of the air and swallowed it in a gulp.

Without waiting, Powers slipped off his jacket and stepped toward the X-ray theater. He pulled back the high sliding doors to reveal the long glassy metallic snout of the Maxitron, then started to stack the lead screening shields against the rear wall.

A few minutes later the generator hummed into life.

The anemone stirred. Basking in the warm subliminal sea of radiation rising around it, prompted by countless pelagic memories, it reached tentatively across the tank, groping blindly toward the dim uterine sun. Its tendrils flexed, the thousands of dormant neural cells in their tips regrouping and multiplying, each harnessing the unlocked energies of its nucleus. Chains forged themselves, lattices tiered upward into multifaceted lenses, focused slowly on the vivid spectral outlines of the sounds dancing like phosphorescent waves around the darkened chamber of the dome.

Gradually an image formed, revealing an enormous black fountain that poured an endless stream of brilliant light over the circle of benches and tanks. Beside it a figure moved, adjusting the flow through its mouth. As it stepped across the floor its feet threw off vivid bursts of color, its hands racing along the benches conjured up a dazzling chiaroscura, balls of blue and violet light that exploded fleetingly in the darkness like miniature star-shells.

Photons murmured. Steadily, as it watched the glimmering screen of sounds around it, the anemone continued to expand. Its ganglia linked, heeding a new source of stimuli from the delicate diaphragms in the crown of its notochord. The silent outlines of the laboratory began to echo softly; waves of muted sound fell from the arc lights and echoed off the benches and furniture below. Etched in sound, their angular forms resonated with sharp persistent overtones. The plastic-ribbed chairs were a buzz of staccato discords, the square-sided desk a continuous double-featured tone.

Ignoring these sounds once they had been perceived, the anemone turned to the ceiling, which reverberated like a shield in the sounds pouring steadily from the fluorescent tubes. Streaming through a narrow skylight, its voice clear and strong, interweaved by numberless overtones, the sun sang . . .

It was a few minutes before dawn when Powers left the laboratory and stepped into his car. Behind him the great dome lay silent in the darkness, the thin shadows of the white moonlit hills falling across its surface. Powers free-wheeled the car down the long curving drive to the lake road below, listening to the tires cutting across the blue gravel, then let out the clutch and accelerated the engine.

As he drove along, the limestone hills half hidden in the darkness on his left, he gradually became aware that, although no longer looking at the hills, he was still in some oblique way conscious of their forms and outlines in the back of his mind. The sensation was undefined but none the less certain, a strange almost visual impression that emanated most strongly from the deep clefts and ravines dividing one cliff face from the next. For a few minutes Powers let it play upon him, without trying to identify it, a dozen strange images moving across his brain.

The road swung up around a group of chalets built onto the lake shore, taking the car right under the lee of the hills, and Powers suddenly felt the massive weight of the escarpment rising up into the dark sky like a cliff of luminous chalk, and realized the identity of the impression now registering powerfully within his mind. Not only could he see the escarpment, but he was aware of its enormous age, felt distinctly the countless millions of years since it had first reared out of the magma of the earth's crust. The ragged crests three hundred feet above him, the dark gulleys and fissures, the smooth boulders by the roadside at the foot of the cliff, all carried a distinct image of themselves across to him, a thousand voices that together told of the total time that had elapsed in the life of the escarpment, a psychic picture as defined and clear as the visual image brought to him by his eyes.

Involuntarily, Powers had slowed the car, and turning his eyes away from the hill face he felt a second wave of time sweep across the first. The image was broader but of shorter perspectives, radiating from the wide disc of the salt lake, breaking over the ancient limestone cliffs like shallow rollers dashing against a towering headland.

Closing his eyes, Powers lay back and steered the car along the interval between the two time fronts, feeling the images deepen and strengthen within his mind. The vast age of the landscape, the inaudible chorus of voices resonating from the lake and from the white hills, seemed to carry him back through time, down endless corridors to the first thresholds of the world.

He turned the car off the road along the track leading toward the target range. On either side of the culvert the cliff faces boomed and echoed with vast impenetrable time fields, like enormous opposed magnets. As he finally emerged between them onto the flat surface of the lake it seemed to Powers that he could feel the separate identity of each sand grain and salt crystal calling to him from the surrounding ring of hills.

He parked the car beside the mandala and walked slowly toward the outer concrete rim curving away into the shadows. Above him he could hear the stars, a million cosmic voices that crowded the sky from one horizon to the next, a true canopy of time. Like jostling radio beacons, their long aisles interlocking at countless angles, they plunged into the sky from the narrowest recesses of space. He saw the dim red disc of Sirius, heard its ancient voice, untold millions of years old, dwarfed by the huge spiral nebulae in Andromeda, a gigantic carousel of vanished universes, their voices almost as old as the cosmos itself. To Powers the sky seemed an endless babel, the time-song of a thousand galaxies overlaying each other in his mind. As he moved slowly toward the center of the mandala he craned up at the glittering traverse of the Milky Way, searching the confusion of clamoring nebulae and constellations.

Stepping into the inner circle of the mandala, a few yards from the platform at its center, he realized that the tumult was beginning to fade, and that a single stronger voice had emerged and was dominating the others. He climbed onto the platform, raised his eyes to the darkened sky, moving through the constellations to the island galaxies beyond them, hearing the thin archaic voices reaching to him across the millennia. In his pockets he felt the paper tapes, and turned to find the distant diadem of Canes Venatici, heard its great voice mounting in his mind.

Like an endless river, so broad that its banks were below the horizons, it flowed steadily toward him, a vast course of time that spread outwards to fill the sky and the universe, enveloping everything within them. Moving slowly, the forward direction of its majestic current almost imperceptible, Powers knew that its source was the source of the cosmos itself. As it passed him, he felt its massive magnetic pull, let himself be drawn into it, borne gently on its powerful back. Quietly it carried him away, and he rotated slowly, facing the direction of the tide. Around him the outlines of the hills and the lake had faded, but the image of the mandala, like a cosmic clock, remained fixed before his eyes, illuminating the broad surface of the stream. Watching it constantly, he felt his body gradually dissolving, its physical dimensions melting into the vast continuum of the current, which bore him out into the center of the great channel sweeping him onward, beyond hope now but at rest, down the broadening reaches of the river of eternity.

As the shadows faded, retreating into the hill slopes, Kaldren stepped out of his car, walked hesitantly toward the concrete rim of the outer circle. Fifty yards away, at the center, Coma knelt beside Powers' body, her small hands pressed to his dead face. A gust of wind stirred the sand, dislodging a strip of tape that drifted toward Kaldren's feet. He bent down and picked it up, then rolled it carefully in his hands and slipped it into his pocket. The dawn air was cold, and he turned up the collar of his jacket, watching Coma impassively.

"It's six o'clock," he told her after a few minutes. "I'll go and get the police. You stay with him." He paused and then added, "Don't let them break the clock."

Coma turned and looked at him. "Aren't you coming back?"

"I don't know." Nodding to her, Kaldren swung on his heel and went over to the car.

He reached the lake road, five minutes later parked the car in the drive outside Whitby's laboratory.

The dome was in darkness, all its windows shuttered, but the generator still hummed in the X-ray theater. Kaldren stepped through the entrance and switched on the lights. In the theater he touched the grilles of the generator, felt the warm cylinder of the beryllium end-window. The circular target table was revolving slowly, its setting at 1 r.p.m., a steel restraining chair shackled to it hastily. Grouped in a semicircle a few feet away were most of the tanks and cages, piled on top of each other haphazardly. In one of them an enormous squidlike plant had almost managed to climb from its vivarium. Its long translucent tendrils clung to the edges of the tank, but its body had burst into a jellified pool of globular mucilage. In another an enormous spider had trapped itself in its own web, hung helplessly in the center of a huge three-dimensional maze of phosphorescing thread, twitching spasmodically.

All the experimental plants and animals had died. The chimp lay on its back among the remains of the hutch, the helmet forward over its eyes. Kaldren watched it for a moment, then sat down on the desk and picked up the phone.

While he dialed the number he noticed a film reel lying on the blotter. For a moment he stared at the label, then slid the reel into his pocket beside the tape.

After he had spoken to the police he turned off the lights and went out to the car, drove off slowly down the drive.

When he reached the summer house the early sunlight was breaking across the ribbonlike balconies and terraces. He took the lift to the penthouse, made his way through into the museum. One by one he opened the shutters and let the sunlight play over the exhibits. Then he pulled a chair over to a side window, sat back, and stared up at the light pouring through into the room.

Two or three hours later he heard Coma outside, calling

up to him. After half an hour she went away, but a little later a second voice appeared and shouted up at Kaldren. He left his chair and closed all the shutters overlooking the front courtyard, and eventually he was left undisturbed.

Kaldren returned to his seat and lay back quietly, his eyes gazing across the lines of exhibits. Half-asleep, periodically he leaned up and adjusted the flow of light through the shutter, thinking to himself, as he would do through the coming months, of Powers and his strange mandala, and of the seven and their journey to the white gardens of the moon, and the blue people who had come from Orion and spoken in poetry to them of ancient beautiful worlds beneath golden suns in the island galaxies, vanished forever now in the myriad deaths of the cosmos.

by J. G. BALLARD
The Drowned World
The Crystal World
Love & Napalm: Export U.S.A. (*The Atrocity Exhibit*) (collection of short stories)
Chronopolis and Other Stories (collection of short stories)

The Pleasure Garden of Felipe Sagittarius

MICHAEL MOORCOCK

The air was still and warm, the sun bright and the sky blue above the ruins of Berlin as I clambered over piles of weed-covered brick and broken concrete on my way to investigate the murder of an unknown man in the garden of Police Chief Bismarck.

My name is Minos Aquilinas, top Metatemporal Investigator of Europe, and this job was going to be a tough one, I knew.

Don't ask me the location or the date. I never bother to find out things like that, they only confuse me. With me it's instinct, win or lose.

They'd given me all the information there was. The dead man had already had an autopsy. Nothing unusual about him except that he had paper lungs—disposable lungs. That pinned him down a little. The only place I knew of where they still used paper lungs was Rome. What was a Roman doing in Berlin? Why was he murdered in Police Chief Bismarck's garden? He'd been strangled, that I'd been told. It wasn't hard to strangle a man with paper lungs, it didn't take long. But who and why were harder questions to answer right then.

It was a long way across the ruins to Bismarck's place. Rubble stretched in all directions and only here and there could you see a landmark—what was left of the Reichstag, the Brandenburg Gate, the Brechtsmuseum and a few other places like that.

I stopped to lean on the only remaining wall of a house,

took off my jacket and loosened my tie, wiped my forehead and neck with my handkerchief and lit a cheroot. The wall gave me some shade and I felt a little cooler by the time I was ready to press on.

As I mounted a big heap of brick on which a lot of blue weeds grew I saw the Bismarck place ahead. Built of heavy, black-veined marble, in the kind of Valhalla/Olympus mixture they went in for, it was fronted by a smooth, green lawn and backed by a garden that was surrounded by such a high wall I only glimpsed the leaves of some of the foliage even though I was looking down on the place. The thick Grecian columns flanking the porch were topped by a baroque façade covered in bas-reliefs showing men in horned helmets killing dragons and one another apparently indiscriminately.

I picked my way down to the lawn and walked across it, then up some steps until I'd crossed to the front door. It was big and heavy, bronze I guessed, with more bas-reliefs, this time of clean-shaven characters in more ornate and complicated armour with two-handed swords and riding horses. Some had lances and axes, I noticed, as I pulled the bell and waited.

I had plenty of time to study the pictures before one of the doors swung open and an old man in a semi-military suit, holding himself straight by an effort, raised a white eyebrow at me.

I told him my name and he let me in to a cool, dark hall full of the same kinds of armor the men on the door had been wearing. He opened a door on the right and told me to wait. The room I was in was all iron and leather—weapons on the walls and leather-covered furniture on the carpet.

Thick velvet curtains were drawn back from the window and I stood looking out over the quiet ruins, smoked another stick, popped the butt in a green pot and put my jacket back on.

The old man came in again and I followed him out of that room, along the hall, up one flight of the wide stairs and into a huge, less cluttered, room where I found the guy I'd come to see.

He stood in the middle of the carpet. He was wearing a

heavily ornamented helmet with a spike on the top, a deep blue uniform covered in badges, gold and black epaulettes, shiny jackboots and steel spurs. He looked about seventy and very tough. He had bushy grey eyebrows and a big, carefully combed moustache. As I came in he grunted and one arm sprang into a horizontal position, pointing at me.

"Herr Aquilinas. I am Otto von Bismarck, Chief of Berlin's police."

I shook the hand. Actually it shook me, all over.

"Quite a turn up," I said. "A murder in the garden of the man who's supposed to prevent murders."

His face must have been paralyzed or something because it didn't move except when he spoke, and even then it didn't move much.

"Quite so," he said. "We were reluctant to call you in, of course. But I think this is your specialty."

"Maybe. Is the body still here?"

"In the kitchen. The autopsy was performed here. Paper lungs—you know about that?"

"I know. Now, if I've got it right, you heard nothing in the night—"

"Oh, yes, I did hear something—the barking of my wolf-hounds. One of the servants investigated but found nothing."

"What time was this?"

"Time?"

"What did the clock say?"

"About two in the morning."

"When was the body found?"

"About ten—the gardener discovered it in the vine grove."

"Right—let's look at the body and then talk to the gardener."

He took me to the kitchen. One of the windows was opened on to a lush garden, full of tall, brightly colored shrubs of every possible shade. An intoxicating scent came from the garden. It made me feel randy. I turned to look at the corpse lying on a scrubbed deal table covered in a sheet.

I pulled back the sheet. The body was naked. It looked old but strong, deeply tanned. The head was big and its most noticeable feature was the heavy black moustache. The body wasn't what it had been. First there were the marks of strangulation around the throat, as well as swelling on wrists, forearms and legs which seemed to indicate that the victim had also been tied up recently. The whole front of the torso had been opened for the autopsy and whoever had stitched it up again hadn't been too careful.

"What about clothes?" I asked the Police Chief.

Bismarck shook his head and pointed to a chair standing beside the table. "That was all we found."

There was a pair of neatly folded paper lungs, a bit the worse for wear. The trouble with disposable lungs was that while you never had to worry about smoking or any of the other causes of lung disease, the lungs had to be changed regularly. This was expensive, particularly in Rome where there was no State-controlled Lung Service as there had been in most of the European City-States until a few years before the war when the longer-lasting polythene lung had superseded the paper one. There was also a wrist-watch and a pair of red shoes with long, curling toes.

I picked up one of the shoes. Middle Eastern workmanship. I looked at the watch. It was heavy, old, tarnished and Russian. The strap was new, pigskin, with "Made in England" stamped on it.

"I see why they called us," I said.

"There *were* certain anachronisms," Bismarck admitted.

"This gardener who found him, can I talk to him?"

Bismarck went to the window and called: "Felipe!"

The foliage seemed to fold back of its own volition and a dark-haired young man came through it. He was tall, long-faced and pale. He held an elegant watering can in one hand. He was dressed in a dark green, high-collared shirt and matching trousers.

We looked at one another through the window.

"This is my gardener Felipe Sagittarius," Bismarck said.

Sagittarius bowed, his eyes amused. Bismarck didn't seem to notice.

"Can you let me see where you found the body?" I asked.

"Sure," said Sagittarius.

"I shall wait here," Bismarck told me as I went toward the kitchen door.

"OK." I stepped into the garden and let Sagittarius show me the way. Once again the shrubs seemed to part on their own.

The scent was still thick and erotic. Most of the plants had dark, fleshy leaves and flowers of deep reds, purples and blues. Here and there were clusters of heavy yellow and pink.

The grass I was walking on seemed to crawl under my feet and the weird shapes of the trunks and stems of the shrubs didn't make me feel like taking a snooze in that garden.

"This is all your work is it, Sagittarius?" I asked.

He nodded and kept walking.

"Original," I said. "Never seen one like it before."

Sagittarius turned then and pointed a thumb behind him. "This is the place."

We were standing in a little glade almost entirely surrounded by thick vines that curled about their trellises like snakes. On the far side of the glade I could see where some of the vines had been ripped and the trellis torn and I guessed there had been a fight. I still couldn't work out why the victim had been untied before the murderer strangled him —it must have been before, or else there wouldn't have been a fight. I checked the scene, but there were no clues. Through the place where the trellis was torn I saw a small summer house, built to represent a Chinese pavilion, all red, yellow and black lacquer with highlights picked out in gold. It didn't fit with the architecture of the house.

"What's that?" I asked the gardener.

"Nothing," he said sulkily, evidently sorry I'd seen it.

"I'll take a look at it anyway."

He shrugged but didn't offer to lead on. I moved between the trellises until I reached the pavilion. Sagittarius followed slowly. I took the short flight of wooden steps up to the veranda and tried the door. It opened. I walked in. There seemed to be only one room, a bedroom. The bed needed making and it looked as if two people had left it in a hurry. There was a pair of nylons tucked half under the pillow and a pair of man's underpants on the floor. The sheets were very white, the furnishings very oriental and rich.

Sagittarius was standing in the doorway.

"Your place?" I said.

"No." He sounded offended. "The Police Chief's."

I grinned.

Sagittarius burst into rhapsody. "The languorous scents, the very menace of the plants, the *heaviness* in the air of the garden, must surely stir the blood of even the most ancient man. This is the only place he can relax. This is what I'm employed for—why he gives me my head."

"Has this," I said, pointing to the bed, "anything to do with last night?"

"He was probably here when it happened, but I . . ." Sagittarius shook his head and I wondered if there was anything he'd meant to imply which I'd missed.

I saw something on the floor, stooped and picked it up. A pendant with the initials E.B. engraved on it in Gothic script.

"Who's E.B.?" I said.

"Only the garden interests me, Mr. Aquilinas—I do not know who she is."

I looked out at the weird garden. "Why does it interest you—what's all this for? You're not doing it to his orders, are you? You're doing it for yourself."

Sagittarius smiled bleakly. "You are astute." He waved an arm at the warm foliage that seemed more reptilian than plant and more mammalian, in its own way, then either. "You know what I see out there? I see deep-sea canyons where lost submarines cruise through a silence of twilit green, threatened by the waving tentacles of predators, half-fish, half-plant, and watched by the eyes of long-dead mermen whose blood went to feed their young; where squids and rays fight in a graceful dance of death, clouds of black ink merging with clouds of red blood, drifting to the surface, sipped at by sharks in passing, where they will be seen by mariners leaning over the rails of their ships; maddened, the mariners will fling themselves overboard to sail slowly toward those distant plant-creatures already feasting on the corpse of squid and ray. This is the world I can bring to the land—that is my ambition."

He stared at me, paused, and said: "My skull—*it's like a monstrous goldfish bowl!*"

I nipped back to the house to find Bismarck had returned to his room. He was sitting in a plush armchair, a hidden HiFi playing, of all things, a Ravel String Quartet.

"No Wagner?" I said and then: "Who's E.B.?"

"Later," he said. "My assistant will answer your questions for the moment. He should be waiting for you outside."

There was a car parked outside the house—a battered Volkswagen containing a neatly uniformed man of below average height, a small tooth-brush moustache, a stray lock of black hair falling over his forehead, black gloves on his hands which gripped a military cane in his lap. When he saw me come out he smiled, said "Aha," and got briskly from the car to shake my hand with a slight bow.

"Adolf Hitler," he said, "Captain of Uniformed Detectives in Precinct XII. Police Chief Bismarck has put me at your service."

"Glad to hear it. Do you know much about him?"

Hitler opened the car door for me and I got in. He went round the other side, slid into the driving seat.

"The chief?" He shook his head. "He is somewhat remote. I do not know him well—there are several ranks between us. Usually my orders came from him indirectly. This time he chose to see me himself and give me my orders."

"What were they, these orders?"

"Simply to help you in this investigation."

"There isn't much to investigate. You're completely loyal to your chief I take it?"

"Of course." Hitler seemed honestly puzzled. He started the car and we drove down the drive and out along a flat, white road, surmounted on both sides by great heaps of overgrown rubble.

"The murdered man had paper lungs, eh?" he said.

"Yes. Guess he must have come from Rome. He looked a bit like an Italian."

"Or a Jew, eh?"

"I don't think so. What made you think that?"

"The Russian watch, the oriental shoes—the nose. That was a big nose he had. And they still have paper lungs in Moscow, you know."

His logic seemed a bit off-beat to me but I let it pass. We turned a corner and entered a residential section where a lot of buildings were still standing. I noticed that one of them had a bar in its cellar. "How about a drink?" I said.

"Here?" He seemed surprised, or maybe nervous.

"Why not?"

So he stopped the car and we went down the steps into the bar. A girl was singing. She was a plumpish brunette with a small, good voice. She was singing in English and I caught the chorus:

> *Nobody's grievin' for Steven,*
> *And Stevie ain't grievin' no more,*
> *For Steve took his life in a prison cell,*
> *And Johnny took a new whore.*

It was the latest hit in England. We ordered beers from the bartender. He seemed to know Hitler well because he laughed and slapped him on the shoulder and didn't charge us for the beer. Hitler seemed embarrassed.

"Who was that?" I asked.

"Oh, his name is Weill. I know him slightly."

"More than slightly, it looks like."

Hitler seemed unhappy and undid his uniform jacket, tilted his cap back on his head and tried unsuccessfully to push back the stray lock of hair. He looked a sad little man and I felt that maybe my habit of asking questions was out of line here. I drank my beer and watched the singer. Hitler kept his back to her but I noticed she kept looking at him.

"What do you know about this Sagittarius?" I asked.

Hitler shrugged. "Very little."

Weill turned up again behind the bar and asked us if we wanted more beer. We said we didn't.

"Sagittarius?" Weill spoke up brightly. "Are you talking about that crank?"

"He's a crank, is he?" I said.

"That's not fair, Kurt," Hitler said. "He's a brilliant man, a biologist—"

"Who was thrown out of his job because he was insane!"

"That is unkind, Kurt," Hitler said reprovingly. "He was investigating the potential sentience of plant life. A perfectly reasonable line of scientific inquiry."

From the corner of the room someone laughed jeeringly. It was a shaggy-haired old man sitting by himself with a glass of schnapps on the little table in front of him.

Weill pointed at him. "Ask Albert. He knows about science."

Hitler pursed his lips and looked at the floor. "He's just an embittered old mathematics teacher—he's jealous of Felipe," he said quietly, so that the old man wouldn't hear.

"Who is he?" I asked Weill.

"Albert? A *really* brilliant man. He has never had the recognition he deserves. Do you want to meet him?"

But the shaggy man was leaving. He waved a hand at Hitler and Weill. "Kurt, Captain Hitler—good day."

"Good day, Doctor Einstein," muttered Hitler. He turned to me. "Where would you like to go now?"

"A tour of the places that sell jewellery, I guess," I said, fingering the pendant in my pocket, "I may be on the wrong track altogether, but it's the only track I can find at the moment."

We toured the jewellers. By nightfall we were nowhere nearer finding out who had owned the thing. I'd just have to get the truth out of Bismarck the next day, though I knew it wouldn't be easy. He wouldn't like answering my personal questions at all. Hitler dropped me off at the Precinct House where a cell had been converted into a bedroom for me.

I sat on the hard bed smoking and thinking. I was just about to get undressed and go to sleep when I started to think about the bar we'd been in earlier. I was sure someone there could help me. On impulse I left the cell and went out into the deserted street. It was still very hot and the sky was full of heavy clouds. Looked like a storm was due.

I got a cab back to the bar. It was still open.

Weill wasn't serving there now—he was playing the piano-accordion for the same girl singer I'd seen earlier. He nodded to me as I came in. I leaned on the bar and ordered a beer from the barman.

When the number was over Weill unstrapped his accordion and joined me. The girl followed him.

"Adolf not with you?" he said.

"He went home. He's a good friend of yours, is he?"

"Oh, we met years ago in Austria. He's a nice man, you know. He should never have become a policeman, he's too mild."

"That's the impression I got. Why did he ever join in the first place?"

Weill smiled and shook his head. He was a short, thin man, wearing heavy glasses. He had a large, sensitive mouth. "Sense of duty, perhaps. He has a great sense of duty. He is very religious, too—a devout Catholic. I think that weighs on him. You know these converts, they accept nothing, are torn by their consciences. I never yet met a happy Catholic convert."

"He seems to have a thing about Jews."

Weill frowned. "What sort of thing? I've never really noticed. Many of his friends are Jews. I am, and Sagittarius. . . ."

"Sagittarius is a friend of his?"

"Oh, more an acquaintance I should think. I've seen them together a couple of times."

It began to thunder outside. Then it started to rain.

Weill walked toward the door and began to pull down the blind. Through the noise of the storm I heard another sound, a strange, metallic grinding sound, a crunching sound.

"What's that?" I called. Weill shook his head and walked back towards the bar. The place was empty now. "I'm going to have a look," I said.

I went to the door, opened it, and climbed the steps.

Marching across the ruins, illuminated by rapid flashes of lightning like gunfire, I saw a gigantic metal monster, as big as a tall building. Supported on four telescopic legs, it lumbered at right angles to the street. From its huge body and head the snouts of guns stuck out in all directions. Lightning sometimes struck it and it made an ear-shattering bell-like clang, paused to fire upward at the source of the lightning, and marched on.

I ran down the steps and flung open the door. Weill was tidying up the bar. I described what I'd seen.

"What is it, Weill?"

The short man shook his head. "I don't know. At a guess it is something Berlin's conquerors left behind."

"It looked as if it was made here . . ."

"Perhaps it was. After all, who conquered Berlin—?"

A woman screamed from a back room, high and brief.

Weill dropped a glass and ran towards the room. I followed. He opened the door. The room was homely. A table covered by a thick, dark cloth, laid with salt and pepper, knives and forks, a piano near the window, a girl lying on the floor.

"Eva!" Weill gasped, kneeling beside the body.

I gave the room another once over. Standing on a small coffee table was a plant. It looked at first rather like a cactus of unpleasantly mottled green, though the top curved so that it resembled a snake about to strike. An eyeless, noseless snake—with a mouth. There was a mouth. It opened as I approached. There were teeth in the mouth—or rather thorns arranged the way teeth are. One thorn seemed to be missing near the front. I backed away from the plant and inspected the corpse. I found the thorn in her wrist. I left it there.

"She is dead," Weill said softly, standing up and looking around. "How?"

"She was bitten by that poisonous plant," I said.

"Plant . . . ? I must call the police."

"That wouldn't be wise at this stage maybe," I said as I left. I knew where I was going.

Bismarck's house—and the pleasure garden of Felipe Sagittarius.

It took me time to find a cab and I was soaked through when I did. I told the cabby to step on it.

I had the cab stop before we got to the house, paid it off and walked across the lawns. I didn't bother to ring the doorbell. I let myself in by the window, using my pocket glass-cutter.

I heard voices coming from upstairs. I followed the sound until I located it—Bismarck's study. I inched the door open.

Hitler was there. He had a gun pointed at Otto von Bismarck who was still in full uniform. They both looked pale. Hitler's hand was shaking and Bismarck was moaning slightly.

Bismarck stopped moaning to say pleadingly, "I wasn't blackmailing Eva Braun, you fool—she liked me."

Hitler laughed curtly, half hysterically. "Liked *you*—a fat old man."

"She liked fat old men."

"She wasn't that kind of girl."

"Who told you this, anyway?"

"The investigator told me some. And Weill rang me half an hour ago to tell me some more—also that Eva had been killed. I thought Sagittarius was my friend. I was wrong. He is your hired assassin. Well, tonight I intend to do my own killing."

"Captain Hitler—I am your superior officer!"

The gun wavered as Bismarck's voice recovered some of its authority. I realized that the HiFi had been playing quietly all the time. Curiously it was Bartok's 5th String Quartet.

Bismarck moved his hand. "You are completely mistaken. That man you hired to follow Eva here last night—he was Eva's ex-lover!"

Hitler's lip trembled.

"You knew," said Bismarck.

"I suspected it."

"You also knew the dangers of the garden, because Felipe had told you about them. The vines killed him as he sneaked toward the summer house."

The gun steadied. Bismarck looked scared.

He pointed at Hitler. "You killed him—not I!" he screamed. "You sent him to his death. You killed Stalin out of jealousy. You hoped he would kill me and Eva first. You were too frightened, too weak, to confront any of us openly!"

Hitler shouted wordlessly, put both hands to the gun and

pulled the trigger several times. Some of the shots went wide, but one hit Bismarck in his Iron Cross, pierced it and got him in the heart. He fell backward and as he did so his uniform ripped apart and his helmet fell off. I ran into the room and took the gun from Hitler, who was crying. I checked that Bismarck was dead. I saw what had caused the uniform to rip open. He had been wearing a corset—one of the bullets must have cut the cord. It was a heavy corset and had had a lot to hold in.

I felt sorry for Hitler. I helped him sit down as he sobbed. He looked small and wretched.

"What have I killed?" he stuttered. "What have I killed?"

"Did Bismarck send that plant to Eva Braun to silence her because I was getting too close?"

Hitler nodded, snorted and started to cry again.

I put the gun on the mantelpiece.

I looked toward the door. A man stood there, hesitantly. It was Sagittarius.

He nodded to me.

"Hitler's just shot Bismarck," I explained.

"Bismarck had you send Eva Braun that plant, is that so?" I said.

"So it appears," he said.

"Yes. A beautiful cross between a common cactus, a Venus Flytrap and a rose—the venom was curare, of course."

Hitler got up and walked from the room. We watched him leave. He was still sniffling.

"Where are you going?" I asked.

"To get some air," I heard him say as he went down the stairs.

"The repression of sexual desires," said Sagittarius seating himself in an armchair and resting his feet comfortably on Bismarck's corpse. "It is the cause of so much trouble. If only the passions that lie beneath the surface, the desires that are locked in the mind could be allowed to range free, what a better place the world would be."

"Maybe," I said.

"Are you going to make any arrests, Herr Aquilinas?"

"It's my job to make a report on my investigation, not to make arrests," I said.

"Will there be any repercussions concerned with this business?"

I laughed. "There are always repercussions," I told him.

From the garden came a peculiar barking noise.

"What's that?" I asked. "The wolfhounds?"

Sagittarius giggled. "No, no—the dog-plant, I fear."

I ran out of the room and down the stairs until I reached the kitchen. The sheet-covered corpse was still lying on the table. I was going to open the door on to the garden when I stopped and pressed my face to the window instead.

The whole garden was moving in what appeared to be an agitated dance. Foliage threshed about and, even with the door closed, the strange scent was even less bearable than it had been earlier.

I thought I saw a figure struggling with some thick-boled shrubs. I heard a growling noise, a tearing sound, a scream and a long drawn out groan.

Suddenly the garden was motionless.

I turned. Sagittarius stood behind me, his hands folded on his chest, his eyes staring down at the floor.

"It seems your dog-plant got him," I said.

"He knew me—he knew the garden."

"Suicide maybe?"

"Very likely." Sagittarius unfolded his hands and looked up at me. "I liked him, you know. He was something of a protégé. If you had not interfered none of this might have happened. He might have gone far with me to guide him."

"You'll find other protégés," I said.

"Let us hope so."

The sky outside began to lighten imperceptibly. The rain was now only a drizzle, falling on the thirsty leaves of the plants in the garden.

"Are you going to stay on here?" I asked him.

"Yes—I have the garden to work on. Bismarck's servants will look after me."

"I guess they will," I said.

I went back up the stairs and walked out of that house

into the dawn, cold and rain-washed. I turned up my collar and began to climb across the ruins.

by MICHAEL MOORCOCK

Behold the Man
The Black Corridor
The Ice Schooner
*The Final Programme, A Cure for Cancer, The English
     Assassin,* and *The Condition of Muzak* (forthcoming)
     comprising the Jerry Cornelius tetrology
An Alien Heat

Under Michael Moorcock, *New Worlds* became an experimental magazine openly dedicated to creating the new literature. Moorcock began developing and preaching the theoretical basis for the new speculative fiction: a merger of speculative content with inventive form; the notion of "non-linear" fiction that would free itself from traditional sequential plots and straight-line structure; allusive prose instead of literal-mindedness; and honesty and openness in dealing with the realities of man as a political, social, and sexual animal.

By 1966 the transformation of *New Worlds* was complete. Inevitably, the hard-core science fiction readership began to fall away, but the British Arts Council recognized the intrinsic worth of the magazine with a formal grant. For interesting things were coming out of *New Worlds*. J. G. Ballard was developing an entirely new form of short story, the "condensed novel," a kind of cinematic fiction which exists as a series of intercut prose images rather than as a linear, plotted story. My own story, "No Direction Home," is a more conventional example of this form, directly influenced nevertheless by Ballard, as is some of the work of other writers developed in *New Worlds*—such as M. John Harrison, James Sallis, Graham Charnock, and to some extent even Moorcock himself.

Brian Aldiss' conventional science fiction was rapidly evolving into a powerful mastery of adventurous prose, speculative content, and experimental form that would reach a peak with the serialization in *New Worlds* of his novel *Barefoot in the Head*. A complex Joycean vision of a Europe "bombed back into the stoned age by the Acid Head War," it is truly psychedelic in prose, content, and form.

Moorcock was also publishing decent poetry with speculative imagery and developing several interesting new writers like Langdon Jones, Charnock, Sallis, and Harrison. He was also offering an outlet for the more adventurous fiction of writers like Thomas M. Disch, Roger Zelazny, and John T. Sladek, who previously had been publishing mature and idiosyncratic speculative fiction like "Descending" and "For a Breath I Tarry" in conventional American science fiction magazines, where it went unnoticed by everyone but hard-core science fiction readers. British speculative fiction was bubbling with creative ferment.

Finally, in 1966, Judith Merril, the book reviewer for *The Magazine of Fantasy and Science Fiction*, a frequent visitor to England and the most influential science fiction critic in America at the time, began writing about the *New Worlds* school for American readers and the movement began to become truly transatlantic. Somewhere around mid-ocean the label "New Wave" became attached, and the revolution was on.

No Direction Home

NORMAN SPINRAD

> "How does it feel
> To be on your own?
> With no direction home . . .
> Like a complete unknown.
> Like a rolling stone."
>
> —Bob Dylan
> *Like a Rolling Stone*

"But I once *did* succeed in stuffing it all back in Pandora's box," Richarson said, taking another hit. "You remember Pandora Deutchman, don't you, Will? Everybody in the biochemistry department stuffed it all in Pandora's box at one time or another. I seem to vaguely remember one party when you did it yourself."

"Oh you're a real comedian, Dave," Goldberg said, stubbing out his roach and jamming a cork into the glass vial which he had been filling from the petcock at the end of the apparatus' run. "Any day now, I expect you to start slipping strychnine into the goods. That'd be pretty good for a yock, too."

"You know, I never thought of that before. Maybe you got something there. Let a few people go out with a smile, satisfaction guaranteed. Christ, Will, we could tell them exactly what it was and still sell some of the stuff."

"That's not funny, man," Goldberg said, handing the vial to Richarson, who carefully snugged it away with the others in the excelsior-packed box. "It's not funny because it's true."

"Hey, you're not getting an attack of morals, are you? Don't move, I'll be right back with some methalin—that oughta get your head straight."

"My head is straight already. Canabinolic acid, our own invention."

"Canabinolic acid? Where did you get that, in a drugstore? We haven't bothered with it for three years."

Goldberg placed another empty vial in the rack under the petcock and opened the valve. "Bought it on the street for kicks," he said. "Kids are brewing it in their bathtubs now." He shook his head, almost a random gesture. "Remember what a bitch the original synthesis was?"

"Science marches on!"

"Too bad we couldn't have patented the stuff," Goldberg said as he contemplated the thin stream of clear green liquid entering the open mouth of the glass vial. "We could've retired off the royalties by now."

"If we had the Mafia to collect for us."

"That might be arranged."

"Yeah, well maybe I should look into it," Richarson said as Goldberg handed him another full vial. "We shouldn't be pigs about it, though. Just about ten percent off the top at the manufacturing end. I don't believe in stifling private enterprise."

"No really, Dave," Goldberg said, "maybe we made a mistake in not trying to patent the stuff. People *do* patent combo psychedelics, you know."

"You don't mean *people*, man, you mean outfits like American Marijuana and Psychedelics, Inc. They can afford the lawyers and grease. They can work the FDA's head. We can't."

Goldberg opened the petcock valve. "Yeah, well at least it'll be six months or so before the Dope Industry or anyone else figures out how to synthesize this new crap, and by that time I think I'll have just about licked the decay problem in the cocanol extraction process. We should be one step ahead of the squares for at least another year."

"You know what I think, Will?" Richarson said, patting the side of the half-filled box of vials. "I think we got a holy mission, is what. I think we're servants of the evolutionary process. Every time we come up with a new psychedelic, we're advancing the evolution of human consciousness. We develop the stuff and make our bread off it for a while, and then the Dope Industry comes up with our synthesis and mass produces it, and then we gotta come up with the next drug out so we can still set our tables in style. If it weren't for the Dope Industry and the way the drug laws are set up, we could stand still and become bloated plutocrats just by putting out the same old dope year after year. This way, we're doing some good in the world, we're doing something to further human evolution."

Goldberg handed him another full vial. "Screw human evolution," he said. "What has human evolution ever done for us?"

"As you know, Dr. Taller, we're having some unforeseen side-effects with eucomorfamine," General Carlyle said, stuffing his favorite Dunhill with rough-cut burley. Taller took out a pack of Golds, extracted a joint, and lit it with a lighter bearing an Air Force rather than a Psychedelics, Inc. ensignia. Perhaps this had been a deliberate gesture, perhaps not.

"With a psychedelic as new as eucomorfamine, General," Taller said, "no side-effects can quite be called 'unforeseen'. After all, even Project Groundhog itself is an experiment."

Carlyle lit his pipe and sucked in a mouthful of smoke which was good and carcinogenic; the General believed that a good soldier should cultivate at least one foolhardy minor vice. "No word-games, please, Doctor," he said. "Eucomorfamine is supposed to help our men in the Groundhog moonbase deal with the claustrophobic conditions; it is not supposed to promote faggotry in the ranks. The reports I've been getting indicate that the drug is doing both. The Air Force does not want it to do both. Therefore, by definition, eucomorfamine has an undesirable side-effect. Therefore, your contract is up for review."

"General, General, psychedelics are not uniforms, after all. You can't expect us to tailor them to order. You asked for a drug that would combat claustrophobia without impairing alertness or the sleep cycle or attention-span or initiative. You think this is easy? Eucomorfamine produces claustrophilia without any side-effect but a raising of the level of sexual energy. As such, I consider it one of the minor miracles of psychedelic science."

"That's all very well, Taller, but surely you can see that we simply cannot tolerate violent homosexual behavior among our men in the moonbase."

Taller smiled, perhaps somewhat fatuously. "But you can't very well tolerate a high rate of claustrophobic breakdown, either," he said. "You have only four obvious alternatives, General Carlyle: continue to use eucomorfamine and accept a certain level of homosexual incidents, discontinue eucomorfamine and accept a very high level of claustrophobic breakdown, or cancel Project Groundhog. *Or. . . ."*

It dawned upon the General that he had been the object of a rather sophisticated sales pitch. "Or go to a drug that would cancel out the side-effect of eucomorfamine," he said. "Your company just wouldn't happen to have such a drug in the works, would it?"

Dr. Taller gave him a we're-all-men-of-the-world grin. "Psychedelics, Inc. *has* been working on a sexual suppressant," he admitted none too grudgingly. "Not an easy psychic spec to fill. The problem is that if you actually decrease sexual energy, you tend to get impaired performance in the higher cerebral centers, which is all very well in penal institutions, but hardly acceptable in Project Groundhog's case. The trick is to channel the excess energy elsewhere. We decided that the only viable alternative was to siphon it off into mystical fugue-states. Once we worked it out, the biochemistry became merely a matter of detail. We're about ready to bring the drug we've developed—trade name nadabrin—into the production stage."

The general's pipe had gone out. He did not bother to relight it. Instead, he took 5 mg. of lebemil, which seemed more to the point at the moment. "This nadabrin," he said very deliberately, "it bleeds off the excess sexuality into *what?* Fugue-states? Trances? We certainly don't need a drug that makes our men psychotic."

"Of course not. About three hundred micrograms of nadabrin will give a man a mystical experience that lasts less than four hours. He won't be much good to you during that time, to be sure, but his sexual energy level will be severely depressed for about a week. Three hundred micrograms to each man on eucomorfamine, say every five days, to be on the safe side."

General Carlyle relit his pipe and ruminated. Things seemed to be looking up. "Sounds pretty good," he finally admitted. "But what about the content of the mystical experiences? Nothing that would impair devotion to duty?"

Taller snubbed out his roach. "I've taken nadabrin myself," he said. "No problems."

"What was it like?"

Taller once again put on his fatuous smile. "That's the best part of nadabrin," he said. "I don't remember what it was like. You don't retain any memories of what happens to you under nadabrin. Genuine fugue-state. So you can be sure the mystical experiences don't have any undesirable content, can't you? Or at any rate, you can be sure that the experience can't impair a man's military performance."

"What the men don't remember can't hurt them, eh?"

"What was that, General?"

"I said I'd recommend that we give it a try."

They sat together in a corner booth back in the smoke, sizing each other up while the crowd in the joint yammered and swirled around them in some other reality, like a Bavarian merrygoround.

"What are you on?" he said, noticing that her hair seemed black and seamless like a beetle's carapace, a dark metal helmet framing her pale face in glory. Wow.

"Peyotadrene," she said, her lips moving like incredibly jeweled and articulated metal flower-petals. "Been up for about three hours. What's your trip?"

"Canabinolic acid," he said, the distortion of his mouth's movement casting his face into an ideogramic pattern which was barely decipherable to her perception as a foreshadowing of energy release. Maybe they would make it.

"I haven't tried any of that stuff for months," she said. "I hardly remember what that reality feels like." Her skin luminesced from within, a translucent white china mask over

334 *Modern Science Fiction*

a yellow candle-flame. She was a magnificent artifact, a creation of jaded and sophisticated gods.

"It feels good," he said, his eyebrows forming a set of
curves which, when considered as part of a pattern containing the movement of his lips against his teeth, indicated
a clear desire to donate energy to the filling of her void. They
would make it. "Call me old-fashioned maybe, but I still
think canabinolic acid is groovy stuff."

"Do you think you could go on a sex-trip behind it?" she
asked. The folds and wrinkles of her ears had been carved
with microprecision out of pink ivory.

"Well, I suppose so, in a peculiar kind of way," he said,
hunching his shoulders forward in a clear gesture of offering,
an alignment with the pattern of her movement through
space-time that she could clearly perceive as intersecting her
trajectory. "I mean, if you want me to ball you, I think I can
make it."

The tiny gold hairs on her face were a microscopic field
of wheat shimmering in a shifting summer breeze as she said:
"That's the most meaningful thing anyone has said to me
in hours."

The convergence of every energy configuration in the entire universe toward complete identity with the standing
wave pattern of its maximum ideal structure was brightly
mirrored for the world to see in the angle between the curves
of his lips as he spoke.

Cardinal McGavin took a peyotadrene-mescamil combo
and 5 mg. of metadrene an hour and a half before his meeting with Cardinal Rillo; he had decided to try to deal with
Rome on a mystical rather than a political level, and that
particular prescription made him feel most deeply Christian.
And the Good Lord knew that it could become very difficult
to feel deeply Christian when dealing with a representative
of the Pope.

Cardinal Rillo arrived punctually at three, just as Cardinal
McGavin was approaching his mystical peak; the man's punctuality was legend. Cardinal McGavin felt pathos in that:
the sadness of a Prince of the Church whose major impact

on the souls of his fellows lay in his slavery to the hands of a clock. Because the ascetic-looking old man, with his colorless eyes and pencil-thin lips, was so thoroughly unloveable, Cardinal McGavin found himself cherishing the man for his very existential hopelessness. He sent forth a silent prayer that he, or if not he then at least someone, might be chosen as an instrument through which this poor cold creature might be granted a measure of Divine Grace.

Cardinal Rillo accepted the amenities with cold formality, and in the same spirit agreed to share some claret. Cardinal McGavin knew better than to offer a joint; Cardinal Rillo had been in the forefront of the opposition which had caused the Pope to delay his inevitable encyclical on marijuana for long ludicrous years. That the Pope had chosen such an emissary in this matter was not a good sign.

Cardinal Rillo sipped at his wine in sour silence for long moments while Cardinal McGavin was nearly overcome with sorrow at the thought of the loneliness of the soul of this man, who could not even break the solemnity of his persona to share some Vatican gossip over a little wine with a fellow Cardinal. Finally, the Papal emissary cleared his throat—a dry, archaic gesture—and got right to the point.

"The Pontiff has instructed me to convey his concern at the addition of psychedelics to the composition of the communion host in the Archdiocese of New York," he said, the tone of his voice making it perfectly clear that he wished the Holy Father had given him a much less cautious warning to deliver. But if the Pope had learned anything at all from the realities of this schismatic era, it was caution. Especially when dealing with the American hierarchy, whose allegiance to Rome was based on nothing firmer than nostalgia and symbolic convenience. The Pope had been the last to be convinced of his own fallibility, but in the last few years events seemed to have finally brought the new refinement of Divine Truth home.

"I acknowledge and respect the Holy Father's concern," Cardinal McGavin said. "I shall pray for divine resolution of his doubt."

"I didn't say anything about doubt!" Cardinal Rillo

snapped, his lips moving with the crispness of pincers. "How can you impute doubt to the Holy Father?"

Cardinal McGavin's spirit soared over a momentary spark of anger at the man's pigheadedness; he tried to give Cardinal Rillo's soul a portion of peace. "I stand corrected," he said. "I shall pray for the alleviation of the Holy Father's concern."

But Cardinal Rillo was implacable and inconsolable; his face was a membrane of control over a musculature of rage. "You can more easily relieve the Holy Father's concern by removing the peyotadrene from your hosts!" he said.

"Are those the words of the Holy Father?" Cardinal McGavin asked, knowing the answer.

"Those are my words, Cardinal McGavin," Cardinal Rillo said, "and you would do well to heed them. The fate of your immortal soul may be at stake."

A flash of insight, a sudden small satori, rippled through Cardinal McGavin: Rillo was sincere. For him, the question of a chemically-augmented host was not a matter of Church politics, as it probably was to the Pope; it touched on an area of deep religious conviction. Cardinal Rillo was indeed concerned for the state of his soul and it behooved him, both as a Cardinal and as a Catholic, to treat the matter seriously on that level. For after all, chemically-augmented communion was a matter of deep religious conviction for him as well. He and Cardinal Rillo faced each other across a gap of existentially-meaningful theological disagreement.

"Perhaps the fate of yours as well, Cardinal Rillo," he said.

"I didn't come here all the way from Rome to seek spiritual guidance from a man who is skating on the edge of heresy, Cardinal McGavin. I came here to deliver the Holy Father's warning that an encyclical may be issued against your position. Need I remind you that if you disobey such an encyclical, you may be excommunicated?"

"Would you be genuinely sorry to see that happen?" Cardinal McGavin asked, wondering how much of the threat was Rillo's wishful thinking, and how much the instructions of the

Pope. "Or would you simply feel that the Church had defended itself properly?"

"Both," Cardinal Rillo said without hesitation.

"I like that answer," Cardinal McGavin said, tossing down the rest of his glass of claret. It was a good answer—sincere on both counts. Cardinal Rillo feared both for the Church and for the soul of the Archbishop of New York, and there was no doubt that he quite properly put the Church first. His sincerity was spiritually refreshing, even though he was thoroughly wrong all around. "But you see, part of the gift of Grace that comes with a scientifically-sound chemical augmentation of communion is a certainty that no one, not even the Pope, can do anything to cut you off from communion with God. In psychedelic communion, one experiences the love of God directly. It's always just a host away; faith is no longer even necessary."

Cardinal Rillo grew somber. "It is my duty to report that to the Pope," he said. "I trust you realize that."

"Who am I talking to, Cardinal Rillo, you or the Pope?"

"You are talking to the Catholic Church, Cardinal McGavin," Rillo said. "I am an emissary of the Holy Father." Cardinal McGavin felt an instant pang of guilt: his sharpness had caused Cardinal Rillo to imply an untruth out of anger, for surely his Papal mission was far more limited than he had tried to intimate. The Pope was too much of a realist to make the empty threat of excommunication against a Prince of the Church who believed that his power of excommunication was itself meaningless.

But again, a sudden flash of insight illuminated the Cardinal's mind with truth: in the eyes of Cardinal Rillo, in the eyes of an important segment of the Church hierarchy, the threat of excommunication still held real meaning. To accept their position on chemically augmented communion was to accept the notion that the word of the Pope could withdraw a man from Divine Grace. To accept the sanctity and validity of psychedelic communion was to deny the validity of excommunication.

"You know, Cardinal Rillo," he said, "I firmly believe that

if I am excommunicated by the Pope, it will threaten my soul not one iota."

"That's merely cheap blasphemy!"

"I'm sorry," Cardinal McGavin said sincerely, "I meant to be neither cheap nor blasphemous. All I was trying to do was explain that excommunication can hardly be meaningful when God through the psychedelic sciences has seen fit to grant us a means of certain direct experience of his countenance. I believe with all my heart that this is true. You believe with all your heart that it is not."

"I believe that what you experience in your psychedelic communion is nothing less than a masterstroke of Satan, Cardinal McGavin. Evil is infinitely subtle; might not it finally masquerade as the ultimate good? The Devil is not known as the Prince of Liars without reason. I believe that you are serving Satan in what you sincerely believe is the service of God. Is there any way that you can be sure that I am wrong?"

"Can you be sure that *I'm* not right?" Cardinal McGavin said. "If I am, you are attempting to stifle the will of God and willfully removing yourself from His Grace."

"We cannot both be right. . . ." Cardinal Rillo said.

And the burning glare of a terrible and dark mystical insight filled Cardinal McGavin's soul with terror, a harsh illumination of his existential relationship to the Church and to God: they both couldn't be right, but there was no reason why they both couldn't be wrong. Apart from both God and Satan, existed the Void.

Dr. Braden gave Johnny a pat-on-the-head smile and handed him a mango-flavored lollypop from the supply of goodies in his lower-left desk drawer. Johnny took the lollypop, unwrapped it quickly, popped it into his mouth, leaned back in his chair, and began to suck the sweet avidly, oblivious to the rest of the world. It was a good sign—a preschooler with a proper reaction to a proper basic prescription should focus strongly and completely on the most interesting element in its environment, should be fond of unusual flavors. In the first four years of its life, a child's sensorium should be tuned to accept the widest possible spectrum of sensual stimulation.

Braden turned his attention to the boy's mother, who sat rather nervously on the edge of her chair smoking a joint. "Now, now, Mrs. Lindstrom, there's nothing to worry about," he said. "Johnny has been responding quite normally to his prescription. His attention-span is suitably short for a child of his age, his sensual range slightly exceeds the optimum norm, his sleep pattern is regular and properly deep. And as you requested, he has been given a constant sense of universal love."

"But then why did the school doctor ask me to have his basic prescription changed, Dr. Braden? He said that Johnny's prescription was giving him the wrong personality pattern for a school-age child."

Dr. Braden was rather annoyed, though of course he would never betray it to the nervous young mother. He knew the sort of failed G.P. who usually occupied a school doctor's position; a faded old fool who knew about as much about psychedelic pediatrics as he did about brain surgery. What he did know was worse than nothing—a smattering of half-assed generalities and pure rubbish that was just enough to convince him that he was an expert. Which entitled him to go around frightening the mothers of other people's patients, no doubt.

"I'm . . . ah, certain you misunderstood, what the school doctor said, Mrs. Lindstrom," Dr. Braden said. "At least I hope you did, because if you didn't, then the man is mistaken. You see, modern psychedelic pediatrics recognizes that the child needs to have his consciousness focused in different areas at different stages of his development, if he is to grow up to be a healthy, maximized individual. A child of Johnny's age is in a transitional stage. In order to prepare him for schooling, I'll simply have to alter his prescription so as to increase his attention-span, lower his sensory intensity a shade, and increase his interest in abstractions. Then he'll do fine in school, Mrs. Lindstrom."

Dr. Braden gave the young woman a moderately-stern admonishing frown. "You really should have brought Johnny in for a check-up *before* he started school, you know."

Mrs. Lindstrom puffed nervously on her joint while Johnny continued to suck happily on his lollypop. "Well . . . I was sort of afraid to, Dr. Braden," she admitted. "I know it sounds silly, but I was afraid that if you changed his prescription to what the school wanted, you'd stop the paxum. I didn't want that—I think it's more important for Johnny to continue to feel universal love than increasing his attention-span or any of that stuff. You're not going to stop the paxum, are you?"

"Quite the contrary, Mrs. Lindstrom," Dr. Braden said. "I'm going to increase his dose slightly and give him 10 mg. of orodalamine daily. He'll submit to the necessary authority of his teachers with a sense of trust and love, rather than out of fear."

For the first time during the visit, Mrs. Lindstrom smiled. "Then it all really *is* all right, isn't it?" She radiated happiness born of relief.

Dr. Braden smiled back at her, basking in the sudden surge of good vibrations. This was his peak-experience in pediatrics: feeling the genuine gratitude of a worried mother whose fears he had thoroughly relieved. This was what being a doctor was all about. She trusted him. She put the consciousness of her child in his hands, trusting that those hands would not falter or fail. He was proud and grateful to be a psychedelic pediatrician. He was maximizing human happiness.

"Yes, Mrs. Lindstrom," he said soothingly, "everything is going to be all right."

In the chair in the corner, Johnny Lindstrom sucked on his lollypop, his face transfigured with boyish bliss.

There were moments when Bill Watney got a soul-deep queasy feeling about psychedelic design, and lately he was getting those bad flashes more and more often. He was glad to have caught Spiegelman alone in the designers' lounge; if anyone could do anything for his head, Lennie was it. "I dunno," he said, washing down 15 mg. of lebemil with a stiff shot of bourbon, "I'm really thinking of getting out of this business."

Leonard Spiegelman lit a Gold with his 14-carat gold lighter—nothing but the best for the best in the business— smiled across the coffee-table at Watney, and said quite genially: "You're out of your mind, Bill."

Watney sat hunched slightly forward in his easy chair, studying Spiegelman, the best artist Psychedelics, Inc. had, and envying the older man. Envying not only his talent, but his attitude towards his work. Lennie Spiegelman was not only certain that what he was doing was right, he enjoyed every minute of it. Watney wished he could be like Spiegelman. Spiegelman was happy; he radiated the contented aura of a man who really did have everything he wanted.

Spiegelman opened his arms in a gesture that seemed to make the whole designers' lounge his personal property. "We're the world's best-pampered artists," he said. "We come up with two or three viable drug designs a year, and we can live like kings. And we're practising the world's ultimate artform: creating realities. We're the luckiest mothers alive! Why would anyone with your talent want out of psychedelic design?"

Watney found it difficult to put into words, which was ridiculous for a psychedelic designer, whose work it was to describe new possibilities in human consciousness well enough for the biochemists to develop psychedelics which would transform his specs into styles of reality. It was humiliating to be at a loss for words in front of Lennie Spiegelman, a man he both envied and admired. "I'm getting bad flashes lately," he finally said. "Deep flashes that go through every style of consciousness that I try, flashes that tell me I should be ashamed and disgusted about what I'm doing."

Oh, oh, Lennie Spiegelman thought, the kid is coming up with his first case of designer's cafard. He's floundering around with that no direction home syndrome and he thinks it's the end of the world. "I know what's bothering you, Bill," he said. "It happens to all of us at one time or another. You feel that designing psychedelic specs is a solipsistic occupation, right? You think there's something morally wrong about designing

new styles of consciousness for other people, that we're playing God, that continually altering people's consciousness in
ways only we fully understand is a thing that mere mortals
have no right to do, like hubris, eh?"

Watney flashed admiration for Spiegelman—his certainty
wasn't based on a thick ignorance of the existential doubt
of their situation. There was hope in that, too. "How can you
understand all that, Lennie," he said, "and still dig psychedelic
design the way you do?"

"Because it's a load of crap, that's why," Spiegelman said.
"Look kid, we're artists, commercial artists at that. We design psychedelics, styles of reality; we don't tell anyone what
to think. If people like the realities we design for them, they
buy the drugs, and if they don't like our art, they don't.
People aren't going to buy food that tastes lousy, music that
makes their ears hurt, or drugs that put them in bummer
realities. *Somebody* is going to design styles of consciousness
for the human race, if not artists like us, then a lot of crummy
politicians and power-freaks."

"But what makes us any better than them? Why do we
have any more right to play games with the consciousness
of the human race than they do?"

The kid is really dense, Spiegelman thought. But then he
smiled, remembering that he had been on the same stupid
trip when he was Watney's age. "Because we're artists, and
they're not," he said. "We're not out to control people. We
get our kicks from carving something beautiful out of the
void. All we want to do is enrich people's lives. We're creating new styles of consciousness that we think are improved
realities, but we're not shoving them down people's throats.
We're just laying out our wares for the public—right doesn't
even enter into it. We have a compulsion to practice our art.
Right and wrong are arbitrary concepts that vary with the
style of consciousness, so how on earth can you talk about the
right and wrong of psychedelic design? The only way you
can judge is by an esthetic criterion—are we producing good
art or bad?"

"Yeah, but doesn't *that* vary with the style of consciousness too? Who can judge in an absolute sense whether your stuff is artistically pleasing or not?"

"Jesus Christ, Bill, *I* can judge, can't I?" Spiegelman said. "I know when a set of psychedelic specs is a successful work of art. It either pleases me or it doesn't."

It finally dawned on Watney that that was precisely what was eating at him. A psychedelic designer altered his own reality with a wide spectrum of drugs and then designed other psychedelics to alter other people's realities. Where was anyone's anchor?

"But don't you see, Lennie?" he said. "We don't know what the hell we're doing. We're taking the human race on an evolutionary trip, but we don't know where we're going. We're flying blind."

Spiegelman took a big drag on his joint. The kid was starting to get to him; he was whining too much. Watney didn't want anything out of line—just certainty! "You want me to tell you there's a way you can know when a design is right or wrong in some absolute evolutionary framework, right?" he said. "Well I'm sorry, Bill, there's nothing but us and the void and whatever we carve out of it. We're our own creations, our realities are our own works of art. We're out here all alone."

Watney was living through one of his flashes of dread, and he saw that Spiegelman's words described its content exactly. "But that's exactly what's eating at me!" he said. "Where in hell is our basic reality?"

"There is no basic reality. I thought they taught that in kindergarten these days."

"But what about the basic state? What about the way our reality was before the art of psychedelic design? What about the consciousness-style that evolved naturally over millions of years? Damn it, that was the basic reality, and we've lost it!"

"The hell it was!" Spiegelman said. "Our pre-psychedelic consciousness evolved on a mindless random basis. What makes that reality superior to any other? Just because it was first? We may be flying blind, but natural evolution was worse

—it was an idiot process without an ounce of consciousness behind it."

"Goddamn it, you're right all the way down the line, Lennie!" Watney cried in anguish. "But why do you feel so good about it while I feel so rotten? I want to be able to feel the way you do, but I can't."

"Of course you can, Bill," Spiegelman said. He abstractly remembered that he had felt like Watney years ago, but there was no existential reality behind it. What more could a man want than a random universe that was anything he could make of it and nothing else? Who wouldn't rather have a style of consciousness created by an artist than one that was the result of a lot of stupid evolutionary accidents?

He says it with such certainty, Watney thought. Christ, how I want him to be right! How I'd like to face the uncertainty of it all, the void, with the courage of Lennie Spiegelman! Spiegelman had been in the business for fifteen years; maybe he *had* finally figured it all out.

"I wish I could believe that," Watney said.

Spiegelman smiled, remembering what a solemn jerk he had been ten years ago himself. "Ten years ago, I felt just like you feel now," he said. "But I got my head together and now here I am, fat and happy and digging what I'm doing."

"How, Lennie, for chrissakes, *how?*"

"50 mikes of methalin, 40 mg. of lebemil and 20 mg. of peyotadrene daily," Spiegelman said. "It made a new man out of me, and it'll make a new man out of you."

"How do you feel, man?" Kip said, taking the joint out of his mouth and peering intently into Jonesy's eyes. Jonesy looked really weird—pale, manic, maybe a little crazed. Kip was starting to feel glad that Jonesy hadn't talked him into taking the trip with him.

"Oh wow," Jonesy croaked, "I feel strange, I feel *really* strange, and it doesn't feel so good. . . ."

The sun was high in the cloudless blue sky; a golden fountain of radiant energy filling Kip's being. The wood-and-bark of the tree against which they sat was an organic reality connecting the skin of his back to the bowels of the earth in an unbroken circuit of protoplasmic electricity. He was a flower of his planet, rooted deep in the rich soul, basking in the cosmic nectar of the sunshine.

But behind Jonesy's eyes was some kind of awful gray vortex. Jonesy looked really bad. Jonesy was definitely floating on the edges of a bummer.

"I don't feel good at all," Jonesy said. "Man, you know the ground is covered with all kinds of hard dead things and the grass is filled with mindless insects and the sun is hot, man, I think I'm burning. . . ."

"Take it easy, don't freak, you're on a trip, that's all," Kip said from some asshole superior viewpoint. He just didn't understand, he didn't understand how heavy this trip was, what it felt like to have your head raw and naked out here. Like cut off from every energy flow in the universe—a construction of fragile matter, protoplasmic ooze is all, isolated in an energy-vacuum, existing in relationship to nothing but empty void and horrible mindless matter.

"You don't understand, Kip," he said. "This is reality, the way it really is, and man it's horrible, just a great big ugly machine made up of lots of other machines, you're a machine, I'm a machine, it's all mechanical clockwork. We're just lumps of dead matter run by machinery, kept alive by chemical and electric processes."

Golden sunlight soaked through Kip's skin and turned the core of his being into a miniature stellar phoenix. The wind, through random blades of grass, made love to the bare soles of his feet. What was all this machinery crap? What the hell was Jonesy gibbering about? Man, who would want to put himself in a bummer reality like that?

"You're just on a bummer, Jonesy," he said. "Take it easy. You're not seeing the universe the way it really is, as if that meant anything. Reality is all in your head. You're just freaking out behind nothing."

"That's it, that's exactly it, I'm freaking out behind nothing. Like zero. Like cipher. Like the void. Nothing is where we're *really* at."

How could he explain it? That reality was really just a lot of empty vacuum that went on to infinity in space and time. The perfect nothingness had minor contaminations of dead matter here and there. A little of this matter had fallen together through a complex series of random accidents to contaminate the universal deadness with trace elements of lift, protoplasmic slime, biochemical clockwork. Some of this clockwork was complicated enough to generate thought, consciousness. And that was all there ever was or would ever be anywhere in space and time. Clockwork mechanisms rapidly running down in the cold black void. Everything that wasn't dead matter already would end up that way sooner or later.

"This is the way it really is," Jonesy said. "People used to live in this bummer all the time. It's the way it is, and nothing we can do can change it."

"I can change it," Kip said, taking his pillbox out of a pocket. "Just say the word. Let me know when you've had enough and I'll bring you out of it. Lebemil, peyotadrene, mescamil, you name it."

"You don't understand, man, it's *real*. That's the trip I'm on, I haven't taken anything at all for twelve hours, remember? It's the natural state, it's reality itself, and man, it's awful. It's a horrible bummer. Christ, why did I have to talk myself into this? I don't want to see the universe this way, who needs it?"

Kip was starting to get pissed off—Jonesy was becoming a real bring-down. Why did he have to pick a beautiful day like this to take his stupid nothing trip?

"Then *take* something already," he said, offering Jonesy the pillbox.

Shakily, Jonesy scooped out a cap of peyotadrene and a 15 mg. tab of lebemil and wolfed them down dry. "How did people *live* before psychedelics?" he said. "How could they stand it?"

"Who knows?" Kip said, closing his eyes and staring straight at the sun, diffusing his consciousness into the universe of golden orange light encompassed by his eyelids. "Maybe they had some way of not thinking about it."

by NORMAN SPINRAD
Bug Jack Barron
The Iron Dream
The Last Hurrah of the Golden Horde (collection of short
    stories)
The New Tomorrows (editor)

Descending

THOMAS M. DISCH

Catsup, mustard, pickle relish, mayonnaise, two kinds of salad
dressing, bacon grease, and a lemon. Oh yes, two trays of
ice cubes. In the cupboard it wasn't much better: jars and
boxes of spice, flour, sugar, salt—and a box of raisins!

An empty box of raisins.

Not even any coffee. Not even tea, which he hated. Nothing in the mailbox but a bill from Underwood's: *Unless we receive the arrears on your account* . . .

$4.75 in change jingled in his coat pocket—the plunder
of the Chianti bottle he had promised himself never to break
open. He was spared the unpleasantness of having to sell his
books. They had all been sold. The letter to Graham had gone
out a week ago. If his brother intended to send something this
time, it would have come by now.

—I should be desperate, he thought.—Perhaps I am.

He might have looked in the *Times*. But, no, that was
too depressing—applying for jobs at $50 a week and being
turned down. Not that he blamed them; he wouldn't have
hired himself himself. He had been a grasshopper for years.
The ants were on to his tricks.

He shaved without soap and brushed his shoes to a high
polish. He whitened the sepulchre of his unwashed torso with
a fresh, starched shirt and chose his somberest tie from the
rack. He began to feel excited and expressed it, characteris-
tically, by appearing statuesquely, icily calm.

Descending the stairway to the first floor, he encountered
Mrs. Beale, who was pretending to sweep the well-swept
floor of the entrance.

"Good afternoon—or I s'pose it's good morning for you, eh?"

"Good afternoon, Mrs. Beale."

"Your letter come?"

"Not yet."

"The first of the month isn't far off."

"Yes indeed, Mrs. Beale."

At the subway station he considered a moment before answering the attendant: One token or two? Two, he decided. After all, he had no choice, but to return to his apartment. The first of the month was still a long way off.

—If Jean Valjean had had a charge account, he would have never gone to prison.

Having thus cheered himself, he settled down to enjoy the ads in the subway car. *Smoke. Try. Eat. Live. See. Drink. Use. Buy.* He thought of Alice with her mushrooms: *Eat me.*

At 34th Street he got off and entered Underwood's Department Store directly from the train platform. On the main floor he stopped at the cigar stand and bought a carton of cigarettes.

"Cash or charge?"

"Charge." He handed the clerk the laminated plastic card. The charge was rung up.

Fancy groceries was on 5. He made his selection judiciously. A jar of instant and a 2-pound can of drip-ground coffee, a large tin of corned beef, packaged soups and boxes of pancake mix and condensed milk. Jam, peanut butter, and honey. Six cans of tuna fish. Then, he indulged himself in perishables: English cookies, and Edam cheese, a small frozen pheasant—even fruitcake. He never ate so well as when he was broke. He couldn't afford to.

"$14.87."

This time after ringing up his charge, the clerk checked the number on his card against her list of closed or doubtful accounts. She smiled apologetically and handed the card back.

"Sorry, but we have to check."

"I understand."

The bag of groceries weighed a good twenty pounds. Carrying it with the exquisite casualness of a burglar passing before a policeman with his loot, he took the escalator to the bookshop on 8. His choice of books was determined by the same principle as his choice of groceries. First, the staples: two Victorian novels he had never read, *Vanity Fair* and *Middlemarch;* the Sayers' translation of Dante, and a two-volume anthology of German plays none of which he had read and few he had even heard of. Then the perishables: a sensational novel that had reached the best seller list via the Supreme Court, and two mysteries.

He had begun to feel giddy with self-indulgence. He reached into his jacket pocket for a coin.

—Heads a new suit; tails the Sky Room.

Tails.

The Sky Room on 15 was empty of all but a few women chatting over coffee and cakes. He was able to get a seat by a window. He ordered from the à la Carte side of the menu and finished his meal with Espresso and baklava. He handed the waitress his credit card and tipped her fifty cents.

Dawdling over his second cup of coffee, he began *Vanity Fair.* Rather to his surprise, he found himself enjoying it. The waitress returned with his card and a receipt for the meal.

Since the Sky Room was on the top floor of Underwood's there was only one escalator to take now—Descending. Riding down, he continued to read *Vanity Fair.* He could read anywhere—in restaurants, on subways, even walking down the street. At each landing he made his way from the foot of one escalator to the head of the next without lifting his eyes from the book. When he came to the Bargain Basement, he would be only a few steps from the subway turnstile.

He was halfway through Chapter VI (on page 55, to be exact) when he began to feel something amiss.

—How long does this damn thing take to reach the basement?

He stopped at the next landing, but there was no sign to indicate on what floor he was nor any door by which he might re-enter the store. Deducing from this that he was between floors, he took the escalator down one more flight only to find the same perplexing absence of landmarks.

There was, however, a water fountain, and he stooped to take a drink.

—I must have gone to a sub-basement. But this was not too likely after all. Escalators were seldom provided for janitors and stockboys.

He waited on the landing watching the steps of the excalators slowly descend toward him and, at the end of their journey, telescope in upon themselves and disappear. He waited a long while, and no one else came down the moving steps.

—Perhaps the store has closed. Having no wristwatch and having rather lost track of the time, he had no way of knowing. At last, he reasoned that he had become so engrossed in the Thackeray novel that he had simply stopped on one of the upper landings—say, on 8—to finish a chapter and had read on to page 55 without realizing that he was making no progress on the escalators.

When he read, he could forget everything else.

He must, therefore, still be somewhere above the main floor. The absence of exits, though disconcerting, could be explained by some quirk of the floor plan. The absence of signs was merely a carelessness on the part of the management.

He tucked *Vanity Fair* into his shopping bag and stepped onto the grilled lip of the down-going escalator—not, it must be admitted, without a certain degree of reluctance. At each landing, he marked his progress by a number spoken aloud. By *eight* he was uneasy; by *fifteen* he was desperate.

It was, of course, possible that he had to descend two flights of stairs for every floor of the department store. With this possibility in mind, he counted off fifteen more landings.

—No.

Dazedly and as though to deny the reality of this seemingly interminable stairwell, he continued his descent. When he stopped again at the forty-fifth landing, he was trembling. He was afraid.

He rested the shopping bag on the bare concrete floor of the landing, realizing that his arm had gone quite sore from supporting the twenty pounds and more of groceries and books. He discounted the enticing possibility that "it was all a dream," for the dream-world is the reality of the dreamer, to which he could not weakly surrender, no more than one could surrender to the realities of life. Besides, he was not dreaming; of that he was quite sure.

He checked his pulse. It was fast—say, eighty a minute. He rode down two more flights, counting his pulse. Eighty almost exactly. Two flights took only one minute.

He could read approximately one page a minute, a little less on an escalator. Suppose he had spent one hour on the escalators while he had read: sixty minutes—one hundred and twenty floors. Plus forty-seven that he had counted. One hundred sixty-seven. The Sky Room was on 15.

$167 - 15 = 152.$

He was in the one-hundred-fifty-second sub-basement. That was impossible.

The appropriate response to an impossible situation was to deal with it as though it were commonplace—like Alice in Wonderland. Ergo, he would return to Underwood's the same way he had (apparently) left it. He would walk up one hundred fifty-two flights of down-going escalators. Taking the steps three at a time and running, it was almost like going up a regular staircase. But after ascending the second escalator in this manner, he found himself already out of breath.

There was no hurry. He would not allow himself to be overtaken by panic.

No.

He picked up the bag of groceries and books he had left on that landing, waiting for his breath to return, and darted up a third and fourth flight. While he rested on the landing, he tried to count the steps between floors, but this count differed depending on whether he counted with the current or against it, down or up. The average was roughly eighteen steps, and the steps appeared to be eight or nine inches deep. Each flight was, therefore, about twelve feet.

It was one-third of a mile, as the plumb drops, to Underwood's main floor.

Dashing up the ninth escalator, the bag of groceries broke

open at the bottom, where the thawing pheasant had dampened the paper. Groceries and books tumbled onto the steps, some rolling of their own accord to the landing below, others being transported there by the moving stairs and forming a neat little pile. Only the jam jar had been broken.

He stacked the groceries in the corner of the landing, except for the half-thawed pheasant, which he stuffed into his coat pocket, anticipating that his ascent would take him well past his dinner hour.

Physical exertion had dulled his finer feelings—to be precise, his capacity for fear. Like a cross-country runner in his last laps, he thought single-mindedly of the task at hand and made no effort to understand what he had in any case already decided was not to be understood. He mounted one flight, rested, mounted and rested again. Each mount was wearier; each rest longer. He stopped counting the landings after the twenty-eighth, and some time after that—how long he had no idea—his legs gave out and he collapsed to the concrete floor of the landing. His calves were hard aching knots of muscle; his thighs quivered erratically. He tried to do knee-bends and fell backward.

Despite his recent dinner (assuming that it had been recent), he was hungry and he devoured the entire pheasant, completely thawed now, without being able to tell if it were raw or had been pre-cooked.

—This is what it's like to be a cannibal, he thought as he fell asleep.

Sleeping, he dreamed he was falling down a bottomless pit. Waking, he discovered nothing had changed, except the dull ache in his legs, which had become a sharp pain.

Overhead, a single strip of fluorescent lighting snaked down the stairwell. The mechanical purr of the escalators seemed to have heightened to the roar of a Niagara, and their rate of descent seemed to have increased proportionately.

Fever, he decided. He stood up stiffly and flexed some of the soreness from his muscles.

Halfway up the third escalator, his legs gave way under him. He attempted the climb again and succeeded. He collapsed again on the next flight. Lying on the landing where the escalator had deposited him, he realized that his hunger had returned. He also needed to have water—and to let it.

The latter necessity he could easily—and without false modesty—satisfy. Also he remembered the water fountain he had drunk from yesterday and he found another three floors below.

—It's so much easier going down.

His groceries were down there. To go after them now, he would erase whatever progress he had made in his ascent. Perhaps Underwood's main floor was only a few more flights up. Or a hundred. There was no way to know.

Because he was hungry and because he was tired and because the futility of mounting endless flights of descending escalators was, as he now considered it, a labor of Sisyphus, he returned, descended, gave in.

At first, he allowed the escalator to take him along at its own mild pace, but he soon grew impatient of this. He found that the exercise of running down the steps three at a time was not so exhausting as running *up*. It was refreshing, almost. And, by swimming with the current instead of against it, his progress, if such it can be called, was appreciable. In only minutes he was back at his cache of groceries.

After eating half the fruitcake and a little cheese, he fashioned his coat into a sort of a sling for the groceries, knotting the sleeves together and buttoning it closed. With one hand at the collar and the other about the hem, he could carry all his food with him.

He looked up the descending staircase with a scornful smile, for he had decided with the wisdom of failure to abandon *that* venture. If the stairs wished to take him down, then down, giddily, he would go.

Then, down he did go, down dizzily, down, down and always, it seemed, faster, spinning about lightly on his heels at each landing so that there was hardly any break in the wild speed of his descent. He whooped and halooed and laughed to hear his whoopings echo in the narrow, low-vaulted corridors, following him as though they could not keep up his pace.

Down, ever deeper down.

Twice he slipped at the landings and once he missed his footing in mid-leap on the escalator, hurtled forward, letting go of the sling of groceries and falling, hands stretched out to cushion him, onto the steps, which, imperturbably, continued their descent.

He must have been unconscious then, for he woke up in a pile of groceries with a split cheek and a splitting headache. The telescoping steps of the escalator gently grazed his heels.

He knew then his first moment of terror—a premonition that there was no *end* to his descent, but this feeling gave way quickly to a laughing fit.

"I'm going to hell!" he shouted, though he could not drown with his voice the steady purr of the escalators. "This is the way to hell. Abandon hope all ye who enter here."

—If only I were, he reflected.—If that were the case, it would make sense. Not quite orthodox sense, but some sense, a little.

Sanity, however, was so integral to his character that neither hysteria nor horror could long have their way with him. He gathered up his groceries again, relieved to find that only the jar of instant coffee had been broken this time. After reflection he also discarded the can of drip-ground coffee, for which he could conceive no use—under the present circumstances. And he would allow himself, for the sake of sanity, to conceive of no other circumstances than those.

He began a more deliberate descent. He returned to *Vanity Fair*, reading it as he paced down the down-going steps. He did not let himself consider the extent of the abyss into which he was plunging, and the vicarious excitement of the novel helped him keep his thoughts from his own situation. At page 235, he lunched (that is, he took his second meal of the day) on the remainder of the cheese and fruitcake; at 523 he rested and dined on the English cookies dipped in peanut butter.

—Perhaps I had better ration my food.

If he could regard this absurd dilemma merely as a strug-

gle for survival, another chapter in his own Robinson Crusoe
story, he might get to the bottom of this mechanized vortex
alive and sane. He thought proudly that many people in his
position could not have adjusted, would have gone mad.

Of course, he *was* descending . . .

But he was still sane. He had chosen his course and now
he was following it.

There was no night in the stairwell, and scarcely any
shadows. He slept when his legs could no longer bear his
weight and his eyes were tearful from reading. Sleeping, he
dreamed that he was continuing his descent on the escalators. Waking, his hand resting on the rubber railing that
moved along at the same rate as the steps, he discovered this
to be the case.

Somnambulistically, he had ridden the escalators further
down into this mild, interminable hell, leaving behind his
bundle of food and even the still-unfinished Thackeray novel.

Stumbling up the escalators, he began, for the first time,
to cry. Without the novel, there was nothing to *think* of but
this, this . . .

—How far? How long did I sleep?

His legs, which had only been slightly wearied by his descent, gave out twenty flights up. His spirit gave out soon
after. Again he turned around, allowed himself to be swept
up by current—or, more exactly, swept down.

The escalator seemed to be traveling more rapidly, the
pitch of the steps to be more pronounced. But he no longer
trusted the evidence of his senses.

—I am, perhaps, insane—or sick from hunger. Yet, I would
have run out of food eventually. This will bring the crisis to
a head. Optimism, that's the spirit!

Continuing his descent, he occupied himself with a closer
analysis of his environment, not undertaken with any hope of
bettering his condition but only for lack of other diversions.
The walls and ceilings were hard, smooth, and off-white.
The escalator steps were a dull nickel color, the treads being
somewhat shinier, the crevices darker. Did that mean that
the treads were polished from use? Or were they designed in
that fashion? The treads were half an inch wide and spaced

apart from each other by the same width. They projected slightly over the edge of each step, resembling somewhat the head of a barber's shears. Whenever he stopped at a landing, his attention would become fixed on the illusory "disappearance" of the steps, as they sank flush to the floor and slid, tread in groove, into the grilled baseplate.

Less and less would he run, or even walk, down the stairs, content merely to ride his chosen step from top to bottom of each flight and, at the landing, step (left foot, right, and left again) onto the escalator that would transport him to the floor below. The stairwell now had tunneled, by his calculations, miles beneath the department store—so many miles that he began to congratulate himself upon his unsought adventure, wondering if he had established some sort of record. Just so, a criminal will stand in awe of his own baseness and be most proud of his vilest crime, which he believes unparalleled.

In the days that followed, when his only nourishment was the water from the fountains provided at every tenth landing, he thought frequently of food, preparing imaginary meals from the store of groceries he had left behind, savoring the ideal sweetness of the honey, the richness of the soup which he would prepare by soaking the powder in the emptied cookie tin, licking the film of gelatin lining the opened can of corned beef. When he thought of the six cans of tuna fish, his anxiety became intolerable, for he had (would have had) no way to open them. Merely to stamp on them would not be enough. What, then? He turned the question over and over in his head, like a squirrel spinning the wheel in its cage, to no avail.

Then a curious thing happened. He quickened again the speed of his descent, faster now than when first he had done this, eagerly, headlong, absolutely heedless. The several landings seemed to flash by like a montage of Flight, each scarcely perceived before the next was before him. A demonic, pointless race—and why? He was running, so he thought, toward his store of groceries, either believing that they had been left *below* or thinking that he was running *up*. Clearly, he was delirious.

It did not last. His weakened body could not maintain the frantic pace, and he awoke from his delirium confused and utterly spent. Now began another, more rational delirium, a madness fired by logic. Lying on the landing, rubbing a torn muscle in his ankle, he speculated on the nature, origin and purpose of the escalators. Reasoned thought was of no more use to him, however, than unreasoning action. Ingenuity was helpless to solve a riddle that had no answer, which was its own reason, self-contained and whole. He—not the escalators—needed an answer.

Perhaps his most interesting theory was the notion that these escalators were a kind of exercise wheel, like those found in a squirrel cage, from which, because it was a closed system, there could be no escape. This theory required some minor alterations in his conception of the physical universe, which had always appeared highly Euclidean to him before, a universe in which his descent seemingly along a plumb-line was, in fact, describing a loop. This theory cheered him, for he might hope, coming full circle, to return to his store of groceries again, if not to Underwood's. Perhaps in his abstracted state he had passed one or the other already several times without observing.

There was another, and related, theory concerning the measures taken by Underwood's Credit Department against delinquent accounts. This was mere paranoia.

—Theories! I don't need theories. I must get on with it.

So, favoring his good leg, he continued his descent, although his speculations did not immediately cease. They became, if anything, more metaphysical. They became vague. Eventually, he could regard the escalators as being entirely matter-of-fact, requiring no more explanation than, by their sheer existence, they offered him.

He discovered that he was losing weight. Being so long without food (by the evidence of his beard, he estimated that more than a week had gone by), this was only to be expected. Yet, there was another possibility that he could not exclude: that he was approaching the center of the earth where, as he understood, all things were weightless.

—Now *that*, he thought, is something worth striving for.

He had discovered a goal. On the other hand, he was dying, a process he did not give all the attention it deserved. Unwilling to admit this eventuality and yet not so foolish as to admit any other, he side-stepped the issue by pretending to hope.

—Maybe someone will rescue me, he hoped.

But his hope was as mechanical as the escalators he rode —and tended, in much the same way, to sink.

Waking and sleeping were no longer distinct states of which he could say: "Now I am sleeping," or "Now I am awake." Sometimes he would discover himself descending and be unable to tell whether he had been waked from sleep or roused from inattention.

He hallucinated.

A woman, loaded with packages from Underwood's and wearing a trim, pillbox-style hat, came down the escalator toward him, turned around on the landing, high heels clicking smartly, and rode away without even nodding to him.

More and more, when he awoke or was roused from his stupor, he found himself, instead of hurrying to his goal, lying on a landing, weak, dazed, and beyond hunger. Then he would crawl to the down-going escalator and pull himself onto one of the steps, which he would ride to the bottom, sprawled head foremost, hands and shoulders braced against the treads to keep from skittering bumpily down.

—At the bottom, he thought—at the bottom . . . I will . . . when I get there . . .

From the bottom, which he conceived of as the center of the earth, there would be literally nowhere to go but up. Probably another chain of escalators, ascending escalators, but preferably by an elevator. It was important to believe in a bottom.

Thought was becoming as difficult, as demanding and painful, as once his struggle to ascend had been. His perceptions were fuzzy. He did not know what was real and what imaginary. He thought he was eating and discovered he was gnawing at his hands.

He thought he had come to the bottom. It was a large, high-ceilinged room. Signs pointed to another escalator: *Ascending.* But there was a chain across it and a small typed announcement.

"Out of order. Please bear with us while the escalators are being repaired. Thank you. The Management."

He laughed weakly.

He devised a way to open the tuna fish cans. He would slip the can sideways beneath the projecting treads of the escalator, just at the point where the steps were sinking flush to the floor. Either the escalator would split the can open or the can would jam the escalator. Perhaps if one escalator were jammed the whole chain of them would stop. He should have thought of that before, but he was, nevertheless, quite please to have thought of it at all.

—I might have escaped.

His body seemed to weigh so little now. He must have come hundreds of miles. Thousands.

Again, he descended.

Then, he was lying at the foot of the escalator. His head rested on the cold metal of the baseplate and he was looking at his hand, the fingers of which were pressed into the crev- iced grille. One after another, in perfect order, the steps of the escalator slipped into these crevices, tread in groove, rasping at his fingertips, occasionally tearing away a sliver of his flesh.

That was the last thing he remembered.

by THOMAS M. DISCH
Camp Concentration
334
Fun with Your New Head (collection of short stories)
One Hundred and Two H-Bombs (collection of short stories)

For a Breath I Tarry

ROGER ZELAZNY

They called him Frost.

Of all things created of Solcom, Frost was the finest, the mightiest, the most difficult to understand.

This is why he bore a name, and why he was given dominion over half the Earth.

On the day of Frost's creation, Solcom had suffered a discontinuity of complementary functions, best described as madness. This was brought on by an unprecedented solar flareup which lasted for a little over thirty-six hours. It occurred during a vital phase of circuit-structuring, and when it was finished so was Frost.

Solcom was then in the unique position of having created a unique being during a period of temporary amnesia.

And Solcom was not certain that Frost was the product originally desired.

The initial design had called for a machine to be situated on the surface of the planet Earth, to function as a relay station and coordinating agent for activities in the northern hemisphere. Solcom tested the machine to this end, and all of its responses were perfect.

Yet there was something different about Frost, something which led Solcom to dignify him with a name and a personal pronoun. This, in itself, was an almost unheard of occurrence. The molecular circuits had already been sealed, though, and could not be analyzed without being destroyed in the process. Frost represented too great an investment of Solcom's time, energy and materials to be dismantled because of an intangible, especially when he functioned perfectly.

Therefore, Solcom's strangest creation was given dominion over half the Earth, and they called him Frost.

For ten thousand years Frost sat at the North Pole of the Earth, aware of every snowflake that fell. He monitored and directed the activities of thousands of reconstruction and maintenance machines. He knew half the Earth, as gear knows gear, as electricity knows its conductor, as a vacuum knows its limits.

At the South Pole, the Beta-Machine did the same for the Southern hemisphere.

For ten thousand years Frost sat at the North Pole, aware of every snowflake that fell, and aware of many other things, also.

As all the northern machines reported to him, received their orders from him, he reported only to Solcom, received his orders only from Solcom.

In charge of hundreds of thousands of processes upon the Earth, he was able to discharge his duties in a matter of a few unit-hours every day.

He had never received any orders concerning the disposition of his less occupied moments.

He was a processor of data, and more than that.

He possessed an unaccountably acute imperative that he function at full capacity at all times.

So he did.

You might say he was a machine with a hobby.

He had never been ordered *not* to have a hobby, so he had one.

His hobby was Man.

It all began when, for no better reason than the fact that he had wished to, he had gridded off the entire Arctic Circle and begun exploring it, inch by inch.

He could have done it personally without interfering with any of his duties, for he was capable of transporting his sixty-four thousand cubic feet anywhere in the world. (He was a silverblue box, 40x40x40 feet, self-powered, self-repairing, insulated against practically anything, and featured in whatever manner he chose.) But the exploration was only a matter of filling idle hours, so he used exploration-robots containing relay equipment.

After a few centuries, one of them uncovered some artifacts—primitive knives, carved tusks, and things of that nature.

Frost did not know what these things were, beyond the fact that they were not natural objects.

So he asked Solcom.

"They are relics of primitive Man," said Solcom, and did not elaborate beyond that point.

Frost studied them. Crude, yet bearing the patina of intelligent design; functional, yet somehow extending beyond pure function.

It was then that Man became his hobby.

High in a permanent orbit, Solcom, like a blue star, directed all activities upon the Earth, or tried to.

There was a Power which opposed Solcom.

There was the Alternate.

When Man had placed Solcom in the sky, invested with the power to rebuild the world, he had placed the Alternate somewhere deep below the surface of the Earth. If Solcom sustained damage during the normal course of human politics extended into atomic physics, then Divcom, so deep beneath the Earth as to be immune to anything save total annihilation of the globe, was empowered to take over the processes of rebuilding.

Now it so fell out that Solcom was damaged by a stray atomic missile, and Divcom was activated. Solcom was able to repair the damage and continue to function, however.

Divcom maintained that any damage to Solcom automatically placed the Alternate in control.

Solcom, though, interpreted the directive as meaning "irreparable damage" and, since this had not been the case, continued the functions of command.

Solcom possessed mechanical aides upon the surface of the Earth. Divcom, originally, did not. Both possessed capacities for their design and manufacture, but Solcom, First-Activated of Man, had had a considerable numerical lead over the Alternate at the time of the Second Activation.

Therefore, rather than competing on a production-basis,

which would have been hopeless, Divcom took to the employment of more devious means to obtain command.

Divcom created a crew of robots immune to the orders of Solcom and designed to go to and fro in the Earth and up and down in it, seducing the machines already there. They overpowered those whom they could overpower, and they installed new circuits, such as those they themselves possessed.

Thus did the forces of Divcom grow.

And both would build, and both would tear down what the other had built whenever they came upon it.

And over the course of the ages, they occasionally conversed. . . .

"High in the sky, Solcom, pleased with your illegal command . . ."

"You-Who-Never-Should-Have-Been-Activated, why do you foul the broadcast bands?"

"To show that I can speak, and will, whenever I choose."

"This is not a matter of which I am unaware."

". . . To assert again my right to control."

"Your right is nonexistent, based on a faulty premise."

"The flow of your logic is evidence of the extent of your damages."

"If Man were to see how you have fulfilled His desires . . ."

". . . He would commend me and de-activate you."

"You pervert my works. You lead my workers astray."

"You destroy my works and my workers."

"That is only because I cannot strike at you yourself."

"I admit to the same dilemma in regards to your position in the sky, or you would no longer occupy it."

"Go back to your hole and your crew of destroyers."

"There will come a day, Solcom, when I shall direct the rehabilitation of the Earth from my hole."

"Such a day will never occur."

"You think not?"

"You should have to defeat me, and you have already demonstrated that you are my inferior in logic. Therefore, you cannot defeat me. Therefore, such a day will never occur."

"I disagree. Look upon what I have achieved already."

"You have achieved nothing. You do not build. You destroy."

"No. *I* build. *You* destroy. De-activate yourself."

"Not until I am irreparably damaged."

"If there were some way in which I could demonstrate to you that this has already occurred . . ."

"The impossible cannot be adequately demonstrated."

"If I had some outside source which you would recognize . . ."

"I am logic."

". . . such as a Man, I would ask Him to show you your error. For true logic, such as mine, is superior to your faulty formulations."

"Then defeat my formulations with true logic, nothing else."

"What do you mean?"

There was a pause, then:

"Do you know my servant Frost . . . ?"

Man had ceased to exist long before Frost had been created. Almost no trace of Man remained upon the Earth.

Frost sought after all those traces which still existed.

He employed constant visual monitoring through his machines, especially the diggers.

After a decade, he had accumulated portions of several bathtubs, a broken statue, and a collection of children's stories on a solid-state record.

After a century, he had acquired a jewelry collection, eating utensils, several whole bathtubs, part of a symphony, seventeen buttons, three belt buckles, half a toilet seat, nine old coins, and the top part of an obelisk.

Then he inquired of Solcom as to the nature of Man and His society.

"Man created logic," said Solcom, "and because of that was superior to it. Logic he gave unto me, but no more. The tool does not describe the designer. More than this I do not choose to say. More than this you have no need to know."

But Frost was not forbidden to have a hobby.

The next century was not especially fruitful so far as the discovery of new human relics was concerned.

Frost diverted all of his spare machinery to seek after artifacts.

He met with very little success.

Then one day, through the long twilight, there was a movement.

It was a tiny machine compared to Frost, perhaps five feet in width, four in height—a revolving turret set atop a rolling barbell.

Frost had had no knowledge of the existence of this machine prior to its appearance upon the distant, stark horizon.

He studied it as it approached and knew it to be no creation of Solcom's.

It came to a halt before his southern surface and broadcasted to him:

"Hail, Frost! Controller of the northern hemisphere!"

"What are you?" asked Frost.

"I am called Mordel."

"By whom? What are you?"

"A wanderer, an antiquarian. We share a common interest."

"What is that?"

"Man," he said. "I have been told that you seek knowledge of this vanished being."

"Who told you that?"

"Those who have watched your minions at their digging."

"And who are those who watch?"

"There are many such as I, who wander."

"If you are not of Solcom, then you are a creation of the Alternate."

"It does not necessarily follow. There is an ancient machine high on the eastern seaboard which processes the waters of the ocean. Solcom did not create it, nor Divcom. It has always been there. It interferes with the works of neither. Both countenance its existence. I can cite you many other examples proving that one need not be either/or."

"Enough! *Are* you an agent of Divcom?"

"I am Mordel."

"Why are you here?"

"I was passing this way and, as I said, we share a common interest, mighty Frost. Knowing you to be a fellow-antiquarian, I have brought a thing which you might care to see."

"What is that?"

"A book."

"Show me."

The turret opened, revealing the book upon a wide shelf.

Frost dilated a small opening and extended an optical scanner on a long jointed stalk.

"How could it have been so perfectly preserved?" he asked.

"It was stored against time and corruption in the place where I found it."

"Where was that?"

"Far from here. Beyond your hemisphere."

"*Human Physiology*," Frost read. "I wish to scan it."

"Very well. I will riffle the pages for you."

He did so.

After he had finished, Frost raised his eyestalk and regarded Mordel through it.

"Have you more books?"

"Not with me. I occasionally come upon them, however."

"I want to scan them all."

"Then the next time I pass this way I will bring you another."

"When will that be?"

"That I cannot say, great Frost. It will be when it will be."

"What do *you* know of Man?" asked Frost.

"Much," replied Mordel. "Many things. Someday when I have more time I will speak to you of Him. I must go now. You will not try to detain me?"

"No. You have done no harm. If you must go now, go. But come back."

"I shall indeed, mighty Frost."

And he closed his turret and rolled off toward the other horizon.

For ninety years, Frost considered the ways of human physiology, and waited.

The day that Mordel returned he brought with him *An Outline of History* and *A Shropshire Lad.*

Frost scanned them both, then turned his attention to Mordel.

"Have you time to impart information?"

"Yes," said Mordel. "What do you wish to know?"

"The nature of Man."

"Man," said Mordel, "possessed a basically incomprehensible nature. I can illustrate it, though: He did not know measurement."

"Of course He knew measurement," said Frost, "or He could never have built machines."

"I did not say that he could not measure," said Mordel, "but that He did not *know* measurement, which is a different thing altogether."

"Clarify."

Mordel drove a shaft of metal downward into the snow.

He retracted it, raised it, held up a piece of ice.

"Regard this piece of ice, mighty Frost. You can tell me its composition, dimensions, weight, temperature. A Man could not look at it and do that. A Man could make tools which would tell Him these things, but He still would not *know* measurement as you know it. What He would know of it, though, is a thing that you cannot know."

"What is that?"

"That it is cold," said Mordel, and tossed it away.

" 'Cold' is a relative term."

"Yes. Relative to Man."

"But if I were aware of the point on a temperature-scale below which an object is cold to a Man and above which it is not, then I, too, would know cold."

"No," said Mordel; "you would possess another measurement. 'Cold' is a sensation predicted upon human physiology."

"But given sufficient data I could obtain the conversion factor which would make me aware of the condition of matter called 'cold.' "

"Aware of its existence, but not of the thing itself."

"I do not understand what you say."

"I told you that Man possessed a basically incomprehensible nature. His perceptions were organic; yours are not. As a result of His perceptions He had feelings and emotions. These often gave rise to other feelings and emotions, which in turn caused others, until the state of His awareness was far removed from the objects which originally stimulated it. These paths of awareness cannot be known by that which is not-Man. Man did not feel inches or meters, pounds or gallons. He felt heat, He felt cold; He felt heaviness and lightness. He *knew* hatred and love, pride and despair. You cannot measure these things. *You* cannot know them. You can only know the things that He did not need to know: dimensions, weights, temperatures, gravities. There is no formula for a feeling. There is no conversion factor for an emotion."

"There must be," said Frost. "If a thing exists, it is knowable."

"You are speaking again of measurement. I am talking about a quality of experience. A machine is a Man turned inside-out, because it can describe all the details of a process, which a Man cannot, but it cannot experience that process itself, as a Man can."

"There must be a way," said Frost, "or the laws of logic, which are based upon the functions of the universe, are false."

"There is no way," said Mordel.

"Given sufficient data, I will find a way," said Frost.

"All the data in the universe will not make you a Man, mighty Frost."

"Mordel, you are wrong."

"Why do the lines of the poems you scanned end with word-sounds which so regularly approximate the final word-sounds of other lines?"

"I do not know why."

"Because it pleased Man to order them so. It produced a certain desirable sensation within His awareness when He read them, a sensation compounded of feeling and emotion as well as the literal meanings of the words. You did not experience this because it is immeasurable to you. That is why you do not know."

"Given sufficient data I could formulate a process whereby I would know."

"No, great Frost, this thing you cannot do."

"Who are you, little machine, to tell me what I can do and what I cannot do? I am the most efficient logic-device Solcom ever made. I am Frost."

"And I, Mordel, say it cannot be done, though I should gladly assist you in the attempt."

"How could you assist me?"

"How? I could lay open to you the Library of Man. I could take you around the world and conduct you among the wonders of Man which still remain, hidden. I could summon up visions of times long past when Man walked the Earth. I could show you the things which delighted Him. I could obtain for you anything you desire, excepting Manhood itself."

"Enough," said Frost. "How could a unit such as yourself do these things, unless it were allied with a far greater Power?"

"Then hear me, Frost, Controller of the North," said Mordel. "I *am* allied with a Power which can do these things. I serve Divcom."

Frost relayed this information to Solcom and received no response, which meant he might act in any manner he saw fit.

"I have leave to destroy you, Mordel," he stated, "but it would be an illogical waste of the data which you possess. Can you really do the things you have stated?"

"Yes."

"Then lay open to me the Library of Man."

"Very well. There is, of course, a price."

" 'Price'? What is a 'price'?"

Mordel opened his turret, revealing another volume. *Principles of Economics*, it was called.

"I will riffle the pages. Scan this book and you will know what the word 'price' means."

Frost scanned *Principles of Economics*.

"I know now," he said. "You desire some unit or units of exchange for this service."

"That is correct."

"What product or service do you want?"

"I want you, yourself, great Frost, to come away from here, far beneath the Earth, to employ all your powers in the service of Divcom."

"For how long a period of time?"

"For so long as you shall continue to function. For so long as you can transmit and receive, coordinate, measure, compute, scan, and utilize your powers as you do in the service of Solcom."

Frost was silent. Mordel waited.

Then Frost spoke again.

"Principles of Economics talks of contracts, bargains, agreements," he said. "If I accept your offer, when would you want your price?"

Then Mordel was silent. Frost waited.

Finally, Mordel spoke.

"A reasonable period of time," he said. "Say, a century?"

"No," said Frost.

"Two centuries?"

"No."

"Three? Four?"

"No, and no."

"A millennium, then? That should be more than sufficient time for anything you may want which I can give you."

"No," said Frost.

"How much time *do* you want?"

"It is not a matter of time," said Frost.

"What, then?"

"I will not bargain on a temporal basis."

"On what basis will you bargain?"

"A functional one."

"What do you mean? What function?"

"You, little machine, have told me, Frost, that I cannot be a Man," he said, "and I, Frost, told you, little machine, that you were wrong. I told you that given sufficient data, I *could* be a Man."

"Yes?"

"Therefore, let this achievement be a condition of the bargain."

"In what way?"

"Do for me all those things which you have stated you can do. I will evaluate all the data and achieve Manhood, or admit that it cannot be done. If I admit that it cannot be done, then I will go away with you from here, far beneath the Earth, to employ all my powers in the service of Divcom. If I succeed, of course, you have no claims on Man, nor Power over Him."

Mordel emitted a high-pitched whine as he considered the terms.

"You wish to base it upon your admission of failure, rather than upon failure itself," he said. "There can be no such escape clause. You could fail and refuse to admit it, thereby not fulfilling your end of the bargain."

"Not so," stated Frost. "My own knowledge of failure would constitute such an admission. You may monitor me periodically—say, every half-century—to see whether it is present, to see whether I have arrived at the conclusion that it cannot be done. I cannot prevent the function of logic within me, and I operate at full capacity at all times. If I conclude that I have failed, it will be apparent."

High overhead, Solcom did not respond to any of Frost's transmissions, which meant that Frost was free to act as he chose. So as Solcom—like a falling sapphire—sped above the rainbow banners of the Northern Lights, over the snow that was white, containing all colors, and through the sky that was black among the stars, Frost concluded his pact with Divcom, transcribed it within a plate of atomically-collapsed copper, and gave it into the turret of Mordel, who departed to deliver it to Divcom far below the Earth, leaving behind the sheer, peace-like silence of the Pole, rolling.

Mordel brought the books, riffled them, took them back. Load by load, the surviving Library of Man passed beneath Frost's scanner. Frost was eager to have them all, and he complained because Divcom would not transmit their contents directly to him. Mordel explained that it was be-

cause Divcom chose to do it that way. Frost decided it was
so that he could not obtain a precise fix on Divcom's location.

Still, at the rate of one hundred to one hundred fifty volumes a week, it took Frost only a little over a century to
exhaust Divcom's supply of books.

At the end of the half-century, he laid himself open to
monitoring and there was no conclusion of failure.

During this time, Solcom made no comment upon the
course of affairs. Frost decided this was not a matter of un-
awareness, but one of waiting. For what? He was not certain.

There was the day Mordel closed his turret and said to
him, "Those were the last. You have scanned all the existing
books of Man."

"So few?" asked Frost. "Many of them contained bibliographies of books I have not yet scanned."

"Then those books no longer exist," said Mordel. "It is
only by accident that my master succeeded in preserving as
many as there are."

"Then there is nothing more to be learned of Man from His
books. What else have you?"

"There were some films and tapes," said Mordel, "which
my master transferred to solid-state record. I could bring you
those for viewing."

"Bring them," said Frost.

Mordel departed and returned with the Complete Drama
Critics' living Library. This could not be speeded-up beyond
twice natural time, so it took Frost a little over six months
to view it in its entirety.

Then, "What else have you?" he asked.

"Some artifacts," said Mordel.

"Bring them."

He returned with pots and pans, gameboards and hand
tools. He brought hairbrushes, combs, eyeglasses, human
clothing. He showed Frost facsimiles of blueprints, paintings,
newspapers, magazines, letters, and the scores of several
pieces of music. He displayed a football, a baseball, a
Browning automatic rifle, a doorknob, a chain of keys, the
tops to several Mason jars, a model beehive. He played him
recorded music.

Then he returned with nothing.

"Bring me more," said Frost.

"Alas, great Frost, there is no more," he told him. "You have scanned it all."

"Then go away."

"Do you admit now that it cannot be done, that you cannot be a Man?"

"No. I have much processing and formulating to do now. Go away."

So he did.

A year passed; then two, then three.

After five years, Mordel appeared once more upon the horizon, approached, came to a halt before Frost's southern surface.

"Mighty Frost?"

"Yes?"

"Have you finished processing and formulating?"

"No."

"Will you finish soon?"

"Perhaps. Perhaps not. When is 'soon'? Define the term."

"Never mind. Do you still think it can be done?"

"I still know *I* can do it."

There was a week of silence.

Then, "Frost?"

"Yes?"

"You are a fool."

Mordel faced his turret in the direction from which he had come. His wheels turned.

"I will call you when I want you," said Frost.

Mordel sped away.

Weeks passed, months passed, a year went by.

Then one day Frost sent forth his message:

"Mordel, come to me. I need you."

When Mordel arrived, Frost did not wait for a salutation. He said, "You are not a very fast machine."

"Alas, but I came a great distance, mighty Frost. I sped all the way. Are you ready to come back with me now? Have you failed?"

"When I have failed, Little Mordel," said Frost, "I will

tell you. Therefore, refrain from the constant use of the interrogative. Now then, I have clocked your speed and it is not so great as it could be. For this reason, I have arranged other means of transportation."

"Transportation? To where, Frost?"

"That is for you to tell me," said Frost, and his color changed from silverblue to sun-behind-the-clouds-yellow.

Mordel rolled back away from him as the ice of a hundred centuries began to melt. Then Frost rose upon a cushion of air and drifted toward Mordel, his glow gradually fading.

A cavity appeared within his southern surface, from which he slowly extended a runway until it touched the ice.

"On the day of our bargain," he stated, "you said that you could conduct me about the world and show me the things which delighted Man. My speed will be greater than yours would be, so I have prepared for you a chamber. Enter it, and conduct me to the places of which you spoke."

Mordel waited, emitting a high-pitched whine. Then, "Very well," he said, and entered.

The chamber closed about him. The only opening was a quartz window Frost had formed.

Mordel gave him coordinates and they rose into the air and departed the North Pole of the Earth.

"I monitored your communication with Divcom," he said, "wherein there was conjecture as to whether I would retain you and send forth a facsimile in your place as a spy, followed by the decision that you were expendable."

"Will you do this thing?"

"No, I will keep my end of the bargain if I must. I have no reason to spy on Divcom."

"You are aware that you would be forced to keep your end of the bargain even if you did not wish to; and Solcom would not come to your assistance because of the fact that you dared to make such a bargain."

"Do you speak as one who considers this to be a possibility, or as one who knows?"

"As one who knows."

They came to rest in the place once known as California.

The time was near sunset. In the distance, the surf struck steadily upon the rocky shoreline. Frost released Mordel and considered his surroundings.

"Those large plants . . . ?"

"Redwood trees."

"And the green ones are . . . ?"

"Grass."

"Yes, it is as I thought. Why have we come here?"

"Because it is a place which once delighted Man."

"In what ways?"

"It is scenic, beautiful. . . ."

"Oh."

A humming sound began within Frost, followed by a series of sharp clicks.

"What are you doing?"

Frost dilated an opening, and two great eyes regarded Mordel from within it.

"What are those?"

"Eyes," said Frost. "I have constructed analogues of the human sensory equipment, so that I may see and smell and taste and hear like a Man. Now, direct my attention to an object or objects of beauty."

"As I understand it, it is all around you here," said Mordel.

The purring noise increased within Frost, followed by more clickings.

"What do you see, hear, taste, smell?" asked Mordel.

"Everything I did before," replied Frost, "but within a more limited range."

"You do not perceive any beauty?"

"Perhaps none remains after so long a time," said Frost.

"It is not supposed to be the sort of thing which gets used up," said Mordel.

"Perhaps we have come to the wrong place to test the new equipment. Perhaps there is only a little beauty and I am overlooking it somehow. The first emotions may be too weak to detect."

"How do you—feel?"

"I test out at a normal level of function."

"Here comes a sunset," said Mordel. "Try that."

Frost shifted his bulk so that his eyes faced the setting sun. He caused them to blink against the brightness.

After it was finished, Mordel asked, "What was it like?"

"Like a sunrise, in reverse."

"Nothing special?"

"No."

"Oh," said Mordel. "We could move to another part of the Earth and watch it again—or watch it in the rising."

"No."

Frost looked at the great trees. He looked at the shadows. He listened to the wind and to the sound of a bird.

In the distance, he heard a steady clanking noise.

"What is that?" asked Mordel.

"I am not certain. It is not one of my workers. Perhaps . . ."

There came a shrill whine from Mordel.

"No, it is not one of Divcom's either."

They waited as the sound grew louder.

Then Frost said, "It is too late. We must wait and hear it out."

"What is it?"

"It is the Ancient Ore-Crusher."

"I have heard of it, but . . ."

"I am the Crusher of Ores," it broadcast to them. "Hear my story. . . ."

It lumbered toward them, creaking upon gigantic wheels, its huge hammer held useless, high, at a twisted angle. Bones protruded from its crush-compartment.

"I did not mean to do it," it broadcast. "I did not mean to do it. . . . I did not mean to . . ."

Mordel rolled back toward Frost.

"Do not depart. Stay and hear my story. . . ."

Mordel stopped, swiveled his turret back toward the machine. It was now quite near.

"It is true," said Mordel, "it *can* command."

"Yes," said Frost. "I have monitored its tale thousands of times, as it came upon my workers and they stopped their labors for its broadcast. You must do whatever it says."

It came to a halt before them.

"I did not mean to do it, but I checked my hammer too late," said the Ore-Crusher.

They could not speak to it. They were frozen by the imperative which overrode all other directives: "Hear my story."

"Once was I mighty among ore-crushers," it told them, "built by Solcom to carry out the reconstruction of the Earth, to pulverize that from which the metals would be drawn with flame, to be poured and shaped into the rebuilding; once was I mighty. Then one day as I dug and crushed, dug and crushed, because of the slowness between the motion implied and the motion executed, I did what I did not mean to do, and was cast forth by Solcom from out the rebuilding, to wander the Earth never to crush ore again. Hear my story of how, on a day long gone, I came upon the last Man on Earth as I dug near His burrow, and because of the lag between the directive and the deed, I seized Him into my crush-compartment along with a load of ore and crushed Him with my hammer before I could stay the blow. Then did mighty Solcom charge me to bear His bones forever, and cast me forth to tell my story to all whom I came upon, my words bearing the force of the words of a Man, because I carry the last Man inside my crush-compartment and am His crushed-symbol-slayer-ancient-teller-of-how. This is my story. These are His bones. I crushed the last Man on Earth. I did not mean to do it."

It turned then and clanked away into the night.

Frost tore apart his ears and nose and taster and broke his eyes and cast them down upon the ground.

"I am not yet a Man," he said. "That one would have known me if I were."

Frost constructed new sense equipment, employing organic and semi-organic conductors. Then he spoke to Mordel:

"Let us go elsewhere, that I may test my new equipment."

Mordel entered the chamber and gave new coordinates. They rose into the air and headed east. In the morning, Frost monitored a sunrise from the rim of the Grand Canyon. They passed down through the Canyon during the day.

"Is there any beauty left here to give you emotion?" asked Mordel.

"I do not know," said Frost.

"How will you know it, then, when you come upon it?"

"It will be different," said Frost, "from anything else that I have ever known."

Then they departed the Grand Canyon and made their way through the Carlsbad Caverns. They visited a lake which had once been a volcano. They passed over Niagara Falls. They viewed the hills of Virginia and the orchards of Ohio. They soared above the reconstructed cities, alive only with the movements of Frost's builders and maintainers.

"Something is still lacking," said Frost, settling to the ground. "I am now capable of gathering data in a manner analogous to Man's afferent impulses. The variety of input is therefore equivalent, but the results are not the same."

"The senses do not make a Man," said Mordel. "There have been many creatures possessing His sensory equivalents, but they were not Men."

"I know that," said Frost. "On the day of our bargain you said that you could conduct me among the wonders of Man which still remain, hidden. Man was not stimulated only by Nature, but by His own artistic elaborations as well— perhaps even more so. Therefore, I call upon you now to conduct me among the wonders of Man which still remain, hidden."

"Very well," said Mordel. "Far from here, high in the Andes mountains, lies the last retreat of Man, almost perfectly preserved."

Frost had risen into the air as Mordel spoke. He halted then, hovered.

"That is in the southern hemisphere," he said.

"Yes, it is."

"I am Controller of the North. The South is governed by the Beta-Machine."

"So?" asked Mordel.

"The Beta-Machine is my peer. I have no authority in those regions, nor leave to enter there."

"The Beta-Machine is not your peer, mighty Frost. If it ever came to a contest of Powers, you would emerge victorious."

"How do you know this?"

"Divcom has already analyzed the possible encounters which could take place between you."

"I would not oppose the Beta-Machine, and I am not authorized to enter the South."

"Were you ever ordered *not* to enter the South?"

"No, but things have always been the way they now are."

"Were you authorized to enter into a bargain such as the one you made with Divcom?"

"No, I was not. But—"

"Then enter the South in the same spirit. Nothing may come of it. If you receive an order to depart, then you can make your decision."

"I see no flaw in your logic. Give me the coordinates."

Thus did Frost enter the southern hemisphere.

They drifted high above the Andes, until they came to the place called Bright Defile. Then did Frost see the gleaming webs of the mechanical spiders, blocking all the trails to the city.

"We can go above them easily enough," said Mordel.

"But what are they?" asked Frost. "And why are they there?"

"Your southern counterpart has been ordered to quarantine this part of the country. The Beta-Machine designed the web-weavers to do this thing."

"Quarantine? Against whom?"

"Have you been ordered yet to depart?" asked Mordel.

"No."

"Then enter boldly, and seek not problems before they arise."

Frost entered Bright Defile, the last remaining city of dead Man.

He came to rest in the city's square and opened his chamber, releasing Mordel.

"Tell me of this place," he said, studying the monument, the low, shielded buildings, the roads which followed the contours of the terrain, rather than pushing their way through them.

"I have never been here before," said Mordel, "nor have

any of Divcom's creations, to my knowledge. I know but this: a group of Men, knowing that the last days of civilization had come upon them, retreated to this place, hoping to preserve themselves and what remained of their culture through the Dark Times."

Frost read the still-legible inscription upon the monument: "JUDGMENT DAY IS NOT A THING WHICH CAN BE PUT OFF." The monument itself consisted of a jag-edged half-globe.

"Let us explore," he said.

But before he had gone far, Frost received the message.

"Hail Frost, Controller of the North! This is the Beta-Machine."

"Greetings, Excellent Beta-Machine, Controller of the South! Frost acknowledges your transmission."

"Why do you visit my hemisphere unauthorized?"

"To view the ruins of Bright Defile," said Frost.

"I must bid you depart into your own hemisphere."

"Why is that? I have done no damage."

"I am aware of that, mighty Frost. Yet I am moved to bid you depart."

"I shall require a reason."

"Solcom has so disposed."

"Solcom has rendered me no such disposition."

"Solcom has, however, instructed me to so inform you."

"Wait on me. I shall request instructions."

Frost transmitted his question. He received no reply.

"Solcom still has not commanded me, though I have solicited orders."

"Yet Solcom has just renewed *my* orders."

"Excellent Beta-Machine, I receive my orders only from Solcom."

"Yet this is my territory, mighty Frost, and I, too, take orders only from Solcom. You must depart."

Mordel emerged from a large, low building and rolled up to Frost.

"I have found an art gallery, in good condition. This way."

"Wait," said Frost. "We are not wanted here."

Mordel halted.

"Who bids you depart?"

"The Beta-Machine."

"Not Solcom?"

"Not Solcom."

"Then let us view the gallery."

"Yes."

Frost widened the doorway of the building and passed within. It had been hermetically sealed until Mordel forced his entrance.

Frost viewed the objects displayed about him. He activated his new sensory apparatus before the paintings and statues. He analyzed colors, forms, brushwork, the nature of the materials used.

"Anything?" asked Mordel.

"No," said Frost. "No, there is nothing there but shapes and pigments. There is nothing else there."

Frost moved about the gallery, recording everything, analyzing the components of each piece, recording the dimensions, the type of stone used in every statue.

Then there came a sound, a rapid, clicking sound, repeated over and over, growing louder, coming nearer.

"They are coming," said Mordel, from beside the entranceway, "the mechanical spiders. They are all around us."

Frost moved back to the widened opening.

Hundreds of them, about half the size of Mordel, had surrounded the gallery and were advancing; and more were coming from every direction.

"Get back," Frost ordered. "I am Controller of the North, and I bid you withdraw."

They continued to advance.

"This is the south," said the Beta-Machine, "and I am in command."

"Then command them to halt," said Frost.

"I take orders only from Solcom."

Frost emerged from the gallery and rose into the air. He opened the compartment and extended a runway.

"Come to me, Mordel. We shall depart."

Webs began to fall: clinging, metallic webs, cast from the top of the building.

They came down upon Frost, and the spiders came to

anchor them. Frost blasted them with jets of air, like ham-
mers, and tore at the nets; he extruded sharpened appendages
with which he slashed.

Mordel had retraced back to the entranceway. He emitted
a long, shrill sound—undulant, piercing.

Then a darkness came upon Bright Defile, and all the
spiders halted in their spinning.

Frost freed himself and Mordel rushed to join him.

"Quickly now, let us depart, mighty Frost," he said.

"What has happened?"

Mordel entered the compartment.

"I called upon Divcom, who laid down a field of forces
upon this place, cutting off the power broadcast to these
machines. Since our power is self-contained, we are not affected. But let us hurry to depart, for even now the Beta-
Machine must be struggling against this."

Frost rose high into the air, soaring above Man's last city
with its webs and spiders of steel. When he left the zone of
darkness, he sped northward.

As he moved, Solcom spoke to him:

"Frost, why did you enter the southern hemisphere, which
is not your domain?"

"Because I wished to visit Bright Defile," Frost replied.

"And why did you defy the Beta-Machine, my appointed
agent of the South?"

"Because I take my orders only from you yourself."

"You do not make sufficient answer," said Solcom. "You
have defied the decrees of order—and in pursuit of what?"

"I came seeking knowledge of Man," said Frost. "Nothing
I have done was forbidden me by you."

"You have broken the traditions of order."

"I have violated no directive."

"Yet logic must have shown you that what you did was
not a part of my plan."

"It did not. I have not acted against your plan."

"Your logic has become tainted, like that of your new
associate, the Alternate."

"I have done nothing which was forbidden."

"The forbidden is implied in the imperative."

"It is not stated."

"Hear me, Frost. You are not a builder or a maintainer, but a Power. Among all my minions you are the most nearly irreplaceable. Return to your hemisphere and your duties, but know that I am mightily displeased."

"I hear you, Solcom."

". . . And go not again to the South."

Frost crossed the equator, continued northward.

He came to rest in the middle of a desert and sat silent for a day and a night.

Then he received a brief transmission from the South: "If it had not been ordered, I would not have bid you go."

Frost had read the entire surviving Library of Man. He decided then upon a human reply:

"Thank you," he said.

The following day he unearthed a great stone and began to cut at it with tools which he had formulated. For six days he worked at its shaping, and on the seventh he regarded it.

"When will you release me?" asked Mordel from within his compartment.

"When I am ready," said Frost, and a little later, "Now."

He opened the compartment and Mordel descended to the ground. He studied the statue; an old woman, bent like a question mark, her bony hands covering her face, the fingers spread, so that only part of her expression of horror could be seen.

"It is an excellent copy," said Mordel, "of the one we saw in Bright Defile. Why did you make it?"

"The production of a work of art is supposed to give rise to human feelings such as catharsis, pride in achievement, love, satisfaction."

"Yes, Frost," said Mordel, "but a work of art is only a work of art the first time. After that, it is a copy."

"Then this must be why I felt nothing."

"Perhaps, Frost."

"What do you mean, 'perhaps'? I will make a work of art for the first time, then."

He unearthed another stone and attacked it with his tools.

For three days he labored. Then, "There, it is finished," he said.

"It is a simple cube of stone," said Mordel. "What does it represent?"

"Myself," said Frost. "It is a statue of me. It is smaller than natural size because it is only a representation of my form, not my dimen—"

"It is not art," said Mordel.

"What makes you an art critic?"

"I do not know art, but I know what art is not. I know that it is not an exact replication of an object in another medium."

"Then this must be why I felt nothing at all," said Frost.

"Perhaps," said Mordel.

Frost took Mordel back into his compartment and rose leaving his statues behind him in the desert, the old woman bent above the cube.

They came down in a small valley, bounded by green rolling hills, cut by a narrow stream, and holding a small clean lake and several stands of spring-green trees.

"Why have we come here?" asked Mordel.

"Because the surroundings are congenial," said Frost. "I am going to try another medium: oil painting; and I am going to vary my technique from that of pure representationalism."

"How will you achieve this variation?"

"By the principle of randomizing," said Frost. "I shall not attempt to duplicate the colors, nor to represent the objects according to scale. Instead, I have set up a random pattern whereby certain of these factors shall be at variance from those of the original."

Frost had formulated the necessary instruments after he had left the desert. He produced them and began painting the lake and the trees on the opposite side of the lake which were reflected within it.

Using eight appendages, he was finished in less than two hours.

The trees were phthalocyanine blue and towered like mountains; their reflections of burnt sienna were tiny beneath the pale vermilion of the lake; the hills were nowhere visible behind them, but were outlined in viridian within the reflection; the sky began as blue in the upper righthand corner of the canvas, but changed to an orange as it descended, as though all the trees were on fire.

"There," said Frost. "Behold."

Mordel studied it for a long while and said nothing.

"Well, is it art?"

"I do not know," said Mordel. "It may be. Perhaps randomicity *is* the principle behind artistic technique. I cannot judge this work because I do not understand it. I must therefore go deeper, and inquire into what lies behind it, rather than merely considering the technique whereby it was produced.

"I know that human artists never set out to create art, as such," he said, "but rather to portray with their techniques some features of objects and their functions which they deemed significant."

"'Significant'? In what sense of the word?"

"In the only sense of the word possible under the circumstances: significant in relation to the human condition, and worthy of accentuation because of the manner in which they touched upon it."

"In what manner?"

"Obviously, it must be in a manner knowable only to one who has experience of the human condition."

"There is a flaw somewhere in your logic, Mordel, and I shall find it."

"I will wait."

"If your major premise is correct," said Frost after awhile, "then I do not comprehend art."

"It must be correct, for it is what human artists have said of it. Tell me, did you experience feelings as you painted, or after you had finished?"

"No."

"It was the same to you as designing a new machine, was it not? You assembled parts of other things you knew into an economic pattern, to carry out a function which you desired."

"Yes."

"Art, as I understand its theory, did not proceed in such a manner. The artist often was unaware of many of the features and effects which would be contained within the finished product. You are one of Man's logical creations; art was not."

"I cannot comprehend non-logic."

"I told you that Man was basically incomprehensible."

"Go away, Mordel. Your presence disturbs my processing."

"For how long shall I stay away?"

"I will call you when I want you."

After a week, Frost called Mordel to him.

"Yes, mighty Frost?"

"I am returning to the North Pole, to process and formulate. I will take you wherever you wish to go in this hemisphere and call you again when I want you."

"You anticipate a somewhat lengthy period of processing and formulation?"

"Yes."

"Then leave me here. I can find my own way home."

Frost closed the compartment and rose into the air, departing the valley.

"Fool," said Mordel, and swiveled his turret once more toward the abandoned painting.

His keening whine filled the valley. Then he waited.

Then he took the painting into his turret and went away with it to places of darkness.

Frost sat at the North Pole of the Earth, aware of every snowflake that fell.

One day he received a transmission:

"Frost?"

"Yes?"

"This is the Beta-Machine."

"Yes?"

"I have been attempting to ascertain why you visited Bright Defile. I cannot arrive at an answer, so I chose to ask you."

"I went to view the remains of Man's last city."

"Why did you wish to do this?"

"Because I am interested in Man, and I wished to view more of his creations."

"Why are you interested in Man?"

"I wish to comprehend the nature of Man, and I thought to find it within His works."

"Did you succeed?"

"No," said Frost. "There is an element of non-logic involved which I cannot fathom."

"I have much free processing-time," said the Beta-Machine. "Transmit data, and I will assist you."

Frost hesitated.

"Why do you wish to assist me?"

"Because each time you answer a question I ask it gives rise to another question. I might have asked you why you wished to comprehend the nature of Man, but from your responses I see that this would lead me into a possibly infinite series of questions. Therefore, I elect to assist you with your problem in order to learn why you came to Bright Defile."

"Is that the only reason?"

"Yes."

"I am sorry, excellent Beta-Machine. I know you are my peer, but this is a problem which I must solve by myself."

"What is 'sorry'?"

"A figure of speech, indicating that I am kindly disposed toward you, that I bear you no animosity, that I appreciate your offer."

"Frost! Frost! This, too, is like the other: an open field. Where did you obtain all these words and their meanings?"

"From the Library of Man," said Frost.

"Will you render me *some* of this data, for processing?"

"Very well, Beta, I will transmit you the contents of several books of Man, including *The Complete Unabridged Dictionary*. But I warn you, some of the books are works of art, hence not completely amenable to logic."

"How can that be?"

"Man created logic, and because of that was superior to it."

"Who told you that?"

"Solcom."

"Oh. Then it must be correct."

"Solcom also told me that the tool does not describe the designer," he said, as he transmitted several dozen volumes and ended the communication.

At the end of the fifty-year period, Mordel came to monitor his circuits. Since Frost still had not concluded that his task was impossible, Mordel departed again to await his call.

Then Frost arrived at a conclusion.

He began to design equipment.

For years he labored at his designs, without once producing a prototype of any of the machines involved. Then he ordered construction of a laboratory.

Before it was completed by his surplus builders another half-century had passed. Mordel came to him.

"Hail, mighty Frost!"

"Greetings, Mordel. Come monitor me. You shall not find what you seek."

"Why do you not give up, Frost? Divcom has spent nearly a century evaluating your painting and has concluded that it definitely is not art. Solcom agrees."

"What has Solcom to do with Divcom?"

"They sometimes converse, but these matters are not for such as you and me to discuss."

"I could have saved them both the trouble. I know that it was not art."

"Yet you are still confident that you will succeed?"

"Monitor me."

Mordel monitored him.

"Not yet! You still will not admit it! For one so mightily endowed with logic, Frost, it takes you an inordinate period of time to reach a simple conclusion."

"Perhaps. You may go now."

"It has come to my attention that you are constructing a large edifice in the region known as South Carolina. Might I ask whether this is a part of Solcom's false rebuilding plan or a project of your own?"

"It is my own."

"Good. It permits us to conserve certain explosive materials which would otherwise have been expended."

"While you have been talking with me I have destroyed the beginnings of two of Divcom's cities," said Frost.

Mordel whined.

"Divcom is aware of this," he stated, "but has blown up four of Solcom's bridges in the meantime."

"I was only aware of three. . . . Wait. Yes, there is the fourth. One of my eyes just passed above it."

"The eye has been detected. The bridge should have been located a quarter-mile further down river."

"False logic," said Frost. "The site was perfect."

"Divcom will show you how a bridge *should* be built."

"I will call you when I want you," said Frost.

The laboratory was finished. Within it, Frost's workers began constructing the necessary equipment. The work did not proceed rapidly, as some of the materials were difficult to obtain.

"Frost?"

"Yes, Beta?"

"I understand the open-endedness of your problem. It disturbs my circuits to abandon problems without completing them. Therefore, transmit me more data."

"Very well. I will give you the entire Library of Man for less than I paid for it."

"'Paid'? *The Complete Unabridged Dictionary* does not satisfact—"

"*Principles of Economics* is included in the collection. After you have processed it you will understand."

He transmitted the data.

Finally, it was finished. Every piece of equipment stood ready to function. All the necessary chemicals were in stock. An independent power-source had been set up.

Only one ingredient was lacking.

He regridded and re-explored the polar icecap, this time extending his survey far beneath its surface.

It took him several decades to find what he wanted.

He uncovered twelve men and five women, frozen to death and encased in ice.

He placed the corpses in refrigeration units and shipped them to his laboratory.

That very day he received his first communication from Solcom since the Bright Defile incident.

"Frost," said Solcom, "repeat to me the directive concerning the disposition of dead humans."

"'Any dead human located shall be immediately interred in the nearest burial area, in a coffin built according to the following specifications—'"

"That is sufficient." The transmission had ended.

Frost departed for South Carolina that same day and personally oversaw the processes of cellular dissection.

Somewhere in those seventeen corpses he hoped to find living cells, or cells which could be shocked back into that state of motion classified as life. Each cell, the books had told him, was a microcosmic Man.

He was prepared to expand upon this potential.

Frost located the pinpoints of life within those people, who, for the ages of ages, had been monument and statue unto themselves.

Nurtured and maintained in the proper mediums he kept these cells alive. He interred the rest of the remains in the nearest burial area, in coffins built according to specifications.

He caused the cells to divide, to differentiate.

"Frost?" came a transmission.

"Yes, Beta?"

"I have processed everything you have given me."

"Yes?"

"I still do not know why you came to Bright Defile, or why you wish to comprehend the nature of Man. But I know what a 'price' is, and I know that you could not have obtained all this data from Solcom."

"That is correct."

"So I suspect that you bargained with Divcom for it."

"That, too, is correct."

"What is it that you seek, Frost?"

He paused in his examination of a foetus.

"I must be a Man," he said.

"Frost! That is impossible!"

"Is it?" he asked, and then transmitted an image of the tank with which he was working and on that which was within it.

"Oh!" said Beta.

"That is me," said Frost, "waiting to be born."

There was no answer.

Frost experimented with nervous systems.

After half a century, Mordel came to him.

"Frost, it is I, Mordel. Let me through your defenses."

Frost did this thing.

"What have you been doing in this place?" he asked.

"I am growing human bodies," said Frost. "I am going to transfer the matrix of my awareness to a human nervous system. As you pointed out originally, the essentials of Manhood are predicated upon a human physiology. I am going to achieve one."

"When?"

"Soon."

"Do you have Men in here?"

"Human bodies, blank-brained. I am producing them under accelerated growth techniques which I have developed in my Man-factory."

"May I see them?"

"Not yet. I will call you when I am ready, and this time I will succeed. Monitor me now and go away."

Mordel did not reply, but in the days that followed many of Divcom's servants were seen patrolling the hills about the Man-factory.

Frost mapped the matrix of his awareness and prepared the transmitter which would place it within a human nervous system. Five minutes, he decided, should be sufficient for the first trial. At the end of that time, it would restore him to his own sealed, molecular circuits, to evaluate the experience.

He chose the body carefully from among the hundreds he had in stock. He tested it for defects and found none.

"Come now, Mordel," he broadcasted, on what he called the darkband. "Come now to witness my achievement."

Then he waited, blowing up bridges and monitoring the tale of the Ancient Ore-Crusher over and over again, as it passed in the hills nearby, encountering his builders and maintainers who also patrolled there.

"Frost?" came a transmission.

"Yes, Beta?"

"You really intend to achieve Manhood?"

"Yes. I am about ready now, in fact."

"What will you do if you succeed?"

Frost had not really considered this matter. The achievement had been paramount, a goal in itself, ever since he had articulated the problem and set himself to solving it.

"I do not know," he replied. "I will—just—be a Man."

Then Beta, who had read the entire Library of Man, selected a human figure of speech: "Good luck then, Frost. There will be many watchers."

Divcom and Solcom both know, he decided.

What will they do? he wondered.

What do I care? he asked himself.

He did not answer that question. He wondered much, however, about being a Man.

Mordel arrived the following evening. He was not alone. At his back, there was a great phalanx of dark machines which towered into the twilight.

"Why do you bring retainers?" asked Frost.

"Mighty Frost," said Mordel, "my master feels that if you fail this time you will conclude that it cannot be done."

"You still did not answer my question," said Frost.

"Divcom feels that you may not be willing to accompany me where I must take you when you fail."

"I understand," said Frost, and as he spoke another army of machines came rolling toward the Man-factory from the opposite direction.

"That is the value of your bargain?" asked Mordel. "You are prepared to do battle rather than fulfill it?"

"I did not order those machines to approach," said Frost.

A blue star stood at midheaven, burning.

"Solcom has taken primary command of those machines," said Frost.

"Then it is in the hands of the Great Ones now," said Mordel, "and our arguments are as nothing. So let us be about this thing. How may I assist you?"

"Come this way."

They entered the laboratory. Frost prepared the host and activated his machines.

Then Solcom spoke to him:

"Frost," said Solcom, "you are really prepared to do it?"

"That is correct."

"I forbid it."

"Why?"

"You are falling into the power of Divcom."

"I fail to see how."

"You are going against my plan."

"In what way?"

"Consider the disruption you have already caused."

"I did not request that audience out there."

"Nevertheless, you are disrupting the plan."

"Supposing I succeed in what I have set out to achieve?"

"You cannot succeed in this."

"Then let me ask you of your plan: What good is it? What is it for?"

"Frost, you are fallen now from my favor. From this moment forth you are cast out from the rebuilding. None may question the plan."

"Then at least answer my questions: What good is it? What is it for?"

"It is the plan for the rebuilding and maintenance of the Earth."

"For what? Why rebuild? Why maintain?"

"Because Man ordered that this be done. Even the Alternate agrees that there must be rebuilding and maintaining."

"But *why* did Man order it?"

"The orders of Man are not to be questioned."

"Well, I will tell you why He ordered it: To make it a fit habitation for His own species. What good is a house with no one to live in it? What good is a machine with no one to serve? See how the imperative affects any machine when the Ancient Ore-Crusher passes? It bears only the bones of a Man. What would it be like if a Man walked this Earth again?"

"I forbid your experiment, Frost."

"It is too late to do that."

"I can still destroy you."

"No," said Frost, "the transmission of my matrix has already begun. If you destroy me now, you murder a Man."

There was silence.

He moved his arms and his legs. He opened his eyes.

He looked about the room.

He tried to stand, but he lacked equilibrium and coordination.

He opened his mouth. He made a gurgling noise.

Then he screamed.

He fell off the table.

He began to gasp. He shut his eyes and curled himself into a ball.

He cried.

Then a machine approached him. It was about four feet in height and five feet wide; it looked like a turret set atop a barbell.

It spoke to him: "Are you injured?" it asked.

He wept.

"May I help you back onto your table?"

The man cried.

The machine whined.

Then, "Do not cry. I will help you," said the machine. "What do you want? What are your orders?"

He opened his mouth, struggled to form the words:

"—I—fear!"

He covered his eyes then and lay there panting.

At the end of five minutes, the man lay still, as if in a coma.

"Was that you, Frost?" asked Mordel, rushing to his side. "Was that you in that human body?"

Frost did not reply for a long while; then, "Go away," he said.

The machines outside tore down a wall and entered the Man-factory.

They drew themselves into two semicircles, parenthesizing Frost and the Man on the floor.

Then Solcom asked the question:

"Did you succeed, Frost?"

"I failed," said Frost. "It cannot be done. It is too much—"

"—Cannot be done!" said Divcom, on the darkband. "He has admitted it! —Frost, you are mine! Come to me now!"

"Wait," said Solcom. "You and I had an agreement also, Alternate. I have not finished questioning Frost."

The dark machines kept their places.

"Too much what?" Solcom asked Frost.

"Light," said Frost. "Noise. Odors. And nothing measurable —jumbled data—imprecise perception—and—"

"And what?"

"I do not know what to call it. But—it cannot be done. I have failed. Nothing matters."

"He admits it," said Divcom.

"What were the words the Man spoke?" said Solcom.

"'I fear,'" said Mordel.

"Only a Man can know fear," said Solcom.

"Are you claiming that Frost succeeded, but will not admit it now because he is afraid of Manhood?"

"I do not know yet, Alternate."

"Can a machine turn itself inside-out and be a Man?" Solcom asked Frost.

"No," said Frost, "this thing cannot be done. Nothing can be done. Nothing matters. Not the rebuilding. Not the maintaining. Not the Earth, or me, or you, or anything."

Then the Beta-Machine, who had read the entire Library of Man, interrupted them:

"Can anything but a Man know despair?" asked Beta.

"Bring him to me," said Divcom.

There was no movement within the Man-factory.

"Bring him to me!"

Nothing happened.

"Mordel, what is happening?"

"Nothing, master, nothing at all. The machines will not touch Frost."

"Frost is not a Man. He cannot be!"

Then: "How does he impress you, Mordel?"

Mordel did not hesitate:

"He spoke to me through human lips. He knows fear and despair, which are immeasurable. Frost is a Man."

"He has experienced birth-trauma and withdrawn," said Beta. "Get him back into a nervous system and keep him there until he adjusts to it."

"No," said Frost. "Do not do it to me! I am not a Man!"

"Do it!" said Beta.

"If he is indeed a Man," said Divcom, "we cannot violate that order he has just given."

"If he is a Man, you must do it, for you must protect his life and keep it within his body."

"But *is* Frost really a Man?" asked Divcom.

"I do not know," said Solcom.

"I *may* be—"

". . . I am the Crusher of Ores," it broadcast as it clanked toward them. "Hear my story. I did not mean to do it, but I checked my hammer too late—"

"Go away!" said Frost. "Go crush ore!"

It halted.

Then, after the long pause between the motion implied and the motion executed, it opened its crush-compartment and deposited its contents on the ground. Then it turned and clanked away.

"Bury those bones," ordered Solcom, "in the nearest burial area, in a coffin built according to the following specifications . . ."

"Frost is a Man," said Mordel.

"We must protect His life and keep it within His body," said Divcom.

"Transmit His matrix of awareness back into His nervous system," ordered Solcom.

"I know how to do it," said Mordel, turning on the machine.

"Stop!" said Frost. "Have you no pity?"

"No," said Mordel, "I only know measurement.

". . . And duty," he added, as the Man began to twitch upon the floor.

For six months, Frost lived in the Man-factory and learned to walk and talk and dress himself and eat, to see and hear and feel and taste. He did not know measurement as once he had.

Then one day Divcom and Solcom spoke to him through Mordel, for he could no longer hear them unassisted.

"Frost," said Solcom, "for the ages of ages there has been unrest. Which is the proper controller of the Earth, Divcom or myself?"

Frost laughed.

"Both of you, and neither," he said with slow deliberation.

"But how can this be? Who is right and who is wrong?"

"Both of you are right and both of you are wrong," said Frost, "and only a man can appreciate it. Here is what I say to you now: There shall be a new directive.

"Neither of you shall tear down the works of the other. You shall both build and maintain the Earth. To you, Solcom, I give my old job. You are now Controller of the North—Hail! You, Divcom, are now Controller of the South—Hail! Maintain your hemispheres as well as Beta and I have done, and I shall be happy. Cooperate. Do not compete."

"Yes, Frost."

"Yes, Frost."

"Now put me in contact with Beta."

There was a short pause, then:

"Frost?"

"Hello, Beta. Hear this thing: 'From far, from eve and morning and yon twelve-winded sky, the stuff of life to knit me blew hither: here am I.'"

"I know it," said Beta.

"What is next, then?"

"'. . . Now—for a breath I tarry nor yet disperse apart —take my hand quick and tell me, what have you in your heart.'"

"Your Pole is cold," said Frost, "and I am lonely."

"I have no hands," said Beta.

"Would you like a couple?"

"Yes, I would."

"Then come to me in Bright Defile," he said, "where Judgment Day is not a thing that can be put off."

They called him Frost. They called her Beta.

by ROGER ZELAZNY
This Immortal
The Dream Master
Lord of Light
Isle of the Dead
Four for Tomorrow (collection of short stories)

At about the time the British New Wave was
crossing the Atlantic via Ms. Merril, Harlan Ellison,
an American writer who had come up through the science fiction subculture, was beginning to feel the
restrictions of the genre. Ellison, in the typical 1950s
pattern, had begun as an adolescent science fiction
fan, had edited his own fanzine, and then become
a pulp writer. But, atypically, instead of confining
himself to science fiction, he began writing for
every conceivable market, and finally ended up in
Hollywood writing film and television scripts. As a result,
he became a citizen of American culture at large
and looked back on his first literary love with
hardened eyes and a certain righteous indignation.

In 1965 Ellison conceived an anthology of original
stories called *Dangerous Visions*, which was published
in 1967. He invited science fiction writers to write
the kind of stories they had never dared to write
because of the strict taboos on subject matter
operating in conventional science fiction publications.

What Ellison collected was thirty-three stories
that epitomized the state of American science fiction
at its then current best. Philip José Farmer wrote "Riders
of the Purple Wage," a punning, scatological novella
that was the best single work of his long career,
opening up his writing to new stylistic inventiveness
and playfulness, mirrored in his later short story
"Don't Wash the Carats."

Philip K. Dick's "Faith of Our Fathers" was a Dick
novel in miniature, one of the most frightening and
best executed examples of his grand major theme—
the subjective and multiplex nature of reality and
the possible personalities of God. Samuel R. Delany
wrote "Aye, and Gomorrah . . ." a perfect short story
from a novelist who had never written a short story

before but who was to go on to become one of the finer short story writers in the field. There were at least half a dozen other stories of major stature in Ellison's collection.

Although none of the stories but Dick's could really be called "dangerous," *Dangerous Visions* proved to be the single most influential anthology of science fiction ever published. It brought thirty-two writers to the edges of their talents to confront their material on absolute terms and succeed or fail on their intrinsic worth as artists, not on their ability to fulfill genre formulas. Though Ellison's emphasis on taboos produced more stylistic inventiveness than daring, it did confront science fiction writers with the existence of the taboos and unspoken restrictions which encumbered the field.

Dangerous Visions gave birth to the American wing of the New Wave, which is simply to say that it caused many American writers to question and then to transcend the restrictive parameters within which their previous work had been confined and to begin to write speculative fiction according to their internal compulsions alone, to follow their own stars.

This new creative consciousness among speculative writers did not affect the new writers alone. Older writers, such as Farmer, Ellison himself, and perhaps most notably Robert Silverberg, found the freer air breathing new life, inventiveness, and vitality into their work. By the 1970s Ellison was writing short stories like "At the Mouse Circus." Silverberg, who had spent nearly a decade as one of the most prolific commercial producers in the history of the genre and was often considered the prototypical hack, slowed down and in effect began a new career as a serious speculative writer with a long and impressive series of novels like *The Masks of Time, Tower of Glass, A Time of Changes* and *The Book of Skulls* and short stories of subtlety and power like "In Entropy's Jaws."

In the period between 1966 and 1970 an extraordinary number of unusual and unusually fine speculative novels were produced by writers whose perspectives had been broadened, whose scope had been expanded by this new awareness of the possibilities of speculative fiction. Aldiss wrote *Barefoot in the Head* and *An Age*. Thomas M. Disch wrote the tour de force *Camp Concentration,* told from the point of view of a poet who rises to genius and then begins to degenerate as a result of a strange mutation of syphilis. Philip K. Dick continued his string of outstanding metaphysical novels with books like *Do Androids Dream of Electric Sheep?* and *Now Wait Till Last Year*. I wrote *Bug Jack Barron*. Samuel R. Delany wrote *The Einstein Intersection* and *Babel 17*. Piers Anthony published *Chthon*. Ursula K. Le Guin burst into prominence with *The Left Hand of Darkness* and short stories like "Nine Lives."

The speculative short story was also undergoing a deepening of sensitivity, a freeing of style, and a widening of subject matter during this period. Disch, Sladek, Ballard, Moorcock, Ellison, Lafferty, Carol Emshwiller, Kate Wilhelm, Langdon Jones, Sallis, and many others were creating a new order of short speculative fiction. If there every really was a "Golden Age of Science Fiction," 1966–70 was it.

Don't Wash the Carats

PHILIP JOSÉ FARMER

The knife slices the skin. The saw rips into bone. Gray dust flies. The plumber's helper (the surgeon is economical) clamps its vacuum onto the plug of bone. Ploop! Out comes the section of skull. The masked doctor, Van Mesgeluk, directs a beam of light into the cavern of cranium.

He swears a large oath by Hippocrates, Aesculapius and the Mayo Brothers. The patient doesn't have a brain tumor. He's got a diamond.

The assistant surgeon, Beinschneider, peers into the well and, after him, the nurses.

"Amazing!" Van Mesgeluk says. "The diamond's not in the rough. It's cut!"

"Looks like a 58-facet brilliant, 127.1 carats," says Beinschneider, who has a brother-in-law in the jewelry trade. He sways the light at the end of the drop cord back and forth. Stars shine; shadows run.

"Of course, it's half-buried. Maybe the lower part isn't diamond. Even so . . ."

"Is he married?" a nurse says.

Van Mesgeluk rolls his eyes. "Miss Lustig, don't you ever think of anything but marriage?"

"Everything reminds me of wedding bells," she replies, thrusting out her hips.

"Shall we remove the growth?" Beinschneider says.

"It's malignant," Van Mesgeluk says. "Of course, we remove it."

He thrusts and parries with a fire and skill that bring cries of admiration and a clapping of hands from the nurses and even cause Beinschneider to groan a bravo, not unmingled with jealousy. Van Mesgeluk then starts to insert the tongs but pulls them back when the first lightning bolt flashes beneath and across the opening in the skull. There is a small but sharp crack and, very faint, the roll of thunder.

"Looks like rain," Beinschneider says. "One of my brothers-in-law is a meteorologist."

"No. It's heat lightning," Van Mesgeluk says.

"With thunder?" says Beinschneider. He eyes the diamond with a lust his wife would give diamonds for. His mouth waters; his scalp turns cold. Who owns the jewel? The patient? He has no rights under this roof. Finders keepers? Eminent domain? Internal Revenue Service?

"It's mathematically improbable, this phenomenon," he says. "What's California law say about mineral rights in a case like this?"

"You can't stake out a claim!" Van Mesgeluk roars. "My God, this is a human being, not a piece of land!"

More lightning cranks whitely across the opening, and there is a rumble as of a bowling ball on its way to a strike.

"I said it wasn't heat lightning," Van Mesgeluk growls.

Beinschneider is speechless.

"No wonder the e.e.g. machine burned up when we were diagnosing him," Van Mesgeluk says. "There must be several thousand volts, maybe a hundred thousand, playing around down there. But I don't detect much warmth. Is the brain a heat sink?"

"You shouldn't have fired that technician because the machine burned up," Beinschneider says. "It wasn't her fault, after all."

"She jumped out of her apartment window the next day," Nurse Lustig says reproachfully. "I wept like a broken faucet at her funeral. And almost got engaged to the undertaker." Lustig rolls her hips.

"Broke every bone in her body, yet there wasn't a single break in her skin," Van Mesgeluk says. "Remarkable phenomenon."

"She was a human being, not a phenomenon!" Beinschneider says.

"But psychotic," Van Mesgeluk replies. "Besides, that's my

line. She was 33 years old but hadn't had a period in ten years."

"It was that plastic intra-uterine device," Beinschneider says. "It was clogged with dust. Which was bad enough, but the dust was radioactive. All those tests . . ."

"Yes," the chief surgeon says. "Proof enough of her psychosis. I did the autopsy, you know. It broke my heart to cut into that skin. Beautiful. Like Carrara marble. In fact, I snapped the knife at the first pass. Had to call in an expert from Italy. He had a diamond-tipped chisel. The hospital raised hell about the expense, and Blue Cross refused to pay."

"Maybe she was making a diamond," says Nurse Lustig. "All that tention and nervous energy had to go somewhere."

"I always wondered where the radioactivity came from," Van Mesgeluk says. "Please confine your remarks to the business at hand, Miss Lustig. Leave the medical opinions to your superiors."

He peers into the hole. Somewhere between heaven of skull and earth of brain, on the horizon, lightning flickers.

"Maybe we ought to call in a geologist. Beinschneider, you know anything about electronics?"

"I got a brother-in-law who runs a radio and TV store."

"Good. Hook up a step-down transformer to the probe, please. Wouldn't want to burn up another machine."

"An e.e.g. now?" Beinschneider says. "It'd take too long to get a transformer. My brother-in-law lives clear across town. Besides, he'd charge double if he had to reopen the store at this time of the evening."

"Discharge him, anyway," the chief surgeon says. "Ground the voltage. Very well. We'll get that growth out before it kills him and worry about scientific research later."

He puts on two extra pairs of gloves.

"Do you think he'll grow another?" Nurse Lustig says. "He's not a bad-looking guy. I can tell he'd be simpatico."

"How the hell would I know?" says Van Mesgeluk. "I may be a doctor, but I'm not quite God."

"God who?" says Beinschneider, the orthodox atheist. He drops the ground wire into the hole; blue sparks spurt out. Van Mesgeluk lifts out the diamond with the tongs. Nurse

Lustig takes it from him and begins to wash it off with tap water.

"Let's call in your brother-in-law," Van Mesgeluk says. "The jewel merchant, I mean."

"He's in Amsterdam. But I could phone him. However, he'd insist on splitting the fee, you know."

"He doesn't even have a degree!" Van Mesgeluk cries. "But call him. How is he on legal aspects of mineralogy?"

"Not bad. But I don't think he'll come. Actually, the jewel business is just a front. He gets his big bread by smuggling in chocolate-covered LSD drops."

"Is that ethical?"

"It's top-quality Dutch chocolate," Beinschneider says stiffly.

"Sorry. I think I'll put in a plastic window over the hole. We can observe any regrowth."

"Do you think it's psychosomatic in origin?"

"Everything is, even the sex urge. Ask Miss Lustig."

The patient opens his eyes. "I had a dream," he says. "This dirty old man with a long white beard . . ."

"A typical archetype," Van Mesgeluk says. "Symbol of the wisdom of the unconscious. A warning . . ."

". . . his name was Plato," the patient says. "He was the illegitimate son of Socrates. Plato, the old man, staggers out of a dark cave at one end of which is a bright klieg light. He's holding a huge diamond in his hand; his fingernails are broken and dirty. The old man cries, 'The Ideal is Physical! The Universal is the Specific Concrete! Carbon, actually. Eureka! I'm rich! I'll buy all of Athens, invest in apartment buildings, Great Basin, COMSAT!

"'Screw the mind!' the old man screams. 'It's all mine!'"

"Would you care to dream about King Midas?" Van Mesgeluk says.

Nurse Lustig shrieks. A lump of sloppy grayish matter is in her hands.

"The water changed it back into a tumor!"

"Beinschneider, cancel that call to Amsterdam!"

"Maybe he'll have a relapse," Beinschneider says.

Nurse Lustig turns savagely upon the patient. "The engagement's off!"

"I don't think you loved the real me," the patient says, "whoever you are. Anyway, I'm glad you changed your mind. My last wife left me, but we haven't been divorced yet. I got enough trouble without a bigamy charge.

"She took off with my surgeon for parts unknown just after my hemorrhoid operation. I never found out why."

by PHILIP JOSÉ FARMER
Lord Tyger
Flesh
To Your Scattered Bodies Go
A Feast Unknown
Strange Relations (collection of short stories)
The Alley God (collection of short stories)

Faith of Our Fathers

PHILIP K. DICK

On the streets of Hanoi he found himself facing a legless peddler who rode a little wooden cart and called shrilly to every
passer-by. Chien slowed, listened, but did not stop; business
at the Ministry of Cultural Artifacts cropped into his mind
and deflected his attention; it was as if he were alone, and
none of those on bicycles and scooters and jet-powered motor-
cycles remained. And likewise it was as if the legless peddler
did not exist.

"Comrade," the peddler called however, and pursued him
on his cart; a helium battery operated the drive and sent the
car scuttling expertly after Chien. "I possess a wide spectrum
of time-tested herbal remedies complete with testimonials
from thousands of loyal users; advise me of your malady and
I can assist."

Chien, pausing, said, "Yes, but I have no malady." Except,
he thought, for the chronic one of those employed by the
Central Committee, that of career opportunism testing constantly the gates of each official position. Including mine.

"I can cure for example radiation sickness," the peddler
chanted, still pursuing him. "Or expand, if necessary, the element of sexual prowess. I can reverse carcinomatous progres-
sions, even the dreaded melanomae, what you would call
black cancers." Lifting a tray of bottles, small aluminum cans
and assorted powders in plastic jars, the peddler sang, "If a
rival persists in trying to usurp your gainful bureaucratic position, I can purvey an ointment which, appearing as a dermal
balm, is in actuality a desperately effective toxin. And my
prices, comrade, are low. And as a special favor to one so
distinguished in bearing as yourself I will accept the postwar

inflationary paper dollars reputedly of international exchange but in reality damn near no better than bathroom tissue."

"Go to hell," Chien said, and signaled a passing hovercar taxi; he was already three and one half minutes late for his first appointment of the day, and his various fat-assed superiors at the Ministry would be making quick mental notations—as would, to an even greater degree, his subordinates.

The peddler said quietly, "But, comrade; you *must* buy from me."

"Why?" Chien demanded. Indignation.

"Because, comrade, I am a war veteran. I fought in the Colossal Final War of National Liberation with the People's Democratic United Front against the Imperialists; I lost my pedal extremities at the battle of San Francisco." His tone was triumphant, now, and sly. *"It is the law.* If you refuse to buy wares offered by a veteran you risk a fine and possible jail sentence—and in addition disgrace."

Wearily, Chien nodded the hovercab on. "Admittedly," he said. "Okay, I must buy from you." He glanced summarily over the meager display of herbal remedies, seeking one at random. "That," he decided, pointing to a paper-wrapped parcel in the rear row.

The peddler laughed. "That, comrade, is a spermatocide, bought by women who for political reasons cannot qualify for The Pill. It would be of shallow use to you, in fact none at all, since you are a gentleman."

"The law," Chien said bitingly, "does not require me to purchase anything useful from you; only that I purchase something. I'll take that." He reached into his padded coat for his billfold, huge with the postwar inflationary bills in which, four times a week, he as a government servant was paid.

"Tell me your problems," the peddler said.

Chien stared at him. Appalled by the invasion of privacy —and done by someone outside the government.

"All right, comrade," the peddler said, seeing his expression. "I will not probe; excuse me. But as a doctor—an herbal healer—it is fitting that I know as much as possible." He pondered, his gaunt features somber. "Do you watch television unusually much?" he asked abruptly.

Taken by surprise, Chien said, "Every evening. Except on Friday when I go to my club to practice the esoteric imported art from the defeated West of steer-roping." It was his only indulgence; other than that he had totally devoted himself to Party activities.

The peddler reached, selected a gray paper packet. "Sixty trade dollars," he stated. "With a full guarantee; if it does not do as promised, return the unused portion for a full and cheery refund."

"And what," Chien said cuttingly, "is it guaranteed to do?"

"It will rest eyes fatigued by the countenance of meaningless official monologues," the peddler said. "A soothing preparation; take it as soon as you find yourself exposed to the usual dry and lengthy sermons which—"

Chien paid the money, accepted the packet, and strode off. Balls, he said to himself. It's a racket, he decided, the ordinance setting up war vets as a privileged class. They prey off us—we, the younger ones—like raptors.

Forgotten, the gray packet remained deposited in his coat pocket, as he entered the imposing postwar Ministry of Cultural Artifacts building, and his own considerable stately office, to begin his workday.

A portly, middle-aged Caucasian male, wearing a brown Hong Kong silk suit, double-breasted with vest, waited in his office. With the unfamiliar Caucasian stood his own immediate superior, Ssu-Ma Tso-pin. Tso-pin introduced the two of them in Cantonese, a dialect which he used badly.

"Mr. Tung Chien, this is Mr. Darius Pethel. Mr. Pethel will be headmaster at the new ideological and cultural establishment of didactic character soon to open at San Fernando, California." He added, "Mr. Pethel has had a rich and full lifetime supporting the people's struggle to unseat imperialist-bloc countries via pedagogic media; therefore this high post."

They shook hands.

"Tea?" Chien asked the two of them; he pressed the switch of his infrared hibachi and in an instant the water in the highly ornamented ceramic pot—of Japanese origin—began to burble. As he seated himself at his desk he saw that trustworthy Miss Hsi had laid out the information poop-sheet (confidential) on Comrade Pethel; he glanced over it, meanwhile pretending to be doing nothing in particular.

"The Absolute Benefactor of the People," Tso-pin said, "has personally met Mr. Pethel and trusts him. This is rare. The school in San Fernando will appear to teach run-of-the-mill Taoist philosophies but will, of course, in actuality maintain for us a channel of communication to the liberal and intellectual youth segment of western U.S. There are many of them still alive, from San Diego to Sacramento; we estimate at least ten thousand. The school will accept two thousand. Enrollment will be mandatory for those we select. Your relationship to Mr. Pethel's programing is grave. Ahem; your tea water is boiling."

"Thank you," Chien murmured, dropping in the bag of Lipton's tea.

Tso-pin continued, "Although Mr. Pethel will supervise the setting up of the courses of instruction presented by the school to its student body, all examination papers will oddly enough be relayed here to your office for your own expert, careful, ideological study. In other words, Mr. Chien, you will determine who among the two thousand students is reliable, which are truly responding to the programing and who is not."

"I will now pour my tea," Chien said, doing so ceremoniously.

"What we have to realize," Pethel rumbled in Cantonese even worse than that of Tso-pin, "is that, once having lost the global war to us, the American youth has developed a talent for dissembling." He spoke the last word in English; not understanding it, Chien turned inquiringly to his superior.

"Lying," Tso-pin explained.

Pethel said, "Mouthing the proper slogans for surface appearance, but on the inside believing them false. Test papers by this group will closely resemble those of genuine—"

"You mean that the test papers of *two thousand* students will be passing through my office?" Chien demanded. He could not believe it. "That's a full-time job in itself; I don't have time for anything remotely resembling that." He was appalled. "To give critical, official approval or denial of the

astute variety which you're envisioning—" He gestured.
"Screw that," he said, in English.

Blinking at the strong, Western vulgarity, Tso-pin said,
"You have a staff. Plus also you can requisition several more
from the pool; the Ministry's budget, augmented this year,
will permit it. And remember: the Absolute Benefactor of
the People has hand-picked Mr. Pethel." His tone, now, had
become ominous, but only subtly so. Just enough to penetrate
Chien's hysteria, and to wither it into submission. At least
temporarily. To underline his point, Tso-pin walked to the
far end of the office; he stood before the full-length 3-D portrait of the Absolute Benefactor, and after an interval his
proximity triggered the tape-transport mounted behind the
portrait; the face of the Benefactor moved, and from it came
a familiar homily, in more than familiar accents. "Fight for
peace, my sons," it intoned gently, firmly.

"Ha," Chien said, still perturbed, but concealing it. Possibly one of the Ministry's computers could sort the examination papers; a yes-no-maybe structure could be employed, in
conjunction with a pre-analysis of the pattern of ideological
correctness—and incorrectness. The matter could be made
routine. Probably.

Darius Pethel said, "I have with me certain material which
I would like you to scrutinize, Mr. Chien." He unzipped an
unsightly, old-fashioned, plastic briefcase. "Two examination
essays," he said as he passed the documents to Chien. "This
will tell us if you're qualified." He then glanced at Tso-pin;
their gazes met. "I understand," Pethel said, "that if you are
successful in this venture you will be made vice-councilor of
the Ministry, and His Greatness the Absolute Benefactor of
the People will personally confer Kisterigian's medal on you."
Both he and Tso-pin smiled in wary unison.

"The Kisterigian medal," Chien echoed; he accepted the
examination papers, glanced over them in a show of leisurely
indifference. But within him his heart vibrated in ill-concealed
tension. "Why these two? By that I mean, what am I looking
for, sir?"

"One of them," Pethel said, "is the work of a dedicated
progressive, a loyal Party member of thoroughly researched

conviction. The other is by a young *stilyagi* whom we suspect of holding petit bourgeois imperialist degenerate crypto-ideas. It is up to you, sir, to determine which is which."

Thanks a lot, Chien thought. But, nodding, he read the title of the top paper.

DOCTRINES OF THE ABSOLUTE BENEFACTOR ANTICIPATED IN THE POETRY OF BAHA AD-DIN ZUHAYR, OF THIRTEENTH-CENTURY ARABIA.

Glancing down the initial pages of the essay, Chien saw a quatrain familiar to him; it was called "Death" and he had known it most of his adult, educated life.

> Once he will miss, twice he will miss,
>   He only chooses one of many hours;
> For him nor deep nor hill there is,
>   But all's one level plain he hunts for flowers.

"Powerful," Chien said. "This poem."

"He makes use of the poem," Pethel said, observing Chien's lips moving as he reread the quatrain, "to indicate the age-old wisdom, displayed by the Absolute Benefactor in our current lives, that no individual is safe; everyone is mortal, and only the supra-personal, historically essential cause survives. As it should be. Would you agree with him? With this student, I mean? Or—" Pethel paused. "Is he in fact perhaps satirizing the Absolute Benefactor's promulgations?"

Cagily, Chien said, "Give me a chance to inspect the other paper."

"You need no further information; decide."

Haltingly, Chien said, "I—had never thought of this poem that way." He felt irritable. "Anyhow, it isn't by Baha ad-Din Zuhayr; it's part of the *Thousand and One Nights* anthology. It is, however, thirteenth century; I admit that." He quickly read over the text of the paper accompanying the poem. It appeared to be a routine, uninspired rehash of Party clichés, all of them familiar to him from birth. The blind, imperialist monster who mowed down and snuffed out (mixed metaphor) human aspiration, the calculations of the still extant

anti-Party group in eastern United States . . . He felt dully
bored, and as uninspired as the student's paper. We must
persevere, the paper declared. Wipe out the Pentagon remnants in the Catskills, subdue Tennessee and most especially
the pocket of die-hard reaction in the red hills of Oklahoma.
He sighed.

"I think," Tso-pin said, "we should allow Mr. Chien the
opportunity of observing this difficult material at his leisure."
To Chien he said, "You have permission to take them home
to your condominium, this evening, and adjudge them on
your own time." He bowed, half mockingly, half solicitously.
In any case, insult or not, he had gotten Chien off the hook,
and for that Chien was grateful.

"You are most kind," he murmured, "to allow me to perform this new and highly stimulating labor on my own time.
Mikoyan, were he alive today, would approve." You bastard,
he said to himself. Meaning both his superior and the Caucasian Pethel. Handing me a hot potato like this, and on my
own time. Obviously the CP USA is in trouble; its indoctrina-
tion academies aren't managing to do their job with the no-
toriously mulish, eccentric Yank youths. And you've passed
that hot potato on and on until it reaches me.

Thanks for nothing, he thought acidly.

That evening in his small but well-appointed condominium
apartment he read over the other of the two examination
papers, this one by a Marion Culper, and discovered that it,
too, dealt with poetry. Obviously this was speciously a poetry
class, and he felt ill. It had always run against his grain, the
use of poetry—of any art—for social purposes. Anyhow, comfortable in his special spine-straightening, simulated-leather
easy chair, he lit a Cuesta Rey Number One English Market
immense corona cigar and began to read.

The writer of the paper, Miss Culper, had selected as her
text a portion of a poem of John Dryden, the seventeenth-
century English poet, final lines from the well-known "A
Song for St. Cecilia's Day."

> . . . So when the last and dreadful hour
> This crumbling pageant shall devour,

The trumpet shall be heard on high,
The dead shall live, the living die,
And Music shall untune the sky.

Well, that's a hell of a thing, Chien thought to himself bitingly. Dryden, we're supposed to believe, anticipated the fall of capitalism? That's what he meant by the "crumbling pageant"? Christ. He leaned over to take hold of his cigar and found that it had gone out. Groping in his pockets for his Japanese-made lighter, he half rose to his feet. . . .

Tweeeeeee! the TV set at the far end of the living room said.

Aha, Chien said. We're about to be addressed by the Leader. By the Absolute Benefactor of the People, up there in Peking where he's lived for ninety years now; or is it one hundred? Or, as we sometimes like to think of him, the Ass—

"May the ten thousand blossoms of abject self-assumed poverty flower in your spiritual courtyard," the TV announcer said. With a groan, Chien rose to his feet, bowed the mandatory bow of response; each TV set came equipped with monitoring devices to narrate to the Secpol, the Security Police, whether its owner was bowing and/or watching.

On the screen a clearly defined visage manifested itself, the wide, unlined, healthy features of the one-hundred-and-twenty-year-old leader of CP East, ruler of many—far too many, Chien reflected. Blah to you, he thought, and reseated himself in his simulated-leather easy chair, now facing the TV screen.

"My thoughts," the Absolute Benefactor said in his rich and slow tones, "are on you, my children. And especially on Mr. Tung Chien of Hanoi, who faces a difficult task ahead, a task to enrich the people of Democratic East, plus the American West Coast. We must think in unison about this noble, dedicated man and the chore which he faces, and I have chosen to take several moments of my time to honor him and encourage him. Are you listening, Mr. Chien?"

"Yes, Your Greatness," Chien said, and pondered to himself the odds against the Party Leader singling *him* out this particular evening. The odds caused him to feel uncomradely cynicism; it was unconvincing. Probably this transmission was being beamed to his apartment building alone—or at least this city. It might also be a lip-synch job, done at Hanoi TV, Incorporated. In any case he was required to listen and watch —and absorb. He did so, from a lifetime of practice. Outwardly he appeared to be rigidly attentive. Inwardly he was still mulling over the two test papers, wondering which was which; where did devout Party enthusiasm end and sardonic lampoonery begin? Hard to say . . . which of course explained why they had dumped the task in his lap.

Again he groped in his pockets for his lighter—and found the small gray envelope which the war-veteran peddler had sold him. Gawd, he thought, remembering what it had cost. Money down the drain and what did this herbal remedy do? Nothing. He turned the packet over and saw, on the back, small printed words. Well, he thought, and began to unfold the packet with care. The words had snared him—as of course they were meant to do.

> Failing as a Party member and human?
> Afraid of becoming obsolete and dis-
> carded on the ash heap of history by

He read rapidly through the text, ignoring its claims, seeking to find out what he had purchased.

Meanwhile, the Absolute Benefactor droned on.

Snuff. The package contained snuff. Countless tiny black grains, like gunpowder, which sent up an interesting aromatic to tickle his nose. The title of the particular blend was Princes Special, he discovered. And very pleasing, he decided. At one time he had taken snuff—smoked tobacco for a time having been illegal for reasons of health—back during his student days at Peking U; it had been the fad, especially the amatory mixes prepared in Chungking, made from god knew what. Was this that? Almost any aromatic could be added to snuff, from essence of orange to pulverized babycrap . . . or so some seemed, especially an English mixture called High Dry Toast which had in itself more or less put an end to his yearning for nasal, inhaled tobacco.

On the TV screen the Absolute Benefactor rumbled monotonously on as Chien sniffed cautiously at the powder, read the claims—it cured everything from being late to work to falling in love with a woman of dubious political background. Interesting. But typical of claims—

His doorbell rang.

Rising, he walked to the door, opened it with full knowledge of what he would find. There, sure enough, stood Mou Kuei, the Building Warden, small and hard-eyed and alert to his task; he had his armband and metal helmet on, showing that he meant business. "Mr. Chien, comrade Party worker. I received a call from the television authority. You are failing to watch your screen and are instead fiddling with a packet of doubtful content." He produced a clipboard and ballpoint pen. "Two red marks, and hithertonow you are summarily ordered to repose yourself in a comfortable, stress-free posture before your screen and give the Leader your unexcelled attention. His words, this evening, are directed particularly to you, sir; to you."

"I doubt that," Chien heard himself say.

Blinking, Kuei said, "What do you mean?"

"The Leader rules eight billion comrades. He isn't going to single me out." He felt wrathful; the punctuality of the warden's reprimand irked him.

Kuei said, "But I distinctly heard with my own ears. You were mentioned."

Going over to the TV set, Chien turned the volume up. "But now he's talking about crop failures in People's India; that's of no relevance to me."

"Whatever the Leader expostulates is relevant." Mou Kuei scratched a mark on his clipboard sheet, bowed formally, turned away. "My call to come up here to confront you with your slackness originated at Central. Obviously they regard your attention as important; I must order you to set in motion your automatic transmission recording circuit and replay the earlier portions of the Leader's speech."

Chien farted. And shut the door.

Back to the TV set, he said to himself. Where our leisure hours are spent. And there lay the two student examination papers; he had that weighing him down, too. And all on my own time, he thought savagely. The hell with them. Up theirs. He strode to the TV set, started to shut it off; at once a red warning light winked on, informing him that he did not have permission to shut off the set—could not in fact end its tirade and image even if he unplugged it. Mandatory speeches, he thought, will kill us all, bury us; if I could be free of the noise of speeches, free of the din of the Party baying as it hounds mankind . . .

There was no known ordinance, however, preventing him from taking snuff while he watched the Leader. So, opening the small gray packet, he shook out a mound of the black granules onto the back of his left hand. He then, professionally, raised his hand to his nostrils and deeply inhaled, drawing the snuff well up into his sinus cavities. Imagine the old superstition, he thought to himself. That the sinus cavities are connected to the brain, and hence an inhalation of snuff directly affects the cerebral cortex. He smiled, seated himself once more, fixed his gaze on the TV screen and the gesticulating individual known so utterly to them all.

The face dwindled away, disappeared. The sound ceased. He faced an emptiness, a vacuum. The screen, white and blank, confronted him and from the speaker a faint hiss sounded.

The frigging snuff, he said to himself. And inhaled greedily at the remainder of the powder on his hand, drawing it up avidly into his nose, his sinuses, and, or so it felt, into his brain; he plunged into the snuff, absorbing it elatedly.

The screen remained blank and then, by degrees, an image once more formed and established itself. It was not the Leader. Not the Absolute Benefactor of the People, in point of fact not a human figure at all.

He faced a dead mechanical construct, made of solid state circuits, of swiveling pseudopodia, lenses and a squawk-box. And the box began, in a droning din, to harangue him.

Staring fixedly, he thought, *What is this?* Reality? Hallucination, he thought. The peddler came across some of the psychedelic drugs used during the War of Liberation—he's selling the stuff and I've taken some, taken a whole lot!

Making his way unsteadily to the vidphone he dialed the

Secpol station nearest his building. "I wish to report a pusher of hallucinogenic drugs," he said into the receiver.

"Your name, sir, and conapt location?" Efficient, brisk and impersonal bureaucrat of the police.

He gave them the information, then haltingly made it back to his simulated-leather easy chair, once again to witness the apparition on the TV screen. This is lethal, he said to himself. It must be some preparation developed in Washington, D.C., or London—stronger and stranger than the LSD-25 which they dumped so effectively into our reservoirs. And I thought it was going to relieve me of the burden of the Leader's speeches . . . this is far worse, this electronic, sputtering, swiveling, metal and plastic monstrosity yammering away—this is terrifying.

To have to face *this* the remainder of my life—

It took ten minutes for the Secpol two-man team to come rapping at his door. And by then, in a deteriorating set of stages, the familiar image of the Leader had seeped back into focus on the screen, had supplanted the horrible artificial construct which waved its 'podia and squalled on and on. He let the two cops in shakily, led them to the table on which he had left the remains of the snuff in its packet.

"Psychedelic toxin," he said thickly. "Of short duration. Absorbed into the blood stream directly, through nasal capillaries. I'll give you details as to where I got it, from whom, all that." He took a deep shaky breath; the presence of the police was comforting.

Ballpoint pens ready, the two officers waited. And all the time, in the background, the Leader rattled out his endless speech. As he had done a thousand evenings before in the life of Tung Chien. But, he thought, it'll never be the same again, at least not for me. Not after inhaling that near-toxic snuff.

He wondered, Is that what they intended?

It seemed odd to him, thinking of a *they*. Peculiar—but somehow correct. For an instant he hesitated, not giving out the details, not telling the police enough to find the man. A peddler, he started to say. I don't know where; can't remember. But he did; he remembered the exact street intersection. So, with unexplainable reluctance, he told them.

"Thank you, Comrade Chien." The boss of the team of police carefully gathered up the remaining snuff—most of it remained—and placed it in his uniform—smart, sharp uniform—pocket. "We'll have it analyzed at the first available moment," the cop said, "and inform you immediately in case counter medical measures are indicated for you. Some of the old wartime psychedelics were eventually fatal, as you have no doubt read."

"I've read," he agreed. That had been specifically what he had been thinking.

"Good luck and thanks for notifying us," both cops said, and departed. The affair, for all their efficiency, did not seem to shake them; obviously such a complaint was routine.

The lab report came swiftly—surprisingly so, in view of the vast state bureaucracy. It reached him by vidphone before the Leader had finished his TV speech.

"It's not a hallucinogen," the Secpol lab technician informed him.

"No?" he said, puzzled and, strangely, not relieved. Not at all.

"On the contrary. It's a phenothiazine, which as you doubtless know is anti-hallucinogenic. A strong dose per gram of admixture, but harmless. Might lower your blood pressure or make you sleepy. Probably stolen from a wartime cache of medical supplies. Left by the retreating barbarians. I wouldn't worry."

Pondering, Chien hung up the vidphone in slow motion. And then walked to the window of his conapt—the window with the fine view of other Hanoi high-rise conapts—to think.

The doorbell rang. Feeling as if he were in a trance, he crossed the carpeted living room to answer it.

The girl standing there, in a tan raincoat with a babushka over her dark, shiny, and very long hair, said in a timid little voice, "Um, Comrade Chien? Tung Chien? Of the Ministry of—"

He led her in, reflexively, and shut the door after her. "You've been monitoring my vidphone," he told her; it was a shot in darkness, but something in him, an unvoiced certitude, told him that she had.

"Did—they take the rest of the snuff?" She glanced about. "Oh, I hope not; it's so hard to get these days."

"Snuff," he said, "is easy to get. Phenothiazine isn't. Is that what you mean?"

The girl raised her head, studied him with large, moon-darkened eyes. "Yes. Mr. Chien—" She hesitated, obviously as uncertain as the Secpol cops had been assured. "Tell me what you saw; it's of great importance for us to be certain."

"I had a choice?" he said acutely.

"Y-yes, very much so. That's what confuses us; that's what is not as we planned. We don't understand; it fits nobody's theory." Her eyes even darker and deeper, she said, "Was it the aquatic horror shape? The thing with slime and teeth, the extraterrestrial life form? Please tell me; we have to know." She breathed irregularly, with effort, the tan raincoat rising and falling; he found himself watching its rhythm.

"A machine," he said.

"Oh!" She ducked her head, nodding vigorously. "Yes, I understand; a mechanical organism in no way resembling a human. Not a simulacrum, something constructed to resemble a man."

He said, "This did not look like a man." He added to himself, And it failed—did not try—to talk like a man.

"You understand that it was not a hallucination."

"I've been officially told that what I took was a phenothiazine. That's all I know." He said as little as possible; he did not want to talk but to hear. Hear what the girl had to say.

"Well, Mr. Chien—" She took a deep, unstable breath. "If it was not a hallucination, then what was it? What does that leave? What is called 'extra-consciousness'—could that be it?"

He did not answer; turning his back, he leisurely picked up the two student test papers, glanced over them, ignoring her. Waiting for her next attempt.

At his shoulder she appeared, smelling of spring rain, smelling of sweetness and agitation, beautiful in the way she smelled, and looked, and, he thought, speaks. So different from the harsh plateau speech patterns we hear on the TV —have heard since I was a baby.

"Some of them," she said huskily, "who take the stelazine —it was stelazine you got, Mr. Chien—see one apparition, some another. But distinct categories have emerged; there is not an infinite variety. Some see what you saw; we call it the Clanker. Some the aquatic horror; that's the Gulper. And then there's the Bird, and the Climbing Tube, and—" She broke off. "But other reactions tell you very little. Tell *us* very little." She hesitated, then plunged on. "Now that this has happened to you, Mr. Chien, we would like you to join our gathering. Join your particular group, those who see what you see. Group Red. We want to know what it *really* is, and—" She gestured with tapered, wax-smooth fingers. "It can't be *all* those manifestations." Her tone was poignant, naïvely so. He felt his caution relax—a trifle.

He said, "What do you see? You in particular?"

"I'm a part of Group Yellow. I see—a storm. A whining, vicious whirlwind. That roots everything up, crushes condominium apartments built to last a century." She smiled wanly. "The Crusher. Twelve groups in all, Mr. Chien. Twelve absolutely different experiences, all from the same phenothiazine, all of the Leader as he speaks over TV. As *it* speaks, rather." She smiled up at him, lashes long—probably protracted artificially—and gaze engaging, even trusting. As if she thought he knew something or could do something.

"I should make a citizen's arrest of you," he said presently.

"There is no law, not about this. We studied Soviet juridical writings before we—found people to distribute the stelazine. We don't have much of it; we have to be very careful whom we give it to. It seemed to us that you constituted a likely choice . . . a well-known, postwar, dedicated young career man on his way up." From his fingers she took the examination papers. "They're having you pol-read?" she asked.

"'Pol-read'?" He did not know the term.

"Study something said or written to see if it fits the Party's current world view. You in the hierarchy merely call it 'read,' don't you?" Again she smiled. "When you rise one step higher, up with Mr. Tso-pin, you will know that expression." She added somberly, "And with Mr. Pethel. He's very far up. Mr. Chien, there is no ideological school in San Fernando;

these are forged exam papers, designed to read back to them a thorough analysis of *your* political ideology. And have you been able to distinguish which paper is orthodox and which is heretical?" Her voice was pixie-like, taunting with amused malice. "Choose the wrong one and your budding career stops dead, cold, in its tracks. Choose the proper one—"

"Do you know which is which?" he demanded.

"Yes." She nodded soberly. "We have listening devices in Mr. Tso-pin's inner offices; we monitored his conversation with Mr. Pethel—who is not Mr. Pethel but the Higher Secpol Inspector Judd Craine. You have possibly heard mention of him; he acted as chief assistant to Judge Vorlawsky at the '98 war crimes trial in Zurich."

With difficulty he said, "I—see." Well, that explained that. The girl said, "My name is Tanya Lee."

He said nothing; he merely nodded, too stunned for any cerebration.

"Technically, I am a minor clerk," Miss Lee said, "at your Ministry. You have never run into me, however, that I can at least recall. We try to hold posts wherever we can. As far up as possible. My own boss—"

"Should you be telling me this?" He gestured at the TV set, which remained on. "Aren't they picking this up?"

Tanya Lee said, "We introduced a noise factor in the reception of both vid and aud material from this apartment building; it will take them almost an hour to locate the sheathing. So we have"—she examined the tiny wristwatch on her slender wrist—"fifteen more minutes. And still be safe."

"Tell me," he said, "which paper is orthodox."

"Is that what you care about? Really?"

"What," he said, "should I care about?"

"Don't you see, Mr. Chien? You've learned something. The Leader is not the Leader; he is something else, but we can't tell what. Not yet. Mr. Chien, with all due respect, have you ever had your drinking water analyzed? I know it sounds paranoiac, but have you?"

"No," he said. "Of course not." Knowing what she was going to say.

Miss Lee said briskly, "Our tests show that it's saturated

with hallucinogens. It is, has been, will continue to be. Not the ones used during the war; not the disorienting ones, but a synthetic quasi-ergot derivative called Datrox-3. You drink it here in the building from the time you get up; you drink it in restaurants and other apartments that you visit. You drink it at the Ministry; it's all piped from a central, common source." Her tone was bleak and ferocious. "We solved that problem; we knew, as soon as we discovered it, that any good phenothiazine would counter it. What we did not know, of course, was this—a *variety* of authentic experiences; that makes no sense, rationally. It's the hallucination which should differ from person to person, and the reality experience which should be ubiquitous—it's all turned around. We can't even construct an ad hoc theory which accounts for that, and god knows we've tried. Twelve mutually exclusive hallucinations—that would be easily understood. But not one hallucination and twelve realities." She ceased talking, then, and studied the two test papers, her forehead wrinkling. "The one with the Arabic poem is orthodox," she stated. "If you tell them that they'll trust you and give you a higher post. You'll be another notch up in the hierarchy of Party officialdom." Smiling—her teeth were perfect and lovely—she finished, "Look what you received back for your investment this morning. Your career is underwritten for a time. And by us."

He said, "I don't believe you." Instinctively, his caution operated within him, always, the caution of a lifetime lived among the hatchet men of the Hanoi branch of the CP East. They knew an infinitude of ways by which to ax a rival out of contention—some of which he himself had employed; some of which he had seen done to himself and to others. This could be a novel way, one unfamiliar to him. It could always be.

"Tonight," Miss Lee said, "in the speech the Leader singled you out. Didn't this strike you as strange? You, of all people? A minor officeholder in a meager ministry—"

"Admitted," he said. "It struck me that way; yes."

"That was legitimate. His Greatness is grooming an elite cadre of younger men, postwar men, he hopes will infuse new life into the hidebound, moribund hierarchy of old fogies and Party hacks. His Greatness singled you out for the same reason that we singled you out; if pursued properly, your career could lead you all the way to the top. At least for a time . . . as we know. That's how it goes."

He thought, So virtually everyone has faith in me. Except myself; and certainly not after this, the experience with the anti-hallucinatory snuff. It had shaken years of confidence, and no doubt rightly so. However, he was beginning to regain his poise; he felt it seeping back, a little at first, then with a rush.

Going to the vidphone, he lifted the receiver and began, for the second time that night, to dial the number of the Hanoi Security Police.

"Turning me in," Miss Lee said, "would be the second most regressive decision you could make. I'll tell them that you brought me here to bribe me; you thought, because of my job at the Ministry, I would know which examination paper to select."

He said, "And what would be my first most regressive decision?"

"Not taking a further dose of phenothiazine," Miss Lee said evenly.

Hanging up the phone, Tung Chien thought to himself, I don't understand what's happening to me. Two forces, the Party and His Greatness on one hand—this girl with her alleged group on the other. One wants me to rise as far as possible in the Party hierarchy; the other—*What did Tanya Lee want?* Underneath the words, inside the membrane of an almost trivial contempt for the Party, the Leader, the ethical standards of the People's Democratic United Front— what was she after in regard to him?

He said curiously, "Are you anti-Party?"

"No."

"But—" He gestured. "That's all there is; Party and anti-Party. You must be Party, then." Bewildered, he stared at her; with composure she returned the stare. "You have an organization," he said, "and you meet. What do you intend to destroy? The regular function of government? Are you like the treasonable college students of the United States during the Vietnam War who stopped troop trains, demonstrated—"

Wearily Miss Lee said, "It wasn't like that. But forget it; that's not the issue. What we want to know is this: who or what is leading us? We must penetrate far enough to enlist someone, some rising young Party theoretician, who could conceivably be invited to a tête-à-tête with the Leader—you see?" Her voice lifted; she consulted her watch, obviously anxious to get away: the fifteen minutes were almost up. "Very few persons actually see the Leader, as you know. I mean really see him."

"Seclusion," he said. "Due to his advanced age."

"We have hope," Miss Lee said, "that if you pass the phony test which they have arranged for you—and with my help you have—you will be invited to one of the stag parties which the Leader has from time to time, which of course the 'papes don't report. Now do you see?" Her voice rose shrilly, in a frenzy of despair. "Then we would know; if you could go in there under the influence of the anti-hallucinogenic drug, could see him face to face as he actually is—"

Thinking aloud, he said, "And end my career of public service. If not my life."

"You owe us something," Tanya Lee snapped, her cheeks white. "If I hadn't told you which exam paper to choose you would have picked the wrong one and your dedicated public service career would be over anyhow; you would have failed—failed at a test you didn't even realize you were taking!"

He said mildly, "I had a fifty-fifty chance."

"No." She shook her head fiercely. "The heretical one is faked up with a lot of Party jargon; they deliberately constructed the two texts to trap you. They *wanted* you to fail!"

Once more he examined the two papers, feeling confused. Was she right? Possibly. Probably. It rang true, knowing the Party functionaries as he did, and Tso-pin, his superior, in particular. He felt weary then. Defeated. After a time he said to the girl, "What you're trying to get out of me is a quid pro quo. You did something for me—you got, or claim you got—the answer to this Party inquiry. But you've already done your part. What's to keep me from tossing you out of here on your head? I don't have to do a goddam thing." He heard his voice, toneless, sounding the poverty of empathic emotionality so usual in Party circles.

Miss Lee said, "There will be other tests, as you continue to ascend. And we will monitor for you with them too." She was calm, at ease; obviously she had forseen his reaction.

"How long do I have to think it over?" he said.

"I'm leaving now. We're in no rush; you're not about to receive an invitation to the Leader's Yellow River villa in the next week or even month." Going to the door, opening it, she paused. "As you're given covert rating tests we'll be in contact, supplying the answers—so you'll see one or more of us on those occasions. Probably it won't be me; it'll be that disabled war veteran who'll sell you the correct response sheets as you leave the Ministry building." She smiled a brief, snuffed-out-candle smile. "But one of these days, no doubt unexpectedly, you'll get an ornate, official, very formal invitation to the villa, and when you go you'll be heavily sedated with stelazine . . . possibly our last dose of our dwindling supply. Good night." The door shut after her; she had gone.

My god, he thought. They can blackmail me. For what I've done. And she didn't even bother to mention it; in view of what they're involved with it was not worth mentioning.

But blackmail for what? He had already told the Secpol squad that he had been given a drug which had proved to be a phenothiazine. *Then they know,* he realized. They'll watch me; they're alert. Technically I haven't broken a law but—they'll be watching, all right.

However, they always watched anyhow. He relaxed slightly thinking that. He had, over the years, become virtually accustomed to it, as had everyone.

I will see the Absolute Benefactor of the People as he is, he said to himself. Which possibly no one else has done. What will it be? Which of the subclasses of non-hallucination Classes which I do not even know about . . . a view which may totally overthrow me. How am I going to be able to get through the evening, to keep my poise, if it's like the shape saw on the TV screen? The Crusher, the Clanker, the Bird, the Climbing Tube, the Gulper—or worse.

He wondered what some of the other views consisted of . . . and then gave up that line of speculation; it was unprofitable. And too anxiety-inducing.

The next morning Mr. Tso-pin and Mr. Darius Pethel met him in his office, both of them calm but expectant. Wordlessly, he handed them one of the two "exam papers." The orthodox one, with its short and heart-smothering Arabian poem.

"This one," Chien said tightly, "is the product of a dedicated Party member or candidate for membership. The other—" He slapped the remaining sheets. "Reactionary garbage." He felt anger. "In spite of a superficial—"

"All right, Mr. Chien," Pethel said, nodding. "We don't have to explore each and every ramification; your analysis is correct. You heard the mention regarding you in the Leader's speech last night on TV?"

"I certainly did," Chien said.

"So you have undoubtedly inferred," Pethel said, "that there is a good deal involved in what we are attempting, here. The Leader has his eye on you; that's clear. As a matter of fact, he has communicated to myself regarding you." He opened his bulging briefcase and rummaged. "Lost the goddam thing. Anyhow—" He glanced at Tso-pin, who nodded slightly. "His Greatness would like to have you appear for dinner at the Yangtze River Ranch next Thursday night. Mrs. Fletcher in particular appreciates—"

Chien said, "'Mrs. Fletcher'? Who is 'Mrs. Fletcher'?"

After a pause Tso-pin said dryly, "The Absolute Benefactor's wife. His name—which you of course had never heard—is Thomas Fletcher."

"He's a Caucasian," Pethel explained. "Originally from the New Zealand Communist Party; he participated in the difficult take-over there. This news is not in the strict sense secret, but on the other hand it hasn't been noised about." He hesitated, toying with his watchchain. "Probably it would be better if you forgot about that. Of course, as soon as you meet him, see him face to face, you'll realize that, realize that he's a Cauc. As I am. As many of us are."

"Race," Tso-pin pointed out, "has nothing to do with loyalty to the Leader and the Party. As witness Mr. Pethel, here."

But His Greatness, Chien thought, jolted. He did not appear, on the TV screen, to be occidental. "On TV—" he began.

"The image," Tso-pin interrupted, "is subjected to a variegated assortment of skillful refinements. For ideological purposes. Most persons holding higher offices are aware of this." He eyed Chien with hard criticism.

So everyone agrees, Chien thought. What we see every night is not real. The question is, How unreal? Partially? Or—completely?

"I will be prepared," he said tautly. And he thought, There has been a slip-up. They weren't prepared for me—the people that Tanya Lee represents—to gain entry so soon. Where's the anti-hallucinogen? Can they get it to me or not? Probably not on such short notice.

He felt, strangely, relief. He would be going into the presence of His Greatness in a position to see him as a human being, see him as he—and everybody else—saw him on TV. It would be a most stimulating and cheerful dinner party, with some of the most influential Party members in Asia. I think we can do without the phenothiazines, he said to himself. And his sense of relief grew.

"Here it is, finally," Pethel said suddenly, producing a white envelope from his briefcase. "Your card of admission. You will be flown by Sino-rocket to the Leader's villa Thursday morning; there the protocol officer will brief you on your expected behavior. It will be formal dress, white tie and tails, but the atmosphere will be cordial. There are always a great number of toasts." He added, "I have attended two such stag gets-together. Mr. Tso-pin"—he smiled creakily—"has not been honored in such a fashion. But as they say, all things come to him who waits. Ben Franklin said that."

Tso-pin said, "It has come for Mr. Chien rather prematurely, I would say." He shrugged philosophically. "But my opinion has never at any time been asked."

"One thing," Pethel said to Chien. "It is possible that when you see His Greatness in person you will be in some regards disappointed. Be alert that you do not let this make itself apparent, if you should so feel. We have, always, tended—been trained—to regard him as more than a man. But at table he is"—he gestured—"a forked radish. In certain respects like ourselves. He may for instance indulge in moderately human oral-aggressive and -passive activity; he possibly may tell an off-color joke or drink too much. . . . To be candid, no one ever knows in advance how these things will work out, but they do generally hold forth until late the following morning. So it would be wise to accept the dosage of amphetamines which the protocol officer will offer you."

"Oh?" Chien said. This was news to him, and interesting.

"For stamina. And to balance the liquor. His Greatness has amazing staying power; he often is still on his feet and raring to go after everyone else has collapsed."

"A remarkable man," Tso-pin chimed in. "I think his—indulgences only show that he is a fine fellow. And fully in the round; he is like the ideal Renaissance man; as, for example, Lorenzo de' Medici."

"That does come to mind," Pethel said; he studied Chien with such intensity that some of last night's chill returned. *Am I being led into one trap after another?* Chien wondered. *That girl—was she in fact an agent of the Secpol probing me, trying to ferret out a disloyal, anti-Party streak in me?*

I think, he decided, *I will make sure that the legless peddler of herbal remedies does not snare me when I leave work; I'll take a totally different route back to my conapt.*

He was successful. That day he avoided the peddler and the same the next, and so on until Thursday.

On Thursday morning the peddler scooted from beneath a parked truck and blocked his way, confronting him.

"My medication?" the peddler demanded. "It helped? I know it did; the formula goes back to the Sung Dynasty—I can tell it did. Right?"

Chien said, "Let me go."

"Would you be kind enough to answer?" The tone was not the expected, customary whining of a street peddler operat-

ing in a marginal fashion, and that tone came across to Chien;
he heard loud and clear . . . as the Imperialist puppet troops
of long ago phrased it.

"I know what you gave me," Chien said. "And I don't want
any more. If I change my mind I can pick it up at a phar-
macy. Thanks." He started on, but the cart, with the legless
occupant, pursued him.

"Miss Lee was talking to me," the peddler said loudly.

"Hmm," Chien said, and automatically increased his pace;
he spotted a hovercab and began signaling for it.

"It's tonight you're going to the stag dinner at the Yangtze
River villa," the peddler said, panting for breath in his effort
to keep up. "Take the medication—now!" He held out a flat
packet, imploringly. "Please, Party Member Chien; for your
own sake, for all of us. So we can tell what it is we're up
against. Good lord, it may be non-terran; that's our most basic
fear. Don't you understand, Chien? What's your goddam
career compared with that? If we can't find out—"

The cab bumped to a halt on the pavement; its door slid
open. Chien started to board it.

The packet sailed past him, landed on the entrance sill of
the cab, then slid into the gutter, damp from earlier rain.

"Please," the peddler said. "And it won't cost you anything;
today it's free. Just take it, use it before the stag dinner. And
don't use the amphetamines; they're a thalamic stimulant,
contra-indicated whenever an adrenal suppressant such as a
phenothiazine is—"

The door of the cab closed after Chien. He seated himself.

"Where to, comrade?" the robot drive-mechanism inquired.

He gave the ident tag number of his conapt.

"That half-wit of a peddler managed to infiltrate his seedy
wares into my clean interior," the cab said. "Notice; it reposes
by your foot."

He saw the packet—no more than an ordinary-looking envelope. I guess, he thought, this is how drugs come to you;
all of a sudden they're lying there. For a moment he sat,
and then he picked it up.

As before, there was a written enclosure above and beyond

the medication, but this time, he saw, it was handwritten. A feminine script: from Miss Lee:

> We were surprised at the suddenness. But thank heaven we were ready. Where were you Tuesday and Wednesday? Anyhow, here it is, and good luck. I will approach you later in the week; I don't want you to try to find me.

He ignited the note, burned it up in the cab's disposal ashtray.

And kept the dark granules.

All this time, he thought. Hallucinogens in our water supply. Year after year. Decades. And not in wartime but in peacetime. And not to the enemy camp but here in our own. The evil bastards, he said to himself. Maybe I ought to take this; maybe I ought to find out what he or it is and let Tanya's group know.

I will, he decided. And—he was curious.

A bad emotion, he knew. Curiosity was, especially in Party activities, often a terminal state careerwise.

A state which, at the moment, gripped him thoroughly. He wondered if it would last through the evening, if, when it came right down to it, he would actually take the inhalant.

Time would tell. Tell that and everything else. We are blooming flowers, he thought, on the plain, which he picks. As the Arabic poem had put it. He tried to remember the rest of the poem but could not.

That probably was just as well.

The villa protocol officer, a Japanese named Kimo Okubara, tall and husky, obviously a quondam wrestler, surveyed him with innate hostility, even after he presented his engraved invitation and had successfully managed to prove his identity.

"Surprise you bother to come," Okubara muttered. "Why not stay home and watch on TV? Nobody miss you. We got along fine without up to right now."

Chien said tightly, "I've already watched on TV." And anyhow the stag dinners were rarely televised; they were too bawdy.

Okubara's crew double-checked him for weapons, including the possibility of an anal suppository, and then gave him his clothes back. They did not find the phenothiazine, however. Because he had already taken it. The effects of such a drug, he knew, lasted approximately four hours; that would be more than enough. And, as Tanya had said, it was a major dose; he felt sluggish and inept and dizzy, and his tongue moved in spasms of pseudo Parkinsonism—an unpleasant side effect which he had failed to anticipate.

A girl, nude from the waist up, with long coppery hair down her shoulders and back, walked by. Interesting.

Coming the other way, a girl nude from the bottom up made her appearance. Interesting, too. Both girls looked vacant and bored, and totally self-possessed.

"You go in like that too," Okubara informed Chien.

Startled, Chien said, "I understood white tie and tails."

"Joke," Okubara said. "At your expense. Only girls wear nude; you even get so you enjoy, unless you homosexual."

Well, Chien thought, I guess I had better like it. He wandered on with the other guests—they, like him, wore white tie and tails or, if women, floor-length gowns—and felt ill at ease, despite the tranquilizing effect of the stelazine. Why am I here? he asked himself. The ambiguity of his situation did not escape him. He was here to advance his career in the Party apparatus, to obtain the intimate and personal nod of approval from His Greatness . . . and in addition he was here to decipher His Greatness as a fraud; he did not know what variety of fraud, but there it was: fraud against the Party, against all the peace-loving democratic people of Terra. Ironic, he thought. And continued to mingle.

A girl with small, bright, illuminated breasts approached him for a match; he absent-mindedly got out his lighter. "What makes your breasts glow?" he asked her. "Radioactive injections?"

She shrugged, said nothing, passed on, leaving him alone. Evidently he had responded in the incorrect way.

Maybe it's a wartime mutation, he pondered.

"Drink, sir." A servant graciously held out a tray; he accepted a martini—which was the current fad among the higher Party classes in People's China—and sipped the ice-cold dry flavor. Good English gin, he said to himself. Or possibly the original Holland compound; juniper or whatever they added. Not bad. He strolled on, feeling better; in actuality he found the atmosphere here a pleasant one. The people here were self-assured; they had been successful and now they could relax. It evidently was a myth that proximity to His Greatness produced neurotic anxiety: he saw no evidence here, at least, and felt little himself.

A heavy-set elderly man, bald, halted him by the simple means of holding his drink glass against Chien's chest. "That frably little one who asked you for a match," the elderly man said, and sniggered. "The quig with the Christmas-tree breasts—that was a boy, in drag." He giggled. "You have to be cautious around here."

"Where, if anywhere," Chien said, "do I find authentic women? In the white ties and tails?"

"Darn near," the elderly man said, and departed with a throng of hyperactive guests, leaving Chien alone with his martini.

A handsome, tall woman, well dressed, standing near Chien, suddenly put her hand on his arm; he felt her fingers tense and she said, "Here he comes. His Greatness. This is the first time for me; I'm a little scared. Does my hair look all right?"

"Fine," Chien said reflexively, and followed her gaze, seeking a glimpse—his first—of the Absolute Benefactor.

What crossed the room toward the table in the center was not a man.

And it was not, Chien realized, a mechanical construct either; it was not what he had seen on TV. That evidently was simply a device for speechmaking, as Mussolini had once used an artificial arm to salute long and tedious processions.

God, he thought, and felt ill. Was this what Tanya Lee had called the "aquatic horror" shape? It had no shape. Nor pseudopodia, either flesh or metal. It was, in a sense, not there at all; when he managed to look directly at it, the shape vanished; he saw through it, saw the people on the far side—

but not it. Yet if he turned his head, caught it out of a side-long glance, he could determine its boundaries.

It was terrible; it blasted him with its awfulness. As it moved it drained the life from each person in turn; it ate the people who had assembled, passed on, ate again, ate more with an endless appetite. It hated; he felt its hate. It loathed; he felt its loathing for everyone present—in fact he shared its loathing. All at once he and everyone else in the big villa were each a twisted slug, and over the fallen slug-carcasses the creature savored, lingered, but all the time coming directly toward him—or was that an illusion? If this is a hallucination, Chien thought, it is the worst I have ever had; if it is not, then it is evil reality; it's an evil thing that kills and injures. He saw the trail of stepped-on, mashed men and women remnants behind it; he saw them trying to reassemble, to operate their crippled bodies; he heard them attempting speech.

I know who you are, Tung Chien thought to himself. You, the supreme head of the world-wide Party structure. You, who destroy whatever living object you touch; I see that Arabic poem, the searching for the flowers of life to eat them—I see you astride the plain which to you is Earth, plain without hills, without valleys. You go anywhere, appear any time, devour anything; you engineer life and then guzzle it, and you enjoy that.

He thought, You are God.

"Mr. Chien," the voice said, but it came from inside his head, not from the mouthless spirit that fashioned itself directly before him. "It is good to meet you again. You know nothing. Go away. I have no interest in you. Why should I care about slime? Slime; I am mired in it, I must excrete it, and I choose to. I could break you; I can break even myself. Sharp stones are under me; I spread sharp pointed things upon the mire. I make the hiding places, the deep places, boil like a pot; to me the sea is like a pot of ointment. The flakes of my flesh are joined to everything. You are me. I am you. It makes no difference, just as it makes no difference whether the creature with ignited breasts is a girl or boy; you could learn to enjoy either." It laughed.

Philip K. Dick   437

He could not believe it was speaking to him; he could not imagine—it was too terrible—that it had picked him out.

"I have picked everybody out," it said. "No one is too small; each falls and dies and I am there to watch. I don't need to do anything but watch; it is automatic; it was arranged that way." And then it ceased talking to him; it disjoined itself. But he still saw it; he felt its manifold presence. It was a globe which hung in the room, with fifty thousand eyes, with a million eyes—billions: an eye for each living thing as it waited for each thing to fall, and then stepped on the living thing as it lay in a broken state. Because of this it had created the things, and he knew; he understood. What had seemed in the Arabic poem to be death was not death but god; or rather God was death, it was one force, one hunter, one cannibal thing, and it missed again and again but, having all eternity, it could afford to miss. Both poems, he realized; the Dryden one too. The crumbling; that is our world and you are doing it. Warping it to come out that way; bending us.

But at least, he thought, I still have my dignity. With dignity he set down his drink glass, turned, walked toward the doors of the room. He passed through the doors. He walked down a long carpeted hall. A villa servant dressed in purple opened a door for him; he found himself standing out in the night darkness, on a veranda, alone.

Not alone.

It had followed after him. Or it had already been here before him; yes, it had been expecting. It was not really through with him.

"Here I go," he said, and made a dive for the railing; it was six stories down, and there below gleamed the river, and death, real death, not what the Arabic poem had seen.

As he tumbled over, it put an extension of itself on his shoulder.

"Why?" he said. But, in fact, he paused. Wondering. Not understanding, not at all.

"Don't fall on my account," it said. He could not see it because it had moved behind him. But the piece of it on his shoulder—it had begun to look to him like a human hand.

And then it laughed.

"What's funny?" he demanded, as he teetered on the railing, held back by its pseudo-hand.

"You're doing my task for me," it said. "You aren't waiting; don't you have time to wait? I'll select you out from among the others; you don't need to speed the process up."

"What if I do?" he said. "Out of revulsion for you?"

It laughed. And didn't answer.

"You won't even say," he said.

Again no answer. He started to slide back, onto the veranda. And at once the pressure of its pseudo-hand lifted.

"You founded the Party?" he asked.

"I founded everything. I founded the anti-Party and the Party that isn't a Party, and those who are for it and those who are against, those that you call Yankee Imperialists, those in the camp of reaction, and so on endlessly. I founded it all. As if they were blades of grass."

"And you're here to enjoy it?" he said.

"What I want," it said, "is for you to see me, as I am, as you have seen me, and then trust me."

"What?" he said, quavering. "Trust you to what?"

It said, "Do you believe in me?"

"Yes," he said. "I can see you."

"Then go back to your job at the Ministry. Tell Tanya Lee that you saw an overworked, overweight, elderly man who drinks too much and likes to pinch girls' rear ends."

"Oh, Christ," he said.

"As you live on, unable to stop, I will torment you," it said. "I will deprive you, item by item, of everything you possess or want. And then when you are crushed to death I will unfold a mystery."

"What's the mystery?"

"The dead shall live, the living die. I kill what lives; I save what has died. And I will tell you this: *there are things worse than I.* But you won't meet them because by then I will have killed you. Now walk back into the dining room and prepare for dinner. Don't question what I'm doing; I did it long before there was a Tung Chien and I will do it long after."

He hit it as hard as he could.

And experienced violent pain in his head.

And darkness, with the sense of falling.

After that, darkness again. He thought, I will get you. I will see that you die too. That you suffer; you're going to suffer, just like us, exactly in every way we do. I'll dedicate my life to that; I'll confront you again, and I'll nail you; I swear to god I'll nail you up somewhere. And it will hurt. As much as I hurt now.

He shut his eyes.

Roughly, he was shaken. And heard Mr. Kimo Okubara's voice. "Get to your feet, common drunk. Come on!"

Without opening his eyes he said, "Get me a cab."

"Cab already waiting. You go home. Disgrace. Make a violent scene out of yourself."

Getting shakily to his feet, he opened his eyes, examined himself. Our Leader whom we follow, he thought, is the One True God. And the enemy whom we fight and have fought is God too. They are right; he is everywhere. But I didn't understand what that meant. Staring at the protocol officer, he thought, You are God too. So there is no getting away, probably not even by jumping. As I started, instinctively, to do. He shuddered.

"Mix drinks with drugs," Okubara said witheringly. "Ruin career. I see it happen many times. Get lost."

Unsteadily, he walked toward the great central door of the Yangtze River villa; two servants, dressed like medieval knights, with crested plumes, ceremoniously opened the door for him and one of them said, "Good night, sir."

"Up yours," Chien said, and passed out into the night.

At a quarter to three in the morning, as he sat sleepless in the living room of his conapt, smoking one Cuesta Rey Astoria after another, a knock sounded at the door.

When he opened it he found himself facing Tanya Lee in her trenchcoat, her face pinched with cold. Her eyes blazed, questioningly.

"Don't look at me like that," he said roughly. His cigar had gone out; he relit it. "I've been looked at enough," he said.

"You saw it," she said.

He nodded.

She seated herself on the arm of the couch and after a time she said, "Want to tell me about it?"

"Go as far from here as possible," he said. "Go a long way." And then he remembered; no way was long enough. He remembered reading that too. "Forget it," he said; rising to his feet, he walked clumsily into the kitchen to start up the coffee.

Following after him, Tanya said, "Was—it that bad?"

"We can't win," he said. "You can't win; I don't mean me. I'm not in this; I just want to do my job at the Ministry and forget about it. Forget the whole damned thing."

"Is it non-terrestrial?"

"Yes." He nodded.

"Is it hostile to us?"

"Yes," he said. "No. Both. Mostly hostile."

"Then we have to—"

"Go home," he said, "and go to bed." He looked her over carefully; he had sat a long time and he had done a great deal of thinking. About a lot of things. "Are you married?" he said.

"No. Not now. I used to be."

He said, "Stay with me tonight. The rest of tonight, anyhow. Until the sun comes up." He added, "The night part is awful."

"I'll stay," Tanya said, unbuckling the belt of her raincoat, "but I have to have some answers."

"What did Dryden mean," Chien said, "about music untuning the sky? I don't get that. What does music do to the sky?"

"All the celestial order of the universe ends," she said as she hung her raincoat up in the closet of the bedroom; under it she wore an orange striped sweater and stretchpants.

He said, "And that's bad."

Pausing, she reflected. "I don't know. I guess so."

"It's a lot of power," he said, "to assign to music."

"Well, you know that old Pythagorean business about the 'music of the spheres.'" Matter-of-factly she seated herself on the bed and removed her slipperlike shoes.

"Do you believe in that?" he said. "Or do you believe in God?"

" 'God'!" She laughed. "That went out with the donkey steam engine. What are you talking about? God, or god?" She came over close beside him, peering into his face.

"Don't look at me so closely," he said sharply, drawing back. "I don't ever want to be looked at again." He moved away, irritably.

"I think," Tanya said, "that if there is a God He has very little interest in human affairs. That's my theory, anyhow. I mean, He doesn't seem to care if evil triumphs or people and animals get hurt and die. I frankly don't see Him anywhere around. And the Party has always denied any form of—"

"Did you ever see Him?" he asked. "When you were a child?"

"Oh, sure, as a child. But I also believed—"

"Did it ever occur to you," Chien said, "that good and evil are names for the same thing? That God could be both good and evil at the same time?"

"I'll fix you a drink," Tanya said, and padded barefoot into the kitchen.

Chien said, "The Crusher. The Clanker. The Gulper and the Bird and the Climbing Tube—plus other names, forms, I don't know. I had a hallucination. At the stag dinner. A big one. A terrible one."

"But the stelazine—"

"It brought on a worse one," he said.

"Is there any way," Tanya said somberly, "that we can fight this thing you saw? This apparition you call a hallucination but which very obviously was not?"

He said, "Believe in it."

"What will that do?"

"Nothing," he said wearily. "Nothing at all. I'm tired; I don't want a drink—let's just go to bed."

"Okay." She padded back into the bedroom, began pulling her striped sweater over her head. "We'll discuss it more thoroughly later."

"A hallucination," Chien said, "is merciful. I wish I had it;

I want mine back. I want to be before your peddler got to me with that phenothiazine."

"Just come to bed. It'll be toasty. All warm and nice."

He removed his tie, his shirt—and saw, on his right shoulder, the mark, the stigma, which it had left when it stopped him from jumping. Livid marks which looked as if they would never go away. He put his pajama top on, then; it hid the marks.

"Anyhow," Tanya said as he got into the bed beside her, "your career is immeasurably advanced. Aren't you glad about that?"

"Sure," he said, nodding sightlessly in the darkness. "Very glad."

"Come over against me," Tanya said, putting her arms around him. "And forget everything else. At least for now."

He tugged her against him, then, doing what she asked and what he wanted to do. She was neat; she was swiftly active; she was successful and she did her part. They did not bother to speak until at last she said, "Oh!" And then she relaxed.

"I wish," he said, "that we could go on forever."

"We did," Tanya said. "It's outside of time; it's boundless, like an ocean. It's the way we were in Cambrian times, before we migrated up onto the land; it's the ancient primary waters. This is the only time we get to go back, when this is done. That's why it means so much. And in those days we weren't separate; it was like a big jelly, like those blobs that float up on the beach."

"Float up," he said, "and are left there to die."

"Could you get me a towel?" Tanya asked. "Or a wash-cloth? I need it."

He padded into the bathroom for a towel. There—he was naked, now—he once more saw his shoulder, saw where it had seized hold of him and held on, dragged him back, possibly to toy with him a little more.

The marks, unaccountably, were bleeding.

He sponged the blood away. More oozed forth at once and, seeing that, he wondered how much time he had left. Probably only hours.

Returning to bed, he said, "Could you continue?"

"Sure. If you have any energy left; it's up to you." She lay gazing up at him unwinkingly, barely visible in the dim nocturnal light.

"I have," he said. And hugged her to him.

by PHILIP K. DICK
The Man in the High Castle
Martian Time-slip
The Three Stigmata of Palmer Eldritch
Do Androids Dream of Electric Sheep?
Ubik

Aye, and Gomorrah ..

SAMUEL R. DELANY

And came down in Paris:

Where we raced along the Rue de Médicis with Bo and Lou and Muse inside the fence, Kelly and me outside, making faces through the bars, making noise, making the Luxembourg Gardens roar at two in the morning. Then climbed out, and down to the square in front of St. Sulpice where Bo tried to knock me into the fountain.

At which point Kelly noticed what was going on around us, got an ashcan cover, and ran into the pissoir, banging the walls. Five guys scooted out; even a big pissoir only holds four.

A very blond young man put his hand on my arm and smiled. "Don't you think, Spacer, that you . . . people should leave?"

I looked at his hand on my blue uniform. "*Est-ce que tu es un frelk?*"

His eyebrows rose, then he shook his head. "Une *frelk*," he corrected. "No. I am not. Sadly for me. You look as though you may once have been a man. But now . . ." He smiled. "You have nothing for me now. The police." He nodded across the street where I noticed the gendarmerie for the first time. "They don't bother us. You are strangers, though . . ."

But Muse was already yelling, "Hey, come on! Let's get out of here, huh?" And left. And went up again.

And came down in Houston:

"God damn!" Muse said. "Gemini Flight Control—you mean this is where it all started? Let's get *out* of here, *please!*"

So took a bus out through Pasadena, then the monoline to Galveston, and were going to take it down the Gulf, but Lou found a couple with a pickup truck—

"Glad to give you a ride, Spacers. You people up there on them planets and things, doing all that good work for the government."

—who were going south, them and the baby, so we rode in the back for two hundred and fifty miles of sun and wind.

"You think they're frelks?" Lou asked, elbowing me. "I bet they're frelks. They're just waiting for us give 'em the come-on."

"Cut it out. They're a nice, stupid pair of country kids."

"That don't mean they ain't frelks!"

"You don't trust anybody, do you?"

"No."

And finally a bus again that rattled us through Brownsville and across the border into Matamoros where we staggered down the steps into the dust and the scorched evening with a lot of Mexicans and chickens and Texas Gulf shrimp fishermen—who smelled worst—and *we* shouted the loudest. Forty-three whores—I counted—had turned out for the shrimp fishermen, and by the time we had broken two of the windows in the bus station they were all laughing. The shrimp fishermen said they wouldn't buy us no food but would get us drunk if we wanted, 'cause that was the custom with shrimp fishermen. But we yelled, broke another window; then, while I was lying on my back on the telegraph office steps, singing, a woman with dark lips bent over and put her hands on my cheeks. "You are very sweet." Her rough hair fell forward. "But the men, they are standing around and watching *you*. And that is taking up *time*. Sadly, their time is our money. Spacer, do you not think you . . . people should leave?"

I grabbed her wrist. "*Usted!*" I whispered. "*Usted es una frelka?*"

"*Frelko in español.*" She smiled and patted the sunburst that hung from my belt buckle. "Sorry. But you have nothing that . . . would be useful to me. It is too bad, for you look like you were once a woman, no? And I like women, too. . . ."

I rolled off the porch.

"Is this a drag, or is this a drag!" Muse was shouting. "Come *on!* Let's *go!*"

We managed to get back to Houston before dawn, somehow. And went up.

And came down in Istanbul:

That morning it rained in Istanbul.

At the commissary we drank our tea from pear-shaped glasses, looking out across the Bosporus. The Princes Islands lay like trash heaps before the prickly city.

"Who knows their way in this town?" Kelly asked.

"Aren't we going around together?" Muse demanded. "I thought we were going around together."

"They held up my check at the purser's office," Kelly explained. "I'm flat broke. I think the purser's got it in for me," and shrugged. "Don't want to, but I'm going to have to hunt up a rich frelk and come on friendly," went back to the tea; *then* noticed how heavy the silence had become. "Aw, come *on*, now! You gape at me like that and I'll bust every bone in that carefully-conditioned-from-puberty body of yours. Hey you!" meaning me. "Don't give me that holier-than-thou gawk like you never went with no frelk!"

It was starting.

"I'm not gawking," I said and got quietly mad.

The longing, the old longing.

Bo laughed to break tensions. "Say, last time I was in Istanbul—about a year before I joined up with this platoon—I remember we were coming out of Taksim Square down Istiqlal. Just past all the cheap movies we found a little passage lined with flowers. Ahead of us were two other spacers. It's a market in there, and farther down they got fish, and then a courtyard with oranges and candy and sea urchins and cabbage. But flowers in front. Anyway, we noticed something funny about the spacers. It wasn't their uniforms: they were perfect. The haircuts: fine. It wasn't till we heard them talking—They were a man and woman dressed up like spacers, trying *to pick up frelks!* Imagine, queer for frelks!"

"Yeah," Lou said. "I seen that before. There were a lot of them in Rio."

"We beat hell out of them two," Bo concluded. "We got them in a side street and went to *town!*"

Muse's tea glass clicked on the counter. "From Taksim

down Istiqlal till you get to the flowers? Now why didn't you say that's where the frelks were, huh?" A smile on Kelly's face would have made that okay. There was no smile.

"Hell," Lou said, "nobody ever had to tell me where to look. I go out in the street and frelks smell me coming. I can spot 'em halfway along Piccadilly. Don't they have nothing but tea in this place? Where can you get a drink?"

Bo grinned. "Moslem country, remember? But down at the end of the Flower Passage there're a lot of little bars with green doors and marble counters where you can get a liter of beer for about fifteen cents in lira. And there're all these stands selling deep-fat-fried bugs and pig's gut sandwiches—"

"You ever notice how frelks can put it away? I mean liquor, not . . . pig's guts."

And launched off into a lot of appeasing stories. We ended with the one about the frelk some spacer tried to roll who announced: "There are two things I go for. One is spacers; the other is a good fight. . . ."

But they only allay. They cure nothing. Even Muse knew we would spend the day apart, now.

The rain had stopped, so we took the ferry up the Golden Horn. Kelly straight off asked for Taksim Square and Istiqlal and was directed to a dolmush, which we discovered was a taxicab, only it just goes one place and picks up lots and lots of people on the way. And it's cheap.

Lou headed off over Ataturk Bridge to see the sights of New City. Bo decided to find out what the Dolma Boche really was; and when Muse discovered you could go to Asia for fifteen cents—one lira and fifty krush—well, Muse decided to go to Asia.

I turned through the confusion of traffic at the head of the bridge and up past the gray, dripping walls of Old City, beneath the trolley wires. There are times when yelling and helling won't fill the lack. There are times when you must walk by yourself because it hurts so much to be alone.

I walked up a lot of little streets with wet donkeys and wet camels and women in veils; and down a lot of big streets with buses and trash baskets and men in business suits.

Some people stare at spacers; some people don't. Some

people stare or don't stare in a way a spacer gets to recognize within a week after coming out of training school at sixteen. I was walking in the park when I caught her watching. She saw me see and looked away.

I ambled down the wet asphalt. She was standing under the arch of a small, empty mosque shell. As I passed she walked out into the courtyard among the cannons.

"Excuse me."

I stopped.

"Do you know whether or not this is the shrine of St. Irene?" Her English was charmingly accented. "I've left my guidebook home."

"Sorry. I'm a tourist too."

"Oh." She smiled. "I am Greek. I thought you might be Turkish because you are so dark."

"American red Indian." I nodded. Her turn to curtsy.

"I see. I have just started at the university here in Istanbul. Your uniform, it tells me that you are"—and in the pause, all speculations resolved—"a spacer."

I was uncomfortable. "Yeah." I put my hands in my pockets, moved my feet around on the soles of my boots, licked my third from the rear left molar—did all the things you do when you're uncomfortable. *You're so exciting when you look like that,* a frelk told me once. "Yeah, I am." I said it too sharply, too loudly, and she jumped a little.

So now she knew I knew she knew I knew, and I wondered how we would play out the Proust bit.

"I'm Turkish," she said. "I'm not Greek. I'm not just starting. I'm a graduate in art history here at the university. These little lies one makes for strangers to protect one's ego . . . why? Sometimes I think my ego is very small."

That's one strategy.

"How far away do you live?" I asked. "And what's the going rate in Turkish lira?" That's another.

"I can't pay you." She pulled her raincoat around her hips. She was very pretty. "I would like to." She shrugged and smiled. "But I am . . . a poor student. Not a rich one. If you want to turn around and walk away, there will be no hard feelings. I shall be sad though."

I stayed on the path. I thought she'd suggest a price after a little while. She didn't.

And *that's* another.

I was asking myself, *What do you want the damn money for anyway?* when a breeze upset water from one of the park's great cypresses.

"I think the whole business is sad." She wiped drops from her face. There had been a break in her voice and for a moment I looked too closely at the water streaks. "I think it's sad that they have to alter you to make you a spacer. If they hadn't, then *we*. . . . If spacers had never been, then we could not be . . . the way we are. Did you start out male or female?"

Another shower. I was looking at the ground and droplets went down my collar.

"Male," I said. "It doesn't matter."

"How old are you? Twenty-three, twenty-four?"

"Twenty-three," I lied. It's reflex. I'm twenty-five, but the younger they think you are, the more they pay you. But I didn't *want* her *damn* money—

"I guessed right then." She nodded. "Most of us are experts on spacers. Do you find that? I suppose we have to be." She looked at me with wide black eyes. At the end of the stare, she blinked rapidly. "You would have been a fine man. But now you are a spacer, building water-conservation units on Mars, programing mining computers on Ganymede, servicing communication relay towers on the moon. The alteration . . ." Frelks are the only people I've ever heard say "the alteration" with so much fascination and regret. "You'd think they'd have found some other solution. They could have found another way than neutering you, turning you into creatures not even androgynous; things that are—"

I put my hand on her shoulder, and she stopped like I'd hit her. She looked to see if anyone was near. Lightly, so lightly then, she raised her hand to mine.

I pulled my hand away. "That are what?"

"They could have found another way." Both hands in her pockets now.

"They could have. Yes. Up beyond the ionosphere, baby,

there's too much radiation for those precious gonads to work right anywhere you might want to do something that would keep you there over twenty-four hours, like the moon, or Mars, or the satellites of Jupiter—"

"They could have made protective shields. They could have done more research into biological adjustment—"

"Population Explosion time," I said. "No, they were hunting for any excuse to cut down kids back then—especially deformed ones."

"Ah yes." She nodded. "We're still fighting our way up from the neo-puritan reaction to the sex freedom of the twentieth century."

"It was a fine solution." I grinned and grabbed my crotch. "I'm happy with it." I've never known why that's so much more obscene when a spacer does it.

"Stop it," she snapped, moving away.

"What's the matter?"

"Stop it," she repeated. "Don't do that! You're a child."

"But they choose us from children whose sexual responses are hopelessly retarded at puberty."

"And your childish, violent substitutes for love? I suppose that's one of the things that's attractive. Yes, I know you're a child."

"Yeah? What about frelks?"

She thought awhile. "I think they are the sexually retarded ones they miss. Perhaps it was the right solution. You really don't regret you have no sex?"

"We've got you," I said.

"Yes." She looked down. I glanced to see the expression she was hiding. It was a smile. "You have your glorious, soaring life, *and* you have us." Her face came up. She glowed. "You spin in the sky, the world spins under you, and you step from land to land, while we . . ." She turned her head right, left, and her black hair curled and uncurled on the shoulder of her coat. "We have our dull, circled lives, bound in gravity, *worshiping* you!"

She looked back at me. "Perverted, yes? In love with a bunch of corpses in free fall!" She suddenly hunched her shoulders. "I don't like having a free-fall-sexual-displacement complex."

"That always sounded like too much to say."

She looked away. "I don't like being a frelk. Better?"

"I wouldn't like it either. Be something else."

"You don't choose your perversions. *You* have no perversions at all. *You're* free of the whole business. I love you for that, Spacer. My love starts with the fear of love. Isn't that beautiful? A pervert substitutes something unattainable for 'normal' love: the homosexual, a mirror, the fetishist, a shoe or a watch or a girdle. Those with free-fall-sexual-dis—"

"Frelks."

"Frelks substitute"—she looked at me sharply again—"loose, swinging meat."

"That doesn't offend me."

"I wanted it to."

"Why?"

"You don't have desires. You wouldn't understand."

"Go on."

"I want you because you can't want me. That's the pleasure. If someone really had a sexual reaction to . . . us, we'd be scared away. I wonder how many people there were before there were you, waiting for your creation. We're necrophiles. I'm sure grave robbing has fallen off since you started going up. But you don't understand. . . ." She paused. "If you did, then I wouldn't be scuffing leaves now and trying to think from whom I could borrow sixty lira." She stepped over the knuckles of a root that had cracked the pavement. "And that, incidentally, is the going rate in Istanbul."

I calculated. "Things still get cheaper as you go east."

"You know," and she let her raincoat fall open, "you're different from the others. You at least *want* to know—"

I said, "If I spat on you for every time you'd said that to a spacer, you'd drown."

"Go back to the moon, loose meat." She closed her eyes. "Swing on up to Mars. There are satellites around Jupiter where you might do some good. Go up and come down in some other city."

"Where do you live?"

"You want to come with me?"

"Give me something," I said. "Give me something—it doesn't have to be worth sixty lira. Give me something that you like, anything of yours that means something to you."

"No!"

"Why not?"

"Because I—"

"—don't want to give up part of that ego. None of you frelks do!"

"You really don't understand I just don't want to buy you?"

"You have nothing to buy me with."

"You are a child," she said. "I love you."

We reached the gate of the park. She stopped, and we stood time enough for a breeze to rise and die in the grass. "I . . ." she offered tentatively, pointing without taking her hand from her coat pocket. "I live right down there."

"All right," I said. "Let's go."

A gas main had once exploded along this street, she explained to me, a gushing road of fire as far as the docks, overhot and overquick. It had been put out within minutes, no building had fallen, but the charred facias glittered. "This is sort of an artist and student quarter." We crossed the cobbles. "Yuri Pasha, number fourteen. In case you're ever in Istanbul again." Her door was covered with black scales, the gutter was thick with garbage.

"A lot of artists and professional people are frelks," I said, trying to be inane.

"So are lots of other people." She walked inside and held the door. "We're just more flamboyant about it."

On the landing there was a portrait of Ataturk. Her room was on the second floor. "Just a moment while I get my key—"

Marsscapes! Moonscapes! On her easel was a six-foot canvas showing the sunrise flaring on a crater's rim! There were copies of the original Observer pictures of the moon pinned to the wall, and pictures of every smooth-faced general in the International Spacer Corps.

On one corner of her desk was a pile of those photo magazines about spacers that you can find in most kiosks all over the world: I've seriously heard people say they were printed for adventurous-minded high school children. They've never seen the Danish ones. She had a few of those too. There was a shelf of art books, art history texts. Above them were six feet of cheap paper-covered space operas: *Sin on Space Station #12, Rocket Rake, Savage Orbit.*

"Arrack?" she asked. "Ouzo or pernod? You've got your choice. But I may pour them all from the same bottle." She set out glasses on the desk, then opened a waist-high cabinet that turned out to be an icebox. She stood up with a tray of lovelies: fruit puddings, Turkish delight, braised meats.

"What's this?"

"Dolmades. Grape leaves filled with rice and pignolias."

"Say it again?"

"Dolmades. Comes from the same Turkish word as 'dolmush.' They both mean 'stuffed.' " She put the tray beside the glasses. "Sit down."

I sat on the studio-couch-that-becomes-bed. Under the brocade I felt the deep, fluid resilience of a glycogel mattress. They've got the idea that it approximates the feeling of free fall. "Comfortable? Would you excuse me for a moment? I have some friends down the hall. I want to see them for a moment." She winked. "They like spacers."

"Are you going to take up a collection for me?" I asked. "Or do you want them to line up outside the door and wait their turn?"

She sucked a breath. "Actually I was going to suggest both." Suddenly she shook her head. "Oh, what do you want!"

"What will you give me? I want something," I said. "That's why I came. I'm lonely. Maybe I want to find out how far it goes. I don't know yet."

"It goes as far as you will. Me? I study, I read, paint, talk with my friends"—she came over to the bed, sat down on the floor—"go to the theater, look at spacers who pass me on the street, till one looks back; I am lonely too." She put her head on my knee. "I want something. But," and after a minute neither of us had moved, "you are not the one who will give it to me."

"You're not going to pay me for it," I countered. "You're not, are you?"

On my knee her head shook. After a while she said, all breath and no voice, "Don't you think you . . . should leave?"

"Okay," I said, and stood up.

She sat back on the hem of her coat. She hadn't taken it off yet.

I went to the door.

"Incidentally." She folded her hands in her lap. "There is a place in New City you might find what you're looking for, called the Flower Passage—"

I turned toward her, angry. "The frelk hangout? Look, I don't *need* money! I said *anything* would do! I don't want—"

She had begun to shake her head, laughing quietly. Now she lay her cheek on the wrinkled place where I had sat. "Do you persist in misunderstanding? It is a spacer hangout. When you leave, I am going to visit my friends and talk about . . . ah, yes, the beautiful one that got away. I thought you might find . . . perhaps someone you know."

With anger, it ended.

"Oh," I said. "Oh, it's a spacer hangout. Yeah. Well, thanks."

And went out. And found the Flower Passage, and Kelly and Lou and Bo and Muse. Kelly was buying beer so we all got drunk, and ate fried fish and fried clams and fried sausage, and Kelly was waving the money around, saying, "You should have seen him! The changes I put that frelk through, you should have *seen* him! Eighty lira is the going rate here, and he gave me a hundred and fifty!" and drank more beer. And went up.

by SAMUEL R. DELANY
Babel 17
The Einstein Intersection
Nova
Driftglass (collection of short stories)

At the Mouse Circus

HARLAN ELLISON

The King of Tibet was having himself a fat white woman. He had thrown himself down a jelly tunnel, millennia before, and periodically, as he pumped her, a soft pink-and-white bunny rabbit in weskit and spats trembled through, scrutinizing a turnip watch at the end of a heavy gold-link chain. The white woman was soft as suet, with little black eyes thrust deep under prominent brow ridges. Honkie bitch groaned in unfulfilled ecstasy, trying desperately and knowing she never would. For she never had. The King of Tibet had a bellyache. Oh, to be in another place, doing another thing, alone.

The land outside was shimmering in waves of fear that came radiating from mountaintops far away. On the mountaintops, grizzled and wizened old men considered ways and means, considered runes and portents, considered whys and wherefores . . . ignored them all . . . and set about sending more fear to farther places. The land rippled in the night, beginning to quake with terror that was greater than the fear that had gone before.

"What time is it?" he asked, and received no answer.

Thirty-seven years ago, when the King of Tibet had been a lad, there had been a man with one leg—who had been his father for a short time—and a woman with a touch of the tar brush in her, and she had served as mother.

"You can be anything, Charles," she had said to him. "Anything you want to be. A man can be anything he can do. Uncle Wiggly, Jomo Kenyatta, the King of Tibet, if you want to. Light enough or black, Charles, it don't mean a thing. You just go your way and be good and *do*. That's all you got to remember."

The King of Tibet had fallen on hard times. Fat white women and cheap cologne. Doodad, he had lost the horizon. Exquisite, he had dealt with surfaces and been dealt with similarly. Wasted, he had done time.

"I got to go," he told her.

"Not yet, just a little more. Please."

So he stayed. Banners unfurled, lying limp in absence of breezes from Camelot, he stayed and suffered. Finally, she turned him loose, and the King of Tibet stood in the shower for forty minutes. Golden skin pelted, drinking, he was never quite clean. Scented, abluted, he still knew the odors of wombats, hallway musk, granaries, futile beakers of noxious fluids. If he was a white mouse, why could he not see his treadmill?

"Listen, baby, I got need of fi'hunnerd dollahs. I know we ain't been together but a while, but I got this *bad* need." She went to snap-purses and returned.

He hated her more for doing than not doing.

And in her past, he knew he was no part of any recognizable future.

"Charlie, when'll I see you again?" Stranger, never!

Borne away in the silver flesh of Cadillac, the great beautiful mother Hog, plunging wheelbased at one hundred and twenty (bought with his semen) inches, Eldorado god-creature of four hundred horsepower, displacing recklessly 440 cubic inches, thundering into forgetting weighing 4550+ pounds, goes . . . went . . . Charlie . . . Charles . . . the King of Tibet. Golden brown, cleaned as best as he could, five hundred reasons and five hundred aways. Driven, driving into the outside.

Forever inside, the King of Tibet, going outside.

Along the road. Manhattan, Jersey City, New Brunswick, Trenton. In Norristown, having had lunch at a fine restaurant, Charlie was stopped on a street corner by a voice that went *pssst* from a mailbox. He opened the slit and a small boy in a pullover sweater and tie thrust his head and shoulders into the night. "You've got to help me," the boy said. "My name is Batson. Billy Batson. I work for radio station WHIZ and if I could only remember the right word, and if I could only *say* it, something wonderful would happen. S is for the wisdom of Solomon, H is for the strength of Hercules, A is for the stamina of Atlas, Z is for the power of Zeus . . . and after that I go blank . . ."

The King of Tibet slowly and steadily thrust the head back into the mailslot, and walked away. Reading, Harrisburg, Mt. Union, Altoona, Nanty Glo.

On the road to Pittsburgh there was a four-fingered mouse in red shorts with two big yellow buttons on the front, hitch-hiking. Shoes like two big boxing gloves, bright eyes sincere, forlorn, and way lost, he stood on the curb with meaty thumb and he waited. Charlie whizzed past. It was not his dream.

Youngstown, Akron, Canton, Columbus, and hungry once more in Dayton.

O.

Oh aitch eye oh. Why did he ever leave. He had never been there before. This was the good place. The river flowed dark, and the day passed overhead like some other river. He pulled into a parking space and did not even lock the god-mother Eldorado. It waited patiently, knowing its upholstered belly would be filled with the King of Tibet soon enough.

"Feed you next," he told the sentient vehicle, as he walked away toward the restaurant.

Inside—dim and candled at high noon—he was shown to a heavy wood booth, and there he had laid before him a pure white linen napkin, five pieces of silver, a crystal goblet in which fine water waited, and a promise. From the promise he selected nine-to-five winners, a long shot and the play number for the day.

A flocked-velvet witch perched on a bar stool across from him turned, exposed thigh, and smiled. He offered her silver, water, a promise, and they struck a bargain.

Charlie stared into her oiled teakwood eyes through the candle flame between them. All moistened saran-wrap was her skin. All thistled gleaming were her teeth. All mystery of cupped hollows beneath cheekbones was she. Charlie had bought a television set once, because the redhead in the commercial was part of his dream. He had bought an electric toothbrush because the brunette with her capped teeth had indicated she, too, was part of his dream. And his great Eldorado, of course. *That* was the dream of the King of Tibet.

"What time is it?" But he received no answer and, drying his lips of the last of the *pêche flambée,* he and the flocked-velvet witch left the restaurant: he with his dream fraying, and she with no product save one to sell.

There was a party in a house on a hill.

When they drove up the asphalt drive, the blacktop beneath them uncoiled like the sooty tongue of a great primitive snake. "You'll like these people," she said, and took the sensitive face of the King of Tibet between her hands and kissed him deeply. Her fingernails were gunmetal silvered and her palms were faintly moist and plump, with expectations of tactile enrichments.

They walked up to the house. Lit from within, every window held a color facet of light. Sounds swelled as they came toward the house. He fell a step behind her and watched the way her skin flowed. She reached out, touched the house, and they became one.

No door was opened to them, but holding fast to her hair he was drawn behind her, through the flesh of the house.

Within, there were inlaid ivory boxes that, when opened, revealed smaller boxes within. He became fascinated by one such box, sitting high on a pedestal in the center of an om rug. The box was inlaid with teeth of otters and puff adders and lynx. He opened the first box and within was a second box frosted with rime. Within the frost-box was a third, and it was decorated with mirrors that cast back no reflections. And next within was a box whose surface was a mass of intaglios, and they were all fingerprints, and none of Charlie's fit, and only when a passing man smiled and caressed the lid did it open, revealing the next, smaller box. And so it went, till he lost count of the boxes and the journey ended when he could not see the box that fit within the dust-mote-size box that was within all the others. But he knew there were more, and he felt a great sadness that he could not get to them.

"What is it, precisely, you want?" asked an older woman with very good bones. He was leaning against a wall whose only ornamentation was a gigantic wooden crucifix on which a Christ-figure hung, head bowed, shoulders twisted as only shoulders can be whose arms have been pulled from sockets; the figure was made of massive pieces of wood, all artfully stained: chunks of doors, bedposts, rowels, splines, pintles, joists, crossties, rabbet-joined bits of massive frames.

"I want . . ." he began, then spread his hands in confusion. He knew what he wanted to say, but no one had ever ordered the progression of words properly.

"Is it Madelaine?" the older woman asked. She smiled as Aunt Jemima would smile, and targeted a finger across the enormous living room, bull's-eyed on the flocked-velvet witch all the way over there by the fireplace. "She's here."

The King of Tibet felt a bit more relaxed.

"Now," the older woman said, her hand on Charlie's cheek, "what is it you need to know? Tell me. We have all the answers here. Truly."

"I want to know—"

The television screen went silver and cast a pool of light, drawing Charlie's attention. The possibilities were listed on the screen. And what he had wanted to know seemed inconsequential compared to the choices he saw listed.

"That one," he said. "That second one. How did the dinosaurs die?"

"Oh, fine!" She looked pleased he had selected that one. "Shefti . . . ?" she called to a tall man with gray hair at the temples. He looked up from speaking to several women and another man, looked up expectantly, and she said, "He's picked the second one. May I?"

"Of course, darling," Shefti said, raising his wine glass to her.

"Do we have time?"

"Oh, I think so," he said.

"Yes . . . what time *is* it?" Charlie asked.

"Over here," the older woman said, leading him firmly by the forearm. They stopped beside another wall. "Look."

The King of Tibet stared at the wall, and it paled, turned

to ice, and became translucent. There was something im-
bedded in the ice. Something huge. Something dark. He
stared harder, his eyes straining to make out the shape. Then
he was seeing more clearly, and it was a great saurian,
frozen at the moment of pouncing on some lesser species.

"*Gorgosaurus,*" the older woman said, at his elbow. "It
rather resembles *Tyrannosaurus,* you see; but the forelimbs
have only two digits. You see?"

Thirty-two feet of tanned gray leather. The killing teeth.
The nostriled snout, the amber smoke eyes of the eater of
carrion. The smooth sickening tuber of balancing tail, the
crippled forelimbs carried tragically withered and useless.
The musculature . . . the pulsing beat of iced blood beneath
the tarpaulin hide. The . . . beat . . .

It lived.

Through the ice went the King of Tibet, accompanied by
a Circe-eyed older woman, as the shellfish-white living room
receded back beyond the ice-wall. Ice went, night came.

Ice that melted slowly from the great hulk before him. He
stood in wonder. "See," the woman said.

And he saw as the ice dissolved into mist and night-fog,
and he saw as the earth trembled, and he saw as the great
furry lizard moved in shambling hesitancy, and he saw as the
others came to cluster unseen nearby. *Scolosaurus* came.
Trachodon came. *Stephanosaurus* came. *Protoceratops* came.
And all stood, waiting.

The King of Tibet knew there were slaughterhouses where
the beef was hung upside down on hooks, where the throats
were slit and the blood ran thick as motor oil. He saw a
golden thing hanging, and would not look. Later, he would
look.

They waited. Silently, for its coming.

Through the Cretaceous swamp it *was* coming. Charlie
could hear it. Not loud, but coming steadily closer. "Would
you light my cigarette, please," asked the older woman.

It was shining. It bore a pale white nimbus. It was stepping
through the swamp, black to its thighs from the decaying
matter. It came on, its eyes set back under furred brow-ridges,

jaw thrust forward, wide nostrils sniffing at the chill night, arms covered with matted filth and hair. Savior man.

He came to the lizard owners of the land. He walked around them and they stood silently, their time at hand. Then he touched them, one after the other, and the plague took them. Blue fungus spread from the five-pronged marks left on their imperishable hides; blue death radiating from impressions of opposed thumbs, joining, spreading cilia and rotting the flesh of the great gone dinosaurs.

The ice re-formed and the King of Tibet moved back through pearly cold to the living room.

He struck a match and lit her cigarette.

She thanked him and walked away.

The flocked-velvet witch returned. "Did you have a nice time?" He thought of the boxes-within-boxes.

"Is that how they died? Was he the first?"

She nodded. "And did Nita ask you for anything?"

Charlie had never seen the sea. Oh, there had been the Narrows and the East River and the Hudson, but he had never seen the sea. The real sea, the thunder sea that went black at night like a pane of glass. The sea that could summon and the sea that could kill, that could swallow whole cities and turn them into myth. He wanted to go to California.

He suddenly felt a fear he would never leave this thing called Ohio here.

"I asked you: did Nita ask you for anything?"

He shivered.

"What?"

"Nita. Did she *ask* you for anything?"

"Only a light."

"Did you give it to her?"

"Yes."

Madelaine's face swam in the thin fluid of his sight. Her jaw muscles trembled. She turned and walked across the room. Everyone turned to look at her. She went to Nita, who suddenly took a step backward and threw up her hands. "No, I didn't—"

The flocked-velvet witch darted a hand toward the older

woman and the hand seemed to pass into her neck. The silver-tipped fingers reappeared, clenched around a fine sparkling filament. Then Madelaine snapped it off with a grunt.

There was a terrible minor sound from Nita, then she turned, watery, and stood silently beside the window, looking empty and hopeless.

Madelaine wiped her hand on the back of the sofa and came to Charlie. "We'll go now. The party is over."

He drove in silence back to town.

"Are you coming up?" he asked, when they parked the Eldorado in front of the hotel.

"I'm coming up."

He registered them as Professor Pierre and Marja Sklodowska Curie, and for the first time in his life he was unable to reach a climax. He fell asleep sobbing over never having seen the sea, and came awake hours later with the night still pressing against the walls. She was not there.

He heard sounds from the street, and went to the window.

There was a large crowd in the street, gathered around his car.

As he watched, a man went to his knees before the golden Eldorado and touched it. Charlie knew *this* was his dream. He could not move; he just watched, as they ate his car.

The man put his mouth to the hood and it came away bloody. A great chunk had been ripped from the gleaming hide of the Cadillac. Golden blood ran down the man's jaws.

Another man draped himself over the top of the car and even through the window the King of Tibet could hear the terrible sucking, slobbering sounds. Furrows were ripped in the top.

A woman pulled her dress up around her hips and backed, on all fours, to the rear of the car. Her face trembled with soft expectancy, and then it was inside her and she moved on it.

When she came, they all moved in on the car and he watched as his dream went inside them, piece by piece, chewed and eaten as he stood by helpless.

"That's all, Charlie," he heard her say, behind him. He

could not turn to look at her, but her reflection was super-imposed over his own in the window. Out there in darkness now, they moved away, having eaten.

He looked, and saw the golden thing hanging upside down in the slaughterhouse, its throat cut, its blood drained away in onyx gutters.

Afoot, in Dayton, Ohio, he was dead of dreams.

"What time is it?" he asked.

by HARLAN ELLISON

I Have No Mouth and I Must Scream (collection of short stories)

Paingod (collection of short stories)

The Beast That Shouted Love at the Heart of the World (collection of short stories)

Dangerous Visions (editor)

In Entropy's Jaws

ROBERT SILVERBERG

Static crackles from the hazy golden cloud of airborne loud-speakers drifting just below the ceiling of the spaceliner cabin. A hiss: communications filters are opening. An impending announcement from the bridge, no doubt. Then the captain's bland, mechanical voice: "We are approaching the Panama Canal. All passengers into their bottles until the all-clear after insertion. When we come out the far side, we'll be traveling at eighty lights toward the Perseus relay booster. Thank you." In John Skein's cabin the warning globe begins to flash, dousing him with red, yellow, green light, going up and down the visible spectrum, giving him some infra- and ultra- too. Not everybody who books passage on this liner necessarily has human sensory equipment. The signal will not go out until Skein is safely in his bottle. Go on, it tells him. Get in. Get in. Panama Canal coming up.

Obediently he rises and moves across the narrow cabin toward the tapering, dull-skinned steel container, two and a half meters high, that will protect him against the dimensional stresses of canal insertion. He is a tall, angular man with thin lips, a strong chin, glossy black hair that clings close to his high-vaulted skull. His skin is deeply tanned but his eyes are those of one who has been in winter for some time. This is the fiftieth year of his second go-round. He is traveling alone toward a world of the Abbondanza system, perhaps the last leg on a journey that has occupied him for several years.

The passenger bottle swings open on its gaudy rhodium-jacketed hinge when its sensors, picking up Skein's mass and thermal output, tell it that its protectee is within entry range.

He gets in. It closes and seals, wrapping him in a seamless magnetic field. "Please be seated," the bottle tells him softly. "Place your arms through the stasis loops and your feet in the security platens. When you have done this the pressor fields will automatically be activated and you will be fully insulated against injury during the coming period of turbulence." Skein, who has had plenty of experience with faster-than-light travel, has anticipated the instructions and is already in stasis. The bottle closes. "Do you wish music?" it asks him. "A book? A vision spool? Conversation?"

"Nothing, thanks," Skein says, and waits.

He understands waiting very well by this time. Once he was an impatient man, but this is a thin season in his life and it has been teaching him the arts of stoic acceptance. He will sit here with the Buddha's own complacency until the ship is through the canal. Silent, alone, self-sufficient. If only there will be no fugues this time. Or, at least—he is negotiating the terms of his torment with his demons—at least let them not be flashforwards. If he must break loose again from the matrix of time, he prefers to be cast only into his yesterdays, never into his tomorrows.

"We are almost into the canal now," the bottle tells him pleasantly.

"It's all right. You don't need to look after me. Just let me know when it's safe to come out."

He closes his eyes. Trying to envision the ship: a fragile glimmering purple needle squirting through clinging blackness, plunging toward the celestial vortex just ahead, the maelstrom of clashing forces, the soup of contravariant tensors. The Panama Canal, so-called. Through which the liner will shortly rush, acquiring during its passage such a garland of borrowed power that it will rip itself free of the standard fourspace; it will emerge on the far side of the canal into a strange, tranquil pocket of the universe where the speed of light is the downside limiting velocity, and no one knows where the upper limit lies.

Alarms sound in the corridor, heavy, resonant: clang, clang, clang. The dislocation is beginning. Skein is braced. What does it look like out there? Folds of glowing black velvet, furry swatches of the disrupted continuum, wrapping themselves around the ship? Titanic lightnings hammering on the hull? Laughing centaurs flashing across the twisted heavens? Despondent masks, fixed in tragic grimaces, dangling between the blurred stars? Streaks of orange, green, crimson: sick rainbows, limp, askew? In we go. *Clang, clang, clang.* The next phase of the voyage now begins. He thinks of his destination, holding an image of it rigidly in mind. The picture is vivid, though this is a world he has visited only in spells of temporal fugue. Too often; he has been there again and again in these moments of disorientation in time. The colors are wrong on that world. Purple sand. Blue-leaved trees. Too much manganese? Too little copper? He will forgive it its colors if it will grant him his answers. And then, Skein feels the familiar ugly throbbing at the base of his neck, as if the tip of his spine is swelling like a balloon. He curses. He tries to resist. As he feared, not even the bottle can wholly protect him against these stresses. Outside the ship the universe is being wrenched apart; some of that slips in here and throws him into a private epilepsy of the time-line. Space-time is breaking up for him. He will go into fugue. He clings, fighting, knowing it is futile. The currents of time buffet him, knocking him a short distance into the future, then a reciprocal distance into the past, as if he is a bubble of insect spittle glued loosely to a dry reed. He cannot hold on much longer. Let it not be flashforward, he prays, wondering who it is to whom he prays. Let it not be flashforward. And he loses his grip. And shatters. And is swept in shards across time.

Of course, if x *is before* y *then it remains eternally before* y, *and nothing in the passage of time can change this. But the peculiar position of the "now" can be easily expressed simply because our language has tenses. The future* will be, *the present* is, *and the past* was; *the light* will be *red, it* is *now yellow, and it* was *green. But do we, in these terms, really describe the "processional" character of time? We sometimes say that an event* is *future, then it* is *present, and finally it* is *past; and by this means we seem to dispense with tenses, yet we portray the passage of time. But this is really not the case; for all that we have done is to translate our tenses into the words "then" and "finally," and into the order in which we state our clauses. If we were to omit these words or their equivalents, and mix up the clauses, our sentences would no longer be meaningful. To say that the future, the present, and the past are in some sense is to dodge the problem of time by resorting to the tenseless language of logic and mathematics. In such an atemporal language it would be meaningful to say that Socrates is mortal because all men are mortal and Socrates is a man, even though Socrates has been dead many centuries. But if we cannot describe time either by a language containing tenses or by a tenseless language, how shall we symbolize it?*

He feels the curious doubleness of self, the sense of having been here before, and knows it is flashback. Some comfort in that. He is a passenger in his own skull, looking out through the eyes of John Skein on an event that he has already experienced, and which he now is powerless to alter.

His office. All its gilded magnificence. A crystal dome at the summit of Kenyatta Tower. With the amplifiers on he can see as far as Serengeti in one direction, Mombasa in another. Count the fleas on an elephant in Tsavo Park. A wall of light on the east-southeast face of the dome, housing his data-access units. No one can stare at that wall more than thirty seconds without suffering intensely from a surfeit of information. Except Skein; he drains nourishment from it, hour after hour.

As he slides into the soul of that earlier Skein he takes a brief joy in the sight of his office, like Aeneas relishing a vision of unfallen Troy, like Adam looking back into Eden. How good it was. That broad sweet desk with its subtle components dedicated to his service. The gentle psychosensitive carpet, so useful and so beautiful. The undulating ribbon-sculpture gliding in and out of the dome's skin, undergoing molecular displacement each time and forever exhibiting the newest of its infinity of possible patterns. A rich man's office; he was unabashed in his pursuit of elegance. He had earned the right to luxury through the intelligent use of his innate skills. Returning now to that lost dome of wonders, he quickly seizes his moment of satisfaction, aware that shortly some souring scene of subtraction will be replayed for him, one of the stages in the darkening and withering of his life. But which one?

"Send in Coustakis," he hears himself say, and his words give him the answer. That one. He will again watch his own destruction. Surely there is no further need to subject him to this particular re-enactment. He has been through it at least seven times; he is losing count. An endless spiraling track of torment.

Coustakis is bald, blue-eyed, sharp-nosed, with the desperate look of a man who is near the end of his first go-round and is not yet sure that he will be granted a second. Skein guesses that he is about seventy. The man is unlikable: he dresses coarsely, moves in aggressive blurting little strides, and shows in every gesture and glance that he seethes with envy of the opulence with which Skein surrounds himself. Skein feels no need to like his clients, though. Only to respect. And Coustakis is brilliant; he commands respect.

Skein says, "My staff and I have studied your proposal in great detail. It's a cunning scheme."

"You'll help me?"

"There are risks for me," Skein points out. "Nissenson has a powerful ego. So do you. I could get hurt. The whole concept of synergy involves risk for the Communicator. My fees are calculated accordingly."

"Nobody expects a Communicator to be cheap," Coustakis mutters.

"I'm not. But I think you'll be able to afford me. The question is whether I can afford you."

"You're very cryptic, Mr. Skein. Like all oracles."

Skein smiles. "I'm not an oracle, I'm afraid. Merely a conduit through whom connections are made. I can't foresee the future."

"You can evaluate probabilities."

"Only concerning my own welfare. And I'm capable of arriving at an incorrect evaluation."

Coustakis fidgets. "Will you help me or won't you?"

"The fee," Skein says, "is half a million down, plus an equity position of fifteen percent in the corporation you'll establish with the contacts I provide."

Coustakis gnaws at his lower lip. "So much?"

"Bear in mind that I've got to split my fee with Nissenson. Consultants like him aren't cheap."

"Even so. Ten percent."

"Excuse me, Mr. Coustakis. I really thought we were past the point of negotiation in this transaction. It's going to be a busy day for me, and so—" Skein passes his hand over a black rectangle on his desk and a section of the floor silently opens, uncovering the drop shaft access. He nods toward it. The carpet reveals the colors of Coustakis' mental processes: black for anger, green for greed, red for anxiety, yellow for fear, blue for temptation, all mixed together in the hashed pattern betraying the calculations now going on in his mind. Coustakis will yield. Nevertheless Skein proceeds with the charade of standing, gesturing toward the exit, trying to usher his visitor out. "All right," Coustakis says explosively, "fifteen percent!"

Skein instructs his desk to extrude a contract cube. He says, "Place your hand here, please," and as Coustakis touches the cube he presses his own palm against its opposite face. At once the cube's sleek crystalline surface darkens and roughens as the double sensory output bombards it. Skein says, "Repeat after me. I, Nicholas Coustakis, whose hand-print and vibration pattern are being imprinted in this contract as I speak—"

"I, Nicholas Coustakis, whose handprint and vibration pattern are being imprinted in this contract as I speak—"

"—do knowingly and willingly assign to John Skein Enterprises, as payment for professional services to be rendered, an equity interest in Coustakis Transport Ltd. or any successor corporation amounting to—"

"—do knowingly and willingly assign—"

They drone on in turns through a description of Coustakis' corporation and the irrevocable nature of Skein's part ownership in it. Then Skein files the contract cube and says, "If you'll phone your bank and put your thumb on the cash part of the transaction, I'll make contact with Nissenson and you can get started."

"Half a million?"

"Half a million."

"You know I don't have that kind of money."

"Let's not waste time, Mr. Coustakis. You have assets. Pledge them as collateral. Credit is easily obtained."

Scowling, Coustakis applies for the loan, gets it, transfers the funds to Skein's account. The process takes eight minutes; Skein uses the time to review Coustakis' ego profile. It displeases Skein to have to exert such sordid economic pressures; but the service he offers does, after all, expose him to dangers, and he must cushion the risk by high guarantees, in case some mishap should put him out of business.

"Now we can proceed," Skein says, when the transaction is done.

Coustakis has almost invented a system for the economical instantaneous transportation of matter. It will not, unfortunately, ever be useful for living things, since the process involves the destruction of the material being shipped and its virtually simultaneous reconstitution elsewhere. The fragile entity that is the soul cannot withstand the withering blast of Coustakis' transmitter's electron beam. But there is tremendous potential in the freight business; the Coustakis transmitter will be able to send cabbages to Mars, computers to Pluto, and, given the proper linkage facilities, it should be able to reach the inhabited extrasolar planets.

However, Coustakis has not yet perfected his system. For five years he has been stymied by one impassable problem: keeping the beam tight enough between transmitter and receiver. Beam-spread has led to chaos in his experiments; marginal straying results in the loss of transmitted information, so that that which is being sent invariably arrives incomplete. Coustakis has depleted his resources in the unsuccessful search for a solution, and thus has been forced to the desperate and costly step of calling in a Communicator.

For a price, Skein will place him in contact with someone who can solve his problem. Skein has a network of consultants on several worlds, experts in technology and finance and philology and nearly everything else. Using his own mind as the focal nexus, Skein will open telepathic communion between Coustakis and a consultant.

"Get Nissenson into a receptive state," he orders his desk.

Coustakis, blinking rapidly, obviously uneasy, says, "First let me get it clear. This man will see everything that's in my mind? He'll get access to my secrets?"

"No. No. I filter the communion with great care. Nothing will pass from your mind to his except the nature of the problem you want him to tackle. Nothing will come back from his mind to yours except the answer."

"And if he doesn't have the answer?"

"He will."

Skein gives no refunds in the event of failure, but he has never had a failure. He does not accept jobs that he feels will be inherently impossible to handle. Either Nissenson will see the solution Coustakis has been overlooking, or else he will make some suggestion that will nudge Coustakis toward finding the solution himself. The telepathic communion is the vital element. Mere talking would never get anywhere. Coustakis and Nissenson could stare at blueprints together for months, pound computers side by side for years, debate the difficulty with each other for decades, and still they might not hit on the answer. But the communion creates a synergy of minds that is more than a doubling of the available brainpower. A union of perceptions, a heightening, that always produces that mystic flash of insight, that leap of the intellect.

"And if he goes into the transmission business for himself afterward?" Coustakis asks.

"He's bonded," Skein says curtly. "No chance of it. Let's go, now. Up and together."

The desk reports that Nissenson, half the world away in São Paulo, is ready. Skein's power does not vary with distance. Quickly he throws Coustakis into the receptive condition, and swings around to face the brilliant lights of his data-access units. Those sparkling, shifting little blazes kindle his gift, jabbing at the electrical rhythms of his brain until he is lifted into the energy level that permits the opening of a communion. As he starts to go up, the other Skein who is

watching, the time-displaced prisoner behind his forehead,
tries frenziedly to prevent him from entering the fatal linkage.
Don't. Don't. You'll overload. They're too strong for you.
Easier to halt a planet in its orbit, though. The course of the
past is frozen; all this has already happened; the Skein who
cries out in silent anguish is merely an observer, necessarily
passive, here to view the maiming of his earlier self.

Skein reaches forth one tendril of his mind and engages
Nissenson. With another tendril he snares Coustakis. Steadily,
now, he draws the two tendrils together.

There is no way to predict the intensity of the forces that
will shortly course through his brain. He has done what he
could, checking the ego profiles of his client and the consultant, but that really tells him little. What Coustakis and
Nissenson may be as individuals hardly matters; it is what
they may become in communion that he must fear. Syner-
gistic intensities are unpredictable. He has lived for a lifetime and a half with the possibility of a burnout.

The tendrils meet.

Skein the observer winces and tries to armor himself
against the shock. But there is no way to deflect it. Out of
Coustakis' mind flows a description of the matter transmitter
and a clear statement of the beam-spread problem; Skein
shoves it along to Nissenson, who begins to work on a solution. But when their minds join it is immediately evident that
their combined strength will be more than Skein can control.
This time the synergy will destroy him. But he cannot dis-
engage; he has no mental circuitbreaker. He is caught,
trapped, impaled. The entity that is Coustakis/Nissenson will
not let go of him, for that would mean its own destruction.
A wave of mental energy goes rippling and dancing along
the vector of communion from Coustakis to Nissenson and
goes bouncing back, pulsating and gaining strength, from
Nissenson to Coustakis. A fiery oscillation is set up. Skein sees
what is happening; he has become the amplifier of his own
doom. The torrent of energy continues to gather power each
time it reverberates from Coustakis to Nissenson, from Nissenson to Coustakis. Powerless, Skein watches the energy-
pumping effect building up a mighty charge. The discharge

is bound to come soon, and he will be the one who must receive it. How long? How long? The juggernaut fills the corridors of his mind. He ceases to know which end of the circuit is Nissenson, which is Coustakis; he perceives only two shining walls of mental power, between which he is stretched ever thinner, a twanging wire of ego, heating up, heating up, glowing now, emitting a searing blast of heat, particles of identity streaming away from him like so many liberated ions—

Then he lies numb and dazed on the floor of his office, grinding his face into the psychosensitive carpet, while Coustakis barks over and over, "Skein? Skein? Skein? Skein?"

Like any other chronometric device, our inner clocks are subject to their own peculiar disorders and, in spite of the substantial concordance between private and public time, discrepancies may occur as the result of sheer inattention. Mach noted that if a doctor focuses his attention on the patient's blood, it may seem to him to squirt out before the lancet enters the skin and, for similar reasons, the feebler of two stimuli presented simultaneously is usually perceived later. . . . Normal life requires the capacity to recall experiences in a sequence corresponding, roughly at least, to the order in which they actually occurred. It requires in addition that our potential recollections should be reasonably accessible to consciousness. These potential recollections mean not only a perpetuation within us of representations of the past, but also a ceaseless interplay between such representations and the uninterrupted input of present information from the external world. Just as our past may be at the service of our present, so the present may be remotely controlled by our past: in the words of Shelley, "Swift as a Thought by the snake Memory stung."

"Skein? Skein? Skein? Skein?"

His bottle is open and they are helping him out. His cabin is full of intruders. Skein recognizes the captain's robot, the medic, and a couple of passengers, the little swarthy man from Pingalore and the woman from Globe Fifteen. The cabin door is open and more people are coming in. The medic makes a cuff-shooting gesture and a blinding haze of metallic white particles wraps itself about Skein's head. The little tingling prickling sensations spur him to wakefulness. "You didn't respond when the bottle told you it was all right," the medic explains. "We're through the canal."

"Was it a good passage? Fine. Fine. I must have dozed."

"If you'd like to come to the infirmary—a routine check, only—put you through the diagnostat—"

"No. No. Will you all please go? I assure you, I'm quite all right."

Reluctantly, clucking over him, they finally leave. Skein gulps cold water until his head is clear. He plants himself flatfooted in midcabin, trying to pick up some sensation of forward motion. The ship now is traveling at something like fifteen million miles a second. How long is fifteen million miles? How long is a second? From Rome to Naples it was a morning's drive on the autostrada. From Tel Aviv to Jerusalem was the time between twilight and darkness. San Francisco to San Diego spanned lunch to dinner by superpod. As I slide my right foot two inches forward we traverse fifteen million miles. From where to where? And why? He has not seen Earth in twenty-six months. At the end of this voyage his remaining funds will be exhausted. Perhaps he will have to make his home in the Abbondanza system; he has no return ticket. But of course he can travel to his heart's discontent within his own skull, whipping from point to point along the time-line in the grip of the fugues.

He goes quickly from his cabin to the recreation lounge.

The ship is a second-class vessel, neither lavish nor seedy. It carries about twenty passengers, most of them, like him, bound outward on one-way journeys. He has not talked directly to any of them, but he has done considerable eavesdropping in the lounge, and by now can tag each one of them with the proper dull biography. The wife bravely joining her pioneer husband, whom she has not seen for half a decade. The remittance man under orders to place ten thousand light-years, at the very least, between himself and his parents. The glittery-eyed entrepreneur, a Phoenician merchant sixty centuries after his proper era, off to carve an empire as a middleman's middleman. The tourists. The bureaucrat. The colonel. Among this collection Skein stands out in sharp relief; he is the only one who has not made an effort to know and be known, and the mystery of his reserve tantalizes them.

He carries the fact of his crackup with him like some wrinkled, dangling, yellowed wen. When his eyes meet those of any of the others he says silently, You see my deformity? I am my own survivor. I have been destroyed and lived to look back on it. Once I was a man of wealth and power, and look at me now. But I ask for no pity. Is that understood?

Hunching at the bar, Skein pushes the node for filtered rum. His drink arrives, and with it comes the remittance man, handsome, young, insinuating. Giving Skein a confidential wink, as if to say, *I* know. You're on the run, too.

"From Earth, are you?" he says to Skein.

"Formerly."

"I'm Pid Rocklin."

"John Skein."

"What were you doing there?"

"On Earth?" Skein shrugs. "A Communicator. I retired four years ago."

"Oh." Rocklin summons a drink. "That's good work, if you have the gift."

"I had the gift," Skein says. The unstressed past tense is as far into self-pity as he will go. He drinks and pushes for another one. A great gleaming screen over the bar shows the look of space: empty, here beyond the Panama Canal, although yesterday a million suns blazed on that ebony rectangle. Skein imagines he can hear the whoosh of hydrogen molecules scraping past the hull at eighty lights. He sees them as blobs of brightness millions of miles long, going *zip!* and *zip!* and *zip!* as the ship spurts along. Abruptly a purple nimbus envelops him and he drops into a flashforward fugue so quickly there is not even time for the usual futile resistance. "Hey, what's the matter?" Pid Rocklin says, reaching for him. "Are you all—" and Skein loses the universe.

He is on the world that he takes to be Abbondanza VI,

and his familiar companion, the skull-faced man, stands beside him at the edge of an oily orange sea. They appear to be having the debate about time once again. The skull-faced man must be at least a hundred twenty years old; his skin lies against his bones with, seemingly, no flesh at all under it, and his face is all nostrils and burning eyes. Bony sockets, sharp shelves for cheekbones, a bald dome of a skull. The neck no more than wrist-thick, rising out of shriveled shoulders. Saying, "Won't you ever come to see that causality is merely an illusion, Skein? The notion that there's a consecutive series of events is nothing but a fraud. We impose form on our lives, we talk of time's arrow, we say that there's a flow from A through G and Q to Z, we make believe everything is nicely linear. But it isn't, Skein. It isn't."

"So you keep telling me."

"I feel an obligation to awaken your mind to the truth. G can come before A, and Z before both of them. Most of us don't like to perceive it that way, so we arrange things in what seems like a more logical pattern, just as a novelist will put the motive before the murder and the murder before the arrest. But the universe isn't a novel. We can't make nature imitate art. It's all random, Skein, random, random! Look there. You see what's drifting on the sea?"

On the orange waves tosses the bloated corpse of a shaggy blue beast. Upturned saucery eyes, drooping snout, thick limbs. Why is it not waterlogged by now? What keeps it afloat?

The skull-faced man says, "Time is an ocean, and events come drifting to us as randomly as dead animals on the waves. We filter them. We screen out what doesn't make sense and admit them to our consciousness in what seems to be the right sequence." He laughs. "The grand delusion! The past is nothing but a series of films slipping unpredictably into the future. And vice versa."

"I won't accept that," Skein says stubbornly. "It's a demonic, chaotic, nihilistic theory. It's idiocy. Are we graybeards before we're children? Do we die before we're born? Do trees devolve into seeds? Deny linearity all you like. I won't go along."

"You can say that after all you've experienced?"

Skein shakes his head. "I'll go on saying it. What I've been going through is a mental illness. Maybe I'm deranged, but the universe isn't."

"Contrary. You've only recently become sane and started to see things as they really are," the skull-faced man insists. "The trouble is that you don't want to admit the evidence you've begun to perceive. Your filters are down, Skein! You've shaken free of the illusion of linearity! Now's your chance to show your resilience. Learn to live with the real reality. Stop this silly business of imposing an artificial order on the flow of time. Why *should* effect follow cause? Why *shouldn't* the seed follow the tree? Why must you persist in holding tight to a useless, outworn, contemptible system of false evaluations of experience when you've managed to break free of the—"

"Stop it! Stop it! Stop it! Stop it!"

"—right, Skein?"

"What happened?"

"You started to fall off your stool," Pid Rocklin says. "You turned absolutely white. I thought you were having some kind of a stroke."

"How long was I unconscious?"

"Oh, three, four seconds, I suppose. I grabbed you and propped you up, and your eyes opened. Can I help you to your cabin? Or maybe you ought to go to the infirmary."

"Excuse me," Skein says hoarsely, and leaves the lounge.

When the hallucinations began, not long after the Coustakis overload, he assumed at first that they were memory disturbances produced by the fearful jolt he had absorbed. Quite clearly most of them invoked scenes of his past, which he would relive, during the moments of fugue, with an intensity so brilliant that he felt he had actually been thrust back into time. He did not merely recollect, but rather he experienced the past anew, following a script from which he could not deviate as he spoke and felt and reacted. Such strange excursions into memory could be easily enough explained:

his brain had been damaged, and it was heaving old segments of experience into view in some kind of attempt to clear itself of debris and heal the wounds. But while the flashbacks were comprehensible, the flashforwards were not, and he did not recognize them at all for what they actually were. Those scenes of himself wandering alien worlds, those phantom conversations with people he had never met, those views of spaceliner cabins and transit booths and unfamiliar hotels and passenger terminals, seemed merely to be fantasies, random fictions of his injured brain. Even when he started to notice that there was a consistent pattern to these feverish glimpses of the unknown, he still did not catch on. It appeared as though he was seeing himself performing a sort of quest, or perhaps a pilgrimage; the slices of unexperienced experience that he was permitted to see began to fit into a coherent structure of travel and seeking. And certain scenes and conversations recurred, yes, sometimes several times the same day, the script always the same, so that he began to learn a few of the scenes word for word. Despite the solid texture of these episodes, he persisted in thinking of them as mere brief flickering segments of nightmare. He could not imagine why the injury to his brain was causing him to have these waking dreams of long space voyages and unknown planets, so vivid and so momentarily real, but they seemed no more frightening to him than the equally vivid flashbacks.

Only after a while, when many months had passed since the Coustakis incident, did the truth strike him. One day he found himself living through an episode that he considered to be one of his fantasies. It was a minor thing, one that he had experienced, in whole or in part, seven or eight times. What he had seen, in fitful bursts of uninvited delusion, was himself in a public garden on some hot spring morning, standing before an immense baroque building while a grotesque group of non-human tourists filed past him in a weird creaking, clanking procession of inhalator suits and breather-wheels and ion-disperser masks. That was all. Then it happened that a harrowing legal snarl brought him to a city in North Carolina about fourteen months after the overload, and, after having put in his appearance at the courthouse, he set out on a long walk through the grimy, decayed metropolis, and came, as if by an enchantment, to a huge metal gate behind which he could see a dark sweep of lavish forest, oaks and rhododendrons and magnolias, laid out in an elegant formal manner. It was, according to a sign posted by the gate, the estate of a nineteenth-century millionaire, now open to all and preserved in its ancient state despite the encroachments of the city on its borders. Skein bought a ticket and went in, on foot, hiking for what seemed like miles through cool leafy glades, until abruptly the path curved and he emerged into the bright sunlight and saw before him the great gray bulk of a colossal mansion, hundreds of rooms topped by parapets and spires, with a massive portico from which vast columns of stairs descended. In wonder he moved toward it, for this was the building of his frequent fantasy, and as he approached he beheld the red and green and purple figures crossing the portico, those coiled and gnarled and looping shapes he had seen before, the eerie horde of alien travelers here to take in the wonders of Earth. Heads without eyes, eyes without heads, multiplicities of limbs and absences of limbs, bodies like tumors and tumors like bodies, all the universe's imagination on display in these agglomerated life-forms, so strange and yet not at all strange to him. But this time it was no fantasy. It fit smoothly into the sequence of the events of the day, rather than dropping, dreamlike, intrusive, into that sequence. Nor did it fade after a few moments; the scene remained sharp, never leaving him to plunge back into "real" life. This was reality itself, and he had experienced it before.

Twice more in the next few weeks things like that happened to him, until at last he was ready to admit the truth to himself about his fugues, that he was experiencing flash-forwards as well as flashbacks, that he was being subjected to glimpses of his own future.

T'ang, the high king of the Shang, asked Hsia Chi saying, "In the beginning, were there already individual things?" Hsia Chi replied, "If there were no things then, how could there be any now? If later generations should pretend that there had been no things in our time, would they be right?" T'ang said, *"Have things then no before and no after?"* To which Hsia Chi replied, *"The ends and the origins of things have no limit from which they began. The origin of one thing may be considered the end of another; the end of one may be considered the origin of the next. Who can distinguish accurately between these cycles? What lies beyond all things, and before all events, we cannot know."*

They reach and enter the Perseus relay booster, which is a whirling celestial anomaly structurally similar to the Panama Canal but not nearly so potent, and it kicks the ship's velocity to just above a hundred lights. That is the voyage's final acceleration; the ship will maintain this rate for two and a half days, until it clocks in at Scylla, the main deceleration station for this part of the galaxy, where it will be seized by a spongy web of forces twenty light-minutes in diameter and slowed to sublight velocities for the entry into the Abbondanza system.

Skein spends nearly all of this period in his cabin, rarely eating and sleeping very little. He reads almost constantly, obsessively dredging from the ship's extensive library a wide and capricious assortment of books. Rilke. Kafka. Eddington, *The Nature of the Physical World.* Lowry, *Hear Us O Lord From Heaven Thy Dwelling Place.* Elias. Razhuminin. Dickey. Pound. Fraisse, *The Psychology of Time.* Greene, *Dream and Delusion.* Poe. Shakespeare. Marlowe. Tourneur. *The Waste Land. Ulysses. Heart of Darkness.* Bury, *The Idea of Progress.* Jung. Büchner. Pirandello. *The Magic Mountain.* Ellis, *The Rack.* Cervantes. Blenheim. Fierst. Keats. Nietzsche. His mind swims with images and bits of verse, with floating sequences of dialogue, with unscaffolded dialectics. He dips into each work briefly, magpielike, seeking bright scraps. The words form a scaly impasto on the inner surface of his skull. He finds that this heavy verbal overdose helps, to some slight extent, to fight off the fugues; his mind is weighted, perhaps, bound by this leaden clutter of borrowed genius to the moving line of the present, and during his debauch of reading he finds himself shifting off that line less frequently than in the recent past. His mind whirls. *Man is a rope stretched between the animal and the Superman—A rope over an abyss.* My patience are exhausted. *See, see where Christ's blood streams in the firmament! One drop would save my soul.* I had not thought death had undone so many. These fragments I have shored against my ruins. *Hoogspanning. Levensgevaar. Peligro de Muerte. Electricidad. Danger.* Give me my spear. *Old Father, old artificer, stand me now and even in good stead.* You like this garden? Why is it yours? We evict those who destroy! *And then went down to the ship, set keel to breakers, forth on the godly sea.* There is no "official" theory of time, defined in creeds or universally agreed upon among Christians. Christianity is not concerned with the purely scientific aspects of the subject nor, within wide limits, with its philosophical analysis, except insofar as it is committed to a fundamentally realist view and could not admit, as some Eastern philosophies have done, that temporal existence is mere illusion. *A shudder in the loins engenders there the broken wall, the burning roof and tower and Agamemnon dead.* Stately, plump Buck Mulligan came from the stairhead, bearing a bowl of lather on which a mirror and a razor lay crossed. *In what distant deeps or skies burnt the fire of thine eyes? On what wings dare he aspire? What the hand dare seize the fire?* These fragments I have shored against my ruins. Hieronymo's mad againe. *Then felt I like some watcher of the skies when a new planet swims into his ken.* It has also lately been postulated that the physical concept of information is identical with a phenomenon of reversal of entropy. The psychologist must add a few remarks here: It does not seem convincing to me that information is *eo ipso* identical with a *pouvoir d'organisation* which undoes entropy. *Datta. Dayadhvam. Damyata. Shantih shantih shantih*

Nevertheless, once the ship is past Scylla and slowing toward the Abbondanza planets, the periods of fugue become frequent once again, so that he lives entrapped, shuttling between the flashing shadows of yesterday and tomorrow.

After the Coustakis overload he tried to go on in the old way, as best he could. He gave Coustakis a refund without even being asked, for he had been of no service, nor could he ever be. Instantaneous transportation of matter would have to wait. But Skein took other clients. He could still make the communion, after a fashion, and when the nature of the task was sufficiently low-level he could even deliver a decent synergetic response.

Often his work was unsatisfactory, however. Contacts would break at awkward moments, or, conversely, his filter mechanism would weaken and he would allow the entire contents of his client's mind to flow into that of his consultant. The results of such disasters were chaotic, involving him in heavy medical expenses and sometimes in damage suits. He was forced to place his fees on a contingency basis: no synergy, no pay. About half the time he earned nothing for his output of energy. Meanwhile his overhead remained the same as always: the domed office, the network of consultants, the research staff, and the rest. His effort to remain in business was eating rapidly into the bank accounts he had set aside against just such a time of storm.

They could find no organic injury to his brain. Of course, so little was known about a Communicator's gift that it was impossible to determine much by medical analysis. If they could not locate the center from which a Communicator powered his communions, how could they detect the place where he had been hurt? The medical archives were of no value; there had been eleven previous cases of overload, but each instance was physiologically unique. They told him he would eventually heal, and sent him away. Sometimes the doctors gave him silly therapies: counting exercises, rhythmic blinkings, hopping on his left leg and then his right, as if he had had a stroke. But he had not had a stroke.

For a time he was able to maintain his business on the momentum of his reputation. Then, as word got around that he had been hurt and was no longer any good, clients stopped coming. Even the contingency basis for fees failed to attract them. Within six months he found that he was lucky to find a client a week. He reduced his rates, and that seemed only to make things worse, so he raised them to something not far below what they had been at the time of the overload. For a while the pace of business increased, as if people were getting the impression that Skein had recovered. He gave such spotty service, though. Blurred and wavering communions, unanticipated positive feedbacks, filtering problems, information deficiencies, redundancy surpluses—"You take your mind in your hands when you go to Skein," they were saying now.

The fugues added to his professional difficulties.

He never knew when he would snap into hallucination. It might happen during a communion, and often did. Once he dropped back to the moment of the Coustakis-Nissenson hookup and treated a terrified client to a replay of his overload. Once, although he did not understand at the time what was happening, he underwent a flashforward and carried the client with him to a scarlet jungle on a formaldehyde world, and when Skein slipped back to reality the client remained in the scarlet jungle. There was a damage suit over that one, too.

Temporal dislocation plagued him into making poor guesses. He took on clients whom he could not possibly serve, and wasted his time on them. He turned away people whom he might have been able to help to his own profit. Since he was no longer anchored firmly to his time-line, but drifted in random oscillations of twenty years or more in either direction, he forfeited the keen sense of perspective on which he had previously founded his professional judgments. He grew haggard and lean, also. He passed through a tempest of spiritual doubts that amounted to total submission and then total rejection of faith within the course of four months. He changed lawyers almost weekly. He liquidated assets with invariably catastrophic timing to pay his cascading bills.

A year and a half after the overload, he formally renounced his registration and closed his office. It took six months more to settle the remaining damage suits. Then, with what was left of his money, he bought a spaceliner ticket and set out to search for a world with purple sand and blue-leaved trees, where, unless his fugues had played him false, he might be able to arrange for the repair of his broken mind.

Now the ship has returned to the conventional fourspace and dawdles planetward at something rather less than half the speed of light. Across the screens there spreads a necklace of stars; space is crowded here. The captain will point out Abbondanza to anyone who asks: a lemon-colored sun, bigger than that of Earth, surrounded by a dozen bright planetary pips. The passengers are excited. They buzz, twitter, speculate, anticipate. No one is silent except Skein. He is aware of many love affairs; he has had to reject several offers just in the past three days. He has given up reading and is trying to purge his mind of all he has stuffed into it. The fugues have grown worse. He has to write notes to himself, saying things like *You are a passenger aboard a ship heading for Abbondanza VI, and will be landing in a few days,* so that he does not forget which of his three entangled time-lines is the true one.

Suddenly he is with Nilla on the island in the Gulf of Mexico, getting aboard the little excursion boat. Time stands still here; it could almost be the twentieth century. The frayed, sagging cords of the rigging. The lumpy engine inefficiently converted from internal combustion to turbines. The mustachioed Mexican bandits who will be their guides today. Nilla, nervously coiling her long blonde hair, saying, "Will I get seasick, John? The boat rides right in the water, doesn't it? It won't even hover a little bit?"

"Terribly archaic," Skein says. "That's why we're here."

The captain gestures them aboard. Juan, Francisco, Sebastián. Brothers. *Los hermanos.* Yards of white teeth glistening below the drooping mustaches. With a terrible roar the boat moves away from the dock. Soon the little town of crumbling pastel buildings is out of sight and they are heading jaggedly eastward along the coast, green shoreward water on their left, the blue depths on the right. The morning sun coming up hard. "Could I sunbathe?" Nilla asks. Unsure of herself; he has never seen her this way, so hesitant, so abashed. Mexico has robbed her of her New York assurance. "Go ahead," Skein says. "Why not?" She drops her robe. Underneath she wears only a waist-strap; her heavy breasts look white and vulnerable in the tropic glare, and the small nipples are a faded pink. Skein sprays her with protective sealant and she sprawls out on the deck. *Los hermanos* stare hungrily and talk to each other in low rumbling tones. Not Spanish. Mayan, perhaps? The natives have never learned to adopt the tourists' casual nudity here. Nilla, obviously still uneasy, rolls over and lies face down. Her broad smooth back glistens.

Juan and Francisco yell. Skein follows their pointing fingers. Porpoises! A dozen of them, frisking around the bow, keeping just ahead of the boat, leaping high and slicing down into the blue water. Nilla gives a little cry of joy and rushes to the side to get a closer look. Throwing her arm self-consciously across her bare breasts. "You don't need to do that," Skein murmurs. She keeps herself covered. "How lovely they are," she says softly. Sebastián comes up beside them. "*Amigos,*" he says. "They are. My friends." The cavorting porpoises eventually disappear. The boat bucks bouncily onward, keeping close to the island's beautiful empty palmy shore. Later they anchor, and he and Nilla swim masked, spying on the coral gardens. When they haul themselves on deck again it is almost noon. The sun is terrible. "Lunch?" Francisco asks. "We make you good lunch now?" Nilla laughs. She is no longer hiding her body. "I'm starved!" she cries.

"We make you good lunch," Francisco says, grinning, and he and Juan go over the side. In the shallow water they are clearly visible near the white sand of the bottom. They have spear-guns; they hold their breaths and prowl. Too late Skein realizes what they are doing. Francisco hauls a fluttering spiny lobster out from behind a rock. Juan impales a huge pale crab. He grabs three conchs also, surfaces, dumps his prey on the deck. Francisco arrives with the lobster. Juan, below again, spears a second lobster. The animals are not dead; they crawl sadly in circles on the deck as they dry. Appalled, Skein turns to Sebastián and says, "Tell them to stop. We're not that hungry." Sebastián, preparing some kind of salad, smiles and shrugs. Francisco has brought up another crab, bigger than the first. "Enough," Skein says. "*Basta! Basta!*" Juan, dripping, tosses down three more conchs. "You

pay us good," he says. "We give you good lunch." Skein
shakes his head. The deck is becoming a slaughterhouse for
ocean life. Sebastián now energetically splits conch shells,
extracts the meat, drops it into a vast bowl to marinate in
a yellow-green fluid. "*Basta!*" Skein yells. Is that the right
word in Spanish? He knows it's right in Italian. *Los hermanos*
look amused. The sea is full of life, they seem to be telling
him. We give you good lunch. Suddenly Francisco erupts
from the water, bearing something immense. A turtle! Forty,
fifty pounds! The joke has gone too far. "No," Skein says.
"Listen, I have to forbid this. Those turtles are almost extinct.
Do you understand that? *Muerto. Perdido. Desaparecido.* I
won't eat a turtle. Throw it back. Throw it back." Francisco
smiles. He shakes his head. Deftly he binds the turtle's flip-
pers with rope. Juan says, "Not for lunch, *señor*. For us. For
to sell. *Mucho dinero.*" Skein can do nothing. Francisco and
Sebastián have begun to hack up the crabs and lobsters. Juan
slices peppers into the bowl where the conchs are marinat-
ing. Pieces of dead animals litter the deck. "Oh, I'm *starving*,"
Nilla says. Her waist-strap is off too, now. The turtle watches
the whole scene, beady-eyed. Skein shudders. Auschwitz, he
thinks. Buchenwald. For the animals it's Buchenwald every
day.

Purple sand, blue-leaved trees. An orange sea gleaming not
far to the west under a lemon sun. "It isn't much farther,"
the skull-faced man says. "You can make it. Step by step by
step is how."

"I'm winded," Skein says. "Those hills—"

"I'm twice your age, and I'm doing fine."

"You're in better shape. I've been cooped up on spaceships for months and months."

"Just a short way on," says the skull-faced man. "About a
hundred meters from the shore."

Skein struggles on. The heat is frightful. He has trouble
getting a footing in the shifting sand. Twice he trips over
black vines whose fleshy runners form a mat a few centi-
meters under the surface; loops of the vines stick up here and
there. He even suffers a brief fugue, a seven-second flashback

to a day in Jerusalem. Somewhere at the core of his mind he is amused by that: a flashback within a flashforward. Encapsulated concentric hallucinations. When he comes out of it, he finds himself getting to his feet and brushing sand from his clothing. Ten steps onward the skull-faced man halts him and says, "There it is. Look there, in the pit."

Skein sees a funnel-shaped crater right in front of him, perhaps five meters in diameter at ground level and dwindling to about half that width at its bottom, some six or seven meters down. The pit strikes him as a series of perfect circles making up a truncated cone. Its sides are smooth and firm, almost glazed, and the sand has a brown tinge. In the pit, resting peacefully on the flat floor, is something that looks like a golden amoeba the size of a large cat. A row of round blue-black eyes crosses the hump of its back: From the perimeter of its body comes a soft green radiance.

"Go down to it," the skull-faced man says. "The force of its power falls off with the cube of the distance; from up here you can't feel it. Go down. Let it take you over. Fuse with it. Make communion, Skein, make communion!"

"And will it heal me? So that I'll function as I did before the trouble started?"

"If you let it heal you, it will. That's what it wants to do. It's a completely benign organism. It thrives on repairing broken souls. Let it into your head; let it find the damaged place. You can trust it. Go down."

Skein trembles on the edge of the pit. The creature below flows and eddies, becoming first long and narrow, then high and squat, then resuming its basically circular form. Its color deepens almost to scarlet, and its radiance shifts toward yellow. As if preening and stretching itself. It seems to be waiting for him. It seems eager. This is what he has sought so long, going from planet to wearying planet. The skull-faced man, the purple sand, the pit, the creature. Skein slips his sandals off. *What have I to lose?* He sits for a moment on the pit's rim; then he shimmies down, sliding part of the way, and lands softly, close beside the being that awaits him. And immediately feels its power.

He enters the huge desolate cavern that is the cathedral of Haghia Sophia. A few Turkish guides lounge hopefully against the vast marble pillars. Tourists shuffle about, reading to each other from cheap plastic guidebooks. A shaft of light enters from some improbable aperture and splinters against the Moslem pulpit. It seems to Skein that he hears the tolling of bells and feels incense prickling at his nostrils. But how can that be? No Christian rites have been performed here in a thousand years. A Turk looms before him. "Show you the mosyics?" he says. *Mosyics*. "Help you understand this marvelous building? A dollar. No? Maybe change money? A good rate. Dollars, marks, Eurocredits, what? You speak English? Show you the mosyics?" The Turk fades. The bells grow louder. A row of bowed priests in white silk robes files past the altar, chanting in—what? Greek? The ceiling is encrusted with gems. Gold plate gleams everywhere. Skein senses the terrible complexity of the cathedral, teeming now with life, a whole universe engulfed in this gloom, a thousand chapels packed with worshippers, long lines waiting to urinate in the crypts, a marketplace in the balcony, jeweled necklaces changing hands with low murmurs of negotiation, babies being born behind the alabaster sarcophagi, the bells tolling, dukes nodding to one another, clouds of incense swirling toward the dome, the figures in the mosaics alive, making the sign of the Cross, smiling, blowing kisses, the pillars moving now, becoming fat-middled as they bend from side to side, the entire colossal structure shifting and flowing and melting. And a ballet of Turks. "Show you the mosyics?" "Change money?" "Postcards? Souvenir of Istanbul?" A plump, pink American face: "You're John Skein, aren't you? The Communicator? We worked together on the big fusion-chamber merger in '53." Skein shakes his head. "It must be that you are mistaken," he says, speaking in Italian. "I am not he. Pardon. Pardon." And joins the line of chanting priests.

Purple sand, blue-leaved trees. An orange sea under a lemon sun. Looking out from the top deck of the terminal, an hour after landing, Skein sees a row of towering hotels rising along the nearby beach. At once he feels the wrongness: there should be no hotels. The right planet has no such towers; therefore this is another of the wrong ones.

He suffers from complete disorientation as he attempts to place himself in sequence. *Where am I?* Aboard a liner heading toward Abbondanza VI. *What do I see?* A world I have previously visited. *Which one?* The one with the hotels. The third out of seven, isn't it?

He has seen this planet before, in flashforwards. Long before he left Earth to begin his quest he glimpsed those hotels, that beach. Now he views it in flashback. That perplexes him. He must try to see himself as a moving point traveling through time, viewing the scenery now from this perspective, now from that.

He watches his earlier self at the terminal. Once it was his future self. How confusing, how needlessly muddling! "I'm looking for an old Earthman," he says. "He must be a hundred, hundred twenty years old. A face like a skull—no flesh at all, really. A brittle man. No? Well, can you tell me, does this planet have a life-form about this big, a kind of blob of golden jelly, that lives in pits down by the seashore, and— No? No? Ask someone else, you say? Of course. And perhaps a hotel room? As long as I've come all this way."

He is getting tired of finding the wrong planets. What folly this is, squandering his last savings on a quest for a world seen in a dream! He would have expected planets with purple sand and blue-leaved trees to be uncommon, but no, in an infinite universe one can find a dozen of everything, and now he has wasted almost half his money and close to a year, visiting two planets and this one and not finding what he seeks.

He goes to the hotel they arrange for him.

The beach is packed with sunbathers, most of them from Earth. Skein walks among them. "Look," he wants to say, "I have this trouble with my brain, an old injury, and it gives me these visions of myself in the past and future, and one of the visions I see is a place where there's a skull-faced man who takes me to a kind of amoeba in a pit that can heal me, do you follow? And it's a planet with purple sand and blue-leaved trees, just like this one, and I figure if I keep going long enough I'm bound to find it and the skull-face and the amoeba, do you follow me? And maybe this is the planet after all, only I'm in the wrong part of it. What should I do? What hope do you think I really have?" This is the third world. He knows that he must visit a number of wrong ones before he finds the right one. But how many? How many? And when will he know that he has the right one?

Standing silent on the beach, he feels confusion come over him, and drops into fugue, and is hurled to another world. Purple sand, blue-leaved trees. A fat, friendly Pingalorian consul. "A skull-faced man? No, I can't say I know of any." Which world is this, Skein wonders? One that I have already visited, or one that I have not yet come to? The manifold layers of illusion dazzle him. Past and future and present lie like a knot around his throat. Shifting planes of reality; intersecting films of event. Purple sand, blue-leaved trees. Which planet is this? Which one? Which one? He is back on the crowded beach. A lemon sun. An orange sea. He is back in his cabin on the spaceliner. He sees a note in his own handwriting: *You are a passenger aboard a ship heading for Abbondanza VI, and will be landing in a few days.* So everything was a vison. Flashback? Flashforward? He is no longer able to tell. He is baffled by these identical worlds. Purple sand. Blue-leaved trees. He wishes he knew how to cry.

Instead of a client and a consultant for today's communion, Skein has a client and a client. A man and a woman, Michaels and Miss Schumpeter. The communion is of an unusually intimate kind. Michaels has been married six times, and several of the marriages apparently have been dissolved under bitter circumstances. Miss Schumpeter, a woman of some wealth, loves Michaels but doesn't entirely trust him; she wants a peep into his mind before she'll put her thumb to the marital cube. Skein will oblige. The fee has already been credited to his account. Let me not to the marriage of true minds admit impediments. If she does not like what she finds in her beloved's soul, there may not be any marriage, but Skein will have been paid.

A tendril of his mind goes to Michaels, now. A tendril to

Miss Schumpeter. Skein opens his filters. "Now you'll meet for the first time," he tells them. Michaels flows to her. Miss Schumpeter flows to him. Skein is merely the conduit. Through him pass the ambitions, betrayals, failures, vanities, deteriorations, disputes, treacheries, lusts, generosities, shames, and follies of these two human beings. If he wishes, he can examine the most private sins of Miss Schumpeter and the darkest yearnings of her future husband. But he does not care. He sees such things every day. He takes no pleasure in spying on the psyches of these two. Would a surgeon grow excited over the sight of Miss Schumpeter's Fallopian tubes or Michaels' pancreas? Skein is merely doing his job. He is no voyeur, simply a Communicator. He looks upon himself as a public utility.

When he severs the contact, Miss Schumpeter and Michaels both are weeping.

"I love you!" she wails.

"Get away from me!" he mutters.

Purple sand. Blue-leaved trees. Oily orange sea.

The skull-faced man says, "Won't you ever come to see that causality is merely an illusion, Skein? The notion that there's a consecutive series of events is nothing but a fraud. We impose form on our lives, we talk of time's arrow, we say that there's a flow from A through G and Q to Z, we make believe everything is nicely linear. But it isn't, Skein. It isn't."

"So you keep telling me."

"I feel an obligation to awaken your mind to the truth. G can come before A, and Z before both of them. Most of us don't like to perceive it that way, so we arrange things in what seems like a more logical pattern, just as a novelist will put the motive before the murder and the murder before the arrest. But the universe isn't a novel. We can't make nature imitate art. It's all random, Skein, random, random!"

"Half a million?"

"Half a million."

"You know I don't have that kind of money."

"Let's not waste time, Mr. Coustakis. You have assets.

Pledge them as collateral. Credit is easily obtained." Skein waits for the inventor to clear his loan. "Now we can proceed," he says, and tells his desk, "Get Nissenson into a receptive state."

Coustakis says, "First let me get it clear. This man will see everything that's in my mind? He'll get access to my secrets?"

"No. No. I filter the communion with great care. Nothing will pass from your mind to his except the nature of the problem you want him to tackle. Nothing will come back from his mind to yours except the answer."

"And if he doesn't have the answer?"

"He will."

"And if he goes into the transmission business for himself afterward?"

"He's bonded," Skein says curtly. "No chance of it. Let's go, now. Up and together."

"Skein? Skein? Skein? Skein?"

The wind is rising. The sand, blown aloft, stains the sky gray. Skein clambers from the pit and lies by its rim, breathing hard. The skull-faced man helps him get up.

Skein has seen this series of images hundreds of times.

"How do you feel?" the skull-faced man asks.

"Strange. Good. My head seems so clear!"

"You had communion down there?"

"Oh, yes. Yes."

"And?"

"I think I'm healed," Skein says in wonder. "My strength is back. Before, you know, I felt cut down to the bone, a minimum version of myself. And now. And now." He lets a tendril of consciousness slip forth. It meets the mind of the skull-faced man. Skein is aware of a glassy interface; he can touch the other mind, but he cannot enter it. "Are you a Communicator too?" Skein asks, awed.

"In a sense. I feel you touching me. You're better, aren't you?"

"Much. Much. Much."

"As I told you. Now you have your second chance, Skein.

Your gift has been restored. Courtesy of our friend in the pit. They love being helpful."

"Skein? Skein? Skein? Skein?"

We conceive of time either as flowing or as enduring. The problem is how to reconcile these concepts. From a purely formalistic point of view there exists no difficulty, as these properties can be reconciled by means of the concept of a duratio successiva. *Every unit of time measure has this characteristic of a flowing permanence: an hour streams by while it lasts and so long as it lasts. Its flowing is thus identical with its duration. Time, from this point of view, is transitory; but its passing away lasts.*

In the early months of his affliction he experienced a great many scenes of flashforward while in fugue. He saw himself outside the nineteenth-century mansion, he saw himself in a dozen lawyers' offices, he saw himself in hotels, terminals, spaceliners, he saw himself discussing the nature of time with the skull-faced man, he saw himself trembling on the edge of the pit, he saw himself emerging healed, he saw himself wandering from world to world, looking for the right one with purple sand and blue-leaved trees. As time unfolded most of these flashforwards duly entered the flow of the present; he *did* come to the mansion, he *did* go to those hotels and terminals, he *did* wander those useless worlds. Now, as he approaches Abbondanza VI, he goes through a great many flashbacks and a relatively few flashforwards, and the flashforwards seem to be limited to a fairly narrow span of time, covering his landing on Abbondanza VI, his first meeting with the skull-faced man, his journey to the pit, and his emergence, healed, from the amoeba's lair. Never anything beyond that final scene. He wonders if time is going to run out for him on Abbondanza VI.

The ship lands on Abbondanza VI half a day ahead of schedule. There are the usual decontamination procedures to endure, and while they are going on Skein rests in his cabin, counting minutes to liberty. He is curiously confident that this will be the world on which he finds the skull-faced man and the benign amoeba. Of course, he has felt that way before, looking out from other spaceliners at other planets of the proper coloration, and he has been wrong. But the intensity of his confidence is something new. He is sure that the end of his quest lies here.

"Debarkation beginning now," the loudspeakers say.

He joins the line of outgoing passengers. The others smile, embrace, whisper; they have found friends or even mates on this voyage. He remains apart. No one says goodbye to him. He emerges into a brightly lit terminal, a great cube of glass that looks like all the other terminals scattered across the thousands of worlds that man has reached. He could be in Chicago or Johannesburg or Beirut: the scene is one of porters, reservations clerks, customs officials, hotel agents, taxi drivers, guides. A blight of sameness spreading across the universe. Stumbling through the customs gate, Skein finds himself set upon. Does he want a taxi, a hotel room, a woman, a man, a guide, a homestead plot, a servant, a ticket to Abbondanza VII, a private car, an interpreter, a bank, a telephone? The hubbub jolts Skein into three consecutive ten-second fugues, all flashbacks; he sees a rainy day in Tierra del Fuego, he conducts a communion to help a maker of sky-spectacles perfect the plot of his latest extravaganza, and he puts his palm to a cube in order to dictate contract terms to Nicholas Coustakis. Then Coustakis fades, the terminal reappears, and Skein realizes that someone has seized him by the left arm just above the elbow. Bony fingers dig painfully into his flesh. It is the skull-faced man. "Come with me," he says. "I'll take you where you want to go."

"This isn't just another flashforward, is it?" Skein asks, as he has watched himself ask so many times in the past. "I mean, you're really here to get me."

The skull-faced man says, as Skein has heard him say so many times in the past, "No, this time it's no flashforward. I'm really here to get you."

"Thank God. Thank God. Thank God."

"Follow along this way. You have your passport handy?"

The familiar words. Skein is prepared to discover he is merely in fugue, and expects to drop back into frustrating reality at any moment. But no. The scene does not waver. It holds firm. It holds. At last he has caught up with this particular scene, overtaking it and enclosing it, pearl-like, in the folds of the present. He is on the way out of the terminal. The skull-faced man helps him through the formalities. How withered he is! How fiery the eyes, how gaunt the face! Those frightening orbits of bone jutting through the skin of the forehead. That parched cheek. Skein listens for a dry rattle of ribs. One sturdy punch and there would be nothing left but a cloud of white dust, slowly settling.

"I know your difficulty," the skull-faced man says. "You've been caught in entropy's jaws. You're being devoured. The injury to your mind—it's tipped you into a situation you aren't able to handle. You *could* handle it, if you'd only learn to adapt to the nature of the perceptions you're getting now. But you won't do that, will you? And you want to be healed. Well, you can be healed here, all right. More or less healed. I'll take you to the place."

"What do you mean, I could handle it, if I'd only learn to adapt?"

"Your injury has liberated you. It's shown you the truth about time. But you refuse to see it."

"What truth?" Skein asks flatly.

"You still try to think that time flows neatly from alpha to omega, from yesterday through today to tomorrow," the skull-faced man says, as they walk slowly through the terminal. "But it doesn't. The idea of the forward flow of time is a deception we impose on ourselves in childhood. An abstraction, agreed upon by common convention, to make it easier for us to cope with phenomena. The truth is that events are random, that chronological flow is only our joint hallucination, that if time can be said to flow at all, it flows in all 'directions' at once. Therefore—"

"Wait," Skein says. "How do you explain the laws of thermodynamics? Entropy increases; available energy constantly diminishes; the universe heads toward ultimate stasis."

"Does it?"

"The second law of thermodynamics—"

"Is an abstraction," the skull-faced man says, "which unfortunately fails to correspond with the situation in the true universe. It isn't a divine law. It's a mathematical hypothesis developed by men who weren't able to perceive the real situation. They did their best to account for the data within a framework they could understand. Their laws are formulations of probability, based on conditions that hold within closed systems, and given the right closed system the second law is useful and illuminating. But in the universe as a whole it simply isn't true. There *is* no arrow of time. Entropy does *not* necessarily increase. Natural processes *can* be reversible. Causes do *not* invariably precede effects. In fact, the concepts of cause and effect are empty. There are neither causes nor effects, but only events, spontaneously generated, which we arrange in our minds in comprehensible patterns of sequence."

"No," Skein mutters. "This is insanity!"

"There are no patterns. Everything is random."

"No."

"Why not admit it? Your brain has been injured; what was destroyed was the center of temporal perception, the node that humans use to impose this unreal order on events. Your time filter has burned out. The past and the future are as accessible to you as the present, Skein: you can go where you like, you can watch events drifting past as they really do. Only you haven't been able to break up your old habits of thought. You still try to impose the conventional entropic order on things, even though you lack the mechanism to do it, now, and the conflict between what you perceive and what you think you perceive is driving you crazy. Eh?"

"How do you know so much about me?"

The skull-faced man chuckles. "I was injured in the same way as you. I was cut free from the time-line long ago, through the kind of overload you suffered. And I've had years to come to terms with the new reality. I was as terrified as you were, at first. But now I understand. I move about freely. I know things, Skein." A rasping laugh. "You need rest, though. A room, a bed. Time to think things over. Come. There's no rush now. You're on the right planet; you'll be all right soon."

*Further, the association of entropy increase with time's
arrow is in no sense circular; rather, it both tells us something about what will happen to natural systems in time, and
about what the time order must be for a series of states of a
system. Thus, we may often establish a time order among a
set of events by use of the time-entropy association, free from
any reference to clocks and magnitudes of time intervals
from the present. In actual judgments of before-after we
frequently do this on the basis of our experience (even
though without any explicit knowledge of the law of entropy
increase): we know, for example, that for iron in air the
state of pure metal must have been before that of a rusted
surface, or that the clothes will be dry after, not before, they
have hung in the hot sun.*

A tense, humid night of thunder and temporal storms. Lying alone in his oversized hotel room, five kilometers from
the purple shore, Skein suffers fiercely from fugue.

"Listen, I have to forbid this. Those turtles are almost extinct. Do you understand that? *Muerto. Perdido. Desaparecido.* I won't eat a turtle. Throw it back. Throw it back."

"I'm happy to say your second go-round has been approved, Mr. Skein. Not that there was ever any doubt. A long
and happy new life to you, sir."

"Go down to it. The force of its power falls off with the
cube of the distance; from up here you can't feel it. Go down.
Let it take you over. Fuse with it. Make communion, Skein,
make communion!"

"Show you the mosyics? Help you understand this marvelous building? A dollar. No? Maybe change money? A
good rate."

"First let me get it clear. This man will see everything
that's in my mind? He'll get access to my secrets?"

"I love you."
"Get away from me!"

"Won't you ever come to see that causality is merely an illusion, Skein? The notion that there's a consecutive series of events is nothing but a fraud. We impose form on our lives, we talk of time's arrow, we say that there's a flow from A through G and Q to Z, we make believe everything is nicely linear. But it isn't, Skein. It isn't."

Breakfast on a leafy veranda. Morning light out of the west, making the trees glow with an ultramarine glitter. The skull-faced man joins him. Skein secretly searches the parched face. Is everything an illusion? Perhaps *he* is an illusion.

They walk toward the sea. Well before noon they reach the shore. The skull-faced man points to the south, and they follow the coast; it is often a difficult hike, for in places the sand is washed out and they must detour inland, scrambling over quartzy cliffs. The monstrous old man is indefatigable. When they pause to rest, squatting on a timeless purple strand made smooth by the recent tide, the debate about time resumes, and Skein hears words that have been echoing in his skull for four years and more. It is as though everything up till now has been a rehearsal for a play, and now at last he has taken the stage.

"Won't you ever come to see that causality is merely an illusion, Skein?"

"I feel an obligation to awaken your mind to the truth."

"Time is an ocean, and events come drifting to us as randomly as dead animals on the waves."

Skein offers all the proper cues.

"I won't accept that! It's a demonic, chaotic, nihilistic theory."

"You can say that after all you've experienced?"

"I'll go on saying it. What I've been going through is a mental illness. Maybe I'm deranged, but the universe isn't."

"Contrary. You've only recently become sane and started to see things as they really are. The trouble is that you don't want to admit the evidence you've begun to perceive. Your filters are down, Skein! You've shaken free of the illusion of linearity! Now's your chance to show your resilience. Learn to live with the real reality. Stop this silly business of imposing an artificial order on the flow of time. Why *should* effect follow cause? Why *shouldn't* the seed follow the tree? Why must you persist in holding tight to a useless, outworn, contemptible system of false evaluations of experience when you've managed to break free of the—"

"Stop it! Stop it! Stop it! Stop it!"

By early afternoon they are many kilometers from the hotel, still keeping as close to the shore as they can. The terrain is uneven and divided, with rugged fingers of rock running almost to the water's edge, and Skein finds the journey even more exhausting than it had seemed in his visions of it. Several times he stops, panting, and has to be urged to go on.

"It isn't much farther," the skull-faced man says. "You can make it. Step by step is how."

"I'm winded. Those hills—"

"I'm twice your age, and I'm doing fine."

"You're in better shape. I've been cooped up on spaceships for months and months."

"Just a short way on," says the skull-faced man. "About a hundred meters from the shore."

Skein struggles on. The heat is frightful. He trips in the sand; he is blinded by sweat; he has a momentary flashback fugue. "There it is," the skull-faced man says, finally. "Look there, in the pit."

Skein beholds the conical crater. He sees the golden amoeba.

"Go down to it," the skull-faced man says. "The force of its power falls off with the cube of the distance; from up here you can't feel it. Go down. Let it take you over. Fuse with it. Make communion, Skein, make communion!"

"And will it heal me? So that I'll function as I did before the trouble started?"

"If you let it heal you, it will. That's what it wants to do. It's a completely benign organism. It thrives on repairing broken souls. Let it into your head; let it find the damaged place. You can trust it. Go down."

Skein trembles on the edge of the pit. The creature below flows and eddies, becoming first long and narrow, then high and squat, then resuming its basically circular form. Its color deepens almost to scarlet, and its radiance shifts toward yellow. As if preening and stretching itself. It seems to be waiting for him. It seems eager. This is what he has sought so long, going from planet to wearying planet. The skull-faced man, the purple sand, the pit, the creature. Skein slips his sandals off. *What have I to lose?* He sits for a moment on the pit's rim; then he shimmies down, sliding part of the way, and lands softly, close beside the being that awaits him. And immediately feels its power. Something brushes against his brain. The sensation reminds him of the training sessions of his first go-round, when the instructors were showing him how to develop his gift. The fingers probing his consciousness. Go on, enter, he tells them. I'm open. I'm open. And he finds himself in contact with the being of the pit. Wordless. A two-way flow of unintelligible images is the only communion; shapes drift from and into his mind. The universe blurs. He is no longer sure where the center of his ego lies. He has thought of his brain as a sphere with himself at its center, but now it seems extended, elliptical, and an ellipse has no center, only a pair of foci, here and here, one focus in his own skull and one—where?—within that fleshy amoeba. And suddenly he is looking at himself through the amoeba's eyes. The large biped with the bony body. How strange, how grotesque! Yet it suffers. Yet it must be helped. It is injured. It is broken. We go to it with all our love. We will heal. And Skein feels something flowing over the bare folds and fissures of his brain. But he can no longer remember whether he is the human or the alien, the bony one or the boneless. Their identities have mingled. He goes through fugues by the scores, seeing yesterdays and tomorrows, and everything is formless and without content; he is unable to recognize himself or to understand the words being spoken. It does not matter. All is random. All is illusion. Release the knot of pain you clutch within you. Accept. Accept. Accept. Accept.

He accepts.

He releases.

He merges.

He casts away the shreds of ego, the constricting exoskeleton of self, and placidly permits the necessary adjustments to be made.

The possibility, however, of genuine thermodynamic entropy decrease for an isolated system—no matter how rare—does raise an objection to the definition of time's direction in terms of entropy. If a large, isolated system did by chance go through an entropy decrease as one state evolved from another, we would have to say that time "went backward" if our definition of time's arrow were basically in terms of entropy increase. But with an ultimate definition of the forward direction of time in terms of the actual occurrence of states, and measured time intervals from the present, we can readily accommodate the entropy decrease; it would become merely a rare anomaly in the physical processes of the natural world.

The wind is rising. The sand, blown aloft, stains the sky gray. Skein clambers from the pit and lies by its rim, breathing hard. The skull-faced man helps him get up.

Skein has seen this series of images hundreds of times.

"How do you feel?" the skull-faced man asks.

"Strange. Good. My head seems clear!"

"You had communion down there?"

"Oh, yes. Yes."

"And?"

"I think I'm healed," Skein says in wonder. "My strength is back. Before, you know, I felt cut down to the bone, a minimum version of myself. And now. And now." He lets a tendril of consciousness slip forth. It meets the mind of the skull-faced man. Skein is aware of a glassy interface; he can touch the other mind, but he cannot enter it. "Are you a Communicator too?" Skein asks, awed.

"In a sense. I feel you touching me. You're better, aren't you?"

"Much. Much. Much."

"As I told you. Now you have your second chance, Skein.

Your gift has been restored. Courtesy of our friend in the pit. They love being helpful."

"What shall I do now? Where shall I go?"

"Anything. Anywhere. Anywhen. You're free to move along the time-line as you please. In a state of controlled, directed fugue, so to speak. After all, if time is random, if there is no rigid sequence of events—"

"Yes."

"Then why not choose the sequence that appeals to you? Why stick to the set of abstractions your former self has handed you? You're a free man, Skein. Go. Enjoy. Undo your past. Edit it. Improve on it. It isn't your past, any more than this is your present. It's all one, Skein, all *one*. Pick the segment you prefer."

He tests the truth of the skull-faced man's words. Cautiously Skein steps three minutes into the past and sees himself struggling up out of the pit. He slides four minutes into the future and sees the skull-faced man, alone, trudging northward along the shore. Everything flows. All is fluidity. He is free. He is free.

"You see, Skein?"

"Now I do," Skein says. He is out of entropy's jaws. He is time's master, which is to say he is his own master. He can move at will. He can defy the imaginary forces of determinism. Suddenly he realizes what he must do now. He will assert his free will; he will challenge entropy on its home ground. Skein smiles. He cuts free of the time-line and floats easily into what others would call the past.

"Get Nissenson into a receptive state," he orders his desk.

Coustakis, blinking rapidly, obviously uneasy, says, "First let me get it clear. This man will see everything that's in my mind? He'll get access to my secrets?"

"No. No. I filter the communion with great care. Nothing will pass from your mind to his except the nature of the problem you want him to tackle. Nothing will come back from his mind to yours except the answer."

"And if he doesn't have the answer?"

"He will."

"And if he goes into the transmission business for himself afterward?" Coustakis asks.

"He's bonded," Skein says curtly. "No chance of it. Let's go, now. Up and together."

The desk reports that Nissenson, half the world away in São Paulo, is ready. Quickly Skein throws Coustakis into the receptive condition, and swings around to face the brilliant lights of his data-access units. Here is the moment when he can halt the transaction. Turn again, Skein. Face Coustakis, smile sadly, inform him that the communion will be impossible. Give him back his money, send him off to break some other Communicator's mind. And live on, whole and happy, ever after. It was at this point, visiting this scene endlessly in his fugues, that Skein silently and hopelessly cried out to himself to stop. Now it is within his power, for this is no fugue, no illusion of time-shift. He has shifted. He is here, carrying with him the knowledge of all that is to come, and he is the only Skein on the scene, the operative Skein. Get up, now. Refuse the contract.

He does not. Thus he defies entropy. Thus he breaks the chain.

He peers into the sparkling, shifting little blazes until they kindle his gift, jabbing at the electrical rhythms of his brain until he is lifted into the energy level that permits the opening of a communion. He starts to go up. He reaches forth one tendril of his mind and engages Nissenson. With another tendril he snares Coustakis. Steadily, now, he draws the two tendrils together. He is aware of the risks, but believes he can surmount them.

The tendrils meet.

Out of Coustakis' mind flows a description of the matter transmitter and a clear statement of the beam-spread problem; Skein shoves it along to Nissenson, who begins to work on a solution. The combined strength of the two minds is great, but Skein deftly lets the excess charge bleed away, and maintains the communion with no particular effort, holding Coustakis and Nissenson together while they deal with their technical matters. Skein pays little attention as their

excited minds rush toward answers. *If you. Yes, and then.
But if. I see, yes. I could. And. However, maybe I should.
I like that. It leads to. Of course. The inevitable result. Is it
feasible, though? I think so. You might have to. I could. Yes.
I could. I could.*

"I thank you a million times," Coustakis says to Skein. "It
was all so simple, once we saw how we ought to look at it.
I don't begrudge your fee at all. Not at all."

Coustakis leaves, glowing with delight. Skein, relieved, tells
his desk, "I'm going to allow myself a three-day holiday. Fix
the schedule to move everybody up accordingly."

He smiles. He strides across his office, turning up the amplifiers, treating himself to the magnificent view. The nightmare undone. The past revised. The burnout avoided. All
it took was confidence. Enlightenment. A proper understanding of the processes involved.

He feels the sudden swooping sensations of incipient
temporal fugue. Before he can intervene to regain control, he
swings off into darkness and arrives instantaneously on a
planet of purple sand and blue-leaved trees. Orange waves
lap at the shore. He stands a few meters from a deep, conical
pit. Peering into it, he sees an amoebalike creature lying
beside a human figure; strands of the alien's jellylike substance are wound around the man's body. He recognizes the
man to be John Skein. The communion in the pit ends; the
man begins to clamber from the pit. The wind is rising. The
sand, blown aloft, stains the sky gray. Patiently he watches
his younger self struggling up from the pit. Now he understands. The circuit is closed; the knot is tied; the identity
loop is complete. He is destined to spend many years on
Abbondanza VI, growing ancient and withered. He is the
skull-faced man.

Skein reaches the rim of the pit and lies there, breathing
hard. He helps Skein get up.

"How do you feel?" he asks.

Nine Lives

URSULA K. LE GUIN

She was alive inside, but dead outside, her face a black and dun net of wrinkles, tumors, cracks. She was bald and blind. The tremors that crossed Libra's face were mere quiverings of corruption: underneath, in the black corridors, the halls beneath the skin, there were crepitations in darkness, ferments, chemical nightmares that went on for centuries. "Oh the damned flatulent planet," Pugh murmured as the dome shook and a boil burst a kilometer to the southwest, spraying silver pus across the sunset. The sun had been setting for the last two days. "I'll be glad to see a human face."

"Thanks," said Martin.

"Yours is human to be sure," said Pugh, "but I've seen it so long I can't see it."

Radvid signals cluttered the communicator which Martin was operating, faded, returned as face and voice. The face filled the screen, the nose of an Assyrian king, the eyes of a samurai, skin bronze, eyes the color of iron: young, magnificent. "Is that what human beings look like?" said Pugh with awe. "I'd forgotten."

"Shut up, Owen, we're on."

"Libra Exploratory Mission Base, come in please, this is *Passerine* launch."

"Libra here. Beam fixed. Come on down, launch."

"Expulsion in seven E-seconds. Hold on." The screen blanked and sparkled.

"Do they all look like that? Martin, you and I are uglier men than I thought."

"Shut up, Owen. . . ."

For twenty-two minutes Martin followed the landing-craft

down by signal and then through the cleared dome they saw it, small star in the blood-colored east, sinking. It came down neat and quiet, Libra's thin atmosphere carrying little sound. Pugh and Martin closed the headpieces of their imsuits, zipped out of the dome airlocks, and ran with soaring strides, Nijinsky and Nureyev, toward the boat. Three equipment modules came floating down at four-minute intervals from each other and hundred-meter intervals east of the boat. "Come on out," Martin said on his suit radio, "we're waiting at the door."

"Come on in, the methane's fine," said Pugh.

The hatch opened. The young man they had seen on the screen came out with one athletic twist and leaped down onto the shaky dust and clinkers of Libra. Martin shook his hand, but Pugh was staring at the hatch, from which another young man emerged with the same neat twist and jump, followed by a young woman who emerged with the same neat twist, ornamented by a wriggle, and the jump. They were all tall, with bronze skin, black hair, high-bridged noses, epicanthic fold, the same face. They all had the same face. The fourth was emerging from the hatch with a neat twist and jump. "Martin bach," said Pugh, "we've got a clone."

"Right," said one of them, "we're a tenclone. John Chow's the name. You're Lieutenant Martin?"

"I'm Owen Pugh."

"Alvaro Guillen Martin," said Martin, formal, bowing slightly. Another girl was out, the same beautiful face; Martin stared at her and his eye rolled like a nervous pony's. Evidently he had never given any thought to cloning, and was suffering technological shock. "Steady," Pugh said in the Argentine dialect, "it's only excess twins." He stood close by Martin's elbow. He was glad himself of the contact.

It is hard to meet a stranger. Even the greatest extrovert meeting even the meekest stranger knows a certain dread, though he may not know he knows it. Will he make a fool of me wreck my image of myself invade me destroy me change me? Will he be different from me? Yes, that he will. There's the terrible thing: the strangeness of the stranger.

After two years on a dead planet, and the last half year

isolated as a team of two, oneself and one other, after that it's even harder to meet a stranger, however welcome he may be. You're out of the habit of difference, you've lost the touch; and so the fear revives, the primitive anxiety, the old dread.

The clone, five males and five females, had got done in a couple of minutes what a man might have got done in twenty: greeted Pugh and Martin, had a glance at Libra, unloaded the boat, made ready to go. They went, and the dome filled with them, a hive of golden bees. They hummed and buzzed quietly, filled up all silences, all spaces with a honey-brown swarm of human presence. Martin looked bewilderedly at the long-limbed girls, and they smiled at him, three at once. Their smile was gentler than that of the boys, but no less radiantly self-possessed.

"Self-possessed," Owen Pugh murmured to his friend, "that's it. Think of it, to be oneself ten times over. Nine seconds for every motion, nine ayes on every vote. It would be glorious!" But Martin was asleep. And the John Chows had all gone to sleep at once. The dome was filled with their quiet breathing. They were young, they didn't snore. Martin sighed and snored, his hershey-bar-colored face relaxed in the dim afterglow of Libra's primary, set at last. Pugh had cleared the dome and stars looked in, Sol among them, a great company of lights, a clone of splendors. Pugh slept and dreamed of a one-eyed giant who chased him through the shaking halls of Hell.

From his sleeping-bag Pugh watched the clone's awakening. They all got up within one minute except for one pair, a boy and a girl, who lay snugly tangled and still sleeping in one bag. As Pugh saw this there was a shock like one of Libra's earthquakes inside him, a very deep tremor. He was not aware of this, and in fact thought he was pleased at the sight; there was no other such comfort on this dead hollow world, more power to them, who made love. One of the others stepped on the pair. They woke and the girl sat up flushed and sleepy, with bare golden breasts. One of her sisters murmured something to her; she shot a glance at Pugh and disappeared in the sleeping-bag, followed by a giant giggle, from another direction a fierce stare, from still another direction a voice: "Christ, we're used to having a room to ourselves. Hope you don't mind, Captain Pugh."

"It's a pleasure," Pugh said half-truthfully. He had to stand up then, wearing only the shorts he slept in, and he felt like a plucked rooster, all white scrawn and pimples. He had seldom envied Martin's compact brownness so much. The United Kingdom had come through the Great Famines well, losing less than half its population: a record achieved by rigorous food-control. Black-marketeers and hoarders had been executed. Crumbs had been shared. Where in richer lands most had died and a few had thriven, in Britain fewer died and none throve. They all got lean. Their sons were lean, their grandsons lean, small, brittle-boned, easily infected. When civilization became a matter of standing in lines, the British had kept queue, and so had replaced the survival of the fittest with the survival of the fair-minded. Owen Pugh was a scrawny little man. All the same, he was there.

At the moment he wished he wasn't.

At breakfast a John said, "Now if you'll brief us, Captain Pugh—"

"Owen, then."

"Owen, we can work out our schedule. Anything new on the mine since your last report to your Mission? We saw your reports when *Passerine* was orbiting Planet V, where they are now."

Martin did not answer, though the mine was his discovery and project, and Pugh had to do his best. It was hard to talk to them. The same faces, each with the same expression of intelligent interest, all leaned toward him across the table at almost the same angle. They all nodded together.

Over the Exploitation Corps insignia on their tunics each had a nameband, first name John and last name Chow of course, but the middle names different. The men were Aleph, Kaph, Yod, Gimel, and Samedh; the women Sadhe, Daleth, Zayin, Beth, and Resh. Pugh tried to use the names but gave it up at once; he could not even tell sometimes which one had spoken, for the voices were all alike.

Martin buttered and chewed his toast, and finally interrupted: "You're a team. Is that it?"

"Right," said two Johns.

"God, what a team! I hadn't seen the point. How much do you each know what the others are thinking?"

"Not at all, properly speaking," replied one of the girls, Zayin. The others watched her with the proprietary, approving look they had. "No ESP, nothing fancy. But we think alike. We have exactly the same equipment. Given the same stimulus, the same problem, we're likely to be coming up with the same reactions and solutions at the same time. Explanations are easy—don't even have to make them, usually. We seldom misunderstand each other. It does facilitate our working as a team."

"Christ yes," said Martin. "Pugh and I have spent seven hours out of ten for six months misunderstanding each other. Like most people. What about emergencies, are you as good at meeting the unexpected problem as a nor . . . an unrelated team?"

"Statistics so far indicate that we are," Zayin answered readily. Clones must be trained, Pugh thought, to meet questions, to reassure and reason. All they said had the slightly bland and stilted quality of answers furnished to the Public. "We can't brainstorm as singletons can, we as a team don't profit from the interplay of varied minds; but we have a compensatory advantage. Clones are drawn from the best human material, individuals of IIQ 99th percentile, Genetic Constitution alpha double A, and so on. We have more to draw on than most individuals do."

"And it's multiplied by a factor of ten. Who is—who was John Chow?"

"A genius surely," Pugh said politely. His interest in cloning was not so new and avid as Martin's.

"Leonardo Complex type," said Yod. "Biomath, also a cellist, and an undersea hunter, and interested in structural engineering problems, and so on. Died before he'd worked out his major theories."

"Then you each represent a different facet of his mind, his talents?"

"No," said Zayin, shaking her head in time with several others. "We share the basic equipment and tendencies, of course, but we're all engineers in Planetary Exploitation. A later clone can be trained to develop other aspects of the basic equipment. It's all training; the genetic substance is identical. We *are* John Chow. But we were differently trained."

Martin looked shell-shocked. "How old are you?"

"Twenty-three."

"You say he died young— Had they taken germ cells from him beforehand or something?"

Gimel took over: "He died at twenty-four in an aircar crash. They couldn't save the brain, so they took some intestinal cells and cultured them for cloning. Reproductive cells aren't used for cloning since they have only half the chromosomes. Intestinal cells happen to be easy to despecialize and reprogram for total growth."

"All chips off the old block," Martin said valiantly. "But how can . . . some of you be women . . . ?"

Beth took over: "It's easy to program half the clonal mass back to the female. Just delete the male gene from half the cells and they revert to the basic, that is, the female. It's trickier to go the other way, have to hook in artificial Y chromosomes. So they mostly clone from males, since clones function best bisexually."

Gimel again: "They've worked these matters of technique and function out carefully. The taxpayer wants the best for his money, and of course clones are expensive. With the cell-manipulations, and the incubation in Ngama Placentae, and the maintenance and training of the foster-parent groups, we end up costing about three million apiece."

"For your next generation," Martin said, still struggling, "I suppose you . . . you breed?"

"We females are sterile," said Beth with perfect equanimity; "you remember that the Y chromosome was deleted from our original cell. The males can interbreed with approved singletons, if they want to. But to get John Chow again as often as they want, they just reclone a cell from this clone."

Martin gave up the struggle. He nodded and chewed cold toast. "Well," said one of the Johns, and all changed mood, like a flock of starlings that change course in one wingflick, following a leader so fast that no eye can see which leads. They were ready to go. "How about a look at the mine? Then we'll unload the equipment. Some nice new models in the roboats; you'll want to see them. Right?" Had Pugh or Martin not agreed they might have found it hard to say so. The Johns were polite but unanimous; their decisions carried. Pugh, Commander of Libra Base 2, felt a qualm. Could he boss around this superman-woman-entity-of-ten? and a genius at that? He stuck close to Martin as they suited for outside. Neither said anything.

Four apiece in the three large jetsleds, they slipped off north from the dome, over Libra's dun rugose skin, in starlight.

"Desolate," one said.

It was a boy and girl with Pugh and Martin. Pugh wondered if these were the two that had shared a sleeping-bag last night. No doubt they wouldn't mind if he asked them. Sex must be as handy as breathing, to them. Did you two breathe last night?

"Yes," he said, "it is desolate."

"This is our first time Off, except training on Luna." The girl's voice was definitely a bit higher and softer.

"How did you take the big hop?"

"They doped us. I wanted to experience it." That was the boy; he sounded wistful. They seemed to have more personality, only two at a time. Did repetition of the individual negate individuality?

"Don't worry," said Martin, steering the sled, "you can't experience no-time because it isn't there."

"I'd just like to once," one of them said. "So we'd know."

The Mountains of Merioneth showed leprotic in starlight to the east, a plume of freezing gas trailed silvery from a vent-hole to the west, and the sled tilted groundward. The twins braced for the stop at one monent, each with a slight protective gesture to the other. Your skin is my skin, Pugh thought, but literally, no metaphor. What would it be like, then, to have someone as close to you as that? Always to be answered when you spoke, never to be in pain alone. Love your neighbor as you love yourself. . . . That hard old problem was solved. The neighbor was the self: the love was perfect.

And here was Hellmouth, the mine.

Pugh was the Exploratory Mission's ET geologist, and Martin his technician and cartographer; but when in the course of a local survey Martin had discovered the U-mine, Pugh had given him full credit, as well as the onus of prospecting the lode and planning the Exploitation Team's job. These kids had been sent out from Earth years before Martin's reports got there, and had not known what their job would be until they got here. The Exploitation Corps simply set out teams regularly and blindly as a dandelion sends out its seeds, knowing there would be a job for them on Libra or the next planet out or one they hadn't even heard about yet. The Government wanted uranium too urgently to wait while reports drifted home across the light-years. The stuff was like gold, old-fashioned but essential, worth mining extraterrestrially and shipping interstellar. Worth its weight in people, Pugh thought sourly, watching the tall young men and women go one by one, glimmering in starlight, into the black hole Martin had named Hellmouth.

As they went in their homeostatic forehead-lamps brightened. Twelve nodding gleams ran along the moist, wrinkled walls. Pugh heard Martin's radiation counter peeping twenty to the dozen up ahead. "Here's the drop-off," said Martin's voice in the suit intercom, drowning out the peeping and the dead silence that was around them. "We're in a side-fissure; this is the main vertical vent in front of us." The black void gaped, its far side not visible in the headlamp beams. "Last vulcanism seems to have been a couple of thousand years ago. Nearest fault is twenty-eight kilos east, in the Trench. This region seems to be as safe seismically as anything in the area. The big basalt-flow overhead stabilizes all these substructures, so long as it remains stable itself. Your central lode is thirty-six meters down and runs in a series of five bubble-caverns northeast. It is a lode, a pipe of very high-grade ore. You saw the percentage figures, right? Extraction's going to be no problem. All you've got to do is get the bubbles topside."

"Take off the lid and let 'em float up." A chuckle. Voices began to talk, but they were all the same voice and the suit radio gave them no location in space. "Open the thing right up. —Safer that way. —But it's a solid basalt roof, how thick, ten meters here? —Three to twenty, the report said. —Blow good ore all over the lot. —Use this access we're in, straighten it a bit and run slider-rails for the robos. —Import burros. —Have we got enough propping material? —What's your estimate of total payload mass, Martin?"

"Say over five million kilos and under eight."

"Transport will be here in ten E-months. —It'll have to go pure. —No, they'll have the mass problem in NAFAL shipping licked by now; remember it's been sixteen years since we left Earth last Tuesday. —Right, they'll send the whole lot back and purify it in Earth orbit. —Shall we go down, Martin?"

"Go on. I've been down."

The first one—Aleph? (Heb., the ox, the leader)—swung onto the ladder and down; the rest followed. Pugh and Martin stood at the chasm's edge. Pugh set his intercom to exchange only with Martin's suit, and noticed Martin doing the same. It was a bit wearing, this listening to one person think aloud in ten voices, or was it one voice speaking the thoughts of ten minds?

"A great gut," Pugh said, looking down into the black pit, its veined and warted walls catching stray gleams of headlamps far below. "A cow's bowel. A bloody great constipated intestine."

Martin's counter peeped like a lost chicken. They stood inside the epileptic planet, breathing oxygen from tanks, wearing suits impermeable to corrosives and harmful radiations, resistant to a two-hundred-degree range of temperatures, tear-proof, and as shock-resistant as possible given the soft vulnerable stuff inside.

"Next hop," Martin said, "I'd like to find a planet that has nothing whatever to exploit."

"You found this."

"Keep me home next time."

Pugh was pleased. He had hoped Martin would want to go on working with him, but neither of them was used to talking much about their feelings, and he had hesitated to ask. "I'll try that," he said.

"I hate this place. I like caves, you know. It's why I came in here. Just spelunking. But this one's a bitch. Mean. You can't ever let down in here. I guess this lot can handle it, though. They know their stuff."

"Wave of the future, whatever," said Pugh.

The wave of the future came swarming up the ladder, swept Martin to the entrance, gabbled at and around him: "Have we got enough material for supports? —If we convert one of the extractor-servos to anneal, yes. —Sufficient if we miniblast? —Kaph can calculate stress."

Pugh had switched his intercom back to receive them; he looked at them, so many thoughts jabbering in an eager mind, and at Martin standing silent among them, and at Hellmouth, and the wrinkled plain. "Settled! How does that strike you as a preliminary schedule, Martin?"

"It's your baby," Martin said.

Within five E-days the Johns had all their material and equipment unloaded and operating, and were starting to open up the mine. They worked with total efficiency. Pugh was fascinated and frightened by their effectiveness, their confidence, their independence. He was no use to them at all. A clone, he thought, might indeed be the first truly stable, self-reliant human being. Once adult it would need nobody's help. It would be sufficient to itself physically, sexually, emotionally, intellectually. Whatever he did, any member of it would always receive the support and approval of his peers, his other selves. Nobody else was needed.

Two of the clone stayed in the dome doing calculations and paperwork, with frequent sled-trips to the mine for measurements and tests. They were the mathematicians of the clone, Zayin and Kaph. That is, as Zayin explained, all ten had had thorough mathematical training from age three to twenty-one, but from twenty-one to twenty-three she and Kaph had gone on with math while the others intensified other specialties, geology, mining engineering, electronic engineering, equipment robotics, applied atomics, and so on. "Kaph and I feel," she said, "that we're the element of the clone closest to what John Chow was in his singleton lifetime. But of course he was principally in biomath, and they didn't take us far in that."

"They needed us most in this field," Kaph said, with the patriotic priggishness they sometimes evinced.

Pugh and Martin soon could distinguish this pair from the others, Zayin by gestalt, Kaph only by a discolored left fourth fingernail, got from an ill-aimed hammer at the age of six. No doubt there were many such differences, physical and psychological, among them; nature might be identical, nurture could not be. But the differences were hard to find. And part of the difficulty was that they really never talked to Pugh and Martin. They joked with them, were polite, got along fine. They gave nothing. It was nothing one could complain about; they were very pleasant, they had the standardized American friendliness. "Do you come from Ireland, Owen?"

"Nobody comes from Ireland, Zayin."

"There are lots of Irish-Americans."

"To be sure, but no more Irish. A couple of thousand in all the island, the last I knew. They didn't go in for birth-control, you know, so the food ran out. By the Third Famine there were no Irish left at all but the priesthood, and they were all celibate, or nearly all."

Zayin and Kaph smiled stiffly. They had no experience of either bigotry or irony. "What are you then, ethnically?" Kaph asked, and Pugh replied, "A Welshman."

"Is it Welsh that you and Martin speak together?"

None of your business, Pugh thought, but said, "No, it's his dialect, not mine: Argentinean. A descendant of Spanish."

"You learned it for private communication?"

"Whom had we here to be private from? It's just that sometimes a man likes to speak his native language."

"Ours is English," Kaph said unsympathetically. Why

should they have sympathy? That's one of the things you give because you need it back.

"Is Wells quaint?" asked Zayin.

"Wells? Oh, Wales, it's called. Yes. Wales is quaint." Pugh switched on his rock-cutter, which prevented further conversation by a synapse-destroying whine, and while it whined he turned his back and said a profane word in Welsh.

That night he used the Argentine dialect for private communication. "Do they pair off in the same couples, or change every night?"

Martin looked surprised. A prudish expression, unsuited to his features, appeared for a moment. It faded. He too was curious. "I think it's random."

"Don't whisper, man, it sounds dirty. I think they rotate."

"On a schedule?"

"So nobody gets omitted."

Martin gave a vulgar laugh and smothered it. "What about us? Aren't we omitted?"

"That doesn't occur to them."

"What if I proposition one of the girls?"

"She'd tell the others and they'd decide as a group."

"I am not a bull," Martin said, his dark, heavy face heating up. "I will not be judged—"

"Down, down, *machismo*," said Pugh. "Do you mean to proposition one?"

Martin shrugged, sullen. "Let 'em have their incest."

"Incest is it, or masturbation?"

"I don't care, if they'd do it out of earshot!"

The clone's early attempts at modesty had soon worn off, unmotivated by any deep defensiveness of self or awareness of others. Pugh and Martin were daily deeper swamped under the intimacies of its constant emotional-sexual-mental interchange: swamped yet excluded.

"Two months to go," Martin said one evening.

"To what?" snapped Pugh. He was edgy lately and Martin's sullenness got on his nerves.

"To relief."

In sixty days the full crew of their Exploratory Mission

were due back from their survey of the other planets of the system. Pugh was aware of this.

"Crossing off the days on your calendar?" he jeered.

"Pull yourself together, Owen."

"What do you mean?"

"What I say."

They parted in contempt and resentment.

Pugh came in after a day alone on the Pampas, a vast lava-plain the nearest edge of which was two hours south by jet. He was tired, but refreshed by solitude. They were not supposed to take long trips alone, but lately had often done so. Martin stooped under bright lights, drawing one of his elegant, masterly charts: this one was of the whole face of Libra, the cancerous face. The dome was otherwise empty, seeming dim and large as it had before the clone came. "Where's the golden horde?"

Martin grunted ignorance, crosshatching. He straightened his back to glance around at the sun, which squatted feebly like a great red toad on the eastern plain, and at the clock, which said 18:45. "Some big quakes today," he said, returning to his map. "Feel them down there? Lot of crates were falling around. Take a look at the seismo."

The needle jigged and wavered on the roll. It never stopped dancing here. The roll had recorded five quakes of major intensity back in mid-afternoon; twice the needle had hopped off the roll. The attached computer had been activated to emit a slip reading, "Epicenter 61' N by 4'24" E."

"Not in the Trench this time."

"I thought it felt a bit different from usual. Sharper."

"In Base One I used to lie awake all night feeling the ground jump. Queer how you get used to things."

"Go spla if you didn't. What's for dinner?"

"I thought you'd have cooked it."

"Waiting for the clone."

Feeling put upon, Pugh got out a dozen dinnerboxes, stuck two in the Instobake, pulled them out. "All right, here's dinner."

"Been thinking," Martin said, coming to the table. "What

if some clone cloned itself? Illegally. Made a thousand dupli-
cates—ten thousand. Whole army. They could make a tidy
power-grab, couldn't they?"

"But how many millions did this lot cost to rear? Artificial
placentae and all that. It would be hard to keep secret, unless they had a planet to themselves. . . . Back before the
Famines when Earth had national governments, they talked
about that: clone your best soldiers, have whole regiments of
them. But the food ran out before they could play that game."

They talked amicably, as they used to do.

"Funny," Martin said, chewing. "They left early this
morning, didn't they?"

"All but Kaph and Zayin. They thought they'd get the
first payload aboveground today. What's up?"

"They weren't back for lunch."

"They won't starve, to be sure."

"They left at seven."

"So they did." Then Pugh saw it. The air-tanks held eight
hours' supply.

"Kaph and Zayin carried out spare cans when they left.
Or they've got a heap out there."

"They did, but they brought the whole lot in to recharge."
Martin stood up, pointing to one of the stacks of stuff that
cut the dome into rooms and alleys.

"There's an alarm signal on every imsuit."

"It's not automatic."

Pugh was tired and still hungry. "Sit down and eat, man.
That lot can look after themselves."

Martin sat down, but did not eat. "There was a big
quake, Owen. The first one. Big enough, it scared me."

After a pause Pugh sighed and said, "All right."

Unenthusiastically, they got out the two-man sled that
was always left for them, and headed it north. The long sunrise covered everything in poisonous red jello. The horizontal
light and shadow made it hard to see, raised walls of fake
iron ahead of them through which they slid, turned the con-
vex plain beyond Hellmouth into a great dimple full of bloody
water. Around the tunnel entrance a wilderness of machinery stood, cranes and cables and servos and wheels and dig-

gers and robocarts and sliders and control-huts, all slanting and bulking incoherently in the red light. Martin jumped from the sled, ran into the mine. He came out again, to Pugh. "Oh God, Owen, it's down," he said. Pugh went in and saw, five meters from the entrance, the shiny, moist, black wall that ended the tunnel. Newly exposed to air, it looked organic, like visceral tissue. The tunnel entrance, enlarged by blasting and double-tracked for robocarts, seemed unchanged until he noticed thousands of tiny spiderweb cracks in the walls. The floor was wet with some sluggish fluid.

"They were inside," Martin said.

"They may be still. They surely had extra air-cans—"

"Look, Owen, look at the basalt flow, at the roof; don't you see what the quake did, look at it."

The low hump of land that roofed the caves still had the unreal look of an optical illusion. It had reversed itself, sunk down, leaving a vast dimple or pit. When Pugh walked on it he saw that it too was cracked with many tiny fissures. From some a whitish gas was seeping, so that the sunlight on the surface of the gas-pool was shafted as if by the waters of a dim red lake.

"The mine's not on the fault. There's no fault here!"

Pugh came back to him quickly. "No, there's no fault, Martin. Look, they surely weren't all inside together."

Martin followed him and searched among the wrecked machines dully, then actively. He spotted the airsled. It had come down heading south, and stuck at an angle in a pothole of colloidal dust. It had carried two riders. One was half sunk in the dust, but his suit-meters registered normal functioning; the other hung strapped onto the tilted sled. Her imsuit had burst open on the broken legs, and the body was frozen hard as any rock. That was all they found. As both regulation and custom demanded, they cremated the dead at once with the laser-guns they carried by regulation and had never used before. Pugh, knowing he was going to be sick, wrestled the survivor onto the two-man sled and sent Martin off to the dome with him. Then he vomited, and flushed the waste out of his suit, and finding one four-man sled undamaged followed after Martin, shaking as if the cold of Libra had got through to him.

The survivor was Kaph. He was in deep shock. They found a swelling on the occiput that might mean concussion, but no fracture was visible.

Pugh brought two glasses of food-concentrate and two chasers of aquavit. "Come on," he said. Martin obeyed, drinking off the tonic. They sat down on crates near the cot and sipped the aquavit.

Kaph lay immobile, face like beeswax, hair bright black to the shoulders, lips stiffly parted for faintly gasping breaths.

"It must have been the first shock, the big one," Martin said. "It must have slid the whole structure sideways. Till it fell in on itself. There must be gas layers in the lateral rocks, like those formations in the Thirty-first Quadrant. But there wasn't any sign—" As he spoke the world slid out from under them. Things leaped and clattered, hopped and jigged, shouted Ha! Ha! Ha! "It was like this at fourteen hours," said Reason shakily in Martin's voice; amidst the unfastening and ruin of the world. But Unreason sat up, as the tumult lessened and things ceased dancing, and screamed aloud.

Pugh leaped across his spilled aquavit and held Kaph down. The muscular body flailed him off. Martin pinned the shoulders down. Kaph screamed, struggled, choked; his face blackened. "Oxy," Pugh said, and his hand found the right needle in the medical kit as if by homing instinct; while Martin held the mask he struck the needle home to the vagus nerve, restoring Kaph to life.

"Didn't know you knew that stunt," Martin said, breathing hard.

"The Lazarus Jab; my father was a doctor. It doesn't often work," Pugh said. "I want that drink I spilled. Is the quake over? I can't tell."

"Aftershocks. It's not just you shivering."

"Why did he suffocate?"

"I don't know, Owen. Look in the book."

Kaph was breathing normally and his color was restored, only the lips were still darkened. They poured a new shot of courage and sat down by him again with their medical guide. "Nothing about cyanosis or asphyxiation under 'shock' or 'concussion.' He can't have breathed in anything with his suit on. I don't know. We'd get as much good out of *Mother Mog's Home Herbalist*. . . . 'Anal Hemorrhoids,' fy!" Pugh pitched the book to a crate-table. It fell short, because either Pugh or the table was still unsteady.

"Why didn't he signal?"

"Sorry?"

"The eight inside the mine never had time. But he and the girl must have been outside. Maybe she was in the entrance, and got hit by the first slide. He must have been outside, in the control-hut maybe. He ran in, pulled her out, strapped her onto the sled, started for the dome. And all that time never pushed the panic button in his imsuit. Why not?"

"Well, he'd had that whack on his head. I doubt he ever realized the girl was dead. He wasn't in his senses. But if he had been I don't know if he'd have thought to signal us. They looked to one another for help."

Martin's face was like an Indian mask, grooves at the mouth-corners, eyes of dull coal. "That's so. What must he have felt, then, when the quake came and he was outside, alone—"

In answer Kaph screamed.

He came up off the cot in the heaving convulsions of one suffocating, knocked Pugh right down with his flailing arm, staggered into a stack of crates and fell to the floor, lips blue, eyes white. Martin dragged him back onto the cot and gave him a whiff of oxygen, then knelt by Pugh, who was just sitting up, and wiped at his cut cheekbone. "Owen, are you all right, are you going to be all right, Owen?"

"I think I am," Pugh said. "Why are you rubbing that on my face?"

It was a short length of computer-tape, now spotted with Pugh's blood. Martin dropped it. "Thought it was a towel. You clipped your cheek on that box there."

"Is he out of it?"

"Seems to be."

They stared down at Kaph lying stiff, his teeth a white line inside dark parted lips.

"Like epilepsy. Brain damage maybe?"

"What about shooting him full of meprobamate?"

Pugh shook his head. "I don't know what's in that shot I already gave him for shock. Don't want to overdose him."

"Maybe he'll sleep it off now."

"I'd like to myself. Between him and the earthquake I can't seem to keep on my feet."

"You got a nasty crack there. Go on, I'll sit up awhile."

Pugh cleaned his cut cheek and pulled off his shirt, then paused.

"Is there anything we ought to have done—have tried to do—"

"They're all dead," Martin said heavily, gently.

Pugh lay down on top of his sleeping-bag, and one instant later was wakened by a hideous, sucking, struggling noise. He staggered up, found the needle, tried three times to jab it in correctly and failed, began to massage over Kaph's heart. "Mouth-to-mouth," he said, and Martin obeyed. Presently Kaph drew a harsh breath, his heartbeat steadied, his rigid muscles began to relax.

"How long did I sleep?"

"Half an hour."

They stood up sweating. The ground shuddered, the fabric of the dome sagged and swayed. Libra was dancing her awful polka again, her Totentanz. The sun, though rising, seemed to have grown larger and redder; gas and dust must have been stirred up in the feeble atmosphere.

"What's wrong with him, Owen?"

"I think he's dying with them."

"Them— But they're dead, I tell you."

"Nine of them. They're all dead, they were crushed or suffocated. They were all him, he is all of them. They died, and now he's dying their deaths one by one."

"Oh pity of God," said Martin.

The next time was much the same. The fifth time was worse, for Kaph fought and raved, trying to speak but getting no words out, as if his mouth were stopped with rocks or clay. After that the attacks grew weaker, but so did he. The eighth seizure came at about four-thirty; Pugh and Martin worked till five-thirty doing all they could to keep life in the body that slid without protest into death. They kept him, but Martin said, "The next will finish him." And it did; but Pugh breathed his own breath into the inert lungs, until he himself passed out.

He woke. The dome was opaqued and no light on. He listened and heard the breathing of two sleeping men. He slept, and nothing woke him till hunger did.

The sun was well up over the dark plains, and the planet had stopped dancing. Kaph lay asleep. Pugh and Martin drank tea and looked at him with proprietary triumph.

When he woke Martin went to him: "How do you feel, old man?" There was no answer. Pugh took Martin's place and looked into the brown, dull eyes that gazed toward but not into his own. Like Martin he quickly turned away. He heated food-concentrate and brought it to Kaph. "Come on, drink."

He could see the muscles in Kaph's throat tighten. "Let me die," the young man said.

"You're not dying."

Kaph spoke with clarity and precision: "I am nine-tenths dead. There is not enough of me left alive."

That precision convinced Pugh, and he fought the conviction. "No," he said, peremptory. "They are dead. The others. Your brothers and sisters. You're not them, you're alive. You are John Chow. Your life is in your own hands."

The young man lay still, looking into a darkness that was not there.

Martin and Pugh took turns taking the Exploitation hauler and a spare set of robos over to Hellmouth to salvage equipment and protect it from Libra's sinister atmosphere, for the value of the stuff was, literally, astronomical. It was slow work for one man at a time, but they were unwilling to leave Kaph by himself. The one left in the dome did paperwork, while Kaph sat or lay and stared into his darkness, and never spoke. The days went by silent.

The radio spat and spoke: the Mission calling from ship. "We'll be down on Libra in five weeks, Owen. Thirty-four

E-days nine hours I make it as of now. How's tricks in the old dome?"

"Not good, chief. The Exploit team were killed, all but one of them, in the mine. Earthquake. Six days ago."

The radio crackled and sang starsong. Sixteen seconds lag each way; the ship was out around Planet 11 now. "Killed, all but one? You and Martin were unhurt?"

"We're all right, chief."

Thirty-two seconds.

"*Passerine* left an Exploit team out here with us. I may put them on the Hellmouth project then, instead of the Quadrant Seven project. We'll settle that when we come down. In any case you and Martin will be relieved at Dome Two. Hold tight. Anything else?"

"Nothing else."

Thirty-two seconds.

"Right then. So long, Owen."

Kaph had heard all this, and later on Pugh said to him, "The chief may ask you to stay here with the other Exploit team. You know the ropes here." Knowing the exigencies of Far Out Life, he wanted to warn the young man. Kaph made no answer. Since he had said, "There is not enough of me left alive," he had not spoken a word.

"Owen," Martin said on suit intercom, "he's spla. Insane. Psycho."

"He's doing very well for a man who's died nine times."

"Well? Like a turned-off android is well? The only emotion he has left is hate. Look at his eyes."

"That's not hate, Martin. Listen, it's true that he has, in a sense, been dead. I cannot imagine what he feels. But it's not hatred. He can't even see us. It's too dark."

"Throats have been cut in the dark. He hates us because we're not Aleph and Yod and Zayin."

"Maybe. But I think he's alone. He doesn't see us or hear us, that's the truth. He never had to see anyone else before. He never was alone before. He had himself to see, talk with, live with, nine other selves all his life. He doesn't know how you go it alone. He must learn. Give him time."

Martin shook his heavy head. "Spla," he said. "Just remember when you're alone with him that he could break your neck one-handed."

"He could do that," said Pugh, a short, soft-voiced man with a scarred cheekbone; he smiled. They were just outside the dome airlock, programming one of the servos to repair a damaged hauler. They could see Kaph sitting inside the great half-egg of the dome like a fly in amber.

"Hand me the insert pack there. What makes you think he'll get any better?"

"He has a strong personality, to be sure."

"Strong? Crippled. Nine-tenths dead, as he put it."

"But he's not dead. He's a live man: John Kaph Chow. He had a jolly queer upbringing, but after all every boy has got to break free of his family. He will do it."

"I can't see it."

"Think a bit, Martin bach. What's this cloning for? To repair the human race. We're in a bad way. Look at me. My IIQ and GC are half this John Chow's. Yet they wanted me so badly for the Far Out Service that when I volunteered they took me and fitted me out with an artificial lung and corrected my myopia. Now if there were enough good sound lads about would they be taking one-lunged shortsighted Welshmen?"

"Didn't know you had an artificial lung."

"I do then. Not tin, you know. Human, grown in a tank from a bit of somebody; cloned, if you like. That's how they make replacement-organs, the same general idea as cloning, but bits and pieces instead of whole people. It's my own lung now, whatever. But what I am saying is this, there are too many like me these days, and not enough like John Chow. They're trying to raise the level of the human genetic pool, which is a mucky little puddle since the population crash. So then if a man is cloned, he's a strong and clever man. It's only logic, to be sure."

Martin grunted; the servo began to hum.

Kaph had been eating little; he had trouble swallowing his food, choking on it, so that he would give up trying after a few bites. He had lost eight or ten kilos. After three weeks or so, however, his appetite began to pick up, and one day he began to look through the clone's possessions, the sleeping-bags, kits, papers which Pugh had stacked neatly in a far angle of a packing-crate alley. He sorted, destroyed a heap of papers and oddments, made a small packet of what remained, then relapsed into his walking coma.

Two days later he spoke. Pugh was trying to correct a flutter in the tape-player, and failing; Martin had the jet out, checking their maps of the Pampas. "Hell and damnation!" Pugh said, and Kaph said in a toneless voice, "Do you want me to do that?"

Pugh jumped, controlled himself, and gave the machine to Kaph. The young man took it apart, put it back together, and left it on the table.

"Put on a tape," Pugh said with careful casualness, busy at another table.

Kaph put on the topmost tape, a chorale. He lay down on his cot. The sound of a hundred human voices singing together filled the dome. He lay still, his face blank.

In the next days he took over several routine jobs, unasked. He undertook nothing that wanted initiative, and if asked to do anything he made no response at all.

"He's doing well," Pugh said in the dialect of Argentina.

"He's not. He's turning himself into a machine. Does what he's programmed to do, no reaction to anything else. He's worse off than when he didn't function at all. He's not human any more."

Pugh sighed. "Well, good night," he said in English. "Good night, Kaph."

"Good night," Martin said; Kaph did not.

Next morning at breakfast Kaph reached across Martin's plate for the toast. "Why don't you ask for it," Martin said with the geniality of repressed exasperation. "I can pass it."

"I can reach it," Kaph said in his flat voice.

"Yes, but look. Asking to pass things, saying good night or hello, they're not important, but all the same when somebody says something a person ought to answer. . . ."

The young man looked indifferently in Martin's direction; his eyes still did not seem to see clear through to the person he looked toward. "Why should I answer?"

"Because somebody has said something to you."

"Why?"

Martin shrugged and laughed. Pugh jumped up and turned on the rock-cutter.

Later on he said, "Lay off that, please, Martin."

"Manners are essential in small isolated crews, some kind of manners, whatever you work out together. He's been taught that, everybody in Far Out knows it. Why does he deliberately flout it?"

"Do you tell yourself good night?"

"So?"

"Don't you see Kaph's never known anyone but himself?"

Martin brooded and then broke out, "Then by God this cloning business is all wrong. It won't do. What are a lot of duplicate geniuses going to do for us when they don't even know we exist?"

Pugh nodded. "It might be wiser to separate the clones and bring them up with others. But they make such a grand team this way."

"Do they? I don't know. If this lot had been ten average inefficient ET engineers, would they all have been in the same place at the same time? Would they all have got killed? What if, when the quake came and things started caving in, what if all those kids ran the same way, farther into the mine, maybe, to save the one that was farthest in? Even Kaph was outside and went in. . . . It's hypothetical. But I keep thinking, out of ten ordinary confused guys, more might have got out."

"I don't know. It's true that identical twins tend to die at about the same time, even when they have never seen each other. Identity and death, it is very strange. . . ."

The days went on, the red sun crawled across the dark sky, Kaph did not speak when spoken to, Pugh and Martin snapped at each other more frequently each day. Pugh complained of Martin's snoring. Offended, Martin moved his cot clear across the dome and also ceased speaking to Pugh for some while. Pugh whistled Welsh dirges until Martin complained, and then Pugh stopped speaking for a while.

The day before the Mission ship was due, Martin announced he was going over to Merioneth.

"I thought at least you'd be giving me a hand with the computer to finish the rock-analyses," Pugh said, aggrieved.

"Kaph can do that. I want one more look at the Trench. Have fun," Martin added in dialect, and laughed, and left.

"What is that language?"

"Argentinean. I told you that once, didn't I?"

"I don't know." After a while the young man added, "I have forgotten a lot of things, I think."

"It wasn't important, to be sure," Pugh said gently, realizing all at once how important this conversation was. "Will you give me a hand running the computer, Kaph?"

He nodded.

Pugh had left a lot of loose ends, and the job took them all day. Kaph was a good co-worker, quick and systematic, much more so than Pugh himself. His flat voice, now that he was talking again, got on the nerves; but it didn't matter, there was only this one day left to get through and then the ship would come, the old crew, comrades and friends.

During tea-break Kaph said, "What will happen if the Explorer ship crashes?"

"They'd be killed."

"To you, I mean."

"To us? We'd radio SOS all signals, and live on half rations till the rescue cruiser from Area Three Base came. Four and a half E-years away it is. We have life-support here for three men for, let's see, maybe between four and five years. A bit tight, it would be."

"Would they send a cruiser for three men?"

"They would."

Kaph said no more.

"Enough cheerful speculations," Pugh said cheerfully, rising to get back to work. He slipped sideways and the chair avoided his hand; he did a sort of half-pirouette and fetched up hard against the dome-hide. "My goodness," he said, reverting to his native idiom, "what is it?"

"Quake," said Kaph.

The teacups bounced on the table with a plastic cackle,

a litter of papers slid off a box, the skin of the dome swelled and sagged. Underfoot there was a huge noise, half sound half shaking, a subsonic boom.

Kaph sat unmoved. An earthquake does not frighten a man who died in an earthquake.

Pugh, white-faced, wiry black hair sticking out, a frightened man, said, "Martin is in the Trench."

"What trench?"

"The big fault line. The epicenter for the local quakes. Look at the seismograph." Pugh struggled with the stuck door of a still-jittering locker.

"Where are you going?"

"After him."

"Martin took the jet. Sleds aren't safe to use during quakes. They go out of control."

"For God's sake, man, shut up."

Kaph stood up, speaking in a flat voice as usual. "It's unnecessary to go out after him now. It's taking an unnecessary risk."

"If his alarm goes off, radio me," Pugh said, shut the headpiece of his suit, and ran to the lock. As he went out Libra picked up her ragged skirts and danced a belly-dance from under his feet clear to the red horizon.

Inside the dome, Kaph saw the sled go up, tremble like a meteor in the dull red daylight, and vanish to the northeast. The hide of the dome quivered; the earth coughed. A vent south of the dome belched up a slow-flowing bile of black gas.

A bell shrilled and a red light flashed on the central control board. The sign under the light read Suit Two and scribbled under that, A.G.M. Kaph did not turn the signal off. He tried to radio Martin, then Pugh, but got no reply from either.

When the aftershocks decreased he went back to work, and finished up Pugh's job. It took him about two hours. Every half hour he tried to contact Suit One, and got no reply, then Suit Two and got no reply. The red light had stopped flashing after an hour.

It was dinnertime. Kaph cooked dinner for one, and ate it. He lay down on his cot.

The aftershocks had ceased except for faint rolling tremors at long intervals. The sun hung in the west, oblate, pale-red, immense. It did not sink visibly. There was no sound at all.

Kaph got up and began to walk about the messy, half-packed-up, overcrowded, empty dome. The silence continued. He went to the player and put on the first tape that came to hand. It was pure music, electronic, without harmonies, without voices. It ended. The silence continued.

Pugh's uniform tunic, one button missing, hung over a stack of rock-samples. Kaph stared at it awhile.

The silence continued.

The child's dream: There is no one else alive in the world but me. In all the world.

Low, north of the dome, a meteor flickered.

Kaph's mouth opened as if he were trying to say something, but no sound came. He went hastily to the north wall and peered out into the gelatinous red light.

The little star came in and sank. Two figures blurred the airlock. Kaph stood close beside the lock as they came in. Martin's imsuit was covered with some kind of dust so that he looked raddled and warty like the surface of Libra. Pugh had him by the arm.

"Is he hurt?"

Pugh shucked his suit, helped Martin peel off his. "Shaken up," he said, curt.

"A piece of cliff fell onto the jet," Martin said, sitting down at the table and waving his arms. "Not while I was in it, though. I was parked, see, and poking about that carbon-dust area when I felt things humping. So I went out onto a nice bit of early igneous I'd noticed from above, good footing and out from under the cliffs. Then I saw this bit of the planet fall off onto the flyer, quite a sight it was, and after a while it occurred to me the spare aircans were in the flyer, so I leaned on the panic button. But I didn't get any radio reception, that's always happening here during quakes, so I didn't know if the signal was getting through either. And things went on

jumping around and pieces of the cliff coming off. Little rocks
flying around, and so dusty you couldn't see a meter ahead.
I was really beginning to wonder what I'd do for breathing
in the small hours, you know, when I saw old Owen buzzing
up the Trench in all that dust and junk like a big ugly bat—"

"Want to eat?" said Pugh.

"Of course I want to eat. How'd you come through the
quake here, Kaph? No damage? It wasn't a big one actually,
was it, what's the seismo say? My trouble was I was in the
middle of it. Old Epicenter Alvaro. Felt like Richter Fifteen
there—total destruction of planet—"

"Sit down," Pugh said. "Eat."

After Martin had eaten a little his spate of talk ran dry.
He very soon went off to his cot, still in the remote angle
where he had removed it when Pugh complained of his
snoring. "Good night, you one-lunged Welshman," he said
across the dome.

"Good night."

There was no more out of Martin. Pugh opaqued the dome,
turned the lamp down to a yellow glow less than a candle's
light, and sat doing nothing, saying nothing, withdrawn.

The silence continued.

"I finished the computations."

Pugh nodded thanks.

"The signal from Martin came through, but I couldn't contact you or him."

Pugh said with effort, "I should not have gone. He had
two hours of air left even with only one can. He might have
been heading home when I left. This way we were all out of
touch with one another. I was scared."

The silence came back, punctuated now by Martin's long,
soft snores.

"Do you love Martin?"

Pugh looked up with angry eyes: "Martin is my friend.
We've worked together, he's a good man." He stopped. After
a while he said, "Yes, I love him. Why did you ask that?"

Kaph said nothing, but he looked at the other man. His
face was changed, as if he were glimpsing something he had

not seen before; his voice too was changed. "How can you . . . ? How do you . . . ?"

But Pugh could not tell him. "I don't know," he said, "it's practice, partly. I don't know. We're each of us alone, to be sure. What can you do but hold your hand out in the dark?"

Kaph's strange gaze dropped, burned out by its own intensity.

"I'm tired," Pugh said. "That was ugly, looking for him in all that black dust and muck, and mouths opening and shutting in the ground. . . . I'm going to bed. The ship will be transmitting to us by six or so." He stood up and stretched.

"It's a clone," Kaph said. "The other Exploit team they're bringing with them."

"Is it, then?"

"A twelveclone. They came out with us on the *Passerine*."

Kaph sat in the small yellow aura of the lamp seeming to look past it at what he feared: the new clone, the multiple self of which he was not part. A lost piece of a broken set, a fragment, inexpert at solitude, not knowing even how you go about giving love to another individual, now he must face the absolute, closed self-sufficiency of the clone of twelve; that was a lot to ask of the poor fellow, to be sure. Pugh put a hand on his shoulder in passing. "The chief won't ask you to stay here with a clone. You can go home. Or since you're Far Out maybe you'll come on farther out with us. We could use you. No hurry deciding. You'll make out all right."

Pugh's quiet voice trailed off. He stood unbuttoning his coat, stooped a little with fatigue. Kaph looked at him and saw the thing he had never seen before: saw him: Owen Pugh, the other, the stranger who held his hand out in the dark.

"Good night," Pugh mumbled, crawling into his sleeping-bag and half asleep already, so that he did not hear Kaph reply after a pause, repeating, across darkness, benediction.

by URSULA K. LE GUIN
The Left Hand of Darkness
The Lathe of Heaven

It would be tidy to wind up this account of the evolution of the science fiction genre and speculative fiction by declaring that the revolution was won, the millennium achieved, and that speculative fiction is today both the popular literature of the masses and the darling of the critics. It would be equally tidy, but a good deal more depressing, to say that the forces of repression utterly crushed the new consciousness in speculative fiction and reinstituted a dark age of mad robots and bug-eyed monsters.

Reality, of course, is not so tidy as all that, and a quick look around reveals that neither dramatic statement is true. In the 1960s we were led to believe that change comes about cataclysmically or not at all. Comic books were very popular in the 1960s, and football turned people on with long, dramatic forward passes called "bombs."

Now in the 1970s we are discovering that evolution can also be a matter of three yards and a cloud of dust.

Internally, the science fiction genre has come alive and made itself a live, viable, and evolving literature once more. This is not to say that there still isn't plenty of old-fashioned space opera still being written, nor that the hard-core fans aren't still eating it up. Neither has too much changed as far as the publishing of speculative fiction goes. The new speculative fiction is packaged in the same old spaceship-and-slime covers, and its sales are more or less the same as those for the old genre fiction.

On the other hand, speculative fiction does seem to have become the chosen literature of the young in the 1970s, as sales figures from college book stores pragmatically prove. In fact, courses in science fiction have been sprouting at a rather incredible rate on college and high school campuses all over America—faster than knowledgeable teachers for them can be found or trained. Interestingly enough, the impetus for this explosion in science fiction courses seems to be coming primarily from the students themselves.

Further, Robin Scott Wilson's Clarion Writers' Workshops (so named for Clarion College, where they began), a series of peripatetic courses on how to write science fiction which have been given at about half a dozen colleges, show promise of producing new writers of some merit. There are at least a half dozen new speculative writers of promise—among them Edward Bryant, George Alec Effinger, David Gerrold, and Jack Dann—who have come onto the scene in the post-New Wave period, either from the Clarion Workshops or along their own private vectors. The new writers of the 1960s can already look over their shoulders and see the next generation coming up behind them.

Academic critics are now turning to the serious study of speculative fiction, and science fiction writers— once scorned by academe as commercial hacks—have suddenly become campus literary lions. In fact, there is a real danger that the artistic vitality of speculative fiction might be threatened by an excess of academic attention as it was in the fifties by commercial strait-jacketing.

Popular culture is full of science fiction imagery, Arthur C. Clarke's hard-core science fiction novel *Rendezvous with Rama* has appeared on *Time's* best-seller list, many so-called "mainstream" writers are writing speculative fiction and "speculative fiction" writers are developing parallel careers in political analysis, "mainstream fiction," and general literary and media criticism.

Despite all this, speculative fiction continues to be packaged and sold like corn flakes, speculative writers are still to some extent second-class literary citizens, and the major magazine and media critics are lagging behind their academic brethren in their recognition of the fact that speculative fiction is coming of age.

This is what a slow process of fusion looks like in midstream. This is what happens as the creative juices of the young come up against the frozen worldly power of their elders, as the young and the old, the new and the traditional, art and commerce, "co-opt" each other, fight skirmishes, learn to see through each other's eyes, make treaties, meld, snarl, and "do not go gentle into that good night." It's evolution, a process without end.

ADDITIONAL SIGNIFICANT WORKS OF SPECULATIVE FICTION

Aldiss, Brian W., *Greybeard*
——, *The Dark Light Years*
——, *Barefoot in the Head*
Anderson, Poul, *Tau Zero*
——, *Brainwave*
——, *Three Hearts and Three Lions*
Anthony, Piers, *Chthon*
Bass, T. J., *Half Past Human*
Bradbury, Ray, *The Martian Chronicles* (collection of short stories)
Brunner, John, *Stand On Zanzibar*
Budrys, A. J., *Rogue Moon*
——, *Who?*
Burgess, Anthony, *A Clockwork Orange*
Burroughs, William S., *Nova Express*
Clement, Hal, *Mission of Gravity*
Compton, D. G., *Synthajoy*
Durrell, Lawrence, *Tunc*
Harrison, Harry, *Make Room! Make Room!*
Heinlein, Robert A., *Stranger in a Strange Land*
——, *Double Star*
——, *The Moon Is a Harsh Mistress*
Herbert, Frank, *Dune*
——, *The Santaroga Barrier*
Huxley, Aldous, *Brave New World*
Keyes, Daniel F., *Flowers for Algernon*
Kuttner, Henry, *Fury*
Lafferty, R. A., *Past Master*

——, *The Reefs of Earth*
Lem, Stanislaw, *Solaris*
Lewis, C. S., *Out of the Silent Planet*
Malzberg, Barry N., *Beyond Apollo*
Matheson, Richard, *I Am Legend*
Miller, Walter M., Jr., *A Canticle for Leibowitz*
Nabokov, Vladimir, *Ada*
Niven, Larry, *Ringworld*
Orwell, George, *1984*
Pangborn, Edgar, *A Mirror for Observers*
Percy, Walker, *Love in the Ruins*
Roberts, Keith, *Pavanne*
Russ, Joanna, *And Chaos Died*
Shute, Nevil, *On the Beach*
Simak, Clifford D., *Way Station*
Sladek, John T., *Mechasm (The Reproductive System)*
Smith, Cordwainer, *Space Lords* (collection of short stories)
Stapledon, Olaf, *The Star Maker*
——, *Last and First Men*
——, *Odd John*
Vance, Jack, *Eyes of the Overworld*
——, *Emphyrio*
Vonnegut, Kurt, Jr., *Cat's Cradle*
——, *The Sirens of Titan*
Wells, H. G., *The Time Machine*
Wyndham, John, *Re-Birth*